By Dorothy Uhnak

LAW AND

a novel by

ORDER

DOROTHY UHNAK

SIMON AND SCHUSTER • NEW YORK

PART ONE

The Father:
Sergeant
Brian O'Malley
1937

ONE

Patrolman Aaron Levine kept his eyes on the traffic ahead of him as he tried to gauge the mood of the sergeant. The thin tuneless whistling was neither irritable nor cheerful. It was just the automatic sound of breath forced through the slightly parted lips of Sergeant Brian O'Malley. Levine risked a quick glance to his right and his eyes flicked the hard clear-cut profile.

"Thinking of making a turn, are you?" Sergeant O'Malley asked while staring straight ahead.

"Oh, no, Sergeant, I was just checking that cab. He came kind of close."

"Them cabbies can handle themselves in traffic. They're not about to hit a patrol car. Let's take a left on 117th. We've got us some bad jigaboos on that block."

Levine's long bony fingers tightened on the steering wheel. Eight months and he still could not get used to it, this feeling of being an alien in an alien land; a silent witness, incredulous and always slightly afraid of the men with whom he worked.

Jesus, the niggers are hot stuff when they got their load on. You ought to see them on a Saturday night. Christ, you never seen anyone's eyes roll around, like they was going to pop the sockets.

Hey, them wops is mean, vicious sons a' bitches when they got one of them vendettas of theirs going. But you gotta give them credit. They take care of their own and don't bother outsiders unless someone messes with them.

What kind of shit is this? How come I got the sheeny driving for me? How the hell did the little Ikey-kike work that?

"Take it nice and slow now. Let's give them the opportunity to get a good long look at us," O'Malley instructed. He pushed his hat up off his forehead, ran his finger under the sweatband. "Hot for October, Jesus, isn't it though?"

He started whistling softly again, turned to stare past his driver to the other side of the street. "Played basketball, did you, at City College?" he asked without preliminaries.

"Well, yes. Not varsity, that is. You have to be a junior to get on varsity." Levine seemed unable to stop repeating the word, which acted as an immediate irritant.

"The *varsity?*" Sergeant O'Malley twisted the word tightly. "And what the hell might that be: the varsity?"

The soft Irish voice posed the question with an innocence that Aaron Levine had learned to be wary of; anything to do with his two years at City College had to be handled with a degree of caution.

"Well, varsity is the regular college team. That gets to play against the other colleges. The rest of us, well, we're in squads and play against each other."

"Well, sounds like great sport. Takes stamina, then, all that runnin'?"

"I got the long legs for running, Sergeant," Levine said. He always tried to make the comment himself; his long pole legs were a sore point with him.

"As long as they run in the right direction," O'Malley said in his soft, ambiguous, accusatory way. "Let's pull up here, in front of the huge Packard. It's a living crime, isn't it, these jigs and their big cars while their kids roam the streets for food. Now Patrolman Levine"—Sergeant O'Malley shifted his compact body slightly and waited until the patrolman met his gaze—"this here is one of those stops which is what we will call 'unofficial.' Is my meaning perfectly clear to you?"

Aaron nodded. "Yes, Sergeant."

The sergeant's eyes studied him for a moment, unreadable in the darkness of the patrol car. "Well, let's just see how clear. What does it mean when I tell you this is an 'unofficial' stop?"

Aaron licked his dry lips with a dry tongue. Involuntarily his hands traced empty patterns in the air. "Well, Sergeant, it means that . . . that we don't put it in the memo book. That you're . . . taking a personal or something—"

O'Malley's voice cut him off. "It don't mean I'm 'taking a personal or something.' It means we didn't stop at all, so how the fuck could I be taking a personal if we didn't stop at all?"

The young patrolman responded quickly in what he hoped was an earnest, good-natured tone. "Yes, sir, Sergeant. We didn't stop at all. Right."

The sergeant smiled at him tightly, as though he was a stupid child who had just learned a simple lesson. "Well, that's fine now, just fine. What else did they teach up at the City College besides basketball? Well, don't worry about it, son, you'll learn out here before you know it." He got out of the patrol car, looked around, then leaned in the window. "Look at them little pickaninnies, will you, ten o'clock at night and them all over the place like little cockaroaches. Damn shame."

Aaron cut the motor but his fingers lingered on the ignition key for a moment. He glanced at his wristwatch. God. Two more hours to go. Then two more tours of four to twelve, then a swing, then midnights. Whoever thought they were doing him a favor was wrong. Not that it was much of a choice, but given a choice, he'd prefer to patrol his tour alone, on foot.

He rubbed his tired eyes carefully with his fingertips and wondered, as he had wondered maybe a million times these last eight months: What in God's name am I doing here, a policeman, in a uniform, with a gun at my side?

Sergeant O'Malley opened the pack of Chesterfields. With his thumb, he pushed the bottom of the pack, then grasped a cigarette between his teeth. Restlessly, his eyes searched the barroom. Narrowed against the smoke and heavy acrid odors of human beings, his eyes were two dark-blue slashes, barely visible but aware of everyone around him. He hunched his broad shoulders forward, cupped his hands around the flickering match, inhaled deeply, blew the smoke straight out from his lungs.

"Pretty quiet tonight, Jappy. Where's the action?"

The bartender, a brown-skinned man with strangely slanted Oriental eyes, a fighter's flat nose and taut purple lips, turned as though to confirm the sergeant's observation. "Sure is quiet, Sergeant. Ain't much action, not nowhere. Middle of the week.

13

Business been bad, Sergeant, real bad. You can know that for a fact."

O'Malley swallowed exactly half of the shot of whiskey and carefully replaced the glass directly over the small wet circle before him. "Don't give me none of that shit, now, Jappy." He spoke without malice, absently, by rote.

The bartender ran his hands down the front of his body, which was covered by a dirty grayish apron. "Ain't no shit, Sergeant. Ain't nobody with money to spend. Not round here. Don't know myself how I gonna make the rent this month. That's a fact."

"Well, you just worry about making your 'rent' to yours truly and other things will take care of themselves, lad." He finished the whiskey and pulled his mouth down. "This must be pure kerosene. Likely take the lining off my stomach."

"Now, Sergeant, you know I keeps a special bottle just for you and your men."

"Sure you do, Jappy, sure you do. And someday I'm going to catch you putting something into it. You watch yourself and see if I don't."

O'Malley pulled himself from the bar and extended his hand. He gestured impatiently, his fingers snapping. "I haven't got all night, Jappy." He regarded the bill which was placed in his hand and shook his head. "Ah, now, you're having sport with me. Is that it?"

Jappy turned, hit the no-sale key and the drawer of the cash register slid open. He pointed to the small pile of bills. "Sergeant, I swear to God, I'm coming up most empty. Hell, ain't enough to put bread on my table."

O'Malley sighed and his fingers snapped inexorably. "Let's not exchange tales of woe, Jappy my boy. It's too late and I've got to get out and look this neighborhood over and keep the peace in the still of night."

Two single dollar bills were handed over, added mournfully to the five. O'Malley regarded the currency bleakly before his fist closed over it. "Ah, you've got to put some effort into it, lad. It's not much of a place you've got here, what with all the violations you've not taken care of, and what with stories around about tiny little kids, not bigger than this here bar" — he held his hand, palm down, level with the bar — "drinking their fill. Have a care, Jappy my boy. It's not much, but it is

14

all you've got, after all. And *I've* got a lot of people over me who don't want to know your problems; they just want to see the green."

"Next week, Sergeant," Jappy said blandly, "things goin' to pick up for sure." He grinned, a wide, joyless but nonmalicious showing of his teeth. "Like the man say on the radio, good times just around the corner. Just don't know where that corner is, but sure would like to take my turn at it." He reached beneath the counter, moved his head sideways. "One for the road, Sergeant."

"No, no thanks the same, lad. One shot of that poison will do me. Stay out of trouble now, Jappy."

Jappy watched the large blue-uniformed man walk slowly, steadily along the bar and out the door. He watched O'Malley without anger or resentment or feelings of any kind. O'Malley was just a fact of life, and as the facts of Jappy's life went, O'Malley was neither particularly good nor particularly bad.

Sergeant O'Malley tossed a pack of cigarettes to the young patrolman beside him.

Levine returned the cigarettes. "Thanks, Sergeant, but I don't smoke."

"Ah, don't smoke? Is it smoking seems like a bad thing to you?"

Carefully, trying to avoid offense, Aaron said, "Well, I still play a little ball, and smoking cuts my wind."

"I was afraid you might be worrying it would stunt your growth," O'Malley said caustically. "Take a right at the next corner. Fine. There now, see the little candy store down the street? Pull over just across from it." O'Malley, between puffs of smoke, regarded his driver thoughtfully for a moment. "Take a walk over there, lad, and say good evening to Mr. Horowitz. He's a nice enough old gent and always glad to see the boys in blue. He'll be especially glad to see one speaks his own language, in a manner of speaking."

Aaron nodded. "Right, Sergeant."

Sergeant O'Malley held out Aaron's nightstick. "Take it along with you, officer. Puts the fear of God into the niggers and makes Mr. Horowitz feel a little more secure. See he gives you a nice glass of that egg-cream soda you people like so much."

Aaron could feel O'Malley's hard stare along the back of his

15

neck as he walked with his long, crazy-legged strides. He was conscious of the weight of the stick in his hand and the thumping of the .38 against his thigh.

The candy store was dimly lit, small, scruffy, dirty. A bell jingled as he opened the door. Two black men turned to regard him, their faces stiff, sullen, disinterested. Their eyes slid from Aaron to each other and as though by silent, mutual agreement, they concentrated once more on the heavy, chipped mugs of coffee.

The old man was short, round, frazzled. His hair stood in thin bushy clumps around his skullcap; his wire-framed glasses magnified watery, colorless eyes. His brows were thick and unruly and dominated a broad, wrinkled forehead. He leaned from behind the chipped marble counter, raised his hands in a familiar gesture of greeting that seemed almost supplication.

"So, *nu*, officer, what you'd like to have? A nice ice-cream soda, it's such a hot night for October." As he spoke, his hands snatched at a tall glass, grabbed eagerly at an ice-cream scoop.

"Make it a plain seltzer, please."

"A plain seltzer?" The old man seemed offended. "You should have a little something in it, maybe a little milk and some syrup, so we make you nice chocolate or vanilla egg cream maybe?"

Aaron shook his head, glanced at the two black men who were listening but pretending not. "Just plain seltzer, really." His fingers slid two pennies across the marble counter.

Surprised, the old man carefully slid the pennies back toward Aaron's hand and looked fully into his face for the first time. "*Nu*, you insult me. You come here to insult me, you can't take a glass of seltzer by me." The round magnified eyes blinked rapidly, then held steady, puzzled by Aaron's face. "*Gott in himmel*, a *landsman*. So what are you doing in that? That blue, a boy like you."

The two Negroes slid their attention between the two white men, one old and funny-talking, the other nothing but a policeman. They couldn't understand the old man's surprise or what he was talking about or what connection had suddenly sprung between them. Whatever it was, the two black men didn't get it; whatever it was, the two white men seemed comfortable with each other, like old friends.

16

"Everyone has to live," Aaron told the old man apologetically.

Mr. Horowitz held his head to one side for a moment as he considered Aaron's words. Then he nodded and turned away. "Yah, yah, true. Everyone got to live." He reached up, withdrew a pack of Camels from the cigarette rack. "So, I hope this is the right brand for you. If not, you tell me. I got others." His gnarled fingers indicated his wares.

Aaron shook his head. "Thanks, but I don't smoke."

"You don't smoke?" the old man asked incredulously. "What's you don't smoke got to do with the price of apples?" He reached for Aaron's hand, pressed the package of cigarettes into the large palm along with a five-dollar bill. "*Nu*, you got something to learn maybe they didn't teach you yet?" He jerked his head to one side, turned his body away from his customers, cupped his hand around his mouth and motioned Aaron closer to him.

"You tell them, please, you tell them not six this month. My wife, she had to go to the doctor twice this week." He held up two fingers for emphasis. "Twice this week alone and that *shtunk*, the fees he charges, he should die choking on money."

Aaron placed the cigarettes and the money back into the old man's hand and shook his head. "I just came in for a seltzer," he said.

The old man shrugged. "Look, *boychik*, it ain't nothin' to do with you. Ain't nothin' to do with me neither if you want to know the truth. I'm *glad* the boys come around. This way *everyone* knows they have to behave themselves." His eyes moved sideways toward the two men, still hunched over coffee cups. "It ain't you who picks up, then it's somebody else. It's the way of life. You'll do yourself a favor, you'll do me a favor, just do what's expected." He pressed Aaron's fingers tightly around the pack of cigarettes and the money, held his hand for a moment, gave it a squeeze and released it. "It's the way things are. I'm grateful God should be so good to me I got my health." He turned now to the two black men and smiled. "You're finished the coffee now, gentlemen, you'll give me, please, that's five cents each, and I'll wash up the cups and tell you good night so I can go home and go to bed."

The two men stood slowly, regarded the old man, then Aaron, then each other. Wordless, the taller of the two dug into a torn pocket, fingered around inside the lining and came up with a dime, which he placed, somewhat regretfully, on the counter. Then they left and the bell on the door jangled as they shut it behind them.

"So, *nu*, a Jewish policeman. When I think of policemen in the old country . . ." Mr. Horowitz put his hands on either side of his face and rocked his head from side to side. He studied Aaron for a moment, his face softened and he said kindly, "Look, don't be so upset by this, this with the cigarette package. A little here, a little there, things run nice and smooth. The *schwartzes* know the police look after things, so I ain't got no problems with them. It's worth it to me, you fellas stop in now and then, have a soda and a *shmooz*."

Aaron's hand felt clammy and sticky on the cellophane package. The bill was damp against his palm. "This"—he held the pack up—"this is regular?"

The old man laughed; his face registered an old man's sympathy for the innocence before him. "Ah, you're just a baby, *mein kind,* a little boy in that big, tall policeman uniform. How old, twenty-one, twenty-two? Me, I'm an old man. I lived a long time already. Things is the way they are. You're a good boy, a nice boy. You come back next time, I make you a real nice egg cream. Now, ah, now, I close up and go home and go to sleep. At six A.M. I open, six A.M., and it's very late now. You go now, go now."

Aaron felt the weight of the graft in the palm of his hand, wet, sticky, unclean. He handed it to O'Malley without looking at him.

"That little cheap son of a bitch," O'Malley said. "Five? What'd he tell ya, that his wife was sick?"

Aaron stared straight ahead through the windshield. "Yes," he said, "Mr. Horowitz said his wife was sick."

"Ah, well, I'll see him myself tomorrow night." He held the cigarettes before Aaron's face, close to his nose. "And you *still* don't smoke?" he asked ambiguously.

Aaron turned his face to the sergeant. "No," he said coldly, not trusting his voice; it had thinned with tension. "No, I *still* don't smoke."

"Well, aren't I the lucky one then, getting all these nice packs of butts for myself. Drive straight on down the avenue."

O'Malley leaned comfortably back against the seat and

loosened the collar of his tunic. The plaid shirt beneath his uniform was too damn heavy and warm for the weather and the weather was too heavy and warm for the time of year. He would be glad when it turned cold and raw. The hard winds would clear the streets of the damn black niggers, all leaning against the lampposts, sprawled the length of outdoor stairways, leaning and sitting and lounging on garbage cans or on the curb or along the running boards and fenders of cars like they were glued in place. He'd never seen a race for just leaning on things like these people.

As Aaron Levine carefully followed his directions, O'Malley scanned the scene through the side window. A bum hurriedly hid the brown paper bag behind his back, nodded his head toward the patrol car in that funny, silly way they had about them. Ah, the hell with that damn fool. O'Malley was not about to collar some jig for drinking from a common bottle. Not at ten-thirty at night. He glared at the son of a bitch just long enough and hard enough to let him know he had fooled no one, especially not Sergeant O'Malley. Couldn't let them think you weren't on to them at all times. Well, they knew him up here at any rate. A hard man. Yeah, watch out for Sergeant O'Malley, he's a ball breaker. Damn right too they were to think it; it was the only way to deal with them. It was what they expected and what he gave them.

"What the hell is that up ahead there?" O'Malley asked. He pointed to the left side of the street.

"Looks like a jump-rope game," Levine said. He braked lightly and waited for the sergeant's instruction.

"Ah, for Christ's sake, now look at them. All them little girls should be home and asleep. Just pull up here for a minute and I'll have a word with them."

There were four of them: two steady enders and two steady jumpers. The steady enders were the smallest, no more than seven or eight years old, with big, dark evasive eyes. The tiniest dropped her hand and the rope dangled from it as she watched, from beneath her lowered face, the police sergeant approach.

"Now what are you little girls doing out this time of night?" Brian O'Malley asked in what he thought was a warm and friendly tone.

The three smallest girls studied the sidewalk intently, then

19

looked up, not at Brian but at the oldest girl. She was a slim light-tan girl with a head full of tiny tight braids which stuck out at all angles from her skull.

She spoke for all of them in a lazy blurred voice. "We just jumpin'. Ain't doin' no harm." She mumbled but her expression was sharp and defiant and her tan eyes met him without wavering.

"Just jumpin', is it? And do you know what time of night it is? You should be home in your beds asleep."

The smallest girl turned and ran, dragging the rope behind her. The oldest girl called after her, "You let that rope go, you dum' Lainie. You drop it, hear? That *my* rope we wuz usin'."

She ran forward swiftly and gracefully and snatched the rope from the sidewalk, and as she returned to where Brian and the two other girls stood, she slowly and deliberately wound the rope around her arm and over her shoulder into a loop. She returned her gaze to O'Malley and waited.

"Well, where do you live?"

The second-smallest girl giggled, pointed across the street.

"Well, get going home then. Right now, missy."

The child grabbed the other girl's arm and pulled her. "She my sister. She live there too."

"Well, isn't that a wonder. Get off home, then, the two of you and quick." He turned from the sight of them running into their building. This was another matter altogether standing here confronting him. Thirteen, maybe fourteen, she stood, feet wide apart in broken shoes, flimsy sweater and dirty skirt over thin body, head raised slightly, fingers threading the rope over her shoulder restlessly.

"Well, now, what about you?"

"Didn't do nothin'. Just standing out here. Didn't do nothin'."

There was a stretched tension about the girl. Her body, thin and limber, seemed about to spring, either at him or from him. Her voice was tight and challenging. The little bitch didn't come high as his shoulder, and though she'd said nothing openly defiant, there was nothing but defiance and insolence coming from her.

"You watch that mouth of yours or it's liable to feel some knuckles," O'Malley said quietly. "Where do you live, or don't you have a home? You some little alley cat, or what?"

She seemed to go pale. It was an odd thing but sometimes these yellow ones went pale and it never failed to surprise him.

"Ain't no alley cat," she said tightly. "Got a home like everybody else."

She didn't flinch or grimace or make a sound when he wrapped his strong hand around the slender arm and squeezed, deliberately inflicting a hard, mean pain.

"Then turn your black ass around and head for your home before I take my nightstick and start knocking some of them braids off a' your kinky little head."

He shoved her from him and watched her closely. Her eyes glassed over with stark hatred; her mouth twitched but she raised her head and walked past him slowly, with that deliberateness he had noticed before. The rope hung over one thin shoulder and she rested her hand inside the loop. He watched her walk down the block, a child but not a child. Nearer to a woman; nearer to a black woman. Her backside swayed, high-assed, with that peculiar sway-back that emphasized the hard, lean but rounded buttocks. Christ, it got to him. Made him think of someone else. Some other high-assed black woman with black firm flesh.

He watched the girl turn toward the entrance of a tenement, stop, face toward him. He couldn't see her clearly, just the dark outline of her slim young body, but the contempt was in the rigid posture and the sudden way she turned, head high, dismissing him by entering the doorway. He ought to follow after her and give her a taste of his nightstick. Right across that high black little ass. Little bitch. Little black bitch.

Brian O'Malley returned to the patrol car. He strained to get his voice normal. "Little bastards ought to be home in bed instead of out on the streets this time of night. Well, what can you expect anyways? Look what they come from. Drive along 118th, give us a right on Lenox."

O'Malley removed his hat and wiped his forehead with the back of his hand and sleeve. He could feel sweat down his back, under his arms, in his crotch. Memory, moist and hot, flooded him.

The first real attraction had been the over-all darkness of her skin: all over her body, a smooth, even brown, her breasts as dark as her arms, her arms as dark as her stomach, one

21

smooth stretch of color. Rounded, all of her rounded, all of her a wondrous combination of hardness and softness. Firm flesh which was not like any flesh he had ever known: it was flesh which had moved *toward* him, at him.

O'Malley shoved his hat on, pulled the visor low over his forehead. Levine slowed down, anticipating a red light.

O'Malley turned his attention to the Jew. Who the hell did this long-legged little kike know anyway, to get his ass in a patrol car not even a full year on the job? He should be out pounding his shoes, not resting his behind.

Raucous laughter, female, high and sustained and uninhibited, cut through all other street noises and thoughts and brought O'Malley back to the inside of his brain, to contemplation of that despised, degraded and degrading body. His hands rested lightly on his knees, moved, his fingers cupped kneecaps which turned into dark, hard, mysterious breasts. His tongue flicked his lips dreamily.

You wanna taste, baby? Go ahead, baby. Ain't you never tasted? Man, you ain't never lived. You poor policeman, think you know everything when you don't know nothing. But Lola will teach you.
Moist, thick, sour, sticky, repellent. But still . . .

His large hands kneaded his kneecaps but they were not pliant and wildly obscene: she had a marvelous obscenity of flesh beneath the skin, nipples leaping hard at his touch. Belly round and flat at the same time. Muscular. Muscles moving easily, drawing in the flesh so that her whole rib cage seemed to pierce the surface of dark skin when she writhed in a certain way.

You like to see tricks, baby lover man? Ain't nobody showed you no tricks? Just one, two, three, out and away. Shit, honey, that's nothin'. That's not even getting there. Getting there's the most fun, the ride, the trip on the way. Let Lola show you, take you there. Oh, nice, nice, not yet, slow down, lover man, slow torture, let it be, right to your toes. Feel it, lover, feel it where you didn't know you could. Lola gonna make you feel. Oh, baby, can't you just die, what Lola do for you?

22

• •

There was static on the car radio, a voice spoke some incomprehensible message, but they ignored it since it hadn't been prefaced by their car number.

"You want me to continue along Lenox, Sarge?"

O'Malley snapped his head around. "Huh? Oh. Yeah, yeah, just move along some. Let's give Patrolman Fitzgerald a see."

Patrolman Fitzgerald was where he was supposed to be, clearly visible, clearly on the job.

He saluted casually. "Hot night, Sarge, for the time of the year."

"Yeah, it is." He scanned the memorandum book which was presented for his initialing. Fitzgerald had a nice round clear hand. "Here, what's this all about? Here, at nine-twenty you found Jones's grocery store opened? What was that all about?"

"The old man is getting a bit absent-minded, Sergeant. He left the light burning and the door on the latch. I sent a neighborhood kid up to his flat to fetch him. He's getting on to seventy-six or seventy-seven, you know. Just took himself off to bed without locking up. I gave him a talking-to, you know."

O'Malley peered brightly from beneath his visor. "And what did he give you in return?"

Fitzgerald clutched his breast theatrically. "Oh, now, Sergeant O'Malley, what is it you're thinking? Would I be accepting anything from the poor old gent?"

"You'd accept his eyeballs if you could sell them to a blind man."

Fitzgerald said bitterly, "Ah, the old man is so damn old he hasn't the sense he was born with. Didn't even have the decency to tell me 'thank you, officer' and that's a fact."

"It's facts I go by, Fitz," O'Malley told him. "And they have a way of making themselves known."

"Sergeant, you know me." Fitzgerald spread his hands wide and his nightstick dangled from its leather thong.

"Yeah, I do and that's the trouble. Well, good night, Fitz. And watch yourself, lad, because you never know who else might be doing just that."

Again, innocence accused, Fitzgerald's tone was injured. "Ah, Sergeant O'Malley, I've no idea at all what you mean."

23

O'Malley didn't respond. He'd gone through the routine with Fitzgerald automatically. He tried to distract himself with words but the images and memories and flesh-longing encompassed him again as he settled in the patrol car and he could not distract himself from his body. His brain filled with remembered sensuality and he sat, slightly dazed, in the dank, sour automobile.

"Sergeant O'Malley, you want me to take a left on 127th?"

It was the second time Aaron had asked the question, but O'Malley still didn't answer. Since he could only go right or left and stay within their precinct, Aaron pumped the brake pedal and signaled for a left turn.

"Go straight ahead," O'Malley said in a strange thick voice.

"But we're on 127th."

"Go straight ahead. Do what you're told."

Aaron didn't ask any questions but he felt a slow creeping chill down his spine as they crossed the barrier into the 32nd Precinct. The city was defined by precinct lines: each territory marked out, assigned, defined. He felt as threatened as though he were in a foreign land where an incomprehensible language was spoken. The simple fact was that a radio car from the 28th had no legitimate reason to casually patrol the streets of the 32nd. At each corner he hesitated, slowed, waited for the order to turn around and head back.

"Keep going to 129th," O'Malley instructed.

At 129th, O'Malley directed a right turn. "Pull up here. No, a bit farther down, in back of that Dodge. All right, all right, cut the motor, Levine."

O'Malley was tense and irritated but more tense than anything else. He blotted sweat from his upper lip, glanced through the windshield, then through the back window. His tension was contagious and Aaron looked around too, afraid of what might be coming.

"I'll not be gone more than a few minutes," O'Malley said.

Aaron had to suppress a crazy urge to plead with O'Malley not to leave. What if a precinct car came by? What would he say? What the hell was he doing here anyway?

"I just have to take care of a personal matter," O'Malley said. "Sit tight and keep your eyes straight ahead. You don't know nothin' about this. Just take it easy."

24

"But, Sergeant, what if a precinct car comes by?" he couldn't resist asking.

O'Malley glanced at his wristwatch. A quarter to eleven. Good timing. "There'll be no precinct car. Relax and keep your trap shut, Levine. And your eyes straight ahead."

O'Malley disappeared somewhere behind the car. Aaron couldn't resist the urge to watch him through the rear-view mirror. He entered the second building behind the car before Aaron turned around and stared out the back window.

Swell. Now the stupid Irish bastard was shaking down people *outside* his precinct. All Aaron needed was for the regular precinct man to come along and start asking questions. He wouldn't know what to say. What do you say to these crazy dumbbells?

In a whisper loud enough for God to hear, Aaron prayed, "Please, please. Let him come back in a minute. Let him just take a leak in the hallway and come back and let us get out of here before one of those other *gonifs* comes and starts asking *me* questions. What do I know about all this? *Please!*"

TWO

The strong sharp odor of black enveloped Brian O'Malley completely. He filled his lungs in short hard gasps, breathed through his mouth, tried to avoid the repugnant sourness of the tenement hallway but the urine, sweat, grease, body, animal smell encompassed him, clung to him, entered him. He stopped halfway up the wooden staircase and listened, not to the muffled sounds of radios behind the walls or of people moving about.

His hand moved down, gently pressed against the hardness which had, unbidden, throbbed against the fabric of his trousers. It was the first time he had touched himself since the sight of the girl and he was not surprised. The hardness was from within the center of himself, where no resolve or regret could ever penetrate; there was only the one destroying desire for the soft-hard body of the flat-bellied brown woman on the top floor.

He rapped his knuckles sharply on her door, pressed his face close to the fetid wood. He heard a shuffling movement, a sigh, and then her voice, heavy as he remembered it.

"Who dere?"

His lips practically tasted the rotting wood. "Open up, Lola, it's me. It's Sergeant O'Malley. Open up the door."

The voice seemed to whisper from within the wood itself into his ear. "What you want?"

His shoulder leaned heavily with a terrible physical awareness of the barrier between them. "Open up before I rip the door off."

He heard the lock turn, felt the metal doorknob turn within the palm of his hand. She stepped back and watched him as he entered the room.

26

Added to all the other odors, there now assaulted him the odor of the woman. Beads of sweat stood on her broad dark forehead. There were large wet half-moons under each arm of the shapeless, colorless wrapper. She drank deeply from the glass of gin and that too filtered through her body, came from the pores of the skin, mixed with other smells, blatant, repellent, maddening, mysterious.

She leaned against the table at the center of the small dark room and said without expression, "Ain't seen you in a long time." She moved to the sink, poured more liquor into her glass, leaned back. It was a crazy room: a kitchen, but at the same time a living room, with heavy upholstered furniture.

The sink, the fact that she stood there, leaned against the sink, made Brian feel that they were in a kitchen and that, too, added to his growing sense of excitement. There was only one small light in the room, a yellowish bulb which hung from a wire in the ceiling and which moved slightly from side to side, as though she'd brushed it with her hand. It cast shadows over everything, cast her face into ugly shadow. It was an ugly face, wide, placid, unfocused. Her very placidity and ugliness excited him. The richness of her naked arm, the knowledge that beneath the thin fabric of her wrapper was that brown moist mystery of flesh, choked him. His hand moved along the buttons of his tunic; he slid his belt around so that his holstered gun pressed the small of his back.

Watching him, she moved now; she moved her head back and forth slightly, but so slightly he wasn't sure he had seen it, and if he had seen it, the movement, of denial, only increased his sense of purpose and his growing sense of brutality.

Here, in the kitchen, standing up, clothed, her, pressed against the sink, shaking her head, no no no. His eyes stayed on her full lips as his fingers undid the buttons of his fly.

"Don't shake your head at me, you bitch," he told her and grabbed her heavy face, held it still.

"You don't understand, baby," she said. The lazy slurred speech, not alarmed, reconciled, explained. "I been trying to tell you something, man, but you ain't listening." Her voice breathed into his face with the hot steaming smell of her. She moved from him, a step away, looked down at her own body. "Okay, man, see for yourself, then."

She held the robe wide from her naked body, showed herself to him. She hooked her thumbs inside the narrow band of elastic which encircled her waist and she jutted her pelvis forward. He watched, repelled, fascinated, drawn by the openness with which she displayed the stained sanitary napkin. He was appalled by her frankness; more appalled by the quickening of his own lust.

It was some primal force, unknown, unknowable, that made the hot flesh within his hand swell and throb, pound with blood toward the blood he had seen, whose tantalizing pungent odor entered his nostrils with the familiar earthiness of an animal beckoning him. It was the powerful awareness of the presence of that forbidden blood that drove him toward her again.

There was a different tone in her voice now, something urgent, bordering on fear. "Hey, listen there a minute, man. Ain't what you think. Ain't the monthly blues, honey. See, I had to get me this operation. Got me socked up and this old woman down the street, she done this job on me just two days ago." She turned, lifted the glass, held it for him to see, to confirm her story. "See, I been drinking gin steady." She swallowed hugely, eyes closed, head tossed back, then jerked forward to assure him. "Well, you know I don't drink like this. But she didn't do me so good, that old woman, and I got me plenny pain and trouble." The slurring voice tightened and she seemed suddenly, starkly sober. "Hey, man, you ain't listenin' what I been telling you. I been hurt pretty bad. I been cut up inside."

He heard nothing but the sound of her voice; not her words; not her plea; not her meaning. He reached out and ripped the wrapper from her. The pleading sound reached some dark corner of his need; he responded in a rough, hoarse, grating voice, and this too, this hard sound of himself, was what he needed.

"Don't give me no shit, Lola. We done it before when you were like this."

Bodily memory of that other time overwhelmed him. One hand felt his own flesh, smooth, swelling, burning. His other hand tore the narrow elastic band from her body, tossed the bloody napkin with its reeking gelatinous fumes away from her.

28

"No, no, that was different. Please, oh, God, no, listen, I'm all tore up inside."

He responded relentlessly to the begging panic sound of her with his own deep-throated unbearable hardness. "Stand still, you whore. I'm gonna come out the other bloody side of you. Damn it, stand still!"

His hand dug at the wire-strong hairy wetness of her body, fingers felt the heavy pollution of blood. His eyes locked tight. He inhaled the terrible blackness of every part of her and he tried to plunge into her body, but she moved, writhed away. Brutally, he grabbed at a firm full breast and twisted.

Her words fell about his head, her mouth touched his ear, the wetness of her pleas fell about his cheeks, his neck, as she tried to fight him off. "Oh, Gawd, no, Gawd, no, Gawd, no!"

Over and over, it seemed, the phrase was repeated. He heard the breaking of glass, somewhere. She held up a jagged slash of glass before his eyes but he didn't see it. It disappeared from his view too swiftly, just the faint vapor of gin drifted into his awareness and the moist and rubbery feel of her flesh within his fingers and the feel of his own slippery hardness meeting her.

The woman's muffled scream covered his own terrible gasp but he knew he had made some strangulated sound. He felt sound travel through his chest and throat, felt it inside his mouth. Not a sound of pain; there was no real pain, just an instantaneous numbness which shot down his thighs and into his navel and filled his groin.

The flesh within his hand, his flesh, changed; no longer hard and firm and throbbing.

Brian O'Malley raised his right hand to his face, stared at the bloody mutilated part of his body in total nonrecognition and disbelief. He looked dumbly at the gushing blood which spouted through his opened fly, ran ceaselessly down his legs. He clutched both hands over the open wound, pressed the severed flesh back into place, moved his head slowly from side to side, would not look down, could not view the nightmare come true.

"No. No. No. No."

It was a prayer, a plea, an incantation.

"Please. Please. Please. Please."

The girl watched him in horror and she moaned with him, mistook his careful, glassy-eyed movement toward her, and, to save herself from whatever she feared of him at this point, she lunged once more with the jagged piece of broken glass and ripped open Brian O'Malley's jugular vein.

She moved blindly backwards from what she had done, from the new fountain of blood, from the terrible cackling sound of the dying man. As she moved, she shook her head, whispered, much as he had done, "No. No. No. No." Tried to deny reality. She covered her eyes with both of her arms, threw her head back, her arms high in the air over her head.

As she took another step back, her thighs hit against the window sill and her large body stumbled backwards, fell backwards, crashed backwards through the opened window. Lola Jason landed four stories below with a sharp crash into the garbage-laden air shaft of the tenement house.

THREE

Aaron Levine stared vacantly through the windshield of the patrol car, transfixed by a spot of light which was reflected from his own dimmed headlights on the shiny bumper of the Dodge in front of him. Enclosed in a magic childhood incantation, he was protected from whatever dangers the surly, unpleasant Sergeant O'Malley might inflict.

"What the hell are you doing here?"

Levine, taken totally by surprise, twisted to his left and was confronted by the anger and suspicion of a ranking officer. A lieutenant? A captain? Which?

"Just . . . sitting here, Captain." The higher rank was safer. It was strange, some part of Aaron's brain, the spectator, remote and removed from events, noted how automatically he had chosen the higher rank even in the middle of his terror.

The face which glared from the window of the precinct patrol car directly beside him was large, broad, topped by unruly red eyebrows. The lips, set into the heavy face, were thin and pulled back, almost animal-like, in tight anger.

"You're from the Twenty-eighth and you're 'just sitting' in *my* precinct?"

A foreign invader. My God, I'm a foreign invader. Aaron literally could not think of anything to say. For the past fifteen minutes, he had been trying to think up excuses should just such an event occur. But he was not devious. He had failed to come up with a single plausible or even implausible reason for this gross departmental violation and so had let himself lapse into vacuity and magic.

The captain spoke to his driver, then heavily pulled himself from his car and leaned in to examine Aaron's face with a narrow-eyed look of accusation that made guilt roil in the pit of Aaron's stomach.

"Who is it you're driving for?"

The captain's voice had a familiar, baiting quality; the hard grating assurance of a man who knew everything and you'd better not try to kid him.

There must be some accepted and acceptable response besides the truth. But Aaron, his brain racing over the emptiness of his experience, could only search fruitlessly and finally admit the truth.

"For Sergeant O'Malley. Sergeant Brian O'Malley."

Aaron Levine felt the vaporous guilt solidify now. He was now an informer and would be forever marked informer. He had violated a code he did not understand, would never understand, had not been made a party to and did not even know for sure existed.

"Oh, for Christ's sake, that stupid son of a bitch. Did he go up to that nigger whore's apartment?"

The captain's tone changed. There was a definite relaxing of the suspicious belligerence. Still tight, still hard, there was beneath his words a sense of amused scorn. Aaron didn't know what to answer and kept his mouth locked.

The captain, grossly fat, stuck his face close to Aaron's. "He'll never learn to stay away from trouble. Well, maybe it's for the best I go myself."

Aaron nodded dumbly.

The captain considered Aaron for a moment. He was a miserable-looking policeman and hardly could meet his eye. "Take it easy, lad," the captain said. "You only done what your sergeant told you to do. I'll straighten out the sergeant. You just keep your mouth shut about this. Got that now?"

It was what everyone kept telling him: Keep your mouth shut.

"Yes, sir, Captain."

Again the captain regarded him and this time he frowned. "What's your name anyway, officer?"

Aaron felt nailed: identified now. "Patrolman Aaron Levine, sir."

The captain's lips pulled back into what was probably a smile. "Aaron Levine is it? Mother of God, we've got us an Aaron Levine. And driving for Brian. Well, well." He leaned heavily close. "Keep your nose clean and your mouth shut, son."

"I will. Oh, I will," Aaron assured him and the captain, assured, left.

The precinct patrol car backed into the space behind Aaron. The driver had given no sign of friendliness, he was no commiserator. That's okay, Aaron thought; I'm not looking for friends. Just to get out of here. Idly, nervously trying not to think of the moment when he would be alone in the car with Sergeant O'Malley again, he turned the radio up a bit.

The captain's voice, hollow, loud, strange, filled the air. At first, Aaron didn't know where it was coming from; then. he got out of the car and looked up.

"Charlie! Charlie, for the love of God, come up here. In a hurry!"

The other policeman ran toward the tenement and Aaron started after him, but a second later, the captain's head reappeared and his voice ordered, "You. You get back in your car and don't leave it!"

That's okay with me, Aaron thought; I don't want any part of it. He nibbled on a piece of cuticle around the edge of his left index finger, bit too deeply, felt a sharp needle of pain. God, he wished they were on their way back to the precinct house. It was nearly time for the tour to end. He never thought that filthy precinct would feel like home, but it was where he wanted to be right now.

The voice from the radio speaker was thin but insistent and caught his attention through the heavy customary static by its urgency. Patrolman Aaron Levine leaned forward and strained to pick out the words.

"Assist patrolman. Armed robbery in progress. All cars in vicinity of Lenox Avenue and 131st Street respond immediately. Approach with caution. Two armed men."

Words penetrated: liquor store; two armed men; patrolman in need of assistance; approach with caution; all cars in vicinity. The call was being repeated as Aaron turned the key, turned over the motor. He left Sergeant O'Malley to the fat captain and the patrolman named Charlie. He gave no thought whatever to what he was riding toward. He knew only that he wanted to get away from whatever O'Malley had become involved in.

Patrolman Charles Gannon could not take it in. He could not make sense of what he saw and he turned his face, mouth opened, to Captain Peter Hennessy.

"Get a blanket," the captain told him, and when he failed to move, the captain's heavy hand shoved him toward a closet or another small room, Gannon couldn't distinguish which. "Look in there, look around, there must be a blanket somewhere. Move, man, move!"

Gannon dragged a thin gray blanket from beneath a cot. The yellow light cast by the single bulb moved and swung in crazy directions as the cord became tangled somehow in the captain's hand. Captain Hennessy reached up to steady it, burned his fingers, cursed. The light cast terrible crazy patterns over the blood-covered body of Brian O'Malley.

"Is he dead?" Gannon asked stupidly. Of course, he knew Brian was dead. Not just the frozen eyes, the heavy pools of blood, but everything about him spelled death.

Captain Hennessy didn't bother to answer. He bent, breathed short heavy gasps, motioned to Gannon. "Get him on the blanket, for God's sake. We've got to get him out of here."

That seemed the necessary and urgent and vital thing. Charlie Gannon, completely unaware of the mess on his own uniform, lifted O'Malley's head and shoulders, felt the captain lift the dead legs. They placed the body on the blanket, which Gannon pulled close and neatly tucked in loose edges. Charlie bit the tip of his tongue in concentration; he wanted to make the bundle firm and secure and tight.

"Stand up now, Charlie. Stand up, man, and listen to me."

Captain Hennessy's face was red with exertion but there was a yellow circle around his mouth and his lips had an almost bluish cast in the peculiar light.

"Did you see what she did to Brian?" Charlie Gannon nodded; he had seen blood. He wasn't sure, exactly, what else he'd seen. "We've got to get him out of here completely. Do you understand what I'm telling you, Charlie?"

Charlie Gannon nodded, then stopped, then slowly shook his head from side to side. He was a slight, wiry man, and when he looked at the captain, he had to lean back somewhat. "What is it that happened here, anyway, Cap?" Some slow and terrible realization of unnamable deeds began to fill him. His small eyes began to rotate as though to encompass the event.

Captain Hennessy cut him off swiftly. His hands grasped the collar of Gannon's jacket and jerked at him so that they stared into each other's eyes.

"We've got to get Brian out of here. The black whore who did this to him is down in the alley. I don't know what went on here and I don't want to find out. The thing is, we've got to get Brian out of here. Whatever happened didn't happen here, Charlie. You got that now, lad? Good boy, good boy." He released Gannon and nodded.

"Yes, Captain, you're right, you're right. Let's get him out."

Gannon was very strong. His small size was deceptive. "I can manage him nicely," he said, speaking to the bundle on the floor. He braced his legs, balanced as the weight was placed across his back and shoulders, swayed a moment, balanced again. Irrationally, Gannon said, "I could have been a fireman had I chosen, Captain. Did you know that? But instead I chose the Department."

Hennessy went first, shielding the patrolman and the dead sergeant with the bulk of his own body. His voice was murderous and he roared at the few dark curious faces which peered from behind slightly opened doors. "Get the fuck back inside, you bastards, or I'll take a club to your skulls." They believed him and doors closed quickly. He slammed the butt of his jack against a door or two, just to be sure they believed him.

He turned once at the sound of a door reopening and Gannon stumbled into him and nearly lost his burden. The sight of the stumbling policeman, the strangeness of the lurchings of the large captain, terrified whoever had ventured to look and the door slammed and locked above them.

They reached street level, and in the dark, the captain leaned against the hall wall for a moment and said to Gannon, though more to himself, "Let me think now, let me think a minute. Oh, Jesus, let me think a minute."

There was no one on the street. The patrol car stood, empty and dark and waiting. He walked quickly to it, opened the back door, scanned the block, signaled to Gannon, then stood back and watched as the patrolman placed the body in the back of the car.

Captain Hennessy settled into the front seat without glancing behind him. He heard a soft hiccuping from Gannon, who grasped the steering wheel with both hands, stared straight ahead and asked him, almost querulously, "What are we to do with him, Captain? Now we've got him, what are we to do with him?"

"Shut up and let me think, will you, just shut up, Charlie."

He stared straight ahead into the empty space before them, then turned to face Gannon and said, "Jesus, Mary and Joseph, where the hell is the sheeny?"

The sound was not as loud as when he practiced shooting targets in the firing range. There the report of his revolver was enlarged by the closed-in area and echoed and re-echoed inside his head. But here the noise was dissipated by the openness of the street and sounded like firecrackers or a car back-firing or a kid's cap gun.

Patrolman Levine held the heavy .38 in his right hand, carefully kept his finger off the trigger. He crouched behind his patrol car, bounced on his long legs just enough to enable him to see into the liquor store. There was one other patrol car beside his and the occupants of that car, two patrolmen, lay sprawled on the sidewalk outside the liquor store. Through the brightly lit window, in his quick bouncing rise and then crouch, Aaron saw another policeman inside the store, on his back. Dead, from what Aaron, in some cool, dispassionate judgment, could determine. With a surprising, shocking sense of recognition, he had a quick glimpse of the two gunmen: the two Negroes who had sat in Horowitz' candy store, hunched over coffee cups. That made it all the more unreal: he *recognized* them. How could they have caused all this carnage?

Carnage. It was the word that formed inside Aaron's brain. He could see blood, inside the store, where the owner was probably dead or dying; outside, the policemen. One of the Negroes, Aaron observed in a quick bounce, was bleeding from a wounded arm; in one split-second observation, Aaron saw blood oozing between the man's fingers as he held the wound.

There was a soft, low moan, a whimper which drifted from one of the policemen on the sidewalk. He's alive; he needs help. Aaron wanted to stand up, hold up his hands: fins. Hey,

36

guys, fins, time out, let me see to this guy, okay. He's out of it, okay. As though this was all just some kind of game and not real and he would play peacemaker or referee or whatever. But the sense of crazy reality kept him from standing up, from approaching the wounded man.

There were the two Negroes. Aaron wondered why they hadn't thought to turn out the lights in the liquor store. The lights blazed and every time the men moved he could catch a glimpse of them. He tried not to wonder anything at all about them; he slid his long body along the gutter; he became sharply aware of the smell of dog dirt on his clothing. The policeman began to cry now, to mumble and sob the way a confused child would. Aaron felt a new surge of emotion now: anger. Hey, listen, you bastards, this guy is really hurt. Enough is enough.

Suddenly they burst through the front door of the liquor store. They stared down at him; their eyes went wild. One of them, the taller, raised his hand quickly, too quickly and carelessly, for Aaron timed his shot, controlled the aim before he cocked the hammer and squeezed the trigger. He felt the rebound up along his arm. The gunman fell. His shoulder brushed Aaron's leg. His falling gun hit Aaron's foot.

The second man, the one who had been wounded, crouched behind some garbage cans. Instead of running, he crouched behind the garbage cans and shot in Aaron's direction. He had more than one gun and he fired quickly, first one then the other.

There was a loud whistling ping along the sidewalk and a chip of cement must have cut into Aaron Levine's shoulder: he felt a sharp, clean, cutting sensation. Snakelike, with an instinct he'd never tested before, he writhed to take cover behind his patrol car. There were sirens, somewhere in the distance, or close up, he couldn't judge exactly because there was a ringing sensation in his head now. He took quiet, steady and accurate aim at the exact spot where the remaining gunman would appear, and when he did, just as Aaron had calculated, Aaron squeezed the trigger and watched, without emotion and without much understanding, as the second gunman fell dead to the sidewalk.

He stood up, somewhat unsteadily, legs shaky, ice-cold. He

held the revolver in the palm of his hand, uncocked it carefully. Another patrol car was on the scene now. It was the fat captain with the hard and penetrating stare.

"That one, over there, Captain, that officer is still alive, I think," Aaron heard himself say.

"Put the revolver in your holster, son," the captain said and he did as he was told.

Other patrol cars arrived. Blue-uniformed men moved all around him. The captain told everyone what to do and Aaron didn't have to think or act anymore. He leaned against the fender of his patrol car and waited. He felt pain along his shoulder and reached up to rub the pain away. He looked with surprise at his fingers; they were wet and sticky with his own blood. Just before he lost consciousness, Aaron Levine thought, Oh, my God. I've been shot. I'm going to throw up.

The call had come insistently over the car radio and broke into the consciousness of Captain Peter Hennessy. Without looking at Brian O'Malley's body, in a calm and terrible voice that was not to be denied, he had ordered Patrolman Charlie Gannon to proceed to the scene of the liquor store holdup.

When they arrived, there were just the two cars on the scene: one was that of the two men who were lying outside the store; the other was Brian O'Malley's.

As he opened the door and sniffed the air, which was acrid with spent gunfire and the smell of dead and dying men, Captain Hennessy took a deep breath and saw his way clear.

"Now, just follow what I tell you from here on in, Charlie," he said to Gannon, "and we'll get Brian a hero's funeral out of all this."

FOUR

Automatically, Margaret O'Malley's fingers counted off the stitches: knit seven, purl two, knit two, slip one, knit one, pass the slipped stitch over. The intricate pattern took shape beneath her touch but her eyes were on some inner vision. Her brain absorbed all the various noises of her household, sorted them, then, satisfied, was able to disregard them. Her sons had quieted down. Kevin finally tossed and lunged himself into restless sleep; Martin had placidly settled in and wouldn't move again until morning.

The soft snoring of her mother-in-law was steady, though God knew, the old woman could awaken at the drop of a stitch. Margaret tried, very hard, not to look at the clock. The radio announcer gave the time, though, softly through the fabric of the speaker. She kept the radio tuned so low she could hardly hear it, but she caught the words: 10 P.M. And Roseanne not home yet.

She held the piece of work before her eyes, sighed, started the next row, then gave it up as a bad job. Her mind was too filled with her oldest daughter, Roseanne.

Mother of God, she intoned silently, let her come home within the minute. An hour over the time her father set for her and he'd kill her if he knew. And me keeping the secret for her. Wrong. It's wrong. Billy Delaney was wrong and that was the whole matter clear and simple. A great strong fair-haired boy, with a strong jaw and clear blue eyes and a way about him: that was all Roseanne cared to see. He'd come to no good, everyone else could see that. The boy'd been nothing but trouble from grade school on, and here he was, eighteen years old and put out of St. Simon's in his last year. Well,

Father Donlon was not harsh; he'd kept Billy on years more than he should have, if the truth were known. The boy had been arrested when he was twelve, stealing money from a cash register in a drugstore. If it hadn't been for his uncles and Father Donlon, he'd have been sent to reform school right then. There were other things, all along, and Father Donlon had resisted. He knew the boy's aching background. Who didn't? Poor Eileen Murphy got nothing but trouble and kids from Tommy Delaney and him nothing but a thief and a deserter. That was what was the worst thing of all. It wasn't only the men in the neighborhood agreed on that point. The women too: a deserter, left his wife and children to fend for themselves and lose the bail money that friends and relatives and neighbors, including, God knew, the O'Malleys, had put up for him, and him charged with some crime or other. Took himself off and never came back, neither alive nor dead.

But it was Tommy Delaney all over again, for hadn't he been the handsome, wise and charming boy that his oldest son, Billy Delaney, now appeared. And, oh, how could she tell Roseanne how little all that meant, how quickly it disappeared and the ugliness beneath came through.

Brian had turned to stone when first he saw the boy walking down Ryer Avenue with Roseanne. There'll be none of that one, he said; both mother and daughter avoided his cold fierce expression and the girl ran crying to her bed. It was to her that Brian issued his instructions: Keep her away from that bad piece of business, Margaret. You're the mother, that's your job.

There was the soft sound of voices just outside the window. The O'Malley apartment, at street level, opened with its own private door into a little private hallway and Margaret heard the doorknob turn, waited, strained into the strange sound-filled silence. She thanked the Holy Mother that the girl was home and vowed she would try not to say angry things, not to say all the wrong things to the girl. But, oh, sweet Jesus, it was so hard. The girl had become a stranger to her these last few months, someone she'd never known, never laughed with or cried over or rocked in her arms.

"Is that you, Roseanne?"

The door closed softly, there was a stifled cough and then

her daughter's voice, sullen, muffled, speaking from behind her hands. "Yeah, Ma." When she came into the room, pretending to be coughing, Margaret knew she was hiding her smeared lipstick. Her eyes blazed defiance and she said, before she could be accused, "Look, I know I'm late, I'm sorry. My watch is slow or something. I'm tired, Ma, I'm going to bed."

"You'll stay here and let me look at you." It wasn't the tone of voice she'd intended, but this wasn't the girl she wanted desperately to see. This was a taut, angry young girl, with blazing eyes confronting her as though she was an enemy.

"Roseanne," she tried in a softer voice, "if your dad knew what you've been up to—"

Quickly, as though she'd been waiting to attack, Roseanne said, "I haven't been 'up to' anything. For Pete's sake, I went for a walk. I'm not a child anymore. Can't I even go for a walk?"

"You've been out with Billy Delaney, haven't you?"

The deep-blue eyes, shimmering, closed; the pale full lips tightened; the girl turned her face toward the ceiling with an insulting glance of supplication.

She was so filled with herself and her own newly discovered feelings. The anger made the girl's delicate beauty intensify; the fine bones of her high cheeks showed through the stretched white skin, her delicate nostrils dilated, her dark eyes sought her mother's and held the glare without the slightest awareness or concern for the pain she could inflict.

"Oh, Roseanne," Margaret said wearily, unable to speak to the girl the way she wanted to. "You've truly time, Roseanne. You've the whole of your life before you. Billy Delaney is just one boy in all this whole wide world."

"*You* were married at seventeen." It was an accusation and a challenge and a justification. The seventeen-year-old girl shifted her weight, her hand went to a thin sharp hipbone, her chin went up.

"Yes," Margaret said sharply. "I married at seventeen but not to the likes of Billy Delaney."

"You don't know anything about Billy. You *don't*. Everyone's always been down on him because of his father."

"Everyone's down on him because of his own sweet self

41

now, Roseanne. He's not living on his father's bad name anymore. He's doing just fine making his own bad name."

"It's not fair, Ma, it's not! Everyone always picked on Billy. In the street, at school. Brother Andrew was beating him up. What did anyone expect him to do anyway?"

Margaret held her hand up and lowered her own voice. "For the love of God, Roseanne, if you don't care about the neighbors, at least let your young brothers and sister and poor old grandmother sleep undisturbed." She pretended not to see the quickly wiped at tears and choking swallow back of sobs: all this for a great thug of a boy not worth her daughter's thumbnail. She'd have to be careful; Brian didn't understand it wasn't all that easy. "Well, would you like a cup of hot tea with me and some poundcake I baked fresh this afternoon? It's a bit heavy but the flavor's nice."

"I'm not hungry."

"Ah, you're falling away to skin and bone." She bit her lip, tried to be light and casual. "But I guess that's fashionable these days, isn't it?"

The girl seemed to be turning words over in her mind; her mouth worked for a moment, then finally she said, "You might as well know, Ma. He wants to marry me. And I want to marry him."

Margaret shook her head and felt a little more sure of herself. That was such nonsense she could deal with it. "No, no," she said. "We'll hear no such talk in this house. Why, you're a mere slip of a girl and you've just the year to finish at St. Simon's and you've a chance to get out into the world a little bit. Why, you're the champion in your typing class. Think of the nice office you can work in. Ah, Roseanne, you're a silly little girl still, sometimes. Off to bed now and mind you don't wake your sister."

The tears spilled down Roseanne's face now and she rubbed at them so hard with the back of her hand it seemed she was trying to jam them back into her eyes. "Oh, Ma, I love him. I *love* him. Have you forgotten what it's like to be young and in love?" Through the tears, there was a hard glint in Roseanne's eyes; a woman's smile flashed on her child lips, mean and unpleasant, and her voice was small and unfamiliar. "Have you forgotten what it's like to be *loved?*"

42

Margaret's hands held the knitting; her fingers trembled over the wool and she spoke very softly, aware that the old woman's snores had taken a false, uneven turn. "It's a quickly passing thing, Roseanne, and seventeen is a quickly passing age. It isn't *just* Billy Delaney, though God knows your dad wouldn't let him in this house." She looked up sharply. "Now, just hold your tongue and don't give me one of your killing looks. You stay away from him for he's a boy with no future and nothing good in mind for you. A kiss feels nice for a short time, Roseanne, and then it's gone."

Roseanne stood before her mother, filled with explosive emotions which she could not convey. How could she describe the sudden strange unfamiliar surge of feeling that kept her in a constant state of excitement and alarm? How could she risk having everything she was experiencing being discounted with a shrug, a sigh, an "Oh, Roseanne"? She looked about the room wildly, needing to find some way of inflicting pain on this maddeningly ignorant woman, her mother. Her eyes found the letter on top of the radio, wedged under the cut-glass vase, where her father had put it the day it arrived.

"What about Brian, Ma? Has Dad decided to let him come back?"

The knitting flew from Margaret's hands; the needles seemed to have a life of their own. She kept her face down, collected the various items. "Brian will come back. He'll come back home."

"Well, he's crazy to want to come back here, if you ask me."

Margaret's face froze. She dropped her work and moved toward her daughter, but stopped herself, hands clenched together before her. A terrible, implacable fierceness, seldom seen, but once seen, remembered, replaced her normal gentle, placid, resigned expression. "Don't you ever *dare* to say such a thing to me again, Roseanne. This is Brian's home and we are his family and I thank God on my knees that my son had the sense finally to write to us and that finally he knows where he belongs on this earth." Her hands went to her mouth, fingers trembled at her lips.

Roseanne, breathless from the intensity of her mother's emotion, startled, alarmed that she had caused the transformation, reached her hand toward her mother's shoulder, but

43

stopped just short of contact and let it drop to her side. "Ma, I'm sorry for what I said. About Brian. Honest, Ma, I'm sorry."

Margaret nodded without looking up. She sat, gathered her knitting. "All right, then. Go off to bed now before your old gran starts complaining of the noise."

She longed for the return of her oldest son as much as she dreaded it. With God's help, Father Donlon said, with God's help, Margaret, it will all work out. After all, didn't he write the lovely letter from—where was it? Georgia?—the south of the United States, and wasn't it God's miracle that he was alive at all?

He'd had a terrible fever there in that strange place and the doctor in the hospital sent for a priest and he'd made his good confession and been given the rites and vowed that if he recovered he'd beg his father and his mother to let him come home. He would be the son his father wanted him to be and wouldn't be off leaving home, pretending to be a man when he was just a mere boy still.

She tried to forget her husband's face, his words, the hard smile as he read the tumble of words written in the large familiar hand of their oldest living child.

But as she had faced everything else in her life, Margaret O'Malley would have to face this too and she could not change fact by trying to alter memory.

"So the little bastard wants to come running home, does he? Thought he was on his deathbed, did he?"

"Oh, Brian, please. It's what I've prayed these last terrible months, day and night, it's what I've prayed for."

"Yeah and that's the point, isn't it, Margaret? We're to send him a reply through this priest—Father Concertta, an Eye-talian, for Christ's sake—and tell him to come on home and we'll forget the whole thing, the grief he's caused his mother, the worry, not knowing if he was alive or dead in some ditch. We're to forget the things that were said in this house by that *boy*." He made the word a terrible insult. He tapped the letter in the palm of his hand, glanced at it, folded it back into its envelope and placed it under the vase, where it stayed for the week.

She knew he'd wait until his own good time; she knew there was no way she could prevail on him until he was ready.

44

And she knew that it would be hard when her son finally came home.

"Oh, Blessed Mother," she prayed, her eyes on the large framed print on the wall over the radio, "oh, Sweet Mother of God, I know I've no right to ask more. You've watched over him all this time, you've watched over him. Just this one thing more, Blessed Mother." She bit her lower lip, pressed her hands against her breast, her eyes on the sad, upturned eyes of the print. *She* knew how Margaret felt, as no man could ever know. She, whose hands and feet and heart ached with an anguish greater than nails and spikes could inflict. She would make it possible for Margaret to get through the hard time ahead. Her son would come home and her husband would relent and she would draw her family around her once again.

An unexpected memory caught at her: the three small dead ones. Oh, Holy Mother, the three precious little ones. Look after them for me, kiss their sweet faces, smooth their brows. Oh, God, the years seemed to dissolve and the pain of their loss was as raw and new as the pain of their birth.

Margaret stood up abruptly, rolled the yarn, plunged the needles into the ball. She blinked and cleared her mind. No sense at all to suffer old pain. She'd see about some late supper, for Brian's tour would be over before long. Indeed, wasn't that him already at the door?

FIVE

But it was not; and it was with the old one, Brian's mother, that they had the most trouble. She'd buried enough of her own flesh to know ritual and rite, and was not easily denied.

"I washed the blood from his body the day I brought him into this world and I'll wash the blood from off him the day he leaves it."

Margaret, his widow, not fully comprehending, concerned with the rising anguish of the old woman, involved with her rather than with herself, held the old woman's arms and shook her head. "Hush, now, they'll bring him home soon. Let them do it their way, for the love of God. They're trying to spare you."

"To spare me? To spare me?" Brian's mother whirled her strong compact old body away from her daughter-in-law. She planted her feet wide apart. Her eyes blazed with anger as she whirled back in time and filled the room with her accusations. "And who was there to spare me the birth pangs? Tell me that, will you? Alone but for the other small ones, alone without your fancy hospitals and doctors and nurses, if you please, and I birthed all twelve and kept my jaws locked together the whole time. And washed the blood from them and buried them when I had to!"

Margaret turned, uncertain and anxious, to Father Donlon and Captain Hennessy. "Couldn't they bring him here direct, then?" It was a soft, tentative question, without thought or consideration of what she was asking.

"Ah, Margaret, let Tommy Farley do the job. We'll bring Brian home to you all fixed up grand and just as you'd want to see him," Hennessy said, oblivious of the shudder that suddenly shook the young widow. To the old one, he said,

"Come on now, Mother, don't be making it harder on yourself. Spare yourself a bit of the hardship."

"Don't call me Mother; I'm no mother of yours," Brian's mother said sharply. The old face became shrewd and knowing. "Ah, Tommy Farley is it? And isn't he a cousin of yours, Peter Hennessy? A fine relation that is to have, and him living off of the dead."

Margaret raised a helpless hand but Captain Hennessy moved his head to one side: it was all right. He knew how difficult an old woman could be.

Father Donlon asked, "Do you suppose you could fetch me a cup of tea, Mrs. O'Malley?"

"Do you suppose you could fetch me my son home, Father Donlon?"

The priest sighed. "He'll be home by noon and it will ease you to see how fine he'll look."

She muttered something they could not make out and walked off to the kitchen. Captain Hennessy wiped a hand over his face. It came away wet with perspiration. His eyes darted to Margaret's face, then away.

"Well, I'd best get back to Tommy's, Margaret. I'll just take along the uniform I came to fetch."

She brought the uniform, neat and brushed, on a heavy wooden hanger and handed it to him with a vague, polite smile. There was a blank, uncomprehending look about her.

"And how are the children, Margaret?" Hennessy asked.

"Fine, just fine," she answered automatically, then stopped. Her hand touched lightly at her heavy dark hair and she shrugged. "Oh. You mean about Brian? Well. They're young, you know. They'll be just fine." Her eyes sought Father Donlon.

"Yes, yes, of course," Father Donlon said. "The young get over things. They're healthy, fine, strong children." He turned to Hennessy. "Well, Peter, you've had a long night of it yourself and here it is almost daylight. You'd better be off to Tommy Farley's."

"Yes, Father. I'll see you later in the day, Margaret. When we bring Brian home."

"Yes," she said with that vague disbelief. "Yes, thank you very much, Peter. We'll see you later. Yes."

• •

"You should at least have the decency to tell me what the hell happened, Peter. There's not a sign of a gunshot wound, and you must admit that the corpse is certainly in a strange condition."

Peter Hennessy viewed the tiny wisp of a man who was somehow the son of his mother's brother with the scorn reserved for one who fed on the dead. Every day of his life, Tommy Farley had some total stranger stretched out in his front parlor and sat himself down in the next room and ate his dinner with his wife and kiddies ranged around him. He even tried to talk families out of waking their dead within the confines of their own homes, argued that his facilities could accommodate great numbers of mourners comfortably. He had endless folding chairs, baskets just waiting to be filled with flowers, and he would highly recommend Gallegher's as florist, for which Gallegher would of course give him a handsome kickback. It had even been whispered about that if the deceased was an unloved bastard, Tommy Farley could, for a price, provide a fair number of loud weepers and wailers, and, indeed, he wore a professionally mournful expression himself, regardless of his acquaintance with the corpse.

"What exactly seems to be bothering you, Tommy?" Hennessy asked. He knew the effect he had on his small wizened cousin; he enjoyed watching the quick, intimidated licking of dry lips, the shift in expression, the attempt to set matters right.

The shrug was nervous and uncertain and self-effacing. "Well, after all, I'm no coroner and I suppose it isn't my business at all."

"Well, you're right on both counts, Tommy." Hennessy leaned back heavily in the small wooden kitchen chair. His large hands, folded and motionless, rested on the table before him and he offered nothing more, just waited.

Tommy's pale eyes darted about the kitchen, as though searching for some friendly item, perhaps the loudly ticking clock or the silent radio, to vouch for him. "You know me, Peter. I'm not one to be blabbering. But . . . but there's no gunshot wounds on the man at all. And, you know, there's . . . well—" He stopped speaking abruptly. The frightened eyes raced crazily, came back for just an instant to meet his cousin's, then fled around the room again. His small, almost dainty

48

hand formed a cup around his mouth and he leaned forward and whispered, straining for some delicacy, "Well, Peter, the thing of it is, Mother of God, but there's a part of Brian that appears to be missing."

This terrible confidence given, Tommy Farley seemed to hunch into himself. His small, frail shoulders rose up and forward as though to protect his chest against some expected blow.

Peter Hennessy leaned farther into the chair, felt the joints give a little inside the glued sockets. "And is that what it is that's got you all concerned, Tommy?"

Farley nodded, not just once or twice, but eagerly, his head bobbing up and down.

Hennessy stood up and looked down from his great height. "Well now, Tommy, surely we can remedy your problem and give some peace to your agitation. The last thing, man, I want to do is cause you any agitation."

"Well now, that's very kind of you, very kind indeed." Farley had absolutely no idea what his cousin was up to but every instinct warned him and the warning systems of his body tightened all his muscles and sent blood pounding through him with alarm. "Well now, Peter, wait, now just a moment. Where are you off to?"

He lurched after his cousin, who calmly opened the door to the basement and didn't look over his shoulder at Tommy Farley or acknowledge that he was even there.

"Here now, Peter, that's my preparation room down there. Here, now, you don't want to see him just yet."

He ran after Hennessy, amazed at how quickly he moved once he'd a mind to.

"Jesus, it stinks down here," Hennessy said.

"Well, it's the chemicals and such, you see," Farley told him with a mixture of nervousness and pride. It was a unique and special thing he did; it was his profession. He reached up to adjust the shade of the light and stood beside Hennessy and looked down at the naked and chalk-white body that had once been Brian O'Malley. Unasked, he began explaining what was taking place. "You see, it takes a while to drain all the natural fluids from the body, and then we replace the fluid with a preservative. Peter! Peter, what are you doing?"

Calmly, wordlessly, Peter Hennessy slid his revolver from

his holster. He pulled the hammer back, squeezed the trigger twice. One bullet entered the corpse in the area of the groin. The second bullet entered the throat. With each shot, the corpse jumped slightly on the table.

Hennessy put the revolver back in his holster, then for the first time looked at his cousin. "Well now, do you have any other problems, Tommy? Speak up, lad. Is there anything else I can do to ease your mind?"

Tommy Farley shook his head rapidly and his voice, thin and reedy, assured Hennessy, "No, no. Oh, no. No, no problems at all. Everything is just fine, Peter, yes, just fine. No, no, no problems."

"Well, isn't that grand, then. I guess you'd better go and finish your breakfast, Tommy, and then get to work on poor Brian here. I promised his family you'd have him home by noon."

SIX

Whatever sense of herself she had was mercifully fleeting because it was a deep sense of shame at her reaction to those who tried to be kind to her. She tried not to stiffen against the hands and arms that reached out to embrace her, tried not to go deaf against words whispered in her ear, tried not to go blind against the sight of all the sad faces which were thrust at her. She told herself that all of those who entered and took possession of her home did so with the best of intentions.

The men, Brian's brothers and friends, were strong and certain, each knowing exactly what to do, as though they'd rehearsed it. The furniture had to be moved, some of it taken from the house completely, and they assured her it was stored safely and she was not to worry about it. She wanted to tell them she had not a worry in the world about her furniture and what in God's name were they talking about anyway?

Whatever she touched turned out badly. The tea spilled as she poured from kettle to cup and no one allowed her to wipe up the mess she'd made. They took cloths from her hand, told her to sit and not worry about it. She cut a piece of bread and the knife somehow went deep into her index finger and someone, yes, Brian's brother Gene, grasped her hand, applied pressure, then wrapped the cut so tightly that it throbbed and pounded inside the gauze. She'd cut her fingers many times before; all her fingers had scars of one kind or another. Why then was this cut so special and such a fuss made of it? They all fussed about her so, she wanted them to let her be.

In the center of all that was happening around her, Margaret O'Malley had one wish, one swift vision of escape. If only she could walk, alone, alone, along the narrow high road of home.

51

If only she could sit where she wanted to sit, her knees up to her chin, the cool late breeze on her face, the green smell sharp and clean; scan the pale purple covering the rich lodes of peat, the bright-yellow flowers, appearing all innocent but harboring their cruel little thorns to protect themselves. If only she could reach out and run her hand through the thick and matted coat of some beige glassy-eyed, sweet-faced, stupid and complaining young sheep and gentle it with her own soft voice and lead it back down the hillside to its own mother to be chided and bleated over and pushed against in that funny way they had.

"They're bringing him in now, Margaret," Father Donlon said. His voice was crackling and old. Father Donlon was getting old and she hadn't noticed it until this very moment. She studied his face with alarm; he had a terrible look of anxiety. She reached out, took his arm and he patted her hand, misunderstanding. She sought to comfort him.

"It's all right, Father. I'm fine, truly."

He pressed his rosary on her and she took it absently. Her eyes sought her children. Kevin stood, slouched in that new way of his, face down but his eyes not missing anything. Martin stood straight and tall and solemn; he held his small sister's hand, while she, Kit, stood awkwardly in her Sunday dress, biting on her lower lip and blinking. The scabs at her knees looked bloody again. She must have been picking at them.

Roseanne stood just behind the others. The girl was so thin and pale with nothing to fall back on but her own bony self and memories of harsh words with her father: about that boy. Oh, God, it was strange, but Margaret could not remember the boy's name; could see his face but not find his name. She studied Roseanne intently, as though the name would come from her daughter's face. Instead, the girl misread her searching gaze and came to her side, put an arm about her.

"Ma," she said in her familiar little-girl voice, "oh, Ma, what's going to happen to us now?"

From her depth of calmness, Margaret found Roseanne's hand and squeezed it, and without even being aware of her words, she said, "Sure, now, we'll be fine, won't we though, dear? Sure, now, we'll be just fine."

Chant words, crooned to a sick child, over and over, the sound of them more important than the words themselves. Automatic mothering words which filled her with a sense of herself and the beginning of reality. Wasn't she the fool, thinking herself a small child again when here she was, mother of this lovely girl and those other fine children?

The women suddenly swelled around her as though the worst part of all of this would be for her to see the men place the large coffin in the room. Margaret let them surround and comfort her for it made them feel useful. Her own sister Ellen, married to Brian's brother Matthew, pressed against her, shielded her face, spoke to her in the same crooning way she had spoken to Roseanne.

"There's no need for you to watch this part. Sure, it's just men's work, darling. Sure, it will be all right, darling. Just hold to my hand; it'll be all right now, sure."

She felt remote and untouched. "I'm all right, Ellen, really, dear. How is the old woman, poor soul?"

Ellen's broad clear good face had to work at sadness; her natural manner was happy and her natural voice contained a laugh. She bent close to her sister and whispered about their mutual mother-in-law, "Ah, that one. Sure, she's just in there making a great fuss about herself. We'll let her have her moment, then quiet her with a bit of whiskey. Don't let her upset you, now you know what to expect."

They let the old woman, the mother, have her moment first and they were all prepared and she didn't let them down and then they took her into one of the bedrooms to quiet her. During the lament, the piercing cry, Margaret held to her sister and drew herself inside, all tight and dry.

"Ellen," she said in a suddenly vital, real panic, as the thought occurred to her. "Ellen," she repeated into her sister's ear, as Ellen leaned to her, "what about my Brian?" There was a terrible impatience as her sister drew back and stared as though she'd gone mad. She shook her sister's hand. "Young Brian, I'm talking of. My God, his letter. It was on the top of the radio and they've carried it off somewhere and it contained the address and . . ."

Ellen's strong hands held her to the chair. "It's taken care of, love. I'd forgotten to tell you. No, truly, now, it's all taken

53

care of. Peadar telephoned the priest your Brian named in the letter."

Anxiety filled her, a sense of time lost. "But there's money to be sent for train fare. The boy hasn't the fare home and he's got to see his dad before . . . before . . ."

"It's all done, Margaret, it's all taken care of. He'll be here; he's on his way this very minute. I swear he'll be here."

"All right, then. All right," Margaret said.

After the old woman was taken from the room, everyone seemed to move back, to press away and clear a path for her. Father Donlon helped her to stand and again she was stricken with a sense of his fragility; his old man's arm beneath her fingers was so surprisingly slender and she didn't know if the trembling was from her or from him.

She knelt on the little velvet-cushioned prayer stool, her eyes locked against the sight of her husband. She prayed quickly, without a sense of words, then, finally, she opened her eyes and stared at the locked stranger's face inside the massive coffin. He wore Brian's uniform but he wasn't Brian at all. Too small. She looked away from the body; it was surrounded by flowers. Baskets and wreaths ranged alongside and behind, all about, carefully placed as decorations. Standing at the head of the coffin, she just noticed, was Tommy Farley, looking sad but somehow eager and expectant. His small eyes were bright on hers and she felt he wanted something from her but couldn't imagine what until his glance flicked from her to the corpse and then back to her.

She moved toward Tommy Farley and said, "Thank you very much, Mr. Farley. You've done very nicely with him."

Tommy Farley glowed, his eyes sparked with an expression of pleasure. He reached for her hand, muttered, "Sorry for your trouble, Mrs. O'Malley."

Margaret withdrew her hand sharply. His palm was terribly cold and moist.

Each of her children knelt before the coffin, said a prayer, then moved away, and Margaret O'Malley knew without knowing how she knew: None of this has come home to us yet; we don't really accept it yet as something that's happened.

SEVEN

Aaron Levine tensed against his parents' visit to the hospital room. Through the warm, floating nothingness, his mother's voice penetrated. She pounced on him not with actual words, but with sounds, deep, strangulating laments. Her face went from red to dead white; her eyes, focused on him, rolled back in her head and she passed out cold on the floor. He tried to lean over, to see, but he was bound to the bed not only by his total lack of energy but by a series of tubes that had been inserted into and out of his body at various locations.

After the commotion with his mother, when she had been removed, revived, quieted, secreted away to some remote room where she wouldn't upset anyone or herself, his father returned alone, slightly embarrassed, slightly apologetic. As always.

"Aaron. So. How are you?"

His father looked a little blurred. Aaron moved the fingers of his uninjured hand and his father took the hint and reached for it and stood awkwardly. Generally, he stood behind his wife; it was she who held hands and touched and surrounded. Alone, he seemed slightly at a loss.

"So, you're okay, Aaron?"

There was a deadness in his father's voice as he searched for words; his father was not an articulate man but Aaron sensed what was happening to him. He was struggling, choking on words that did not come easy.

"Papa, I'm okay. Look, this whole thing—it's going to be all right."

David Levine fingered the brim of his hat restlessly. "Everything is going to be all right," he said flatly. He addressed the floor or the bed or his hat. "Bullets in my son's body, and everything is going to be all right."

"Papa, it was just one bullet. Not bullets."

His father spoke to the floor again. "Not bullets. Just one bullet in my son's body. That makes a big difference."

He began to choke, the words turned into one huge but silent sob, and he pressed his hands and his hat over his face. The sounds that escaped, the words, were what Aaron had been afraid of. "Mine fault . . . my son . . . a policeman . . . wrong . . . from the start . . . mine fault."

Finally, his father snorted into his handkerchief, pushed at his reddened eyes, turned to Aaron, patted his cheek. "They taking good care of you here, Aaron? You need something maybe?"

"Not a thing, Pop. Listen, Pop. I'm gonna say it. Don't turn away from me. Look, it was my decision to take this job . . ."

"Sure, sure, your own decision. I maybe could have made enough money to pay Morris' medical school, you maybe wouldn't have made your own decision to have such a life for yourself."

"Papa, it was all worked out; it was all discussed. For two years, then Morris will finish and I'll go back to school and he'll help me. Papa, please, don't start. Don't make it harder."

His father nodded briskly. "Okay. Okay, I won't start. But I'll say this, two years. No more, Aaron. And then, your turn." His father took a deep breath and whispered, "This I *swear* to you!"

"Right, Papa, then a lawyer I'll be." He lapsed easily into his father's pattern of speech. "And the father you'll be of a doctor and a lawyer. All you'll need is an Indian chief."

"What? What Indian chief?"

"A joke, Pa."

"A joke. He lies in that bed and makes jokes at me. A bullet in his body, he makes jokes." He kept his face down and spoke quickly. "Aaron, this morning I went to *schul,* Aaron, and I thanked God you were not killed because if that had happened to you . . . all those other men killed . . ."

His father leaned over quickly, pressed his wet face against Aaron's, kissed his cheek. "Later, Aaron. I see you later. I come back more calm, I promise. You rest now. You rest."

56

When he was a little boy, when his family had just moved to Flatbush, there was a boy named Sheldon Cohen who caused terror in the heart of Aaron Levine and all of his other playmates. He was a tough, swaggering, muscular bully who enjoyed punching and twisting and jabbing at others, and though Aaron and his friends took pains to avoid this boy, Aaron had been secretly fascinated by his behavior.

Patrolman Sam Feldman, president of the Sholem Society, could have been Sheldon Cohen, all grown up. He was a compact, solid, lithe man of about forty. His gray hair was neatly clipped close to the scalp of a large round head; his eyes were the same steely gray. His nose was short and pugnacious and he held his head slightly to one side so that he seemed always to be regarding those about him with a wary, suspicious glance. He had been a semiprofessional boxer in his youth and there was a persistent, if unfounded, rumor that he had once killed a man in the ring. Aaron didn't know which of the stories he'd heard about Feldman were true but there was definitely an aura of controlled violence and secret anger surrounding the man who stood beside his bed.

"Well, hero, how you doing, kid?"

Aaron shrugged without thinking and the gesture sent pain shooting down from his shoulder to his wrist. He bit his lip and tried not to let Feldman see his discomfort but Feldman seemed to feed on it.

"Hurts, huh, kid? Damn right it hurts. Gonna hurt for a long time, too. You did some job last night, kid, I'm here to tell you."

Aaron wondered if Feldman knew his name; he was sure he'd been told, but probably forgot; or maybe he called everyone kid; Aaron wished he'd just give his message and leave.

Feldman leaned close and spoke in a deep-throated rasp. "Listen, kid, there's stories going around, you know? Rumors. There's always rumors from these bastards, which is why I want to get it direct. Like from the horse's mouth, you know. They're trying to downgrade your part of last night, which is why *I'm* here. They take care of their own, *we* take care of our own. There aren't many of us, kid, but we got it up here." His index finger tapped his forehead. He spun around, moved

57

on the balls of his feet across the room, picked up a chair which he carried to the bedside. "Okay, Levine, what's the story?"

He arrived on the scene; there were wounded, dead and dying all around; he exchanged shots with the culprits; he was hit; they were hit; they died; he woke up in the hospital. What more story? That's what happened.

Feldman, restless, filled with a thoughtful energy, drew himself from the chair, paced around the room, scratched his scalp vigorously. "What they wanna do is, they wanna give all the big awards to the dead guys and hand you off a Class B commendation. Make them all big heroes posthumously; which is okay with me, don't get me wrong, as long as they take care of you. If it was one of them survived and one of us killed, they'd switch it around, you can bet your ass."

Aaron felt exhausted and disinterested and puzzled over Sam Feldman's apparent agitation and anger. A medal, a commendation; let the dead have it; he just wanted to rest, to sleep a little, but it seemed to mean so much to Sam, like they were personally cheating *him*. If the truth were known, Aaron didn't want to think too much about last night; didn't want to think about the fact that he, Aaron Levine, had killed two men.

Feldman was going on and on and only sporadically did his words penetrate Aaron's growing lethargy.

". . . they figure maybe a Class A for Sullivan, but they're set on the Honor Legion for O'Malley."

"O'Malley?" O'Malley? What happened to Sergeant O'Malley? "What about Sergeant O'Malley?"

Feldman shrugged. "Well, being he *was* the sergeant on the scene, I don't object to his getting the posthumous. My main concern is just that they don't screw *you* . . ."

"Posthumous? For Sergeant O'Malley? He's dead?"

"Ya didn't know? Yeah, sure, he was killed too."

Aaron remembered sitting in the patrol car, hearing the call, driving away. And leaving Sergeant O'Malley behind. "But . . . how was he killed, Sam?"

Feldman squinted at him. "How the hell do I know, kid? I wasn't there."

But neither was Sergeant O'Malley, Aaron thought.

EIGHT

Patrolman Patrick Quade, president of the Irish Society, felt the blood fill his face. "The stupid dumb son of a bitch," he said for the third time.

"If you're looking for an argument on that point, you'll not get one from anyone here, so why don't you just sit down?" Captain Peter Hennessy said. He watched as Quade dropped into a chair and twitched his fingers over the kitchen table. "We're all agreed, Pat. Brian O'Malley was a dumb bastard. Alive or dead, Brian was a certain lad for causing trouble to those around him. The point now is that we've got to go about getting him safely buried with all the honors we'd want our families to see for ourselves. He was our past president and we've that to consider."

At a signal from Hennessy, Patrolman Charlie Gannon reached for the bottle of whiskey and poured a generous amount into each of the four glasses on the kitchen table. He caught a sharp look from the captain and pushed his own glass toward the center of the table. "I don't really think I'll have anymore myself, Captain."

It was Charlie Gannon's kitchen and Charlie Gannon's whiskey, but still and all, it wasn't a social gathering. It was a meeting, if unofficial and closed and secret, it was still a meeting and there was a certain decorum prevailed.

"Well, let's hear your thinking in the matter, Ed," the captain said to the fourth man present. "You've been silent and thoughtful for a while. What are you turning over in your mind?"

Lieutenant Ed Shea was a lean man, with black hair and

59

brows and dark-brown eyes and a thoughtful, careful way of speaking. "We've two things to attend to, seems to me."

"And what might those two things be?"

Carefully, Ed Shea took a swallow from his glass, exhaled with a sigh. "Aside from everyone getting nice and calm, that is," he said to Pat Quade, who nodded. "Yes. Well, the first thing is, we've to pay a little visit to our young Jewish friend in the hospital and offer him our congratulations on a nice job well done. And have a friendly little conversation with him. The Jews are a sentimental race and very understanding about families. He'd not be denying that Brian, for the sake of the family that's left, should be given all suitable honors. Brian being such a hero and all that."

Captain Hennessy moved his hand in a gesture of dismissal. He wasn't worried about the Jew. "What's the second thing, then, Ed?"

"Well, this might be a bit risky." He turned to Pat Quade. "We got someone in the Property Office, someone who doesn't have a big mouth?"

Quade's hand covered his eyes for a moment, then his face brightened. "Yes, sure, we've got Michael Smith. You could leave your life in Michael's hand and it'd be safe."

"What's this all about then, Ed?" Captain Hennessy asked.

"Well, here's what I've been turning over in my mind, Captain. Brian's revolver and Patrolman Levine's revolver are being held in the Property Office, along with the guns of all the other poor lads was shot last night, may they rest in peace."

Automatically, around the table, the men murmured "Amen."

"Well, then, just to be on the safe side all around, I think that when young Levine is on his feet again, and goes to reclaim his revolver, I think he should be handed Brian's revolver in place of his own weapon."

Pat Quade nodded slowly; Charlie Gannon looked blank; Peter Hennessy frowned. "Now, why the hell would we do that, Ed?"

"Because, Captain," Pat Quade said, "the bullets in the dead niggers came from the sheeny's gun. If he should decide to make any trouble, why the bullets can just be dug out of them bodies and matched up to the gun they came from and it won't be the gun Levine is holding." He had latched on to the logic immediately and approved.

"What a devious mind you do have, Ed," the captain said quietly. "I personally don't think it will be necessary at all because that Jew cop looked scared of his own shadow when I seen him behind the wheel of Brian's car last night."

"That was before he killed two men, Captain," Ed Shea pointed out.

"True. Yes, that's true, very true," Hennessy said quietly. "However, it's been my experience, you understand, that a Jew is a Jew. But, as you say, we might as well touch all the bases and do the job properly, so to speak." He turned to Pat Quade. "And the matter of the registration of the weapons we're speaking of?"

"It'll be taken care of, Captain."

"Good. Good." There was a heavy silence in the small kitchen before the captain spoke again. "Well, now, I guess there's no need to say to anyone in this room that what we've spoken of this day goes no farther than is absolutely necessary, which is to say"—he raised his face toward Quade for confirmation—"just Michael Smith, and no one else is party to anything said here. You all take my meaning?"

No one said anything, except Charlie Gannon, who said loudly in the silence, "Oh, yes, absolutely, Captain."

Captain Hennessy said, "Drink your whiskey, Charlie."

Marvin Gutterman pushed his eyeglasses up along his nose but they slid down again the half inch to the thin line across the bridge of his nose. He considered his cousin, Aaron Levine, a faraway look across his face. If you didn't know him, you'd think it was a blankness, but Aaron knew Marvin and Marvin's steel trap of a mind.

"And you didn't tell this joker, this Sam Feldman, not a thing about your sergeant staying behind?"

"No, like I told you, Marvin, when it started to come back to me, I just told Sam my head hurt and I had to go to sleep and then I had the nurse call you."

"And nobody's seen you; just me, after Sam?"

"Right, right."

Marvin sucked at his eyetooth a few times, then pointed at Aaron. "Answer, please, as carefully as you can. First, you're positive of the address where your sergeant went in?"

Aaron nodded. "Yeah. I was sitting in front of 212. He went two doors past that: 210, 208. Yeah, it was 208."

Marvin nodded. "Good. Good. Now, you're sure that the fat captain said something about a 'nigger whore' in connection with Sergeant O'Malley?"

"That's what he said. Marvin, by now I'm sure of everything I told you. I just don't understand how you connected it to some woman falling to her death."

"Look, I'm in Legal Aid; I read the *Daily News*, the *Mirror*; I read every rag in the city. You never know who you're going to have to defend, so I like to read about prospective clients in advance. You know me, with this crazy trick brain filled with all kinds of useless garbage. Occasionally, something worthwhile is tucked away with all the rest."

While he had been telling Marvin of the night's events, soliciting his cousin's advice, since Marvin was his closest friend as well as his cousin, there had come a sudden moment when Marvin held his hand up, squinted, frowned, left the room, returned with a wrinkled copy of the morning paper, searched frantically for an item and read it to him: "'An unidentified colored female, age about thirty to thirty-five, was found in the air shaft of 208 East 129th Street early this morning. Police say she apparently jumped or fell from the top-floor flat.'"

"But assuming that Sergeant O'Malley was up there with that woman, we still don't know what happened, Marvin."

Marvin Gutterman ran his fingertips lightly along a tube which was filled with colorless fluid which filtered into his cousin's arm. "But we do know one thing, Aaron. He wasn't on the scene last night where all the shooting took place. I want you to listen to me, Aaron, and then think very carefully about what I'm going to suggest."

Aaron Levine listened in alert and respectful and awed silence for the next half hour while his cousin gave him detailed advice regarding his future.

Lieutenant Shea carried a chair across the room for the

captain. Aaron could feel the animal heat rise from the fat man next to him. It was amazing the way he gave off such a strong essence of himself. The captain's face was a dark flat red and he pursed his lips several times and said, "Well, well, well, now. He's looking very well, wouldn't you say so, Lieutenant?"

Lieutenant Edward Shea stood at the foot of the bed and nodded. "Yes, Captain, I would."

"We're just on our way to the wake of poor Sergeant O'Malley. We've spent most of our day just visiting with bereaved families. And how is *your* family, Patrolman Levy?" At some slight sound from Ed Shea, Captain Hennessy swung around. "What? What? *Levine* is it, yes, of course. They must be proud of you, your people, eh?"

"Yes. Well, you know. They were a little upset."

"Well, certainly, why wouldn't they be? If it'd been you was killed, your people would have you in the ground already, or that's my understanding of the situation. Is that the way your people do it?"

Aaron wasn't sure how to answer. The captain spoke with a barrage of words; his statements were like so many challenges. Aaron's arm and shoulder ached, his head hurt, his stomach was loose and making noises. "Well, yes. It's our religious custom to bury the dead within twenty-four hours."

"Seems fast, seems like a fast way to do things."

The small beadlike eyes glistened; the heavy face tilted, waited for an explanation.

"Well," Aaron explained, "then after the funeral, we sit *shivah* for seven days."

"Sit and shiver do you?" Hennessy said, deliberately misunderstanding and taking no pains to hide the fact.

Lieutenant Shea, unexpectedly, spoke. "Much the same as a wake, Captain, but the corpse isn't present. Everyone comes to the deceased's house to pay respect to the family."

Aaron was unnerved by the conversation; he could almost see Captain Hennessy handing a cakebox offering to his mother; scanning the room, noting the strange customs: all the mirrors covered, are they? sit on little wooden boxes, do you? no shoes on your feet? hair all undone? Strange people, ah, yes.

He studied Hennessy now as though all that he had visualized was true and he felt anger along with repulsion but
Hennessy seemed totally unaware of any feeling directed at
him. He was oblivious to anything except his own purpose
and everything that had gone before was part of the process
leading up to what was to follow.

"Well, you've done a nice bit of work, officer," Hennessy
said, "and it was a sad night. Yes, very sad for all concerned.
Well, are you comfortable here, is the room all right, are they
treating you well? You see," he continued without pause,
"the Department takes care of its own. And you *are* one of our
own, Patrolman Levine."

Dully, Aaron said, "Thank you, Captain."

"It's us owes you the thanks, lad," Hennessy said. He
shifted his weight, relieved first one heavy buttock, then the
other, resettled, squinted toward Shea, then stared back at
Aaron. "Yes, your name has been put in for a commendation
and you can be assured you'll receive . . . Class B was it, Ed?
Yes. Now, that's a fine start for a young man like yourself. I
imagine you'll be looking forward to taking promotion examinations as they come along. You people are good at that, and
the commendation will provide you with an additional point
right at the start." He slapped his knee with the flat of his
fleshy hand as an indication that he was finished; the matter
was finished.

Right up until the exact moment he opened his mouth and
spoke, Aaron Levine didn't know he was going to speak,
hadn't decided, hadn't felt strong enough to confront them.
Maybe it was because they were so sure of him or because
Captain Hennessy had been so blatant and crude, his every
remark piercing through, below, some surface of Aaron's
being. Maybe because of some loyalty to his cousin, who had
talked to him so logically. Or maybe in some tired, weary recognition that what at first had seemed to him so unbelievably
corrupt an action for him to attempt now seemed to him
merely pragmatic.

At first, it was just a sound in his throat, his attempt to speak,
to tell Captain Hennessy and Lieutenant Shea that matters
were not quite settled. Captain Hennessy had actually stood
up, turned from him. It was Ed Shea who studied him, whose

face tightened with recognition at something he saw on Aaron Levine's tired but tense face.

"Captain," Shea said softly, "I think there's something Patrolman Levine wants to say."

"What? What's that?" Hennessy turned ponderously, toweringly, peered forward as though at some audacious bit of misconduct. "Something *you* want to say?"

Though he felt his voice thin and wavery, though his head floated and spun and nausea rocked and lurched in his stomach, through all the misery, Aaron felt a sharp, clear joy. Just as Marvin had told him, he was going to beat these bastards at their own game.

NINE

It was not the presence of death which caused the strangeness, for he had seen death before. His dead father merely added to the aura of strangeness which emanated from the living who surrounded the coffin. He viewed them all from the remoteness of his absence; perhaps that was a large part of it. They were, after all, his family, grandmother, mother, sisters, brothers, aunts, uncles, cousins; but the year and a half he had been away from all of them gave him a sharply piercing clearer vision of them than he had ever realized possible and he felt a shock of recognition with each face he encountered.

Toward the corpse he felt a numb indifference for it had no relation to the hard and powerful man who had driven him from this home and family. It was too diminished and characterless to have anything at all to do with those strong hands, the sharp voice, the piercing, knowing eyes which had seen into the deepest, most hidden places of his very being. It was an effigy and a poor effigy at that, not even suggesting the man his father had been. He knelt, prayed, was conscious of the eyes taking in the scene; he felt only a fleeting guilt-laden sense of weariness because he could feel nothing at all.

His mother's face, familiar, known, unchanged, was at the same time a different face, or confronted him now in a different way. The light-gray eyes sought something he did not understand. He realized, though, that something was being asked of him.

He was now Brian O'Malley.

The kids, his brothers and sisters, had grown and changed in the period of time he'd been away; Roseanne most of all, Martin least.

66

Roseanne seemed cut out of her own flesh, fine carved as though she'd formerly been an indication of the woman she would become. She embraced him with a quick, mature hug and she whispered in his ear, as though she'd rehearsed it carefully and selected the words she liked best, "Oh, God, Bri, it's good to have you home." She had never said anything even remotely personal to him before. He sensed a feeling of relief on her part, a passing of responsibility. With him home, she was no longer the oldest.

His brother Martin had gotten larger, but he'd always been a large, solid boy, older beyond his years. At fifteen, he was nearly as tall as Brian's six feet; broader in the shoulder and hip. Martin hugged him, held his shoulders for a moment. He was the natural member of the family, who didn't think primarily of himself, of what impression he might be making on any observer.

His brother Kevin was undersized at thirteen, with bad skin and a weak, wet handshake. A tic played at the corner of his nose and he didn't meet Brian's gaze but ducked his head and peered up at him fleetingly.

His youngest sister, Kit, stared at him warily. She was a small, tense girl of ten and even before he'd left they'd been strangers. There were eight years between them and he had no idea what, if anything, went on inside her head.

It was his grandmother who thrust him into the center of this lagging wake, which had gone into the third day by the time he arrived. She cast aside her exhaustion and with a great surge of energy she tied him irrevocably into the history of his family.

"Jesus, look at him," she instructed and they all fastened eyes on him. "He's the living image of his dead father. Sweet Mother of God, and don't I remember my own son just turned eighteen and didn't he have the exact face and size of this one here?"

She searched among her remaining children for confirmation. Peadar and Matthew O'Malley agreed with her, assured her. The other members of the family stared first at the dead father, then at the living son, and the judgment was rendered: he was that same Brian. No more and no less, a continuation of his father.

He felt a deep choking cry but there were no sensible words

to tell them who he was. He stood quietly for their inspection and said nothing.

Old Mrs. Kerrigan, a friend of his grandmother's came, ʾaited for him to walk her to the coffin. He knew she must have been there before, but she nodded brightly, eyes from corpse to son. She was nearly deaf and her voice was unnaturally loud.

"Sorry for your trouble, Brian."

Her hand, given first to his grandmother and then to him, was misshapen and dry. The two old women lingered and peered down together and nodded their heads up and down. Their eyes met for a brief instant and Brian caught something between them, something which appeared and disappeared so instantaneously that he might have imagined it, but he knew he had seen it. It was a knowing, shrewd look, almost triumphant, and it sent a shiver through him.

Mrs. Kerrigan made a deep sound in her throat. "God's will, Mrs. O'Malley. Ah, yes, well, that's the way of it, isn't it?"

There was a firm hand clasped on his shoulder and he turned, expecting a man, one of his uncles or one of his father's friends. It was his Aunt Ellen and she leaned close to him and whispered, "Come on into the kitchen now. Let's get some food into you."

He wouldn't have believed he could eat, but as his aunt put the plate of food on the kitchen table before him he was overwhelmed by hunger. He ate without tasting; just the physical act of shoving food into his mouth, gulping it down, seemed to fill a vast pit of emptiness which had opened up inside of him.

"Here, lad, you'll have a glass of beer to wash it all down." She sat across the table from him, then turned and brusquely chased away the collection of boys, including his brother Kevin, who stood in the doorway watching him. "Go on outside now in the courtyard and keep your voices down. I don't want to be hearing any of you again."

They jostled and pushed each other, five or six of them, as they scrambled into the courtyard, which was O'Malley territory for the simple reason that the O'Malley apartment was on the ground floor and the bedroom windows faced the first small courtyard.

"They're close to exhaustion," she explained. "You must be tired yourself, Brian. Oh, you're that thin. You've been sick, have you?"

He nodded, wiped his mouth. "I'm fine, Aunt Ellen, really I am. Thanks again for arranging things, for seeing I got the fare and all."

Her hand pressed his arm, dismissed any trouble she might have gone to. She studied him frankly, openly, the way she did everything. "Well, it's a full-grown man, despite the thinness. You'll fill out quickly enough. Your ma is going to need you, Brian. Listen, in a few days' time, stop upstairs and see your Uncle Matt. He's going to offer you a bit of a job helping him on the milk wagon, but don't tell him I told you. Let him think he's telling you for the first time. I just want to set your mind at ease in case you were worrying about how you'd manage and all. Ah, eat up now, eat up, you need something to sustain you."

His Uncle Peadar sat across the table from him next. He was a thin man and his reddish hair was shot through with gray. His light-blue eyes were red-rimmed from weariness. Peadar O'Malley was a fireman and he told Brian, "The boys from my house will be out in force for your dad's funeral tomorrow. He'll have his full inspector's funeral, will Brian, and it's only fitting. But he was that well thought of that the lads from my house will be there too. Did Father Donlon have a chance to tell you the details?"

"Yes. Yes, he did, Uncle Peadar."

Peadar reached for a water tumbler which was half filled with whiskey. He drank deeply, sighed. "Ah, yes. And the radio says it'll be a clear day and mild. Thank God for small blessings, I always say." Then, after carefully searching his memory for something to say, he added, "The mayor himself came to the wake the first day, did you know that? Yes. A fine little man he is, for all his faults. They say he's a little bit crazy, but it's hard to tell with them Italians, isn't it? They say his wife is a Jew. Now isn't that a strange thing for an Italian, to have a Jewish wife? But then, I guess you'd not have to go too far, for isn't my own sister Maureen married to John Kinelli and him a wop himself. Ah, yes, well."

His mother entered the kitchen finally, stopped at the doorway, surprised to see him completely alone at the table. "I came to fetch some tea," she said, as though she needed some excuse. She moved to the stove, fussed at the kettle, filled it with water, lit a match and held it to the pilot light. "Did you have enough to eat, Brian?"

Her eyes and hands moved constantly, neither making contact with him. "There's the cups to wash. I'd best wash the cups, they get used up and needed so quickly. Will you have some tea, Brian? The water will boil before you know it. Well, will you just look at the mess of this kitchen. You've never seen it look like this before, have you now?"

She moved about, collected and scraped and stacked. He got up, brought his plate to the sink and began to scrape it clean. She tried to take it from him.

"Here," she said, "what are you doin'? You've no need, I'll do that for you," she said, as though he was a stranger or a guest.

"That's okay, Ma, I'll do it."

"No. No, I'll take care."

They stood for a moment, the plate held between them. She bit down on her lip and turned away quickly, her attention taken completely by the running water.

He came behind her, touched her shoulder lightly. "Ma, listen. I want to tell you . . ."

Without facing him, she leaned her cheek against his hand, then shook her head. "Not now, Bri. Not now."

He knew she couldn't turn to him; if she did, if they faced each other, she would shatter; she had to hold together and she had to do it completely. His hand moved down her arm and he was surprised by the sharpness of her bones, a deep sense of physical surprise. He wondered if she had always existed this way. Beneath the calm solidity of her outward self, had this other vulnerable woman been present all the time? He was shocked by her youth; her face in profile was a girl's, unlined, untouched. He had remembered her older, fuller, and she seemed diminished by grief; vulnerable, innocent.

"Thanks for waiting for me, Ma. Father Donlon told me how you even waited the Rosary service until I got here."

Her head nodded quickly and she said sharply, "It was only proper."

"Listen, do you think Kevin is strong enough to carry . . ." He faltered, unable to continue.

She turned to him now and her face was totally without expression. Her words were matter of fact, as though she was discussing an ordinary circumstance. "I think he'll find his strength and I think all three of you boys should help to carry your dad. There'll be your uncles Peadar and Gene and Matt and some men from the Department as needed. Since Kev is so small, your Uncle Matt said something about him walking at the front. That way he won't get too much of the weight, but he won't feel he's being left out of it."

"Okay, Mom."

She dried her red hands on her apron. "I told the boys they were not to stand watch tonight, Brian. They've not slept much these last days. Everything's been so . . . so . . ." Her hand waved vaguely. "But Martin says he'll take his turn with you; he has the strength, God knows. We'll be all right, Brian." She searched his face with a sudden look of desperation, as though reality cut through ritual unexpectedly and caught her unprepared. Her voice went small, tiny, chilled him. *"Won't we be all right, Brian?"*

It was what he had been waiting for without knowing: her turning to him. "We'll be just fine, Mom. Don't you worry about it. We'll all be just fine."

He listened to the diminishing household sounds with a growing sense of uneasiness for he was now completely alone with his father. He knew it had been planned and that this was supposed to be a totally significant moment, this last private meeting with his father.

Brian felt only a sense of his own sinful awfulness: he could not feel grief. He fingered his rosary and recited prayers but some true sense of himself would not allow him to deceive himself. He was merely going through the ritual; there was no true piety, no grief involved, and he did not know why. He stayed on his knees, prayed, but neither for his father's nor his own immortal soul. He was too numb.

As his fingers moved, he began an Our Father, but his lips fell open and soundless as he gazed, finally, on the visage of the man who had fathered him. The dark hair, combed neatly off the wide forehead, was slightly wrong; the part was too high and threw the face off balance slightly. The black brows were stiff and immobile, and that too distorted the face, for his father's face was constantly in a state of animation; it had been a listening, watching, expressive face and now it was wooden and masklike.

Where was it gone? The life of the man, his flash, his spark, his anger, his sound, all the things he had been?

He had been begotten by this now dead man within the body of the woman in the other room, and he knew now, from the lusts and sins of his own body, that his creation had taken place in a steamy, wet and forceful physicality. And this dead man himself had been sinfully thrust into the body of the old woman whose light moans punctuated the silence even now, through her fitful and uneasy sleep.

This corpse had been a child and a man and a father.

Why hadn't he ever realized this before? And what did it have to do with him, anyway?

It had to do with him because child he had been and man he was and therefore: *therefore* the fact of death had to do directly with himself. Brian felt the beads tremble as he let them dangle over his hand and he tried to pray but couldn't; he was appalled at himself, at the terribleness of the uncontrollable thoughts about his father's body, his own conception, his father's conception. He shuddered, felt the tears wet his face and he moved and formed words, prayed quickly, hoping to latch on to the sense of prayer.

He moved to the next bead, heard the noise beside him.

"He doesn't look very natural, does he, Brian?" his brother Martin asked.

Brian turned away, smeared his face with his arm, blinked hard. Brian studied the round, placid face. There was a sprinkling of light freckles across Martin's nose and wide cheeks. His eyes were almost navy blue, startling in their darkness because his hair and lashes were so fair.

"He doesn't even look like Dad," Brian said.

"Oh, he's long since gone from here," Martin said with a calm certainty. "Pray for him, Brian. He needs all our prayers. But yours are special."

"Why? Why do you say that?"

"He was a hard man, Bri. Harder on you than on the rest of us because you were the oldest. I think he wanted to make you hard because he always knew you might have to share the responsibility."

Brian was puzzled and curious at the strangely mature explanation. He'd never thought of anything like that; he had just assumed that his father wasn't too fond of him.

As though reading his thoughts, Martin added, "It was never anything more personal than that, Bri."

Because he wanted to believe him, Brian nodded, and side by side, the brothers knelt, prayed, stood quietly and kept the watch by their father's coffin through the night.

PART TWO

The O'Malleys

TEN

Margaret O'Malley expertly worked the thread back and forth, in and out. Beneath her skilled fingers, the hole closed so perfectly that no one could say for sure just where the tear had been. They were hard on clothes, she thought, but God's love, what youngsters weren't?

Her hands fell still. How many tears and rips and holes had she mended? How many clothes had she cut down, shaped, taken in, let out, made do with, for brothers older and younger, sisters yet to be taught, and then for her own children? With deep and quiet pride, she knew that not one of hers, no matter how poor they'd ever been, no matter how empty the pot, not one ever walked about in clothes which advertised their need.

It was something her mother had taught her when she was just a small girl: We may be dirt poor, Margaret, but we're not dirt.

She hadn't thought of that for years; nor of her mother. Strange, to think of it now, this quiet night. She gathered the clothing and her needles and threads. There was no need to be mending now, this time of night. She just liked to keep her hands busy until the last child was home; she'd better start getting over that, with Brian practically a man. And whatever was he up to half the time, she didn't know, acting so secret, storming out of the house, so hard on the younger ones at times, then at times, so like the young boy again. She didn't know how to be mother to a man; she'd never been before. She turned the lamplight low and gazed through the sheer curtains to the quiet street.

Sweet Jesus of the Sorrows, be my strength.

Margaret gasped and her hands tightened on the arms of the chair.

Why, that was my mother's prayer and never my own. Never, in all my thirty-eight years, until this very moment. Sweet Jesus of the Sorrows, be my strength. Through all the hunger and pain and ache of death, her mother had leaned on that prayer. She'd had nine born, four miscarried, three buried and six raised, her mother.

Three of us here, so far from home: me with my brood, little Ellen all grown with her passel of kiddies, and Jimmie John with that strange, unholy life he'd entered into.

And all the others still at home.

God forgive me, twenty years I've been here and the other place is still what I think of as home. Well, it's what's in my secret heart and there it stays: home.

Ground, hard and rock-covered and unyielding, filled with earth-starved corpses it was, and offering nothing to the living but its own sweet beauty and you can't eat the beauty of the hills nor drink the sparkle of the evening waters as they rushed back from the day's journey to the sea. But wasn't it strange and wonderful though, the way the waters came back to where they belonged, no matter how far they poured away from shore, leaving the vast shallow mudholes, thick and gummy and good for nothing but muck on bare feet; yes, the waters came streaming back all silver-sparkled each evening, as though they knew they'd belong in this place only.

Margaret's people, the O'Briens, were a gentler people than the O'Malleys. They had about them the soft, shy, quiet ways of a people accustomed for generations to listening to the sound of the land beneath their feet and the wind about their heads. The harsh, querulous complaints of sheep were more familiar to their ears, and comfortable for that matter, than the loud, boisterous, hearty commotion of the O'Malleys, who settled among them in a clatter of arrival.

No one moved to the west; the west was the barren place, its voids filled only with sorrows too bitter to mention. Clare and Galway and Mayo were the places of wild beauty from which people came and held only in memory, with the hard and cold and hungry days mellowed and gentled by time and distance.

But the O'Malleys, father and mother and sons and daughters, came, thrust themselves upon the quiet wind-swept hills, moved into a deserted, half-destroyed hut, collected stones from odd places, filled the holes, turfed the roof, washed down the walls and set the peat to burning without anyone's by-your-leave. There was no one really to send them packing, for the former tenant, gone so long none could recall his name or story, had no claim to the house. The actual owner, far from his property, had no informer or agent to set or collect rent from the dead ruins which had been so heartily resurrected by the O'Malley clan.

The O'Malleys filled places in their lives that no one in Clifden had dreamed were empty. They brought an excitement which was more than just the rare intrusion of strangers. They brought with them a certain daring and determination and sense of life which the bleak, weary, drained and emptied villagers and countrymen around the tiny town watched with wariness at first, then with interest, then, gradually, with a reviving enthusiasm of their own toward life.

The O'Malleys had no intention whatever of rotting or dying off in silence. They let it be known they were just biding time until they would be able to retrace their steps across the face of the land to the Irish Sea, to embarkation, to the New World. What had brought them, in obvious flight, to the west, was a mystery to which they never referred, nor permitted any in their hearing to refer, and it was a matter of much speculation.

The O'Malleys let it be known that their plan was a migration: the whole lot of them, not just an eldest son, or daughter with a position waiting, but the whole bunch of them, part and parcel, from parents to oldest son, Peadar, to youngest girl, Maureen. They'd go when the time and cash came together, and if they'd be damned, well, then, they'd go and be damned and so be it.

Kevin O'Malley, the father, was a large red-haired and red-faced man who announced himself in the town's main pub to be a man of all trades and entertainments. He briskly listed his accomplishments to an unimpressed gathering: tradesman and craftsman; common laborer or skilled; a head for facts and figures; a teller of stories to hold the listener spellbound; a player of tunes and a singer of songs. To prove the last boast,

79

he motioned to his oldest son, a tall, vague, reddish-haired shadow of the father, who provided a fiddle which Kevin fondled for a moment and then briskly played.

He cajoled them all to join him in singing but they held back until his own voice, strong and clear, reached into them, surrounded them, embraced them, until they could feel the very tune reel inside their blood. One by one, the younger men first, uncertain and shy, glances cast at their elders, who finally moved their own lips, unloosed their own voices, joined in, unable to remain silent in the face of Kevin O'Malley's singing.

No one had any money to speak of, yet, carefully, eyes averted, as though they might be committing an offense, they placed the large copper pennies in the hat which rested, upturned, upon the bar.

"Don't be shy, lads," Kevin O'Malley roared at them. "Jasus knows, there's none to hear the dumb man and doesn't it bring joy to your hearts to hear the gifted!"

He traveled the countryside, his sons with him, his wife and girls awaiting him at home. He returned with his wagon filled with kindling or grain or a sheep or goat or two. Sometimes, he brought a rare bag of coins. Rarely did he return empty-handed, and when he did, he would embrace his wife and girls with rough heartiness and sit over mugs of tea and plan for future encounters with fate.

They acquired, somehow, through shrewd trade or dumb luck, a lean and fragile greyhound with haunted eyes and trembling frame. They raced him and won; raced him and lost; purchased a mate for him; raised some pups; sold some; raced others. Won and lost, but won more than lost.

Occasionally, Kevin and his sons disappeared for long periods of time and then returned home silent and thoughtful, reluctant to join the men in the pub or around the open fire in someone's hut. There were rumors went about at those times: that the O'Malleys had been up to a bad day's work to the north. But whatever the bad day's work might be, no one would care to speculate out loud, and the rumors, dark and dour and curious, would hang over them for a while until Kevin appeared, all gloom cast off, with a generous offer of a sup and a swallow and all such talk would cease. Yet there was always that about them: an aura of unspoken deeds done in the black of night, mysterious, unknowable and vastly intriguing.

Kevin brought into the town great surly brutes of men who hammered at each other's bodies and heads with mallet fists to the amazed and excited shouts of the men of five neighboring communities who traveled upward of ten miles by foot and wagon and paid their bread money to watch the matches.

Kevin sold and traded and acquired and dispensed: animals, goods, services, arrangements of all kinds. The O'Malleys seemed to live off the land or from up their sleeves for they were never known to spend hard coin. Cash was for the family's migration to America and for nothing else in this world or the other.

Kevin O'Malley's last great spectacle was not intended by him to be his last; it was as his fate decreed without consulting himself.

On his travels, he had come upon a huge beast of a man, nearer to seven feet tall than six, with shoulders wide enough for two men and legs as stout around as solid old trees and arms to match. He managed to convince the lad—he was a simple farm boy—to test his strength by lifting heavy things: stones and logs and man and animal. Kevin caught the basic flaw; while the lad had strength, he had no technique. He bent from his ample waist, so that when he lifted, all the exertion went to his back. Huge and strong though he was, he was no great weight lifter and Kevin took care not to teach him too much: just enough for Kevin's purpose.

His purpose was to match the boy against the strong men in various villages, to hold events and spectacles and have the wagering fall in such a way that Kevin O'Malley would, in a manner of speaking, emerge the strongest man of all of them. To convince the crowd that the great lad—his name was Aiden Doyle—could be beaten, for his mere size might discourage strong men to try him, Kevin, though a large man, no larger than those who might be reluctant, though tempted, would first oppose the lad. Because he knew the tricks and techniques of how to lift and shift and balance (for hadn't he and his own brothers performed for crowds when he was just a lad himself?), Kevin could handle a surprisingly great weight.

81

The lad's strength alone, without technique, could either come close to or beat Kevin, but the difference in their performance was slight enough to encourage men, who now measured themselves by Kevin's performance.

Kevin held his matches and won his coins, as he'd expected. The big fellows of each village could not resist the challenge. Encouraged by their chums, they proved their manhood by breaking their backs and soothed their injured pride by cooling their losers' thirsts in the local pub, whose owner, by arrangement and in appreciation, but mostly by arrangement, paid a certain fee to Kevin for each drink sold. For wasn't his spectacle the reason for the heavy drink in the middle of the week?

However, something happened that Kevin had not anticipated. Aiden Doyle, who worshiped Kevin completely, had taken to watching him carefully, emulating him, learning from him. Bending deeply at his knees, he taught himself to lift as skillfully as did Kevin O'Malley. In the process, he rendered himself unbeatable and no one wanted to match against him. Frantic to prove him beatable, for he was earning a nice coin from the events, Kevin offered himself against Aiden, but the word went around: "Sure, O'Malley, but he'd let you win to lure an unsuspecting opponent."

Livid at the accusation of dishonesty—which in this particular case was totally unwarranted—Kevin, on the spot, devised a test of strength which none could call dishonest.

He ordered his sons to release the horse from the wagon, and before anyone could believe what the man was doing, O'Malley was stretched face down under the wagon from where he declared he would lift the wagon six inches off the ground. "Then let's see if the lad can do the same. I'll warrant he can't, for though he's stronger than me on the surface, he's no technique. To prove me good faith, I'll take no bets on this event at all."

The crowd decided that no one at all, O'Malley or Doyle, could perform such a feat and they drew around astonished and impressed. If Kevin O'Malley could perform such a task, who among them couldn't take on the farm lad?

It wasn't as difficult as it would appear on the surface of it. It was a trick he'd worked out many years ago, a stunt he and his brothers had devised. It had to do with balance and force and technical things which didn't involve strength so much as skill, and Kevin knew young Aiden wouldn't be able to budge the wagon, and that his great failure would be an attractive lure to the men to try again.

Kevin O'Malley, aged forty-eight, positioned himself in the way he remembered from some thirty years past. He drew his breath in sharply, stiffened his body, pressed his hands flat into the face of the earth, dug the tips of his boots in and arched his body.

For one incredible instant, the wagon rose from the hard soil, balanced unbelievably, six inches from the ground, on the back of Kevin O'Malley, whose face, purple and stunned, seemed to freeze, turned black and collapsed at the same moment his outraged heart burst within his chest, failing, in its outrage, his otherwise fine and healthy body.

The newly widowed mother gathered her clan about her and bitterly informed them that their recently deceased father had been a damned and bloody fool but that didn't mean the rest of them should be stuck for all time in this empty and dying land scrounging for their pennies. She snapped her fingers at her eldest son, Peadar, who carefully placed a familiar canvas bag on top of the table. The mother knew, to the exact penny, how much hard cash the bag contained. More importantly, she knew what it represented.

"We leave at the end of this very week," she told them and they did.

There were a few unforeseen things prior to leaving, but they were cleared up to the widow's satisfaction if no one else's.

Matthew, the quietest of her five sons and two daughters, sought her out and with great stammering and blushing mentioned that he'd like very much to marry young Anne Foley from down the glen, and she a wild slip of a girl with a very bad temper. Widow O'Malley considered carefully, chewed her lip and advised him to speak with the younger O'Brien girl, Ellen, who was placid enough and had large blue eyes and a gentle expression.

Matthew did as he was advised, and though he was a great deal older than the girl, she thought him quite handsome and the idea of going to America seemed great fun. For his part, Matthew thought it probably would all work out pretty much the same in the end, and this way, his mother was pleased with him.

The next thing was with her son Brian, and a different lad from his older brother, though him only nineteen, but a will of iron. He was much taken, though God alone knew why, with the next O'Brien girl, Margaret, not quite eighteen, yet seeming younger than her sixteen-year-old sister. The mother knew she could not put Brian off, so there was no point to deny him. In a way, it would be good for the lad to have a steady country girl for a wife, for he'd need the protection from the trollops and wild girls in America.

Brian O'Malley's shadow fell on her before she heard the sound of him and she grabbed a handful of thick wool to keep her hands from trembling. The beige-eyed lamb protested the unexpected indignity loudly with much bleating. She concentrated then on gentling it and tried not to look up into his handsome face, but it became impossible.

"Well," he said bluntly, "we're off at last, now the dad's been done. The whole damned pack of us, off to the New World."

"What will you do there?" she asked shyly.

"Why, live, of course, and grow rich and powerful. My old mother's a brother there, in America, in Bronx City, that's in New York somehow. And he's to get us all into the Police Department there for he's a great many connections." His hand reached idly into the animal's coat, his fingers moved, caught hers and held. "Well then, Margaret. Your sister Ellen's accepted Matthew and he's nowhere near the catch that I am; here's your chance. Are you comin' with us or not?"

That was his proposal and she accepted.

They were married, two brides and two grooms, by Father McSweeney at the village church and he was secretly glad to be done with the whole mob of O'Malleys for he'd feared from the first they'd bring the wrath of the authorities on the whole village for their secret comings and goings through the years.

The O'Briens, mother and father, brothers, sisters, pressed the girls briefly in final embrace: they'd never come home, nor see them again. Ellen stared straight ahead, but Margaret watched over her shoulder as the land fell back and far away as they jogged in the O'Malley wagon to the sea.

The early years in New York City were a time of unrelenting terror for Margaret O'Brien O'Malley. They were a totally wild bunch, the O'Malleys, the girls as much as the boys, given to terrible bursts of temper and angry words which led directly to flying fists. They didn't care what harm they did each other or themselves for that matter. In their fights they wrecked the few sticks of furniture which were jammed into the long, dark and heavy-smelling rooms up three flights of stairs from the cement-covered world of New York's West Side. It was one of the things that bothered her terribly: that her feet never touched earth. But it didn't bother any of them at all. Nothing bothered the O'Malleys: not their surroundings; not the curious neighbors who spoke in an assortment of strange tongues and didn't like them any better than they were liked in return; not the reeking hallways which seemed just recently abandoned by pigs, for what other animals would foul their own living quarters. They walked through life with blackened eyes, bleeding noses, loosened teeth and declared with broad smiles that they'd given as good as they got in the long series of battles they encountered with life.

Ellen and Matt moved out first, to a flat somewhere "uptown," and Margaret had no idea how to get about the city to visit with her sister, who seemed content and perfectly satisfied. Margaret kept house for the others; Brian's mother and his other brothers and sisters were all in the same building with them. The old woman took care of children for some rich lady on Riverside Drive, though where that could be Margaret could only wonder.

The old one rushed off each morning, filled with her own importance, braving buses or subways without a thought. She returned home each night with an odd assortment of things which she distributed among them: a warm sweater the missus didn't need no more; a fine scarf, if a bit threadbare; no need to mend it, Margaret. Ah, Christ, the girl's so damn fussy and proud, you'd think her descended from the kings directly. Here, eat these damn things. They're tomatoes, the lady in the market said, and delicious even if they are filled with vicious little seeds. Swallow them down or spit them out, suit yourself.

The boys all went to work, but not in the Police Department, for they had to be citizens and it turned out the old woman's brother couldn't arrange things as easily as they'd expected, but in some mysterious manner, and in a short period of time, they each of them came marching in with heavy, fine printed documents which did indeed declare them now citizens of the United States and they began watching out for when various examinations could be taken to get them the jobs they wanted and in the meantime worked where they could for whoever would have them.

The older sister, Ann, a deep-voiced, two-fisted girl with the flashing blue O'Malley eyes, found herself a fine young man named Daniel Reilly, already situated in the Police Department, and pleased for a girl from home, and they got married and settled into an apartment in Brooklyn.

The younger sister, a holy terror named Maureen, was more than a match for the Sisters in the local parochial school and even the public school threw her out, she was so much trouble, with her bad temper and fierce wish to make trouble for herself and anyone who crossed her path. Her mother could beat her head bloody and her brothers could strap her sore but the crazy girl said she was bound to become a singer on the stage. She had a fine voice, inherited from her father and his father before him, but they'd not allow her to even think of such a terrible life and they had their hands filled with the girl and her bad temper.

But it all turned out in the end the way the O'Malleys said it would, *knew* it would all along.

Brian and Eugene, the youngest boy, did get into the Police Department when they reached the age. Peadar and John, for reasons that Margaret could never fathom, were declared suitable for the Fire Department but not the police, but this seemed to please them just as well.

Neither department would have Matt, for his eyesight was that bad and he had a very slight limp besides, but he'd found a position with a milk company that was to his liking.

They all moved to the Bronx eventually and Margaret

thought it was a fine place, with its great broad thoroughfare, tree-lined streets, quiet, peaceful parks. She and Brian found a fine apartment in the same building where Ellen and Matt lived, with Gene and his new wife taking an apartment in the very next house and the John O'Malleys eventually around the corner.

There were many Jews on the block, but mostly they lived on one side of the street or inhabited one particular apartment house or the other and didn't mingle much with any except their own. They seemed to Margaret a nice enough people, quiet and very fussy about their children.

Brian and his brothers called them various names—kikes and sheenies—but there seemed nothing malicious about it for they called everyone by various names, the niggers and the Polacks and the hunkies and the guineas and wops.

About the Italians, it was a very odd thing that Brian and his brothers called them so many names and made their jokes, for didn't their own wild little sister, Maureen, settle down and marry John Kinelli, even though they'd one and all vowed it would be over their dead bodies. But Maureen married John Kinelli in church with all of them present and not one of them dead.

All of them were settled and growing families of their own, fine large families of boys and girls. The Reillys, with their five redheaded sons, all with their dad's pleasant, mild face; and the Kinellis, with their brood of dark-eyed children, looking more like their dad but acting more like their wild-tempered mother and she getting mad at them and telling them they'd better watch it or they'd turn into a passel of damn guineas. And all the O'Malleys, nearly taking over the block, ranging from fine grown boys like Margaret's Brian and Ellen's Billy to toddlers like Gene's twin baby girls.

It was an odd thing, the way she'd think of that other place as home every now and then, when she'd buried her tiny infants here and raised her children here. And buried her husband; didn't that make this place truly her home? And yet, the pull and tug were there, and sometimes, in thought, she'd wander back and dwell there again.

Margaret O'Malley gathered her handwork and put it out of the way, where no one would sit on a needle or a pin. It was foolish to stay up, waiting for Brian to come home. It wasn't all that late and he'd be annoyed at the sight of her, as though he was some little boy. She walked quietly into the girls' room and put Kit's mended socks on her dresser.

The light from the hallway caught Roseanne's sleeping face and Margaret had to admit to herself, though it might seem sinful pride, that this girl had a special rare beauty which sometimes nearly took her breath away. She had fine fragile bones and flawless white skin and dark brows and heavy lashes, surprising with her light hair.

If she could have one wish for the girl now, at this time in her life, it would be that she could have the sense to get some understanding of life; that all was not of the moment; that it went by you so fast you've got to learn to pick and choose and savor. That Billy Delaney was not the world.

Margaret O'Malley bit her lip and turned abruptly from the room. She thought she heard Brian at the door and she'd best go and put some tea to boil.

ELEVEN

A raw blast of wind penetrated his jacket and Brian felt a chill mingle with the sweat that ran down his back. He clicked his tongue against his front teeth three times and moved toward the milk wagon.

"Come on, move, you damn bag of bones." He spoke without any real rancor; it was just a natural impatience toward the slow-moving horse as well as toward his slow-moving uncle. They were perfectly teamed and tuned to each other, and in some funny way, Brian thought, they resembled each other: Matt O'Malley and the horse, Cutter.

Each seemed to be constantly speaking to himself. Matt went on with a soft stream of words which contained portions of songs, complaints against the weather, his aching cold fingers, the company; he mused over orders, commented on the disrespect of young people, how everything was going to the dogs anyway. Everything, pleasant, unpleasant, said in the same monotone.

The horse, an unevenly gaited fat nag, lurched in sudden starts and fits which suited itself and never in response to the clicking and whistling signals to which it was supposed to respond. A deep rumbling sound constantly emanated from the horse's throat, and every now and then, it would toss its head wildly from side to side, as though commenting on its own discourse.

"Oh, takes me for a damn fool, does she? Well, we'll just see, then, we'll just see," Matt whispered to himself as he scowled over a note scrawled on a piece of brown wrapping paper. "Hey, Brian, take a look here. What do you think?"

Brian hopped onto the wagon easily. "About what, Uncle Matt?"

"Well, here, take a look at this note from Mrs. Flynn back at 2280. Thinks I'm a damned fool. Well, we'll see about it."

The note was concise and to the point. "No cream delivered on Tuesday. No money for no cream!!!"

Matt shook his head morosely, bent, sorted his orders. "I'm wise to her, lad. She had her cream, all right, delivered it myself. What she does is, gets a bit short of the cash, you see, and instead of mentioning it, she pretends the cream got stolen, or not delivered at all. Too proud to admit being a bit short, but not too proud to drink the damn stuff down." A smile pulled across his creased, weathered face. "I'm going to ring her bell next Tuesday morning, her regular day for a pint of cream. At five-thirty I'll ring her damn bell and present the damn bottle right into her hands." He laughed at his own cleverness, then noticed where the horse was pulling them. "Ho, you stubborn damn fool, get yourself off the sidewalk now. You've no brains at all in your great empty head."

The horse came to a halt, stood, implacable, front hooves on the sidewalk, head lowered: unmoving and immovable.

"I'll take 2308, Uncle Matt." Brian leaped from the wagon, hoisted the heavy wooden crate to his shoulder. He entered the darkened silent apartment house and moved rapidly to the fifth floor. He didn't mind the weight on his shoulder at all anymore. At first he'd had a shocking ache down his arms and legs and back but now he took pleasure in the awareness of his growing strength. He moved swiftly, distributed the orders, placed the bottles outside the apartment doors in the dimly lit hallway. He liked the way the bottles sounded when they tapped together lightly; it was a special early-morning sound that probably annoyed hell out of the people who were still trying to sleep. It was a reminder to them that their day was about to begin.

Brian's day began at three-thirty in the morning and he was surprised at how quickly he had become used to it. By six, he felt glowingly alive and strong; by eight, his first job of the day was over.

There was something special, mysterious, exotic about working when everyone else was still asleep, though he could not have explained what it was. It was a vague sense of owning some secret portion of the world, of being alive when everyone else was dead.

It would be like that when he was on the job. Someday. The next examination for patrolman wasn't scheduled for three years and that worked out exactly right because in three years Brian would be twenty-one. That gave him three years to study all the manuals, to enroll in Delehanty's and to build up a good work record on the milk truck with his uncle and at his job ushering in the Loew's Paradise. He knew that every aspect of his life had to be accounted for; the year and a half he'd been on his own could be discounted. His family would close ranks and the Civil Service people would never know he'd bummed around the country.

He stood for a moment in the doorway of the apartment building, surveyed the empty, barely light street. Christ, he wished time away, wished all the obstacles away, wished he could be part of the Department now, start proving himself *now*. It was funny about the Department. He'd never discussed it with anyone, never made any kind of decision, yet Brian always knew that someday he'd become a policeman, in the same way he knew, someday, he'd become a man. Maybe they were one and the same thing. Maybe the time he'd spent, alone and cut off and hungry, away from his family, the terrible unconnected time, maybe that made him realize what it was that he wanted to do with his life. He knew that the Department was more than a job; it was like being part of a strong, untouchable family. He'd heard his father say it, and his uncles: "We take care of our own."

He was taking care of his own now, of his mother and grandmother and sisters and brothers, but on nickels and dimes. When he was on the job, when he was in the Department, he'd make good money and it would be steady and regular and he would be a part of that vast mysterious masculine world where no one, not ever again, could ever consider him a boy. He visualized himself, dressed smartly in a blue uniform, the visor of his hat tilted just slightly over one eye; the gun heavy against his thigh, the way he'd seen it on his father's thigh. His hand slid around his narrow leather belt and he imagined it wider, with a little attachment containing six bullets which he might need, Christ, you might have to reload at any time; and the heavy gleaming handcuffs would be clipped to the left side of his belt.

Brian heard his uncle's voice, softly chiding to himself, and it brought him back to reality. Shit, three more years of lugging milk bottles and flashing a beam of light over worn carpeting down the long aisle of the movie theater. For one terrible, unbearable moment, the thought occurred to Brian: What if he didn't make it? What if he didn't pass the examination, or if he did pass, what if he didn't come out high enough on the list to get appointed during the life of the list? Or what if he came out high enough but didn't get appointed for three years or more? Each list lasted for four years. Just because the exam was timed exactly right for him, exactly timed to his twenty-first birthday, that didn't mean anything.

Brian O'Malley dug in his pocket, found half a stick of Juicy Fruit gum, unwrapped it and chewed it slowly between his back teeth and decided that there would be no goddamn "what ifs" in his life. He would do whatever the hell he had to do, study whatever the hell he had to study, learn whatever the hell he had to learn, and when he took that damn Police Department examination, he would come out so goddamn high on the list that he'd be appointed with the first group of recruits.

As suddenly as the unexpected terror came over him, it was gone and he felt strong and sure of himself. Hell, he was no snot-nosed kid; he'd survived on his own and he was taking care of his own. He flexed his shoulders slightly, felt the strength of his arms and legs, and on a sudden impulse, he spit the gum in a high arcing circle into the middle of the sidewalk.

Brian grinned at the sight in the middle of the street. The horse stood stubbornly in the center of the sidewalk and his Uncle Matt stood in the gutter, fists clenched and waving at the animal's nose. "Get your stupid damned gray arse off the sidewalk because I've had enough of your nonsense. You'll end up in the meat factory and the glue factory and be damned to you this time." In final exasperation, Matt thrust his face at the horse and said, "You're just making a damned fool of yourself, and that's the truth of the matter."

92

He turned to Brian and sought an ally against the animal. "Would you just look at this fool? Well, the Borden's people will be putting out more trucks before you know it, and this time I'm going to sign up for one. I've had it with this great nut all these years past."

The gray morning light hit Matt's hair and the horse's rump at uneven angles and it seemed odd and interesting to Brian. The two, man and horse, seemed the same color in this light— old musty gray.

Matt said, "Ah, to hell with you then, go off your own way if you've a mind to. I certainly don't care." Matt turned, winked at Brian and with feigned indifference he walked straight down the center of the street. The animal stood for a moment or two, shifted weight from one leg to the other, bobbed its head up and down, then plunged along after Matt, slowly at first, then it picked up its pace until its muzzle pushed and prodded against Matt's shoulder.

"Ah, begone with you, you stubborn old fool, you. I want nothing more to do with you. Now come on, who wants your ugly old face under his arm?"

It was a conversation between them and Brian watched each morning as they fussed and argued as they had for more than twelve years. There was a deep and mysterious bond which drew man and animal together. It was at once something very simple and something very complicated and at times Brian felt, seeing them, that he had come upon something private and personal.

The sounds they made, the men, the horse, the wagon, the bottles and wooden crates, were part of the early-morning-world sounds. Iron wheels were hard and nearly silent on smoothly paved tar, but there were wide streets still cobbled and the wagon rattled and groaned on those streets. The tentative beginning songs of early-rising, tough, ruffled little Bronx sparrows were interrupted by the sudden eruptions of clanging alarm clocks and the scrape of windows being raised or lowered and the far-off sound of trolley cars and the less frequent sound of car engines being turned over. Arriving shop-keepers invariably spoke louder in the silent morning streets, exchanging complaints with each other, comparing aches, predicting weather.

Brian caught up to the wagon and trotted beside the horse. He smacked his hand flatly, resoundingly on the animal's rump and it turned to stare at him, sad and offended. A sudden gust of cold air filled Brian with an almost unbearable sense of strength and happiness. He ran backwards before the horse, jutted his face up tauntingly.

"Hey, come on, you old nag, you. I could outrun you backwards, you horse meat!"

His uncle, at the rear among his bottles, felt the lurch and was thrown forward as the animal picked up speed. "What are you doing, Bri? For the love of God, lad, stop teasing the poor beast. Here, now, you Cutter, stop playing the fool and just ignore him or you're dumb as he is."

As soon as he tried to turn the doorknob, he knew there was something wrong. The door was locked and he'd left it on the latch as always. Only his grandmother ever locked the door and it was his grandmother who opened it even before he rang the bell.

Her eyes leaped wildly over his face. "Ah, Brian, thank God you've come home, thank God."

Her fingers dug into his arm, pulled at him. She studied his face intently, shook her head sharply as some sensible part took hold of her and dissipated her confusion. It was a mistake she'd made several times in the months since his father's death and it never failed to unnerve him when she thought him to be his father.

"What is it, Nana? What's wrong?"

"It's your mother, Brian. She's off to the hospital. She'll be all right. You hear, she'll be all right. Come and have some hot breakfast."

Roseanne looked up at him, her face taut, her hands busy portioning out breakfast. "Go ahead now, Kit. And you too, Kevin. Stop making faces at me."

"It's lumpy," Kevin protested, sullen as always.

"Your head'll be lumpy if I hear another sound out of you," she warned. She signaled Brian to wait, poured coffee for the two of them and led him to the living room. She put her own cup on top of the radio and handed him his.

He felt cold and numb as he watched her. "Well?" he asked finally, not wanting to ask, not wanting to be told.

94

Roseanne sipped from her cup, put it down again, wiped her mouth with her fingertips. "She's in Morrisania Hospital, Brian. About four-thirty this morning I guess it was. I heard Ma making strange sounds out in the kitchen, like she was crying or like she was sick, you know, vomiting or gagging. She was trying not to make a sound. You know her, never a word when she's not feeling well."

Roseanne had deep black rings under her eyes and her face looked pale and sick and drawn.

Brian put his cup down on the radio, next to hers. He kept his back to his sister and in an empty, hollow, reconciled terror he asked, "Is she dead, Roseanne? Is that what you're trying to tell me?"

He heard her gasp. She pulled him around to face her. "Oh, my God, Brian. No. No, don't even say . . ." She clamped her hand over her mouth for a moment, closed her eyes and shook her head. Then she breathed deeply and, not meeting his eyes, she spoke quickly and quietly. "She's had a miscarriage, Bri. We called Aunt Ellen and she and I took Mom by cab to the hospital. Aunt Ellen stayed and I came home to take care of the kids. Aunt Ellen's home now; she stopped by a few minutes ago to say it's over and Ma is resting."

"A *miscarriage?*" he asked incredulously. "*Mom?*"

Roseanne studied the coffee in her cup; she tilted the cup from side to side and watched the dark liquid as though fascinated by it. "She was four months pregnant. She had a miscarriage last year, just about this time."

Dumbly, he said, "I didn't know . . . she was pregnant."

"It was none of your business," his sister flashed at him. There was something angry and hostile, something he had never seen before. Confronting him, she seemed to be daring him to make any kind of comment, to say anything at all about their mother. There was something overwhelmingly female about her; the way she held herself, one hand clutched at the collar of her wrapper, the other arm across her body protectively. Her eyes, tired and troubled, watched him intently. She touched at the flat bobby-pinned circles still wound around her head and she looked older than she was.

"You go and see her this afternoon," Roseanne said.

He turned away. "I've got to go to work this afternoon."

"Brian, go and see her."

It was an odd, undeniable demand such as she'd never spoken to him before. There were deep, unmentionable things surrounding them all now, and in order to make it tolerable, for whatever reason, he knew he had to take that step: visit his mother, act natural, not let his mind wander on dangerous thoughts. Brian shrugged and returned to the kitchen.

Kit spooned at her cereal; it was a sugar-encrusted mess. Her large deep-blue eyes, replicas of his, of Roseanne's, of their father's, searched his face. She stopped the spoon midway to her mouth, let it drop with a splash into her plate. In a low voice, she asked him, "Brian, is Mom *really* gonna die?"

Brian twisted around to Roseanne. "For God's sake, didn't you tell them Mom'll only be gone a few days?"

"Of course I told her." Roseanne's fingers pinched Kit's shoulder. "I *told* you Ma had an attack of her gallstones again and that she'd be home in a day or two. I *told* you."

There was a sudden, explosive commotion as Kit O'Malley recklessly flung her small wiry body against Kevin. She knocked him backwards out of his chair and sent him sprawling across the kitchen floor in a clatter of broken dishes, spilled cereal and coffee.

Brian grabbed at her roughly, pulled and yanked at her. Her red face, damp with fury, struggled against tears. "Let go of me. Get your damn hands off of me. I'll kill you, Kevin, I'll kill you!"

Kevin leaped to his feet, his face white with rage and anticipation. "I didn't tell her nothing like that. She's a rotten little lying troublemaker."

"You said she was gonna die," Kit yelled and tried to break free of Brian's hold.

Brian turned to his brother and Kevin yelled, "Liar! You asked and I said *everybody* dies sometime or other."

Brian shoved Kit from him and reached for Kevin's shirt front. "You little bastard," he said in a harsh whisper. He shook his brother savagely with a surge of violence. "How would you like to get your ass kicked from one end of the street to the other?"

Kevin blinked compulsively and tried to pull himself free. "I didn't, I swear, Bri. She's a liar. I didn't tell her anything bad."

96

His sister swung past him at Kevin and he put himself between them. "Cut it out. Damn it, now cut it out!" He shook them both to gasping silence. "If there's another sound from either one of you"—he jostled them both—"I'll crack your skulls together, you got that?" Kevin nodded and he was released. "Go and change your clothes; you look like a damn slob. And you," he told his sister, "you go and wash your face and comb your hair and get to school." He pushed Kit from him and she stalked away, turned at the door, put her hands low on her hips and glared at him.

"I'm not afraid of you, Brian," she said in a furious voice.

Brian shook his head and sighed. "Oh, for Christ's sake."

TWELVE

He didn't want to think about the visit to his mother, and so on the trolley ride to the hospital, he let his mind become vacant. The wheels of the trolley car hummed along the tracks and the hum rumbled through the floor, through the soles of his shoes, up his legs and along his thighs. The vibrations became a part of him and he floated along, encased in vague sensation.

Sensation led to memory: fragmented memories, unbidden, each connected to the other through the medium of his flesh. As the streets of the Bronx slid and jerked past his unseeing gaze, Brian let himself be possessed by other times.

Everyone called her "Mad Sister Louise." It was a known and established fact that she was mad but her madness did not noticeably interfere with her teaching ability until the time of Kathleen Gagan's murder.

Sixth grade. Twelve years old.

She had been a totally unexceptional girl who resembled every other girl in Sister Louise's class. Neither heavy nor thin, her body unremarkable beneath the shapeless brown jumper, arms and throat concealed by the light-tan school blouse. What had there been about Kathleen Gagan that had caused some insane devil of a man to snatch out at her as she walked home from some errand? Her small bag of spilled groceries had been found outside of the alley which led to the basement which contained her battered and violated body. The man had been caught within hours; had been dragged away moaning and crying, his sounds dimmed beneath the screams and terrible voices of the neighborhood women. He had disappeared from Brian's life in a flash, lost behind unknowable walls of adult silence and glances. But Kathleen Gagan remained. The tantalizing mystery of Kathleen Gagan remained.

They had attended a Mass of the Angels for Kathleen, all thirty-five of her classmates. Stretched out in her small white box, her Sacred Heart Medal on a bright-red velvet ribbon flat against the whiteness of her confirmation dress, she did not look either murdered or violated, merely asleep. They all said their prayers and a lightheaded hysteria traveled from one child to the other for there was at the center of all this something no one would explain to them.

Sister Louise made a shrine out of Kathleen Gagan's desk and each day for the remainder of the school year, each day for nearly seven months, the small candle flickered throughout the school day and each school day began with each of them in turn offering at Kathleen Gagan's shrine a Hail Mary on her behalf.

But while his lips automatically formed the words, Brian's brain attempted visions of Kathleen and Kathleen's body, violated. Because he had no true idea of what her violation consisted of, what he imagined were gross mutilations, as shown in comic books, which he devoured in great gulps. Whatever he imagined, however, totally failed to satisfy some deep inexplicable need to know.

It was an eighth grader who eventually told him: a dirty, sly, cigarette-puffing eighth grader.

Then the praying over Kathleen's desk became more and more of an ordeal and the vision of Kathleen which appeared to him terrified him and he offered additional prayers for his own salvation rather than hers.

At the end of the term, Sister Louise was sent away for a rest and the shrine to Kathleen Gagan was removed from the sixth-grade room, but the shrine and all its implications remained forever in his brain.

He had ridden far past his destination. It was just as well. He needed to walk, to get some air, to physically move away from his memory.

But it was not the amorphous flesh of the violated Kathleen Gagan from which he tried to escape; it was the reality of his own flesh which sent Brian O'Malley plunging along the

Bronx afternoon streets. His sense of being a physical entity overwhelmed him and he drove himself, hard, mercilessly, until his hard-pressed lungs gasped for air, the tight-chested pain distracted him; he slowed down, jammed his hands into his pockets, felt the thump of his heart against his rib cage, felt the sweat down his back and the dryness of his mouth.

He dogtrotted, eyes straight ahead, but he didn't miss anything. He saw girls along the sidewalks, outside the houses, leaning against stairways; in idle conversation with each other, fingers raking short, waved hair, casual and nonchalant. But their eyes caught his, held for some brief instant of contact, signaled that mysterious quality of sexuality with no more than a glance.

The street he was on, no farther than a mile from his own neighborhood, had an exotic foreign flavor. Italian. Bathgate Avenue, Arthur Avenue. Heavy black-clothed women; dark hair and dark eyes and moist olive skin. Strange foods; long cylindrical cheeses tied with heavy string, which bit into the substance, like flesh, hung in grocery windows; salamis, hard and black; huge loaves of crusty bread, all tossed together, all piled up in a heap in the corner of a store window. Fragrance of spices, unknown, unfamiliar, wafted from a shop as a door opened for a moment; sound of a strange, dark, succinct language, some phrase that seemed significant, but which he could not grasp, intrigued him.

He watched as a woman, neither young nor old from his point of view, with a strong Madonna face, seized a small struggling boy by the collar and landed blows on the back of his head and shoulders. The sound of her words was fierce and hissing and the boy hunched his shoulders against the onslaught, but beneath the burst of the woman's anger and wrath, through the unintelligible words, Brian sensed how held in was the power of the woman. The blows were not intended to destroy; the boy yelled because it was expected of him, not because he was in real pain. The woman shoved her son, ordered him into the house, then turned, surprised that she had been observed. She shrugged, a universal movement of her shoulders, and Brian felt the impact of the gesture which had been directed to him. He was removed forever from the hunched shoulders of childhood and included now in the world of the adult. She stared at him for a moment, puz-

100

zled, then turned her dark liquid eyes from him and hurried about her business.

Brian stood nervously at the entrance to the long, narrow hospital ward, the visitor's pass held tightly in the grasp of his fingers, and searched for his mother. She was in the third bed to his left, her face turned from him; she seemed to be asleep. The room was warm, overheated, and she was covered with a thin white blanket which outlined the contours and divisions of her body. She was on her back and her legs were slightly parted and the blanket clung to her as though it were a sheet and he stood, fascinated, unable to move either toward the bed or away from it as some terribleness overwhelmed him. He had never seen his mother in bed, never, not once in his life, and he saw her now, absolutely, totally vulnerable and female.

"Who are you here to see?"

He turned, his face burning with guilt, and he tried to meet the narrowed suspicious eyes of a heavy-set nurse. He held his pass up as though to exonerate himself from accusation. She snatched the pass, then jerked her head and led him to his mother's bed.

The nurse leaned over and shook his mother's foot from side to side.

"Mrs. O'Malley? You awake? This your son here to see you?"

Her face was pale and she blinked in confusion and seemed to be trying to sit up but the nurse said, "You just stay put now. And you," she said brusquely to Brian, "don't you be tiring her out."

He leaned over awkwardly and kissed her cheek and felt her hand, fragile and weak on his. There was a white metal chair beside the bed and he sat on it, then handed her the box of cookies his grandmother had prepared.

"You okay, Ma?" he asked.

Her voice was thin and the smile was forced and her eyes seemed dark and filled with pain. "Now don't you go worryin', Bri. You'd no need to come at all. Sure I'll be home in a few days and there's an end to it. You're not to come again, what with all your workin' hours."

"Listen, is there anything you need?"

101

She moved her head listlessly, her eyes stayed closed for a moment, and when she opened them, she seemed to gaze past him. It occurred to him that they were avoiding each other's eyes, that there was something between them now that had never existed before: a knowledge which neither of them could even begin to approach. Instinctively, he realized the best way to handle it was to ignore it, to pretend whatever ignorance she needed from him.

"Don't you worry about anything, Ma, okay? The kids are fine. Boy, Roseanne bosses them around more than you ever did."

She smiled thinly. "They're all good kids, Brian. All my children are good." Her hand moved slightly and he pressed it. "Thank you for coming, son. I guess I'd best get some sleep now."

He was grateful to her, released from the nearness of her, from the discomfort they felt in each other's presence under these strange circumstances. He didn't look back, but left the room quickly, in long strides. He had to control an urge to run from the building. He rubbed his eyes against the strong, piercing unexpected December sunlight which glinted from remnants of ice on the sidewalk. He bent against the wind and lit a cigarette but the image was engraved inside his brain and neither sunlight nor glare of ice nor rapidly inhaled nicotine could erase it or relieve him of the deep terror which assaulted him; he would live with it forever, through all of burning eternity he would live with the knowledge that he had stood and seen his mother, and that her body, mysterious and forbidden, had aroused him.

In a sudden impulse, Brian crushed the cigarette into the palm of his hand, clenched his teeth at the burning sensation. He felt his stomach churn with nausea, his head ached, his throat was dry; his whole body pounded with an anxiety that seemed to have no beginning and no end. He walked blindly, inhaled a faintly familiar fragrance, stopped in front of a small stone church: St. Lucia of the Cross. As some elderly women entered, a whiff of incense mingled with the air and he breathed it deeply and felt an odd sense of relief. He could be free of the strangulating sense of guilt which he had avoided facing these past few months. He had known all along that his

102

confession to that nodding Italian priest hadn't been a good confession, hadn't been a true confession, hadn't been the cleansing confession which could truly save him.

He'd convinced himself that he'd truly repented and received absolution and that would be the end of it, but Brian O'Malley knew better, and the sad-faced, brown-eyed Father Concertta, cool hand on his burning forehead, had soothed him, asked only, "Do you truly repent all your sins, my son?" and Brian had whispered from his hot, dry mouth, "Yes, Father," and was given absolution: deathbed absolution.

Brian felt cold sweat chill his body. Dear Sweet Christ, if he'd died then, he'd have been condemned for all eternity because his sins went untold. He clenched his teeth because they began to chatter with cold and inexplicable fear and certainty such as he hadn't known since he was a small child enraptured by the graphic pictures in his textbook of all the souls in hell. His sins had been worse than those described in his third-grade textbook.

Flesh. The sins of the flesh.

By the time he reached Father Donlon's study, Brian O'Malley was bathed in the sweat of his own terror. The housekeeper took one look at his gray face, decided he must have come directly from murdering someone and ran to interrupt Father at his reading of the missal.

Father Donlon plucked off his wire-framed eyeglasses, blinked his small blue eyes in some confusion for the light in his study was dim. "Oh. Is that you then, Brian? For the instant, you looked so like your father, may he rest in peace, that you gave me a start." He squinted tightly, sensed the boy's state of mind and said calmly, "Well now, Brian, I've been rather expecting you'd come to see me sooner or later."

"Father Donlon, I . . . Father . . . I . . ."

Father Donlon was a small man, short and fragile, and his strong face seemed misplaced on his delicate body as his deep voice seemed to come from someone else altogether.

"Brian," he said firmly, "go down into the confessional, lad, and say five Hail Marys to calm yourself and then I'll be along."

Brian shook his head, distracted, but Father Donlon's hand guided him firmly and he did what he was told.

The prayers calmed him and when he heard the priest enter the confessional he felt more in control of himself. They went through the opening rituals quietly, by rote, and Brian began to feel a sense of security within the familiar ritual of confession: there was some sense of safety at last. He locked his eyes closed and resolved, with every fiber of his life, to make a good and true confession.

"Sins of the flesh, Father," he began haltingly.

"Did you commit acts of self-abuse, my son?"

"That, too, Father, but worse. I . . . I . . . When I left home, Father, there was a time, a period of time. In the south. I hitched a ride in a boxcar, Father, and I thought I was alone, and after a while, two . . . there were two other people in the car with me, Father."

"Who were they, my son?"

"Well, I thought at first that they were just little kids. They looked like little kids, but they were . . . not so little. They were a brother and a sister, Father; they were twins. Fifteen years old. And . . . and . . ."

"Did you commit a sin of the flesh with either of them, my son?"

Brian bit his knuckle until he gasped, but the priest waited patiently, soundlessly, without judging. His question was calmly put, unstartled, uncondemning.

"With the girl, Father. I . . . I had sexual intercourse with the girl. But it was worse than that. The boy . . . the boy watched. He leaned close and he watched and then . . . and then . . ."

"Did you have sexual relations with the boy, my son?"

"We were together in that boxcar for three days and three nights, Father. The car was sealed and we were locked in. They had been on the road for three years. I didn't know about . . . I swear, Father, I didn't know some of the things. They were younger than me, but they knew all kinds of . . . of terrible things, Father. Yes." Finally, strangling with the purging of it, Brian said, "Yes, Father, I had sexual relations with both of them."

There was a soft sigh from behind the screen which separated them, a sad, sorrowful sound. "Do you realize, my son, how this has offended God?"

104

"Yes, Father, I do."

"Do you truly repent, my son, not only the awfulness of the sins of your flesh, but the terrible pain you inflicted on our Savior through this weakness?"

"Yes, Father, I do."

"Have you anything more to confess, my son? God is merciful beyond our comprehension, beyond anything we deserve. He will grant you absolution if you truly repent."

He could not find words. There were no words to describe the constant, tantalizing, omnipresent sexuality which seemed to fill his brain more and more. There were specific and vaporous things. He tried to speak. "Father . . . I am locked in my flesh. I feel sexual desire. I can't seem to . . . to . . ."

Father Donlon said softly, for the first time speaking to him personally, "We are all made of flesh, Brian. We are all mortal and therefore imperfect. God never demands perfection, only that we truly *try*. Are you capable of truly *trying*, Brian?"

"I *want* to be free of it, Father, truly I do." He locked his eyes and the vision came to him: his mother's body, covered with the thin white blanket, outlined, female. He clenched his fists and hammered them on his knees fiercely. "Oh, Father Donlon, I think I'm beyond redemption."

"If you were beyond redemption, my child, you wouldn't be here, now would you?" He sighed quietly, patiently, and spoke in the measured tones of one who has heard all things, expected all things, was shocked by nothing. "You're at an age, my child, where the devil will mock and torment you through your awakening sex. It is a time of terrible testing for some, my child, and you must be equal to it. You've been given a heavy responsibility, Brian, at a very young age, and you've been chosen to set a good example for your brothers and sisters. You must give yourself more to your work, my child, keep yourself busy. You *can*, Brian, for I know your strength and I also know that God never sends us a burden greater than we can bear." It was a strong, determined, reasonable voice and Brian began to find some comfort, some reassurance.

"But, Father, sins of the imagination. Sometimes my thoughts drift off, they are so . . . so . . ."

"Yes, there are sins of the mind too, Brian; you've learned

that. But is there any other specific *act* that you should confess? Search your soul, my child."

He sat quietly hunched over, slowly shaking his head. "No, Father Donlon."

"Then make a general good confession, my child, and resolve to do better, to try harder." And then, in a gentle, sad voice, Father Donlon said, "Brian, don't let the sins of your imagination rule you, lad. Control both your mind *and* your body. Both were gifts to you from our Lord and given in trust. Don't abuse either of them."

Father Donlon assigned him penance and gave him absolution. Brian felt the heavy lump of pain in his chest ease and lift; as he knelt, praying his rosary, he felt an extraordinary sense of peace and resolve descend about him.

THIRTEEN

John O'Malley was nearly fifteen years old, but because he had been left back several times, he was in the same class as his younger cousin Kevin. He was a large, gawky, lumbering giant of a boy, with close-cropped reddish hair, a round, smooth, mild face with rich high color, somewhat blank, puzzled eyes and a broad and ready smile. No one had ever seen any display of temper, no mild anger or even annoyance, even when poor John had every right to such emotions. He had an enduring quality of unquestioning acceptance which caused some to think him saintly but most to think him simple.

His father, John O'Malley, Sr., had been a fireman. He had braved dense acrid smoke on the last day of his life, had entered the burning tenement building again and again, each time retrieving half-conscious little children and delivering them into the arms of burned, hysterical parents who blabbed in a language he didn't understand at all; whether Polish or Slovak or Ukrainian, it was all one to him, for he didn't understand any of it. What he and the men with him understood was that within the intense heat of the burning building were some others, dead or dying; it was their job to save the dying. He reached the last small child in a back bedroom; it had crept under a bed and died in the smoke, but he clasped the child against his chest—at least the mother would have the body—and as he reached the staircase to the street, it gave way and he tumbled to his death without even knowing that his young wife had newly conceived his own and only child.

She was a bride for only four months when they took to calling her Mary the Widow to distinguish her from other Marys among them. Mary the Widow she remained forever. She was a strange and lonely girl, remote, cast inward. For

107

long periods of time, she would sit and stare at a blank wall
as though seeing a picture show, while her infant son howled
and screamed for food or a change of clothing or just some
arms to hold him. Her only blood relative in the country was a
nun of the Order of Perpetual Help, a first cousin and dour
but helpful. She arranged for Mary the Widow to have care
and the infant to have comfort, first within the confines of their
own small apartment and then, when it became apparent that
wasn't working too well, a place was found for them at the
Order's hospital, which served an assortment of poor women
with terrible problems of one kind and another.

But it was Mary the Widow needed the hospitalizing and
the O'Malley clan took John in among them. He stayed first
with one bunch of them and then the other, but his true home
seemed to be with his Uncle Brian and Aunt Margaret, partly
because Margaret mothered him more than anyone, partly
because it was where his grandmother lived, and she claimed
him as her blood more directly than anyone else.

Mary the Widow had taken to long and solitary pulls directly
from the bottle, until her tired body would fall to the floor and
there she would stay until her son, poor John, would summon
help; then off she'd go and he'd appear and stay with his
cousins.

"For the love of Jesus, Johnnie," his grandmother said now,
"did the madwoman go off again?"

It always amazed them the way their grandmother spoke
about Mary the Widow to her own son. But John hadn't the
sense to either defend or blame his mother. He shrugged
good-naturedly. "Aunt Ellen said I should stay with her and
Uncle Matt and all because Aunt Margaret'll be just home
from the hospital and all . . . but . . ." He stood, grinned at
them all sheepishly.

"You'll stay here where you belong," their grandmother
said with a warning glare at Brian, who shrugged. "Now get
inside and wash your hands. Aren't you a huge hulk of a boy
to go about so filthy all the time."

Nodding toward Brian, the boy meekly went off to wash.
When he returned, the old woman, sighing, but not unpleased
to be surrounded by family, rose to her feet.

"Ah, well, I'll fix us all up with some good hot tea and cake.

And maybe there might be a story or two. You'd never know about that, now would you?" their grandmother said.

It was rare and special for her to gather them around her and spin one of her stories, to have both the chance and the inclination at the same time. She and Roseanne and Kit carried trays of sandwiches and cookies and cake and milk and hot tea into the living room and Brian put away his books.

Kevin, on his stomach, rested his face on his hands; his bony elbows dug into the rug. John sat on the floor, his back against the couch, feet pulled up, chin to knees. Martin sat on the arm of the couch, next to Kit. Roseanne sat on the hassock, which she'd pulled from under Brian's legs; her thin shoulders· hunched forward and she nibbled daintily on a small piece of sandwich one of the boys had left.

There was an expectant silence in the room. They all watched their grandmother's hands as she worked in the near-darkness. They heard the thin thready sound of the little bone instrument that plucked the string from one hand and twisted and weaved it intricately and precisely and ceaselessly as a spider. Her tatted webs covered all the chair arms and backs and tabletops of their home, but still she continued to spin the delicate secret designs whenever her hands were free of other things. As she spoke, her fingers worked quickly or slowly, according to the tempo of the story.

"Ah, yes," she said, looking at Kit. "She's Kate, indeed. And wouldn't I be the one to know, when it was myself seen her die that terrible morning?"

A shudder, a quick passing chill, went around the room. It was merely a story, what was to come. They had all, except possibly John, become aware of that through the years, that what she passed along to them as fact was largely fiction. What had confused them was the way she tied family into her tales: mothers and fathers, sons and daughters; she named them all. In truth, some portion of what she told had some basis in the family history, but through the years, time and places became confused in her narratives. What she stated happened, some great event, was historically inaccurate, and if questioned, called to task, the story, ruined, would fall about their heads. The telling, the listening, the being taken into the heart and substance of the tale, were what was important, not the picking up of fallacies and inaccuracies. Brian had learned that years before when he'd questioned some point of a story that didn't agree with a previous version. He'd been dragged from the room by his father, had his face smacked for calling his grandmother a liar and got shoved off to bed. After that, he kept his questions to himself and accepted the stories for what they were.

"A wild girl she was, my sister, Kate. Me father himself was after telling her she'd best settle down. 'Settle down, Kate,' sez he, 'there's other lads a plenty and that Johnnie Driscoll you've an eye for is as good as dead for didn't the Black and Tans catch him and his crew and will shoot him dead come mornin'.'

"And didn't she get a look in her eye then and tossed her head at my father himself and sez, all cheeky and tart and so fresh it would make your blood turn cold, she sez, shrewd now, 'Well, mebbe yes and mebbe no. Mebbe they'll be some others dead come mornin' as well.' Well, himself, may he rest in peace, terrifying man that he was, didn't the man pounce on the slip of a girl and plant his fist on her mouth and knock her half across the room and the poor old mother cryin' all the time. 'Oh, now, Patrick,' sez my mother, 'oh, now, Paddy me love, she's just a small girl and you'll be killin' her.'"

With each character, her voice changed. She was young and smart and bold for Kate, a low, hard growl for her father, a weak, pathetic whine for her mother.

The tatting bone moved constantly, click and pull and twist.

"'She'll be done with all that foolish talk then,' sez me dad. 'I'll have no trouble inside this house of that sort,' and off he goes for his pint and bit with the boys. Kate waits him out, shrewd she is, then stands up fresh as ever and the blood still wet on her mouth. 'Good-by, Mother,' sez she, 'for you'll not see me again.' 'Oh, Jasus,' cries me poor mother, 'don't say that, Kate, for there's some that says you've been made wild by that Driscoll boy and he's to be shot in the mornin', and let the devil take his own but don't bring down trouble and shame on your poor old mother's head.'

"'Tis not disgrace but glory,' says Kate." The old woman's hands stopped for the first time, immobilized by her words. She repeated the phrase in wonder and her grandchildren

110

seemed to lean forward slightly to catch it the second time. *" 'Tis not disgrace but glory."*

The hands moved again, spinning, creating. "Ah, God love us, but she ran from the house and the mother pulled a shawl about me and sez, 'Follow her, Mary. Follow your mad, wild sister. Don't let her get herself into something terrible. Your dad'll kill her for her wildness one day.' Well, I followed her but she ran so quickly, Kate did, always faster even than my brothers, and headed straight as an arrow to where the lads held their dark secret meetings, and weren't the English always trying to find out where, but couldn't.

"Well, I waited the long cold night, not knowing what I feared the most, those crazy plotters inside or the English outside or my own father himself waiting at home. I was a slip of a girl then, yes.

"And then the dawn came, all cold and shining hard. Out they came, the plotters, all sleepless and frozen-eyed from plotting their terrible plans all the night long. At first, I didn't even know me own big sister, she seemed for all the world some fierce dread stranger, her hair loose and wild, her eyes all large and seeing things not there and not seeing what was. I caught her arm. 'Kate,' I sez, 'for the love of God, Kate, it's your own sweet sister Mary and the mother sent me to fetch you home.' And she turned to me and sez in so strange and lovely a voice it sent the shivers along me spine, 'I'm goin' to me own home with Johnnie Driscoll this mornin' and we're to take some of them with us, but they'll go their own separate road from us. It's hell for them this morning', dear.'

"And, oh, holy saints protect and love us but she was a sly one and kept her arms locked tight inside her shawl for that was where she carried the sticks of dynamite.

"And marched proud she did, right to the encampment where they had the poor lads all tied up to their death stakes and themselves lined up and facing them with their great long guns. And I stood shaking with the fear of death, and not ashamed to admit it." The old face looked up, scanned them, dared any to call her coward but no one did. "Well," she continued, "anyone with any sense at all in their heads would have feared that dreaded place, but not Kate. Went right up to that British commander and all his soldiers there about him.

111

Shook her head of wild black curls in all directions and he was taken by the astonishing beauty of the girl. He sez to his men, 'Well who's this beautiful thing here?'

"'Well, Captain,' sez my Kate, all soft and sweet, 'why don't you and your good lads go on about to your homes and tend to your chores? Sure, what is it you're about this early in the mornin'?'

"He laughed, the captain, and sez, 'I'll tend my chores, girl, and then have some time for you.' And at this, doesn't Johnnie Driscoll, at the stake, let out a terrible earth-ripping cry to reach heaven and hell and it stopped only by the louder sound, the sound of guns going off all in the row, for the captain had given his signal behind Kate's back and the men fell dead and dying at their stakes and then the captain gave his orders and they was all finished off.

"Kate walked all smooth and floating like to Johnnie Driscoll, then turns and faces the British captain, who followed close behind. Jasus, save us, but her face was like white marble, all cold and lovely and composed, and her voice, sweet and lovely and calm. All the more terrible, for there was her own sweet love, Johnnie Driscoll, dead at her feet, his blood all over her skirt.

"'Come over close to me, Captain dear, do, for I've something nice to show you.'"

The tatting ceased. Abruptly, she put the ivory-colored thread to her mouth and bit at it. Carefully, she smoothed the bit of lace on her lap, then looked up. "And show them something she did, God love us. The simple fools clustered about the girl. Oh, Jasus, they flocked to see what it was she had to show the captain and it was the blinding flash of hell. Then there were bursts of dynamite and guns all around for wasn't my poor sister Kate's explosion the very signal the other lads, hidden all about, were waiting for? And they blew up all the artillery the troops had stored there and the explosions went on for all those many hours until your head was like to break from the noise. And many a lad died there that day."

There was a fragile, thoughtful silence and a thin, tired, dreamy voice asked, "And they never did find a single trace of Kate's body, did they, Nana?"

No one turned or glanced at Kit. Her voice was eerie, not

her own, and it was easy in the dimness to dream many things about their own wild sister.

"Ah, they never did at all, love, they never did at all. Nor of Johnnie Driscoll either, for though he was seen to be shot, all trace of him disappeared in the explosions, and that's strange, isn't it?"

The old woman rocked back in her chair and studied the ceiling, then said, "And there was some who said they've seen the two of them, wild and happy as you please, racin' up and down a mountainside and laughin' and carryin' on in the devil's own way." She hugged her body, arms close, hands on elbows. "Well, I'll not say nothin' about it, one way or the other, not havin' seen for myself. But I've heard about such things. Yes, I've heard tell of such things."

Kit drowsed, warm and distant, holding the wild, brave girl deep inside herself till she fell asleep where she was on the sofa, and Brian heard her call out once during the night from inside of a dream. He couldn't make out what name she'd cried. He folded his arms beneath his head and stared at the black space and heard the sounds of breathing, each one so individual from the other, marking and defining the sleeper.

His grandmother shouldn't tell Kit the stories about that wild dead Kate; the kid was wild enough as it was. But it was strange, when he thought about it. It was strange. All of them, each of them, part of each other and part of people who had lived and felt and been angry and been brave and been cowardly. Whatever truth there was or whatever Nana made up, they *had* come from a long, unknowable line of people whose names they carried. Kevin O'Malley, who danced and sang and fiddled, married the old woman, who was young then, and who it was said Roseanne resembled; and Martin it was said bore the same solemn face of some other Martin, long buried in distant hills. All of them carried lines and threads as intricately woven as his grandmother's tatting and tales.

All of them contained within them not just themselves but parts and pieces of each other and of the strangers whose names they bore. Brian watched the darkness become heavier and heavier and he rocked his head from side to side, puzzled by his gentle and contemplative mood.

113

FOURTEEN

Peadar O'Malley leaned his long body against the back of the wooden chair and flexed his shoulder muscles. They were good muscles still, fireman-strong and flexible and reliable. Barely moving, just turning his head toward the hallway, he said softly, "If I catch any of you damn kids out of your beds, I'll whip the bejesus out of you and give you a second dose tomorrow." He waited, allowed the bare feet to run almost soundlessly before he checked the hallway. "Lucky for them," he called out loudly through the apartment, then turned back into the kitchen.

"Damn little bastards," he said good-naturedly, "always think they're missing something. Well, Brian, is it some beer you'll be drinking?"

Brian knew they were all a little uncomfortable with him. It gave him the edge he needed for the advantage was all too much with his uncles. He moved his hand vaguely. "Nothing just yet, Uncle Peadar, but thanks."

"All around for the rest?"

Matthew O'Malley reached for his glass and sipped his beer and wished to hell Peadar would get on with it. It was well enough for him, he'd worked an afternoon shift and had all morning to sleep away.

Eugene O'Malley, the youngest of the brothers at thirty-four, turned his dark-blue gaze to his nephew. "Matt treating you all right, Brian? He's getting on for an old fella is Matt, but we can't let him take advantage of your youth and inexperience."

Brian slid a cigarette from his pack and hunched over the match which Gene extended. "Thanks. Well, I think I can handle my end of it, Uncle Gene."

114

"That was quite a spell of time you were on your own altogether, Bri, wasn't it? Well, you've fit in back home and done a good job of it too, haven't you? And you managed well enough when you was on your own, I guess?"

Peadar had his father's voice; Gene had his father's eyes and dark hair. Only Matt, quiet, thoughtful, somewhat vague, demanded nothing from him, no explanation. Brian's voice was a little taut and dry.

"Well, I managed, yeah. And learned a few things too, I guess. I guess you'd say I learned the hard way — on my own."

"Well, that's the way a man's got to learn things, isn't that so, Peadar?" Gene's eyes stayed on his nephew though he'd addressed his brother.

Peadar took a long swallow then put his glass on the table. "Well now, then, Brian. I guess we've a few things to clear up here, haven't we, lad? Is there anything you'd like to say, anything on your mind that we might like to hear about before we get to the business at hand?"

It was the old challenge voice: Go ahead, kid, go ahead. Try. We're ready for you, you cute little bastard.

But Peadar wasn't his father and he'd gone through what he had had to go through with his father. It was strange; he felt they were trying to bait him and he felt no need to rise to their bait.

"I thought there was something *you* wanted to say to *me*, Uncle Peadar. Hell, that's why we're all here, isn't it? Ma said you wanted to talk to me."

Gene narrowed his eyes and studied him, then said, "He's sharp, Peadar, is our young Bri."

Brian nodded. "That's what I am, Uncle Gene. Sharp. A little young maybe; a little damp behind the ears still. But sharp enough."

What his mother had told him was that they were out of money. They had managed for nearly six months on what Brian brought home from his two jobs, on the small amounts Kevin and Martin kicked in occasionally from their odd jobs, on the few dollars Roseanne contributed from her evening job in Loehmann's department store.

It had come as a surprise; whenever he'd tried to discuss their financial situation, she'd brushed it aside and he'd assumed they were okay. Then she'd told him: the insurance

115

money was nearly gone except for the sum set aside, irrevocably, for Martin's seminary studies. That was untouchable. It had been a small sum to start with and there had been the expenses: her hospitalization and clothes outgrown and food eaten and all sorts of things.

The only thing they had left was a piece of property which his dad had bought along with his brothers.

"They bought this lovely bit of land, Bri," his mother said, "not an hour's drive from here. We were all to build summer cottages. There's a lovely sparkling lake and all and it will all be private, Brian, just the family. Peadar and Eileen and Matt and Ellen and Gene and his family and your Aunt Ann and Uncle Dan Reilly and Maureen and John Kinelli, the whole mob of us was planning to have cottages and keep it for the family to spend summers together."

When his uncles questioned Margaret about her financial situation, though she'd been reluctant, she had finally revealed that they were low and in need of some cash. His uncles had offered to buy out the piece of land his father had bought.

"It was decent of them to offer, Bri. They've even offered a bit higher price than your dad paid. And of course we'd all still be welcome to use any of the cottages any of them finally build. We are part of the family, even so."

He was angry, first, that she'd discussed their situation with them; it touched a raw edge of pride in him. He was either the head of his family or still one of the boys and he had to have it established once and for all.

It was his grandmother who fixed it in his mind, whispered crazily into his ear, dug his arm with her long, hard, bony fingers. "Hold on to that piece of land any way you can. I don't give a damn in hell whose house you're to be welcomed into; hold the land yourself."

That was exactly what he intended to do, though they'd no notion of it yet.

They were treating him as though he were still a boy; they kidded with him, prodded him a bit, provoked him a bit in the way of men, but he wasn't fooled. They considered him a boy.

"Well, Brian, we're all family here and there's no need for any of us not to speak right up," Peadar, the oldest, told him.

116

"Hell, that's why we didn't have John the Wop here tonight or even Ann's husband for that matter either, but just the O'Malley men." Peadar kept his eyes on the beer as he poured into his glass from the small jug. "I understand you've signed up at Delehanty's, lad, and you're studying for the Department examination. It's a long way off yet, isn't it?"

"I figure that'll give me a long enough time to prepare myself, Uncle Peadar. I'll take the exam when I've just turned twenty-one. Maybe I'll get lucky and get right to the top of the list."

"Jasus, Matty," Gene said, "but don't the time go by fast. Here's our Brian's son and talking about making the list. I look at you, Brian, and I see myself not all that many years ago. It goes fast, the years, lad."

"I guess so. But that's not what we're here to talk about tonight, right?"

Gene clicked his tongue sharply and nodded. "He's a sharp guy, right, Peadar?"

"All right then," said Peadar, finally. "We've been keeping our eyes open, lad, and, God knows, we realize how hard things've been. You've done a good job, keeping your heads above water, but you know, there's nothin' to be ashamed of at all in running out of the cash on hand. And you're just a lad and you've done a fine job. We know you've been near to killing yourself working that hard—"

Matt observed dryly, "He doesn't exactly kill himself on my wagon. So if he's near death from overwork, it must be from whatever the hell he does in the Loew's Paradise at night."

"Ah, well, when we get him in the Department, Matt, he'll learn what hard work is," Gene said. "Unless he becomes one of the forty thieves, like Peadar here, and learns to sleep a lot."

"Oh, for Christ's sake," Peadar said, "can't we get on with the matter at hand without your interruptin' every minute or so?" He glowered around the table and his brothers shrugged and drank their beer. "Well now, Brian, as you know, we all got together more than a year ago, your dad and your uncles and me, and all of us bought this nice land your mother told you about. And we've started some of us putting up our little cottages and all." He cast a far-off glance, over the top of the refrigerator, his eye fixed on another scene. "It's a grand

117

place, truly. And your dad had a nice plan for his house." He shook his head. "Ah, may he rest in peace, Brian had some plans of his own."

"May he rest in peace" circled the table.

It was Brian who brought them sharply back. "Mom says you want to buy our piece of land and divide it amongst yourselves."

Peadar watched him closely. "Well, that's a sharp choice of words, lad, for the reason we've offered to buy is to give *you* a bit of cash rather than *us* a bit of land." He raised his chin slightly, ready to see if any offense was intended.

"I realize that, Uncle Peadar."

"It isn't that we're givin' you something for nothing, Brian. God knows, we're all family here and we've all our pride and don't take something for nothing. We've offered your ma a fair price, so there's no problem and everyone should be happy," Peadar said. "And of course, lad, as I've told your ma, why you're all of you to come to the lake any time—"

"Well, there's just one thing, Uncle Peadar."

Peadar leaned forward; they all sensed the tension emanating from the boy. His finely cut profile held very still and he met Peadar's eye straight on. He seemed a little straighter in his chair; something had definitely changed in the room and the change had to do with young Brian. It was as though they all understood: there was something of importance about to occur.

Peadar leaned back in his chair and gave his nephew his complete attention. "And what might that one thing be, lad? Eh?"

He took a quick breath, then said, "I'm not selling."

"*You're* not selling?"

"That's right."

Gene said, "Well, that's interesting, but the land isn't in your name, Brian, so it's your mother's decision to make, isn't it?"

Brian shook his head slowly and turned to Gene's bright stare: his father's narrowed hard look. "It's in *my* name now. I thought it would be a good idea, since I'm the head of my family. Mom signed it over to me."

"Signed it over to you? What's that mean?" Peadar de-

118

manded, for it meant more than he had been prepared to concede.

"It means the deed has been transferred to my name. It means that I'm the owner of the acre of land which is smack in the center of your property, Uncle Peadar." He licked his lips and tightened his fingers along the edge of the table. "And I've decided I don't want to sell." He waited but held their attention so that they knew he wasn't finished. Quietly, he added, "Just now, that is. And not to any of you."

"Well, exactly what's that supposed to mean, Brian?" Peadar asked in his soft, low, intimidating voice. "The choice of words has me a bit puzzled, lad, you're not wanting to sell 'just now' to any of *us*. I seem to hear something beneath the words and you're working your way toward whatever the hell it is you really want to say, so since we're all family here, suppose you just cut out all the baloney and tell us what you've got in mind."

Quickly, Brian said, "Okay." The hard image of his father glared at him, surrounded him, from Gene, from Peadar, now even from Matt, who revealed some inner hardness. Brian cast around quickly at them, found no special face to focus on, kept himself from lighting a cigarette and plunged ahead. "The first thing is that I'll offer you the land for *rent*. Five dollars a month from each of you."

"You'll *rent* it to us? *Rent it?*" Peadar asked, incredulous.

Brian studied his fingernails before he risked the rest of it. "If you don't want to rent it from me, my alternative would be to sell it." He looked directly at Peadar now, the challenge finally out in the open. *"But not to the family."*

"Holy Mother of God," Peadar intoned and they stared at their dead brother's son and absorbed what he had just said.

"Brian," Gene said, "you ought to get your goddamn head shoved right through that wall."

"You're talkin' a bit of blackmail, sounds like," Matt observed thoughtfully.

It was Peadar who reached out finally and punched him roughly on the side of the arm with the side of his fist. It was a man's gesture to a man, respectfully, grudgingly admiring. "You sure are a cute son of a bitch, Bri," he admitted. "Is that what you learned all that time out on the road?"

"I learned how to survive," Brian said. "Could I have that beer now, Uncle Peadar? I could stand to wet the whistle now."

"I think we'll have a good belt of whiskey all around," Peadar said. "I think we could use it at this juncture."

It was a mark of passage and he swallowed the hard shot of whiskey down the back of his throat and blinked the rush of tears back and absorbed the new way his uncles looked at him with a growing sense of his own place among them.

Finally, Matt O'Malley said to his brothers, "Sweet Mother of God, if the old man could see his grandson, oh, wouldn't he ever spin in his grave. The little bastard's turned himself into a *landlord* of all things!"

FIFTEEN

It had been known from his earliest childhood that Jimmie
John O'Brien was marked with a special gift: the gift of joy.
It was not a wild and frightening joy, tinged with the constant
threat of violent action such as surrounded the O'Malleys. It
had a special quality and it was all his own.

Jimmie John had been a somewhat quiet, contemplative
child who had done all chores willingly if somewhat absent-
mindedly. If rebuked or walloped by his father, it was all the
same to Jimmie John for he was not given to grudges or
brooding.

Mostly, his failings were caused by his being taken to things
most people didn't even notice, and so he forgot what it was
he was about. He saw and held to all the minutiae of his daily
life. He found a special beauty in sights and sounds and smells
and was entranced by the vast unknowable connectedness of
things one to the other. He could stand for hours, his eyes
scanning and counting and recognizing each of his flock; he
knew the relationship each bore to the other, for though they
might seem identical, each animal was special and had its own
special and particular way of viewing life. Jimmie John saw
and knew what others could not be bothered with.

It was this special vision and awareness which filled him,
lifted him, enabled him to catch the sudden hint of spring air
that wafted through a dark winter morning before anyone else
had any idea that winter was indeed coming to an end.

Jimmie John sang nearly all the time. His was a clear, pure
voice which could rise and fall with ease, which caressed and
tasted and savored and enjoyed equally the saddest of songs or

121

the gayest. His instinct for melody was true; he could sing anything he'd heard just once and return the song with something extra added to it: a part of himself.

He joined the O'Malleys, to whom he was twice connected by his two sisters, when he was a fair-haired lad of twenty-two. Even then his look marked him out as special, for at that tender age, his hair, which was long and silky, was as purely white as if he were a man of sixty, yet his heavy brows were black and his eyes a clear grass-green. He had been a gangling boy at home, all large knobby wrists and raw hands, and he'd seemed constantly stooped against the wind. But he had grown into himself and held himself tall and straight in a manner that might be called proud by those who did not know his gentle nature.

The O'Malleys immediately tried to take possession of him. They found him a job as a dishwasher for a small but honest wage, with lunch thrown in, at Schrafft's restaurant on Madison Avenue. His large hands were reddened even more by the harsh water and soap but the constant good nature of the boy was always evident. Before long, Jimmie John, decked out in clean starched white trousers and shirt, neat little black bow tie clipped to his collar, jaunty little hat perched over one eye, was serving in the position of sandwich man behind the gleaming dark wood counter. The manager had guessed, quite rightly, that the lad had a quality which was good for business. He had a lovely politeness and bright pleasant smile and happy manner which came over as great vitality and he was attractive to the lady lunchers.

Jimmie John became a focal point at the counter and he was seemingly unaware of the watchful, hopeful, hungry eyes which followed his swift, graceful, effective movements as he delivered the little toasty sandwiches from the dumb-waiter to the counter, unfailingly delivering the right sandwich to the right lady.

None of the O'Malleys knew how it had come about, though they had all speculated through many hours of fanciful calculation. Jimmie John's extreme discretion was a source of annoyance to them and they were left entirely to their own imaginations as to what took place in Jimmie John's life at a certain point. It just came about, somehow, that one of the

122

lady diners, a rich widow with more than fifteen years on him, had taken a fancy to him. Jimmie John must have returned her feelings, for he did a totally incomprehensible thing.

At age twenty-five, and just at the time an examination for the Police Department opened for filing, and the O'Malleys had arranged an application for him so that he could join them in their chosen career, the lad packed his meager belongings —a collection of clean underwear, several pairs of socks, an extra pair of trousers besides those he wore, two clean shirts, one warm sweater and one light jacket—and informed them all that he was off to start a new life.

"But what the hell are you talkin' about then?" Peadar demanded.

Jimmie John, considerate as always, said, "Why, it's a life you'd not approve, Peadar, so why should I burden you with it?"

"Well, I've some right to know, seein' as how you've been under my roof for nearly two years and seein' as how was me arranged yer fine job for you in the first place," Peadar reasoned.

Jimmie John conceded to some extent. "Well, all right then, but I'd rather not say too much, you understand. You see, Peadar, a fine lady has taken an interest in me."

"A fine lady? *Taken an interest in you?* Now what the devil does that mean?"

Amiably, Jimmie John said, "Why, Peadar, it's that which I'm off to find out."

That was it. It was all he would say and he left them to ponder without a further word of explanation ever.

When next they saw him, it was not a beaten, shamed boy but a quietly relaxed, subtly changed man. Any lesser than the O'Malleys would have been in awe of him for he arrived, unannounced and unexpected, with the beam of good health glowing from his handsome face. He wore obviously expensive clothes: a handsome dark-gray sharkskin suit, crisp white shirt and dark tie. His shoes gleamed not only with high polish but from the quality of the leather.

They had predicted, darkly, that he would return with his tail between his legs and his sins to account for. It had taken two years and he came laden with gifts for one and all, unmistakably thoughtful gifts, each chosen specifically for the one for whom it was intended.

It was clear once and for all that no power on earth could force, cajole or jolly any more information from Jimmie John than he cared to relay and where his personal life was concerned he was pleasantly tight-lipped.

Through the years, Jimmie John appeared and disappeared in and out of their lives. Sometimes he'd stay with Ellen and Matt, but more often with Margaret and Brian, for his bonds of kinship were stronger and more natural with Margaret. She had a discretion close to his own and a deep inborn loyalty which respected his own strange loyalty to the unknown woman.

There were times, though Jimmie John never let slip a word of complaint or concern, but there were times Margaret knew her brother's visit was because he'd had some falling out with the woman. He'd arrive, somewhat pale and hesitant, empty-handed and with just the clothes on his back, and stay a week or so, rarely more. Each night he'd wash his shirt and under-wear carefully, not letting Margaret do his laundry. Bedded down in a pair of borrowed pajamas, which he'd wash each morning, Jimmie John would sleep, rise and shower and press his shirt and dress and get the kettle up before anyone in the house was awake.

Another thing he insisted on: he'd help with the household chores. He'd perch on a window sill and sing and polish the panes to a high gleam, then go to work on the floor to make it shine as well.

"For Christ's sake," Brian would say about his brother-in-law, "is that what he does for *her*, then? Is *that* his special talent?"

But Margaret knew there was no work that did not give Jimmie John pleasure; yet there was more than the joy of doing involved. He had to have some way to pay for his bed and board. In the evenings, he sang and told stories to the children and just kept them all good company and they'd feel better for his presence.

As suddenly as he arrived, Jimmie John would depart with just a word, a quick hug and a whisper in his sister's ear. "Thanks, darlin', for your kindness. God watch over and love you until next time."

And then he'd be gone and that was the way of him.

He'd come in October, when Brian had been killed, stayed a few days, filled himself with a thousand chores Margaret didn't even know of but couldn't have done without. Then he departed from their lives with nothing but a postcard at Christmas with the words "My love to all from Jimmie John" scrawled in his beautiful fancy hand across the entire message space. The picture on the other side of the card was from some place called Hollywood, Florida: a big pink hotel with all tall, thin feathery palm trees lining a white beach with blue water.

Now here he was, on a June evening right in the midst of them and keeping them all from killing each other.

"Oh, I've got some surprises for all of you, but first let me get my fill of you," Jimmie John said. They were just as anxious to get their fill of him, though the two youngest, Kit and Kevin, still red-faced and panting from their fight, were anxious to have a look at their presents.

For the first time, Brian considered him as more than the glowing, cheerful apparition who periodically brought a sense of excitement and adventure into their lives. He found himself now somewhat puzzled and confused and curious and even somewhat anxious and resentful. All the overheard discussions, all the tossed-off, scornful, admiring jokes, all the mystery of his uncle's life, came to mind and he studied Jimmie John intently as though the answer might appear on his face.

Brian felt the blood rush furiously to his cheeks when Jimmie John turned his green eyes on him, cocked his head to one side as though he'd just been asked a question.

Jimmie John smiled and said softly, "Ah, his father's son. In your build and in your features, Bri, you've got his looks. But you're yourself too, aren't you?" He nodded slowly and smiled. "Yes, that's the important thing, isn't it?"

Brian had to get off to work but he left them all in a bubbling excitement: Roseanne, finished her crying and sulking and easily wooed by her uncle's kind words; Kit and Kevin, all rivalries forgotten, bursting with greed for their presents; his mother, glowing with the softness of her love for her brother; his grandmother, muttering darkly but still eager and curious; Martin, quietly among them, accepting all their

125

wild angers and bursting joys. He'd have to think about Jimmie John; he'd have to contemplate the mystery of him a bit more.

"Can we look, Jimmie John?" Kit begged, her hands plucking at his sleeve. He was their only relative to discard the title that marked his elevation over them. He was never one of the vast army of grownups who seemed to be free to correct them, yell at them, smack them, tell them what to do and how to do it, to catalog what they did wrong, to tell them they had to shut up, or get up, or get out or get in.

He was for all his tall and shining and immaculate elegance one of *them* and understood their driving impatience to get on with important things.

"Of course, love," he told Kit and opened one of the suitcases he brought. "Dig in, then, until you find something marked with your name."

They tossed aside various packages done up in fancy paper, shoved away what wasn't for them, rummaged through yards of heavy linen and filmy, almost vaporous, material which was seized by Roseanne with small shrieks of delight. Margaret tried to contain them, warned they'd break a fragile glass or scratch a fine piece of silver, for the suitcase contained all kinds of treasures.

"Well, Jimmie John, they're going mad for sure," Margaret said and enjoyed her youngest ripping open their packages.

"Merry Christmas in June," Jimmie John told them. "You've each found your best gift, but have no doubt there's other booty to share. Well, open up then, open up."

Kevin held the black hard circle in his hands uncertainly and looked at Jimmie John, who took it, deftly tapped and snapped it into a high silk hat. "All you need is the cane and you'll be a regular Fred Astaire," Jimmie John told him.

Kevin tipped the hat rakishly over one eye, did a fast two-step and danced out into the hallway to admire himself in the tall narrow mirror.

"It's a ring," Kit said without any effort to disguise her disappointment.

Jimmie John motioned her close; his words were for her ears only. "Ah, but it's a special ring, Kit darlin', and I've been

126

saving it a very long time just especially for you." He glanced around to assure the privacy of their conversation. "You see, but doesn't it look just a small gold signet ring, on the face of it? Well, see, there's a secret catch here, just at the edge, if you know about it. And there's this little flat compartment inside, do you see?"

It was too tiny for a photograph, yet it must have a purpose. Kit touched the hollow space with her fingertip. "For . . . code messages?"

Jimmie John shrugged, not ready to commit himself too quickly. "Some might think that, maybe. Some who listen, maybe, to them radio programs like *Little Orphan Annie* with all their fine code rings and think that's all there is to secret chambers in gold rings." He stared at the ring with grave attention. "But there's others might put this to another use, if you take my meaning."

"*Poison*," Kit whispered dramatically. "It could hold just enough poison for a spy to swallow if he got caught. Right, Jimmie John?"

"Or maybe enough poison, depending on how powerful a substance it is, to wipe out a whole nation of enemies, was it placed in their food or drinking water. And the spy could emerge, alive and victorious." Carefully, he slid the ring on Kit's finger. "A perfect fit and didn't I know. Now there's just this one last thing, Kit." He leaned close to her face and solemnly told her, "I'm not saying I know the history of this ring or nothin' like that, love, but for the love of God, be sure you wash your fingertip thoroughly before it finds its way into your mouth, after having touched that little secret chamber." He nodded and winked. "A word to the wise, love, a word to the wise."

Jimmie John stayed until the day after Roseanne's wedding. To her plaintive wail that her only sister had nothing but a tacky Sunday dress to wear, Jimmie John responded with the purchase of yards and yards of soft light-blue velvet—"to contrast with Kit's dark eyes." He managed to get Kit to stand still long enough to be draped and fitted and finally admired in her floor-length member-of-the-wedding gown ("Which can be cut down and hemmed, later, Margaret, for Sunday wear").

His skill with a needle was as mysterious and wonderful as his sense of what looked right on any of them. He added lace and filmy gauze to Roseanne's borrowed dress, fitted it closer to her long slender waist, made it truly her own wedding gown.

Over her protests, he marched Margaret off to a dress shop and refused to let her look at price tags, only at color and style, until they had selected a soft, bluish-gray crepe.

The old woman insisted she'd wear black, with her own dead son not a year in his grave, but Jimmie John fashioned a lovely deep collar for her from some leftover blue velvet from Kit's dress. He convinced her it would be in keeping with her mourning, and once the old woman saw how the color picked up the color of her eyes, she consented and even stopped complaining and accusing them all of disrespect and sacrilege.

Roseanne's wedding day was exactly as it should have been: bright and sunny, without too much warmth for discomfort, a clean, clear, cloudless deep-blue sky. Brian brought his sister down the aisle and he felt mysteriously transformed by his part in the ritual, for through some mysterious magic transformation everyone present, parent or grandparent, brother or sister, aunt, uncle, friend, became an integral part of the event, drawn by the familiar chant of words, hushed and enthralled at the presence of the Host and the solemn irrevocability of the vows exchanged.

The beauty of the bride was so fragile, pure and ghostly pale, then suddenly, joyously, radiantly flushed, that everyone felt breath catch in the back of his throat and everyone prayed for the happiness of the girl and her large and blushing groom.

"And to the health of the groom's father, wherever he might be, the bastard," Peadar rasped over the rim of his glass.

"Ah, none of that now, Peadar, for the love of God, not on the girl's wedding day," his brother Gene said. However, he touched glasses and drank the toast. He leaned against the refrigerator and poked his chin toward Jimmie John across the room and busy with trays of food. "Well, what do you think, brother? He still 'active on the job' or what?"

"I wish to hell I knew and that's a fact. There's just one thing I'm sure of where that fancy man's concerned."

Brian tried to be casual but it was difficult. The floor moved first toward him and then away. The next rush of motion might land him on the floor and he didn't want his uncles to pay any mind to him; he wanted to hear what they had to say.

"Ah, look at the lad, will you, Gene? Is it the first time you've really had at the hard stuff, Brian? By the look of you, you've gone silly on us."

Peadar's grasp was hard but friendly and steadying. Brian's mouth was numbed and his voice didn't really carry out his intentions. He wanted to sound casual and calm; he sounded intense and frantic to his own ears as he leaned close to his uncle. "What is the one thing you're sure of, Peadar?"

Gene laughed sharply. "Well, well, been listenin' to your elders, have you? Seems he's been wonderin' about our Jimmie John, Peadar."

Brian felt confused; he hadn't meant to come right out with it; he was somewhat shocked. He felt as though the words had been lifted from his brain against his will.

Peadar leaned his forehead against the side of Brian's head. "Well, the one thing I'm sure of, lad, is that Her Ladyship, whoever the hell she is, she isn't an *Irish* lass and that's for damn sure, eh, Gene?"

Gene sputtered and nodded. "Oh, Jesus, yes, that's for sure enough. Oh, will you look at the boy, Peadar, trying to figure it out. Sure, you don't know everything yet, now do you, Bri?"

Brian swayed carefully, trying to keep in time with the floor beneath his feet and at the same time synchronize with the wall opposite. "I never said I knew everything, Uncle Gene," he said, careful to move his tongue slowly. "Which is why I'm asking, so that I can learn."

"Good lad," Peadar said. "Good lad, like a lad willing to learn," He winked, tapped the side of his nose and told Brian, "Well, lad, if you'd our knowledge of women, you'd know Jimmie John's lady couldn't be one of our own." He winked broadly at Brian and turned to Gene for confirmation.

"Damned right, damned right. No Irishwoman would ever *pay* for it, oh, God love us, but that's a fact. Damned hard enough to make them *put up* with it half the time."

A sudden thought came to Gene and he stared narrowly at

his nephew. "What did *you* come upon, all those months on your own, Bri, eh? You've never told anyone at all, now did you, lad?"

There was an urgency in his words, a greedy demand to know. He swallowed some more whiskey and pretended to be drunker than he was. "Come on now, lad, tell your Uncle Gene all about it."

"Came upon hard times, Uncle Gene, that's wha' I came upon. Gonna be very sick, very very sick right now . . ."

Brian made it to the bathroom in time to be sick with some degree of privacy. He flushed the toilet, rinsed his mouth with cold water and splashed his forehead and neck before he even noticed Kevin.

"What are you doing there?" Kevin was perched on the side of the bathtub.

Kevin shrugged. His eyes were empty glass marbles: light-blue puries. He balanced on the side of the tub precariously. Brian thought that if he touched Kevin with the tip of one finger, the boy would fall over backwards into the tub, which was filled with ice and kegs of beer. Kevin sighed, a thin whistling sound that carried with it a powerful aroma of whiskey.

"For Christ's sakes, what have you been drinking?" He grabbed Kevin's shirt just in time to keep him from toppling over backwards. Brian's hands trembled but carefully he helped his brother to kneel and face the tub. He managed to get a piece of ice to the boy's chalk-white face. Kevin shuddered once, then passed out. His face was thin and tight and so pale it was almost blue.

"Oh, it's caught up with him, has it?" Peadar said good-naturedly. He leaned over, lifted Kevin lightly to his shoulder, fireman-style. Then he noticed Brian. "You are all right now, aren't you, lad? Wouldn't do for your ma to see both of you passed out."

"Is he okay?" Brian asked dully.

Peadar smacked Kevin on the backside heartily and there was a faint protesting stir. "He'll be as good as fine, don't worry none. He's been draining glasses all day and all night, the rascal. I'll just put him on the bedroom floor next to John the Wop, who passed out an hour ago and is snoring Sweet Jesus. So much for the capacity of the Eye-talians!" Peadar

130

leaned close to Brian and told him, "The thing is, son, you should take your drink slow and steady and by easy stages. It's supposed to make you feel good, not sick." Kevin sighed and shifted slightly; Peadar patted his leg. "Easy, lad, we'll get you down directly. Hey, Brian, listen to that! Hear your old Nana singing? She's just getting herself started, lad. Now we'll hear some of the good old songs, now the old one's all warmed up to go!"

Matthew O'Malley wrapped his arms around his mother in a bear hug. "Give us a good rousin' song about the troubles, Ma. Won't you do that for us, darlin'?"

She shoved him back and sent him sprawling into a collection of nephews and nieces.

"Be damned to you if you'll be tellin' me what to sing. I'll sing me own songs to me own pleasure." Her sharp eyes glittered around the room until she found Jimmie John. "Here, come over here then, lad, and let's hear that fine sweet tenor of yours." She wiped her mouth with the back of her hand and hit the surface of the footstool with a thumping palm. "Stand back and let Jimmie John through, you bunch of roughnecks. C'mon now, darlin', I'll get them all to pipe down." Her voice rose to a roar, subdued them all, dominated them all, sober or drunk. It was the no-nonsense woman they had obeyed from earliest childhood and the silence she demanded was both respectful and affectionate. "Climb up here now, Jimmie John, and give us a song like you give the quality folk."

Jimmie John, in response, lifted the old woman from the floor and placed her on the footstool, then pressed his face close to hers. "Sure, we'll sing harmony, darlin', for I need a strong voice to bolster my own, what with the good whiskey's been thinning it all day."

"Ah, sure, he's the smooth one, isn't he?" the old woman said but her face glowed and she was pleased and flattered that he insisted.

Jimmie John sang softly and sweetly and carefully kept the old woman on key. Skillfully, he let his voice become an echo of hers as she became stronger and more robust. When she faltered, he picked it up. He led her through the old ballads, the romantic, pining, sad, sentimental farewell songs. Then, when the mood of sadness seemed to be affecting the party, he changed to the jaunty, somewhat off-color songs of his youth, and the younger wedding guests cast quick, questioning glances at each other and grinned and giggled as their elders joined in eagerly and without restraint. Finally, she fell against him, exhausted, and snapped her fingers for a drink.

"For the sweet love of Jesus, will you give me something wet before I perish!"

"Ah, Mary me love," Jimmie John said, "we'll all perish before yourself and that's for sure. You're that strong and sly, Mary me dear."

The old woman reached out her hand and touched his cheek and her gaze was thoughtful and puzzled and sad. "Ah, now there's a strange thing, yes, very strange. There's none to call me Mary left anymore. And used to be, all around would call me Mary this and Mary that and none to call me by my name." She studied Jimmie John intently, as though he could solve the mystery, and then, softly, as though it was a secret to keep between them, she said, "I was a young girl once. I truly was, and all who saw me called me Mary."

Jimmie John whispered to her, "Why and so you are Mary and shall always be to me, love. Here now, drink this down and you'll feel the girl you used to be."

The party continued long after the bride and groom departed. It continued so long that hardly anyone remembered what had prompted it in the first place.

Children slept where they fell, exhausted, overfed, overexcited. They woke from time to time, reached for more candy or cake, had hands smacked or shoulders shaken or found themselves hugged tightly and danced about the room and fussed over and then abandoned abruptly to entertain themselves.

Kit O'Malley leaned out of the sixth-floor window of her Uncle Gene's apartment and saw the light from her own home flooding the street in front of the house. Probably everyone forgot she was here, and maybe she'd make it through the night with the rest of her cousins. They had all vowed to stay awake until daylight and were telling each other stories and making up lies to keep awake.

SIXTEEN

Debbie Gladner had long tawny hair which she pushed casually from her face from time to time as stray locks escaped from her pink ribbon. Her skin glowed with good health and her lips, innocent of lipstick, were full and turned up at the corners. She had a strong, limber, athletic body, slender without thinness. She exuded a calm self-confidence that always put Brian O'Malley at a disadvantage.

Brian held up the package of Neccos and waited for Debbie to reappear from behind the candy stand. He could hear her humming to herself as she arranged boxes of candy along the floor behind the counter. She stood up, started at the sight of him.

"Oh, hello, Brian. I didn't know you were there. Want anything beside the Neccos?"

"No, these will be fine."

Brian knew he looked pretty good in his usher's uniform. In fact, some of the girls passed pretty specific remarks relative to his black hair and stark blue eyes. He was just over six feet tall, narrow-hipped, wide-shouldered. The gym workouts three times a week at Delehanty's in preparation for the Police Department's competitive physical exam had firmed and hardened and expanded his body. Yet, when Debbie Gladner looked at him, he felt like a gawky schoolboy. Just another guy.

"Have you seen the picture yet, Debbie?"

Systematically, she arranged the Hershey bars and Planters Peanuts in rows and she didn't look up from her work. "I haven't time to stand around and watch." Debbie was a student at City College and spent most of her working time hunched over a book behind her counter. She put the book aside only when the counter was besieged between pictures.

"Well, since I *have* to be inside most of the time, I might as well watch." Damn it; he was offering her excuses when he owed her nothing. Knowing this, he continued anyway. "I don't watch *everything*. Just that I like John Garfield."

"John Garfield?" The full mouth turned down scornfully and her blunt hand shoved a shining lock from her smooth face. "You mean *Julie Garfinkle*. I get a pain right in the eyes with all these jerks who change their names."

"Is that what his real name is, Julie Garfinkle?"

The straight brows over her dark eyes drew together and she thrust her chin up and regarded him suspiciously. "You think there's something wrong with that name? Well, I happen to think there's something wrong with a Jew who doesn't want to be identified as a Jew."

Brian wasn't sure what to say. He shrugged, then offered, "Well, I guess maybe John Garfield *looks* better on the marquee than Julie Garfinkle."

"*Looks* better? How can one name *look* better than another name? To whose eyes, looks better? We're talking about connotations now, aren't we?"

Brian didn't know what they were talking about and when she sighed scornfully, turned her back on him by way of dismissal and went back to her work, he felt irritated and slightly stupid. His fingers pried a Necco candy wafer from the package and slid it onto his tongue. It was licorice, the one flavor he didn't like. He crunched it between his back teeth, pried the next one loose and into his mouth. That was licorice too.

That damn girl was crazy; no two ways about it. It was impossible to have a friendly conversation with her without her getting all emotional about something. Usually about being Jewish. She was some kind of nut about being Jewish; she was a Zionist or something like that and Brian figured she must be getting fed an awful lot of peculiar stuff.

Brian escorted an elderly couple to a pair of seats midway down the long sloping aisle; he held the beam of his flashlight on the dark-red carpet and stepped back professionally to let them slide in. They took the aisle seats, which would make it harder for other people taking seats: everyone would have to climb over them. It was funny how everyone wanted an aisle seat on Screeno night. Brian couldn't remember even once when a winner came from an aisle seat.

Mr. Gladner flashed his light from the balcony, playing his code game. He was as crazy as his niece in some ways, but all in all, a fairly decent guy. At least he wasn't always sticking his face up at you and telling you how Jewish he was. The blink of the flashlight asked if he had enough Screeno cards for the patrons; he flashed back once: yes.

A hand grasped his arm blindly. "Ah, is that you Brian O'Malley?"

He recognized the plump wheezy woman. "Hey, Mrs. Kelleher, how are you? Want to go down front tonight?" Carefully, he led her along the aisle to the front of the theater and gave her her Screeno cards.

"Oh, thank you, dear, thank you, you're a sweet boy," Mrs. Kelleher said and her eyeglasses glinted with the flashing of light from the screen as the newsreel unwound. "When I hit the jackpot, Brian, I'll treat you to a nice hot chocolate at Strassler's."

"I'll take you up on that, Mrs. Kelleher."

A few patrons, annoyed by the whispering, hissed at them and Brian walked back up the aisle and flashed the light on his wristwatch.

At promptly 9 P.M., houselights flooded the theater, went off, then on, then off again. A bright-blue spot picked up Mr. Gladner as he strode, smiling broadly, across the stage. He reached for the microphone, blew into it, then satisfied by the huge echo which filled the Loew's Paradise, he spoke to the audience in a rich cheerful voice.

"Well, good evening, ladies and gentlemen. It's good to see so many familiar and eager faces." He leaned forward, scanned, smiled. "Ah, ha-ha. I see some previous winners here tonight. Come to test your luck, eh? Well, well, well, here it is again, folks, Friday night, and time to p-l-a-y . . ." He paused as he did at exactly the same moment every Friday night, turned away from the microphone, then raised his right hand, index finger extended, and pointed at the audience. Like a pack of trained seals, they barked at him the magic word: *"SCREENO!"*

135

At this cue, the projectionist flashed the Screeno spinner on the screen. It was a huge green square with a circle of numbers fitted into it. At the center was an arrow which spun crazily, slowed, until finally it pointed to a number. The only difference between this game and Bingo was that the player had to x out seven numbers instead of five. When seven in a row (including a free center) were marked, the winner had to stand up from his seat and yell "Screeno!" All further action was held up until the winning card could be verified.

"Well, tonight, good friends," Mr. Gladner told them, "we're going to have three games of Screeno instead of the customary two. A little something extra from the management tonight, he-he. Does everyone have three cards?"

There was some commotion as the audience moved and shuffled and consulted and checked and looked around.

"Will my assistants please check over to my left?" Mr. Gladner snapped his fingers and Brian moved quickly and provided a gray-haired man with the third card to which he was entitled. "Will my assistants please check over to my right?" He waited a few minutes, then nodded. "Are we all set now?" Mr. Gladner asked. The audience made a low rumbling noise which satisfied Mr. Gladner, who gave a nod toward the projection booth. The spot dimmed and the Screeno game began.

Mr. Gladner called each number with clear and exaggerated diction. There was a growing, audible reaction from the audience with each number that came up and a resigned disappointment from the obvious losers.

"The sixth number will now be spun," Mr. Gladner said softly. He held his hand up to stay the action. "But wait; we might, just might, get a winner on this number, with the free center thrown in, right? Say, did I fail to mention," he asked, deliberately slowing the game, which was running a little too fast, "that there is a bonus of five dollars on this first game? That's right; instead of the usual game prize of ten dollars, we've added a bonus of five dollars." Mr. Gladner held his hand up to stop the applause and added, "But, I must point out that the bonus applies *only* if we have a winner on the next—the sixth—spin. All right now, good luck, and George, let her go!"

The pointer hovered between two numbers, trembled forward and rested on the number 2.

"For the sixth and maybe, maybe, maybe lucky number," Mr. Gladner said loudly into the microphone, "under letter *o*, number two!"

The houselights flashed high, then plunged the theater into total darkness, then flooded the theater with medium intensity.

"Oh, oh, oh, my goodness," Mrs. Kelleher gasped and sputtered and waved her pocketbook over her head. A spot picked her up and she stood up, her face a bright red. Brian O'Malley moved quickly to her side. It was his job to verify the numbers on her card.

He supported her up the five steps; her face was flushed with excitement and pleasure and embarrassment; she glanced toward the sea of faces in the semidarkness. "Oh, Mother of God," she whispered to Brian, "hold on to me, lad, or I'm off my feet for sure."

Mr. Gladner went through his usual routine; he scanned the already verified card through his second set of eyeglasses, which he flourished, as usual, at the audience. "These are my 'mistake catchers,' he-he. No mistakes here, none at all." He presented the $15.00 prize money with a flourish and asked for the winner's name.

Mrs. Kelleher's voice went thin and wavery and she whispered into the mike and acted as silly and foolish as a girl.

"And what will you do with your prize money, Mrs. Kelleher?"

She mopped her sweaty forehead and giggled, then her voice boomed through the microphone unexpectedly, "Oh, there's bills just waitin'."

By nine-thirty it was all over and the coming attractions were on. Those who had already seen the complete show filtered out; Brian stationed himself in the main lobby and held the exit door open. Everyone was chatting; Mrs. Kelleher was hanging on to a friend's arm, and as she went past Brian, she said, "I owe you that hot chocolate now, lad, just as I promised, oh, yes, indeed."

"Oh, now, Maureen"—her friend giggled—"that sounds

like something fishy goin' on. Did young Brian there fix the win for you then?"

They poked and pushed at each other with good humor. Everyone, winners and losers, seemed happy and contented with the evening. As Brian crossed the lobby with his container of used cards, he caught the expression on Debbie Gladner's face.

It was contemptuous and scornful and angry and superior to everything around her. Brian wondered what the hell it would take to get the damn girl to smile.

SEVENTEEN

Mr. Lenihan stood in front of them, placed his hands flat on his concave stomach and sighed. He rocked back slightly on his heels and told the class, "Well, yer all good boys and I wish all of yez good luck on yer big day tomorrow. I wish to God yez could all pass the examination and the only consolation I have for those who don't make it is this: there's to be probably the greatest number of candidates takin' this Department exam as ever took it before in history, and more lads with college degrees and such.

"What I'm tryin' to convey to yez is that there's no disgrace for them who don't get on the list. Remember, there'll always be a new exam in four years!"

It wasn't exactly a high note on which to end the session but the class groaned good-naturedly because everyone liked and respected Mr. Lenihan, a retired police sergeant. He had instructed them during countless sessions on the kind of material they might encounter on the examination for Patrolman, New York City Police Department, and had regaled them with stories of his own experience. In his dry, matter-of-fact, unimpressed and unimpressive voice, Mr. Lenihan related the most intimate, unbelievable aspects of police work to them. He convulsed them with his stories of investigations that went wrong; terrified them with all the possibilities of error in judgment that might confront them when and if the responsibility for such judgment became theirs. Yet, as relaxed and casual and easygoing as he seemed, there was that about Mr. Lenihan that demanded respect and no student in his classroom ever lit the forbidden cigarette or carried on private conversations during class time; at least not more than once.

Tom Gaffney, a beefy, hulking blond longshoreman with heavy reddish eyebrows and eyes nearly the same color, threw an arm over Francis Kelly and one over Brian O'Malley. "Well, boys, wadda ya say, going down to Muldoon's for a good luck beer or two? We've invited Mr. Lenihan to drink a bit of luck with us."

They gathered, six or seven of them; they punched at each other playfully, flexed hardened muscles, bragged, called obscenities and wished each other good luck in the artificial atmosphere of confidence with which they surrounded themselves.

There was a noticeable quieting down when Mr. Lenihan joined them. It was as though they all felt the need to impress him that they were not noisy foolish boys, but men worthy of the position they sought.

Brian nursed his beer carefully and watched some of the hard drinkers: first a shot of raw-tasting whiskey, then a slug of foamy beer. Brian noted how quickly eyes reddened and speech became thick.

Mr. Lenihan knew how to drink, the way he seemed to know how to do everything else. He was a leathery, tough old guy and he didn't miss anything. He talked a lot, listened a lot and drank slowly and carefully. He held his hands around the glass, played with it, caressed it, covered it palm down at the offers of a refill. "Not this round, lads, I'm just fine."

He was fine. They all sensed that there was something in Lenihan that they wanted to find in themselves. He had an authority about him based on experience and knowledge and the testing of himself which none of them had. He was close to sixty, nearly three times Brian's age, yet physically he was pretty near the match of any of them. Occasionally, they would come upon Mr. Lenihan in the gym, easily lapping around, tapping quickly and precisely with darting gloves at the punching bag, doing fast push-ups, sparring delicately with Dugan, one of the instructors. Everything he did seemed to be easily done, with complete confidence that he *could* do it. Maybe that was it, Brian thought; Mr. Lenihan could look upon himself with the certainty of capability.

Mr. Lenihan put his glass on the smooth polished surface of the bar and regarded Francis Kelly tightly through narrowed

140

eyes with a peculiar searching expression. "I've been trying to place you, lad, for the damnedest time, and it just come to me now who it is you reminded me of." They all quieted down. They knew Mr. Lenihan was about to offer them a memory. "Yes, it's come to me now, seeing you here at the bar, with a glass in your hand. You remind me of my first partner, when I was newly made a detective. Name was Clarke, yes, Jimmy Clarke it was." He nodded, smiled and shook his head fondly. "Oh, Jasus, poor James; him and me both trying so hard to do our damnedest best that time, both of us just newly appointed to the division, you understand."

Mr. Lenihan leaned his elbows on the bar and was silent for a moment, setting the event firmly in his mind. "There was a homicide, in a bar, you see." His eyes slowly scanned the length of the bar, giving his story a proper setting; they followed his glance. "Well, the squad commander sent Jimmy and me out on the squeal. We should have had an experienced man with us, one of us or the other, but as luck would have it, the two of us was all that was available that night. Let's see, now, it was a place in the south Bronx." He studied the ceiling for a moment, then nodded. "Yes, on Brook Avenue and 134th Street, a place called . . . yes . . . the Tumble Inn. Jasus, close to thirty-five years ago.

"Well, there were these two dead bodies to greet us on our arrival. The bartender had caught one right through his right eye and, you can imagine, he was a proper mess. And the woman, God knows the poor thing had only been trying to get out of the way, but the holdup man was the nervous type and mistook her movement, and there she was, a thirty-eight smack in the heart. Well then, all we were to do was to stand by and touch nothing and post the uniformed man outside and wait for the Homicide lads. I guess our C.O. felt it a safe enough assignment even for the likes of us. We was of course to talk to the eyewitnesses, if any, and keep them from leaving. And of course we was to keep our ears open and our mouths shut and try to learn something. Sweet Mother of God, we learned a lesson that night."

He glanced up, nodded at the bartender, pointed around. It was his second and last drink of the night and he waited for everyone to be served, slid his ten across the bar and left the change on the counter as he spoke. He lit a cigarette and the smoke circled around his head.

"Well, there was two witnesses. As pretty a scared-lookin' couple of rum-dums you'd ever want to see. Just out for the night's refreshment they were and never did see the gunman's face; I believed them. They couldn't have seen a snowflake in a blizzard, they were that far gone. But it's an odd thing, lads, and remember this," he said reflectively, "that a man can be dead drunk one minute and stone-cold sober the next, depending on events. And these were two stone-cold-sober drunks, if you take my meaning. Well, at any rate, Jimmy Clarke and me went about our business all professional and calm and showing off to each other, all the while trying to avoid the sight of the corpses, they were that bloody and we just finished with our suppers.

"The Homicide fellas came and moved around and took charge just the way they're supposed to and we just kind of hung around and watched and, God Christ Almighty, but wasn't there a great siren blast right out front. The squad commander, looking pretty shaken, arrived and told us that the Chief of Detectives himself was right behind him and, sure enough, he was."

Mr. Lenihan shook his head at memory and smiled.

"Oh, he was a great old guy, don't get me wrong. Never did get the bloodhound out of his system, though he ended up behind a desk, may he rest in peace. Well, he was on his way home from a party, all dressed up nice in formal clothes and his wife outside in the car. He'd heard the call on the car radio and directed his driver to make a U-turn and go to the scene so's he could have a sniff of blood, so to speak. Well, you can believe everyone was being very careful and staying in line to be impressive and all of that. Yes."

Mr. Lenihan took a long, slow swallow and relished the taste, his tongue carefully touching the corner of his mouth before he winked at them and continued. "Well, the Homicide men of course needed but three minutes to size everything up. 'There's no description of the perpetrator, Chief,' they said, 'but we did learn from one of them witnesses that he had himself a drink at the bar before he pulled the holdup.' Now, I'll add that was more than me or Jimmy got from the witnesses. Well, the words were no sooner out of the man's mouth when Jimmy and me exchanged significant glances." Mr. Lenihan fingered an empty shot glass and placed it directly in front of him on the bar and stood up. Everyone stared at the glass, aware of it now and what it meant.

"Well, there was the glass, untouched since touched by the gunman himself."

"With a set of his prints," Brian said.

"With a set of his prints," Mr. Lenihan agreed with a nod. "Well, the Chief was down at that end of the bar." He indicated the far end, to his right. "And me and Jim was standing right here, in front of the only damn evidence. 'Bring the glass down here, lads,' the Chief called out, 'and let's get it dusted for prints.'"

"Oh, Jesus," Tom Gaffney said, "your partner grabbed it up in his hand?"

"Oh, no, no, he never," Mr. Lenihan said quietly. "We was better trained than that." He reached into his jacket and came up with a long yellow pencil. "We knew how to handle evidence, for Christ's sake. We was detectives, weren't we? Jim took out his pencil and placed it, eraser end down, into the empty glass, just as you're supposed to and nice as you'd please." As he spoke, he carefully put the pencil into the glass, deftly twisted his wrist and turned the impaled glass upside down without touching it. "Now, there's the proper way to handle evidence." Mr. Lenihan stepped back from the bar and they moved back, giving him room. "Well, sir, Jimmy Clarke was as pleased with himself as a man can be to have this rare opportunity to demonstrate to the Chief of Detectives himself what a fine clever fella he was and him just new to the division and all, and off he starts toward the boss."

Mr. Lenihan moved slowly, his eyes on the evidence. Suddenly, he stumbled over an imaginary obstacle. They all watched, horrified, as the glass hit the floor and shattered into splinters.

Mr. Lenihan regarded the broken glass for a moment, then turned and pointed to the floor. "The damned woman corpse got in his way and poor James stepped on her arm and lost his footing. He was so damned concerned with the evidence he didn't look where he was going."

143

"My God," Francis Kelly said. "What happened then, Mr. Lenihan?"

"Well, James Clarke turned old right before my eyes. I had an absolute clear preview of what he'd look like when he was an old, old man. And I remember, God forgive me, but all I could think was 'Oh, Jasus, I'm glad it was him and not me.' " He reached into his back pocket, took out a handkerchief, squatted over the broken glass and looked up at them so they knew the story was not quite over.

Carefully, with his fingertips, Mr. Lenihan placed the delicate slivers of glass into the handkerchief and then stood up and extended the broken glass at arm's length. 'Would these be of any use to anybody?' Jimmy Clarke asked the Chief of Detectives!"

They all burst into nervous, sympathetic, understanding laughter, which grew louder and more relaxed.

Mr. Lenihan smiled, took a long swallow from his drink and waited for the laughter to subside.

"You know what, lads? Now I'll tell you something. That is exactly, *exactly* what happened that night. The Chief laughed first and then the squad commander and then the Homicide guys and then I joined in finally and then poor Jim himself. The two witnesses laughed hysterically, as though they feared we'd all gone mad and they'd better play along with it. I swear to God, I believe that if the poor bloody corpses could have joined in, they would have laughed too." Mr. Lenihan shrugged, held his hands out before him and said reasonably, "After all, what the hell else was there we could have done?"

On the morning of the examination, Brian woke up from a terrible dream: He had gotten into the wrong room, had lost his pencil, time ticked by, his examination paper was blank. He sat up in bed, rubbed his eyes and tried to put the dream from his mind. While he was shaving, he developed a tic in his right eye.

Martin was fully dressed and looked as though he'd been up for a long time. He placed a cup of steaming black coffee on the table in front of his brother.

"Hey, thanks, Martin." He sipped the coffee, added some

144

sugar and stirred. "Hey, what are you doing up so early on a Saturday morning anyway? What time is it?" He turned and squinted at the wall clock. It was six-thirty.

Martin shrugged but didn't answer.

Brian regarded his younger brother curiously. "You been to Mass this morning?"

Martin nodded.

"A little early, isn't it?" The soft eyes met his, then blinked. A slow, deep flush of color traveled up Martin's cheeks and Brian, puzzled at first, suddenly realized Martin had attended six o'clock Mass to pray for Brian's intention. Brian swallowed hard. Jesus, he was a funny kid; never had much to say for himself. As far as Brian knew, Martin wasn't even aware of the examination date, let alone how much it meant to Brian. They'd never discussed it. They'd never discussed much of anything. Brian studied the round, freckled face. "Hey, Martin, thanks."

Martin shook his head slightly, neither confirming or denying. He frowned and looked unutterably sad and clenched his hands.

"What's the matter, Martin?"

Martin turned his face away. "I don't know. I guess I can't seem to do things right." Then, to answer Brian's puzzlement, he added, "You weren't supposed to know."

"Hey, kid, that doesn't spoil it for you, does it?"

Helplessly, Martin turned his hands palm up. "It's not supposed to be something for *me*. I don't know, it's hard to explain. But I wish you luck, Brian. You'll do fine."

Brian rubbed at his eye. "Damn it, if I'm able to see maybe."

"I think it's just because your tensed up, Bri. It'll probably stop in a while. You're up pretty early too, aren't you?"

"Yeah. Well, I couldn't sleep. Kept having this stupid dream. God, I'll be glad when this whole thing is over." Impulsively he turned to his younger brother. "Hey, Martin? I'll probably do pretty good, don't you think?"

Martin's grin was broad and mocking; his sadness slipped away and he jutted his chin at Brian and asked, "How can you miss? You're Brian O'Malley, right?"

Brian punched him lightly on the shoulder with the side of

145

his fist. "You're damn right," he said, and somehow they convinced each other.

Francis Kelly inhaled deeply on the stub end of his Chesterfield, then dropped the butt and stepped on it. "Sure is a big school, huh, Brian?"

"Yeah. I've never been in a public school before, have you?"

Smoke curled from Francis' nose. "Now what would *I* be doin' in a public school?" he asked abruptly. "Jesus, there's an awful lot of guys here."

Brian poked him. "Come on, Kelly. You and me, kid, we're gonna ram it home to them, right?"

Francis Kelly nodded weakly. They met Tom Gaffney, smoked more cigarettes, met other guys they knew, exchanged rumors, tried for false courage, then filed into the building to find assigned rooms. Floor monitors sent them all in different directions.

Francis Kelly shook Brian's hand one final time and said, "Gaffney's in bad shape, isn't he, Bri? Well, buddy, we'll show 'em a thing or two, right?"

"You betcha, kid, luck."

The room monitor checked Brian's admission card, compared his signature on the card to the one he'd just signed and assigned him to the last seat in the last row by the window. Brian was glad he could gaze away from all the tense guys shifting around in the tight seats. Jesus, all of them competing for the job he wanted more than he could understand. He'd never even thought of doing anything else with his life; it was always there, just waiting for him to grow up: the Department.

The silence in the room, when the monitor called for it, was stark and unnatural, as though they were all trying to make good impressions. Brian closed his eyes, didn't hear anything the room monitor told them in his flat emotionless voice. He didn't look at the exam booklet or the separate answer sheet; he just let them lie unseen on the surface of the desk, waiting for the signal.

There was a shifting of bodies, movement of feet, stifled coughs, soft sighs, clearing of throats, flexing of shoulders, touching of good luck charms. Brian slipped his fingers to the

146

chain around his neck and discreetly slid the Miraculous Medal to his lips, then dropped it back inside his shirt.

A tall, thin woman entered the room: an additional monitor. She took a piece of chalk in her hand, consulted her stop watch. At exactly the moment when the school bell rang, signaling the start of the exam, she wrote the time on the blackboard with a screech of chalk: 9 A.M.

As he opened the examination booklet, Brian realized for the first time that the throbbing in his right eye had stopped.

EIGHTEEN

Brian brushed his fingertips along the side of the review stands which had been erected outside the Loew's Paradise for the Memorial Day parade to be held the next day. The sky was black and the stars looked exactly like the fake stars in the ceiling of the movie house: bright, piercing little lights which seemed to flash on and off as he stared at them. He stopped at the newsstand on the corner of 184th Street and the Grand Concourse, as he did every night, and picked up his copy of the *Daily News*.

"Ah, that's Brian O'Malley, yes?" The blind newsman, Mr. Samuels, pocketed the two pennies.

"How's things, Mr. Samuels?"

A shrug, smile, noncommittal. "How could it be? A nice night, Brian. Tomorrow should be a good day for the parade."

Brian yawned, leaned his head back. Christ, he was tired. It had been a long day; late show. He turned down 182nd Street and went to Ryer Avenue. As he approached the police station at the corner of 181st Street, he noticed Mr. Gallegher, the tall, thin clerical man he'd known all his life. Gallegher had broken in with his father.

"Hey, Brian, see you a minute?"

"Oh, hi, Mr. Gallegher. Yeah, sure. Nice night, huh?"

Instead of making some small talk, Gallegher came down the five steps and it suddenly occurred to him: Gallegher had been standing there, in front of the precinct house, waiting for him. Gallegher's face was sad and weary, as though he'd spent a lifetime telling people things they'd rather not hear. Light from the green lanterns and from the yellow streetlamp bounced off his bald head and his mouth turned down at the corners. He pulled at his loosened navy-blue tie and rocked back on his heels.

"What's wrong, Mr. Gallegher?" Nameless panic twisted deep inside his stomach.

"Well, Bri, see, we've got your cousin John O'Malley in the house," he said and jerked a thumb toward the police station to make sure Brian understood.

"You've got John inside?" Brian asked, bewildered.

"You know Danny Dunne?"

Everyone in the neighborhood knew Danny Dunne. He was one of the toughest detectives in the precinct and he prided himself on the fact that when he told the neighborhood kids to move their ball game away from the precinct house, he punctuated his requests with a couple of well-aimed kicks in the backside. Brian had been the recipient of a few of Danny Dunne's quick forays when he was a younger boy.

"What about him?"

"Well, Danny spotted poor Johnnie in there with a carton of flags he'd taken from Kruger's candy store. The thing is, I doubt very much that the whole thing was John's idea, Brian."

Brian lit a cigarette, turned away from Mr. Gallegher for a moment, then turned back and asked tersely, "My brother Kevin around?"

Gallegher spread his palms and shrugged. "You know John. The two lads are always together. Dunne said there were two boys on the scene and one ran off."

Brian rubbed the back of his neck roughly. "And left John?"

"He's a good lad, Bri. Wouldn't open his mouth. And I think Danny gave him a bit of a bad time. I kept my eyes on him, but all in all, it might be just as well for Johnnie. Got scared enough I think to stay out of trouble. It could have been bad, though, Brian, if they'd been in another precinct, if you understand me."

Brian nodded. He felt the sweat on his forehead and down his back.

"Well, come on inside a moment. Dunne wants to have a word with you. Don't let him throw you, Bri. Jut take it nice and easy, all right? And then you take your Johnnie off home." He held Brian's arm for a moment. "And I'd have a word with Kevin, if I were you."

149

Brian nodded. "I'll have a word with Kevin, all right."

John O'Malley sat, elbows resting on the long gray table in front of the bench, a resigned if worried expression on his face. He had finished the comic books Mr. Gallegher had given him and when he looked up and saw Brian he grinned widely.

"Hey, Brian. Boy, I'm glad you're here. Can I go home now, Mr. Gallegher?"

"Just sit there until I come back for you," Brian said.

"Oh. Okay, Brian. I will."

Danny Dunne was a tightly built, compact man, with high cheekbones, a fair complexion and beads of glare for eyes. He hardly opened his mouth when he spoke; he forced the words from him grudgingly. "That's a cute cousin you got in there," Dunne said. There was an edge of laughter in his voice, mocking and cruel. "Oh, he's a real beaut."

Dunne pushed his hat over his brow, leaned back in his swivel chair and placed his feet on his desk. Carefully, deliberately, he lit his cigar and filled the air in front of him with billows of acrid smoke.

"Here's the facts of the case," he said. "I was cruising and pulled over to the curb at 183rd Street and Webster Avenue at ten-thirty tonight. I seen a coupla figures movin' in the vestibule of Kruger's store. I know Kruger closes early on Wednesday night, see." He tapped his forehead. "Ya gotta keep this kinda information on tap, so's you know when somethin' ain't kosher, ya know?"

Mr. Gallegher interrupted. "Listen, Danny, why don't you just give the lad the facts and not give us instruction in how to become a detective?"

Danny turned a glazed stare on Gallegher and then on Brian. Brian realized that if it was up to Dunne, poor John would be in very big trouble.

"Mr. Dunne," he said carefully, "I would appreciate it if you tell me what happened."

"Yeah, I'm sure you'd appreciate it. All right, then, as I approached, the 'other kid,'" Dunne said slowly, sitting up, staring hard at Brian, as though there was a guilty secret between them, "the anonymous other culprit, ran like the thief he is and left the big boob out there holding the goods. See,

Kruger's nephew delivered this box of flags from Jersey. For the parade tomorrow. Kruger left the door to the store open; the nephew put the box inside and I guess forgot to snap the lock. So along comes rube-the-boob in there, and another person unknown, and in they go." He held his index finger up. "Breaking and entering, right? And out they come" — he held a second finger up — "lugging the box of flags with them: larceny-felony."

He sat there and waited; let Brian feel it for the full weight. Finally, he said, "Now lucky for your cousin there that Mike Gallegher persuaded me not to book him. And I don't mind tellin' you right now, kid, given five minutes in the right setting, like downstairs, I'd a' made him tell me who the other kid was. Not that we don't just among us have a pretty good idea."

Brian yanked the unlit cigarette from between his lips and said to Danny Dunne, "My cousin might be a little simple, but he wouldn't have told you *balls*."

Danny pulled his feet from the desk, but Gallegher moved quickly and pulled Brain toward the door. Dunne's face was pale and he flicked a quick look to Gallegher. "Dumb seems to run in the family, don't it? Get them all the hell outta here. Tell junior here you're supposed to say thanks when somebody's doin' you a favor."

Brian shook himself free of Gallegher's hold. "Thanks, Dunne," he said tightly. "Thanks a lot."

Dunne pointed toward the door. "Now get your ass the fuck outta here before I change my mind."

Gallegher's hand was steady and strong as he led Brian from the room. Dunne called out again. "Hey, O'Malley? Are you aware of the fact that if it was your brother, I mean, if it just happened to have been your brother, and if he'd a' got himself booked for breaking and entering and grand larceny, why" — Dunne made a fist, popped his thumb up, then turned it over — "you'd be kicked off the P.D. list so fast it would make your head spin?"

Brian's lungs seemed too tight and hard to expand for the oxygen he needed. He walked past John with just a quick nod for John to follow him, then turned to shake Gallegher's hand. "God, Mr. Gallegher. Jesus, thanks."

"Okay, son, now you take it easy." He motioned to John O'Malley. "Go down the steps and wait for your cousin, there's a good boy. Now listen, Brian . . . oh, hell, boys are boys, these things happen."

"If you hadn't been here . . ."

"Well, it was no more than any of us would've done, lad. Just that Danny Dunne being such a bastard. Your dad did many a favor for many a man in his day, Brian. You go on home now and take it easy."

Brian nodded and took the stairs in two bounds and walked past John, who followed close behind him.

"Hey, Brian, you mad at me? Gee, Brian, I'm real sorry. Don't be mad at me. Gee, Bri, why don't you say something? You're mad at me, I can tell."

Brian's hands curled into fists and he moved down the street with John's worried voice pursuing him. They reached the alleyway which led to the courtyard, the "O'Malley courtyard." For the first time, Brian spoke to John.

"We'll go in this way, through the bedroom window. I don't want us to wake Mom."

John bounded ahead of him, walking backwards so that he could face Brian. "I didn't tell them anything, Brian, if that's what you're mad about, honest. Gee, I'm sorry. Please don't be mad at me. You gonna hit me, Brian? It's okay if you wanna hit me, but just don't be mad."

"I'm not gonna hit you, John," Brian said softly. "Look, I want you to do something for me, okay?"

John nodded, eager to placate his cousin. "Sure, Brian, anything you say, sure. Gee, I'm glad you're not mad at me. That Mr. Dunne, he said you'd probably beat me up real bad. I'm glad you're not mad."

"Okay, now look. Go over there and wait in the next alleyway until I tell you." He pointed across the courtyard to the next alley. "And don't make a sound."

John's mouth hung open. "Over there? Don't you want I should go through the window, Bri? Gee, I'm awful tired."

"In a little while. I want to get Kevin out here for a minute, see? When I get Kev out, then you can go to bed. But you stay over there and don't make a sound. Come on, I'll go over with you." They crossed the yard into the next alleyway. Brian looked up at the dim bulb inside the little wire cage. He took out his handkerchief, opened the cage and unscrewed the bulb and waited for a moment until his eyes became accustomed to the dark. "Now just stay quiet and wait here for us, okay?"

"Yeah, okay, Brian. I won't make no noise."

Kevin pretended he was in a deep sleep and Brian leaned close and whispered in his ear, "Hey, Kevin. Come on, kid, wake up." One hand went firmly around his brother's arm, the other over his mouth as Kevin feigned surprised, waking sounds. "Huh? Wha?"

"Quiet, will you? Don't wake Mom."

The only light in the room came from the hallway and Brian's expression was dimly seen: noncommittal, calm. He turned, found Kevin's pants on a chair and handed them to his brother. "Here, slip into these, will you? Look, I need you to help me with something outside."

Warily, Kevin put the pants on over his shorts, but when he reached for a shirt, Brian told him, "You don't need that, Kev. This'll only take a minute. You don't need your shoes either. I just didn't want anyone to look out the window and see you in your drawers. Go on, go through the window; there's just something I need help with out there."

Kevin stood hesitantly inside the window. He couldn't see anything in the courtyard. "Gee, Brian, I'm still asleep. What's this all about?"

"Stop making noise and go on out, Kevin. I'm right behind you."

Brian's hand rested lightly on the back of Kevin's neck as they walked across the courtyard toward the inner, darkened alleyway. A shiver ran down Kevin's spine. He could feel the hairs along the base of his skull stiffen and he stopped abruptly when they were only a few steps into the passageway.

"Hey, Brian, that you?" John asked, his voice happy and relieved.

Kevin was aware that the pressure on the back of his neck had increased; he couldn't turn or run forward. He was between his brother and his cousin.

"What's this all about anyway, Brian?" Kevin asked.

There was no more pretense at being sleepy. He was starkly awake and the hours of waiting and chewing on his fingers and worrying about what he should do brought him to a pitch of stark terror which he had to dispel. He swung his fist into the unseen bulk of his cousin.

"You stupid son of a bitch," he said to John O'Malley. He felt a satisfying pain in his fist as it made contact with the totally vulnerable, unprepared midsection of his cousin.

Brian locked his arm across Kevin's chest and yanked him back.

"Go on into the house now, John," Brian ordered. "Do what I tell you."

John O'Malley moved reluctantly, his hands hugging his stomach. He didn't want to retaliate for the unprovoked blow. He only wanted to reassure Kevin. "Gee, Kevin," he gasped, "gee, Kev, don't be mad. I never told nobody nothin', I swear to God, Kevin. Hey, Brian, I didn't tell on him, did I?"

"Go on in the house, John, and get to bed now. Move!"

Brian shoved his brother from him. Kevin recoiled from the grating rough surface of the stuccoed wall. He realized now, slowly, with terrifying clarity, why Brian had told him not to put on his shirt.

He rubbed at a scraped elbow. "Ah, Brian, ah, gee, it wasn't my fault. I'm the one's gotta be with that half-wit all the time and I swear it wasn't me that . . ."

Brian took a step toward him. His right shoe ground down on Kevin's bare toes and his arm went up swiftly, implacably, and caught Kevin's throat so that the cry was stifled. He had decided not to use his fists. He wanted something that would last longer than a few punches. His own hand scraped briefly against the rough wall and gave some measure of what Kevin must feel down the right side of his shoulder and arm as he shoved him against the wall with more deliberate force this time.

"Don't, Brian, please, don't. Oh, Jesus, that hurts!"

He felt a cold and dispassionate anger. "You are really a sneaky, rotten little son of a bitch, Kevin. Not only are you a lousy thief, but you let poor John hold the bag for you all these hours. What have you been worrying about these last three hours, poor John in the precinct house or your own ass?"

It was senseless to deny anything. It was always senseless, and yet, even now, he tried.

"It . . . it . . . it was all *John's* idea, Brian. Honest. You all think he's so dumb, that he never gets an idea. But we were

154

on our way home from basketball and we saw the truck pull up, see? And John says, 'Let's go see what they left there.'"

Brian backed away and seemed very interested. "*John* said 'Let's go see what they left there'?"

Encouraged, Kevin nodded eagerly. "Yeah, honest, Brian, and I said, 'No, let's go home.'"

"Oh, you wanted to go home, but John insisted you go and look in the box. So one of you . . . opened the door . . ."

"John did," Kevin said quickly. "John opened the door and saw the flags, and he carried the box to the street, Brian."

"John did that?"

Kevin nodded anxiously. "Yeah, and then that Danny Dunne came by and . . . okay, yeah, I ran home. Honest, I got scared, Brian, so I ran home."

"And got into bed."

"Yeah."

"And went to sleep."

"Well . . . yeah."

"Jesus, it was *John* did everything, and not you, Kevin, right? It was *John*?"

The tears, hot and shameful, spilled from Kevin's eyes. The shadow in front of him, all he could see of his brother, was a dark tormenting force against which he had no defense. His words were no defense; they made everything worse, yet they spilled from his mouth almost with a will of their own.

Though he recognized the uselessness of his attempt, and that the penalty which would be exacted because of his very attempt to avoid penalty would increase with each word, Kevin tried to shift the blame. He was overwhelmed by the need to justify himself and he knew of no other way than by blaming someone else for his misdeeds. He stopped speaking, waited for Brian's cold, hard, mocking voice to egg him on to greater lies, but Brian was silent now and the murderous hand was too swift for him. He tried to twist free of Brian's grasp.

"Stand still, damn you, stand still," Brian whispered savagely into his brother's ear. His finger's tightened along the sharp jawline and his arm pressed against the narrow chest, and the rapid heartbeat inside the frightened body was steady against his arm. "You're a thief and a liar and a rotten, sly little son of a bitch," Brian said and he forced the side of Kevin's face against the cement, then jerked it back again. Kevin's neck stiffened against the expected scrape of the other side of his face, but now Brian's shoe ground down on his bare feet. Kevin's whole body jumped beneath his skin, twitching and twisting to avoid sudden assault.

He tasted the salt of his tears; words spilled from him in a torrent of self-pity; and, strangely, he began to believe his own lies and this filled him with a sense of righteousness which led to some small outrage which translated finally into action. His hands went up, tried to pry Brian off him.

"You gonna fight back, Kevin?" Brian asked in an incredulous and insulting tone. "That's very good, Kev. That's really swell. Come on, kid, let's see what you got." Brian slapped him about the face and head but Kevin's hands refused to do more than attempt to ward off the blows. Brian smacked him freely, then finally held him against the wall.

"You had enough, huh? Now listen to me, Kevin, if you step out of line again by so much as one inch I'll kill you. You got that, Kevin?"

Kevin expected the last terrible pain; it was the logical punctuation for the final threat. He closed his eyes instinctively as his face smashed into the cement. The impact sent him to the ground. Brian kicked him hard in the backside then pulled him to his feet and shoved him toward the house.

Kevin lurched from the alleyway, walked painfully on his aching feet. He climbed over the window sill slowly and crept into his bed carefully. He touched at himself with trembling fingertips. His face was sticky and wet with a combination of tears and blood. His shoulders and arms were raw wounds and he couldn't touch them even lightly.

"Kevin? Hey, Kevin?"

Kevin locked his back teeth together, tried to lock out the sound of his cousin's concern. John leaned over him with that worried, sorry, stupid voice. "You okay, Kevin? Hey, Kevin, you all right?"

Kevin watched through the window as Brian moved slowly from the shadows and toward the street. He waited just long enough to be sure Brian wasn't coming into the house yet.

"Come over here, John," he whispered. "I want to tell you something." He motioned John to the foot of his bed and John perched on his heels, expectant.

"Gee, Kev, I swear I never told nobody nothin'. And you

know, Kev, that Detective Dunne, gee, he hit me on the backside with a club when Mr. Gallegher went outside and he said he'd kill me if I said anything about it, but still I didn't say who was with me, Kev, and gee, it hurt something awful but I never let on."

Kevin sat up, locked his hands together and clenched his fingers hard so that they became a solid weapon at the ends of his arms. He straightened his arms and swung in a quick, dangerous motion. He caught John O'Malley on the right temple with such an unexpected force that the large boy toppled from the bed. He went down with a heavy thud, his head against the radiator.

Kevin leaped up, bent over him, but John was silent. In a sudden panic, Kevin ran across the room, closed the door and put the night lamp on. He fell to his knees beside his cousin and shook him.

"John? Come on, John, quit kidding around. Oh, please, Sweet Jesus, Mother of God, let him be all right. Johnnie, don't be dead. Oh, my God, I didn't mean to do it, John. John?"

There was a soft, bewildered moan and then a tentative movement. Puzzled, dizzy, John O'Malley slowly sat up, blinked, mouth opened at the bloody sight of Kevin. His hand went to his head and he felt the blood where his head had hit the pipe.

"Wow, gee, Kevin, what happened?"

Kevin was weightless with a combination of terror and relief. He pressed his cousin's shoulder with a trembling hand. "You're okay, Johnnie, you're okay."

John looked up at the bed. "Gee, how'd I get down here? Was we horsing around?"

Kevin nodded quickly. "Yeah, that's right. We was clowning around and we fell, both of us. Jesus, John, don't say nothing about this to anybody, okay?"

"Well, yeah, okay, Kevin. Jeez, Kevin, what happened to you? You're all scraped and bloody. You fall or something outside?"

"Yeah. I fell." He put the light out and got back into bed. He heard John settle in his own bed across the room. "Go to sleep now, John, okay?"

"Yeah, Kev. Hey, Kevin, you're not mad at me, right?"

"No, I'm not mad at you."

Brian walked rapidly, with long, determined strides, then finally broke into a run. It took a long time before the sharp, hard pain in his throat and chest forced him to slow down. He was keyed up, both physically and emotionally. He was sickeningly aware of what might have happened to him.

Francis Kelly told him, only that morning, about some guy who was about to be appointed and got dumped off the list for some dumb thing or other. His family had moved out of the city and the guy went to stay with them for a month, not even a permanent move, just a visit. But he hadn't reported it and they found out and it was good-by Charlie.

They could do that to you; after all the years of study and hard work, after that damn written test and the killing physical, each of them competing against a field of contenders with more to gain than a trophy. He'd made the top 10 per cent; he'd be called before long; he'd be appointed and admitted to the Police Academy and put on probation. But anything could kill it for him, once and for all.

A dumb little brother stealing a box of flags and the whole thing could go up in smoke.

Jesus, he'd really messed the kid up. He hadn't meant to hurt him that badly. It had gotten a little out of control; something had snapped; he'd just not known when, or how, to stop. He leaned against a collection of empty garbage cans along the sidewalk edge and lit a cigarette.

It had been a dumb kid's prank, really. Hell, Kevin wasn't going to end up an armed robber or something; the boys just happened on the situation. He'd just meant to slap him around a little, make sure he got the message. He hoped Kevin wouldn't look too battered. Jesus, his mother would be upset. Well, that would be Kevin's problem, and knowing Kevin, he'd come up with some story or other that made him look good. Funny, nobody would believe him but everyone would pretend they did because everyone would have a fair idea of the truth and it would be better not to dig too much into it.

Brian tossed the cigarette into the gutter and started for home. He began to feel better: it would be okay. As he walked up the long, twisting hill from the bottom of 181st Street, he remembered all the times he'd zipped down it on roller skates and in scrap-wood wagons and on bikes and sleds. It was a good hill, fast. He walked up, then turned to survey the steepness, remembering, then continued toward home.

In the general darkness, the brightly lit window on the top floor of the three-story old gray clapboard house just behind the police station shone like a beacon. Brian must have passed that old house a million times; he could remember wondering about the crazy old lady the kids used to say lived there. There had been a hundred stories, passed on from older brothers and sisters, circulated among the young, to keep them all in a pleasant state of terror when they passed the house. Jeez, the woman must be long dead, or a hundred years old by now, if there ever was an old woman. Brian rubbed the back of his neck and started to move again but some unexpected slash of light caught his attention.

He became alert and curious and pressed back into the shadows and finally alongside the huge old tree that stood in front of the old house. The light appeared again, a streak of brightness along the sidewalk as the basement door of the station opened, then disappeared as the door closed.

A figure, dark, compact, quick, moved from the door to the car parked by the curb. It was Detective Danny Dunne. He glanced around carelessly, then put down the carton he had under his arm, opened the trunk of his car and put the carton of flags in and slammed it shut. Then he put his foot on the bumper, tied his shoelace, lit a cigarette, surveyed the late sky, got into the car and took off. He drove in the opposite direction from Kruger's candy store.

Brian stepped from behind the tree and watched the car, bearing the flags, disappear. From nowhere, memory filled him — of boxes of candy balls, glass jars of unwrapped candy, sudden windfalls of games and toys, whole cartons of good rubber balls, commercial boxes of baseball-player cards and gum. None of them ever asked where these treats came from; no one would ever dare ask questions.

Just as Detective Dunne's family would not question the box of American flags he brought home with him that night.

PART THREE

The Son:
Patrolman
Brian Thomas O'Malley
1940

NINETEEN

Thirty-three thousand young men took the examination for Patrolman, New York City Police Department. Fewer than twelve hundred survived the written, physical, medical and background check-out. The class at the Police Academy was comprised of the top 10 per cent of the resulting list of eligibles. Eighty-five per cent of them held college degrees. By the time they received their appointments, they all knew they were something special.

The Fordham College and City College men regarded each other with cool suspicion. The former were would-be F.B.I. agents, the latter would-be professionals; all of them had accepted appointment to the Police Department as a necessary economic adjustment: purely a temporary stopover.

The instructors were somewhat uneasy at the composition of the class. Educationally, there had never been a class with so many degrees and professionals; there were lawyers, dentists, even a doctor or two. Ethnically, aside from the Fordham men, there was a noticeable shortage of Irishmen and a statistically large number of Jews. Some farseeing, long-range predictors muttered darkly about bad days ahead; these bright little Jews would take over the Department within fifteen or twenty years; they'd take the exams, get the promotions, put their own in positions of power. Wiser, calmer heads predicted they'd never go the course.

The recruits picked up the Department's method of identification when speaking of someone: you meant the short Jewish guy or the pale Irishman or the dark Italian or the big Dutchman. If you were safely in the midst of your own, you could be a little more specific and to the point: you meant the sheeny or the mick or the wop or the heinie; you spoke about hunkies and niggers or jigs; sometimes you used a variety of inventive names once you knew who you were talking to and he knew you.

Brian noticed that the only guys who seemed uneasy about the constant ethnic references were the Jews, but everyone knew they were ultrasensitive about themselves for some reason or other. And even about other groups. One guy raised an objection during a lecture on description for purposes of identification. The instructor said the suspect was obviously Italian and this guy argued that an Italian from the north of Italy might have light hair, blue eyes, fair skin and that the "obviously Italian" tag could be confusing. The description might apply to a person from Greece, Crete, Spain and on and on.

The guy was very sincere and the instructor, an old-timer with thirty-two years in the Department, ten of them at the Academy, calmly waited him out. When the recruit finished what he thought was a pretty good argument, the instructor pushed himself back from the lectern, rubbed the back of his neck in a puzzled way and said softly, "Well, sonny, all I can say is that in my experience a guinea is a guinea and that's about the only way to put it."

The recruit, who had a year of law school, pursed his lips thoughtfully against further comment, particularly since the Italian sitting next to him laughed as hard as anyone else in the room.

The lectures were about as boring as those they'd had at Delehanty's and covered material they'd had to know in order to pass the exams in the first place. Brian started to copy notes from the guy next to him, a nice, quiet, easygoing C.C.N.Y. graduate named Arthur Pollack. He had a precise method of listening, mentally sorting, selecting and writing down three or four important facts and key phrases to just about cover whatever you needed to retain of any particular lesson.

Arthur Pollack was about five feet nine inches tall, and since he stooped a bit, he looked smaller than he was. He was thin, gray-faced, hollow-chested, and at a certain angle, he appeared to be cross-eyed. He looked like someone who had just recovered from a terrible illness and his slow, lazy smile seemed an indication of a random happiness at just being

164

alive. He was the kind of guy people generally tend to underestimate.

In Arthur Pollack's case, it was a mistake.

During a vigorous class in physical education, the instructor blew his whistle for a five-minute break. Francis Kelly, last man in the class, called after one recruit came down with the mumps, dropped to his stomach beside Brian.

"Christ," Brian complained, "they're going to kill off half of us before they're finished. I thought I was in good shape, but now I think I'm dying."

Francis Kelly propped up his chin on his folded arms and stared in amazement. "Hey, Brian, look at your little buddy."

Several people, including the instructor, were looking at Arthur Pollack. Arthur Pollack, his thin body in perfect balance, the baggy gym shorts sagging, the laces of his high sneakers dangling, was standing on his head. His head balanced comfortably on his folded arms while the rest of his body rose into the air as casually as he could stand on his feet.

His eyes were closed and there was a faint, silly smile on his lips. The instructor, hands on wide hips, glowered at the spectacle as though it somehow offended him. The weary recruits were grateful that there was something, other than themselves, to distract him. They formed a semicircle and waited. Pollack sighed; it was a peaceful dreamy sound.

Brian watched uncomfortably. He was a nice guy and Brian didn't share the general anticipation.

The instructor winked at his audience and extended his soft-soled shoe and pushed steadily against Pollack's buttock. His body swayed slightly, his arms moved fractionally. Instead of toppling over, which is what he was supposed to do, Pollack merely adjusted his body to the change in balance. He also opened his eyes and scanned, in surprise, the hairy legs which surrounded him. He inhaled, closed his eyes, brought his knees down to his chin and neatly flipped himself through the air. He landed on his feet, face to face with the instructor. Rather, Pollack's face was on the level of the instructor's chest.

"Wadda you, a fucking acrobat?" the instructor asked. Without waiting for an answer, he declared, "This here rest period is over. Now, since you're so well rested an' all, you and me can demonstrate some holds and throws."

165

The instructor, a bulging man named Murphy, went through a few holds, in slow motion, without hurting Pollack, who held himself loose and easy and went with the toss. His face, normal gray again after the healthy flush from standing on his head, was unconcerned.

"You do them holds on each other," Murphy told them, "and you be nice and careful not to hurt nobody. First, though, let's test this guy's memory." He returned to Pollack and everyone had the same thought: Here it comes. "Do you remember what I told you yesterday to do when a guy comes at you from behind?"

Pollack shrugged and rubbed his nose and nodded vaguely, uncertain.

"Well, I think we oughta practice because it's especially important for you little guys. Shit, some big guy's gonna see you and think he can take you easy as hell. He's not impressed when he sees you, right?" As he rambled on, moving away from Pollack, distracting him with the wandering chatter, he suddenly grabbed Pollack, who seemed to forget what to do with his hands and legs. He ended flat on his back on the mat. Murphy looked down at him and grinned. "See, that's why a little guy gotta learn better than the big guy because the little guy ain't got no weight. Okay, kid, gimme your hand and I'll help you up."

Pollack remembered what to do with his hands, his legs, his body. The coordination was perfect, quick, graceful, stunning, almost flashy. Murphy, unprepared, was sent sprawling into the crowd of recruits. Pollack was on his feet instantly, leaning over Murphy.

Murphy glared up at him. "You sonuvabitch. You tricky, sly little bastard. I was going to help you up."

Pollack shook his head in boyish innocence. "Gee, Mr. Murphy, I'm awfully sorry. I thought you were going to demonstrate that second fall you showed us yesterday. You called it something . . . I don't remember." Pollack closed his eyes, and when he opened them, the left eye was turned in slightly toward his thin blade of a nose. " 'The helping-hand toss' you called it."

Immediately, Brian O'Malley said, "That's right, Mr. Murphy. That's what you showed us."

"Yeah, Mr. Murphy, you warned us about falling for the offered hand," someone else said.

Several hands reached down to Murphy and he flung a heavy arm at them and he ignored Arthur's offered apology.

Brian felt a warm glow of pride; the other guys moved from easy mockery to easy admiration for Pollack. The guy was small but he sure had balls.

"Get out the goddamn mats," Mr. Murphy roared. "You need nursemaids to tell you what to do. Bunch a' fucking wise guys, huh? Well, I'll make policemen outta you guys yet, if I gotta sweat you dry to do it."

Later, over a beer, Arthur Pollack brushed aside their compliments somewhat guiltily.

"Well, in a way I wasn't fair to poor old Murphy," he confided. "You see, I worked in a circus for nearly three years. That's how I saved enough to put myself through college."

Arthur Pollack had been, among other things, one-third of a trio who called themselves Wynken, Blynken and Nod. "I was Nod, always began by sleeping while standing on my head. On a high wire. It got so that I really could get some rest that way. And the wire wasn't all that high by New York standards, but, boy, they loved us in Iowa." He slurped beer, ordered more, laughed.

"I also worked out with a muscle man named Grunto the Great. Poor guy was practically a Neanderthal. Really, not retarded, but an actual throwback. But a very gentle man if he liked you. I used to read him stories because of course he didn't know how to read. He loved fairy tales and the poor guy used to cry real tears every time I read 'The Snow Queen' to him. He'd sob and sniff but plead with me to continue. Once, I tried to change it around, to give the story a happy ending, but he got very upset, very disoriented and confused about the whole thing, so I went the whole way with it every time, let him have his good old cry and all." Pollack shook his head in wonder. "Here was a guy used to bend steel bars in his bare hands, and he cried at a fairy tale. Isn't it a funny world?"

Pollack was an orphan, twenty-three years old. He had traveled all over the country with the circus. He had sold patent medicine in Tennessee and Kentucky; had done a song-and-dance routine for a short time in a Jersey burlesque house; spent a season as a waiter and house comic in the Catskills; worked as a counselor in a children's camp; served as a group leader at the Educational Alliance, teaching English to elderly immigrants; spent five years getting his bachelor's degree from City College; and looked forward to a long and successful career as a police officer.

"Of course," he told Brian and Francis Kelly, "the trick is to keep taking those exams. There's no point at all in planning to remain a patrolman. Just figure it this way, in twenty years, who'll be at the top?" He spread his arms to include them. "Us!"

"That's okay for you," Francis Kelly said morosely. Arthur Pollack made him feel very sheltered and inexperienced. "You got a college degree and all. But what the hell, lots of us didn't even get a high-school diploma."

"Francis, I'm surprised at you," Arthur said. "Guys like you, and you, too, Brian, you put too much emphasis on academic degrees. Hell, *I'm* impressed by the number of guys without college who got on the list, and near the top, too." He tapped his index finger on his forehead and beamed at them. "You got it up here, native intelligence, something no time spent in a classroom can give a man. You guys got something going on up here. You beat out an awful lot of contenders. Don't sell yourselves short, buddies, we'll all go to the top together!"

At graduation, Pollack walked off with most of the awards for scholarship, proficiency with firearms and physical achievements. No one begrudged him. He was one of the most universally liked of the graduates.

Brian O'Malley was given the shield his father wore as a patrolman and was told, with a firm handshake by the Commissioner, that he had a lot to live up to.

Francis Kelly was assigned to the 23rd Precinct in Harlem. Pollack, who lived two blocks away from the 9th Precinct on Clinton Street, was assigned to a precinct in Washington Heights.

Brian O'Malley was assigned to the 9th Precinct. He was assigned to work his first round of tours, four to twelves, with

168

Patrolman John Tiernan, who was forty-six years old and had eighteen years on the job.

"The first thing is," Patrolman Tiernan told him bluntly, "forget all the shit they taught you at the Academy. Bunch of fucking schoolteachers, them guys. Book smart, yeah, but they don't know fucking-a nothing when it comes to the street."

Patrolman Tiernan knew his streets intimately, and as he sauntered along, he spoke almost nonstop, identifying, instructing, advising.

"What you do is, see, you get to know your sector. Who's who, if you know what I mean. Let 'em see you, let 'em get to know your face, and let 'em get to know *you*, if you know what I mean."

He tapped his baton on the metal doorframe of a jewelry store, peered through the glass window, then jerked his head for Brian to follow. "Come on in and meet old Hymie."

The jeweler was a small straight man with a lined pink face and clear blue eyes and a wide smile which revealed square yellow teeth. He switched off the gooseneck lamp and rolled the jeweler's eyeglass between his fingers. "So, Patrolman Tiernan, you brought me a new policeman, so young they make them now." He nodded at Brian and the yellow teeth gleamed in what seemed more a grimace than a smile.

"This here's Patrolman Brian O'Malley." To Brian he said, "Hymie got some nice stuff here, kid, and he'll give you a good deal, you should wanna buy something."

The jeweler waved his hand expansively. "A nice watch, a ring for the girl. You're not married yet? Ah, when the time comes, I got a nice diamond ring; I can do something special for the boys in blue. Patrolman Tiernan can tell you that."

"Okay, Hymie, we'll be seeing you."

They walked along Delancey Street until Tiernan stopped in front of a tiny, dirty storefront. "Let's go meet Gyppy Lee Sung."

The Chinese restaurant was a hole in the wall. It contained three battered tables, a collection of mismatched chairs. Plaster chipped from the walls and ceiling. The smell of clothing being ironed came at them from the small back room, along with an assortment of cooking smells.

"Old Gyppy Lee lives back there with his family. Jeez, the

169

guy has seven or eight kids." Tiernan turned to the nodding proprietor. "How many you got now, Gyppy?"

The skin was stretched so tightly over Gyppy Lee's face that when he grinned, it was like looking at a death mask. He nodded brightly. "Got seven or eight now, that's right, plenny kids, plenny nough now."

"Gyppy, show Patrolman O'Malley here where they almost took your head off during the tong wars."

The Chinese came toward them and nodded brightly. "Oh, very bad time then. Good time now, no make trouble now, everything fine." He came close to Brian, who towered over him. "You want to see? Here, you look see." He held his head back and exposed his throat. There was a thick, ropy scar which extended from somewhere behind his right ear across his throat. Gyppy Lee pulled his undershirt down along his left shoulder. The sound he made was something like a laugh. "They make almost good job, nearly take off arm, see. Oh, very bad time then, yes, good time now."

"Okay, Gyppy, you keep your nose clean now. And you feed Patrolman O'Malley here when he gets hungry, okay?"

"Anytime, anytime, you come, Gyppy Lee feed real good."

The air outside the shop, by comparison, was clean and fresh. "Gee, do you really eat there? It looks like a ptomaine den."

"Naw, you gotta learn, kid," Tiernan told him. "Gyppy Lee's wife does the cooking and it's really good. Not like the chop-suey crap. See, it's one of the places you get to know about. Now, the average guy, he sees what Gyppy's place looks like, he don't go near it. But a lotta people, you know," Tiernan winked and nodded for emphasis, "a lotta important people, they come down on a Saturday, Sunday, and they get a real feed here, for a buck, a buck-ten. Now what you do is, you feel like eating Chink, you let Gyppy Lee take care of you. And you toss him, say, a quarter or a half dollar," Tiernan said. "What the hell, the guy got seven or eight kids. Not too often, you understand. You don't wanna abuse the guy's hospitality."

Tiernan expounded on the tong wars, which had occurred farther downtown, out of the precinct, but had, on occasion, spilled over to the streets of the 9th.

"I'll tell you this, though," Tiernan said. "Them Chinks

170

keep it all in the family. They're pretty tough bastards; don't let all the noddin' and bobbin' fool you. Jesus, just a couple years ago, there was a lot of dead Chinamen lining the streets of Chinatown. Hatchets and knives them bastards used too. Jesus, buckets a' blood when they got done with each other. But they're settled down real nice now, and you don't get no lip from their kids, neither."

They turned the corner to Sheriff Street and walked down to Rivington Street, which was lined on both sides, as far as they could see in either direction, with pushcarts. Old men and women guarded an assortment of wares with surprisingly quick, hard hands which snatched from prospective customers or idlers alike.

Women of all ages, dragging children of all sizes, foreign-looking older people, all of them speaking an assortment of languages, filled the street: browsed, handled, measured, argued, purchased or moved on.

Brian felt a curious excitement. There was a pace, a vibration, emanating from the tenement-enclosed street which spoke of a life and raw vitality that he wanted to understand with the easy familiarity which Tiernan displayed. He had a fleeting sense of despair that he would never be able to absorb, understand, categorize, sort out and see through the general commotion of merchandise and human beings, which was essential so that he could distinguish the normal from the police-unusual. It all blended into a noisy, directionless, patternless landscape and his eye moved from the street upward, along the tightly ranged, small-windowed tenement buildings which stood as walls overseeing the constant activity.

Women, heavy-armed, heavy-jawed, sat and leaned on window sills and watched. From their windows, crowded onto small lines of cord attached from window frames to the edge of fire escapes, laundry dripped gray bubbles of water, unnoticed, to the street below. Brightly patterned chenille bedspreads were spread along railings of fire escapes, to catch the small breeze or pale sunshine.

Pigeons flew overhead in sudden sweeps of activity from nearby rooftop coops; occasionally a stray gray feather drifted to the sidewalk. More often, their droppings hit the sidewalks and wagons and shoulders and laundry with random splatter-

171

ings. Women turned angry faces and shook furious fists skyward. Others ignored the violations as though they hadn't occurred.

Small children sat, framed within the windows of their home, looking down as though at a spectacle. Others sat with feet resting on the iron slatted fire escapes, watched over by older sisters who warned against the treacherous stairway opening through which children might tumble to their deaths.

Tiernan pushed a hard elbow into Brian's upper arm. There was a tightening, a change in the patrolman's face and in his entire body. He seemed to grow taller, harder. His chin lifted and he peered from beneath half-closed lids. His eyes, which were clear and pale, focused with the intensity of sun-glinted icicles through the crowded streets directly to the target of his sudden interest.

There was a group of boys, dark-haired, dark-eyed, tawny-skinned and muscular, sprawled on the steps of a tenement halfway down the block. They all wore orange-and-purple-satin jackets inscribed with the name of their club, "The Warriors-SAC." As the policemen approached the steps, the boys fell silent. They pulled themselves from easy stretched positions, which blocked the stairway, into huddled sitting positions and they studied their heavy-toed sneakers or their burning cigarettes or their dirty fingernails.

Tiernan spoke to Brian but his eyes never left the boys. He tapped his baton into the palm of his hand and spoke as though the boys were deaf and blind.

"Now these little bums are never up to any good. See them jackets they got themselves decked out in?" He extended his stick, lightly flipped it along the open edge of a jacket. The boy inside the jacket didn't move or raise his head.

"Not one of these little punks ever did a day's honest work in his life, but they managed to get together ten dollars and fifty cents each to get these shit rags custom made." His voice rose slightly and he turned to Brian. "How about that, O'Malley, you ever get yourself a custom-made jacket for ten dollars and fifty cents? Real class, ain't they, orange and purple? What's that, the guinea national colors?" he asked the boys. Tiernan teached forward swiftly, grabbed a handful of jacket and jerked a boy to his feet. "I asked you a question, Angelo. Didn't I ask you a question?"

The boy mumbled something and Brian saw Tiernan's arm pivot down quickly. Without releasing the boy, he jammed a hard elbow into his stomach. The boy gasped softly.

"This here little bastard is Angelo DiSantini. If there's any trouble in the neighborhood, you just look for Angelo. Right, Angelo?"

Angelo DiSantini wet his lips nervously. He glanced at Brian, then at Tiernan and shrugged. "I didn't do nuthin'."

Tiernan tightened his grip along the edge of the jacket. His large knuckles dug into the boy's throat. "You didn't do nuthin, *what*, you little guinea bastard." There was a dangerous edge to Tiernan's voice. His eyes searched the upturned face for something to confirm his suspicion.

Angelo DiSantini was a dark-browed, black-haired boy of about seventeen. He breathed through slightly parted lips and his white teeth flashed, then clenched tightly over the words which nearly slipped out. Brian caught it all: the naked fury, the burning anger, the held-in rippling power of the compact, well-built body.

Thick black lashes closed over his eyes, which had filled with hatred, then opened slowly. With careful, obvious control, in a voice just inside the thin line between respect and contempt, Angelo said to Tiernan, "I didn't do nuthin', *Mr. Tiernan.*"

Tiernan shoved the boy away from him and laughed shortly. "Your father didn't do nuthin' to your mother to bring you into the world."

Angelo's body tensed; his breath came in a slow, whistling intake, and without moving, he seemed to rise and swell. One of his friends, seated on the step above him, reached out, pressed a stubby hand on Angelo's shoulder, warned him, cautioned him, held him.

Tiernan's stick tapped the knuckles of the restraining hand sharply and the hand was withdrawn. "Someday, you little wop bastards. *Someday.*" It was a promise and a warning. Tiernan's eyes ranged over them for a moment. Then he reached out at random, pulled one of the boys to his feet and told them all, "Okay, get lost, you little bums. I'll be passing this dump again in five minutes and I don't want to see none of your greaseball faces around here."

They moved silently, single file, through the crowded

street. The bright shiny colors of their jackets appeared and disappeared, flittered like butterflies through the grays and blacks and then they were gone.

Brian's mouth was dry and he didn't know what to say or think.

When Tiernan spoke to him again, his voice was friendly, pleasant, informative, instructive. "Ya see, kid, ya gotta keep on top of them, know what I mean? Them little bastards, they'd take over if you let them. Bunch a' little thieves and fuckers is all they are. That kid Angelo, his big brother's doing time for stabbing a guy with an ice pick. Their old man was an iceman and he was a hard-working sonuvabitch. Poor bastard slipped one day in the icehouse, musta been a heart attack. Went down like a ton and fractured his skull. Down on Fulton Street, you know? By the fish markets. They never did figure which killed him, the heart or the head. Far as I'm concerned, you can't hurt a guinea if you crack his head and he got no heart to begin with."

Tiernan laughed at his own joke, then continued. "Yeah, he was a hard-workin' guy. But the kids are nothin' but garbage. One of them will end up in the chair; my money's on Angelo. The mother can't manage them. Four more besides the first two. Christ, one time last summer, I caught that little bum helping himself to some plums offa old lady Weissman's fruit stand. Well the mother musta been at the window and seen it too, because she comes runnin' down and gets to the kid the minute I grab him. We was like pullin' him between us back and forth. She gets him loose from me, and Christ, she got one of them big heavy wooden spoons they use to cook their spaghetti. And she began beating the kid with it. She's hitting him on the head and on the back and on the ass and she whacked him one on the face and split his eyebrow. I thought she'd kill the kid. I finally got them into the hallway and told her, okay, I wouldn't take him in that time. See, that's what got her so scared, you know. She's got one up; she don't want to see another go."

Tiernan rolled a piece of Juicy Fruit gum into a wad and shoved it into his mouth. He sighed philosophically. "The kid'll go one day, though. You can make book on it."

He strolled along, nodded at merchants, fingered bolts of

material idly as they went. At a fruit wagon, he selected a small pear, offered one to Brian, who refused.

Brian watched Tiernan pocket another pear for later. He thought about Angelo DiSantini and the encounter left him with a roiling uneasiness which he did not like. There were far more years between him and Tiernan than between him and Angelo DiSantini.

He felt a flash of anger, a sudden sharp understanding and empathy and an awareness that he had been made a party to something which left him vaguely ashamed. He also realized that Angelo DiSantini had displayed not only self-control but a street wariness that Brian would not have been able to manage under similar circumstances.

There had been a hard look of pride in the boy's dark face, and Tiernan's triumph, though on the surface obvious and undisputed, did not really exist for Angelo DiSantini. He had just done what he had to do under the circumstances. Brian felt that the boy was more than the contemptuous punk who Tiernan dismissed so easily.

It was something Brian had seen for himself; something Tiernan hadn't pointed out and didn't know himself. It had been his own first private street lesson, self-observed and self-learned. He felt a little better and turned his attention back to Tiernan.

"You see that old guy there, the real old guy all dressed in black? They say he's ninety-three years old. Old Man Moses they call him. Sharp as a tack though and tough as hell."

The clothing hung on the emaciated frame and seemed to have aged along with the body. There were greenish spots and gray patches and the elbows of the thin black suit were shiny. The small *yarmulkah* was a black spot set on the top of a full head of yellowish white hair. Bobby pins held it in place along the edges.

"So, *nu, vas machst du?*" Tiernan asked the old man solicitously.

"Ah, so who got good things to say?" The old man blinked rapidly and his hand trembled as he wiped his reddened eyes with a filthy handkerchief. "You need maybe some needles?" He dug into the cardboard carton which rested precariously on an orange crate.

175

"Not today, Pop, thanks. See you in *schul*." He told Brian, "The old man's got three sons who are all rabbis. You know, that's like priests. And each of them got three sons, and about half of *them* are rabbis. Very religious people, them. Now, all of them wanted the old man to come and live with them, but he's a very independent guy. He won't go live with nobody. He lives in a room on the first floor, across the street there, at 121. What I do is, if I don't see him for a day or two, and the weather is nice and all, well, I give a tap on his door. See, once about five or six years ago, the old man had a heart attack. He was all alone and his landlady found him. That's how I know about the family and all. See, I had to get in touch with them and notify them. So, I kinda keep an eye on him. Apartment two. It's what's called a *mitzva*."

"What's that?" Brian asked.

Tiernan smiled. "They call it a good deed, the Jews do. You know, like one you do for free. I don't know if it counts for *us*, but what the hell, it can't hurt, right?"

Tiernan pointed out different precinct landmarks. Up there, top floor, that's where "Three-Finger" Louie Klein got caught by the feds during Prohibition; over there, see that corner bar, that's where Ed Kelly, you know Ed Kelly, that's where he took two gunmen, shot it out with them, killed them both but not before Ed got a slug in his right leg.

"You notice the way Ed Kelly walks? He got a slight shuffle. They never did get the slug out of him."

They came upon a quadrangle of weathered benches, occupied by heavy old women and thin old men and women with baby carriages and toddlers.

"See that park over there? You ever heard of Lefty Quinn? Ah, you're just a kid, but Lefty Quinn, Jeez, he was an old-timer. A con man, Christ, the guy made and lost a million bucks in his lifetime and never done a day's work. Well, one time Lefty got mixed up with some heavy stuff. I don't remember exactly; it was to do with passing off some hot money. These were strong-armers, you know, and Lefty got chicken shit and wanted out when he realized he was playing in the wrong league.

"So Lefty played canary to the feds. See, it was a bank caper, and the feds was able to round them all up. It was planned that

Lefty would take a fall too, you know, so the strong-arm pals wouldn't think he'd crossed them. Well, he wasn't a kid no more, and at the last, he did a disappearing act, but it was a dumb move because he tipped his hand to his partners' buddies. Right over there" — Tiernan pointed with his stick — "right where the old woman is sitting, they found old Lefty Quinn. Christ, they left him all propped up, tied him into a sitting position. His head was half blowed off, and they left a bunch a' dead birds in his lap and in his pockets."

Tiernan laughed suddenly. "Jesus, we had a guy then, Kelcy, a real nut on pets and animals and stuff, you know. He seen Lefty Quinn sitting there like that and you know what he says? He says, 'What a fucking shame they had to go and kill all them poor innocent little birds!'"

When they came upon a drunk, more often than not Tiernan knew him by first name if not by last, and in some cases he had a fairly comprehensive history of the man.

"Sometimes we just let them sleep it off," Tiernan told him, "but tonight the sergeant said to round them up. See this here guy, Brian? Would you believe that this bum was once the vice-president of a bank? God's truth, O'Malley. When the crash come, this guy lost everything. His wife walked out on him and his grown kids, just left him."

They peered down at the bundled body; it might have been a heap of old clothing tossed against some garbage cans until a long sigh emanated from beneath what appeared to be folded arms.

Tiernan pushed against the man with the tip of his shoe. "Hey, Johnnie, you okay? Hey, Johnnie, how's tricks? Let's get a look at you."

The man tried to scramble along the sidewalk in a series of frantic, ineffective movements. Tiernan squatted beside him and his tone was surprisingly soft and gentle. "Easy does it, Johnnie, take it easy. Nobody's gonna hurt you." He looked up at Brian. "Take a good look, kid. Ain't he a beaut?"

There were raw patches on the man's forehead and nose. Blood was caked and matted along the stubble of his cheeks and chin. His lips were swollen and dry and split and his eyes, staring into Tiernan's flashlight, were glassy and frightened.

"You ain't gonna be sick on me, are you, pal?" Tiernan drew back slightly. "Don't he smell good, Brian? What'd you do, pee in your pants, Johnnie? Relax, nobody's gonna hurt you. But if you stay here, someone's gonna come along and take them shoes right off your feet, you know that. Tell you what," Tiernan said reasonably, "how about we take you in, judge gives you some time to clean up? McFee is sitting tonight." He turned again to Brian. "He's a real honey. Always asks these guys what they want. You know, how much time they need to straighten out. Johnnie here, from the looks of him, could use sixty days." He winked at Brian.

The man pulled at Tiernan's arm and made an attempt to rise. "Nah, nah, not sixty. Too much. Thirty do me fine. Thirty."

"Atta boy, Johnnie." Tiernan held the man at arm's length and helped pull him to his feet. "You don't smell so good, ya know?"

They rounded up twelve derelicts, sat them on the quadrangle of benches where the infamous Lefty Quinn met his bloody fate and waited for the wagon to collect them.

For days, Brian tried to get the pervasive odor of corroding flesh from his nostrils and skin.

TWENTY

On his first solo four-to-twelve tour, Brian O'Malley was assigned to lock up Molly the Pretzel Lady.

He caught a fleeting glimpse of himself as he strode past the plate-glass window of Ratner's restaurant. He looked pretty damn good in his uniform. He was getting a little accustomed to the strangeness of the Lower East Side; it was at least as different from his own world as the black Harlem to which Francis Kelly had been sent and they consciously collected bits of information to exchange with each other.

Some of the other policemen taught him some essential Yiddish phrases; McGarry and his partner Flynn were both old-timers and both fairly fluent. However, what they taught Brian was a collection of the filthy phrases in the language, with instructions to make friends with the nice old Jewish lady who ran the bakery on Sheriff Street. Her face had gone first white and then red before he realized not what he was saying but that he shouldn't be saying it in the first place.

He hoped to God that Molly the Pretzel Lady spoke English. Even more emphatically, he hoped that Molly the Pretzel Lady had packed her wares and gone somewhere off his post.

She stood with her two huge cartons of thick doughy pretzels against her body and successfully blocked the entrance to the BMT subway station. She was a short, fat, round-faced old woman whose shapeless body was covered by various layers of garments. A faded babushka covered her head and most of her forehead. As people approached the subway entrance, Molly's hand reached out swiftly, grasped a sleeve, jammed a pretzel into an unsuspecting hand. While the one strong hand clung to the sleeve relentlessly, the other turned palm up and

179

waited impatiently for the demanded two cents. Most people gave it to her as the price for their release. Those who refused had the pretzel snatched from them and were given a slight shove along with a few muttered words.

It was five-fifteen, exactly the time Sergeant Weber told Patrolman O'Malley to apprehend Molly the Pretzel Lady.

"Okay, lady," he said quietly, feeling just a little embarrassed. "Business is over for today."

She ignored him completely and continued her operation. She sold three pretzels and snatched back two. Brian finally planted himself firmly between Molly and her prospective customers.

"Look, go avay now, come back lader, den I got my day's in, but not now! Out of my way, move!"

Brian wished she would stop leaning around him and offering her wares for sale. "Sorry, lady. You're in. Right now. Let's go."

Without warning, the old woman threw her head back and opened her mouth and screamed. Brian looked around, alarmed. People stopped along the street and on the subway stairs to watch. Molly's hands clutched at the babushka, pulled it from her head, which was covered with scanty gray hair which she started to pull and yank.

Brian leaned close to her. "Hey, look, lady, calm down, will you?"

Her small eyes blinked rapidly and she squinted up at him. She motioned for him to come closer and Brian caught a whiff of onions and fish and garlic, a sour staleness, as she whispered frantically at him.

"Look, I give you a liddle something, for you should come back one hour, yah?" When he shook his head, Molly clenched her dirty fist at him and screamed over her shoulder to her audience, "This *shmuck,* he wants I should give to him five dollars, this *shmuck.* He should rot in hell, from an old woman he would steal. *Gonif! Gonif!*"

As she spoke, she collected her cartons, wound ropes securely around them; she stopped, reached around Brian and sold two more pretzels and jammed the pennies into the bulging, jangling pocket of her heavy gray sweater. She looped the rough cord through her arms and dragged the large boxes. She

180

stopped every few feet to smack her ample bust, gasp, wheeze, roll her eyes. Brian, towering above the old woman, felt the angry glances around him.

"Here, lady, gimme those damn boxes."

She dropped them, shoved them toward him and muttered, "Sure, sure, he takes from me my living, what does he care?"

At the top of the steps to the precinct, Brian put the cartons down and told Molly to carry them. He was not about to march before the desk with cartons of pretzels dangling from each arm.

Molly shrugged, hoisted them easily, as though they were weightless, and shoved the heavy door open with her shoulder.

"So, Weber, is you den?" she addressed the desk sergeant in a loud, friendly voice. "What's da madder, you got no crime to send your policemen to? They gotta bodder old ladies?"

Sergeant Weber peered over the top of his eyeglasses. "Molly, stop complaining. You ain't been in for a month. Be fair now, you had a nice long run."

She raised her hands to the high desk and strained forward. "So it makes you sleep good you gimme a collar at five-fifteen? I don't pay enough you should let me earn the rush hour?"

Brian waited uncertainly for Molly to finish. She shoved a few pretzels at Weber, but he shoved them back.

"So who's sitting tonight, I should know how much a fine?"

Weber said, "Ya got Glittsman, Molly. Big deal, two-buck fine and you're done for the month."

Reconciled now, Molly turned to Brian. "So, *nu,* what's the matter? Ya don't know what to do next? Come on, I'll show you."

She practically booked herself: Molly Weisfogel; female; white; 64 years; born Kraków, Poland; 5'2"; 173 pounds; 120 Sheriff Street; peddler; no scars.

She sank down on a bench, leaned noisily against the wall and reached for a wrinkled copy of the *Journal-American.* One of the detectives glanced in, waved casually to Brian and continued on his way. Brian opened his tunic, ran his hand inside the collar of his heavy plaid shirt. Sergeant Weber stopped at the doorway, coffeepot in his hand.

"Relax, O'Malley, you gotta long wait until Night Court."

"Yeah, you coulda let me have my rush hour. Weber, you're a regular no-goodnik sometimes I think. So, you got some coffee ya gonna give me?"

Sergeant Weber said, "I'm just making it, Molly. I'll let you know when it's ready."

About a half hour later, the detective Brian had seen before motioned him from the outer room. Brian gestured to Molly to get ready, but the detective shook his head. "Nah, the wagon's not here yet. Listen, could I see you a minute, kid? Come on out here."

Brian looked doubtfully toward Molly but the detective assured him, "Molly ain't going nowhere, are you, Molly?"

The old woman waved an impatient hand at their nonsense and kept her face down into her newspaper, which she read, word by word, finger and lips moving steadily.

The detective was shorter than Brian by several inches, with a balding pate and worried forehead. His eyes moved constantly, alert, on guard against danger from any direction.

"Listen, you're O'Malley, aren't you?"

"Yeah, why? What's doing?"

The detective cupped a hand over his mouth and spoke in a quick sharp whisper. "Listen, kid, it's none of my business, but you ought to keep your lady friends from visitin' ya at the house."

"My lady friends? What . . ."

Detective Schenkel jerked his thumb toward the caged staircase which led to the detectives' squad room. "Jeez, she come up there lookin' for you. What'd you do, tell her you're outta uniform?"

Brian frowned. "I don't know anybody. Looking for *me*?"

"Well, she asked for you by name, kid. Look, take a run up there and straighten it out, okay? Lucky for all of us the squad boss is out sick. He don't take too much to that kind of thing."

For one second, Brian hesitated, turned toward Molly, but Schenkel assured him Molly would stay put and led the way.

Brian bolted up the two flights of iron steps and felt a slight sense of wariness when Schenkel stepped back for Brian to enter the squad room first. Detective Ed Kelly was seated at a desk, hat on the back of his head, which nodded in weary boredom over his telephone conversation. When he saw Brian, he gestured toward the inner room, raised brows and shoulders to indicate ignorance of the matter.

Brian approached the small inner room where the detectives kept a few cots against one wall for when they had double tours or quiet nights and could catch a few hours. There was one small lamp burning a yellow circle on the surface of a desk and Brian's eyes, unaccustomed to the dark, couldn't make out the shape which moved toward him.

"I'm O'Malley," he said. "What's all this about? Who are you?"

The shape moved into him, wrapped itself around him in a tangle of sharp bony arms and legs. He felt the sweet fragrance of cheap perfume and powder scrape along his face. He grappled with thin wrists and tried to pry frantic clawing fingers from his arms. There was a desperate panting flow of words and questions directly into his ear.

"Is it you, my darling? Is it really you? They told me it was. They told me you'd come back to me, but I couldn't be sure. But I've always believed you would, no matter how long it took. I waited, I was true to you, my lover, I was faithful and now you're back . . ."

Brian tried to pull away but the woman clung to him, forced herself against him; fingers, steel-strong, dug into his flesh, tore at his clothing. Incredulously, he felt her hands, fingers, plucking at his trousers, yanking the buttons, reaching for him.

He shoved her away from him and slammed the back of his legs against the desk.

"Jesus," he said. "Jesus, lady. Come on!"

She lunged at him and he fled to the outer room, his hands furiously clutching at his disheveled clothing. He whirled around to confront her in the light of the detectives' squad room.

She stood, open mouthed, staring at him, unmoving now. Her thin, skull-like, ruined face froze; the eyes, burned out with desperation, were black glass, uncomprehending, gazing vacantly now. Her cheeks, sunken and fleshless, were smeared with bright blotches of powdery rouge. Her lips were thickly greased with orange lipstick, sharp points of color reaching nearly to her nostrils and down toward her chin, a mouth for a mad clown. Her hair, dyed black with sprouts of white at the roots, was a tangled mass, filthy, greasy, falling on her bone-thin shoulders. Slowly, she moved her head back and forth, whispered, "No. No. No. No. That's not him. That's not Albert. Not yet. No. No. No. No. That's not him. That's not Albert. Not yet. Not yet."

As she spoke, her eyes still on Brian, she moved about the room, hit into desks, chairs, without noticing, until she reached the doorway. Then she bolted from the room and they could hear the sound of her footsteps as she lunged down the stairs.

"Christ," Brian asked breathlessly, "who the hell was *that?*"

"Jeez," Detective Schenkel said, "that's what we wanted to ask *you,* kid. Hey, O'Malley, Christ, you better button up, kid, before we get you on indecent exposure." He opened the top drawer of his desk, searched around until he found a cake of soap which he tossed to Brian. "Hey, kid, if she touched your pecker, you better give it a real good wash. She looked like she was crawling with all kinda things."

Brian went into the men's room and inspected the damage to his uniform. The crazy bitch had ripped two buttons off his fly and his tunic was smeared with lipstick, rouge and powder. He scrubbed himself, then rubbed a damp paper towel over his uniform. He used his anger, not trusting himself to go back to the squad room to search for his missing buttons. He could hear the two detectives laughing; he knew he'd been had and that the story would make the rounds and that he'd just have to take it.

He checked his pants, decided he could risk it.

"Hey, Schenkel, here's your soap." He tossed the slippery bar just over the detective's head. "Thanks." He stopped at the doorway and grinned. "By the way, Schenkel. That's a lousy way to get rid of your old girl friends. Next time you want to palm one off, try your partner there. He's a lot more her type than me."

He took the steps two at a time, adjusted his collar, entered the ready room and felt a weight in his stomach. Molly, her cartons and pretzels and the newspaper were gone.

He glanced at Sergeant Weber, bent over some papers on his high desk, didn't know what to do until the clerical man

signaled him silently, jerked an index finger toward the back
exit.

Out in the alley, the patrol wagon waited impatiently. A uniformed man opened the cage door and Brian climbed into the
back of the wagon while a motley assortment of pickups complained.

"*Nu*, you got all night maybe, making us wait, you're fooling
around with your friends. Well, I ain't got all night. You should
be ashamed."

Softly, Brian said, "Molly, shut up."

The Night Court detention pen was a Saturday-night madhouse. Through some error, twenty-five derelicts had been
misrouted and their stench permeated the wire-meshed enclosure long after they had been collected and sent to another
court.

"Holy shit, this place smells like a fucking zoo," a patrolman
observed bitterly.

Detective Horowitz, from the Ninth Squad, whom Brian
knew by sight and reputation, commented, "You can always
tell a Catholic; whenever he shits, it's holy." His prisoner, a
young Negro homosexual, kept his face down so that no one
could see that he was crying.

Brian tried to detach himself from Molly and her boxes of
pretzels. There was something big going on downstairs, where
male prisoners were held prior to being brought up to the
detention pen adjacent to the courtroom. Several reporters
and press photographers were circulating and there was a general air of something happening.

Detective Horowitz yanked his prisoner to Brian's side and
asked him, "Hey, Jeffrey, ain't this young patrolman cute?"
He punctuated his question with a light, friendly jab of his
elbow. The homosexual pretended not to be interested but he
raised his face shyly and studied Brian, then smiled and
blinked.

"How do you like this little fickle bastard?" Horowitz asked
with feigned anger. "An hour ago, he had the hots real bad for
me; now he's rolling them big eyes at you, O'Malley. Just
don't go reaching, Jeffrey. Remember, that's how come you're
here in the first place."

Brian had heard that Julie Horowitz was a dangerous man, despite the wide, friendly face. He was about forty, nearly as tall as Brian but much broader, more solid, though not yet fat. He had a thick fringe of yellowish-red hair surrounding a huge freckled skull and his tiny eyes were constantly disappearing into the crinkles of his laughter. He laughed a lot, but the laugh was deceptive: loud, frequent but humorless.

"Hey, O'Malley, you know what they got down there?"

"No, but I've noticed a lot of action. What gives?"

Horowitz leaned into Brian. At the same time, he firmly pushed his prisoner around in back of him. "They got some big jigaboo bastard on a rape. Little kid on a roof. She was a little colored kid, but what the hell, rape is rape." He laughed in anticipation of what he was to say. "The arresting officers seen it that way too. See, they was a couple spade sleuths who took him and they really creamed the guy. I was talking to this guy from the *Journal,* a pal of mine. You know Sid Lewis? Well, he told me they put the cuffs on this guy and they nearly butchered him."

The laugh spilled over the words and Brian had some difficulty in understanding what Horowitz was saying. "Christ, the guy is a real nut, you know? Built like a brick shithouse, and Sid tells me they beat up on him and he keeps trying to fight back. You gotta be crazy, right? They finally knock him cold and he comes to and tries to rise up, roaring like a ruptured bull and wants to take them on. He ended up by smashing his head into the bars downstairs." Horowitz took a deep wheezy breath and sputtered more words in a gush of breath and laughter. "Now get this, get this. This dumb bastard, see, he's all beat the hell up, and he starts ramming his head against the bars in the holding cell. And every time he bangs his head, see, he yells, 'Bang!'; rams his head, yells, 'Bang!' " Horowitz turned away for a moment to regain his composure. "Like he was making music on a drum, only the drum was his stupid head."

"He must be a nut," Brian said, impressed.

"Or pretending to be a nut case. They sent for the nut wagon and he'll get carted off to Bellevue." His thick lashes batted a few times, eyes darted, examined the crowded room. "Well, kid, wadda you got?"

186

Brian ran his finger around the inside of the stiff collar of his tunic and shrugged. "I had to take the old woman. You know. The pretzel seller."

Sound sputtered from Horowitz' mouth. "Oh, kid, you're in for it tonight. We got old Morry Glittsman sitting. You know about him?"

Everyone knew about Magistrate Morris Glittsman. He was the weekend drawing attraction at Night Court and deserved the attention accorded him. He conducted each session with the wit and timing and pace and audience sense of a master showman. Anyone coming before him might be the target of his sudden, biting, searing verbal assault: police officer, alleged culprit, complainant, court clerk, it was all the same to Glittsman. The perpetrator of the most horrendous crime might, for some unknowable reason, bring forth a kind, concerned, gentle bit of fatherly advice and encouragement and the most timid miscreant might be the recipient of a cruel, malicious tongue-lashing.

"I'll give ya some advice, kid," Horowitz offered. "Ya don't say nothin', nothin' at all, no matter what Glittsman pulls. Don't let the mob in the courtroom bother ya neither; they're nothin' but a bunch of fucking cheap-date phonies and don't you provide them with no free entertainment. You just 'Yes, your Honor,' 'No, your Honor' and . . . Jeez, I remember one time a coupla years back . . ."

The broad smile froze on Horowitz' face, his eyes congealed into a glinting bright awareness and he moved swiftly and decisively before Brian realized there was a need to move.

By the time he turned toward the terrible noise which shrieked through the thick stale air, it was difficult to determine what he saw, to understand the sudden, unexpected burst of violence all around him.

The man was some nightmare apparition, a dark face contorted with pain and anguish and madness. Blood streaked unbelievably from heavy lips and flared nostrils, in long smears, bright and startling against the strange garment. He seemed partially encased in a white wrapping, and as he relentlessly raised tremendous arms against Horowitz' onslaught, a collection of belts and buckles clattered against the escaped prisoner's body. He received the impact of Horowitz' strength

187

without a sound and Brian tried to get to the man but found himself caught up amidst the bodies which moved toward the confusion or away from it.

A small hand clutched frantically, childlike, at his sleeve and it was with considerable difficulty that he managed to break free of the terrified grasp which Horowitz' prisoner had on him.

Finally, Horowitz pinned the man's arms from behind and two Negro detectives placed themselves in front of him, one on each side. A team, perfectly coordinated, wordless, soundless, expressionless, they grasped the flapping material, twisted it about the man's body so that his arms were firmly secured. Finally, an animal cry came from deep within the man's throat as he twisted wildly against the restraint. He began to buck his head, bent forward suddenly for balance, and as he did so, one dark hand reached out, pressed on the bloodied wool-matted skull. Two fists raised, hammerlike, crashed down with a sickening, smashing sound. Brian caught a glimpse of the blunt end of a blackjack within one of the clenched fists.

The prisoner lay motionless on his stomach. One of the Negro detectives reached down and turned him over. The man's eyes were rolled back in their sockets and the white that showed was bloodshot and yellow. Horowitz stepped back, disclaiming any part of what might take place. The two detectives breathed heavily with exertion and excitement, regarded the man, then each other. With a curiously passive concentration and a savagery that seemed devoid of anger or passion, they kicked the prisoner's body deliberately and professionally. They stopped, regarded the trussed body, and without a word or signal between them, each in turn delivered one devastating kick to the groin.

Brian clenched his teeth, felt a tightening in the pit of his stomach, a sudden ache along his navel, down into his groin. The homosexual sobbed and pressed his face into his hands. Someone sighed "Oh, Jesus," but whether in supplication or admiration was not clear.

The two detectives reached for their prisoner and dragged him back inside toward the waiting ambulance attendants.

Brian lit a cigarette and tried to hold his hands steady or at least to hide the tremble.

Horowitz' laugh was a little thin and stretched but otherwise he seemed untouched by what had just happened. He jerked his thumb over his shoulders toward the door. "Listen," he said and moved his head to one side, "you are now gonna hear a body make contact with some steps."

His prediction was almost immediately confirmed. There was a heavy dull thudding sound. Horowitz rested a heavy freckled hand on his prisoner's shoulder. "Come on, Jeffrey, stop crying. Aren't you lucky you didn't play games with them boys?"

For a moment, Brian didn't see Molly and he looked around wildly, but before panic set in, she pulled herself heavily to her feet from behind her boxes. She looked better than he felt.

"To be in such company, I had to lose my whole night?" she complained. "Ach, these *schwartzes,* they want to kill each other, they shouldn't do it here."

Horowitz engaged in a loud and friendly conversation with a plain-clothes man. Brian watched the detective with admiration. He was a big, boisterous, laughing man who knew how to move, what to do, how to do it, and when to do it.

The court attendant appeared and announced that the judge would be off the bench for a ten-minute break. This was greeted with groans and curses.

"Shit, there goes another hour. Okay, move your ass," a detective instructed his prisoner back into the detention cells.

"Fifteen, twenty minutes the most," the court attendant assured them. "Look, if he ain't heavy stuff, don't bring him back down. They're loaded already."

"This bastard cut his girl friend's throat, Hennessy. That heavy enough, for Christ's sake?"

There was a shuffle of feet and rearrangement of bodies as some policemen returned prisoners to detention and others, resigned, slumped on available benches or leaned against the wall and lit cigarettes or read folded newspapers or exchanged gossip or opinions with each other.

Brian opened his tunic, rubbed his flat empty stomach and debated briefly whether he ought to risk one of Molly's pretzels. He was pretty hungry but her hard, scarred hands were dirty and he saw her dig her index finger into an ear or her nose from time to time.

Horowitz lit a cigar and told his prisoner he could sit on the

189

floor if he wanted. A young patrolman, pale, tightly buttoned, bewildered, came from the door leading to the holding cells.

"Hey. Hey, Francis," Brian called out.

Francis Kelly looked around, then waved. "Hey, Brian." He came to Brian's side and spoke in a low, tense voice. "Jesus, Brian, it's a madhouse down there. Listen, I gotta go and get commitment papers. I don't know where the hell I'm supposed to get them or who's supposed to give them to me. Jesus, I don't know anything that's going on, Bri, but I'll tell you one thing: I'm getting a royal hosing."

Julie Horowitz blew acrid smoke into the air and studied it thoughtfully. He made no attempt to turn from the two patrolmen; he was frankly interested.

"What do you mean, Francis? What've you got?"

Francis Kelly looked strange. There was a gray circle around his mouth and his skin had a white cast. He blinked a few times and his eyes moved restlessly around the small, crowded enclosure.

"Brian, you know that big colored guy that they took outta here in a strait jacket? Well, I'm the guy that caught him. And those two, those colored detectives, they just barged right in and took the collar offa me."

"*You* got him?" Brian asked incredulously. Francis Kelly was slight, wiry guy, fast and tough, but the prisoner was a gigantic raving maniac. And Francis didn't have a scratch on him.

Francis understood Brian's surprise. "Yeah, well, he wasn't playing King Kong when I collared him, Bri. See, I was doing my post, and I was just looking things over when this colored woman, she comes up to me yelling and all that this guy took her little kid to the roof. And I ran up." Francis Kelly wiped a thumb over his lower lip thoughtfully. "Jesus, I don't even remember taking those steps, I swear I don't. Okay, I hit the roof and there was this guy, standing there, looking down at the little kid and she was, well, the little kid was like spread out, you know. And I had the gun out and the guy, Christ, he *was* a big sonuvabitch, and he sees me, and he just says, 'Okay, okay, okay, no trouble, man, no trouble,' and he comes along. I got the cuffs on him nice as you please and the mother rushes past me to the little kid and starts screaming and down we go and I call for a wagon and for an ambulance.

"I cuffed him around a lamppost. Hell, the guy was so damn big and he was in that funny kind of calm state, like he wasn't really aware of what was happening yet. Well, before anyone else arrives on the scene, wham, up comes these two colored guys, they flash shields at me, one guy says, 'Gimme the key to them cuffs,' he takes the key and all hell busts loose. They get this guy off the lamppost; hell, first I thought they were setting him free, when wham! in the stomach; wham! in the guy's face." Francis Kelly cupped his hand over his mouth and said to Brian, "Jeez, they was using a jack, Brian; they did it so nice though, you couldna told unless you knew. The guy was spitting teeth, just like in the movies.

"Holy God, and then these two take *my prisoner* into their car and I start after them and they tell me, 'You wait for the ambulance; you stay with the little girl and the mother.'"

Brian held out his pack of cigarettes to Francis, held a match to one for him and then to his own. "Jeez, Francis, they took your collar away from you?" He turned to Horowitz. "Can they do that, Julie? I mean, hell, it's Francis' pinch, right?"

Horowitz puckered his lips and blew a narrow stream of smoke toward the ceiling and smiled. "Kid," he said to Francis Kelly, "you seen what that prisoner looked like when they shoved him into the Bellevue ambulance?"

Francis Kelly's pale face nodded and he closed his eyes for a moment. "Man, he was *bad*."

"Kid," Horowitz continued, "did it ever occur to you that that nigger bastard might just kick off from all of them head and body injuries? He looked pretty bad to me."

"You think he might?"

Horowitz threw a friendly arm around Kelly's shoulder. "Kid, you're O'Malley's friend, right? Okay, so I'll give you a little advice for free. When you get something like that and one of them spade sleuths wants it, consider yourself lucky to get out from under. Now, if they came looking for you *after* the way they messed him up, and said to you that *your* prisoner is on the critical at the nut factory and some questions was going to be asked, *then* you got a beef. *Capisce?*" Horowitz winked.

"Well, yeah, I guess, but hell."

"You get the commitment papers from the clerk in the court, he hands them to the judge to sign, you bring them over to Bellevue and give them to the D.C. guy there and you're

191

home free." He gave Kelly's shoulder a friendly rap with his knuckles. "Forget it, kid. There'll be plenty more collars where that came from. What's the matter, they didn't teach you nothing like this at the Academy?"

Francis Kelly pulled his lips back tightly and grimaced. "They didn't teach us *shit* at the Academy."

Brian O'Malley managed to avoid revealing why he was present and he was glad that Francis Kelly was too upset to ask what kind of collar he'd made.

Francis Kelly was right: they didn't teach them shit at the Academy. But Francis was learning what it was all about. He was right in the middle of it. He was getting to be a part of it.

And Brian O'Malley was out locking up crabby old women for selling pretzels.

TWENTY-ONE

There was nothing unusual about the tenement building where Arthur Pollack lived. The only odd thing to Brian was that he'd never before had a friend with an apartment of his own.

Brian took the long narrow staircases easily. On each landing were four doors, behind each door were muffled sounds, cooking odors wafted into the hallway, mingled with other fragrances. The third-floor landing vibrated with a male voice which attempted to keep up with a loud, tinny Caruso record.

On the fourth floor, Brian found 4-C, dropped his cigarette to the linoleum floor, stepped on it, fingered his tie lightly, then tapped. Arthur Pollack opened the door immediately.

"Hey, Brian, great. Come on in, kid, come on in."

The apartment was unexpected. It was brightly lit, the walls were painted white, there were oak-stained bookshelves ranged across one entire wall and they were filled with books and magazines and records. A studio couch against an opposite wall was covered with a dark-red throw and a collection of brightly colored pillows was piled haphazardly to serve as back rests.

The ceilings were very high; Arthur must have used a tall ladder to place his collection of prints on the wall between the molding and the ceiling. The pictures, some framed, others unframed, were mainly bright splotches of color which didn't convey much of anything to Brian. The two windows, wide and tall, were covered with shutters. The slats of the shutters slanted downward to catch the fading early-evening light.

"Hey, this is quite a place, Arthur. Gee, it doesn't look like what you'd expect. You know what I mean."

Arthur beamed. "Yeah, it's pretty good. A matter of letting

the light in. Come on into the kitchen; we'll find something to drink."

The kitchen was also painted white and the old-fashioned potbelly coal stove, freshly painted black, seemed too shining and clean to be in use, but Arthur assured him that was his cooking stove and provided most of the heat in the flat as well. Against one wall, covered with a huge enamel lid, was a bathtub which stood on lion-claw legs. Covered, it served as a combination table and storage unit for groceries.

Arthur held up a bottle of Scotch for Brian's approval, then reached into the top section of the red-enamel icebox and chopped some slivers of ice and dropped them into the glass. Pasted on the upper door of the icebox was a pen-and-ink line drawing, a cartoon of a thin, emaciated policeman who could only be Arthur Pollack.

The shoulders sagged, the knees bent within baggy, ill-fitting trousers, the gun holster was longer than the short legs, the brim of the policeman's hat rested on a sharp, beaky nose. Beneath the drawing were printed the words, "Don't worry about a thing. Arthur is on the job!" There was a long, fragile trailing line and then the signature of the artist, "With love from Arlene."

Brian was both surprised and impressed. "Hey, you got a girl friend who's an artist?"

"Pretty good likeness, isn't it? She's what you call a quick-sketch artist. You know, caricatures. She works Coney Island, the Greenwich Village street show. Wherever she can turn a buck. Mostly though, she works on the second floor of Gimbels, selling ladies' 'you-knows.' Come on, let's get comfortable."

Arthur waved him into the living room and with a flourish offered Brian a modernistic sling chair, which they both stood and studied for a few moments.

"Wrong end to," Arthur explained, "just take a deep breath and lower away."

Arthur sat, shoeless, cross-legged, on the couch. "I hope you're good and hungry, Brian. The girls have been cooking up a storm."

Brian took a long, deep swallow and glanced around appreciatively. The Scotch sent warm, pleasant waves of easi-

194

ness through his head and across his chest. "Jesus, Arthur, this is very nice."

"There's even a toilet over there. It's about the size of a closet, but at least it's inside my own door. If you've ever had to use a common hallway toilet, you'd know what luxury this is."

There was a staccato of sharp taps, the sound of long fingernails, followed by a soft, breathy voice outside the door. "Arthur, are you there, honey?"

Brian was nearly consumed by curiosity. At first when Arthur had invited him for a dinner to be prepared by two "lady friends," he envisioned fat old aunts or motherly neighbors. But Arthur assured him he'd be delighted and surprised. So far, the apartment surprised him, and he managed to wiggle forward in the strange chair, his eyes on Arthur at the door.

The room filled with female sound, laughs, tumbling words and little squeals. Arthur had an arm around each girl and he brought them to Brian. "Here are my two favorite girls of all time. Rita and Stella Wasinski, meet my friend, Brian O'Malley."

Brian tried to rise but the chair seemed to hold him and he couldn't grab on to an arm for balance since there weren't any; he rocked forward, then back again helplessly. The girls grinned, they all laughed and Brian felt color, or the Scotch, rise to his cheeks.

"Hey, he's a good-looking guy," the older girl said frankly. "You didn't say your friend was such a handsome guy, Arthur. Don't he remind you of somebody, Rita?"

The blond girl, Rita, was the quieter of the two. She glanced at him somewhat shyly, then down at the bowl of food she'd brought with her, then back at him, then to Stella. When she spoke, her voice was a small, childish whisper and her words ended in a tentative laugh.

"Yeah, I think he looks like Tyrone Power. You know?"

Arthur and Stella took the assortment of food into the kitchen and the apartment was filled with rich, tempting fragrances, warm tempting spices.

They were cousins; Arthur had told him that much. And they were his neighbors two flights down; lived with an old aunt. But Arthur hadn't told him that Rita smelled of unnamable flowers and was cream-skinned and soft, with high rounded breasts and a waist that curved in sharply and then out again leading to sharp-boned hips and long, long, long thighs and slender legs. Brian's eyes moved slowly over the girl's body, at first measuring, then discounting, the clothing, evaluating. She wore a tight-fitting bright-blue dress which pulled across her bust and hips and hiked up above her knees as she perched on the edge of the couch. One ankle-strapped shoe dangled in the air as she crossed her legs and ran a finger along a stocking. She pulled her mouth down, touched a pinky to her tongue, then to the stocking.

"I get more runs," she said by way of explanation.

"I bet you do," Brian said coolly.

The girl's eyes held on his for a moment; they were dark brown and warm and startled, as though he had said something unexpected. Her lips were full and shining with bright-red lipstick and her mouth opened slightly. The line where her orangey pancake make-up started and her own natural pale-white skin began showed clearly along the side of her face, as though she'd made up in a room with poor lighting. Her hand moved to the top of her low-cut dress, as though to shield herself from Brian's gaze, or to brush away some invisible lint or dust. She seemed about to say something, then looked up at Arthur, who brought them drinks.

"That food smells great, Rita. Brian, these two are about the best cooks in the world."

Stella was bone-skinny and angular, with high cheekbones and a pointy chin. Her hair, which was dyed black, was piled into a high wavy roll along the top of her head. She had small bright eyes, oddly slanted and wide-set, smeared with heavy mascara over the scanty lashes. She sat on the arm of the stuffed easy chair and wrapped long, thin arms around Arthur's neck; her fingers plunged and raked through his tightly curled hair with an almost maternal gesture.

"It's a cinch to cook for this guy. He don't know from good food, so you just give him something hot and he thinks it's great. Arthur, you're gonna make some girl very, very happy someday. She's gonna think she's marvelous; anything she does, you say its great."

Stella laughed raucously and Rita laughed softly and Brian

196

wondered how the hell little Arthur Pollack did it. The girls watched his every move, hung on his every word. They also did his laundry, cleaned up his apartment and cooked for him every chance they had.

"Are you a policeman, same as Arthur?" Rita asked quietly.

Brian was surprised that they knew about Arthur. He said, "Yeah, I'm a policeman." He hesitated, rolled the glass between his palms, then, eyes on the blonde, he asked, "How about you, Rita? What do you do?"

The words sounded exactly as he'd intended them: soft and low and insinuating. An accusation and an acknowledgment rather than a question. Her face, beneath the hardness of too much make-up, was wounded. Her hands clenched together tightly and she turned toward Arthur, who gave her support with a smile and a slow, friendly wink. It wasn't at all what Brian had anticipated.

"Rita is a dancer," Arthur said. "She's really good, Brian. Someday, we'll hear big things about Rita. She can tap holes right through this floor." His eyes stayed on the girl as he spoke and she relaxed a bit. "The last time we had a great big party here, we had the radio on and they had a record of Fred Astaire tap dancing." He turned to Brian and laughed. "Isn't that a silly thing, a record of a tap dancer? Anyway, Rita just tapped along with him, without any preparation at all. She's just got a natural sense of rhythm, and I swear to God, Brian, she was right on beat the whole record."

Rita smiled at him gratefully and pressed the tip of one shoe into the rug. "That was before you got the place fixed up so nice, Arthur. Before you got the rugs on the floor and all."

Arthur had released the girl from the lip-biting tension; he did it easily, naturally, without acknowledging that anything wrong or out of line had been said or indicated.

Brian was more than slightly confused. Hell, the girls were hookers, out and out. Anyone could see that. It wasn't possible that Arthur didn't know what they were. Yet he leaned back and smiled and talked and cracked nice little jokes like they were Saturday-night dates.

Stella collected the glasses for refills and asked Arthur to help her chip some ice.

Rita became tense again. She bent over a fingernail and

studied it and pulled at the cuticle, then she gazed at the walls and bookshelves and finally she came to Brian. A nervous smile pulled at the corners of her full mouth.

"Arthur's place is real nice, isn't it?"

"Uh-huh. You known Arthur a long time?"

Rita shrugged and her hand went inside the neckline of her dress to adjust a slipped shoulder strap. "Oh, well, you know. Since he moved in. I guess about a year. A little less than a year, I think."

"Uh-huh."

Rita picked at her nails, then said raggedly and without looking at him, "Hey, look, you don't have to give me the business, you know?"

The small breathy laugh was strange. It could mean several things: Don't take me too seriously; don't get mad at what I say. Or, okay, so you're wise to me; well, I'm wise to you too.

An expression of sadness accompanied the laugh. Beneath all the obvious things she was, there was something mysterious and remote and Brian felt a puzzling sense of shame and regret but wasn't sure why he should feel either.

Arthur brought the drinks on a tray and told them, "I went very light on these because Stella tells me she's got some wine to go with dinner and we don't want to be so darned looped that we don't enjoy the food."

The girls arranged the table, a shelf which folded down on hinges from the wall, while Arthur and Brian sipped their drinks.

"We're gonna go down for the wine and glasses, Arthur," Stella told him. "Then everything'll be all set. I got the pans in the oven, so's it'll be ready to serve by the time we come back."

"Okay, honey, make it fast or I'll eat everything before you get back. Man, I'm hungry!"

"Oh, Arthur!"

They heard their chatter and high heels on the metal-tipped steps. Brian managed to extricate himself from the sling chair and he shook his head. "Buddy, I don't get this at all."

"What, Brian, what don't you get?"

Brian lit a cigarette and shook the match out with a wave of his arm. "The whole thing. You told me you'd have a couple of 'really nice girls' over. Now, I mean, this Rita is a real *dish* but . . ."

Earnestly, Arthur said, "But they *are* really nice girls, Brian."

Brian squinted down at his friend, then grinned. "Arthur, you've been on the job as long as I have, kid. You've also been *around* a helluva lot more than I have. I mean, *these girls?* Rita, a *dancer? Come on!*"

"Oh. Oh, that. Well, sure I know what they *do*. They're pros. Heck, Brian, that's what they have to do in order to eat. But what they *are*, Brian, see, that's another thing entirely."

"You lost me, Arthur, you just entirely lost me. They're *hookers*, right? Jesus, I don't know, but where I come from a girl is a good girl or a bad girl, right? A *nice* girl or *not* a nice girl. Your little playmates might cook a good dinner, but what the hell, Arthur, they are what they are."

Arthur Pollack walked to the window and adjusted the slats. His face was serious and intense and earnest and he leaned against the window sill. "Look, Brian, I don't want to lecture or anything but it's just that, well, Rita and Stella are *friends* of mine. I guess we became friends because our backgrounds were similar. It's funny, Brian, but an institution kid can always spot another institution kid a mile away."

He folded his arms over his narrow chest and said quietly, "When I was six years old, my mother died in childbirth and my father, gee, Brian, he was twenty-seven years old. Couple more years and I'll be his age. Well, he was left with my baby sister and me, and one day—we lived in Brooklyn then—one day we were walking along Ocean Parkway. He was pushing the baby carriage and I was holding on." Arthur Pollack raised his hand and studied the palm for a moment. "It's funny, I can still remember how that smooth metal felt, where I hung on to my baby sister's carriage. My father let out a funny sound, like he was surprised by something, and fell down. Dropped dead of a heart attack right on Ocean Parkway."

Brian could see the small six-year-old Arthur and he could see the twenty-seven-year-old dead father in his friend's unhealthy face. "Well, my father had one married brother, that's all the relatives we had in the world. He and his wife took in my baby sister and raised her like their own. And me, well, it was no bargain to take in a six-year-old; they came to see me, out in the orphanage in Rockaway Beach. We had lots of ladies used to come and visit with us and we had fresh air and sunshine and sea breezes."

Arthur spoke without self-pity and with a slight hard edge of amusement over life's condition. He shook his head and continued. "But it was worse for Rita. See, her parents were both alive; they split up and put their six kids in an orphanage. And then took out the oldest; the mother brought home her daughters when each was old enough to go to work. And it just never came Rita's turn. The mother disappeared; the father never showed.

"Finally, her cousin Stella remembered her, and took her in when Rita was fifteen or so. She'd been there from the time she was about a year old, Brian. And, in a way, she's been looking for her father. She started with older men; she's a real pushover. Didn't even take money at first, until Stella wised her up, kind of broke her in. How old do you think Rita is, Bri?"

Brian considered for a moment, then guessed, "Twenty-seven, twenty-eight?"

"She'll be twenty in two months, Brian. And underneath that twenty-seven- or twenty-eight-year-old face, Rita's about four or five years old, afraid, hoping something good is gonna happen." He glanced toward the door, then told Brian, "Look, Bri. I don't have any house rules for my friends but one. I expect my friends to be good to each other, okay? You want to make points with Rita, that's up to you, but you treat her right or forget it, okay? I try to give her and Stella a kind of family up here; that's what they give me. She's been kicked around too much and I won't let anybody hurt her if I can do something about it."

"Jesus, Arthur," Brian said admiringly, "you really are something, buddy."

They heard the girls' voices in the hallway and Brian opened the door. "Hey, let me help you. Wow, this is the biggest bottle of wine I've ever seen. Either the food isn't all that good or you think we've got hollow legs."

Rita licked her mouth uncertainly, then smiled. "We can sip it real slow. Arthur says you drink it slow and eat slow and that way it don't make you dizzy."

"Good," Brian said quietly. "I'm getting dizzy enough just looking at a pretty girl."

The first time, a few weeks later, Brian worked another four-to-twelve tour, instead of heading for the subway, he went to Arthur's flat. He found Rita, curled in a chair, wrapped in a large bathrobe, frowning and squinting over a book. She was neither surprised nor alarmed to see him. It was almost as though she had been expecting him.

"Oh. Hi."

"Hi."

She held up the book and wrinkled her nose. "Arthur says I should read more. I don't know why he likes it so much. Most of these books don't make much sense to me. I always ask him to give me an easy book and he always says I should just take something off the shelf and jump right in." She put the book on the lamp table and her fingers fidgeted with the long belt of her robe. "Arthur's working a midnight."

He had known that; somehow, he'd known that.

She drew herself deeper into the chair. "Gee, it's chilly in here, isn't it?"

"You feel cold?"

"Sort of."

"Want to get warm?"

Rita stared at her hands; she wove the plaid flannel belt in and out, in and out, between her fingers. She nodded without looking at Brian. He glanced around, then went into the kitchen where he took off his off-duty revolver and put it into a high cupboard, behind some bowls.

Rita stood up and dropped her hands to her sides. The robe fell open but she was not naked and exotic as he'd half expected to find her; she was bundled into a large, heavy pair of flannel pajamas, with the sleeves and pants cuffs rolled up. The outfit made her seem very small.

She licked her lips and said, "I guess I look pretty dopey in this outfit."

"You don't look dopey. I just think you'd look better out of it," Brian told her. She raised her face and waited and he helped her to undress, slowly. She was not as heavy as she had been the night of Arthur's dinner. Her flesh was smooth and firm and rounded and her skin was startlingly white in comparison with the orange pancake make-up on her face. Brian stepped back and his eyes moved over her appraisingly, deliberately, carefully, lingeringly.

Rita turned from him and went to the couch-bed. She leaned her face against the dark-red fabric discreetly, not watching him, sensing his shyness while he undressed, but when he approached her she turned toward him and reached out for him.

Her incredible warmth and softness and fragrance and sweet fleshiness overwhelmed him. She moved carefully and languidly against his body, and when he wanted to plunge and rip and devour, she pushed a hand against his chest and whispered, "No. Not yet, Brian. Wait a little. A little longer, Brian, just a little longer."

She brought him along slowly, steadily, agonizingly, until he didn't think he could bear another second, another instant. Every part of his body throbbed and ached and pressed against the nerve endings of his skin. His mouth filled with her flesh, sucked in the sweet-tasting whiteness of her shoulder and arm and breast, then pressed against her mouth ravenously in a way he had never done before. He was inside the center of her very being, drawn in and down, pressure against pressure, and he felt, heard, experienced her deep and shuddering, explosive release, which was his release, and a painful sob came from his throat or her throat, he couldn't tell which and he didn't care.

There were things between them that were unstated, yet they were both sharply, willingly, acutely aware of the necessity for certain guidelines. Rita Wasinski existed for Brian O'Malley, totally and completely, within the boundaries of Arthur Pollack's apartment. She came to life on his arrival and vaporized with his departure.

The things she taught Brian were things she herself was learning. They taught each other, explored each other with fingertips, tongues, eyes, bodies, lips. She taught his body to prolong, defer, hold back, wait, build to a tension that was unbearable and bear that tension a little more, just a little more, so that they rose together, ached, swelled, burst together in a passion of movement and sound.

She taught him to control and use his quick-rising animal

instincts and to feel pride in his self-mastery and in the ·
pleasure he afforded her.

She taught Brian not to be shy of his body. He had never
stood naked before a woman, yet he learned to take pleasure
from the frank scrutiny and her evident delight. At first, he
undressed in darkness or turned from her and covered himself afterward, but Rita pulled blankets away, ran her small,
warm hands down the length of his body, as he stretched and
flexed against the sheets of Arthur's studio couch.

Her touch revived his lust over and over again until he
thought of his body as a never-ending explosive, stronger and
more powerful each time it rose from emptiness to new ful-
fillment. Her hands, curious, caressing, appraised parts of him
he thought had no connection with his sexual being, yet
through her touch, all parts of him related to that central force
which throbbed between the two of them: his toes; the arch
of his foot; the calf of his leg, hard-muscled and strong; his
flat belly; her hands touched lightly, traced, brushed, twisted
at black-haired chest, created sensation along his throat, behind his ears.

"Don't move, Brian; don't do anything, Brian. Let me, oh,
Brian, let *me* do for you."

Tongue tip in his eyelids, his eyebrows; tongue torment-
ingly soft and wet and strong and alive; inside his ear, his
brain.

No, Brian, don't move; let *me* do it this time. Let's try it this
way. A million ways, let's try let's try let's try.

He relinquished the sense of himself as someone separate
and apart from his own strong physicality with a sense of
wonder and regarded everything they did together as something apart from any area of self-judgment. He discovered a
deeper dimension than he had thought possible, and rather
than satiety and a devouring sense of guilt, which he knew he
should feel, Brian O'Malley felt a greater and stronger and
more demanding energy and desire.

When he was not with Rita Wasinski, he thought about her,
and when he was with her, he merged himself into her without hesitation, without reservation, without caution and
generally with a wild sense of exaltation.

She made no demands on him other than the physical demands and those she increased steadily in perfect rhythm with his ability to fulfill. The greater the demand, the greater his power to respond. There was nothing he needed to know about her; her body was perfectly tuned with his own and through her body, he learned of his own uniqueness and potential.

One night, carefully, he asked her, "Rita, how come you bleach your hair so light?"

Her small hand touched a strand of almost whitened hair tentatively and a frown pulled her brows down. "I, well, gee, Brian, I guess because, you know, all the pretty movie stars and all." She laughed softly and shrugged at her own audacity. "I guess I had this big thing about . . . you won't laugh if I tell you?"

"I won't laugh."

"Well, I used to have this like daydream, you know, about being Ginger Rogers and dancing with Fred Astaire and all, in all those beautiful dresses and with all the music and all. Gee, isn't she lucky, and all of them other movie stars, to have such pretty blond hair?"

"They're not natural blondes, Rita, none of them are."

Her mouth opened in surprise, almost in protest, but if Brian said something, she knew it for fact. Her fingers raked her bleach-stiffened hair thoughtfully. "But how come they always look so nice and natural, Brian?"

"I guess they spend a fortune at the hairdresser's."

"Gee. I buy this stuff in the five-and-dime. You know, peroxide. I guess it looks it, huh?" She giggled, laughed at herself.

Casually, he pointed to his jacket which he had slung over the back of a chair. "Look in my pocket. Go ahead, in the right-hand side. I bought you something."

Rita stood absolutely still, hand in her hair, and finally she shook her head slightly without looking at him. "Uh-uh. I don't want you to *buy* anything for me, Brian."

He'd expected her to be pleased and eager to see what it was but her face masked over and she hid within herself.

Boundaries between them; pleasures given and received only for the pleasure involved. No gifts. *No payments.*

Brian stood up abruptly and crossed the room, roughly

yanked at his jacket, dug in the pocket for the small package. He reached into the bag and his hand came up with the gift.

"Look, dopey," he said, "real big-deal present."

It was dark-blond Nestle's color rinse: eight capsules for a quarter. Rita emerged again, grinned, stood on her toes, reached for the package which Brian held over her head.

"Now you can't have it."

"Oh, Brian, give me. Oh, Brian, please." She grabbed his arm and brought his hand down and pried the package loose. "Oh, Brian, let's do it now."

His hand cupped her breast and he teased. "Sure, any time, babe, no time like right now. Let's do it now."

"Oh, no, not that. Let's do my *hair*. Oh, please, Brian, please. Look, I could kneel over the tub and give it a fast wash. I only washed it yesterday, so it's really clean, but I'll wash it again and you could do the rinse for me. Oh, please, Brian, *please*."

"My God, you're a little nut, Rita."

But somehow he understood why she wanted him to do her hair immediately. It was for him, to demonstrate her willingness to please him, to make up to him for misunderstanding.

She raced into the kitchen, took all the various items off the top of the tub, knelt, ran the water, scrubbed billows of soap into her hair, rinsed, prepared herself for him.

She made the solution and he poured it over her head and worked it into her hair; he kneaded and pressed and squeezed and felt a deep sensual pleasure, but beneath that was a deeper, calmer, kinder pleasure as his fingers moved slowly along her skull.

"Close your eyes; you'll get this stuff in them. Will you stop peeking at me and close them?"

She squealed at the sharp stinging pain, reached out for the towel he handed her.

"I told you to close your eyes. You're really a baby, Rita, you know that? Why the hell did you take your shoes off to kneel over the tub and wash your hair?"

"Gee, I don't know. I just never washed my hair with my shoes on. Is it time yet, Brian? Can we rinse it off yet? Did you time it? Is it five minutes? Come on, the directions say to rinse it now in cold water until the water runs clear. Oh, Brian, that cold water gives me chills right down to my spine!"

The rinse toned her hair to a golden glow; it softened her, enabled the young girl to shine through. She pulled a comb through the damp hair, then reached for her round compact.

Brian caught her wrist. "Don't, Rita. Don't put any of that stuff on."

"But gee, Brian, I don't want you to see me like this. I feel funny if you look at me and I don't have my 'face' on."

He tilted her clean face upward. "Nothing," he told her, "nothing at all, not even lipstick. Baby, you don't need a thing. You taste like soap and water and Rita." He nuzzled her, tasted her cheeks and neck, then whispered, "No make-up, okay?"

"Anything you say, Brian, anything you say."

He never saw her when he worked the eight-to-four tour. It just didn't seem right: in the daylight. His tours were opposite to Arthur's and they rarely met; if Arthur happened to be home, they spent a few hours just visiting and Rita prepared coffee and sandwiches and they waited until the next time when they knew Arthur wouldn't be around.

She never questioned him; she seemed to receive the part of himself he offered to her with pleasure and gratitude.

She was a simple, generous girl, warm, uncomplicated, easily delighted, somewhat stupid and shallow. Yet, at the same time, she was complex, shrewd, a knowing woman who would withdraw sharply, unexpectedly, completely at something he said, something she interpreted as threatening or an intrusion on the fragile, secret, private part of herself which she would not allow him.

Rita was rarely moody or tense yet on occasion she was both. He resisted the temptation to probe her moods as conscientiously as she tried to conceal or overcome them. They both knew that they could exist for each other only through the voluntary suspension of reality. Any violation of this fantasy, either through his questions or her replies, would shatter and destroy what they had created for and with each other.

It lasted through three cold, bitter winter months and ended as spring invaded winter. The end was directly related to his job.

TWENTY-TWO

Brian liked working the midnight-to-eight tour. There was something exciting and secretive and special about starting out when everyone else was ending the day. The few subway riders he encountered on his way to work were hunched in the corners of wicker seats, eyes heavy, mouths pulled down with weariness, heads nodding, folded newspapers dangling. They traveled toward gray and unexciting routine. He moved toward possibilities they could not begin to imagine.

Though generally nothing very much happened, he knew that anything *could* happen, and more importantly, he knew that if anything *did* happen, *he* would be the one responsible for taking action: would *know* what to do.

The day had been lightly crusted with winter, but beneath the freeze, touches of spring came through. The sky had been blue before it turned gray and the midnight sky was pierced with bright March stars. Some of the men turned out with raingear and complained when the sergeant informed them it wasn't going to rain. They knew damn well it *was* going to rain; they'd be stuck on patrol in heavy, wet uniforms.

Brian walked his post with a growing sense of familiarity and ease. The day and evening people were gone. The night people, arriving, leaving, hanging around, established time as accurately as his wristwatch.

Two cab drivers on Eldridge Street, a father-and-son team, worked twenty hours between them. As the father pulled up to the curb, the son strolled over, listened to whatever instructions or comments his father had, nodded, and took off. The old man, cap pulled over one eye, hands jammed into the pockets of his jacket, shoulders hunched, invariably said the same thing to Brian.

"Tough way to make a buck, huh, officer?"

Invariably, Brian answered, "Yeah, I guess so."

The newsy on Delancey Street put in about fourteen hours a day but half the time he seemed to be asleep. Most people thought he was blind because of the huge German shepherd who shared the booth with him, and he'd confided to Brian that he didn't go out of his way to correct the false impression. "It makes 'em feel they're doin' a good deed. So what's the harm?"

Three old women walked together slowly on feet that ached but their faces were animated and they argued and laughed good-naturedly before they entered three different tenement buildings, all in a row. Cleaning women, returning from a round of office buildings. Brian wondered what they said to each other, what would make three tired, hard-working old women laugh as though they were carefree schoolgirls. They always greeted him in a language he couldn't understand but which sounded friendly and he always touched the brim of his cap to them and slowed his pace until all three were inside their houses.

Rain started without warning and he ducked into a doorway to wait it out. There was a rawness in the wind and he felt his skin pull away from all the heavy layers of his clothing and tingle with coldness. All the street people who had a place to go disappeared; the few derelicts found places for themselves. The empty streets became lonely and he tensed, listening to the sound of running. A man, young, wiry, swift, sure-footed, ran toward him, stopped some distance away, waved his newspaper over his head in a sort of salutation. Brian followed the direction of the gesture; there was a woman, seated at a window, waiting for him, relieved to see him home. A wife or a mother, or whoever she was. Probably had something hot for him to eat, to warm him up.

The rain didn't slacken for more than an hour and a half, but the wind increased and that kept the streets cold and unpleasant. Brian walked from doorway to doorway, slowly down the street. He tossed his nightstick into the air from the leather thong around his wrist and caught it in the palm of his hand. It was a tricky maneuver, not as easy as it looked. He tapped the stick against a lamppost, then flipped it quickly. The end of the nightstick caught him across the bridge of his nose and brought tears to his eyes. Christ, it hurt. Stupid damn thing. Goddamn stupid thing.

Brian jammed his hands into his heavy coat and fought the tears and hoped he wouldn't have a lump on his nose: it felt bruised back to his sinuses. His feet were wet and numb, his ears ached with cold, he was hungry, and Rivington Street was black and slippery and lonely as hell.

A bony, wet tomcat slunk from beneath a parked car and Brian watched him forage expertly through an unpromising garbage can. The cat dropped to the sidewalk, raised his quivering tail and sprayed the can before he disappeared into an alleyway.

Dampness penetrated his bones. His uniform smelled of wet wool. There wasn't a goddamn spot in the whole sector where he could creep in and get warm. He checked a few doorways, entered a hallway briefly and ducked out just as quickly. It smelled of cat piss and worse. There were a few lights up and down the row of tenements. Brian didn't envy any of those occupants their warmth. He had grown familiar with the inside of those houses and understood why the people took to the streets at the first sign of good weather. They were crowded and bug-infested and reeked with a special aura that spoke of time and place.

He dug inside the bulky coat and carefully slid a cigarette from the pack, cupped his hands against the wind and lit it. He held the cigarette between his thumb and index finger, hidden within the palm of his hand against the wind. Shit.

The sergeant seemed to have a way of timing his periodic "look." Brian carefully squeezed the lit end of his cigarette and hastily stepped on the bright embers as they hit the sidewalk. He put the remains into his coat pocket.

Sergeant Horan was a tense man who leaped out of the patrol car almost before it halted completely. He expected, constantly, to come upon evidence of some grossly irremediable dereliction of duty not just from the newer men, but from *all* of the men who worked under him. He saw his mission as one of tremendous responsibility not only to the Department, but toward the men who must be protected from their own shortcomings.

"Well, O'Malley," Sergeant Horan sniffed suspiciously, "how's things?"

"Quiet, Sergeant. Just me and some stray cats on the street tonight."

Horan scanned the street, then examined Brian. "Where are your gloves, officer?"

Brian dug in his coat pocket and pulled on the heavy woolen gloves. "I took them off a few minutes ago, Sergeant. When I made my ring."

The sergeant consulted his memo book and looked up puzzled. "But you made a ring twenty minutes ago."

Brian answered innocently, "Is that a fact? Boy, time sure flies."

Horan leaned closer, wrinkled his nose. "You've been *smoking*, Patrolman O'Malley."

"Since I was thirteen years old, Sergeant."

Horan shook his head impatiently. "No, no. What I mean is, you've been smoking *recently*. I didn't see you do it, O'Malley, but I can smell it on your breath. I assure you, O'Malley, if I *did* see you with a cigarette on your post, I'd write you up. It would be a *violation*. It wouldn't look right for a citizen to see a police officer smoking while in uniform."

O'Malley was about to ask exactly *what* citizens the sergeant was talking about, but decided he'd better keep his mouth shut.

"So you watch yourself, O'Malley, because I might be back; you never know how many looks you might get. Let's have your memo book, so's I can sign it."

He criticized a few of the routine entries before signing his name and the time of his inspection. As soon as Sergeant Horan's patrol car turned the corner, Brian hunched over the butt and inhaled it back to life. He flipped it quickly behind the garbage cans immediately; the patrol car had merely circled the block. Brian saluted the car as it drove past him; a surly Sergeant Horan hadn't caught him.

Shithead, Brian mouthed as the car continued down the street for as long as he could see it. When it finally turned off, Brian glanced around, then went over to the garbage cans and discreetly splattered them with the same disdain the alley cat had shown when he relieved himself.

It started to rain again, hard, long frosty slashes of rain which iced the streets and beat against storefront windows.

210

Brian leaned into the recessed doorway of a dirty-windowed button store and miserably looked at his wristwatch. A half hour until meal relief. The all-night greasy spoon on Delancey Street was no bargain but at least Jake, the owner, kept a pot of soup hot. Probably kept it hot from the end of one week to the beginning of the next, but what the hell.

He stared at the heavy bursts of rain, intermingled with large, shapeless snowflakes as they fell within the yellow glare of the street light. His eyes ranged the black expanse beyond the light. Absently, he counted windows, left to right, top to bottom, six across, four down, cellar windows not counted.

Fire escapes were illegally blocked, cluttered with bottles of milk and cartons of food and other nondescript items. Things. What the hell was that on the third-floor fire escape?

It was a man, hunched down, face to window, back to street. Brian kept his eyes on the figure and moved carefully and silently, though noise wouldn't have mattered. The wind covered all sound. The guy wasn't cautious at all; never looked around, never checked the street, just leaned his face against the window.

Housebreaker? Housebreakers were cautious, quick-moving, alert.

Jesus, was it just a bundle of old clothes or newspapers, after all?

The dark, shapeless figure shifted slightly. Brian caught a flash of lightness; the guy's hands emerged from the sleeves of his dark coat, then he settled again and concentrated at the window.

Brian entered the building, took the stairs two at a time. He could feel the pounding of his heart in his ears, a hard thumping sound which he didn't even feel in his chest. The metal door on the roof flew open at the touch of his palm, caught by a gust of wind. Brian closed it carefully, walked across the roof and peered down among the maze of fire escapes. He saw the figure, squatting and motionless on the third-floor landing, oblivious to anything but whatever he watched inside the window.

Resolutely, Brian lowered himself over the side of the roof. He felt the slippery rungs of the ladder against the heavy leather soles of his shoes and his gloved hands grasped the pipelike ladder which led to the uppermost fire escape. His foot missed one of the rungs; he slid, scraped his uniform coat, felt a button twist off; he grasped frantically to keep from falling.

In spite of a few near slips, his descent had been almost silent. He considered himself very lucky to reach the fire escape without having been detected; he felt clumsy and inept and wondered how the hell firemen could go up and down those damn iron staircases with people over their shoulders. As he reached the fire escape where the suspect was crouched, his nightstick swung loose and hit the railing. He quickly retrieved it, reached out and grabbed the suspect, who turned a stunned, rain-dripping, pale face to him. For about three seconds, the man's long white hands continued to masturbate, but the naked flesh went limp and he hastily tried to cover the front of his body. Brian yanked him to his feet and the man's trousers fell down around his ankles.

"Jesus," Brian said, "pull them up. Now button them. What the hell were you looking at in there?"

The white face was blank and expressionless. Brian had a good grasp; his fingers clung to the leather belt around the man's trousers. He leaned toward the window. Inside the tiny bedroom, two small girls slept, their innocent faces illuminated by a night lamp. The one nearest the window was eight or nine years old; she was partly uncovered, exposed from thigh to ankle. An inch or so of cotton underpants showed beneath her nightgown as she moved in sleep. The smaller child, about five or six, was on her back, one small hand thrown over her forehead.

"You fucking bastard," Brian whispered. "Don't make a sound. You wake them up and I'll drop you to the sidewalk."

The descent was tricky. Brian put handcuffs on the prisoner and descended first, his hand making contact with the man's foot. He hoped at each step the guy wouldn't kick out at him. At the first-floor landing, Brian had to unhook the ladder and lower it to the sidewalk. His prisoner didn't make a sound. He slipped a few times, lost his footing, his ankle turned when he hit the sidewalk, but he went down in a silent heap and Brian stood back and let him get up without touching him.

"Stand there," Brian instructed. He pointed to the wall of

the building. "Face the wall; just stay there while I get this ladder back in place."

The saliva began to flow again. Brian directed the prisoner to walk alongside of him. At the corner call box, he notified the sergeant that he was bringing in a degenerate. When the desk sergeant asked if he wanted a squad car, Brian declined. This guy wasn't any trouble at all.

They went half a block when the man stopped and said, "I want to go home now."

He was a well-built man, about Brian's height. His voice had an odd, flat, persistent quality. His eyeglasses were beaded with water and he peered dully over the rims.

"Can you see without those glasses?" Brian asked solic-itously.

"I can't see without my glasses." The answer came in a singsong cadence.

Brian took out a handkerchief. "Give them here a minute. I'll wipe 'em off for you."

The man handed Brian his eyeglasses and Brian wrapped them up in the handkerchief and put them in his coat pocket. The prisoner's head swung around and his hands came up as though he was preparing for a fall.

"Hey, I can't see. I can't see nothing."

Brian released his breath. "Good. You'll get these back at the station house." He took a firm grip on the prisoner's right arm and felt a little more in command of the situation.

As they entered the station house, the man mumbled some-thing which Brian couldn't understand.

"Go and stand in front of the desk," he instructed the prisoner.

Detectives Kelly and Meehan leaned against the iron rail-ing which separated the high desk from the rest of the hollow, high-ceilinged room.

"This the bum likes to play with it and look at little girls?" Kelly asked conversationally.

"Yeah," Brian said, "this is him."

Kelly sauntered over to the prisoner and thrust his face up, close to the blank, unseeing eyes. "What's the matter, buster, ain't it big enough for real women?"

The prisoner mumbled something, then said calmly, "I want to go home now."

"Why?" Meehan asked. "You got some little girls at home to play with?"

The prisoner shook his head, then said to Sergeant O'Connor, whose long horse face peered down disapprovingly, "My brother is a captain."

"Yeah? Of what? A shithouse?" Sergeant O'Connor asked.

"No," the prisoner told him reasonably. "My brother is a captain. In the Police Department. My brother is a captain in the New York City Police Department. Can I go home now? I'm very tired."

Captain Peter Toomey came within the hour; within another thirty minutes it was all straightened out.

Captain Toomey reached for Brian's hand for a hard, man-to-man grasp, told Brian he "had a friend" and "wouldn't be forgotten." He was a tense, soft-spoken man who exuded an air of complete self-confidence based largely on his complete confidence that everyone would do exactly as he expected him to do.

"I'll take care of Michael," he assured Brian. "He won't be involved in anything like this again." The captain turned to his brother. "Michael, where are your eyeglasses?"

Brian reached into his overcoat pocket, pressed each lens within the folds of his handkerchief until he could feel glass break and shatter between his thumb and index finger. Some glass pierced his finger and he sucked the blood quickly.

Captain Toomey reached for the glasses, frowned, held them up to the light. "What happened to his glasses, O'Malley?"

Brian's face was expressionless and his voice was polite and official. "They were like that when I collared him, Captain. That's why I took them away from him. Figured he might get blinded or something."

Captain Toomey studied Brian for a moment, nodded slightly with a slightly harder acknowledgment. "I see. Yes, very thoughtful of you. Come on, Michael. Let's get you home."

When he worked the four-to-twelve tour, it seemed to Brian that the entire day was a steady, relentless preparation for the

214

moment when, at three-thirty, he reported to the precinct. If he had a collar the previous night, he spent the morning hours waiting in holding pens, complaint rooms or court corridors, gossiping, griping, exchanging rumors and good-natured insults with other policemen.

If he hadn't made a collar, he had a half day to kill one way or another.

Brian heard the kids getting ready for school; he yelled at Kevin to pipe down and stop slamming bureau drawers and doors. He fell asleep again and woke several hours later, slowly, lazily.

He heard his mother moving around the living room and his grandmother in the kitchen. He heard Roseanne, her voice sharp and edgy as she spoke to her son Billy, barely two years old, then crooning as she tried to settle the baby, Tommy.

His mother's voice was low and gentle as she spoke to Billy. "Oh, that's a fine big boy, Billy. Would you like your grandma to give you a nice carrot? I bet Nana has one for you in the kitchen. Roseanne, you shouldn't give him the chewing gum; his teeth will rot. I'm surprised at you."

"It keeps him quiet," Roseanne said sharply. "I think I'd give him poison if it would just keep him quiet."

Brian rolled onto his stomach and held the pillow over his head. He didn't want to hear what would follow. He knew it by heart: the same old story . . .

"Roseanne, Roseanne, how can you say such a terrible thing? God forgive you, they're just innocent babies, of course they cry. What children don't?"

Roseanne, voice ragged and harsh and stretched an inch short of breaking, said, "But they never shut up, Mom. God Almighty, if I could just have one night, just one night, to sleep through, but so help me, Ma, they never stop. It's one or the other. Billy, get your hands off your little brother. Billy!"

Smack. Crying.

"Oh, he's just a baby himself, Roseanne. He doesn't know he's hurt little Tommy. Come on, Billy, let me show you how to scramble some nice eggs."

"Ma. Ma, I think I'm pregnant again. Damn it, Ma, I don't want any more!"

Silence. Silence. Silence.

"Well, well, it's God's will after all, darling. It's what we were meant for, isn't it? Maybe you'll have a little girl. . . ."

"Oh, Mom, I'm sorry, I'm sorry. It's not you I should say that to, not to you."

Firmly: "Not to anyone, Roseanne, least of all, not to your husband."

"Ma, he doesn't come home some nights. I don't know what he's up to, Ma, and I get so scared and I worry all the time. I ask him about the job he's on and he tells me to just shut up and mind my own business."

Beneath the pillow, Brian heard it all. A broken record, and predictable too. Roseanne and her pregnancies; Billy Delaney, the man of many mysterious jobs, the self-proclaimed truck driver.

Uh-huh. For hijackers, thieves, crooks, Christ knows what. A matter of time; Brian knew; a matter of time and Billy Delaney would be in-like-Flynn, no key to the iron door, no way out. And *he'd* be saddled with Roseanne and her crying, screaming, snot-nosed Billy-Delaney-faced little brats.

He wanted to get up but he waited. He knew Roseanne would be persuaded to leave the little ones with their grandma and take herself off for a nice poke around Fordham Road to look in the store windows or take in a movie, just get off by herself a bit.

"Roseanne, will you look at the storybook Billy's found? I used to read that to Kit when she was just a tiny wee thing. Come to Grandma, Billy. God love you, but it's a big boy and just turned two years old."

He moved the palm of his hand along the sheet and thought of Rita: guiltily but languidly. His mother's voice crooned and whispered and the petulant, whining voice of the child turned sweet as she eased him from his bad mood.

Rita, tongue and lips and firm breasts; tongue and wetness, warmth and chill; pull the covers up quick, I got goose bumps. All down the long stretch of torso, skin tight over ribs, tiny bumps of cold, Rita.

He took a long hot shower, let the water run hot on the base of his neck. The hell with the cold-shower routine; he enjoyed heat, body hotness to penetrate his skin and circulate through his bloodstream; steamy water hotness to remind him. Brian stepped back to shake water from his eyes and stepped on something sharp and pointed. He cursed softly and bent to rub his wounded heel and to see what had caused the injury.

It was a small metal warship. Swirls of blue water color ran between his toes. Kit and her collection. Damn it, that kid and her junk. Brian examined it briefly, decided it wouldn't clog the toilet, reached from behind the shower curtain and tossed it into the bowl. So much for that particular warship: down to the deep-blue sea. A few drops of blood from his heel mingled with the pale tint of blue and he moved his foot around until the water came clean.

He shaved and dressed and told his mother not to bother with breakfast, it was nearly lunchtime. He settled into the easy chair by the window, feet on hassock, *Daily News* opened to the sports pages. Margaret stood in the doorway, grandson in her arms. She jiggled the boy up and down as she spoke.

"Did you hear about your cousin Billy O'Malley? Fell off the training ladder and they think he's broken his shoulder."

Billy O'Malley had been appointed to the Fire Department last month after waiting on the list for three years.

"I ran into Uncle Gene last night at Night Court and he told me. Hey, maybe I'll run over and see him. He's at Fordham Hospital, right?"

"Yes, but he'll be home tomorrow. I'd wait until then, Brian, for Ellen said he wasn't well just now. There, there, now, Billy, that's your Uncle Brian over there. Don't you want to say hello? Brian, look up and smile at him."

"Every time I see that kid, he bursts out crying, Mom. There, look at his puss."

"It's just a stage they go through, Brian, and you're always glowering at him so. Give him a pleasant smile and a nice hello. You'll see him smile back."

"I've never seen that kid smile since the day he was born. Okay, Ma, watch." Brian puffed out his cheeks, rolled his eyes and roared, "Ho, ho, ho, Billy boy! Here's your Uncle Brian playing the fool for you. Now *smile!*"

Billy stared, held his breath, stiffened his small body, turned his face toward the ceiling and screamed until he nearly choked.

"See, Ma," Brian said innocently, "what did I tell you? I try to be nice to him, but that kid is plain nasty. He's like his old man."

Margaret pressed the child to her body as she danced around with him. She alternately comforted the child and scolded Brian. "Hush, now, there, there, Billy. There's no one to hurt you. You ought to be ashamed, Brian. He's just a tiny child. It's not funny, teasing a little one like that. There now, there, sweetheart. Uncle Brian didn't mean to frighten you. Come on now, Grandma will dance you right into the kitchen and we'll get lunch all made up. Kit will be home soon, Billy. You'll be seeing Kit."

As though on signal, Kit and Bobby Kelly burst through the entrance hallway, shouting and arguing over who had won the race from school. Little Billy Delaney, at the sound of Kit's voice, changed into a smiling, laughing, slightly hysterical worshiper. He craned his neck for a better view of his young aunt and reached sturdy arms toward her.

Kit swooped down suddenly, grabbed him roughly under the arms and whirled him around the living room. "Hey, Bobby," she yelled, "here, catch!"

Margaret had visions of the child flying through the air and landing on a cracked skull. "Give him here, Kit. Stop playing the fool. He's just a small baby."

Kit crashed her forehead against her nephew's. "I'm gonna throw you on your head, Billy-o-boy! Right on your big dopey head!"

Billy shrieked and gagged with excitement and struggled for Kit when his grandmother pulled him away.

"Oh, now you've waked the baby with your howling and you've gotten this child so worked up he won't eat his lunch."

"Hey, Ma," Kit said, "Bobby left his lunch home this morning and nobody's at his house. Can he eat here?"

"When would there ever not be an extra sandwich or two on the table? But wash your hands or you'll both go hungry. There now, Billy, sit down on the couch for a minute while Grandma gets things in order in the kitchen."

Kit charged from the bathroom and grabbed Billy by the

218

shoulders and shook him. "Did you throw my battleship down the toilet?" She held the dripping toy between her fingers and her nephew's pink face puckered and his lower lip trembled. "Don't you touch my ships, Billy, or I'll put *you* down the toilet and flush you away and you'll drown. Glug! Glug!"

By now Billy was laughing hysterically and Margaret came and dragged him off to the kitchen. Kit carefully blotted the battleship on the inside hem of her jumper.

"Hey, slob," Brian said disgustedly, "what are you doing?"

"It took me a long time to get that painted just the right color. Gee, Brian, that rotten kid. I'll break his arms if he touches my warships."

"Keep those damn things out of the tub, Kit, or the next time the whole fleet will end up down the toilet."

Kit glared at her brother. "*You* did it? Well, listen, Brian, you just keep your hands off my things." She examined the ship carefully. "I bought them all with my *own* money and they're mine, so you just keep your hands off them, that's all."

Brian stretched his legs in front of him. "Or *what?*" he asked provocatively.

"Well, I don't know, but I'll think of something." With a sudden change of pace, Kit scanned his face. "Hey, Brian, are you in a good mood or a bad mood?"

"You know, Kit, you're a dumb kid. That's a helluva dumb question."

"Yeah, yeah," she said impatiently, "but it's important for me to know." She backed away from him and shifted from one foot to the other. "See, if you're in a *bad* mood, then I won't tell you about my shoe." She held her right foot up and the sole of her shoe flapped as she jiggled up and down. "They don't make shoes the way they used to, Brian. Now, if you're in a *good* mood, you'll give me a quarter and I can get the sole sewed back on at the shoemaker's."

"For Christ's sake, didn't you get those shoes new about two weeks ago? Come over here and let me look at that." She tossed the shoe to him. Not only was the sole loose, but there was a large, soft, round worn spot in the center of the sole. "Jesus, Kit, I ought to let you go barefoot. Didn't Mom tell you to change to sneakers after school?"

Kit held her right ankle behind her knee and hopped across

the room. "Hmm. You're in a bad mood. It's okay, Brian. I'll line it with cardboard and paste it with Elmer's Glue and probably become a pathetic cripple by the time you get in a good mood and gimme the money to get it fixed. I gotta go get lunch now before Kelly eats everything on the table."

She was a whirling dynamo, spinning and hopping and wisecracking good-naturedly. There was a smear of dark-blue water paint on her knee, where the hem of her school jumper brushed her leg. She zoomed around the room on one foot, turned her warship into a warplane which dove at tables and lamps.

"Hey," Brian asked suddenly, "where's your brother?"

Kit came to rigid attention, the foot still clamped behind her. She raised her dark brows, let her mouth fall open stupidly. "Huh? Who? Me?"

"No, the girl in back of you. Come on, stop being a little wise guy. Where's Kevin? Doesn't he come home with you at lunchtime?"

Kit shrugged elaborately, released her ankle, tested it for pins and needles. "How do I know where he is?" she asked flippantly. "What am I, my brother's keeper?" She roared at her own joke, then dashed toward the kitchen as Brian tossed the shoe at her.

The shoe missed Kit but caught little Billy Delaney right in the face as he toddled into the living room.

"Oh, for Christ's sake, kid," Brian said miserably. "C'mere, come over here, Billy. I didn't mean to hit you. Hey, Ma, you better come in here. Roseanne's kid is holding his breath and turning blue."

Brian wandered aimlessly up Ryer Avenue, rubbed his neck, which was prickly with dark hair. Good day for a haircut; overdue haircut. Maybe later; maybe tomorrow.

He heard the schoolboy voices, softened by distance, muffled by the three-story tan brick building between Ryer Avenue and the small schoolyard on Valentine Avenue.

He remembered what it felt like being a schoolboy on a spring afternoon with the starched white collar held close to his damp neck by the navy-blue tie. He remembered how the sun filtered through beams of dust in odd-shaped patches through the windows on one side of the room and how the

chalk smell was heavier and mustier and older in spring sunlight.

Sister Mary Philomena would pull the dark-green shades
down to the window sill at the first signs of spring fever in the
fourth grade. Brian gazed toward the grade school and on the
second floor, Room 206, the shades were down, and behind
them, he visualized, were boys and girls in long straight rows
who pretended to care about geography and religion and
arithmetic while Sister Mary Philomena pretended it wasn't
spring.

St. Simon High School was a separate building attached to
the grade school, and the schoolyard was shared by all the
kids from first grade through the twelfth. It was a small, compact building with slightly larger classrooms and larger desks
and the initials carefully cut into the undersides of desks
were done by more expert hands.

Brian raised one hand and his fingers settled on the wire-
mesh fence which surrounded the schoolyard. Kevin didn't
spot him; he was too intent on his game of basketball. He was
quick and sharp and never seemed to get out of breath. He
darted and pivoted and faked it, turned his shoulders and hips
in opposite directions, pretended confusion but never lost
control of the ball or sight of his target. Kevin had shot up
spectacularly in the last year or so; he seemed all long legs
and arms, but he moved with a small boy's coordination. He
brought the ball down the court, looked for a screen, then
finally one-handed it into the basket.

Brother Gerard blew the whistle, then let it fall. It was a
silver glisten against his drab brown monk's habit.

"O'Malley's team, eighteen; Garrett, your guys better get a
hustle on. They're murdering you." He took the whistle from
around his neck and handed it to one of his students. "Here,
Cleary, you ref for a while. And I don't want any arguments.
Cleary's word is *it* while he's the ref."

Brother Gerard walked to the fence and smiled his strange
tight smile at Brian. "Your brother's coming along, Brian. He's
a little too cocky and sure of himself but he's not bad. He's got
to cut out trying to be the whole show but I think I'll be able
to smooth the rough edges."

It was one of Brother Gerard's favorite expressions: smooth
the rough edges.

The soft white hands seemed harmless enough, thumbs hooked inside the thin leather belt which loosely circled the broad waist. The belt was tied in such a way that in one motion Brother Gerard could untie it, double it over and swing on any target with the minimum amount of effort and the maximum amount of effect. Brother Gerard had been Brian's last teacher at St. Simon and even with the years between them and the fence between them and the circumstances of life between them and their last encounter, Brian still remembered the sting of that belt and the terrible, helpless humiliation. He felt a rigid wariness.

The sky-blue eyes peered at him quizzically through the triangular pattern of the fence. "Well, so you're on the job now, are you, Brian?"

"Yeah."

"Well, that's fine, just fine. And what are we going to do about your cousin John O'Malley?"

Brian's fingers tightened and he consciously forced himself to let loose of the fence. "What do you mean, *do* about him, Brother Gerard?"

The large, fleshy face regarded him with an expression that had confronted hundreds of boys behind the closed door of Brother Gerard's study: Don't play dumb with me. Don't play wise guy with me; *not with me.*

In a reasonable voice, Brother Gerard said, "Why, he's getting to be a big boy, Brian. Seventeen years old and sitting in the classroom with boys and girls two years younger. Have you or any of your uncles any trade in mind for the boy?"

Brian pulled away from the fence and shoved his hands into his trouser pockets, then pulled them out again. "Well, my Uncle Peadar and my Uncle Gene have something in mind but they're not set on it just yet." The lie was heavy and thick in his throat and he gazed over Brother Gerard's shoulder to avoid the knowing round stare.

Brother Gerard turned and watched the basketball game for a moment, then called in a hard, clear voice, "All right, Garrett, I saw that. Since you like physical contact so much, I guess basketball isn't the game for you, after all. Stop by my study this afternoon at three. We'll see if we can't come up with a more appropriate game for you."

Brian felt a wave of sympathy for the unfortunate Garrett. The tall, sweaty-faced boy wiped the back of his hand across his mouth, started to protest but thought better of it. He squatted along the sidelines and watched his replacement proceed to complete the loss to Kevin O'Malley's audacious if somewhat showy theft of the ball.

Brother Gerard blew his whistle decisively as soon as they heard the bell inside the school building. "All right, into line. O'Malley, you and Sweeney bring in the equipment. The rest of you, remember you're entering a school building and behave accordingly. I don't want to have to remind you."

He marched into the building and the boys followed.

Kevin held two basketballs against his chest and bounced the third. "Hey, Brian. You see the game? Pretty good, huh?"

"Not all *that* good. But not too bad."

"Not too bad? Listen, by the time I'm a senior, the scouts will be driving St. Simon's crazy with offers for me; phone calls in the middle of the night, all pleading for Flash O'Malley." He dribbled and raced toward the basket, got his shot, then turned to his brother. "Neat, huh?"

Brother Gerard's face appeared from a window on the top floor. "O'Malley, do you need a special invitation to rejoin the class? If you do, I have a special invitation all ready and waiting for you."

Kevin held up the balls and called out, "Gee, Brother Gerard, I'm on my way. They slipped and I been collecting them."

The window slammed down hard and Kevin muttered, "Cheez, he's always riding me. He's a real bastard."

"Kevin, don't let me hear you call Brother Gerard or any other Brother or priest a bastard," Brian said. Kevin's good mood disappeared; his bright grin turned downward; he ducked his head down. "Hey, Kev," Brian called and gestured him toward the fence. Kevin glanced up at the window, then trotted over to Brian. "You know something? Brother Gerard is a real bastard." He winked at Kevin's grin. "*I* can say it, not you. And you better get your ass upstairs or he's really gonna give it to you. Hey, wait a minute. How come you didn't come home to lunch?"

Kevin pivoted quickly and his large bony hand directed

223

the bouncing ball close to his body. "I ate a coupla Yankee Doodles, Bri. Gives me more time to practice."

"Well, let Mom know if you're not coming home. When I ask where you are, I want to *know* where you are."

Kevin caught the ball on a high bounce and pulled his mouth down. "That damn Kit. I *told* her to tell Mom. I'm gonna belt her one, Brian. She never does anything she's told."

The window on the top floor was suddenly flung open and Kevin stood, mouth opened, doom descending.

"O'Malley," Brother Gerard called out coldly, "stop by my study at three o'clock. We'll have a discussion about the proper way to collect athletic equipment."

Kevin whispered, "Oh, shit."

Brian stood in the vestibule of the subway car, and as he watched Debbie Gladner, he experienced a shameful lack of control over his body. He tried to ignore the drawing tightness along the inside of his thighs and into his groin but could not distract himself. Irrevocably, his eyes slid along the row of seated riders but returned to the golden, clean, straight-backed girl.

He tried to discredit her and devaluate her through her choice of companion: a pimple-faced, ferret-eyed, book-toting, nose-twitching, hand-waving, small-boned, Brillo-haired little Jew with one of those round little skullcaps set on the top of his head. What the hell could that guy be saying that would be of any interest to Debbie Gladner?

Her eyes never left her companion's face. She leaned toward him earnestly, nodded frequently, spoke, listened, agreed; at one point, she reached for his sleeve, let her hand linger on the scrawny arm.

Debbie Gladner's touch went unnoticed, totally unregarded by the recipient, which was a measure of his worthlessness and total incapacity to realize the potential of the warm smooth-skinned body, the firm-fleshed legs. Words; that was what the juiceless little bastard seemed to thrive on and what words was he using to create the radiance on Debbie Gladner's face? Christ, Brian would give anything to know.

When the book-clutching, foot-shuffling, round-shouldered

creep got off the train at 86th Street, Brian heard him call back into the car, "Okay, Deb. I'll see you later tonight."

Brian closed his eyes in the darkness of the steel tomb and longed for Debbie's body, alive and eagerly responsive to his own. His hands would cup and hold and shape and teach. The train lurched to a stop and he opened his eyes to reality.

This was kid stuff, no longer necessary. He would go to Arthur's place after his tour. Rita's body could be Debbie's. Or any particular body he desired her to be. It was all in his mind and he could act it out any way he wanted.

He glanced into the car again, drawn by the hazy honey color of her hair. It was strange and he hadn't noticed it before but Debbie Gladner's hair was the color of Rita's hair when Rita used the rinse he'd bought her. Debbie's face was down into her book and she didn't seem to be bothered by the jolting start and stop of the train. But something made her look up, and for one single moment, Debbie Gladner stared, expressionless, directly at him.

Brian stopped himself from leaning back and edging away from her recognition. She blinked rapidly, frowned, then smiled and he casually waved and started toward her, but Debbie stood up and came into the vestibule.

"Well, hello, Brian. How are you?"

He wondered how she could speak in so normal a voice and how he would be able to respond. Yet he answered and he sounded casual and almost normal.

"Hello, Debbie. You on your way to school?"

She pressed her collection of books against her chest. "Very astute observation. But then, you're a policeman now, aren't you?" She held her head to one side and smiled. "What's the matter, Brian? Don't they allow you to ride inside the car? Or are you working now?"

"I like to ride in here," he said. He was grateful for the darkness which hid his shame and self-anger and anger at her. For being. Just for being. He wanted to ask her who the creep was, what they had been talking about, why she had given all her attention, her concern, her promise of a later meeting, her touch, her essence to someone so obviously unworthy.

He wanted to reach out and slowly move his hands through her heavy long hair and down between her shoulder blades and along all the warm and secret places of her body. He wanted to find a way to tell Debbie Gladner that he had something to share with her, that he was worthy of her consideration. He wanted to tell her that she could no longer use that mocking, lilting, knowing tone and small, maddening, derisive smile when she spoke to him.

"Well, how's the cops-and-robbers business, Brian? You a gangbuster yet?"

The wrong words, unbidden, leaped from his mouth: an offering, foolish and unacceptable. "Why don't you stop making fun of the job, Debbie? You know, there were a lot of Jewish guys in my graduating class. In fact, one of my best buddies is a Jew."

"One of your best buddies is a Jew," Debbie said softly. She mouthed the words contemptuously, threw them back at him with a mysterious tough pride which contained an angry secret knowledge he could not even begin to comprehend. She shifted her stance, leaned her books on one hip and twisted her mouth at him.

"And what does that make you, Brian? Something really special, a guy who has a buddy who is a Jew?" She smiled wisely, then her voice went hoarse and she said, *"No Jew should be a cop."*

The conversation made no sense, left no room for other things, other words. His exasperation was so strong and so total that all other feelings toward her left him and anger broke through. "You know, Debbie," Brian said with just an edge of self-righteousness, "if *I* said that, you'd accuse me of being an anti-Semite."

She regarded him coldly, unimpressed by his dark-blue eyes and clear pale complexion and black hair and lean, long hardness and physical splendor and justifiable anger. She said tersely, "If *you* said it, you *would* be an anti-Semite."

"Jesus, I don't get you, Debbie."

"Good," she said. "Fine."

"What the hell are you always so mad about?"

She released her breath slowly and the sound was an insult, almost a bitter laugh. "Oh, Brian. Brian O'Malley, your world is a very fine and happy place, with no injustices and no horrors and no terrors. You'll do all right, Brian. Your kind always does."

"My kind?"

The grossly generalized definition she assigned him infuriated Brian. He was as unknown and unknowable as she. "You are the smuggest little bitch on two feet," he said thickly. "Who the hell do you think you are anyway?"

She leaned back against the wall of the vestibule and her calmness seemed forced and very consciously controlled. She was white around the mouth and nostrils and there was a dry, clacking sound in her voice.

"I'm the hope of my people's future existence, that's who I am. I'm a separatist and a purist and an antiassimilationist. You don't even know what I'm talking about and I don't even care. It doesn't matter. I'm a Zionist and a zealot, and when the time comes and the need arises, I will become a fanatic!" She leaned forward and her eyes blazed at him but she spoke so softly he could hardly hear. "I am a fragment of my past and of the past of my people. I am an unregenerate member of the Diaspora, committed to the future and survival of my people Israel, and I have watched you all stand by in your abysmal ignorance and indifference while that Austrian lunatic is planning the destruction of my people!"

She jutted her face toward him and in a shaking voice she told him, "I am a daughter of Zion and you can just stop looking at me with your sneaky looks, Brian O'Malley, because I won't have anything to do with any gentile, ever. Never!"

The train stopped at 23rd Street and Debbie Gladner, without a glance at him, exited. It was the City College station. Brian gnawed at a loose piece of skin around his thumbnail.

Debbie Gladner was some kind of nut, he thought to himself.

TWENTY-THREE

Brian listened to Sergeant O'Connor's monotonous droning voice and nodded occasionally, not to convince the sergeant that he was listening but to keep himself awake.

Sergeant O'Connor had two passions in life. One was the decorating of his Christmas tree and the other was the preparation of unique hand-tied flies with which to lure trout from mountain streams into his waiting frying pan. Since Christmas had long since come and gone it was hard for Brian to understand what his reaction to the sergeant's detailed, endlessly instructive flow of words should be.

Sergeant O'Connor handled several telephone calls, spoke crisply and authoritatively, then resumed his lecture to Brian and within minutes created a total aura of unreality which Brian was afraid would cause him to drop the pen from his hand and let his head slump on the large sheets of duty charts he had been set to prepare. He wondered if Mackay, the regular clerical man, was forced to listen to the dry and ceaseless voice, night after night, tour after tour. That might be one of the reasons for Mackay's blank, glassy-eyed, expressionless countenance.

"You see," Sergeant O'Connor explained, "the Germans make these fine little light bulbs in the shape of cottages and elves and Santas and such. They call him Father Christmas, you might or might not know. And I've a whole line of them, of the light bulbs, and they're quite rare, you know, and you won't come upon them in the general run of things. I've a feeling, too, that they won't be making them again for a long time, what with their Hitler and their great interest in the military things and all.

"But the point is, O'Malley, that I've probably collected the finest examples of the craft — 'art' might be the better word, for my collection is indeed a fine example of art. Now some might think to put their tree up on Christmas Eve, when the little ones are asleep, and there are those who let the children help, but no one in my house touches the tree but yours truly, and I'll have you know, it takes me over a week to do it up right."

Sergeant O'Connor peered down over the top of his eyeglasses at Brian, who sat, pen poised, neck craning, body aching, at the clerical desk three feet below the sergeant's desk. There was no fooling around with Sergeant O'Connor's Christmas tree, and if he spoke about its decoration at the end of March, it was in loving memory of ornaments that had been polished, caressed, cherished, counted and carefully put away until their resurrection in early December.

Brian wondered how he would ever complete the duty chart he had been set to prepare. He wondered how long Mackay's illness would keep him at home and how in God's name he could convey to Sergeant O'Connor that he would rather be out on the street than stuck behind a desk. Any such indication would be considered sheer ingratitude. After all, the assignment had been given with a series of winks, nods and nonverbal indications that it was by nature of a special favor, an acknowledgment that Patrolman O'Malley knew how the game was played as evidenced by his handling of the case of Captain Toomey's brother (over which he had no control, and if he had, the little bastard would be banging his head against bars somewhere).

By ten o'clock, the pastrami sandwich which he had devoured at nine o'clock caused bitterness along the back of Brian's throat as he bent over the dimly lit desk and blacked out tiny squares in progressive rows of steps along the graph paper. Sergeant O'Connor's meal was taken in the empty office of the captain and Sergeant Horan sat quietly engrossed in his study manual for the lieutenant's examination which would be held some time in the indefinite future.

The duty chart had a look of abstraction. Random lines ran through squares from left lower corner to right upper corner, then switched to the alternate, then moved relentlessly to a series of black steps. Squad 7: Mid-to-8A, Tues.-Wed. RDO; Squad 8: 8A-to-4P, Thurs.-Fri. RDO. Squad 9. Squad 10.

Which squad got the long swing? Which squad got the short swing? What the hell is this all about?

The house was quiet; the detectives were out on a squeal; a couple of them were cruising; a few derelicts were booked; one lost kid, reported found before anyone was sent out; a noisy card party, no action necessary; disorderly kids, warned, admonished, sent on their way.

"I gotta take a personal," Brian told Sergeant Horan, who glanced at his wristwatch and nodded.

Bastard. Go ahead and time me.

He took his time in the bathroom. He washed his face with cold water, rinsed his eyes, swallowed from his cupped palm and felt heavy with boredom. He blotted his face with scratchy toilet paper, stared at his image in the scarred mirror. A dynamic-looking guy, no doubt about it. He glanced around, made certain he was alone, then posed for himself and admired the fierce policeman who regarded him with professional suspicion. A hard face, wise and knowing and shrewd, capable of great earth-shaking things. He turned slightly to one side, then glanced from the corner of his eye to see how he looked sideways.

His hand fled to his chin; he wiped an imaginary spot from his eye as Sergeant O'Connor entered the lavatory.

"Ah, here you are, Brian. Hmm, the lighting in here's not what it should be. I know a great deal about lighting and electricity. When I get interested in something, you see, I pursue it completely. Yes. If I didn't do that, I'd long ago have ruined my Christmas lights and they are irreplaceable, O'Malley, make no mistake about that. Yes, absolutely irreplaceable."

Brian edged toward the door and nodded. "I better get back to the duty chart, Sergeant. I don't seem to be making much progress."

"Oh, well, there's tomorrow night, and the night after, lad," Sergeant O'Connor said and winked. "One thing you can say for certain, O'Malley, nobody's pressuring you, eh? Eh?"

"Right, Sarge. Absolutely right."

Horan watched him closely as he settled at the clerical desk, checked his watch and his mouth tightened but he didn't say anything. After all, he was just a relief; he'd be going out in a few minutes. Even if O'Connor didn't run a tight ship; no skin off him.

Julie Horowitz headed directly for him, as though he'd been waiting for Brian. He clamped a hand on Brian's shoulder. As he spoke, bits of saliva collected at the corners of his mouth and his eyes gleamed. "Hey, kid, you must have some rabbi, getting yourself a desk job, huh? Listen, O'Malley, you missed it, but I want you should see what we got upstairs, me and Kelly. Huh, Sarge? Good stuff up there?"

Horan shrugged and turned the page of his manual.

"What have you got?" Brian asked warily.

Horowitz prodded Brian with an elbow and jerked his head several times toward the iron staircase. "Cute, O'Malley, something pretty damn cute. C'mon, the sergeant can spare you for a minute. Hey, no shit, kid, not that old battle-ax the guys pulled on you when you first started." Horowitz nearly strangled on that one. "They really got you with old 'Filthy Florence' and her Albert routine, huh? Jeez, she's been around so long lookin' for the guy, he must be about sixty by now. Not that he's alive. But listen, kid" — Horowitz cupped his thick hand around his mouth — "look, this is nice stuff. Not that you can have any, not here anyway, but like maybe you can connect later on. Jeez, we had a lieutenant here coupla years back, the damn place was like a regular cat house on midnights." Horowitz laughed and shook his hand in the air. "Them was the days, kid."

Horan ignored them and Brian felt that anything was better than falling under the spell of the graph paper and the inevitable return of Sergeant O'Connor. He figured Horowitz and Kelly were about to pull something on him, to break *their* monotony, but he might be able to pull something off on them.

They had two prostitutes in custody. One of them he had never seen before.

The other one was Rita Wasinski.

Her face went ashen under the bright application of powdery rouge. Her eyes darted from Horowitz to Brian and a small, tentative smile pulled her lips with the regularity of a twitch. Her small hands, first one, then the other, touched and poked and played with the bleached, untoned hair.

Horowitz threw a familiar arm around her shoulders, squeezed her and breathed words into her ear. Rita shrugged, smiled, giggled, then her hands dangled loosely as Horowitz moved so that her hands came to rest on the fly of his trousers.

"Hey, look at that, O'Malley. The kid can't restrain herself when I'm around."

Rita pulled her hands away, bit her lip, closed her eyes for a moment, opened them, avoided Brian. She fidgeted with her dress, her pocketbook, the corners of her lips, her fingernails, the belt which tightly circled her waist. She frowned and worried over a run in her stocking and Horowitz followed her concern and ran his thick finger up along the run and said, "Hey now, that's a shame, kiddo. Where the hell did it start?"

His hand moved slowly and Rita said weakly, "It must have got caught on the edge of the chair when I sat down."

Horowitz' hand disappeared under her dress, his tongue licked at the spittle in the corners of his mouth, and Rita endured, with a slight, uncertain smile, until he finally released her and kissed a fingertip at her.

"In the old days, Brian, we'd a' had a ball. But we gotta get these kids on their way. Rita baby, tell me how many you got on the sheet, and don't shit me, 'cause we're gonna see it by morning anyways."

For a moment, she held her face down, then she breathed deeply, raised her face and said softly, "Only three, Mr. Horowitz."

Horowitz gurgled, hugged her to him, patted her round bottom. "I love this kid. *Only* three, she says. How about you, Viola? Tell me only three and I'll drop my pants and you'll die 'cause I won't let you have it."

Viola was older, maybe thirty. Her face was too heavy for her thin body; it looked misplaced. She moved with the slow, languid, unreal motion of a sleepwalker. "I dunno. What's the difference anyways?"

"What's the difference anyways is right," Horowitz said and laughed as though he'd cracked a tremendous joke. He wrapped an arm around both of them and squeezed the women. "Now, if you see this policeman here, see, this is Patrolman O'Malley, and if he wants some stuff, you take good care of him, right?" Horowitz winked at Brian. "See, O'Malley, we take care of our own. Holy Christ," he said to Kelly, "take a look at junior here. I swear to God, the kid's blushing!"

His mother watched his face anxiously and warned the kids

not to make any commotion and not to bother Brian with their nonsense.

There was a man beneath his smooth boyish face now and he was a stranger to her, as all men are to all women. Whatever caused the hard faraway cast to darken his eyes and pull at his black brows would forever remain secret to her. Even if she were to know, she could have no hand in it.

Margaret wondered if it was the job that did that to them or was it just the very fact of being men. They seemed to turn into themselves at times, become remote and far away, and when they emerged it was in sudden quick bursts of anger which made them slash out at the young ones. She had seen it with her own husband and with his brothers. She didn't like seeing it now with her son.

Mother of God, there were enough things she knew about to cause her worry without poking and prodding into places that could only reveal more trouble.

Roseanne was working herself into a regular state with her endless concerns and complaints. Well, she'd tell Roseanne, over and over again, if Billy is driving those big trucks huge distances, there's every reason he'd be gone for days at a time. For the love of God, child, the man provides the food on the table and the rent to the landlord, so just let him be.

And oh, this thing with poor John. Well, Brian would have to know about that.

Margaret brought the second cup of steaming black coffee to Brian. She hesitated before she removed the untouched plate of scrambled eggs and bacon, but he pushed it toward her with his fingertips and reached for the coffee. He'd *said* he didn't want any breakfast.

"You'll have to go around to see Uncle Peadar today, Brian."

"Uncle Peadar? What for?"

The dishcloth moved rapidly over the spot where the plate of food had been. "Yes. It's about our John. Gene and Matt will be there too. At about noon, Peadar said. There's something needs to be discussed about poor John."

What the hell did they want him in on it for? They were probably going to make a shoemaker out of the kid; he'd sew his damned fingers together. Or maybe they were going to let him work full time with Matt.

"He's been working on the wagon with Uncle Matt before school every morning, hasn't he, Mom?"

Margaret's lips tightened and her face was set. She moved her thin bony shoulders slightly and her hand moved on the table before him in fast, unnecessary circles. "It's not about that, Brian. It's something more."

The furious scrubbing irritated him. He caught at his mother's wrist and tried to break through the small mystery. "Well, how about telling me what it is about then, Ma? Come on, will you quit wiping at that table? There's nothing there."

"And there's nothing in your stomach neither, for you've not touched your breakfast. Let go my hand and don't tell me how to clean my own table." She gave it a few more swipes, then bunched the damp cloth into her hands. "Your uncles will tell you in their own good time. Ah, Brian. The poor simple lad." She turned quickly to the sink and ran water over the dishes.

He spent his morning in aimless rambling but his mind was filled with scenes of wild violence. He would find her tonight, at the end of his tour. She would be waiting at Arthur's apartment. She would scream, cry out, plead, weep. She would throw herself on the floor, grab at his legs, sob and twitch, and tears would cut long seams on her powdery cheeks. With the cold, emotionless wrath of the deeply wronged, he would beat her with his fists and kick at her body, at all the warm, moist, soft, exciting, vulnerable and secret places of her body. Her lips would plead for his touch but his touch would not be what she expected or longed for.

The scene changed. Rita was not on the floor but on the bed, her body stretched and expectant, arched and waiting. He would approach her slowly, his hand to her hair, fingers twisting slowly. Slowly, she would come to realize his intention and slowly the soft corrupted features of her face would freeze with the knowledge of how he was about to destroy her.

He thought of the moment in terrible and endless variations of cruelty and pleasure, but they all ended with the same empty, hollow sense of despair.

He wanted last night not to have happened. He wanted reality not to have ruined a part of his life which he knew he would never be able to recapture. He didn't want to let go, yet he knew he had no choice, and faced with the fact, he wanted revenge.

He wanted to kill her. He wanted to destroy her, to hurt and humiliate her.

At the same time, he wanted the warm, familiar comfort and the unspeakable excitement of her body.

John O'Malley had been caught in what could only be described as a compromising situation with Anna Caprobella by Anna Caprobella's father, Dominick.

"But for Christ's sake, Uncle Peadar," Brian said, "there isn't a guy over seventeen doesn't know about Anna Caprobella."

Gene O'Malley leaned against the refrigerator and raised his brows. "Well, is that a fact now? And what's your particular knowledge of the girl?"

Peadar's large heavy fist smashed down on the table and the coffee cups rattled. "This is not time for a bunch of smart aleck remarks," he said. "We know the girl's reputation, by God. The point of the thing is that the old guinea bastard caught poor John, right outside the door of their apartment. His precious daughter's hand was inside the damn fool's pants and I've no need to tell you what was in her filthy hand or what the condition of that something was."

"And Caprobella actually thinks we'd let John *marry* her?" Brian asked.

"Not just thinks it, lad. He's those three hulking apes of sons of his brought poor John over to Father Donlon at one this morning and woke the poor man with the commotion similar to the end of the world and announced that first banns were to be published this very Sunday. And didn't I have to get over there and fetch our Johnnie home and try to make some sense out of the whole mess." Peadar shook his head in disgust and with weariness. He'd been up half the night.

"He's a simple-minded fool, our John," Gene commented. "Christ, hasn't anyone ever spoken to the kid about . . . 'things'?"

Brian felt accused and angry. "Don't look at *me*, Uncle Gene. I've got enough to do taking care of the kids and giving John houseroom every time his nut mother takes off."

Matthew spoke for the first time, slowly, quietly. "Well now, there's no point in anyone getting all worked up and blaming anyone else. The thing of it is, you see, there's the situation and we've to find the solution to the whole thing as of where it is now."

Gene jerked his thumb toward his older brother and said caustically, "He's all for wedding bells, isn't that a fact, Matt?"

The milkman sucked on his pipe for a moment, shrugged and spread his hands. "Well, I think the girl's been talked about a great deal more than the facts might warrant. She doesn't come from a bad family. They're all hard workers and honest enough and concerned for her future."

"Concerned?" Peadar roared. "And it's us should be concerned. They're trying to palm off used goods on our poor John and that simple boy has no one but us to protect him."

"Well, what did poor Johnnie say to you, Peadar?" Matt asked reasonably.

Peadar made an ugly derisive sound. "What does he know, the poor damn fool. Seventeen and letting himself be caught with that girl. Nineteen if she's a day and the talk of the neighborhood since she's been thirteen. And where was her concerned family all them years?"

"But when did all this happen?" Brian asked.

Matt explained it. The others were too angry to speak in any continuous strain. "Well, the girl was hanging around outside the candy store and our John came along last night on his way home from the rehearsal of the school play. Kevin went on home without him because there was some confusion as to where our John was headed. Mary the Widow's been home for some days now. Peadar's been to see her and Ellen too and your mother. From all reports, she's been sober but 'strange.' "

"Yes," Peadar interjected, "she's strange, indeed, very quiet and far-off."

"Well, but it's John we're discussing now," Matt insisted. "At any rate, Brian, no one really missed John for your mother figured he'd be at his own home. And our Johnnie stood fooling with the lads until there was no one left at all but the girl, and didn't she tell him she was afraid to walk home alone, of all things."

Gene snorted angrily. "*Afraid*, the filthy thing. Ah, Christ, it's our Johnnie should have been afraid."

Matt ignored the interruption. "And he walked the several blocks home with her and she began to get close to him and all that sort of thing, and as luck would have it, the old man opened the door and there was the situation as Peadar described it and as luck would have it." Matt rubbed his neck and told them softly, "It's not as if it was one of our other lads, you know. Any of the others, like Brian here, or my own boys or yours, Peadar, or John the Wop's, were they older, would have had better sense. But the thing here, it seems to me, is that everyone's getting all excited and no one's looking at some side of the whole thing that's occurred to me and to Father Donlon as well."

Peadar stood up angrily and jammed his hands into his trouser pockets. "Father Donlon didn't have any such thing to say to me in the wee hours this morning as you've discussed with him today. He just wanted me to get John out of the rectory and away from the Caprobellas."

Matt remained unruffled. He spoke to Brian. "I went to Father Donlon's after my rounds this morning and we sat quietly and discussed the whole thing without all the passion and the tempers flying. Now, the girl's family has their fruit market over on Bathgate Avenue and the one brother has his own small business in coal. The old man had indicated they'd find a place for our John amongst them, plus he could continue working for me the few hours in the morning."

Gene shook his head. "Jesus God, would you look at this fool, selling his own dead brother's son to the passel of Eyetalians!"

Matt moved with an economy of speed and effort that astonished Brian; he came from his chair, reached for his younger brother's shirt, had it bunched around his throat before Gene's hands could go up reflexively. The large, strong hands did not relent although Gene's face went purple.

Matt's voice revealed none of the passion of his action; it was low and steady and controlled, but deadly. "Now I've had enough of you and your remarks and your useless, stupid insults. I've a mind to throttle you to get some sense into your head, though I'd just as soon not have to bother for it's all rather pointless, but I will if I must." He shook Gene without seeming to exert any effort. Gene's hands couldn't pry the murderous grasp from his throat.

Peadar leaned against the white enamel sink and watched his brothers without a flicker of concern. Brian had never seen his Uncle Matt display even the potential for violence. He felt his heart race and his mouth go dry and he wondered if Peadar realized that Matt held his brother's life within his grasp. It was a long moment before Peadar tapped Matt's shoulder; his hand remained on the milkman's shoulder.

"Let him be, Matt. There's no point our fighting amongst ourselves, is there?"

"There's no point in our fighting at all, is how I see it," Matt said dryly. He dropped his hands and Gene fell back with a gasp, but Matt turned his back on him; any remarks from that quarter would not be worthy of serious attention.

"Well, Brian," Peadar said, "you're more of an age with poor John than any of us. Let's hear from you, then. What would your thoughts be?"

"About letting John marry Anna Caprobella? Uncle Peadar, you've got to be kidding."

Peadar glared at Matt. "Well, between him and Father Donlon they seemed to feel it's not a bad solution."

"Now I didn't say it was a *good* thing, Peadar. I never said that. But after all, we know John can't stay in school forever; he's a good enough boy and willing to work hard. The girl's family is willing to help set them up. He'd be close by and all . . ."

"But, Jesus. What did John say about it?" Brian asked.

Matt rubbed the back of his neck and sighed. "Ah, well, when Father Donlon put it to him straight out, he wrinkled up his nose and said, 'But, Father, she smells so funny.' Christ, with all the garlic and oily things them people eat, who wouldn't smell funny?" Matt slid his pipestem between his teeth and his face was sad. "Ah, as if that's all was involved with marriage. He's just a boy, after all."

"Well, that's what I've been telling you, Matt," Peadar said, quieter now. "We've talked about getting him into the Navy, Brian."

"The Navy? John?"

"Well, it's not a bad idea," Peadar said. "The thing is, it's better than the other side of the coin. Father Donlon's own sister's son has just joined up and Father Donlon could call

238

the Bishop to take a hand and get the boy started on his way immediately, so the two lads would be together. He's a good sort, Tom Steele, the nephew, and he could keep an eye on our John."

"And what about John?" Brian asked. "Did you ask him about it?"

"Ah, Brian, the lad fancies himself in a uniform as much as anything else," Peadar said brightly. "I'd rather he had a bit of a look at the world than end up behind a counter surrounded by those guineas for the rest of his life. And with that Anna Caprobella waiting for him at home."

The idea suddenly encompassed Brian, appealed to him with a force he did not understand. An escape, a way out of everything, of all things, all responsibilities, all entanglements, all known places and faces and lives and routines and memories. It was the offering of a new life, a fresh start, with the cleansing effect of being a newly emerged communicant, all past sins forgiven, washed away, the vile made clean, the broken made whole, the guilty made innocent.

"What is it, lad?" Peadar asked. "You've a strange expression on your face."

Brian reached for a cigarette and brought himself back into the room. It was John, after all, who was being discussed and not himself.

"I think it would be the best thing for John," he said dishonestly for he'd given no thought to his cousin. "I think that really would be the best."

"Well, we've pretty much decided amongst us then," Peadar said. "Matty, you've no *real* objections to this decision, have you?"

Matt shrugged. "No, I just felt we should consider the other possibility. After all, it's the lad's whole future we're talking about here. We want what will be best for our John."

"Ah, the Navy's the good choice, then," Peadar said heartily. "Let's eat these sandwiches the wife's left. I'm due to visit with Father Donlon at one-thirty and he'll get right to the Bishop. Well, Brian, how goes the job with you, lad?"

The eight-hour tour was both endless and timeless, a compression of hours and an expansion of hours, filled with the

239

dim circle of light, hazy and yellow, over the charts which were shadowed by his own hunched shoulders. Sergeant O'Connor's voice droned; his words rose and fell into sound without meaning. The only fact that penetrated was that Patrolman Mackay would return to his job the next tour and Brian would be out on the street again.

Midnight came as a surprise. It was as though he had spent eight hours suspended in limbo.

The fantasy of Rita Wasinski moved through him with the relentlessness of necessity, and as he walked toward Arthur's apartment, he conjured an endless, repetitive series of confrontations, none of them satisfying.

Arthur jerked his head up and his hands spasmodically leaped on the surface of the newspaper which had fallen over his chest. "Oh, Brian. I fell asleep," he explained unnecessarily. His voice was thick and he struggled to snap himself awake.

Brian had never given a moment's thought to the possibility that Arthur might be present. Everything shattered into disoriented splinters; the familiar apartment turned strange, as though Arthur's intrusion turned it into another place altogether.

"I've got a pot of coffee on, Brian. I'll just put a light under it."

Arthur was on his feet, the newspaper still in his hand. He seemed sharp and alert, intensely aware. It was Brian who felt confused and somewhat dizzy, as though he'd been in a deep sleep.

"Sit down, Brian," Arthur said firmly. "We have to talk."

"There's nothing to talk about, Arthur."

"Sit down."

The little son of a bitch actually pushed him; the thought filled Brian with a dull amusement and he let himself fall into the chair.

"We're *going* to talk about it," Arthur said.

Brian leaned into the crazy sling chair. Arthur pulled up a wooden chair, turned it backwards, straddled it, poked his face at Brian. His eyes turned inward and his hands grasped the top of the chair.

"There isn't a damn thing to talk about, Arthur. That fucking little whore!" His clenched fist tapped on his knee lightly,

240

then a little harder. He pounded his knee with a fierce series of blows, totally unaware of the pain, surprised at his lack of self-control, but it was Rita's betrayal he pounded at.

Arthur said nothing. Words suddenly burst from the depths of Brian, from the twenty-four hours of unspoken sorrow and unending visions of Rita's body. He had visualized her beneath the bodies of all the men he had ever known and all the men he had never seen but who had touched her, known her.

"I want to kill her, Arthur," he said thickly. "Goddamn it to hell, she isn't worth it, but if she was here, right now, so help me God, I'd kill her."

Arthur waited him out. The words slowed, fell away finally to silence, then finally Brian was drained. Arthur got him a cup of coffee.

"It's hot, Brian," he said. "Use the handle."

"Yeah. Yeah, sure."

Arthur sipped from his own cup, then carefully placed it on a table. "Brian," he asked carefully, "what is it you expected of her?"

Brian leaned forward, spoke to the floor. "She was in the precinct last night. She was in the goddamn precinct, locked up for prostitution. Did you know that, Arthur? Did she tell you that?"

"I went bail for her, Brian. She called her cousin Stella, and Stell didn't have any money, so she came to me. I gave her the money to get Rita bailed. Rita told me that you were there, that you'd seen her."

"You went *bail* for her? Jesus Christ, you went *bail?*"

"She doesn't have anyone else," Arthur said calmly.

Recklessly, Brian said, "Oh, but she's got *you*, huh, Arthur? Holy Christ, have I been a dumb, stupid bastard. All the time, she's been screwing *both* of us. I never even gave it a thought."

Arthur's gray face tightened; his fingers clenched the edge of the wooden chair. His voice was high and reedy. "You've got it wrong, Brian. I'm going to straighten you out, once and for all. I told you, right at the very beginning. Rita is a *friend*. If you find that hard to understand, I'm sorry for you but that's the truth. I've never touched her, never been to bed with her, never 'screwed' her, if that's how you want me to put it."

"The hell you haven't. Why else would you . . ."

241

Arthur moved his head from side to side but his eyes stayed on Brian's; the movement of his head made his eyes seem to roll within the sockets. The left eye, the weak one, turned in more than Brian had ever seen before.

"Brian, I'm sorry if it's outside your experience, but that's how it is. Rita is my *friend*. Not my lover or my bed partner or my whore or whatever else you choose to believe."

He believed Arthur. It was irrational, not believable, impossible, implausible. Yet he believed Arthur. It puzzled him and mystified him that he *did* believe Arthur.

"You never got around to answering my question, Brian," Arthur demanded relentlessly. "What is it you expected from Rita?"

The unanswerable question cut through all his feelings and all his anger. He shrugged and swallowed some coffee and wiped his mouth and studied the ceiling, the walls, the pictures, the books, looked anywhere but at Arthur, who waited, implacable.

"Oh, shit," Brian said shortly.

Arthur rubbed his eyes with his fingertips, lightly, carefully. "Brian, you still have some growing up to do."

"Oh, but Christ . . ."

"Oh, but Christ," Arthur mimicked him. "You figured Rita would stop turning a buck, stop making her living, stop paying rent, bills, helping to support her old aunt, all because she had something special, something extra going with you?" Arthur reached out roughly for Brian's sleeve. "Don't keep looking at the ceiling, Brian. Damn it, look at me. Look at yourself. Look at reality." It was the closest Brian had ever seen Arthur come to anger. It wasn't really anger either. There was something pained and hurt and sad about Arthur. "Okay, it *was* rotten the way it happened last night. Sooner or later it had to catch up with you, Brian. That was probably the worst way possible. But come on, kid, that's life."

"I really am dumb, you know, Arthur? I mean, I thought we had something really special going. Now that sounds like a goddamn dumb kid, doesn't it?"

"Brian, you *did* have something special. Whatever went on between you and Rita belongs only to the two of you."

"And any guy with two bucks, right?"

Arthur clicked his tongue and stood up. "God, you really *are* a baby, Brian. Exactly what do you think a guy can buy with two bucks?"

Not the endless hours of exploration; the fun and games and creation of a secret private language of sensation and action and reaction and unstated messages and completed communications and feeling of physical wholeness and newness and rising, growing, endless, boundless pleasure.

He followed Arthur into the kitchen, watched him rinse the cups in the chipped square sink.

"Arthur," he said miserably, "I want her. *I still want her.*"

Arthur turned the water off, carefully dried the cups and put them into the cupboard, then dried his hands. He raised a finger at Brian, as though instructing a child.

"You *can't* see her again, Brian. *Not ever.*" Arthur blinked rapidly and wet his lips. "I'm sorry for what happened. I'm sorry for you and I'm sorry for Rita. But it is a part of your life that you had and now . . . it's finished."

Brian started to say something, to argue, to deny, but the words stayed in his throat, strangled him with futility.

Arthur reached out, pressed Brian's arm. "Rita doesn't exist anymore, Brian. It's as simple as that. And as tough as that."

TWENTY-FOUR

Brian signed up for the Holy Name Society weekend retreat to be held in Staten Island. He'd had a terrible time of it in the confessional, finally had confronted his own guilt, his own lustful sins. Father Donlon agreed that the retreat would be of tremendous help. His flesh still yearned, still wanted, still longed with a terribleness he had not anticipated.

His weekly confessions did not leave him purged and cleansed; it left him empty and hollow for within him was the unadmitted, unadmittable knowledge that what he *really* wanted was not to relinquish his sin, but to be held unaccountable for it.

In the cool and burning, hard and tender, known and secret, glowing and murky, beautiful and terrible, vast and minute recesses of his soul, Brian O'Malley longed to be that pure and sinless boy he never was.

Ultimately, he knew it was flesh that held him, possessed him, tormented, intrigued, delighted, encased and encompassed him, and in the desperate futility of his thousandth confession and millionth resolve, it was flesh which mysteriously dominated his every waking and sometimes sleeping moments.

He *knew*, had been taught, truly believed, that flesh would corrode and rot and pass away and be no more and that it was within the tarnished and sin-scarred soul he would be forced to endure for all eternity.

But having been taught and knowing and truly believing were not enough. What he regretted most of all, what he sorrowed after most of all, was the loss of the flesh of Rita Wasinski, whose flesh completed and fulfilled his own.

• •

He walked his tour mechanically, went through the motions of being, but he felt oddly vacant, transparent, outside of himself. He quietly observed his own actions with a feeling of detachment and disinterest.

Brian glanced around the quiet street, dug a stick of Juicy Fruit gum from his pocket, rolled it into a tight wad, bit down on it. He folded the outer wrapping into a small pellet, aimed at a thin, long-legged cat that was perched on the rim of an uncovered garbage can. He missed his target, but the loud ping against the can made the cat jump a good six inches straight up.

He rubbed his flat hard belly and felt hungry. Fish on Friday nights always left him feeling hungry. Well, what the hell, it was a good six hours since he'd eaten anyway; he'd get a break for a meal in about an hour.

It was a mild night. Surprisingly so, for the day had been surprisingly raw. Ten minutes after ten. Brian checked his wristwatch against the collection of clocks in the window of Farbenstein's jewelry store. Ten after ten; ten after ten; ten after ten. There was something in the air, some quality, some elusiveness, that taunted him, stirred him to restlessness and discontent. The sky was very black, pierced by bright stars, pin sharp. The only formation he could ever make out was the Big Dipper.

Two elderly men walked toward him. They spoke loudly at each other, over each other's words, not listening, too busy telling to listen. One waved his small bundle of religious items in front of him as he spoke. The other shook an index finger at his companion. Their words were incomprehensible to Brian but he was accustomed to the endless, vehement, earnest arguments and discussion of the old men on their way home from late-Friday-night services. Sometimes, as he patrolled past their synagogues, the noise was unbelievable and he wondered how they dared to carry on in such loud, angry voices in a house of God. They were peculiar, at least this special tribe, marked by their long dark clothing and flowing beards and side curls and large-brimmed hats.

Brian touched his nightstick to his cap and cocked his head slightly at them. In response, they nodded, but never interrupted themselves or broke the force of their argument. At the corner, Brian rocked back on his heels. He fingered the Indian-nut machine absently, was surprised that the handle turned on an unused penny. Carefully, he cupped his hand under the spout and felt his palm fill with the thin-shelled tiny nuts.

Indian nuts were a pain in the ass to eat. All that delicate biting down, tongue manipulating the tiny white meat from the sharp, broken fragments of shell. For one fleeting, sweet remnant of taste.

Brian carefully spit the shelled nuts into the palm of his hand. He'd collect a handful of nuts before eating them. But there might be one bad nut, one little morsel of black, in the collection; that would ruin the taste. He moved toward the street light, tilted the palm of his hand, then ate the mouthful of little white nuts. They were delicious. He brushed crumbs from the palm of his hand.

The settlement house was closed and quiet from sundown on Friday night to sundown on Saturday because the Jews observed the Sabbath then. The younger directors were trying to get the rule changed; they argued that the kids needed the house on Friday nights and Saturdays and that they didn't want to be bound by old-country traditions. It was a good-sized building and they ran a lot of activities to keep the kids off the streets after school hours.

Brian decided to risk a cigarette. It would cut his hunger, break in on his boredom. He checked the quiet street, then went down the stone stairs which led from the street level to the basement level of the settlement house. He inhaled the damp mustiness beneath the stairs and moved away from the urine odor. He cupped his hand around his match and lit his cigarette.

He leaned against the brick wall and tried to determine which was the North Star. The crown of his hat caught against the wall and didn't move with his head; the peak of his hat covered his forehead and eyes momentarily.

Brian stood absolutely motionless for a second, stopped his tongue from digging at the small piece of Indian nut wedged between his back teeth, held his breath so that he could concentrate and locate the direction of the sound.

It came from within the settlement house; there was no doubt in his mind of that fact. From within the deserted, closed-down, empty, unused Friday-night settlement house.

Brian pinched the glowing ember from the end of his cigarette and dropped the long butt. He shoved his hat to the back of his head, then pulled it tightly against his skull. He slid his right hand into his gun holster, felt the butt of his gun, heavy and familiar in his palm. He slid the flashlight from his belt and moved carefully, silently toward the door directly beneath the staircase. His eyes were accustomed to the dark; he could see that the door was slightly ajar. Gently, carefully, he pushed the door inward. It gave with a loud scraping crunch.

The sudden beam of his flashlight pierced the room and went directly toward the startled voices. Accustomed to blackness, Brian could not immediately make sense of the scene caught in the beam of light: a tangle of bodies, naked legs, buttocks, startled glow of eyes. There was a low sob, a moan, a cry, some words. "Please. Oh, God. Oh, God, please."

Kids.

Slowly, Brian released his breath and brusquely he told them, "Okay, get up. Come on, move."

He found a light switch on the wall and flicked it to produce a dim glow of illumination from the ceiling light fixture. The girl was on her knees; she clumsily hoisted up her light-pink underpants, pulled her slip and brown pleated skirt down. Her blouse was open and she shoved it into the top of her skirt. Her hair stood wildly from her head.

In a panic, stark and complete and terrible, she crawled to Brian and her hands grasped and fumbled at his legs. He stepped back to free himself from her, but she persisted and clung to him, her fingers as sharp as claws. Her face and voice were distorted and pulled by fear.

"Please, oh, please, mister, please don't turn us in, don't tell nobody, my father will kill me, my mother will die, oh, please, I'll do anything you say, oh, please." In a sudden inspiration, she pointed to the boy, who stood, face down, motionless, silent. "Him," the girl shrieked. "He did it to me, he made me, he told me he was gonna kill me if I didn't, he forced me, lock *him* up, it was him!"

The boy raised his face and his dark eyes burned but everything else about him was cold and reconciled. It was Angelo DiSantini.

He knew that he could expect nothing and so he was ready to accept whatever he had to accept. He held his lower lip between his teeth and kept silent as the girl clutched at Brian's legs and hurled frantic accusations.

"Quiet," Brian said finally as the hysteria grew; she pulled at the edge of his jacket as she tried to raise herself. "Listen, take it easy, will you?"

"Listen, shoot him, shoot him. The bastard, he raped me, I swear to God, he raped me. Tell my father that, please, mister, tell my father that he *made* me."

Brian slipped his gun into his holster and tried to shake the girl from him. A strange anger overcame him, a strange sense of circumstance. He knew the girl had better shut up. He told her again to calm down but she continued to rave. Her desperation hid her extreme youth. Only her frantic female agitation came through to him, her desperate attempt at self-preservation and justification.

He hit her across the face with the back of his hand. It was fast and controlled but unexpected. That increased the power of the blow and sent the stunned girl reeling to the concrete floor. She crept back toward Brian, dazed, not understanding. Brian swung his hand back again and the girl cringed and backed away from him, crept into herself like a cowering animal.

"How old are you, you little bitch?" Brian asked her.

"Please. Please, honest, he done it. He made me, I swear to God."

There was a terrible wild abandon in the girl's posture, made more terrible by the quiet composure of Angelo DiSantini, who stood, silent, watching.

Brian turned to the boy decisively. "Tell her to get out of here. *Right now.*"

The boy nodded, just once, reached quickly for the girl and pulled her to her feet. "Get going, Carmen. Get lost."

His voice was a hiss; the girl struggled to her feet, ran backwards into the wall, then found the doorway. They heard her stumble and rush up the outside staircase.

Angelo DiSantini reached inside the pocket of his bright shiny jacket and took out a pack of Camels. Wordlessly, he extended the cigarettes to Brian, then held the trembling match. Finally, he blew at the flame and dropped the dead match to the floor.

"How old is she?" Brian asked softly.

DiSantini shrugged, closed his eyes for a moment, then whispered, "Jailbait. Oh, God. Jailbait."

Brian said to him wonderingly, "You could get maybe three, five years on a statutory rape for screwing that little whore." He stopped speaking abruptly, signaled with his eyes toward the window over their heads. He reached for the light switch and turned the dim light off. In the darkness, each cupped the lit cigarette against any visible glow. The footsteps along the sidewalk grew louder, then receded.

Their unstated conspiracy puzzled Brian more than it did Angelo DiSantini, who accepted salvation wherever he might find it, regardless of how unexpected the source.

"You could have loused up your whole life because of that little bitch," Brian said softly. "I figured you for a smarter kid than that."

Carefully, Angelo said, "I figured you for a different kind of Joe, too. Maybe we was both wrong."

The boy was not as untouched as he appeared. There was a sharp, heavy reek of perspiration emanating from him; it was the sharp odor of fear. In the darkness, Brian felt lightheaded and slightly irrational. It would have been a good collar: he caught them in the act. The distraught girl would have signed a complaint even though that wasn't even necessary.

The DiSantini boy meant nothing to him. He even felt a vague dislike for the dark muscularity of the boy. But his feelings toward the girl were clear and strong and undeniable. He had, for one tightly controlled instant, resisted the tremendous urge to smash her head to a pulp with his nightstick. Bitch. Bitch. Bitch.

Brian said softly, "Okay, DiSantini. You get the hell out of here. I catch you again, at anything, anything at all, you'll wish you'd never been born."

Whatever reaction he might have anticipated was not forthcoming. Angelo DiSantini pressed the cigarette against the wall, stepped on the sparks that flew toward his shoe, and pocketed the stubbed cigarette.

Almost as an afterthought, he said to Brian, "I won't forget this." His voice was totally neutral, his inflection normal.

He made no sound as he went up the iron-tipped stairs and the silence in the basement closed around Brian with a heavy mustiness. He could almost believe that he had just stepped down into this chilly empty room for a smoke, that he had encountered no one, made no serious decision.

When he left the basement, Brian made sure the lock was set and the premises secure. He felt an incomprehensible sense of well-being and the rest of his tour went quickly.

By the time Father Sebastian was finished with them, there wasn't a man among the Holy Name Society retreatants who didn't feel scourged and raw with shame, self-repulsion, guilt and the renewed awareness of the irrevocable fate of unrepentant sinners.

Father Sebastian was a tall, hollow-cheeked, spare-fleshed Jesuit who mesmerized them with his clearly articulated visions of the wrath of God on the one hand and the unfathomable mercy of the Savior, Jesus Christ, on the other.

"Who among you," he asked them in a beautiful, theatrical, hushed, carefully modulated voice, "who among you, sinners all, sinners, who among you deserves forgiveness for the agony you have inflicted on our Innocent Savior? Willingly, He took up the Cross; willingly, He accepted punishment for *your* sins, *your* salvation. And how have you served Him? By inflicting the weight of *your* sins on His suffering and crucified body."

Father Sebastian's knowing blue eyes candidly sought them out and found among them, as they had guessed, not one, none of them, worthy of the sacrifices made on their behalf. He drew in a sad, pained breath, leaned on the lectern for a moment, dropped his fine prematurely silvered head to his arms.

They gazed uneasily at the short-cropped hair; it was as though he could penetrate them through the top of his skull. Resolutely, with great effort, the tall, black-clad figure pulled upright, the long-jawed face confronted them, the blazing stare accused them. But the voice changed subtly to a tone of sadness, edged with concern and regret. And the beginning of understanding.

"Am I too harsh? Am I too harsh? For you are, after all, men. Just men, though fashioned in God's image. Perhaps I aspire for your perfection when we are all of us, after all, imperfect by virtue of our mortality.

"Imperfectly we were conceived in original sin, salvaged through God's mercy by the act of baptism. But are we then

250

cast adrift in the terrifying, abysmal world of unmitigated sin, without hope of ever regaining that fleeting, momentary state of grace given us at the instant of our baptism?"

The question was asked with a rising pitch of hopelessness and despair, his thick silver brows pulled up, puzzled, as though betrayed. His face froze; his hands held in the rigid position, palms up, of asking an unanswerable question.

For the time he let the question hang in the air, every man in the room, young, old, single, married, father, son, every man held his breath, fervently waiting for the next words which would provide them with the mysterious and wonderful, unbelievable yet true means by which they could return to the state of grace they had each of them lost.

"How terrible that would be," Father Sebastian told them. "How unbelievably terrible that would be: a momentary state of true grace, and then everlasting sinfulness and condemnation.

"But we know, you and I, all of us present here in this chapel, we know that our Lord and Savior did not desert us, did not turn from our imperfections. He provided us with the means for a return to grace."

Father Sebastian spoke very softly; his voice went lower and lower and they all leaned forward slightly, unconsciously, to hear the message which they all knew, had known from childhood, but needed to have reaffirmed at this moment.

"Not just one opportunity for a return, not just a second chance but a third and a fourth chance and an endless number of chances, for our Savior's love and mercy are beyond all understanding."

Father Sebastian stood straight and rigid and his head tilted back slightly and his eyes, bright long slits, raked the room from side to side and front to back. He held his long arms upward and his fingers stretched and spread. "We have been given the means for our salvation through the grace and love and charity and suffering of our Lord and Savior, through the medium of our Holy Mother Church, through the suffering and intercession of all the Holy Saints and Martyrs."

Slowly, deliberately, with a hypnotic economy of motion, the long arms were pressed to the thin body and the long white hands were clasped on the lectern.

"Christ gave authority to the Apostles to forgive the sins of the repentant in His name. You know that. You have all been taught how to examine your conscience, how to root out your sins. Each of you knows the obligation to confess and denounce and repent your mortal sins, fully, completely. I charge you with this obligation as Christ charged his Apostles to grant absolution through the sacrament of penance. I charge you with the examination of conscience now, during the next hour which you will spend alone in the cells to which you have been assigned.

"I charge you now," Father Sebastian told them from beneath his brows, "to fulfill your obligations to your Savior as He fulfilled God's obligation to take upon Himself your salvation from the horrors of everlasting hell, from which there is no escape, in which there is no hope, no help, no second chance.

"I will pray for you during this hour," Father Sebastian said, "I will pray that you make a good confession and that the fruits of your confession will lead you closer to the perfection for which our Lord and Savior, in His imponderable wisdom, created us all."

They filed, wordless, silent, thoughtful, appalled, from the chapel without glancing at the priest, who had turned and knelt before the crucifix directly behind the lectern to pray for them.

Brian turned into the small whitewashed, immaculate cell to which he'd been assigned. He sat on the backless stool and held the paper-covered missal which had been presented to him by a young seminarian who had a terrible raw, scabby infection from the corner of his mouth to his chin. As though he'd read Brian's thoughts, the seminarian blinked quickly, ducked his head down.

Who was it had told them that? It wasn't true. Brian knew it wasn't true. Brian knew it because he'd always had a good, clean, clear skin. His sinfulness never showed on his face. He felt sympathy for the poor young seminarian; everybody who looked at the poor kid probably thought the same thing. There was always a priest somewhere, in the ninth or tenth grade, who made every kid with erupted skin feel unclean and vile. Probably on the general assumption that most of them were anyhow.

A pale ray of sunshine shone thin and vaporish as a moonbeam from the small window set high over his head in the thick wall. Too easily distracted, Brian watched the spidery shadows of the new-blossoming tree waver back and forth through the light to create shadows on the wall and along the shiny floor. A bird called out, then was silent. There was nearly total silence all around him. They were in a world removed, apart, remote. He thought of his brother Martin, who had chosen to live forever in such a world, and he felt a new, deep sense of awe and wonder and respect for the courage that such a decision took.

Brian jumped at the approach of the priest, Father McCarthy.

"I didn't mean to startle you, son," he was told in a warm soft brogue. "I just wanted to know if you are in need of any special assistance."

Gentle-voiced, Father McCarthy explained, "I just wanted to see if I could be of any special help and guidance in the examination of conscience. There are some here, you see, who haven't been to church or to confession in a very long time and feel a real sense of fear. I didn't think you were that remote from your Church." Father McCarthy smiled vaguely and told him, "When you hear the bell toll, in about a half hour from now, just come from your cell and take your turn at one of the confessional booths in the chapel, lad."

Then he was gone.

Later, Brian stood inside the chapel, face down, hands clasped before him, patiently shuffling along the slow-moving line, closer to the booth. His lips silently moved in prayer.

"O Lord God, You enlighten every man who comes into this world; enlighten my heart, I pray You, with the light of Your grace that I may fully know my sins, my shortcomings and negligences and may confess them with that true sorrow and contrition of heart which I so much need. I desire to make full amends for all my sins and to avoid them for the future . . ."

The touch on his shoulder was firm. It was Father McCarthy. He kept things moving, directed them into the confessional, led the confessed to some quiet corner for the private recitation of penance.

"Bless me, Father, for I have sinned; it is one week since my last confession."

As he recounted his mortal sins in the sequence he tried to

remember having committed them; the priest interrupted abruptly.

"Using God's name irreverently is a *venial* sin, my son. Now you should know that."

"But I called on God to damn someone, Father," Brian explained. He knew the difference and felt a slight twinge of annoyance.

"Very well, very well. Continue."

The slight edge of impatience put him off a bit; he knew the lines were long, but the minute examination of conscience led to the revealing of unexpected sins and a great desire to confess in detail. He felt a panic he hadn't experienced since the third grade; he didn't want to forget, willingly or unwillingly, any sin which might be crucial.

He spoke of the unmentionable lusts of his flesh without detailing what had already been detailed; yet he'd never felt purged of Rita Wasinski, of his sinful desire for her.

"Father, I . . . I'm not sure about something I did. I know it was wrong, but I'm not sure if it was venial or mortal."

There was a soft patient sigh, then the voice was renewed with kind perseverance. "Tell me about it, my son. Together we will examine it."

Miserably, he told of his encounter with Angelo DiSantini and the girl.

After a short silence, the confessor said, "Neglecting one's job seriously is a doubtful sin, my son. What is it that bothers you most about the fact that you didn't take what you know are prescribed actions?"

"I'm not sure, Father."

"Then I'll pose questions and you find within yourself the answers, my child. Possibly, you are questioning your own motives. Did you feel pity for the boy because of his youth? His circumstances? Did you feel sympathy for the boy? Because you are friends did you grant him special privilege in violation of your vows as a public servant?"

To all questions, rapidly thrown at him, Brian responded in the negative. He hadn't felt pity for Angelo DiSantini. Angelo DiSantini was no friend of his; there had been no special reason he could fathom. And yet, tantalizingly close to the surface of his consciousness lurked the reason and still he could not quite fathom it.

254

Carefully, finally, the priest asked, "You are young, my son, are you not? Not too long on the job?"

"Twenty-two, Father."

"Well. Ah. My son, there are many circumstances you will come upon where you will have to use a special, separate discretion that you will acquire, that I believe you are in the process of acquiring, right now, even though you do not fully understand how or why this is taking place. I think you are sincere and concerned about fulfilling your job obligations with a good conscience, my son?"

"Yes, Father."

"I think you will learn to handle these discretionary actions which will confront you all the years of your life. I think you will make wise decisions which sometimes you will not completely understand yourself. I think you must learn to put yourself more completely in God's hands, for it is truly God's work you seek to do, you in your vineyard, I in mine."

"Yes, Father."

"Have you sincerely made a true confession, my child? Do you sincerely regret your sins?"

"Yes, Father."

Brian knelt quietly in an isolated corner of the chapel, held the beads between his clasped hands, touched the crucifix to his lips briefly after making the sign of the Cross. Silently, lips moving over the words, he prayed.

"I believe in God the Father Almighty, Creator of Heaven and earth: And in Jesus Christ His only Son our Lord: Who was conceived by the Holy Spirit, Born of the Virgin Mary: Suffered under Pontius Pilate, Was crucified, died and was buried: He descended into hell; The third day He rose again from the dead: He ascended into Heaven, and sitteth at the right hand of God the Father Almighty: From thence He shall come to judge the living and the dead. I believe in the Holy Spirit, the Holy Catholic Church, the Communion of Saints, the Forgiveness of sins, the Resurrection of the body and the life everlasting. Amen."

He let the Cross slide from his fingers and he felt the first large bead, which automatically led to the recitation of the "Our Father." Fingers and brain working together, steadily, completely and devoutly determined, Brian prayed the rosary with a slow intensity.

Each word opened and revealed the full depths of meaning which had always been there but which he had taken for granted. Unaware of anyone else present in the chapel, Brian O'Malley felt within himself the presence of his God, his Savior and his Holy Mother Church.

The voices were muffled and indistinct, the kind of voices heard in a dream. Brian knew it wasn't a dream for he was totally, alertly awake. The hard narrow cot provided no comfort for his long body and he shifted restlessly from side to stomach to back until finally the sounds of conversation drew him from the bed to the window, which was high over his head.

He slid the stool against the wall and hoisted himself up for a view into the moonlit garden. There was a group of men some ten feet from his window, some standing, some squatting, some leaning against trees in a semicircle. He couldn't see their faces but there were two unmistakable clerical collars among them. Carefully, soundlessly, he pushed the leaded-glass window outward on its hinges and the voices became sharper and clearer.

"Well, what the hell, there's no need for that kind of organization and I don't care what you say. There's just a handful of Jews so it's natural for them to organize. Everyone knows they want to stay with their own."

"But that's not the point, don't you see? You've got the guineas in their Columbus Society—"

"Columbia, man, *Columbia* Society."

"Ah, well, all right then, whatever it is. Say, pass that bottle will you, Father." A deep laugh followed. "Ah, I think the lads here keep me talking so's I'll miss my turn at that fine Scotch."

"No, Captain Hennessy, not at all, not at all. It's just that it doesn't seem hardly necessary for *us* to organize when, for the love of God, the Irish *are* the Police Department!"

"I'll drink to that!"

"Not on my round you won't."

"And wasn't Father Sebastian in rare form this afternoon, Father?" That was the captain.

Brian recognized Father McCarthy's voice. It seemed somewhat mellowed by whiskey. "Ah, yes, he's a fine one, all right. Gets you so worked up there isn't a man jack of you doesn't want to stay in that confessional booth for an hour and a half.

By the time he gets through with you lads, you've gone all the way back to confessing the time you wondered what was beneath Sister Ann-Jeanine's flowing black habit, and that's a fact. All very well for him," the priest observed dryly, "he comes from his fine Jesuits and talks all hell and fire and leaves the bloody lot of you to us. My head aches for three days after the bunch of youse leave. Well, God knows, I need this bit of relief that you've kindly brought around with you. Here, now Sean, pass that over to me like a good lad."

Carefully, aware of the weight of his body along the straining muscles of his arms, Brian lowered himself to the floor. He leaned his forehead against the rough-textured whitewashed wall for a moment and felt the blood rush painfully with sharp needle bursts through the veins of his arms. He accepted the unpleasant sensation as penance for the unnatural pressure he had exerted on his arms; it was punishment for having listened to talk that did not concern him.

It was an offering in hope that through the graceful acceptance of this physical reminder of his imperfection, he could be restored to the incomprehensible state of innocence and trust and faith and purity and belief in which he had dwelt for most of the evening.

Or that he could fall onto the narrow cot and plunge into dreamless and uncomplicated sleep.

He recognized the bulk and voice of the man from his shadowy view of the garden the night before. He recognized the deep-red flush, the small beads of eyes from some other time he could not immediately recall.

"Jasus, I'd swear his father stood before me, he's that much Brian O'Malley," Captain Peter Hennessy said to the two men flanking him.

"He is, oh, yes, indeed, Captain, he is that," Patrolman Charlie Gannon eagerly agreed.

Brian recognized Lieutenant Shea from his silent, alert presence at his father's funeral more than three years ago.

"Well, Brian," Lieutenant Shea said easily, "you remember Captain Hennessy and Patrolman Gannon of course."

He did it smoothly and easily and Brian shook hands with the three men. "Yes, sir, of course. Captain, how are you, sir?"

"On the job are you, lad?" Captain Hennessy asked pointlessly. His large, soft, fat hand was moist and held Brian's for a moment.

"Well, yes, sir. Class of '40."

Hennessy turned to Shea. "Well, what do you think, Ed? The living image, wouldn't you say?"

Shea nodded. Charlie Gannon's eyes danced over Brian, then darted to Hennessy. He grinned. "Well, well, so here we have Sergeant O'Malley's son. Yes, isn't that fine, then."

"You've a lot to live up to, O'Malley," Captain Hennessy said. "Wouldn't you say so, Ed? Huh, Charlie?"

Shea didn't move or change expression. Gannon's grin pulled uncertainly at the corners of his mouth until he caught the dead earnestness of the captain. "Oh, yes, indeed, Captain, for wasn't poor Sergeant O'Malley a very fine man."

Gannon, at some barely communicated signal, retreated a few steps behind them. Hennessy motioned Brian to walk along the broad tree-lined path through the monastery grounds. Though they were supposed to be spending the hour before lunch in quiet, solitary contemplation, Brian noticed that most of the men had fallen into groups of three or four and some of the conversations were very animated, then suddenly broken off in realization of the inappropriateness of loud voices.

Brian was uncomfortable in the presence of Captain Hennessy. The penetrating stare did not intimidate him though Brian knew it was meant to. But it seemed that something had been indicated without having been expressed, that Gannon and Shea and Hennessy searched him for something known only to them, each in his own way. Hennessy regarded him with a curious, open hardness; Shea with a subtle blankness; Gannon with quick uncertain glances.

"Well, isn't this a lovely place to be?" Hennessy said. "I'll just stop and sit on this little marble bench for a moment and breathe in some of the fine clean air. Well, the Fathers of Holy Contemplation have a fine place here and that's a fact."

Brian took his cue from Shea and remained quiet while Gannon, apparently unable to bear a moment of silence, nodded vigorously and agreed with the captain. "Yes. Oh, yes, indeed, lovely, lovely."

"Take a nice walk for yourself, Charlie, and we'll see you at lunchtime," Captain Hennessy abruptly instructed Gannon. Gannon nodded and took off immediately.

Hennessy was seated in the center of the marble bench, which would accommodate three normal-sized men, but which at the moment accommodated the massive flesh of Peter Hennessy. He studied Brian, then asked him a series of abrupt, unconnected questions, as though testing his alertness.

"And how is your mother getting on?"

"Fine, thank you, Captain."

"There were a great number of Jews in your class at the Academy, weren't there?"

"Yes. I guess so."

"You've some younger children still at home, haven't you?"

"Yes, sir. My oldest sister is married and has two kids of her own. I've a brother in the seminary and a brother and sister in school."

"Where is it they've got you working?"

"Clinton Street station, Captain. Ninth Precinct."

"You've not been active in the Holy Name, have you, O'Malley? And why is that?"

"Well . . . this is my first retreat. I guess I'm just getting around to it, Captain."

"You've got to be tough on the younger ones, lad. Got to keep them in line."

Brian licked his lips and played safe. "Yes, sir."

"Well, you've something fine to live up to, haven't you, O'Malley? Dad was a regular hero then." The small eyes radiated at Brian. "I was with him at the moment he died. You knew that, didn't you?"

Before Brian could respond, Captain Hennessy leaned heavily forward, one hand on each widespread knee. He exhaled a huge gasping sound and said, "We got them nigger bastards, don't worry none about them." His full mouth bunched as though he was about to whistle, but he didn't. "Poor Brian, may he rest in peace. Did you ever see the young Jew was with your dad that night? His driver, if you please?"

Brian could recall nothing and shook his head.

"Levine was the little kike's name. Your dad might be alive today if it hadn't been for him, isn't that a fact, Ed?"

259

Brian noticed that Shea said nothing, neither confirmed nor denied.

"Yes," Hennessy went on as though Shea had given him full agreement, "your dad caught some bullets meant for Levine."

"Well, he got shot too, didn't he, Captain?" Brian asked carefully.

Hennessy's face pulled upwards; his massive cheeks raised and the corners of his mouth pulled into a grimace. His eyes were lost somewhere in the flesh. He raised his arm and grunted as though he was strangling; it took Brian a moment to figure out what the gesture meant: Hennessy was pointing to his own back.

"He caught a bullet all right, lad. He caught a bullet through the back of the shoulder. Notice I said through the *back* of the shoulder. Running from the scene, which shouldn't surprise anyone's had any dealings with the race. Maybe your father, may he rest in peace, maybe had one of his own been on the scene at the crucial time, he'd be alive and well and here with us in this holy place. Ah, isn't this a fine, grand garden though?"

Hennessy gazed around with pleasure, resettled his hands on his knees, then said, "Now this Patrolman Aaron Levine," he drawled the name slowly, with distaste, "he's got himself set up quite nicely. God knows how he pulled it, but somehow or other, he got himself assigned to steady midnights at a clerical job out in Brooklyn. In one of them nice quiet Jew neighborhoods where he can probably sleep his eight hours. And in the daytime, if you please, our Mr. Levine goes off to Brooklyn College. That's where he goes, isn't it, Ed?"

For the first time, Shea spoke. "Yes, Captain. He's got his bachelor's degree and now he's going for his master's degree."

"God love us, whatever they may be, they're not for the likes of us, for we're but simple policemen trying to do our job with God's help. Isn't that the truth of the matter, O'Malley?"

Brian had the uncomfortable feeling that Hennessy was playing with him, that he might be led to say something, anything, at any given moment, which would cause the small sharp eyes to pin him to the wall. He glanced at Shea: noncommittal, expressionless. He nodded senselessly.

"Ah, lads"—Captain Hennessy stood up noisily—"we are most fortunate to be here, to be part of this, hey?" His hand waved expansively and the gesture included not just the garden, the retreat, but the larger domain which Captain Hennessy claimed on their behalf.

"I just thought of something, Captain," Lieutenant Shea said. "I could use young Brian for that special assignment I've got coming up next Friday night."

Hennessy sucked air in, then blew it out through pursed lips before he turned his bright eyes from Brian to Ed Shea. "What might that be, Ed? Remind me; what assignment are we talking about?"

"The senior dance for the girls at the Holy Mary Academy. I was to be on the lookout for some clean-cut young patrolmen for duty at the school that night."

Hennessy nodded vigorously. "Yes, yes, by God. He'll do. He'll just do fine. Give his C.O. a call when we get back, Ed. And you mind yourself, O'Malley, and something might be worked out for you." He pulled his mouth into a wide smile which showed a collection of tiny teeth, then pursed his lips again; it hadn't been a smile, just a characteristic tic. "We owe it to your poor dad, may he rest in peace, to look after his son. Isn't that a fact, Ed?"

By late afternoon Saturday, the second day of the retreat, Captain Hennessy was rushed to the nearest hospital by ambulance for emergency treatment of a bleeding ulcer. As the two ambulance attendants, assisted by a white-faced Charlie Gannon, struggled with the dead weight from infirmary to ambulance, Hennessy turned his face to one side and with hardly a sound vomited a huge puddle from which emanated powerful whiskey fumes.

Rumors of a fistfight between two detectives from the Bronx made the rounds. There are many versions of what had occurred and they ranged from several good punches thrown to a .38 detective special being pressed against the loser's forehead and an apology the price for its withdrawal. Speculation as to the cause of the altercation included mention of a certain female who had bestowed her charms on a rotating basis between both men.

Those who knew the true facts didn't tell; those who didn't know caught on to bits and pieces and concocted their own more complicated versions.

Father McCarthy wandered the grounds distractedly, hands clenched and lips moving. The young seminarians watched from beneath lowered eyelids. Father McCarthy explained to them, though some were the sons of policemen and needed no such explanation, that their weekend retreatants were a rough group of men, used to facing up to violence as a way of life and it was a miracle and a blessing that they even made any attempt at all periodically to try to get their souls in order somewhat.

"We can't judge them harshly and that's a fact," Father McCarthy said as he eyed a group just behind the outdoor statue of St. Francis. The gestures and postures of the men could hardly be mistaken for piety. "Well, there's not many of us would stand in their shoes and it's not for us to judge them, lads."

Brian blinked and squinted against the strong sunlight, made stronger by contrast to the darkness of the small chapel where he had spent the last hour and a half. He had listened in a paralysis of rapidly dissipating good intention and steadily growing boredom to some heavily accented, middle-aged, monotoned monk who called upon them to devote the first Monday of every month to the recitation of a rosary for the conversion of Russia. In a calculating glance at the few others present beside himself, Brian figured maybe one guy would keep the pledge they all made to the monk. And that was a tall, bald guy with rimless glasses named Joseph Burns.

Joseph Burns was born Joseph Bernstein. When he married an Irish girl some twenty years ago, he took instruction and was simultaneously converted and disowned by the Bernstein family. Though legally his name had been changed to Burns, and his six children were all born to that surname and into the faith and were educated in parochial schools, Bernstein the convert was always spoken of, somewhat derisively, as Bernstein the convert. He never missed Mass, attended every Communion breakfast, every retreat, gave to the parish and to the missions. It was said his oldest daughter had a vocation. If at times a somewhat bewildered exasperation filled him, Bernstein the convert could hardly be blamed for not understanding what more it was his colleagues and coreligionists wanted of him.

They could not put it into words themselves.

As Brian walked across the sun-blazing quadrangle toward the meal hall, he was surprised when Tommy Quill, the P.B.A. delegate, caught up with him. Tommy Quill was generally sought after, not a seeker. He could rarely be found alone; he was generally at the center of an earnest circle.

"Hey, O'Malley. How you doing, kid?"

Quill ran to flesh around the middle, which made him look older than he was because of his poor posture; shoulders hunched forward, knees bent, head ducked down. "Hey, you been in there listening to old Brother Reubin having at the Red Communists? Jesus, the stories I heard about him. I heard that he was a distant relative of the Czar of Russia and once tried to claim some of them jewels. You know, like that nutty dame who keeps popping up and claiming to be Anna something, one of the daughters."

"Really?" Brian said, noncommittal, wondering what Quill wanted.

"Well, kid, how's it going?" Quill said again.

Brian shrugged, which was always a safe response when you weren't too sure what the question was. "Nice place here, Tommy."

"Yeah, sure," Tommy said absently. He jabbed at Brian with an elbow and winked. "Hey, you're pretty cute, O'Malley, huh? You catch on fast."

"What do you mean, Quill?" Brian asked in a tone of voice that indicated he knew *exactly* what Quill meant, even though he didn't have the slightest idea. He'd learned that much: Pretend knowledge, never ignorance.

Quill winked again slowly, held the wink, nodded like an owl, snapped his eyelid up on a startled gray eye. "I seen you walking with Captain Hennessy and Lieutenant Shea this morning after Mass. Smart, kid, smart." Quill tapped his forehead. "Them guys are always good to have on your side, if you know what I mean." Quill glanced over his shoulder, jerked a thumb toward the men who waited for him. "Jesus, these guys don't lemme alone for a minute. Everybody got

263

something he wants done. It's good to see a kid who can take care of himself, O'Malley. Well, duty calls." He sighed wearily but Brian knew it was an act. Quill loved every minute of the attention which was showered on him. "Well, back to the wars, God help us. No rest for the worthy, right, O'Malley?"

Everybody was wheeling and dealing. Practically nobody attended any more of the scheduled talks although everyone strolled the grounds with the printed program of events either clutched in a hand or tucked in a back pocket for easy visibility. Men talked in small groups and the sharp observer could quickly size up the key man in any group. He was the one who affected a bored or blank countenance, upon whose shoulder friendly hands were placed, into whose unwilling ears confidences were offered, pleas were whispered, contracts were arranged.

No one looked anyone else directly in the eye; distances were scanned rapidly and continuously as though in search of hidden and deadly enemies. Out of hearing range, it was difficult to ascertain exactly who was talking to whom; men seemed to address vacant space from lips hidden by cupped hands, as though great and terrible secrets were being cast out for grabs.

The informal meetings began as the reluctant participants were en route, in good faith, to a scheduled talk. Slowly, languidly, kicking pebbles from the path in semblance of serious spiritual contemplation, the policemen, dressed casually and comfortably, moved toward one building or another but were detoured by the call of their name, by the touch of a hand; were drawn into discussions of assignments, details, commendations sought, wrongs inflicted, rights demanded, a little favor or consideration to be arranged. They wandered, drifted, vaporized, never reached their sincerely sought original destination.

The cold salt air had a slight tar flavor, and the raindrops, as they mingled with the spray, tasted to Brian of the ferryboat itself. He didn't want to sit inside the smoky cabin where most of the men were. He felt slightly queasy and his head ached with the constant drone of conversation, which somehow, inside his brain, mingled with the toneless chant of prayer.

Too much of anything was bad for you, whether it was whiskey or women or talk. Taken as a large, uninterrupted dose, the retreat had been too much for Brian. He had attended every lecture, every talk, every Rosary, every confession, every Mass, true to the vow he had made his first night. Though his intention had been pure, the actual quality of his presence violated that intention.

Through narrowed aching eyes, Brian looked toward Manhattan: Sunday-dark concrete forms disconnected from the vast green sweep of Staten Island. He fell into a sad, vacant uneasiness, aware yet disinterested that the clumsy vessel made thudding contact with the heavily padded slip, first one side, then the other. There was a decisive roar of engine, a dark churn of water beneath his feet, then he felt the solid joining of ferry to dock.

"Well, it's always good to get away from all this, to have a chance to straighten yourself out with God," Bernstein the convert said quietly at his elbow.

Brian turned toward the rain-dampened, slightly tense face behind the glinting eyeglasses. He nodded and as noncommittally as possible he said, "Yeah. Yeah, sure is."

TWENTY-FIVE

The Holy Mary Academy stood dark and ominous, a medieval stone castle covered with twisting ivy which nearly obscured the stained-glass windows set high and unobtrusively. From where he stood, the building could have been a mausoleum.

Brian ran a finger inside the collar of his tunic, loosened the hook and eye which bound it closely around his throat. For this crummy assignment, he'd gotten his uniform dry-cleaned and pressed. And his mother had washed his white cotton gloves so that they practically shined in the dark. He studied the fingertips; they were filthy from his thoughtless, admiring touch on the fender of a shining black Chrysler. Most of the cars were Chryslers or Oldsmobiles. There were one or two Lincolns and Cadillacs.

From the parking lot behind the school, Brian could see nothing of the bright lights which pierced the damp May night like slashes of jewels, filtered spotlights of red and blue and gold shining from a rotating disk on the ceiling of the gymnasium. He could hear faint bits of music, just a high flight of trumpet occasionally, then, after a while, the hum of faraway applause.

Special assignment. Big-deal special assignment. Standing guard over the fancy shined-up cars of a bunch of spoiled rich girls. The sergeant, a guy named McCallahan, addressed them like they were hand-picked troops, which they were, of course, but what the hell had they been hand-picked for? To be car-lot attendants, doormen, play nursemaid to a bunch of rich kids, make sure nobody got out of line and if some kid had more to drink than he could handle, smooth it over, take care of things.

Well, Jesus, they all looked spit and polish and not one of them under six feet tall or over twenty-five. What the hell did the school do, put in an order, select them to specification?

"Your job," Sergeant McCallahan had said, "is to insure the safety and well-being of these young people, whose parents are some very important people and who will take a personal interest in how well this here assignment is carried out."

Brian kicked his shoe against the heavy rubber tire of a year-old four-door navy-blue Chrysler sedan. Damn parking-lot attendant who couldn't even risk sitting on a back seat for a break because the s.o.b. sergeant gave him a look every forty minutes or so. That's how much *he* had to do.

"Hey, you O'Malley?"

He turned, coughed to cover the fact that he'd been taken by surprise. "Yeah, that's me."

A hand was thrust at him and Brian returned the hard handshake. "Hi ya, I'm Ed Shea," the familiar but slightly off-center face told him.

"Ed Shea?"

"Yeah. I'm from the Forty-eighth. Sergeant McCallahan sent me out to relieve you. They've got some sandwiches for us in the basement." He pulled a mouth, then grinned. "Better than nothing, but that's about what they're better than. I understand the young ladies made them with their own dainty hands. Don't try the devil's food cake — tastes like the devil's revenge."

"Okay, thanks for the warning." Brian hesitated, then asked, "Ed Shea? You related to Lieutenant Shea?"

"Only by birth. He's my father."

"Jesus, you're a ringer for him."

Shea took off his hat and scratched his curly dark head. "I'm himself less twenty years," he said good-naturedly. "Well, what do you think of this special assignment, O'Malley?"

Brian shrugged, careful.

Shea, who was slightly taller than Brian and thinner, jammed his hat back on his head and held out his arms expansively. "Sure it's a wondrous thing, protectin' all them marvelous automobiles from the plunder of pirates and such kind!" His imitation of McCallahan was good and funny. Brian liked Shea.

"What are the girls like, Ed?"

"These are not 'girls,' O'Malley. These are young ladies. In fact, these are the daughters of some of the most very important people on the face of the earth, if you take my meaning, lad." He cupped his hand over his mouth and said, "Mostly a bunch of dry-looking sticks. Half of them go stiff as soon as the music stops, when they realize they're actually in some guy's arms. You never saw such fast disengaging of couples in your life. Not that they get really close, there are more damn parents and nuns fluttering around. In fact and in summation, not a good lay in the house!"

Brian shrugged. "Can't win 'em all. How's the music. I can't hear a damn thing out here."

"Let's put it this way, O'Malley. They *try* very hard. The sax isn't bad but thank God they keep the trumpet muted. The poor bastard gets all revved up for a high note and can't get anywhere near it. They're all pretty good at facial expressions though. You know, all that narrowing of eyes stuff that's supposed to get to the girls."

Shea posed, hands in front of him, fingering keys, eyes narrowed and lashes batting. "You play anything, O'Malley?"

"I used to blow bugle." On a sudden impulse, because Ed Shea was so relaxed and easygoing, because it had been a long and lonely night and he was restless and felt like making noise, Brian brought his fingers to his lips, held the imaginary bugle, tilted his head back and played the invisible instrument. He felt his lips tingle with effort as he forced out "When Johnny Comes Marching Home."

"Oh, Jesus, on Memorial Day, down the length of the Grand Concourse," Ed Shea said. He hoisted a huge weight, sketched with his arms the bass drum, which had been his instrument. "Shea the dum-dum man, boy wonder, who sets the marchin' feet to marchin' for St. Martin's of the Holy Cross!" He made a banging motion and emitted a hollow sound from his chest. "Thud! Thump! Thud! Thump!"

They didn't realize how loud they were in the silence of the parking lot.

Lieutenant Shea had a hand on each of them before either of them was aware of his presence. Brian froze with a terrible sense of humiliation and shame; his hands were poised foolishly at his lips, his head tilted back. He closed his eyes and wished reality away.

"Now you know where the real fun is," Ed Shea said calmly to his father.

Brian opened his eyes as he felt the hard hand relax on his shoulder. He glanced quickly at Ed, then at Lieutenant Shea. He felt his face turn hot.

"Well, I'll tell the pair of you this," Lieutenant Shea said quietly. "You'd be written off as a pair of fools or clowns if it was Sergeant McCallahan and not me came upon you. And you'd be taken as a pair of easy incompetents were I an auto thief. I'd have been able to make off with my choice beneath the beating of your drum and the tooting of your horn. What the hell tune were you attempting, anyway? It sounded nothing but noise to me."

Brian ran a hand quickly across his mouth and said, "Well, I think we were probably playing the 'Fools' March,' Lieutenant. And I guess we made a pretty good job of it."

Lieutenant Shea regarded him for a moment, then smiled tightly and nodded. He looked from Brian to his son, then told them, "Well, the pair of you could end up on report, larking like a pair of schoolboys. I didn't expect better sense out of you," he told his son totally without rancor, "but Brian O'Malley, I thought you were more of a grownup. Go on now, are you on meal relief or what?"

At the entrance to the car lot, Brian met Sergeant McCallahan. "Did you hear some noises back there, O'Malley? Sounded like some kids."

"Couple of kids walking down the street, Sergeant. They were playing parade."

The sergeant's face screwed into a puzzled expression. "Playing parade? What the hell does that mean, 'playing parade'?"

Brian shrugged. "You know how kids are, Sarge. They were tooting on make-believe horns and banging on make-believe drums."

The sergeant made a disgusted sound. "Ought to be home in bed. They'd get their asses kicked if they were mine, out this time of night, playing parade. I'd play them a parade."

"Yes, Sergeant."

The nun behind the long gray-painted table in the basement of the Holy Mary Academy dispensed chopped-egg and tunafish-salad sandwiches as though she were rendering a great charity to those accustomed to grabbing with both hands.

"One of each," she instructed Brian as he held the paper plate over the meager supply of food. "You're entitled to one of each and some potato salad"—a finger pointed out each item as she named it—"and some coleslaw, but go easy on that, please. We've four more policemen besides you to feed and the policemen who ate on the first shift weren't very considerate of their fellow officers. Besides," she advised him, "you're late, seems to me."

She blinked her thick, short red eyelashes over her pale-blue eyes and faced Brian with her accusation. He immediately declined both the potato salad and the coleslaw and her mouth pursed in disapproval for she had no more patience with martyrs than she did with gluttons.

All the physical signs indicated that Sister Margaret St. John was a warm, jolly, robust young woman with a friendly and open manner. She was large-boned, heavy-fleshed and the pale skin of her broad-nosed face was splashed with deep-orange clusters of freckles that looked like water paint. The backs of her hands were similarly stained, and from the heavy dark-orange eyebrows, there was no question that her hair, what was left of it cropped beneath her habit, was as riotously bright as any red hair could be. Physical appearances aside, she was a dour, sharp, cold, alert and antagonistic woman accustomed to dealing with a roomful of adolescent girls who were accustomed to being told what to do, when and how to do it.

"It's been provided for you men," she said as she spooned a scant amount of salad next to Brian's sandwiches, "and we've no wish to have it left over."

Brian murmured, "Thank you, Sister."

He walked across the gray-painted concrete floor to a folding table, managed to get the cup of coffee and paper plate of food set down without dropping his hat, which had been tucked under his arm. He put the hat on his lap. He didn't think Sister Margaret St. John would be too pleased if he put it on the table and he didn't want to put it on the floor, so there was nowhere else to put it.

Music vibrated overhead. They were playing "Moonlight and Roses" and the trumpet was trying a solo with mixed results. The other musicians must have thought so too; they joined in and the trumpet got lost. But the sound was nice; filtered through the ceiling, it had a rich mellow feel. Brian imagined how it would be to hold one of those pink girls against him. He'd had a quick glimpse when he entered the building, not of any particular girl, just of fluffy pink-and-white forms drifting around the room, being led and guided by their carefully selected escorts. As they breezed by the doorway through which he watched, they gave off an essence of soft, sweet femininity and innocence and perfection, but mostly of softness.

The thought of all that softness, of all those female legs moving against the pink material, making contact through the pinkness with the hard masculine legs, the quick suggestive touch, the sudden unexpected whirl in time to a flurry of music, which would bring the pink body close for a fleeting, exciting contact, made Brian nearly gag on the dry egg-salad sandwich.

He was glad that the light was dim, that there was a table between him and Sister Margaret St. John, that he had his hat on his lap. That made it more exciting, the hiddenness of his excitement. It occurred to him that he should have better control, that he should not let the close inaccessibility of faceless young girls get him into this state. At the same time, he felt a warmth and strange pleasure in the fact that he could get an erection so easily.

An unconvincing vocalist wailed "Embrace me, my sweet embraceable you" in a monotone. Brian chewed a hunk of sandwich slowly, visualized how he would stride across the room, reach out for a juicy pink body, show her what it meant to embrace, to hold against each other, to press against each other and crush the billow of pink skirt between them.

Christ. A crumb of egg went into his windpipe. Brian coughed with a chest-deep pain and hacking that brought tears to his eyes and Sister Margaret St. John to his side. She thumped the center of his back soundly several times until he nodded that he was all right. Then she gave him a tremendous blow, right in the small of his back. It nearly knocked him to the floor.

"There," she said, "that will do the trick."

Brian felt pain run down his spine, shoot into his right buttock and knot the calf of his leg. "Sister," he sputtered, "you

271

could paralyze a person hitting him like that." Carefully, he tested his leg and stood up.

"Nonsense," Sister Margaret St. John told him briskly. "That was done scientifically. There's a nerve center between the two vertebrae and a good solid blow, properly done, clears up any difficulties." As she spoke, she gathered the half-filled paper plate, the empty paper cup and brushed a few crumbs from the table. "I take it you're finished eating, officer."

The pale eyes informed him that he *was* finished eating. Brian felt a tingling down to the toes of his right foot, but by the time he climbed the iron stairs to the main floor, he was all right. He put on his hat and pulled the visor so that it was at a slightly jaunty angle.

"O'Malley, step in here a minute," Sergeant McCallahan called to him.

On the door, in gold letters, was the word "Principal." As he approached the door, Brian had the totally irrational feeling of a schoolboy. There was a thud in the pit of his stomach; his heart pumped so hard he could feel a vein pulsating along his temple. An awareness of imperfections, guilt for all his shortcomings, filled him.

"Come over here for a minute." Lieutenant Shea stood near the huge stained-glass window which covered most of one of the thick whitewashed stone walls. Brian tried to assume an expression of innocence. Miraculously, Lieutenant Shea spoke pleasantly; Brian hadn't done anything wrong, or been found out.

"Brian, a bit of a problem has come up. One of the lads seems to have slipped some whiskey into himself along with the punch and it seems he can't handle it. I've sent Patrolman Shea along to see he gets home without killing himself in the process."

Sergeant McCallahan reappeared at the doorway. "Lieutenant, I've your car ready and waiting, sir."

"Right, Sergeant, thanks." With a gesture, he sent the sergeant away. Shea shook his head slightly. "We've a fire at 230th Street. An apartment house, pretty bad from all reports, and I've been dispatched to supervise our lads on the scene. They've had one fireman seriously hurt and two overcome from the smoke. Oh, but here's what I wanted to know, Brian. You've your driver's license, haven't you?"

He didn't but he wasn't about to disappoint Lieutenant Shea. He *did* know how to drive. "Yes, sir."

"Fine, that's fine." He dug in his pocket and came up with a set of keys. "The girl has to be taken home, you see. The lad was in no condition, and we're responsible." He handed the keys to Brian. "Now, these are for my own car, Brian. It's the '38 Ford you'll see off to the left." He grinned. "Hell, it's the *only* Ford you'll see, so no problem in finding it."

"Black Ford, right, sir?" Brian asked, displaying his alertness.

"That's the one. Now, briefly, O'Malley, here's the assignment." The steady brown eyes searched Brian's face and the confidential voice advised him of the importance of the task. "You're to take the girl directly home, see she gets inside the house, and all with no fuss and bother." He reached out and fingered Brian's tunic. "Slip this off, and the hat, and leave them in the car. We wouldn't want the girl's neighbors to start all kinds of stories and speculation about a policeman bringing the girl home. Then just bring my car back here and leave it and I'll get it later. I hope to God there'll be no more injured at that fire. Oh, and, Brian, you can take off for home once you've returned."

Brian touched his cap quickly and felt the weight of the keys inside his palm. That was a break. His whole tour would only have lasted four hours; maybe that was the special part of the special assignment.

The music drifted through the grimly lit corridor and he waited just outside the principal's office. Waited for one of the pink and soft and female bodies to be presented to him.

Brian clenched his hand tightly over the rough edges of the keys. Hell, he had to stop thinking like a goddamn schoolboy.

She was a head taller than the tiny nun who glided along beside her, but to Brian she was as small and delicate as a doll. She had soft, long pale hair, caught up on each side of her face with narrow pink ribbon. Vague, unruly curls, the color of moonlight, cascaded along her shoulders, which were covered by a shawl the same color and material as her dress. In his one encompassing glance, Brian saw the fragility of the girl's body. Her waist was so small his two hands could span it easily.

"Are you Patrolman O'Malley?" the nun asked.

Brian touched his cap respectfully. "Yes, Sister."

The nun patted the girl's arm. "Don't you worry, Mary Ellen. This officer will see you home. You're not to worry now."

The girl nodded and kept her face down as they walked to the parking lot. Brian felt awkward and clumsy. There was too much of him; his feet were too heavy; he was afraid he might brush one of the tiny pink-satin shoes or that his rough arm might brush against her, that he might hurt her in some way. She seemed so vulnerable; if he sneezed, she'd be blown right down the front stairs of the school.

Christ. She was beautiful.

Her face was delicate perfection: high cheekbones clearly outlined by the fine, nearly translucent skin which was just slightly flushed by her agitation; a delicate straight nose; lips just palely pink and moist. Her brows were dark accents for her large mysterious eyes. They slanted slightly and in the dim light were of indeterminate color, the kind of blue that changed to gray or green, protected by long spidery lashes.

She gathered her full skirt into her small hands as they crossed the parking lot. The sound of her legs against layers of exotic material nearly maddened Brian. He wondered what it would be like to carefully, deliberately peel away layer after layer after layer . . .

She walked around the car and waited as he got the driver's door opened, leaned across, pulled the lock up, then raced around the front of the car to help her get settled in.

He leaned down, caught the sweet fragrance that floated from her. He brushed the edge of her skirt. "It'll get caught in the door," he said.

Her hands grabbed and pulled distractedly and he saw her bite her lower lip. Tears shimmered around the rim of her huge eyes and she turned her face away.

Brian started the car without any trouble and pulled out of the parking lot before he realized he hadn't turned on the headlights. He risked a glance at the girl, but she was turned from him, one handkerchief-clutching hand pressed to her face.

"Well, you live up near Manhattan College, right? You'll have to direct me, I'm afraid."

274

"All right. Just keep going up this street to Fort John, then a left turn."

Brian suddenly remembered something. He pulled the car to the curb. She turned to him, her face showing alarm. "I forgot to take off my uniform tunic and hat." He tossed them onto the back seat, felt a little uncomfortable in his checked sports shirt. She had a terrible, stricken look. In the shadowed light from the streetlamp, she seemed like one of those ageless, sexless, beautiful, oddly provocative but eternally untouchable little princesses in storybooks.

Brian dug a cigarette from his shirt pocket, then dug again for the pack and offered her one. She accepted the cigarette and leaned over his cupped hand, touched it lightly as she inhaled. As he lit his own cigarette, the girl suddenly started to choke.

"Hey, you okay?" Brian asked.

She gasped, held her hand over her face for a moment, then handed him the cigarette. In a bewildered, totally helpless voice, she said, "I don't smoke."

Brian regarded her curiously, then said, "Then why did you take a cigarette?"

She stared at him for about two seconds, then her face melted, collapsed. She brought both hands to her face and tried to stifle the sobs.

Brian felt pure panic. She was a small heap of misery. He rolled the window down, tossed both cigarettes away, had a fleeting wave of anxiety: Jesus, what if the sergeant or lieutenant should come by now? This was immediately replaced by a feeling of shame for that unworthy concern.

"Hey, come on," he said softly, "don't cry. Look, it's no big deal. I don't care if you smoke or not." She shook her head from side to side, and Brian said gently, "I'm only teasing. I know that's not why you're crying. What happened, you have a fight with your boy friend?"

She raised her face and her voice surprised him: it was strong and almost angry. "He's *not* my boy friend. I *hate* Teddy Fairley. He's a sloppy, messy *fool* of a boy."

Brian rested his elbow on the steering wheel and his face against his hand. "Well, I'm glad we cleared that up. That means he's not worth crying about, right?"

Brian took out a clean white handkerchief from his back pocket and handed it to her. The gesture made him feel wise and mature and protective and strange. When she refused to accept it, he cupped her small heart-shaped face in the palm of one hand and carefully blotted her cheeks.

"Now, you gonna blow your nose by yourself or do I have to do everything?"

She smiled slightly and took the handkerchief.

"Fine. By the way, now that you've blown your nose into my handkerchief, it's only right that we introduce ourselves properly. I'm Brian O'Malley."

"I'm Mary Ellen Crowley." It was a soft, elegant, musical announcement. He had never heard a voice as clear and sweet.

"Well, Mary Ellen Crowley, would you please tell me how to get to your house because this Bronx boy doesn't know this section of the Bronx at all."

It took less than ten minutes for them to reach the long, steep winding hill which outlined one edge of the Manhattan College campus.

At the top of the hill was the world of Riverdale.

It was a wooded, carefully groomed village of huge English Tudor and sprawling French Normandy houses, with an occasional colonial. Each house was set far back from the street, protected behind thick hedges and stone fences with deep lawns and thick shrubbery. The streets curved and circled and the streetlamps glowed dully from ornate posts. The whole area had a shrouded, mysterious look: foreign, remote.

Brian thought, Nobody really lives in these houses.

"The third house on the right," Mary Ellen Crowley said.

Even as he slowed the car and turned onto the long driveway, he didn't believe it. Even though he caught sight of the numbers on the signpost and they were the same as the numbers on the slip of paper Lieutenant Shea had given him, he couldn't believe that he was sitting beside a girl who actually lived in a huge stone castle in Riverdale. Which was in the Bronx.

She fumbled at her skirt. Her fingers dug and grappled with the billowing material. She asked him not to get out, but he was out and around to her side before she could protest again.

276

A breeze caught at her dress, whipped it around her for a moment. There had been just the smallest hint, suggestion, of a body beneath the material and Brian wanted to plunge his hands through the fabric and find the body that hid within, feel its shape and dimension and warm fleshiness. At the same time, he felt rigidly proper and respectful and didn't even touch her arm as she alighted from the car.

She turned her face from the brightly lighted house and her voice was so thin it almost trembled. "Thanks very much, but you don't have to walk to the door with me." She added "Please" and it sounded almost desperate.

Before he had a chance to reply, the massive front door opened inward, bright lights flashed on overhead so that they were spotlighted from hidden lights all around the driveway. Mary Ellen put her hands over her face and ran into the house. For a split second, Brian imagined a flurry of sympathetic family gathering around her, comforting the stricken princess of the manor.

"Get the hell over here and let's have a look at you, you little bastard!"

The voice was as raw as a flesh wound, ragged and tough and ugly. It didn't go with the house, the lawn, the stone wall. Most of all, it didn't go with anyone connected in any way with Mary Ellen Crowley. Brian felt a stiffening down the back of his neck, a tightening along his throat. He rolled his fingers into the palms of his hands and stepped forward, not in response to the command directed at him, but for some vaguer reasons: curiosity or anger or even from some misguided notion of valor. He was not about to leave Mary Ellen Crowley without finding out to what it was she was abandoned.

"Get over here, in the light where I can see you," the voice ordered.

Since the lights were shining directly on his face, Brian was at a distinct disadvantage. The owner of the raspy voice was seen as a dark faceless outline who leaned, right-handed, on a long walking stick which he abruptly raised toward the interior of the house.

The man turned and limped in without the slightest doubt that Brian would follow and go where directed. Brian entered and found himself in a vast entrance hall, as large as any three

277

ordinary living rooms he'd ever seen. It was high-ceilinged, stone-floored, with a wide stairway which led to upper floors and balconies.

There were arches and heavy polished doors and a feeling of age and wealth and splendor, but Brian wasn't permitted time to look around. The man knocked a door open with the head of his stick and Brian followed as his host limped into a room as massive as the entrance hall. There was a stone fireplace that took up one entire wall, side to side, floor to ceiling.

The man spun around unexpectedly and his face was six inches from Brian's. It was thin and tense and filled with building rage, but the focus of his glare went past Brian, for he hissed, "Get upstairs, you little hussy! You get upstairs. I'll deal with you later!"

Brian turned and caught just the flutter of pink as Mary Ellen Crowley fled, wordless, from the room. She was followed by a silent, tear-stained little woman.

Christ, this crazy old bastard had to be her father.

"Look, Mr. Crowley," he began carefully.

The walking stick was raised to an inch below his chin. "You shut up until I put a question to you, and then you give an answer!"

Brian's mouth fell open in surprise. This dried-up old guy was unbelievable. Brian debated walking out right now and letting the old guy rant and rave. But again, curiosity held him, and beneath the curiosity, a sense of personal assault and violation made him stand and watch as the man hobbled to a dark-brown upholstered chair.

He leaned both hands on the walking stick and rested his chin on his hands as he studied Brian carefully, taking in the black shoes, navy trousers, red-and-white-checked shirt.

Seated, Crowley appeared to be hopelessly deformed; his knees jutted against the fabric of his trousers like gnarled growths. His right shoulder stretched up around his ear while his left shoulder sloped downward. The old man moved about in the chair, seemed to be searching for the proper spot that would conform to his strange contours. He thrust both legs out straight before him, stiff as sticks, then stretched his arms after he leaned the walking stick against the chair, then he folded his limbs as though they were inanimate mechanical objects.

After all of these fascinating maneuvers, he ended up in exactly the same position as when he had started. His eyes, which blinked continuously, were small, pale, watery blue. They searched around Brian, over his head, past his shoulder, to the left side and the right side of him until finally they found Brian's face, fixed on him, stopped blinking.

"Sit down," he said and a long bone of a finger indicated a chair. It was a wooden chair, without arms, slightly lower than that on which Mr. Crowley sat. When Brian hesitated, the old man thumped impatiently on the floor with his stick. "Goddamn it," he said, "sit down, you little bastard, when you're told to sit down."

Brian sat down, filled with an icy sense of wonder at his self-control.

"All right. Now, well, you're not the one she left with," Crowley said shrewdly. "She left with Tom Fairley's lad." He stared somewhere between Brian's lips and throat, as though to seek out the truth from the very source of his voice. Crowley hunched forward and seemed even more lopsided. "All right. You're no college boy." A quick tilt of his head dismissed Brian's clothes in no uncertain terms. "I don't want any shit from you; you answer my questions." The eyes met Brian's with a cold, calculating, knowing gaze. "Who *are* you? What do you *do?* And where the hell did you meet *her?*"

Brian ran his tongue along the inside of his lower teeth and took measure; the old son of a bitch, trying to bullshit him like he was a scared seventeen-year-old kid. He smiled, leaned forward and said very softly, "I'm Brian O'Malley. I'm a *pimp.* And I picked *her* up at a school dance." He jerked his thumb over his shoulder for casual emphasis, then shrugged. "She might have the makings, but I'm not sure yet."

The blue eyes congealed. The thin lips pulled downward and froze. The long-fingered clawlike hand released the stick and rubbed ferociously at the blade-thin sharp nose, then clutched again at the knob of the stick, which balanced between his high knees. His lips split apart in the sudden, irrevocable way the edges of a terrible wound split, but instead of flesh and blood, long, white, unexpectedly dazzling teeth were revealed.

Crowley's strange body was overwhelmed by spasmodic motion over which he seemed to have no control. His feet stamped alternately, causing the high knees to rise and fall in an almost galloping pace. The palms of his hands slapped first at the arms of the dark chair, then at the accelerating knees.

Crowley's face, long and fleshless as a skull, went from dead white to bright pink, then darkened to an alarming shade of purplish blue. Strange gagging, sputtering sound struggled deep inside his scrawny neck, as though he was trying to bring up a bone.

Brian, at first stunned and then appalled by the fantastic contortions, thought the old man was either having some kind of attack or had gone completely mad. The worst part of it was that it was *his* fault. He should have just kept his mouth shut and left. Now it was too late.

My God, Brian thought, what'll I do if this old nut strangles himself or something?

He leaned over the jerking body but couldn't think of a single thing to do except place his hand on a bony shoulder and ask with some alarm, "Hey, Mr. Crowley, are you okay? Can I do anything for you?"

Crowley gasped and wheezed and indicated with a series of head movements that Brian should lean close to his mouth to receive a message which could not travel very far from his lips.

Incredibly, Patrick Crowley, in a hacking, strangulating sound, whispered into Brian O'Malley's unbelieving ear, "You bastard, you bastard, I like you, you little son of a bitch! You're the first little bastard with any *guts!*"

TWENTY-SIX

When Patrick Joseph Crowley arrived as an immigrant from Knockraha, a tiny hamlet just twelve miles from Cork, he was thirty-seven years old and had just buried his widowed mother. He left behind eight brothers and five sisters and too many nephews and nieces to bother counting.

He brought with him a sense of unaccustomed freedom. All prearrangements were canceled. As the oldest son, the scrap of poor land which had become his wasn't worth a damn, never had been, never would be. After the ordeal of watching the old woman through her hard and lingering death, some unknown claim asserted itself within him: he was tired of his hard and lingering life.

For the price of his ticket to New York and a few odd dollars to get started on, Patrick sold his birthright to the brother born ten months after himself, and good luck to him.

The streets of New York, which had filled lesser men than Patrick Joseph Crowley with terror, had an altogether different effect on the tall, leathery, hard-bitten countryman. He walked the island of Manhattan from east to west across its salty tip and breathed in the tarry smell of the waterfront and found the strangeness tantalizing. He walked into the commerce center of the island and the excitement of the frantic streets pounded in him with the intensity of a powerful heart. He paced the city as though he were a great absentee landlord come home at last to examine his possessions. It was a dirty, filthy, knot-hard fist of a place and it was the home for which, unknowingly, he had always yearned. Skeletons of new buildings rose everywhere out of the rubble of dying wooden

281

structures. The monstrous city reeked with potential and Crowley wanted not just aroma but taste.

Of a frugal nature, even in the heart of enforced frugality, he garnered his pennies and nickels and dimes as carefully as he could from an assortment of odd jobs which did not pay more than pennies and nickels and dimes, but Crowley, patient and experienced with life, sought not miracles but opportunity.

He sought solace from the waves of loneliness that assaulted him like a fever in the familiarity of the saloon, where he could hear the range of Irish voices and words and thoughts, from poet to fool to planner and plotter and thief. He watched carefully and listened closely as he nursed his one large glass of beer each evening.

There were those who had come too soon, young boys with empty bellies and dreams too grand to even touch along the edges of reality. They were the ones who drank too much, too fast. He watched them on a Saturday night, fingers caked with factory grease and oil or muscles knotted and aching from the docks. They dug into the little brown pay envelopes and called for whiskey. By Tuesday night, they'd plead for a short beer and pledge future wages against the favor.

There were some sturdy lads who had had some connections to guide and direct them into the various organizations of government: the great city departments, where the boys all wore blue and sounded like home. Well, Crowley was too old for any of that and had a slight stiffness to his right leg besides. He'd had a childhood accident and some nerves had been severed and the thing never moved right but it didn't bother him too much.

There was another group at the saloon that Pat Crowley observed and it was toward this group he was drawn. They were older men, in their late forties or fifties. They seemed a thoughtful group and a sober group. Most important of all, they seemed a successful group. The owner himself, Hardigan, touched his brow in deference to them, and Shanley, the hired bartender, served them immediately that they appeared.

Crowley did not go unnoticed either. He was marked as a quiet and watchful man and as something of a mystery. No one knew exactly what it was he wanted for he never complained or boasted and complaints and boasts were what filled the smoky air of every saloon along Tenth Avenue from the lower 20's to the lower 40's, along with the singing of sad or merry songs. After a time, the noisemakers and bellyachers dismissed Crowley as not worth the bother to wonder over.

The well-dressed important group, who kept to themselves in a neat rear room and were served fresh trays of free lunch directly from the kitchen, thought that Crowley might one day be useful to them, and though they seemed to ignore him, they had marked him.

It turned out that Patrick J. Crowley was useful, although it also turned out that he was more than his benefactors had bargained for.

Among the habitués of Hardigan's rear room was a certain Michael Fleming, who was a councilman, re-elected every time he ran for the simple fact that he had no opposition. One of Michael Fleming's proudest claims was that as an elected representative of the people he regularly kept promises made to them. One of Fleming's most frequent promises was that the sidewalks and streets of the City of New York would be kept paved and free of holes as long as he had anything to say about it. He had a good deal to say about it, since he made it his business to be actively involved in knowing what streets to rip up and put down again.

Each time a major repavement job came along, sealed bids were submitted by contractors eager for the job. The lowest bidder, of course, would receive the contract. Technically.

Actually, the contractor who submitted the lowest bid would be visited by someone with some useful advice to offer. The useful advice was that it would be wise for all concerned to subcontract the job to the firm of Savacco and Walsh. Otherwise, it was highly likely that a great number of violations of the building code would be found in the manner in which the job was done. It was also possible that the men hired to do the job would find the working conditions and the pay not at all to their liking. It might even come about that between labor problems and violations, the firm might fall upon difficult days and might even fail to survive.

On the other hand, if the job was subcontracted to the firm of Savacco and Walsh, why, for their cooperation and decent

283

good sense, it would be seen to that some really choice jobs would be thrown their way, in addition to a fee of about 10 per cent of whatever amount over the estimated bid the job actually ran.

Savacco and Walsh, the subcontractors, generally ran at least 50 per cent over the estimate given by the original contractor, whose firm's name remained on the contracts. On a few grand occasions, they ran nearly 200 per cent over the estimate.

The firm name of Savacco and Walsh never appeared anywhere in connection with city business.

Savacco was a senile cripple without wife or child. He had been paid a generous fee for the use of his signature when the partnership was formed. His signature was no longer necessary since he had long ago given power of attorney to his partner, George Walsh.

George Walsh was the name Michael Fleming used in his dealings as a subcontractor.

Out of nowhere, or so it seemed to Michael Fleming and his colleagues in city government, came a snot-nosed young greaseball of an assistant district attorney who thought to make his name a household word in time for election in the fall, though God knew what the poor bastard hoped to run for. There were long lines of faithful party servants ahead of him and turning on his party was hardly the way to make himself popular, but that was the thing he tried to do.

His name was Anthony Tulisi, and when Mike Fleming sent for him, he cautioned the boys not to call him a greaseball or wop to his face, since the lad had an education and seemed sensitive.

The meeting was held in Fleming's office at City Hall. Tulisi, beneath his dark complexion, was pale with indignation and glowed with the light of youthful righteousness.

He told all assembled that a change was coming and that they were through. They were all a bunch of robbers and thieves. He, Anthony Tulisi, was going to expose them all before the grand jury and the people of the City of New York. Honesty was going to come into style. The crooks were going to jail.

They kept him talking. He was young and emotional

284

enough to let slip the fact that his case against them rested on the evidence of some jackass of a bookkeeper whose hobby, it seemed, was minding other people's business. The bookkeeper worked for the city's Department of Finance, and instead of thanking God he had a steady job, he took it upon himself to worry about how much money was spent over and above the low-contract bid on various jobs. He got himself curious enough to start keeping a regular little record, and finally he brought his little record book to Anthony Tulisi, who happened to be his cousin.

Between them, they seemed to think they were about to rise, in a few spectacular years, from the sons of street fruit peddlers to rulers of the City of New York.

Not by a long shot.

The difficulty was, as Michael Fleming explained to his cohorts, that "family" was involved. If the little bastard bookkeeper wasn't related to the young assistant district attorney, it might be easy enough to just get rid of him and his records, but blood made things tougher. Those Italians were like jungle tribes where it came to family and were known for murdering the children of their enemies for four or five generations when they had one of their feuds going strong. That was the kind of situation to be avoided.

One of Fleming's colleagues, a gifted thinker named Tommy Doolan, said that since family was so all-important, it was through family that the solution was to be found, just given enough thought. He was right, as he generally was.

Several trustworthy people, some professional at the job since they were members of the Police Department, some not professional and valuable for that very reason, did a careful, thorough, 100 per cent complete investigation of the family of Anthony Tulisi and his cousin, Joseph.

Joseph Tulisi, the bookkeeper, had a seventy-two-year-old father who liked little girls. Very little girls, four or five or six years old.

What he liked to do was to touch them on the knee or on the thigh. What he liked best was to duck his hand under a little girl's dress for a quick grab. Then he'd give the little girl a penny or a piece of fruit and a pat on the head.

Since there was nothing better, and since Michael Fleming

and Tommy Doolan both thought it was pretty good, they decided to go with what they had. What they now needed was an impartial witness, someone with no connections or ties with Michael Fleming or anyone else in the city government. Someone who was without malice or reason to bring about catastrophe upon the head of the Tulisi family through discovery of the fact that seventy-two-year-old Louis liked little girls.

That was where Patrick Joseph Crowley came in. He met all the prerequisites of the job. It was learned that he was from Knockraha, and as fate would have it, Tommy Doolan himself was from Dungourney, not fifteen miles east of Crowley's home in the County of Cork. After some hard and amazing concentration, for which he was famous, Doolan remembered that he had a cousin married to a Crowley girl and from all accounts there was nothing bad known of the Crowleys of Knockraha.

It was Tommy Doolan himself struck up a conversation with Crowley, liked the way the man darted and squinted his eyes when spoken to; it showed a sharp sense of caution. Crowley seemed to be his own man. No one had anything to say about him, not one way or another.

Doolan put the deal to him directly. A sober honest man was needed to do a job of observation for four dollars a day, and when a certain dirty old Italian man committed a certain dirty act, of which there was no question he would sooner or later, and likely sooner, why the honest man was merely to call the matter to the attention of a policeman and go before the magistrate.

Mike Fleming agreed with Tommy Doolan that Crowley was a good choice. A younger man in the same situation might be maddened by the old degenerate's action and crack his skull on the sidewalk. Certainly, no one wanted a dead Louis Tulisi. What was wanted was a live Louis Tulisi caught with his hand up a little girl's dress by an outraged stranger.

It went better than they could have hoped. On the second day that Patrick Crowley strolled through the Mulberry Street commotion of Little Italy, idly avoiding crashing into any of the hundreds of pushcarts that lined both sides of the street, he knelt at one point to tie his shoe. In this position, he had a

286

clear view through the spokes of the high-wheeled cart of the shaved-ice peddler. What he saw was the gnarled old hand of Louis Tulisi creep beneath the dress of a little girl who stood on her toes, straining anxiously toward the ice peddler with her penny held high. The child didn't even notice Louis Tulisi next to her.

Patrick Crowley stood up, shot around the wagon and with a tremendous roar he pointed an accusing finger at the culprit. The old man froze in his position of guilt just long enough to be seen by the crowd. Then he collapsed on the sidewalk in trembling terror. People screamed and shrieked, and though their language was incomprehensible, their intention was clear. Crowley protected the frail body from flying fists and pinching fingers and relinquished him only to the arms of a blue-clad policeman.

At the police station, Louis Tulisi pleaded and begged and, above all, he confessed. Before many witnesses and without even being asked, the old man berated himself and cursed himself for his terrible fault and knocked his fists against his forehead, but without enough strength to knock himself out.

The police sergeant leaned down imperially from his high position behind the desk and told Patrick Crowley, "You needn't stay here now. You've seen the old bastard into the station and we'll take it from here."

"No, I'll just stay on a while," Crowley said.

The sergeant's harsh voice might have intimidated another man as he asked, "Oh, you will, will ya? And just who the hell do you think you are?"

Patrick Crowley folded his arms across his chest, each elbow resting in a large palm, country-fashion. "If you just call Tommy Doolan, you might find out," he said.

A different voice came from the sergeant. "Oh, yes, well then, yes, that's different, of course."

There was a deference, a respect, an eagerness to please which had never before been directed to Patrick Crowley. He knew that he had used the name of Doolan to test its power. He had known Doolan was an important man, but didn't know exactly where he fitted into the scheme of things. With a shrewd instinct, Crowley knew he'd been used for more than the capturing of an old man with bad habits.

He hung around the police station and watched the commotion and clamor. There were arrivals and departures of all kinds of people in all stages of excitement and concern. No one questioned him; he was Doolan's man. But Crowley asked a few questions and all concerned were very cooperative. After all, it was assumed that he knew all there was to know already.

What he had no way of knowing was that the bookkeeper, Joseph Tulisi, frantically traded his record book for his father.

But not before his cousin, Anthony Tulisi, was confronted in court with his errant old Uncle Louis. He was struck dumb and could not bring himself to utter a word on behalf of the People of the State of New York relative to the arraignment of the old culprit.

It was officially noted that the young assistant district attorney was temperamentally unsuited to see to the administration of justice without fear, favor or partiality.

Because of his age, the old man's case was dropped by an understanding judge.

Because of *his* lack of integrity, that young district attorney was informed that charges of malfeasance would be brought against him unless he resigned forthwith.

He resigned, forthwith.

Joseph, the bookkeeper, also resigned.

None of the Tulisis was ever heard of again.

Patrick Joseph Crowley was heard of again. On several occasions, he proved his usefulness to Tommy Doolan in various ways. He handled himself with style; he knew when to lean without leaning too hard and without bringing attention to himself. He never asked questions beyond the scope of any given assignment. Not of Tommy Doolan, that is.

What he did was ask questions of those who had no way of knowing that he didn't already possess the information he sought; he gave the impression that he was "checking up" among those eager themselves to be cooperative. Bit by bit, piece by piece, Crowley collected facts and names and an understanding of how the city was really run. When he felt he had a strong enough foundation, he approached Tommy Doolan, with style. No threats or demands, just a statement to the effect that Patrick J. Crowley wanted more than just the odd job thrown, the bone tossed, to a reliable man. He wanted something steady that would lead to something worthwhile.

And he wanted something that wouldn't involve too much sweat for he'd sweated enough in his life already.

A conference was held among those whose affairs had been handled, one way or another, by Pat Crowley. It was pointed out that it would be a perfect waste to get rid of Crowley through an unfortunate accident. The guy had sense and he had balls and he wanted his; as long as he knew the rules and played by them, well, God knew, a good loyal man was worth something. There was a job needed filling in the Building Department and that was where they sent him.

Nine months after he left Knockraha, Patrick J. Crowley was on the payroll of the City of New York.

Within a short time, Tommy Doolan decided that what Pat Crowley needed was a wife and the girl he had in mind just happened to be the daughter of his wife's sister. Elizabeth McNamara, twenty-two years old and newly arrived from Dungourney, was strong and healthy and accustomed to taking care of a home and a family. Since there was a serious shortage of marrying men in Dungourney, she'd come to America not so much to seek her fortune but to find a man to marry and take care of.

While he didn't think much of the girl herself, the whole idea didn't seem too bad to Pat. After all, for most of his life, his mother looked after him and it would be good to have someone to cook a hot meal and see that the holes in his socks were properly mended. It was true that she was a bit beefy but it was all muscle, as Tommy Doolan pointed out. Her nose was far too small and turned up besides, but her eyes were a clear and honest blue, when she raised her face long enough for him to catch a glimpse. All in all, she seemed sensible and didn't have much to say for herself.

Of course, with a wife, he'd need a bit more money to put by and an opportunity to prepare for the responsibilities of a family.

Doolan was ready for Crowley and it worked out fine all around. There was a bit of land, not a large amount at all, in fact it was a wedge-shaped scrap of land up in the Bronx, more of an alley than anything else, and it was up for bid at city auction and could be had dirt-cheap. Of course, no one could know that within two years the city would be building a magistrate's court right at that location and the scrap of land would be essential for the project. But Tommy Doolan knew that particular information for a fact. The parcel was Tommy Doolan's wedding present to the couple.

When his first daughter was born a year later, Pat was too involved in various assignments to acknowledge the slight disappointment that his first-born failed to be a boy. His wife was young and healthy and there would be a son the next time.

Before the first girl could walk steadily, the second daughter was born, and before the first girl could talk clearly, the third daughter was born. By the time the fourth girl was born, the first girl was able to keep her little sisters amused by pushing them around the apartment in the baby buggy which each had tenanted for such a short period of time.

By the time the fifth girl was born, Elizabeth McNamara Crowley had lost the fine hearty, beefy look and had instead a thin, frantic body topped by a pinched, terrified face. She confided to a cousin who came to give her a hand for a few days that her husband, when he viewed the newest girl, went purple, as though he finally realized what it was she was doing to him.

"Goddamn it," he told her, "why the hell can't you get it right, you jackass?"

She didn't know. What Crowley's wife did know was that her husband was possessed of a growing determination that he would have a son. He ignored the house filled with little girls and concentrated on providing himself with a son with a fury that no sooner was spent but that it renewed itself.

Elizabeth prayed constantly for Patrick's son; her lips moved over her prayers as she scrubbed and cleaned and polished the floors and walls of the fine house Patrick had one day moved them into, far up in the country section of the Bronx. She didn't know how they were able to live in such a grand manor house but she wouldn't dream of asking. She took her tasks much to heart, kept the girls clean and out of sight as much as possible when their father and his friends were at home.

Her sixth pregnancy ended in a miscarriage and she knew wearily that it was God's will, as all things are: the unborn child of five months was another girl.

When the sixth girl was born, the first girl was a fine helper and could, at the tender age of nine, practically run the house herself and knew when to round up the girls to keep them from bothering their dad.

At the end of their twelfth year of marriage, Elizabeth miscarried a perfectly formed little boy; at seven months, all the tiny fingernails and toenails were pink and white. Patrick nearly went mad with grief: he'd lost his son.

In all the years of their life together, through many an emotional storm, Elizabeth had never seen him grieve. She vowed and promised on her life that she'd deliver a son to him before she died. The doctor said she couldn't carry another child. It took two years before she became pregnant again, and by the time their seventh and last child, Mary Ellen Crowley, was born, their first-born, Veronica, had declared her vocation. She was hardly missed when she went off to the convent on Long Island since her next sister in line performed all of Veronica's chores with easy capability.

Patrick could never tell them one from the other. They were a bunch of skinny, pale-faced, blinking, silent wraiths, forever marching off to some special novena or other. He hardly knew which of them it was off to join the others in that convent out on Long Island. The one thing that Patrick Crowley finally decided was that his line was not about to come to a complete and fruitless halt within the stone walls of a nunnery.

It came to a choice between the last two and there really was no choice at all. When Kathleen Crowley was barely twelve years old, it was clearly marked upon her frowning forehead and tightly pursed lips exactly what she was to become. The child could hardly wait the year out to bid them a hasty good-by.

That left Mary Ellen. As luck would have it, she was the only beauty among the lot. Somehow, she'd inherited a modification of all the prominent features of the McNamara and Crowley lines. Whereas half her sisters had sharp beaky noses and the rest had little pugs, Mary Ellen showed up with a delicate, finely tipped nose that seemed slightly elegant. All the others had watery gray eyes; Mary Ellen's were green and blue and slate, all at the same time. Instead of tight pale lips, hers were red and soft and full. Their straight mousy hair was not for Mary Ellen; she had a mane of thick hair that reminded Patrick of his sisters and his cousins back home. Clearly, Mary Ellen was a Crowley product, and of all of them, the only one to bear him a Crowley grandson.

She was the only one he took any interest in at all. He let it be clearly understood that she was headed for no convent. The rest could go and be damned to them. This one had to carry on his line.

Besides being pretty, she was a good girl, not too clever at her books, though the Sisters always stressed that she tried hard. He was satisfied, for too many brains were no advantage in a girl. The problem was to find the girl a right husband.

The mealymouthed sons were poor advertisements for their tough, energetic fathers, and Crowley wondered sometimes what the benefits of success were if one were to judge by the products he'd seen recently. The girl was about to graduate from her fine school and go on for a year or so at the Sacred Heart Academy, but what the hell, it was only until a suitable lad turned up.

The college boys who paraded through his hallway were a sorry lot who stumbled over their own tongues if he asked a direct question, turned purple at the sight of the girl and sweated a lot, hands and face. They'd been prompted by anxious fathers and showed it. Crowley knew that a great many men in high and low places would count themselves fortunate to be allied with the Crowley name. *He* was a power; *he* was a man to know. He wasn't about to hand his daughter over to just anyone; he didn't have to.

Patrick Crowley sat for a long time, bent over his walking stick, shoulders and knees aching with arthritis. He stared thoughtfully into the ashes of the huge fireplace and watched a quick flame lick to life for a burst of flame among the ashes. It burned brightly before it died out completely. He thought of new life emerging as the flame had from the ashes. From crippled old age, new vital youth. The soft chimes of the grandfather clock in the hallway interrupted his reverie.

292

The lateness of the hour never occurred to Patrick Crowley. He stood up painfully, his weight on the knob of the stick, crossed the massive room to his desk and picked up the telephone receiver. He dialed a certain number, was annoyed that it took five rings before a sleepy voice whispered into his ear.

"This is Crowley," he said abruptly. "Find out what there is to know about this young Brian O'Malley."

TWENTY-SEVEN

It was a muggy, noisy, hot June morning when Brian found the murdered body of the man known as Old Man Moses. Checking on the old man was routine, as automatic as testing a shop door on a midnight. Yet Brian could never say if he had a premonition or if his tense wariness was strictly in retrospect.

He tapped lightly with the end of his nightstick against the wooden door, then a little harder because the old man was slightly deaf.

"Hey, Mr. Moses? Everything okay in there?"

There was something ominous, almost inevitable, about the door opening at Brian's careful touch on the doorknob, something almost expected about the terrible chaos of destruction that confronted him within the confines of the tiny flat.

He had seen a few murder victims, but this was the first time *he* was first on the scene. The undefined area of crime encompassed him. The walls and floor and ceiling were splattered with the old man's blood. The frail old peddler was a grotesque corpse, slashed and stabbed and hacked as though it was his blood which had been sought. It congealed in a stagnant pool beneath the wooden chair on which he had been tied and gagged. The dead eyes stared in a last, unimaginable passion, and among the thoughts that seared through Brian's brain was, Christ, the poor old man didn't want to die.

The detectives arrived and complimented Brian; he hadn't ruined anything; he had preserved the integrity of the murder scene. That had been his job and he had done it properly.

There was an air of subdued rage among all of the men; not even the Homicide detectives were unaffected. Anyone who lived for ninety-odd years had a right to die unviolated.

"Jesus," one of the Homicide men observed, "how the hell could anyone think this poor old man had anything? All he had was one suit of clothes besides what's on his body now. Jeez, look at all the family pictures, prayer shawls, graduation certificates of his sons and grandsons." He scratched along his jaw and shook his head. "This is gonna be a rough one to tell to a family."

There was nothing but rotten cotton wadding inside the slashed old settee. There was nothing but horsehair stuffing inside the old mattress. There was nothing but old goose feathers inside the worn comforter and stained pillows. Under the pulled-up linoleum there was nothing but rotting wooden flooring. There had been no fortune hidden inside the old man's poverty.

Neighbors cried and pulled their hair. He was a holy man, the father of rabbis, the grandfather of rabbis. The old man had been seen the day before, on the street, with his box of needles. There was no carton of needles anywhere in the small flat. Apparently that and whatever loose change the old man had on him had been taken.

Brian stood back and watched as the experts worked, methodically, professionally, enviably. They photographed the corpse from various angles, though he didn't know why. The old man was dead from wherever you looked. They dusted for fingerprints, circled the room with tiny brushes and envelopes into which they scooped fragments and invisible bits and pieces. Carefully, they scraped black filth from the fingernails of the dead old fingers, and finally gave the okay for the body to be removed from the chalk circle they had drawn.

The stench in the room nauseated Brian but they couldn't open any windows until the lab men were finished. Even then, it wasn't a good idea. There were too many loose feathers to fly around.

The Department brass came and stood and surveyed the scene. Brian was introduced to a deputy inspector, who nodded solemnly, clicked his teeth, curtly complimented Brian for having checked on the old man. The D.I. clicked his teeth, muttered an obscenity and told the men to get the sons of bitches who did this. Then he left.

It was obviously the kind of crime some young punks would

pull. The detectives rounded up every kid who had ever been arrested or who had given anybody lip for whatever reason or whose face they didn't like.

By ten o'clock, Brian was exhausted from the reports he'd had to prepare, from questions he'd had to answer and from the endless hanging around. The precinct would throb with activity in brief bursts of noise, then would fall silent. Angelo DiSantini, along with three of his cohorts, was shoved up the stairs; loud voices called him and his kind nothing but bums and trouble. There were some loud scuffle sounds, a couple of smacks, then a good deal of feet sounds thudding down the iron steps in response to the command, "Get your ass the fuck outta here!" Angelo DiSantini and his friends were only too happy to comply.

Brian walked into the ready room, lit a cigarette, rubbed his sore eyes and wondered if anyone would think to tell him to get his ass out of there. He'd been on duty since eight in the morning and had an eight to four the next day. He looked toward the door and an elderly man with dark bags beneath his eyes, dressed in the strange black outfit of the Orthodox Jew, came to Brian and put out his hand. He was one of the old man's sons.

Brian felt a shiver at the wet, cold, smooth palm which grasped his hand.

"I'm Rabbi Schulman," the man told him. "Thank you very much. Thank you very much for checking on my father. The other policeman, the sergeant—you are Patrolman O'Malley, yes?—he told me how kind you were . . . to . . . to . . . check on my father."

"I'm . . . I'm very sorry for your trouble, Rabbi."

"Yes. Yes, thank you very much for everything," the man said irrationally, with great, warm fervor, as though he had no control over the flow of words. "Well. So. That's how things turned out. Well. Thank you very much."

All the time he spoke, the rabbi held Brian's hand in an iron grasp; he pumped it up and down sporadically.

"Would you like a cup of coffee, Rabbi? We have some hot."

"Coffee? Coffee? No, no, thank you very much. I have things to look after. For my father. The feathers," he said suddenly, and finally released Brian's hand. He raised his arms

296

in a wide empty gesture. "The feathers were all over the place. Did you see the terrible mess in my father's house?" His voice broke into a deep, half-stifled cry. The rabbi ground the back of his hands into his eyes for a moment, regained control and said, "I'm very sorry. I just wanted to say, on behalf of my family and myself, thank you very much for looking after my father. We know you've all looked in on him, and if there's ever anything we can do for you, please, you let me know."

Brian waited until the rabbi walked out of the ready room and across the outer room. Then he went into the bathroom and threw up.

It was nearly one o'clock when the sergeant told him to go home. The air was crisp and clean and Brian didn't get enough of it before he plunged into the clammy dankness of the subway station. He tasted the sharp black steel dust, leaned over and spit onto the tracks. From the receding rumble, it was apparent that he had just missed a train and would have a long wait.

He walked down to the center of the platform and stretched onto the wooden bench. He unrolled the *Daily News*, scanned it for the hundredth time. It was so familiar he could quote paragraphs from memory. He rubbed his eyelids lightly and pressed his tongue against the roof of his mouth; became absolutely still, listened. He gave no indication whatever that he was intensely aware, alert; he seemed to be dozing.

He saw the shadow first, then the dark quick movement as someone slid from behind one pillar to the next, moved steadily toward him. He was ready to move in whatever direction he might have to but he didn't have to move at all. When the figure came to the pillar directly to his left a voice called him by name.

"Hey, Mr. O'Malley. Could I talk to you?"

Angelo DiSantini stood uncertainly in the shadows.

"Yeah, you can talk to me, Angelo. You got something to say to me?"

The boy scanned the station nervously, even though the platform was deserted. "Look, don't get me wrong, Mr. O'Malley, but, well, I don't want to be seen with you. You know? See, I got something you should know, about that old man. Shit, that was a bad thing, but, see, I don't want nobody should see us talking, if you understand what I mean."

Exhaustion slipped away; the long hours of hanging around, repeating the same things endlessly, listening to the others, the theories, the anger, the grief, all of it disappeared and was replaced by a surge of energy and expectation. Without moving, Brian asked quietly, "You know who gave it to the old man?"

DiSantini's voice was hoarse, and before he answered, he tossed his head back, bit his fingernail, looked around. "Yeah, but look, when the train comes, could we maybe ride up a few stations, separate, you know, and then we'll get off and talk there. Jeez, you know how it is, Mr. O'Malley."

They rode up three stations when the train came, Brian in one car, Angelo in another. They got off and walked toward each other. Angelo walked on the balls of his feet, as though ready for instant flight.

"Okay," Brian said, "wanna go for some coffee? Or you wanna talk here or what?"

"Naw, here's fine." He hunched his shoulders up and jammed his hands into the pockets of his dungarees. "Hell, I ain't never done nothing like this before, but this is different. This whole thing. I mean, shit, the old guy was almost a hundred years old, you know, almost like a neighborhood landmark. They had no right to kill no old man almost a hundred years old." Angelo scuffed his sneaker along the platform; his hands fingered the rivets on the dark-green iron pillar as he spoke. "See, nobody in the neighborhood would ever mess with an old man like that. My pals, well, I guess you might say we're kind of rough in some ways. Hell, we don't deserve no medals or nothing, but hell, nothing like that. We got respect for a man like that, know what I mean?"

Brian gave the kid a cigarette. He tried to conceal the growing elation with a calm, slightly impatient exterior. "Okay, Angelo, so you and your buddies are clean. Talk to me."

Angelo took two quick drags on the cigarette, inhaling as though the nicotine were oxygen. "See, there are a coupla real bums, not from the neighborhood. They started hanging around about a coupla weeks ago. Strong-arm types, coupla

298

hustlers, eighteen, nineteen years old. Well, they just show up, see, start hanging around, telling stories about what big men they are and all. And they started messin' with the girls. Not just kiddin' around, but some strong-arm stuff, you know. Like they *like* to hurt people. They think it's funny." Angelo shook his head, then looked directly at Brian. "Jeez, I can't believe it's me here like this, Mr. O'Malley, but, well, you were real fair to me that time. You seen what the score was and you were fair, but I know you coulda really let me have it and you didn't."

"Okay," Brian said, "but we're talking about the murder of the old man. So talk."

Angelo nodded. "They done it, these two guys. Not that they're around bragging about it or nothing, but, you know, everyone was talking about it, you know, feeling real bad. And these two guys, shit, you just gotta look at them. At their faces, like they are grinning at each other and making remarks. I don't know, but you put your hands on these guys and you got the old man's killers."

Brian flipped his cigarette to the tracks and straightened to his full height. "Okay, Angelo. Tell me where they are."

They were holed up like two rats in the basement of a deserted tenement, exactly where Angelo DiSantini said they would be.

Brian caught them totally off guard, and when one of them tried frantically to diminish the oil lamp that provided them with an uncertain, eerie light, he kicked the murderer's temple with absolutely no compunction.

"Move again," Brian said softly, "and I'll put a bullet where my foot was."

They believed him and sat in frozen, watchful silence. He searched them quickly, took the heavy knives from their pockets and told them to sit on the floor.

"How much money did you get from the old man?" he asked.

They looked at each other, then shrugged wordlessly. Brian slid his finger off the trigger of his gun, held the revolver flat in the palm of his hand and brought it down hard on the forehead of the one he had kicked. It made a dull thud of a sound, followed by a harsh gasp from the man.

"Jeez, Jeez, you don't hafta do that. There wuz onny two fuckin' dollars was all. And the box of needles there and that's all, swear to God, that's all."

In the flickering light, he couldn't see them clearly but they were both husky, muscular guys with tough broken faces. The one he pushed around seemed a little simple. He kept touching the stream of blood with his fingertips and examining it with a slight smile. Brian wasn't worried about that one.

The other guy seemed a little brighter and he was too big for comfort. For the first time, Brian realized it was not as easy as just finding these two. The station house was only three blocks away, but he had only a come-along, the chain link that went around the prisoner's wrist while you held it. There sure as hell wasn't any telephone nearby.

The bigger guy kept watching him with sharp little eyes that moved ferretlike from Brian's face to the doorway. He wasn't as bright as Brian thought. His quick furtive glances gave him away. He lunged past Brian for the door. Brian smashed the butt of the gun against the base of the man's skull. The blow landed as hard and solid as a baseball bat against cement. The man landed face down, dead weight.

Christ, Brian thought, the guy'll have a double concussion, front and back. He groaned, rolled onto his back and one hand went to his split forehead.

For sheer size, he was still a dangerous son of a bitch and the only thing to do was to render him as helpless as possible.

Brian clenched his teeth, steeled himself for what he had to do. He didn't think of the terrible, sick, gut-wrenching pain; he did what was necessary. He kicked the big bastard as hard as he could in the groin.

After that, the murderers came along as docile as children.

"Jesus Christ Almighty," the sergeant said, surprised to see him back at the station house. "What the hell have you got here, O'Malley, the walking wounded?"

"What I got here, Sergeant," Brian said, "are the two bums who murdered Old Man Moses."

The Chief of Detectives thought it would be a good idea to give the kid a gold shield. Everything fell into place. The collar was made less than twenty-four hours after the hunky bastards butchered the old man. He got them cold with the goods. There were two signed confessions and two corroborating re-enactments. Murder one, from here straight to the chair.

The newspapers, every single rag in the city, had a chance for just two editions. The first announced and described the crime; the second answered the demand made in the first: the criminals were brought to justice.

It just happened that there was a vacancy in third grade. The kid, O'Malley, seemed tailor-made. He checked out with a good background; his father was killed on the job, Honor Legion. The kid's own record with the Department, in such a short time, was damn good. Generally, the Chief wasn't too enthused about headline promotions but this one looked good. Even the Commissioner thought so. The day before.

The Chief of Detectives held his hand over the burning ulcer pain along his right side. He'd long ago learned when to ask and when to keep shut. The Commissioner had his reasons for his change of heart. Whatever the hell they were.

He picked up the memorandum addressed to him, at his direction, by the captain of Patrolman Brian O'Malley's precinct. It was a recommendation that Patrolman O'Malley be awarded a Class A commendation for effecting the arrest of the two murderers. The Chief of Detectives scrawled his name across the bottom of the page under the word "Approved."

The Police Commissioner of the City of New York leaned back in his swivel chair and wondered what the hell Pat Crowley had against this young patrolman, Brian O'Malley.

The telephone conversation, short and sweet, had been right to the point.

"Well now, Johnnie, it's Pat here. How're the wife and kiddies? Ah, fine, fine. Say, that's a fine lad you've got there, been getting all them favorable headlines for the Department and himself. Good work, fine job."

"Thanks, Pat. Well, yes, it was a damn fine piece of work for that was a dirty bit of business."

"Ah, yes, yes, damn shame. Well, well, now I've read something confusing, too."

"What was that?"

301

"Well, knowing how opposed you are to headline promotions, I was surprised to learn—at least the newspapers quoted you, but then damned to them, the liars, they never get it straight—but seems to me it said you was planning on giving the boy a gold shield? Was that my understanding?"

Warily, warily, "Well, that announcement was premature. We're turning some alternatives over. It was mentioned there was a vacancy. You know how the public loves to see a hero rewarded, Pat."

"And deserves to be, indeed, a fine job. But it's been my feeling, you know, Johnnie, that it's good for the young fellas to season a bit, if you take my meaning. Well, that young O'Malley seems a fine young lad and could make do with a Class A commendation, if it was me had the decision. But listen, Johnnie, you know me. I tend on the conservative side."

"No sense in rushing them, Pat. Plenty of opportunity in the future."

"Ah, sure. And how did you say your dear Maureen was feeling?"

Francis Kelly commiserated with Brian over a glass of beer. "Well, at least, Bri, they didn't take the pinch away from you altogether."

"Don't think they didn't try, the lousy bastards." Brian wrapped his hands around the heavy, sweating glass mug. His head was beginning to feel heavy. "Everyone from the desk sergeant to the clerical man wanted a share. Jesus, they pinned every unsolved homicide for the past ten years on those two sons a' bitches. That would have made them murderers at nine years old. Shit, do you know that Horowitz and his partner got two collars apiece out of it? How about that, they made out better than me."

"Ah, screw 'em, Brian. The hell with it."

"Yeah. Right." He drained the glass, then let his head fall. Then he looked up, filling again with the sense of anger and frustration he had carried around all day. "They can take their Class A commendation and shove it. Jesus, Francis, the captain told me himself I had third grade. He told me he got it right from the Chief of Detectives; they were going to give me the gold shield. Bastards." He turned slowly to study Francis Kelly, then brightened. "Hey, shit, I didn't come out to play

302

crybaby. Screw 'em is right, pal." With elaborate care, because the room seemed to be slowly tipping, Brian faced the bartender. "Hey, Charlie, did you know Francis is getting married in a few weeks, huh? Give us some *real* drinks, we're celebrating. On me, Francis, on me. Some whiskey to drink to Francis Kelly."

Francis Kelly had been matching Brian beer for beer and now started matching whiskey for whiskey. It was a slow and careful process. "Hey, Brian, I just thought of something that just occurred to me. You and me will be related, right?"

"Huh?"

"Well, Marylou is Billy's sister and Billy is your sister's husband. What does that make us, Brian?"

Brian flung an arm around Francis Kelly's shoulder and said, "That makes us fucking cousins, right?"

"I'll drink to that."

They had two boilermakers each before they swayed, arms around each other, from the bar. Older men watched them good-naturedly, toasted the bridegroom-to-be, winked, grinned.

Francis Kelly carefully extracted himself from Brian, pulled himself upright and forced his eyes wide. "Holy Christ, Brian, you know what I just remembered?"

"What did you just remember, pal?"

"I gotta work a midnight tonight. I forgot that I gotta work a midnight tonight. Brian, how the hell can I work a midnight, Brian? The goddamn sidewalk is as soft as oatmeal. And I gotta work a fucking midnight."

Francis Kelly carefully sat down on the curb, dropped his head between his knees and began to groan.

"Got to get it outta you, Francis. It's the only way," Brian decided. "Come on, buddy, gonna take you home and get all the booze outta you."

Kit stood in the middle of the kitchen and asked, "Hey, Ma, how come Francis Kelly is being sick in our bathroom?"

Margaret turned her daughter toward her bedroom. "You go back to bed now and mind your business."

It was rare that Margaret O'Malley's face wore a pinched, tight-lipped, angry expression but there was no question in anyone's mind that she was not to be argued with at such

303

times. She marched after Kit and pulled the bedroom door closed, went back to the kitchen and poured two cups of hot black coffee. The sounds from the bathroom were awful.

"Brian," she called out, "you come in here now."

Her son looked at the cups of coffee he'd asked for and nodded. "Good, Ma, that's good and strong. But we've got to clean him out a little more. I need another big glass of hot soapy water."

Margaret placed herself firmly in front of the sink. "Brian, you'll not be forcing poor Francis to drink any more of that soapy water. For the love of God, what are you trying to do to him?"

Brian's face was flushed and damp and his eyes were glazed, but beneath the slightly thick speech and confusion, some glint of mischief came through. He caught her in a playful hug and lifted her from her post onto a kitchen chair. When he leaned over her, his mother caught the heavy whiskey fumes.

"'Tis trying to save the lad his job I am, Ma. Sure you'll not want our Francis Kelly tossed off the job because he can't perform his tour of duty."

He was quick and she couldn't stop him from taking another glass of hot soapy water into the bathroom. The sounds were terrible; Brian's voice encouraging and insistent; Francis Kelly's, gasping and groaning; then the awful retching which the flushing of the toilet didn't altogether hide. Finally it was quiet in the bathroom; their voices became low. Then the shower was turned on.

After some fifteen minutes, Brian and Francis came into the kitchen. Francis wore a clean shirt of Brian's and he brushed tentatively at his trousers, which weren't any too clean.

"Hello, Mrs. O'Malley," Francis said sheepishly. His face was white as death and his fair hair was wet and plastered slickly over his forehead.

Margaret shook her head and clicked her tongue over the two of them. She poured two cups of fresh coffee, then put a plate of sandwiches in front of them.

Francis Kelly closed his eyes as he ate a few bites and Brian prodded him to eat more.

"Come on now, boy, line your stomach with something. There you go. You'll be as good as new." He looked at the wall

304

clock. "Well, I sobered you up in thirty minutes. You still got an hour to get to work."

Margaret folded her arms over her chest and glared at them. "Where did you learn such goings on, the two of you? What kind of way is that to act in your own home, Brian?"

Francis apologized. "Gee, Mrs. O'Malley, it was my fault. I got to thinking about my wedding and Brian and me were toasting each other. I forgot I had to work a midnight. Gee, sometimes it gets a little confusing, even now, what shift I got."

"Ah, you're as bad as he is, Francis Kelly. The two of you should be ashamed. At least I'm glad your mother didn't see you in that condition. You had sense enough to bring him here," she added to Brian.

"I'd do the same for Brian, Mrs. O'Malley."

"Ah, for the love of God, you'd better not have to. That's all I'll say about it." She shook her head over the two of them. "All that terrible hot soapy water. How could you even swallow it down?"

Francis Kelly's hand clamped over his mouth and he swallowed the flood of saliva before he could speak in a low, muffled voice. "Please, Mrs. O'Malley, don't mention that right now. I can still taste it."

"A guy on the job told me about the hot-soapy-water treatment," Brian said. "You know, I thought the guy was just kidding me, but it really does work. You'll be fine, Francis."

"I'd like to take some soap to *your* mouth, Brian, coming home and carrying on that way, and young children in the house to be set a bad example."

Brian put his finger over his lips, winked at his mother, tiptoed to the hallway where he caught Kit. "Hey, look at the spy I found." He lifted her high, then seated her unceremoniously on the kitchen table.

Kit leaned forward and stared at Francis Kelly.

"Hey, Francis, you look terrible. What was Brian doing to make you sick? You sounded like you were gagging to death."

"Katherine O'Malley, you get yourself to bed this minute, because if I see your face once more tonight, you're goin' to feel the sting of that paddle!"

Even Brian was finally convinced of the intensity of his mother's anger. Her voice went tight and thin but her eyes

305

glared and her chin went up with determination. Kit went back to bed without a sound.

"Hey, Ma," Brian said, "I'm just gonna walk Francis to the subway and then I'll come back and clean up in the bathroom. Look, don't you go in there. I'll be back in five minutes and clean it up, okay?"

Margaret gathered dishes together and finally said, "Don't you be telling me what to do in my own home. You should be ashamed, both of you."

"Good-by, Mrs. O'Malley. Gee, I'm real sorry," Francis Kelly offered, but she shook her head and dismissed the two of them as bad business.

They walked along the Grand Concourse down to Burnside Avenue, then along Burnside to Jerome Avenue. At the foot of the Jerome Avenue el, Francis told Brian, "Don't come up to the platform, for Chrissake. I'm okay. I hope I didn't cause you any trouble at home."

Brian shrugged. "Don't worry about it. Well, bud, how do you feel?"

"I feel like shit but at least I'll get through the tour." He gave Brian a clumsy punch on the arm. "It was a helluva cure, but thanks." He started up the long iron staircase, then turned and came back to the sidewalk with a silly grin on his face. "Hey, Brian, in a few weeks, huh? I'll be getting married. I mean, Christ, *me. Married.* Jesus."

Francis Kelly bolted up the stairs two at a time and they called wild insults back and forth at each other, the way they used to when they were ten years old.

Brian stood for a while, heard the train pull in and then depart. He rubbed his hand across his chin over the rough stubble. His mouth tasted dirty and stale and sour. Watching Francis Kelly vomit buckets of soapy water hadn't done his stomach much good.

But that wasn't what was bothering him.

Brian dug his hands into his trouser pockets and walked slowly along Jerome Avenue with his head bent down. An odd pattern of shadowy tracks and pillars spilled along the gutter from the overhead el. For one odd fleeting moment, Brian stood absolutely still. He had the sensation of being lost, of being somewhere he had never been before without any idea of how he had come to be there.

306

He raised his face and tried to fight away the aching dizziness of too much whiskey and too much beer, both unaccustomed. He didn't particularly like drinking and generally kept to his modest limit.

He took a few deep breaths and let himself fill with it: They screwed him.

So they screwed him, so what?

His family had all been excited and impressed by all the publicity; his mother added his new clippings to the scrapbook filled with clippings about his father. Everyone had made a fuss over the collar; it was a damn good collar. And the captain had *told* him it was all set: a gold shield.

Then the captain was absolutely blank-faced. Told him he was going to get a Class A commendation, and the bastard had the nerve to congratulate him. Period. End of discussion, O'Malley.

Brian dug his feet at the cobbled section of Burnside Avenue, where the trolley tracks were sunk, and walked along, eyes on the shiny track. Sonuvabitching captain. And sonuvabitching Department. The whole goddamn Department was lousy. Someday. Someday he'd show them all. Screw them. Screw all of them.

The thing that rankled, that burned and throbbed, was the mystery of it all. Who the hell had screwed *him* and why?

The captain handed him the heavy package and he had a peculiar look on his thin face. Patrolmen rarely had anything to do with captains and it seemed a good rule to Brian. There were enough sergeants and lieutenants between to keep the captain a myth: the boss who was always teed off about something and to whom, in line, everyone was ultimately responsible.

When Captain Leary sent for him, there were two sergeants and one lieutenant who felt somehow offended. It certainly wasn't the captain who would be called upon to soothe their ruffled feathers. Brian felt the heft of the package and it did indeed seem heavy enough to contain two target pistols.

"Now I want you to get up to that address with them right away. It's been cleared with your sergeant and the trip up and back will just about take care of the rest of your tour."

What Brian wanted to ask was what the hell a patrolman in

the New York City Police Department was doing acting as delivery boy, assigned to transport two target pistols which Captain Leary had obtained for Mr. Crowley up to Riverdale. He kept quiet for a moment, then under the slightly quizzical gaze of Captain Leary, he asked, "Captain, uh . . . who *is* Mr. Crowley?"

Captain Leary carefully nibbled on the cuticle of his right thumb, picked the tiny piece of skin from the tip of his tongue, studied it, flicked it away before he answered.

"Mr. Crowley is a very good man to have as a friend," he said softly. "And a very bad man to have as an enemy."

The house was even more impressive by daylight. What had been shadow now had substance. It was a tremendous handsome structure, with stained-glass windows set in high-rising splendor more suitable for a cathedral than a private residence. As he walked along the broad brick pavement, he studied the house so intently that he didn't see Crowley's daughter until he stepped on her hand and she cried out.

As he bent to comfort her, she started to rise and they crashed into each other, head to head. In an agony of confusion, Mary Ellen Crowley half knelt and seemed to wait for instruction.

"Let me help you up," Brian said. Her hand in his was cold. "I didn't see you down there. Did I hurt you?"

She shook her head, pushed a lock of pale hair from her cheek. "I was trimming the grass along the edge of the walk. It has to be done by hand." She held the heavy scissors toward him as though in affirmation of the words.

"I was so busy looking at your house, I didn't see you. It's a great house."

Mary Ellen examined the house briefly and shrugged. "I guess. Does Daddy know you're here?"

Brian caught the slightly worried, uncertain tone, remembered the night she fled, all pink softness, up the broad stairs.

She didn't look like a storybook princess now. She looked real, and reality gave her a fragile, somewhat pale and puzzling expectancy. It was the first good look Brian had had of Mary Ellen Crowley and he studied her intently.

She was small-boned and delicate, with a long, sloping waist and sharp, narrow hipbones which jutted against the dark-green shorts she wore for gardening. Her firm neat breasts pressed against the starched white school blouse and she fingered the top button nervously, then touched again at the heavy pale hair which had slipped from the band of green ribbon. Her face, heart-shaped, was slightly flushed but the natural pale translucency of fine skin was evident. Her brows were dark in contrast to her light hair and framed her deep-blue, slightly slanted eyes, which were fringed with thick, long, upswept lashes.

Self-conscious, she faltered under his open appraisal, wiped her damp upper lip with a crumpled handkerchief which she then tucked into the waistband of her shorts.

She gestured vaguely toward the house but faced him. "Does . . . is Daddy expecting you?"

He nodded, then reached out toward her. "You've got a smudge on your chin." She reached up instinctively and Brian caught her wrist. "Hey, watch it, Mary Ellen, you'll cut yourself." The scissors nearly made contact with her face.

Startled by his touch, her mouth opened, then she blinked and regarded the scissors. "Oh. Oh, yes." She shifted the shears to her left hand. When she bit on her lower lip, a deep dimple appeared in one cheek. "I'm really a mess, aren't I?"

"I wouldn't say that." It was a softly appraising remark and she accepted it without comment.

"How's your boy friend?" Brian asked abruptly.

There was a slight flare of color and a show of spirit. "I *told* you he wasn't my boy friend."

"That's right, you did." Brian pushed his hat off his forehead, rubbed a finger along the pressure line from the hatband, then readjusted it. "But I bet you *do* have a boy friend. In fact, I'd bet you have a *lot* of boy friends."

Guilelessly, she said, "Oh, but they're just 'boys.'" She wrinkled her nose and shook her head. "The sons of my father's friends."

Unexpectedly, he said, "*I'm* not the son of your father's friend."

Stillness surrounded them, an intimacy created by the oddly intense meaning of his words. Mary Ellen's eyes sought the shears; her fingers investigated the sharp points, the cutting edge. She glanced up at Brian quickly, a small smile ready at the corners of her mouth to prove she understood his words were meant in fun, but there was no answering smile.

"How old are you, Mary Ellen?"

"Eighteen."

"You don't look it, you look younger."

"Oh, no, really," she assured him earnestly. "In fact, I'm nearly eighteen and a half."

"I'm twenty-two," he said, and again it seemed a great intimacy and she reacted with some confusion. Brian reached over and took the shears from her and ran his fingertips lightly over the blades. "You should be careful with these things. Don't want to cut yourself."

There was a sudden loud banging: wooden stick on glass window. The old man was summoning him to the house.

Mary Ellen turned quickly. The color left her face. "Daddy's calling for you. You'd better go. He might know how long you've been standing here."

Brian moved a hand casually toward the house and returned the shears to her. He readjusted his hat again, hefted the weight of his package and started for the house. He stopped and turned. She was kneeling, snipping tentatively at the grass. "Will Saturday night be okay? I mean, you haven't got anything on for this Saturday night that you can't get out of, have you? You see, I only get Saturdays once in a while. The next one won't come up for a month."

The banging at the window started again. Mary Ellen glanced past Brian, then back again. "Saturday? Me?"

Brian nodded. "Yeah. With me. You like to go roller skating? I got some passes for the rink on Fordham Road." He jabbed a thumb over his shoulder and said, as though it was the easiest thing in the world, "Don't worry, I'll clear it with your old man. Okay with you?"

She looked down, nodded, snipped at the grass and cut her finger but held it hidden within the palm of her hand.

"I'll call for you at about seven, okay?"

There was a hard, shattering, crashing sound, followed by the harsh voice shrieking through the broken window, "Goddamn it, O'Malley, if you've come to see me, don't be all day about it!"

Mr. Crowley thumped himself around, thrust his head forward, squinted his eyes as though to test against an impostor. Finally, he nodded abruptly.

"Yes, yes. So it is. Yes." He stood absolutely still for a moment and the only sound was the soft tinkling of stained glass being brushed carefully into a dustpan by Mrs. Crowley. He shouted over his shoulder without looking at his wife, "For Christ's sake, aren't you finished with that yet, goddamn it?"

There was a soft flurry of quick brushing sounds as she hurried, then Mrs. Crowley rose from her knees and hushed apologetic words were aimed nowhere in particular. She left quickly and, with her departure, might never have even been present.

"Well, well, now, you've brought that package for me, have you?"

Brian extended the package but Crowley kept both hands on his stick and with a jerk of his head indicated where the package was to be placed. Brian hesitated for a moment, then moved carefully across the room and put the package on the huge leather-topped desk. He turned and watched Crowley struggle into his chair; he used more gestures and motions than seemed absolutely necessary, as though he enjoyed putting on a show for whatever purposes.

"Tell me something, O'Malley," the old man's voice crackled and the glittering eyes sought Brian's in a calculating, sidelong stare, "what the hell is it you find to talk about with *her?*"

For a moment, a split second, Brian drew a blank but the jerk of Crowley's head toward the broken window recalled Mary Ellen, the golden daughter, totally unmatched to either the whispering mother or the appalling father. It was a question asked with candor and apparent curiosity and it was unexpected and threw Brian off balance.

He debated a quick, smart answer, some fast, fresh wisecrack, but some sense of caution stopped the words in his mouth. Such an answer wouldn't be honest and the question had been.

"She's a very lovely girl, Mr. Crowley," he informed Mary Ellen's father.

Crowley raised his bone of a hand, a long index finger tapped lightly on the broad expanse of tight-skinned forehead. "Not too much up here, I don't think," he said confidingly.

Brian was surprised by the open confidentiality. "She'll do, Mr. Crowley," he said protectively.

Crowley regarded him for a moment, then said, "Ah, well, we'll see. We'll see. Well then, now, it seems to me that I've been reading something about you in the newspapers, eh? Is that right, eh?"

He indicated with a jerky wave of his arm that Brian was to be seated. The chair was several inches lower than Crowley's and the old man stared down at him. There was a slow, slashing exposure of white teeth, a wolflike grin cracked his face and Crowley nodded briskly.

"Yes, I read about your fine job in catching the murderin' bastards of the poor old man. Over a hundred was he, or thereabouts? What the hell, an old son of a gun and a damn, damn shame, yes."

Brian saw the knowing look, the easy, grinning triumph on Crowley's face. He wanted to leap from the chair and smash the grin right off his face. He grasped the wooden arms of the chair and leaned forward.

"It was you," he said softly. "It was *you* who shafted me!"

Crowley's smile stretched, then his lips sprang together and his teeth disappeared. "Well now, 'shafted' is your word, not mine." He struggled and fussed around with the walking stick, pulled himself to his feet and stood over Brian. "And how do you suppose," he asked in an innocent, wondering voice, "however in this whole wide world do you suppose that an old cripple like me could shaft a cute little bastard like you, O'Malley? Now why would I *want* to do a thing like that? Huh? Did you consider that, lad? *Motivation.* Certainly an important word for a police officer to consider."

"I don't know, Mr. Crowley. I'm listening."

Crowley peered down at him and nodded briskly, as though he was pleased, as though some previous judgment had just been confirmed. "Ah, I like a lad willing to listen and willing to learn. There are all kinds of lessons to be learned in this world, O'Malley. Yes, indeed."

Brian released the pressure in his hands, flexed his fingers and leaned back. He watched with an odd mixture of anger, curiosity and fascination.

"For instance, what, Mr. Crowley?"

The old man held a bony finger in the air, then pointed it at Brian. "What would you say is the symbol of power in this room, lad? The most absolute symbol of power? Ah, you're patting the gun at your hip, eh? Or perhaps the blackjack you carry in your hip pocket? Could knock a man senseless and the gun could shoot him dead. Well, look around." Slowly, in a shuffling gait, he turned a full circle, his arm thrust out into space as he surveyed the room. "In this vast room, here, without my having to leave this room at all, is the more powerful weapon. There. *There!*" He pointed a gnarled index finger at the black telephone on the desk, hobbled across the room and let his hand fall caressingly. The other hand idly picked out numbers and spun at random.

"Any strange collection of spins, any particular combination of letters and numbers, and through the magic of modern science, why God love us, but anyone's voice at all comes right into my ear and my voice travels the same magical route and ends directly in that other person's ear. Now wouldn't you call that a powerful, magic weapon?"

"I guess it depends on who's at one end and who's at the other," Brian said carefully.

"I guess you're right," Crowley said in a different voice. There was no longer a bantering tone. The tension which emanated from the old man could be playful and stimulating or could turn vicious and mean. The meanness was not the loud, bellowing, bullying display that Crowley had put on previously. It was a cold, sharp, controlled revealing of what lay, ultimately, at the center of him. It was a careful warning rather than a threat.

"Now, when *I* am at the end of this instrument and when the Police Commissioner is at the other end, this instrument becomes the weapon which can make or break a man, if you understand me."

Brian stood up, licked his lips, sucked in his breath and leaned over the man beneath him. "You're a real mean sonuvabitch, aren't you, Mr. Crowley?"

"I *can* be, if I set my mind to it." Suddenly, the smile cracked his face again and he nodded brusquely, then pointed to the chair. "Ah, sit down, sit down. You've not finished with the lesson of the day. For there's more to it than you seem to understand."

Patrick Crowley preferred to look down at someone. Aside from any symbolic position of power, it was physically more comfortable for his somewhat twisted neck. He caught the tough, wary expression, the slightly amused, puzzled, angry but curious reaction on the young man's face and he nodded. He hadn't underestimated O'Malley; the little bastard was cute and sharp and tough and he liked him.

"Now someone might think me a man to take offense at a fresh-mouthed young guy who gives me a bit of his lip, lad, but that's not the case. Oh, no, not with Pat Crowley it's not." He shifted, arranged himself so that the stick was aligned to hold most of the weight of his long, lanky body. His hands moved, one over the other, on the knob of the stick. "I've never yet in my entire life run into a third-grade detective who was worth a damn. It's a bad thing for a bright young lad to get caught up in the Detective Division."

Brian's mouth opened; he started to say something but couldn't match the words to his confused thoughts. Instead, he made a sound, a laugh, an incredulous gasp, and shook his head.

"Ah, it's not the place for a man capable of better things. See, once they get you in the detectives, it's push and pull, scheme and plan, to get second grade and then the whole damn routine all over again to finally make first, and damn few do make first, and then it's the rest of your life to hold on to what you got." His tone was warm and friendly and confiding, as though they'd known each other a lifetime.

Finally, Brian found words. "You trying to tell me, Mr. Crowley, that . . . that you were doing me a *favor?*"

Crowley regarded him for a long moment, then the wolf grin split his face and his head bobbed in a sidewise motion of assent. "Ah, see now, how things can turn about and change just by the mere considering of a different explanation than that which first occurred? Isn't it interesting though?"

Impulsively, Brian said, "Well, Mr. Crowley, with you doing me favors, I won't need to worry about any enemies."

There was a deep, rumbling, gagging sound in Crowley's chest and it was several seconds before it worked its way up to his throat and finally sputtered out of his split lips. The sound turned Crowley's face purple. Brian was no less alarmed than the first time he'd seen Crowley laugh, but at least this time he knew what it was. The laughter struggled against Crowley's body for a few seconds, then subsided into a rasping hoarseness.

314

"Well, ah, well, there, now, easy does it, eh?" Crowley folded himself into his chair, adjusted his stick, rubbed his nose vigorously and his face froze at the interruption as his daughter tapped lightly on the open door. "Eh? Eh, what the hell do you want?"

She leaned in, glanced quickly from Brian to her father. "Daddy? Daddy, Mr. McHugh is here for his two o'clock appointment with you. I checked, Daddy, he's on your appointment calendar."

"Well, tell him to cool his heels until he's sent for, goddamn it." Crowley's mouth pulled down as he watched his daughter duck out into the hallway. He cocked his head to the side and studied Brian, whose face was still turned toward where Mary Ellen had been.

He coughed loudly, caught Brian's attention fully. "In deciding whether you've been shafted or favored, O'Malley, consider this. When a bright lad makes sergeant, the shield is his; when he makes lieutenant, the shield is his. When he makes captain, the *Department* is his. Take the exams, lad, take the exams."

He struggled to his feet with less difficulty than before, and Brian stood up. Crowley glared at him with a new intensity and the bantering tone was gone, the playfulness was gone, and a cold, raw sound came into his voice. He seemed a total stranger to anyone Brian had previously been confronted by. Before him was a tough, ruthless, bitter survivor.

"It's customary, O'Malley, when someone's done you a favor, to say thanks for it."

It was ultimatum, not needle or sarcasm or taunt. It was real.

Brian knew instinctively that a smart reply at this point would destroy him. He sensed, without the slightest doubt, that he was not a match for the power of Patrick Crowley.

It didn't cost him as much as he would have thought. It hardly cost him anything at all.

"Thanks, Mr. Crowley," he said thickly.

Crowley held it for several seconds with satisfaction, absorbed it like knowledge: the admission, acceptance, recognition. Then the moment broke into fragments of movement, bodily adjustments, sighs, slight groans, curses at knee joints and shoulder pains. His face relaxed, became familiar again.

"On your way out, O'Malley, tell McHugh to get his ass in

315

here. You'll recognize the man by the fat bulk of him and his nervousness of manner. Goddamn, but I hate a man to be early for an appointment almost as much as I hate him to be late."

The bantering, friendly tone was back. Crowley, as Crowley, was back and Brian, sensing safety again, said to him in a tough wise-guy voice, "Right, Mr. Crowley. Oh, by the way, I'm taking Mary Ellen roller skating Saturday night."

Crowley's eyes brightened, glistened; he turned his head to the side and grinned. "Well now, and isn't that fine. Yes, indeed, that's a fine thing for young people to be doing. Roller skating. Yes."

As he walked down the long, winding hill, back to the elevated for his trip downtown, back into reality, Brian was lost deeply in thought. Christ. Holy Christ. He had just thanked old Patrick Crowley for keeping him from getting third grade. The old bastard just came right out and admitted it and Brian had listened to him and actually thanked him.

Yet what the old man had said made sense. What didn't make sense was why he bothered. Why he took an interest in Brian at all. That's what didn't make any sense at all.

On their very first date, Brian realized that Mary Ellen Crowley was like no other girl he had ever gone with. Her total innocence and expectations that he would treat her protectively made him feel strong and superior and mature. He talked more than he had ever talked in his life, for she was a good listener, who hung on every word and glowed at him.

Carefully, he related anecdotes about his job; he altered and censored incidents which might amuse her, careful not to offend. His desire to reach out for her and to press her to him, to hold and caress her, was different from other urges he'd had in the past. It was removed from blatant sexual desire, and while physical, it was part of the encompassing feeling that he must shield her from all unpleasant moments and knowledge.

Mary Ellen Crowley was the embodiment of all the virtues he had been taught through all his parochial school years. She *was* what girls were supposed to be.

He could not help but think of Mary Ellen as he stood beside Francis Kelly and witnessed his marriage to Marylou Delaney. He experienced an inexplicable feeling of guilt, not for anything that had ever passed between them, but because he felt sorry for Francis Kelly with a long lifetime ahead of him as Marylou's husband.

The Kelly apartment was too small and too hot and too crowded with celebrants who drank and ate too much too early in the day. Francis' mother, her face damp and flushed, pulled Brian close to her and embraced him with a special significance; he was part of Francis' past now and her momentary sadness contrasted with the jaunty cheerfulness of the little flowered hat which sat at a slight angle atop her newly permanent-waved iron-colored hair. Absently, she yanked at the stiff corset which was clearly outlined beneath the peach lace dress.

"Oh, Brian," she said, "wasn't it a lovely ceremony, all the girls comin' down the aisle and you lads standing there, so handsome and tall?" Mrs. Kelly wiped her eyes with a little lace-edged handkerchief, turned, distracted by relatives who were demanding more food.

Someone placed a drink in Brian's hand and waved a plate of food in front of him. He was clouted on the back by uncles of the groom who'd known him since he was four or five years old, carefully looked over by female cousins, hugged indiscriminately by neighbors as though this was his wedding day.

A hot, damp hand pressed on his neck and he turned to face Marylou Delaney, now Kelly. Her bride's veil, held by black bobby pins, perched in the mass of her thick dark hair and framed her wide bright-pink face like parted curtains. There were lipstick smudges on her cheeks, where enthusiastic kisses had been placed by girl friends and relatives. Her own mouth was shiny with dark lipstick. Her eyes moved from Brian's mouth to his eyes, then lingered on his lips as her red tongue moistened her lower lip.

"Well, well," she said in a husky, insinuating voice, "if it isn't the best man."

He moved slightly so that he was free of her touch. "Nice party, Marylou."

"How about a good luck kiss from the best man, Brian? Seems to me you didn't get to kiss the bride." She lowered her voice to a thick whisper. "Last chance, Bri."

"Sure, Marylou."

317

He leaned toward her, aimed at a spot between two clearly defined lipstick stains, but Marylou twisted her head, raised her hands and locked her fingers behind his neck and pressed her lips against his.

For one dizzy, confusing moment, he encountered the fullness of her mouth and absorbed the richness of the various emanations of her. She tasted of cheap make-up and sweet perfume and wilted flowers and deodorant cream and sweat and food and whiskey and heavy musty satin. Her strong tongue slid between his parted lips, created a secret between them, which her hands, locked tightly on the back of his neck, emphasized.

"Hey, how about a handshake for the groom?"

Brian pulled back abruptly, faced Francis Kelly's beaming smile and flushed goodhearted innocence, which shone from his slightly glazed eyes. Brian's lips tingled with the taste of Francis' bride. In a burst of confusion and forced heartiness, he hugged his friend in a strong embrace. They exchanged words which neither could hear because of all the noise around them; it was part of an expected established ritual, as was the whole noisy and exhausting celebration.

Brian was glad his family had gone up to the lake right after Francis Kelly's wedding. It was nice having the apartment to himself for a change; he had to work a four to twelve and could sleep late in the morning, which was good. It had been a long day.

Brian sat, head resting against the stiff antimacassar at the back of the easy chair, long legs extended, shoeless feet on the hassock. He felt the contour of the cold brown bottle of beer between his palms, drank without thirst, felt lazy and warm and too tired to do more than gaze in the darkened room at the shadows on the ceiling of the living room.

It was curious and it struck him as curious that the vaguely suggested patterns of cracked plaster and shadow had changed through the years, though in reality, physically, they remained the same. *He* was the one who had changed. What had been a large-bodied, small-headed dinosaur now, under his languid, thoughtful gaze, became some indefinable sexual object: imponderable, illusive, exciting.

The airplane near the corner, which had carried him across

318

cloudless skies in roaring pursuit of fame and glory, now, as he dreamed and drifted, became an extension of himself, of that mysterious part of his body which occupied and preoccupied vast stretches of his consciousness. His right hand relinquished the bottle, moved and touched lightly, held gently the quick-rising cylindrical hardness, so ready to respond.

He experienced a detached sense of wonder rather than the urgent conscience-destroying need which sometimes consumed him.

He shook his head, puzzled at his sexuality: an imaginary design on the ceiling of the living room could stir him.

His fingers slid up and down, not holding, just tracing. Mary Ellen. Did she know that this was what happened to a man? Had she any idea at all? He wondered what she'd think, how she'd feel if he took her hand and gently, carefully, taught her to explore.

He wanted to be her teacher, to lead her slowly through the ritual of physical awakening but without destroying her total innocence and total purity. He didn't know how he could possibly attain both of those opposing goals; in achieving one he'd destroy the other. He wished it would somehow be all right but he knew it couldn't be.

He wondered if Mary Ellen Crowley had even the slightest idea of what tremendous self-control he exerted in her presence. He wanted her to know, yet that knowledge too would infringe upon the complete innocence with which he endowed her.

He closed his eyes and remembered the dreams he'd been having recently after tense and careful dates with Mary Ellen. In sleep, freed totally from the control over which he'd felt so proud, there was nothing gentle or kind or considerate or careful or instructive or loving about him. He mounted her roughly, urgently, brutally, selfishly, explosively and her face beneath him was always remote and serene and trusting and it maddened him that her expression never changed. At the moment of release, just immediately prior to waking, he sought her face but it was never Mary Ellen who stared back at him. It was either Marylou Delaney, with her lipstick-smeared smirk of a mouth, or Debbie Gladner, with her cold, superior, untouched and unrelenting stare.

Brian held the beer in his mouth for a moment, swished it around his teeth and swallowed. He shouldn't be thinking of Marylou, not on her wedding night.

He wondered if girls had wet dreams or sex dreams, if they ever experienced that combination of release and guilt, desire and disgust.

He wondered if Mary Ellen ever thought about him deep into the night when she hovered between wakefulness and sleep. He pictured her clean and cool and peaceful and calm in a crisp white-and-blue nightgown with panties of cool blue or clean white and beneath that garment the triangle of hair would be the color of moonlight

He wondered how many men had screwed Rita Wasinski since the last time he'd screwed her.

Brian stood up abruptly and felt hot shame flood his face. To think of Mary Ellen one instant and Rita Wasinski the next was sacrilege, vile and dirty, as though he'd masturbated in church or in front of a statue of the Holy Mother.

The beer on an already too full stomach, the heat of the air-less June night, all made him feel heavy and dizzy. He went into the bedroom, stripped to his shorts in the dark and eased himself onto the bed.

Rita Wasinski came to him. Memory of her warm, giving body, with all its shared secrets and joys and excitements, engulfed him and in a confusion of unbearable desire not just Rita but other faces and bodies intermingled, intertwined, engulfed him.

All previous innocent, controllable, easy speculation turned into the urgency of that hard, demanding, relentless need and he couldn't excuse it. It was no wet dream. It was a conscious grasping of self and a conscious conjuring of girls he had had and girls he had never had and then it was over and he was left with his self-loathing and his hot, wet, sticky, empty exhaustion.

"Oh, Christ," Brian whispered. "Oh, Jesus, I'm getting too old for this."

TWENTY-EIGHT

In an odd way, Mary the Widow returned to life, even though it was a very limited, circumscribed life, through the death of her cousin, the nun. Sister Louise Matthew lingered for a long and painful time at the understaffed hospital run by the Sisters of the Order of Perpetual Help in Yonkers, New York.

When Mary O'Malley, newly recovered from a bout with the bottle, encountered the pale, small death mask, a miraculous transformation came over her. Her cousin's normally severe and reproachful gray eyes confronted her with an unspoken plea which reached the depths of Mary the Widow. It was arranged that she stay on and assist in the nursing of her dying cousin. The Mother Superior decided it would be a good way to keep Mary off the bottle and at the same time serve a useful purpose.

As it turned out, Mary the Widow indeed found a purpose in life, and if the finding came late, it was a wonder that it came at all.

There was no task she did not perform willingly, lovingly, eagerly and with a quiet, soft affection that the dying nun found comforting beyond words. Her illness was such that her body filled the room with the most unbearable stench. Even the most stoic and dedicated nursing Sisters betrayed by some flicker of nostril, some unconscious downward turn of lip the repulsion for the form of death which systematically claimed Sister Louise Matthew's earthly portion.

But not Mary the Widow. It was as though nothing could touch her. She found life in the fanatical dedication to the dying woman and a slight, sweet smile played about her lips and she hummed softly as she went about the most onerous tasks of cleaning the ruined patient and removing soiled linen and clothing. Her long hands, bone-thin from years of semi-starvation and self-neglect, caressed the damp pained brow, placed an escaped lock of oily gray hair inside the starched white nun's cap and found nothing distasteful. She did not have to steel herself to her service; devotion to task flowed from some vast reservoir within her. The years of formless waiting and mourning for the dead young husband were over. She no longer felt the terrible need to search inside the alcohol confusion and murkiness of her brain for the lover who would come no more.

A peaceful awareness of purpose, the first she had ever experienced, filled her, and when her cousin finally died, it was Mary the Widow who prepared the body with love and dignity.

She moved without grief from the dead cousin to the next sickest patient in the small hospital. Without anything having been discussed or decided, Mary O'Malley took up residence with the Sisters of the Order of Perpetual Help. The nuns regarded her with a special affection. They had seen her through the terrible years of her torment and now she was more dedicated and selfless than any of them. She was, in effect, their own private miracle.

When John O'Malley, home on leave from the Navy, came to visit his mother at the hospital, she regarded him serenely, touched his brow lightly, as though to seek out signs of death or disease. When her fingers came away from his cool, firm, healthy flesh, it wasn't exactly disappointment that she felt, but rather a lack of interest. Her special mystical call came from the presence of Death. Youth and health held nothing for her. She smiled absently at the tall, heavy-set young man but felt no sense of connection with him and was slightly puzzled when he clumsily embraced her and said that he wouldn't see her for a long time because he was going overseas.

She wondered where she had seen him before. She knew she had, somewhere, but it was all very vague and probably locked in that strange, hazy past which drifted through her mind sometimes late at night or early in the morning.

She told him that she hoped he had a very pleasant trip and

322

he promised to send her picture postcards from everywhere he went. She said that would be very nice indeed and thanked him.

"Well, she's a damned nut if you ask me," the old woman said, though no one asked her or intended to ask her opinion of Mary the Widow.

"I think it's fine, John," Margaret told her nephew, "that your mother is with the Sisters like that. It's strange how things work out, isn't it?" She leaned back slightly and regarded his large, steamy face. "If you don't look fine in your uniform, all grown up. I swear I wouldn't know you."

They all acted strangely, all except his grandmother. They watched him, measured him, commented on how much he'd changed, though he hadn't changed at all. Lost some weight, hardened through the belly and chest, but he was still John. That was what he wanted to tell them but he didn't know how.

"Stop standing there with your hat on your head, you big fool," his grandmother said. "Do I still have to teach you manners?"

He swiped at his hat quickly and grinned, grateful to her. He put the hat on Kit's head, pulled it down over her eyes and she clutched at it, begging to keep it.

His uncles and aunts and cousins all came and fussed over him. He felt uneasy, the center of all their attention. He ate and smiled and nodded and answered their questions quickly and was grateful when Brian took him to McCaffery's for some beer and then his uncles came and his older cousins.

They drank whiskey and got him to drink whiskey, which Gene and Matt and Peadar slugged down with beer. But Brian and John and Billy O'Malley, who'd just joined the Marines, couldn't keep up.

John's head spun on his shoulders and sweat dripped from his forehead and his legs felt funny, all unconnected and soft. He laughed at everything and his uncles kept punching him on the shoulders and slapping him on the back. And they kept congratulating themselves on how he had turned out, how they'd been right all along, getting poor Johnnie here into the Navy.

John laughed and agreed with them and laughed. Suddenly

he grabbed Brian's arm and they rushed into the men's room. His mouth filled with a terrible full taste and he vomited and apologized to Brian and vomited some more. Brian held on to his arm tightly and kept telling him it was all right, okay, kid, okay, and John went back with Brian to the bar.

Billy O'Malley bragged that the Marine Corps was the real thing, the Navy was easy stuff compared to the Corps, and John laughed when everyone else did and he drank beer over the burning taste of vomit deep inside his throat. He felt warm and safe and wildly happy when his Uncle Peadar flung an arm around him and said, "Oh, Christ, he's a good kid though, isn't he? Ah, what wouldn't we all give to have our Johnnie the Fireman, may he rest in peace, just get a look at him. He turned out all right, after all, didn't he?"

John O'Malley always knew that he was stupid. He knew that he seemed to see things in slow motion, to continue looking at what was already in the past. He knew he was always just a little out of step, but he bore the slightly out-of-focus feeling with patience and acceptance. When others made fun of him and played tricks on him, he responded with a sweet smile across his broad face, ready to join the laughter because when he did, the laughter of the others turned friendly and the teasing was usually less cruel and more approving.

He wondered what it felt like to be smart, to grasp things, to understand mysteries. He knew that most others did not live surrounded by puzzlement. He knew that when the others filed into the classrooms, seated themselves casually, good-naturedly clowning until the instructor showed up, none of them felt that terrible stomach-aching twist deep inside that he felt. None of them felt sweat, smelly and thick, down the inside of armpits and center of back. For John O'Malley the code classroom was exactly the same as any classroom at St. Simon's: threatening, frightening, a place where he would be revealed once more.

He looked around, a ready smile pulling at the corners of his mouth. He admired the way some of the guys were able to distinguish themselves, even though dressed exactly like everybody else. Some turned the collar of the denim shirt up just slightly along the back of their necks. Some angled the heavy white duck hat over one eyebrow; others shoved the hat back so that it clung precariously to the crown of a newly Navy-shaved skull.

He wished he could be like that, jaunty and calm inside, not all jumpy and feeling like he had to pee. John O'Malley's hat sat squarely across his broad forehead, just the way they told him it should.

The instructor arrived and he was a dapper guy in crisp fatigues that could stand all by themselves. He called the roll and they answered "Yo!" in that sharp way they had learned was the Navy way. Even John could do that, though it didn't make him feel any more comfortable. The instructor lugged a box to the top of his desk and had the first man in each row come forward and count out enough tapping devices for the others in the row. The instructor warned that nobody was to touch the device, just leave it alone for now.

The sounds of clicking and tapping filled the room. Even John lightly fingered the flat little key and depressed it a few times.

"Okay," the instructor said after a few minutes, "what the fuck does it take to convince you jerk-offs that I'm not kidding?"

His face convinced them, and his voice and the threatening tension of his body. They all clasped their hands in their laps as he said to do. Over the blackboard in the front of the room was a shade and the instructor hooked his index finger into the small metal ring and pulled, unrolled the chart to reveal the dots and dashes. John O'Malley felt panic, sick, familiar: the classroom part of himself. It thudded in his chest and down into his stomach. The chart was terrifying, foreign, incomprehensible, unknowable.

"Now this here is what the Morse code looks like," the instructor said, "but it's pure shit to think you're gonna learn anything from looking at a chart even though I'm gonna give each of you a small card with the code on it to study. What you're gonna do," he told them, "is you're gonna *listen*." He stressed the word and it reverberated in the air as he yanked on the metal ring and sent the chart spinning out of sight. As it disappeared, John O'Malley felt a nameless sense of relief.

"You're gonna listen and listen and listen. You're gonna close your goddamn eyes and *listen!*"

Dot dash; dash dot dot dot; dot dot wait dot; dash dot dot dot.

The electrical sounds buzzed through him, not just through his brain, but through his body, his chest and stomach and arms and legs. He could *feel* the sounds at the tip of his fingers, at the ends of his curled toes. He saw the letters beneath his closed eyelids, actually *saw* them as they flashed through him. He chanted in unison with the others, identifying the sounds as letters. His voice rose strangely strong and certain and an odd sense of elation filled every part of John O'Malley's being.

By the end of the introductory lesson, John had absorbed the entire Morse alphabet, effortlessly, naturally, as though all his life he had been waiting for some special language, some clarifying magic which would render the whole mysterious world comprehensible at last.

Through some freak quirk or accidental arrangement of nerve endings, through some blood-borne never-before-encountered natural instinctive rhythm, he, of all of them, had a positive genius for codes.

The instructor said he was a wise guy for failing to answer truthfully when the class was asked if anyone knew the code already. A few of the other guys convinced the instructor that John O'Malley didn't lie, not ever. They also had to convince John O'Malley that the code, the dashes and dots and pauses and flickers, did *not* speak to anyone else the way it spoke to him.

The magic sounds, which spoke to him more clearly than anything he had ever encountered before, were truly a special gift. In his bunk that night, the other guys threw sounds at him, beeps and clicks. With a sense of awe and bemused admiration, they heard him respond accurately, astonishingly.

He lay awake that night, afraid to sleep. He moved his eyes from side to side, traced the sagging bulges of the mattress inches over his face, blinked himself awake time and again so that he wouldn't fall asleep. Because, he reasoned, if he fell asleep, he might lose the gift; it might all drift away. And he had been waiting too long.

But it didn't drift away. It became firmly fixed in his brain and he devoured codes like sustenance, was the first in the class to raise his hand, shyly, to hand in the decoded message which had flashed, singing, through his brain.

The instructor discussed John O'Malley with the Senior Coding Instructor and they went over John O'Malley's records. It was decided that he was one of those rare flukes that turn up from time to time: a nearly retarded boy, messing up at almost everything he touched, but with an absolute gift for codes.

They jumped him into advanced code classes, threw the most complicated codes at him. It was all the same to John O'Malley.

The Senior Coding Instructor scratched his chin and said, "I guess it's because the rest of his head is so damn empty. All his concentration goes into what he hears on the earphones. I guess it's something like the way a blind man can concentrate on sound. Ya know, nothing to distract him."

Cables were sent, thousands of miles away, about John O'Malley's rare and perfect gift. After his leave, because of his facility, he was to be given a very special assignment.

TWENTY-NINE

Kit O'Malley carefully stretched her pistol-holding hand along the branch of the huge old tree and aimed directly into the window of Eileen Fahey's living room. She closed one eye, sighted, and systematically shot all six of the stupid girls dead as they bobbed and ducked into the pan of water and came up with apples stuck in their mouths like pigs.

What a dumb way to spend Halloween. Kit remembered all the things she and Bobby Kelly had planned to do. It hadn't been much fun doing them with some of the other boys; it just wasn't the same. Bobby Kelly had the mumps and there was a whole year of anticipation shot to hell. He'd tried to sneak out the fire escape but his father caught him and whacked him, because, he yelled, "A sneak is a sneak, mumps or no mumps!"

Kit fingered the heavy stocking filled with flour which was tied around her waist; that was for thumping people. Her water pistol was filled with Waterman's ink; there was a bag of rotten eggs, carefully collected, one at a time, from the refrigerator over a period of weeks. She squinted at her Mickey Mouse watch; she still had an hour until she had to be home. Her limit was nine o'clock because it was a special night. She'd run the streets with the boys, knocking over ash cans in front of apartment houses where the janitor was known as a rat, making as much commotion as possible. She'd marked sidewalks and gutters with chalk and hunks of coal; she'd had a few thumping fights with opponents bigger than herself and considered herself victorious.

But there had to be something more, to make up for Bobby Kelly having let her down.

328

Her eyes moved from Eileen Fahey's dumb party to the tin shack on the big lot across the street. The plan came to her, full-blown, as though long conceived and just waiting for her to recognize it. She would blitz the shack; singlehanded she would mess it up so badly that the big guys would talk about nothing else until next year.

Carefully, she eased herself down the branches to the ground. Her heart pounded with building excitement and her mouth went dry from self-inflicted fear. She scanned the block, snatched up her bag of eggs, darted in the shadows to the edge of the street, waited until a car went by, ran across the street and leaped into the shadows on the edge of the lot. She climbed the hill in the big lot, breathless, body close to earth in a slithering motion. She willed herself to become invisible: no one could see her or know of her existence.

She crept to the edge of the silent shack and listened, then released her breath. The world was different from up here, strange and unfamiliar. She pressed her ear against the side of the shack and counted to ten, then waited again and surveyed the shack carefully.

It had been put together from bits and pieces of whatever materials a neighborhood of growing boys could scrounge. There were tin walls and a cutout window with a real wooden window frame. Instead of glass, the window had cardboard panes which kept out nosy people. The roof was flat, either tin or heavy cardboard.

Carefully, Kit O'Malley transferred her water pistol from her right hand to her left. She reached out, tested the doorknob. It turned with a creaking sound and the door opened inward with a sudden lunge. Kit found herself inside a dimly lit room, about ten feet by ten feet. The light came from a small electric bulb which dangled at the end of a cord which had been strung over a hook on the ceiling. The question of how they had ever managed to get electricity into the shack never even occurred to Kit.

She was more immediately concerned with what Timmy Mulcahy was doing here and how to get free of his grasp.

"What the fuck do you want here?" he demanded thickly as he bent her left wrist almost off her arm. "C'mere, lemme get a look at you, kid. Who the hell are you?"

The heavy odor of beer came not only from the row of empties along one side of the room but from Timmy Mulcahy's breath and from the sweaty odor of his body. Kit tried to pull free but Mulcahy held her in a terrible grip.

"Hey, come on, Mulcahy. Come on, will ya? Look, let go. It's me, Kit O'Malley. You know me. Let go, will ya?"

He leaned into her face, his hand went roughly to the back of her head and he jerked her face toward the light so abruptly that her sailor cap fell to the floor. His small eyes narrowed, then widened in appreciation.

"Hey, yeah. I know ya, don't I? You're that little girl plays ball so good, right? Hey, what the fuck you doin' dressed like a sailor boy anyways?"

"For Halloween, ya know. I'm wearin' my brother's Sea Scout shirt and my cousin's sailor cap. Hey, look, Mulcahy, let go of my arm, huh? You're hurting me."

He tightened his grip and moved closer to her face and said suspiciously, "Yeah? Well, what the fuck are you doin' here? What's in that bag? What are you up to?" He shook her with each question.

Kit began to feel afraid. It was one thing for boys her own age to use rough language around her or to jostle her. It was another thing for a grown-up man like Timmy Mulcahy. She moved, an inch at a time, tried to get nearer to the door, which Mulcahy had slammed shut.

"I was just going to . . . kind of . . . you know, just Halloween stuff. I was gonna shake some flour around and smash some eggs on the wall and stuff like that. You know, Timmy, for a Halloween joke on the big guys."

He released her, folded his arms across his chest and flung his head back with a snapping motion so that the heavy hank of greasy black hair was off his forehead for a moment before it fell back again. He studied Kit appraisingly.

"Hey, you know something, kid? You got real balls planning to do something like that."

"Well, look, I won't do anything now. I mean, okay, I got caught and fair is fair, so I'll just leave." Instinctively, she added, "See, my three friends dared me to do this, and they'll be wondering what I'm up to if I don't get back down from the lot, Mulcahy."

He didn't seem to even be aware of her rush of words. He

seemed to be thinking about his own last remark. He made a strange laughing sound down in his throat. "Hey, kid, don't you get it? Ain't that funny? You hear what I just said? Shit, I just said you got *real balls* planning to do something like that." He stopped laughing suddenly and lowered his head to peer at her through his hair. "You ain't got *no* balls at all, have you, girly? Huh, have you?"

Kit looked around quickly, searched for escape. There were no real windows; they were covered dummies. There was just the one door and Timmy Mulcahy's massive bulk covered it completely. On the walls were calendar pictures of half-naked women and a few dirty words neatly printed and repeated with artistic flourishes and a few dirty drawings in crayon. There were some dirty old couch cushions against one wall. And the line of empty beer bottles.

Kit dove for a bottle, clutched it by its long neck. "Get outta my way, Mulcahy."

Mulcahy, lost in his own contemplation, might have been deaf. "If you ain't got no balls down there, girly, then what have you got, huh? Let's have a look at what you got there, kid."

He moved so ponderously, so irrevocably that she hadn't time to elude him. The bottle flew harmlessly from her hand as he knocked her to the hard-packed dirt floor. She felt the bulk of her water pistol press into her buttock, felt the rough, coarse, sandpaper hands grab at her as she whirled and twisted and kicked.

There was a sudden explosion of shock in the pit of her stomach and her breathing stopped. She could neither inhale nor exhale or move or make a sound from the sledge-hammer impact of Timmy Mulcahy's fist.

"Now keep the hell quiet, you little bitch," the dark reddened face over her said. "I'm gonna see for myself what the fuck you got down there."

There were parts of it she would never remember, a totally blank passage of time during which she somehow found her way down the hill of the big lot, crossed the street, walked through the darkness of the small lot, climbed a fence which separated Dr. Fineman's tiny back yard from the lot and fell in a huddle against the back door of the doctor's house.

She remembered that the dog, Murphy, came over to her and

that she reached up and wrapped her arms around his bobbing, nodding head and hid her face against his acrid fur.

That was where Mrs. Fineman found her, bleeding, torn, gray with shock but adamantly refusing to release her rigid grasp of arms and locked fingers which held the dog close to her and kept others away.

It took Brian O'Malley three days to get Timmy Mulcahy.

Had he caught him on the night of the rape, there was no question but that he would have killed him. Dr. Fineman and Dr. Mahoney both sensed that immediately. They fed him a couple of shots of cheap abrasive whiskey, handed him a lit cigarette, tried physically to restrain him.

"We'll not let you go running off into the streets the way you are now, Brian," Dr. Mahoney told him. "We've your family to think of if you're not sane enough to think about them yourself." The large hand was firm on his shoulder and only released him when Brian sat down on one of the stiff wooden chairs in the doctors' inner office.

"Now, Brian," Dr. Mahoney said carefully, "you could arrest him, you know. That's one alternative."

Dr. Fineman's bushy black brows shot up; he yanked the short cigar from between his teeth. "One *alternative?*" he asked his colleague. "Are there *alternatives* in this situation? The man's committed an act of criminal sexual assault on a fourteen-year-old child. O'Malley's a policeman; he knows the law. What are the alternatives to arresting this bum, Peter? I'm really curious."

Mahoney cursed softly, then jabbed an index finger at Fineman. "You'd have the child subjected to a courtroom trial? After what she's been through?"

Fineman lit a match and puffed the dead cigar to life until clouds of foul smoke surrounded him. "No, not necessarily a trial. I don't think it would ever get that far. But, God, this bum should be arrested and charged. It can be handled discreetly. Look, I've got a few friends who could see to it —"

Brian stood up and towered over the doctors. "Fuck your few friends, Dr. Fineman. Look. You both mean well. Okay. Take care of my sister. *I'll* take care of Mulcahy."

• •

Mulcahy disappeared for a while and Brian's search became not so much a physical thing as a carefully controlled emotional ordeal. He took time off from the job, used some overtime that was coming to him, pleaded family illness, and devoted himself to searching and waiting. Mostly waiting, because he considered Mulcahy an animal, and with an animal's instinct, he would head for home.

On the third night, Brian watched as Mulcahy finally returned to his family's flat on Park Avenue and East 180th Street. He felt no change in the dead, still calmness of his brain as he leaned into the wooden doorframe of the tenement next to Mulcahy's and waited. It would have been so easy, right there, in the rain-empty street to confront Mulcahy; his fists clenched and unclenched as he watched his prey lean heavily on the doorknob, then shove himself through the creaking, battered front door.

Brian lit a cigarette and breathed evenly. Now he knew where Mulcahy was, that he felt it was safe to return home, that he was no longer wary. There was the sound of a train as it roared down the tracks of the Central. It was a short train, just a few cars with a few vague passengers returning from Manhattan, heading to Westchester, peering blankly toward the dark walls which lined their passage.

None of them saw Mulcahy as he shuffled out of the house and walked to the middle of the sidewalk and faced the building where he lived and hollered at the blackened windows, "Hey, Patsy, open the fuckin' door, you dummy. I ain't got no key. Patsy, open the fuckin' door or I'll kill ya."

There was a sliding sound, a pale face appeared at a window, the voice was thin and frightened. "Timmy, come back tomorrow. Ya can't come in tonight; ya been away so long and ya scared me just now. Come back in the mornin' when you ain't drunk, Timmy. Me and the kids're sick; ya can't come in tonight." The window closed and Mulcahy lurched toward the house, then back.

He stood, shook his fist in the air at his wife, barricaded with their children against the rage with which he always returned from a drinking bout.

He cried out obscenities and threats, circled uncertainly, then headed up the street. Brian dropped the cigarette, stepped on it, shoved his hands in his pants pockets and followed Timmy Mulcahy at a safe distance.

Mulcahy stopped at a corner bar two blocks away, pounded with heavy fists at the closed door. He ripped a sign off the door and held it toward the streetlamp. "Closed due to death in family" the hand-printed message explained. Mulcahy ripped the cardboard sign into several pieces, dropped the debris onto the sidewalk into a puddle of rain water. Brian hunched against a renewed onslaught of rain and walked close beside the line of parked cars as Mulcahy picked up speed toward a new destination.

It was a dank, tiny bar on Fordham Road and Third Avenue, empty except for an elderly couple who sipped beer wordlessly in one of the two booths and the beefy, bare-armed bartender who glanced at his wristwatch when Mulcahy entered. Brian watched from outside as Mulcahy swallowed a shot, followed by beer, which he guzzled, and reordered. After thirty minutes, the elderly couple emerged, walked stiff-legged and in matched slow stride, silently beneath the Third Avenue el. Then Mulcahy came out onto the black wet street and staggered up the hill of Fordham Road.

It was nearly 1 A.M. All the stores were closed; no loiterers or strollers were tempted by the cold, wet autumn night.

The terrible, building, anguished fury, held tightly within the deliberate coldness with which he regarded Mulcahy, nearly choked Brian. He knew he was going to get Mulcahy now, on this broad deserted street.

Mulcahy missed his footing, slipped on a paper bag, fell, his face hitting the sidewalk. He got to his feet, cursed, kicked at the paper bag, looked up toward the sky, seemed finally to realize that it was raining. He pulled his soaking jacket tightly around him, carefully turned his collar up, then sought some protection in the deep-recessed entrance to a shoe store. He leaned against the showcase of women's shoes for a moment, then moved out of the entranceway and stopped in front of a jewelry store.

The window of the jewelry store glittered with the reflected light of the streetlamp. Small diamond rings glowed and sparkled. Wristwatches took on luster from the gleaming raindrops which ran slowly in long slender rivulets down the length of the window. Mulcahy balanced with his fingers pressed heavily against the window, stared unseeing at the merchandise displayed before him.

"Turn around, Mulcahy," Brian said hoarsely.

"Huh?"

Stupidly, slowly, face thrust forward, eyes narrowed to pierce the dark, Mulcahy turned. "Yeah? Who's that?"

He wasn't as tall as Brian but he was heavier, in the chest and shoulders, through his massive arms and muscled legs. Timmy Mulcahy, twenty-four, father of cretins, ex-amateur light heavyweight, dock-walloper, raper of little girls. It overwhelmed Brian for one shattering moment: the breathing, grunting, stinking physicality of the man.

He delivered the first essential blow swiftly. He hadn't realized how huge Mulcahy was, and in the first breathless instant of confrontation, a cold, clear terror of reality sent Brian's knee to Mulcahy's unprotected and unprepared groin.

The rest was professional and methodical. Brian felt the leather covering of his blackjack grow damp in the palm of his hand as he delivered butt-end blows to Mulcahy's face and throat.

Mulcahy moved heavily, hunched to protect himself, but Brian kicked his head hard enough to flatten Mulcahy to his back.

"You bastard, you bastard, you dirty fucking bastard," Brian whispered over and over again. "I want to kill you, you dirty fucking bastard."

Mulcahy peered at him through swollen lids, shook his head from side to side as though trying to clear it. Unable to defend himself, taken too swiftly and without warning, he absorbed the battering without comprehension.

Who the hell is this guy anyways?

Mulcahy's torn and bloody mouth formed some words and finally Brian heard him say, "A mistake, mister; you're making some mistake. Hey, a mistake, a mistake."

"Yeah, a mistake, Mulcahy. You made a mistake you're not gonna forget for the rest of your life."

Mulcahy's head fell heavily to the sidewalk, unconscious.

Brian, breathing in short, quick, unsatisfying gasps, looked up and down both sides of the street. No one. Silence. Just

335

rain and some wind and his own breathing and some groaning from Mulcahy. He felt a sudden empty hollowness.

It wasn't enough. Beating Mulcahy wasn't enough. He could kill him, right here, right now, but that wouldn't be enough. He wanted to shake Mulcahy conscious, stand him up, start again.

Brian pressed his forehead against the cool wet window and closed his eyes for a moment. When he opened them, his eyes fastened on the small twinkling diamond rings, a display box, right down in the front of the window, with unreadable little price tags attached to each ring.

It came to him full-blown, and as the plan came, he acted on it immediately and without hesitation.

With the butt end of his jack, Brian smashed the jeweler's window three times, four times before the glass cracked and shattered into the display case. Carefully, he reached in, grabbed rings and watches indiscriminately, turned and jammed them into Mulcahy's jacket pocket. He reached for a little jeweled music box, small enough to fit the palm of his hand, and he shoved that into Mulcahy's pocket.

He dragged Mulcahy, dead weight, comatose, halfway to his feet and shoved his right arm along the broken glass edge of the window. Blood burst through Mulcahy's torn wrist and smeared the satin lining on which the jewelry rested inside the window. He forced a few gold rings inside Mulcahy's fist, then let him fall back to the sidewalk.

Brian dug in his back pocket and found his throwaway: the .32 caliber gun he had acquired on advice of his uncles.

Listen, kid, you never know when the hell you'll find yourself in a situation that calls for some quick protective thinking. If you damage some bastard, always make sure he has a weapon on him.

He carefully wiped the gun with his handkerchief, then forced it into Mulcahy's hand, then dropped it inside the jeweler's window: the butt of the gun had served as Mulcahy's burglar tool. Then Brian turned and walked quickly away without turning back.

Two blocks away, Brian walked over to a small green police

call box, opened it, picked up the receiver and in a low muffled voice he said very quickly, "Hey, listen, there's some man
and he's robbing the window of Fox's Jewelry Store on Fordham Road and Webster Avenue. Yeah, he's there right now. I
just went past him on the other side of the street. And hey,
listen, the guy's got a gun."

He hung up without waiting for the inevitable questions,
closed the little metal door, walked across Fordham Road and
down to the Valentine Theater, where he waited and watched
as the patrol car pulled up three minutes later.

He knew just how they felt, the patrolmen, as they leaped
from the patrol car, guns drawn, flashlights picking out the
scene. He knew how tense and excited and ready they were.

"Holy Christ," the patrolman closest to Mulcahy said, "the
guy musta fallen through the window. He's all cut up. Better
call an ambulance, Frank. Hold it a minute till I get the bum's
gun."

Brian moved silently, unseen, along the wet street, up to the
Grand Concourse, where he turned left and headed directly
into the rain and toward home.

They never mentioned it among them. His mother's mouth
tightened, her face went pale when she read about Timmy
Mulcahy's arrest in the *Bronx Home News,* and later when
she read that he had been sentenced to fifteen years in prison
for armed robbery, she said nothing but Brian noticed a
strange, unfamiliar hard glow in her eyes.

Kit was quiet and seemed thoughtful and withdrawn and
she developed an odd hesitation when she spoke, not quite a
stutter but a pause between words. One Saturday, Brian heard
his mother tell Kit to go out and play and he heard his sister's
response, slow and tortured and not like Kit at all.

There was a sudden explosion of sound and Brian lay still
on his back, unable to believe it was his mother's voice.

"Now, you listen to me, Katherine O'Malley, I've put up
with your silences and your whispers and your tripping on
your tongue all I'm going to. I'll shake your head off your
shoulders and take the strap to you myself if you don't quit
this moping around and mooning over yourself. Now take
yourself up to the schoolyard and take your basketball and go

find Bobby Kelly. The poor lad must think you've lost your sense you've neglected him so." There was a softening in the harsh voice, just slightly, "Go on now, Kit. I'm telling you that you *must!*"

Kit ran through the house, slammed out the door. He heard the basketball bounce as she ran, then he heard Kit's voice call out, "Hey, Bobby. Hey, Bobby, wait up, will ya?"

In the silence that followed, Brian heard a gasp, a great swallowing sound, as though his mother had held her hands over her mouth not quite in time. Then he heard the soft sounds of her prayer and he leaned back in bed to wait until she returned to the kitchen.

THIRTY

He hadn't seen Arthur Pollack for a long time and his first impression was that Arthur was lost inside his uniform. The coat was too long at hem and sleeve; the visor of his cap practically covered his forehead and the earflaps obscured most of his neck. Arthur enthusiastically offered Brian half of a mittened hand.

"Hey, Brian, gee, kid. Gee, it's great to see you."

Actually, it seemed that Arthur was having difficulty in seeing anything. He wore small, round steel-rimmed tinted glasses which steamed over as soon as he came into the heated storeroom. Arthur shrugged and his narrow body shivered inside the large coat.

"God, it's cold out there. I don't know how those crazy people can sit through these football games week after week."

"We've got some hot coffee, Arthur. One of the guys keeps a hot plate here. Jesus, you look like you need a bucket of hot coffee."

When Brian handed him a mug of coffee, he felt a surprising warmth of affection for his friend. He shook his head good-naturedly. "Gimme your coat; I'll put it over here with mine. My God, what have you got, five sweaters?"

Arthur held up his fingers. "Three, plus long underwear. I am not what you'd call a fan of winter." He wrapped his hands around the mug and smiled up at Brian. "So. Well, Brian, kid, how are you doing?"

The small gray eyes, one turned in slightly, searched his face candidly and Brian recalled the last time they had met and he remembered vividly, painfully, but now somewhat sadly and wistfully, Rita Wasinski.

It was a funny thing. They hadn't seen each other in more than six months yet Brian felt the exchange, unspoken, between them. He had learned what Arthur had known all along. You live with what you have to live with; time heals; things work out. Wordlessly, Arthur was asking him: Wasn't I right, kid?

Brian smiled, nodded, just the way Arthur had nodded to him. It was a peculiar thing. When he was around Arthur, some essence of Arthur, his mannerisms, his method of communicating, flowed into Brian. While not consciously imitating Arthur, Brian found himself adopting his gestures, his nuances. This seemed to relieve him of the necessity of too many words.

"Things are good, Art. Hey, what's with the glasses? I never saw you with glasses before."

Arthur's hand went up and he touched the frame lightly with his fingertips. "I had some kind of infection in my eyes for a few weeks so I got to wear these tinted glasses for a while. They're actually just windowpanes. You know, Brian, I don't know why everybody is surprised when they hear I got 20-20 vision. Even the eye doctor I went to was surprised. I don't know why."

There was a deep rolling sound rising upward toward the little room where they were. The floorboards rumbled as one team or the other made a good play. Arthur turned toward the door and shrugged.

"Now if it was baseball and it was the Dodgers and the Giants, *then*, I'm interested. Football? Forget it. So, Brian, how come you're up in my precinct? Isn't the Polo Grounds a little far afield for a Clinton Street man?"

Brian shrugged without answering. He'd had a lot of good assignments that Arthur knew nothing about; he'd seen prize fights, the rodeo, the President of the United States, a few movie stars up close.

They exchanged a few bits of gossip about mutual acquaintances, bantered back and forth good-naturedly, then Arthur said, "Well, Brian, I guess you don't know, but I'm getting married."

For one sharp breath-catching instant, Rita Wasinski's face, pale, startled, frightened, flashed through his mind and kept the words of congratulations from getting any farther than his

340

throat. He knew that Arthur had seen the hardly discernible hesitation.

"I'm one hell of a lucky guy, too, I'll tell you," Arthur said smoothly. "Naomi is a schoolteacher and she comes from a complete, large family, the whole works: father, mother, one sister, one brother and even a grandmother. She accuses me of proposing because I want a ready-made family." He reached out, tapped Brian's shoulder and winked. "When you meet her, don't tell her she's right!"

Brian shook Arthur's hand and spoke in a rush of words, all the right things he was supposed to say. He spoke warmly and quickly, as though he owed Arthur an apology for something he could not define.

Surprisingly, he found himself speaking about Mary Ellen Crowley, and as he spoke about her, she became more real than she seemed at times when he was with her.

Arthur studied him carefully, tilted his head to one side and smiled warmly. "Brian, that's great. Really great. I knew there had to be a reason for you to look so good." Arthur straightened up and thrust his head back. "You notice the change in me? Everybody says I look great and that I must be in love!"

"Arthur, you're beautiful. Really, buddy, I hardly knew you."

"So, when are you setting the date, kid?"

"Hell, I'm in no position yet, Arthur. I still got my kid sister and brothers, you know. Family." Unexpectedly, he added, "But I'm pretty sure she's gonna be the one."

He'd never said that before to anyone, never really thought much about it, but as he said the words, he knew them for fact. He'd marry Mary Ellen Crowley sometime, in the future. That was as definite as if it had been decided so long ago he couldn't remember the exact time or place.

A guy named Walsh, big, red-faced, twice as wide as Arthur Pollack, shoved the door open and the room filled with a cold blast of air.

"Shit," Walsh said, "it's almost as cold in here. Some goddamn place they give us for a relief."

"There's some coffee," Arthur offered.

"Shit, that ain't gonna warm me up." He moved clumsily, dug inside his bulky blue-serge coat, came up with a flat can-

341

teen. He unscrewed the cap, took a deep swallow, sighed with appreciation, then offered the others a swallow.

"Thanks, but I've got a look coming from my sergeant in about ten minutes," Brian said.

Walsh opened his tight collar, took off his hat, rubbed a large raw hand over his short red hair and squinted at Brian. He made a deep throat sound which was not quite a laugh. "Shit, no sergeant's gonna go worryin' about what's on *your* breath, O'Malley. Who you kiddin'?"

Brian's eyes glazed and Arthur saw his mouth tighten and his head come up slightly. "I'm not kidding anybody, friend," he said. "There's nobody around worth kidding."

Walsh considered this for a moment, examined it and decided it was not worth bothering with. He scanned the small room and grumbled at the lack of comfort. "Well," he conceded, "at least they got a radio. I wonder if the fucking thing works."

He twisted the knob, then adjusted the tuner. There was some heavy static until Walsh zeroed in on the station he sought. The familiar laugh and narrow metallic voice filled the small room: *Who knows what evil lurks in the hearts of men? (laugh) The Shadow knows! (laugh-laugh-laugh)* . . .

"For Christ's sake, Walsh, you gonna listen to that?"

Walsh puffed his stub of a cigar to life and ignored Brian.

Arthur stretched and flexed his thin arms, ready to do battle with his heavy uniform overcoat. He eyed it sadly. "I wish this was as warm as it is heavy," he said. He seemed to sink an inch or two under its weight. He jotted down his schedule for the next few weeks and handed the scrap of paper to Brian. "Let's get together, kid, maybe with our girls, maybe a little restaurant hopping, huh? Or maybe just the two of us for a drink or something, okay?"

Walsh abruptly turned the volume of the radio up.

Arthur took the hint and said, "I better get back on post."

Brian buttoned his coat. "Wait, I'll go with you. I'm on meal relief. Gotta see if I can catch a hot dog before my time is up."

"Don't eat the hot dogs here, Brian," Arthur advised. "Did I ever tell you about the time I worked for a hot-dog company? Well, it was the company that sells to the stadium and—"

Brian held his hand up. "Don't, Arthur. Please. Because I

got a feeling you're going to tell me about all kinds of terrible things mixed up in the frankfurters."

"Listen, Brian, if you knew what I knew, you'd never eat another one of those poisoned things again."

"I've eaten six so far today, Arthur," Brian said and pressed his hand against his flat stomach. "Don't tell me anything. Not anything at all."

They started down the ramp which led to the interior of the stadium, stopped for a moment to exchange greetings with a couple of patrolmen heading for relief. The two older men were football fans and they were vigorously arguing a point and asked the younger policemen for an opinion.

The discussion became very involved because Arthur started to kid them along, and even though he knew nothing about football, he was convincing. Brian backed him up, taking his cues from him.

There was a sharp blast of cold gray wind from around the corridor that led to an aisle into the upper tier of the Polo Grounds and a roar of human voices rose, the familiar roar of excitement, so familiar it went almost unnoticed by the four policemen.

It was Arthur who noticed first, sensed, felt, something different. He held his mittened hand up for a moment, then grabbed Brian's arm so that the others turned to him in surprise. Arthur tilted his head toward the sound, which had changed somehow, almost imperceptibly. He moved toward the opening, and the others followed.

They stood looking down at the playing field wondering what play had caused the strange, indefinable scene. Incomprehensibly, players on both teams were mingling, hands on each other's arms, shoulders, not teammates, just players mingling with umpires and officials who seemed to wander on the field in a daze. They all stood, puzzled, waiting to absorb what the nearly incoherent voice of the announcer on the loudspeaker had said.

Fans stood up restlessly, leaned forward, questioned, shrugged. Some people yelled for the game to go on, yelled "What the hell is going on?" "What the hell is the delay?" "Come on, what gives?"

"Hey, Jesus, hey, Jesus, you guys."

They turned, the four policemen, and there was Walsh, hat off, coat off, cigar in his hand, his large, normally red face gone white as a sheet.

"What's up, Walsh?" Brian asked.

They moved toward him, the four surrounded him in the corridor. Walsh's face contorted, puzzled. His mouth was dry and his voice crackled when he spoke.

"Jesus, I don't know. See, I was listening to *The Shadow*, you know? Right?" He looked at Brian and then at Arthur as though he needed them to confirm this fact. "Well, then, right in the middle of the story, see, they interrupted the program. This guy just busts right in with a news announcement and he says that the Japanese had just bombed Pearl Harbor. And that all of our warships there got sunk. And that this means that we're at war with Japan. Jeez, you think it's some kinda joke like that nutty guy pulled about the Mars invasion a coupla years back?"

One of the older patrolmen raised his eyebrows and turned to his partner. "Pearl Harbor? Where the hell is Pearl Harbor?"

Only Brian O'Malley knew where Pearl Harbor was and that the U.S.S. *Arizona* was currently in Pearl Harbor and that his cousin Radioman John O'Malley was stationed on the U.S.S. *Arizona*.

Arthur heard the quick choking intake of breath, the gasp as though Brian had been kicked in the stomach. Arthur saw Brian's face drain of color, turn as white as Walsh's.

"Brian, hey, what is it, kid?"

Brian stared at Arthur and moved his head slightly, then said softly as a moan, "Oh, Holy Mother of God. *Poor John!*"

The O'Malleys didn't have much time to grieve for John. Too many things happened too quickly. Secretly, his uncles might have questioned themselves about the ultimate wisdom of their solution for poor John, but among themselves none of them betrayed anything but pride in his heroism as described in the Navy Department's telegram.

Billy O'Malley, a full-fledged Marine, was to receive his mail addressed to him at something called "A.P.O. San Francisco" and his letters home, generally cryptic, were even more so.

Billy Delaney deserted Roseanne two months after their third child was born and joined the Army. After an absence of four months, he showed up, trim and sheepish, and signed over his allotment to Roseanne, and by the time he returned to camp in Kansas, they were reconciled.

Francis Kelly enlisted in the Navy and left behind a bloated, pregnant, self-satisfied Marylou, who promptly put a little rayon flag with a blue star on it in the window of her apartment to show that she was a Navy wife.

Arthur Pollack enlisted in the Army Air Force and was married just before his induction.

One cold and rainy day in March, Kevin came home from school much too early and with a glow of excitement that alarmed Brian the minute he entered the apartment. Kevin, three days after his eighteenth birthday, and three months before high school graduation, joined the Navy. There was no way to persuade him to wait and Margaret gave up the attempt and signed the papers.

All during the months following Pearl Harbor, Brian felt his life suspended in unreality. Only he was not part of everything that was happening around him; the others were all undergoing drastic changes, movement, relinquishing old responsibilities for the excitement of new adventures. Two of his younger cousins joined the Navy when Kevin did.

It was his mother and grandmother and younger sister who stood between Brian and the Army; he wasn't to be drafted because of his dependents.

It was Patrick Crowley who pointed out that there was always a way to do what you want providing you take the time to figure things out sensibly. What Patrick Crowley wanted was Brian O'Malley for a son-in-law; he knew that what Brian wanted was a way to get into the war.

"Well now, did you young people have a good time?" he asked in an artificially solicitous tone. "Why don't you go into the kitchen and help your mother prepare some tea?"

Mary Ellen responded to her father's suggestion as though it were a direct command: it was all the same.

He signaled to Brian and watched, settled in his chair, as Brian poured the two customary shots of whiskey. "Well," he said softly, "let's drink the health of your young brother," Crowley said, intent on Brian. "The girl tells me he's joined up in the Navy. Here's his health then." He tossed the drink to the back of his throat, gasped, swallowed, blinked and twitched, which was also customary. "Well, and have you thought much about your own self, Brian? This is a big war, lad, and you must be itchin' to get into it."

Brian slugged down the drink and carefully rotated the glass between his fingers. He'd known Crowley well enough by now to realize this was no casual conversation. It was the preliminary to something and he felt curiosity as well as caution.

"Well," Crowley said abruptly, "the girl will finish her first year at the Academy come this June."

"Yes, I guess so."

"When do you plan to marry her, if I may ask?"

The question took him totally by surprise. The glass slipped from his fingers and he felt the heat rush to his face as he bent to retrieve it.

"Well, that's been on your mind, I take it?" Crowley said flatly, more statement than question.

"Well, yes, sure. I mean, yes. But I'm not exactly in a position right now to . . . well . . ."

"Well, yes, sure, I mean, yes, but," Crowley mimicked him precisely, then laughed shortly. "God love us, but who the hell ever is in a position? The point is, I see no sense in investing another year on the girl at the Academy while you're cooling your heels and trying to see exactly what your position is." He gestured for another shot of whiskey and held his eye steady on Brian as Brian poured. "Not for yourself, lad? Ah, it's just as well, for you should have a clear head for this little talk. Now, here's what I had in mind, lad. You'd like to get into the fray, in a manner of speaking, lad, wouldn't you? What with even your little brother in the service, and your young cousin among the first killed, it must make it hard on you. If you'd your choice, what would it be?"

He dreamed of being a pilot, but realized the dream was unrealistic. He knew he became seasick, so the Navy was out.

"Marines," he answered, without much thought.

Crowley's head jerked up and down several times. "Well, that would be very fine. Would serve you well in the future, too. Remember this, lad, a man who hadn't a part of this great war, he won't be worth shit in the future. Remember that now."

And then Crowley put it to him, straight out, on the line. So that Brian could enlist in the Marines, he'd give a dowry of a year's tuition; that would more than support Brian's mother and grandmother and sister, along with Brian's allotment. Mary Ellen wouldn't need it; she'd live at home.

As quickly as the old man said the words, the possibility formed inside Brian with a force beyond anything he could protest. He'd have it all: the adventure, the excitement, the freedom of all responsibility, and Mary Ellen, waiting for him at home.

The technicality, easily tended, was asking Mary Ellen. She accepted shyly and he never knew if her father had ever discussed the situation with her and it seemed wiser not to ask.

When he left for war, he left a beautiful young wife, pregnant with their daughter, to spend the next three and a half years under the care of her parents.

PART FOUR

The Grandson:
Patrolman
Patrick Brian O'Malley
1970

THIRTY-ONE

The sound of his parents' voices penetrated the light stage of morning sleep. Sound rather than words washed over him and aroused no particular emotion but slowly memory touched along the edges of his consciousness. There had been other mornings, hundreds of other mornings, and the voices then had been neither soft nor careful. They were according him the status of a guest and he felt strange, as though he were in fact a guest in this house.

There had been mornings of his childhood when the angry words penetrated the walls of his room and forced him to partake of their unknowable mysteries. Force-fed on their secrets, he would emerge blank-faced, sit at the breakfast table with them and with their terrible silences. His sister's pale face, his mother's trembling hands, his father's angry and abrupt movements, filled him with a tension he could scarcely contain.

Under the weight of pretended ignorance, he and his sister were subjected to sudden, unanticipated questions from their father. How did you do on that Latin quiz? You get the math straightened out yet? Tell me again about that dance you want to go to on Friday night. Who did you say was going to chaperon? How the hell did your bike get broken this time?

Each question was a veiled accusation, a probe, an attempt to turn his father's anger to something which could be dealt with openly. He knew that, yet knowing, he always provided the substance.

"Don't, Patrick," Maureen had told him over and over again. Four years older than he, four years of greater endurance or wisdom or whatever it was that kept her eyes carefully down

351

and her mouth tightly closed. While he, Patrick, provided the tight-lipped grudging response to his father's interrogation. For God knew what reason, he would fix his steel-gray eyes on his father's wrath, feel himself freeze into breakable ice, sliver thin, melting in the growing danger, yet unable to stop himself.

Whatever was unfinished between his mother and father always left his father filled with a consuming anger. To restore himself, to purge himself, the force of that emotion would always turn toward his son.

Maureen told Patrick that it was his own fault. Why did he always put himself in the middle by tone of voice, glare of eyes? It was a senseless defiance that could only end badly for him.

He didn't know why. Helplessness. Because of a feeling of abject helplessness. The knowledge that he was totally powerless to heal the rift between them, yet forced to witness and by witnessing, participate, filled him with an anger of his own.

At some distant time in his life there had been the small, twisted, loud-voiced, evil-smelling old man for whom he had been named: Patrick Crowley, his grandfather. Recollection of his grandfather was not of an actual man but of a presence, powerful, terrible, a knowing presence which had somehow, mysteriously, incomprehensibly, controlled their lives, and at some point in that distant time, his grandfather died and Patrick wondered sometimes if he actually remembered the old man or merely remembered stories told him about the old man.

Although his grandmother lived with them until he was nearly twelve, she was no more part of his knowledge than had she been an apparition. When she died, no void was left. It was as though she had never been.

He could conjure nothing of her, no expression, sound, fragrance, essence, quality. There was nothing left of her beyond a few photographs to establish that she had indeed led an existence in close proximity to his own, within the same walls as part of the same family.

Patrick stretched his arms straight into the air, yawned, studied his wristwatch in surprise. He must have fallen asleep or had been so totally involved in fleeting memory that

352

an hour had gone by. They'd probably gone to ten o'clock Mass, which was late for his mother but standard for his father. His mother hadn't asked him about Mass and he felt a slight uneasy sense of shame. Not about missing Mass, but about her unwillingness to face him with it.

That was his mother: Don't mention it and it won't be.

She had aged. Her fine skin, tight over delicate facial structure, had eased somewhat and cracked at the corners of her eyes into a series of hairline wrinkles. He had been surprised; she had always seemed flawless, as flawless as a child actress who is never really young and never really grows old. He felt guilty at having seen, noticed, the signs of her age, as though he had betrayed her somehow. She was still a beautiful woman: forty-seven years old, slim as a girl, favoring blue clothes for her eyes, her hair tinted a discreet silver-soft blond.

He'd seen Henderson cast an appraising eye. Henderson's mother was one of those big women, arms larded and neck thick. Henderson's father looked like her twin.

God, he'd been proud of them, that they were his parents. In the hustle and commotion at Kennedy, that was his first feeling when he caught sight of them. Christ, they looked great.

His father had that finished look, the dark, certain pride of a man who knew who the hell he was: Deputy Chief Inspector in Charge of Public Affairs of the Police Department of the City of New York.

The security guard tried to make a big commotion about it but his father, with just a gesture, just a few quick whispered words, got things under control, managed to slip through the V.I.P. gate without anyone noticing. His father handled things smoothly, was definitely a man accustomed to handling things smoothly.

They looked great, his mother so fair and slight, his father, thick, dark hair gone just a little gray at the temples, lean in a good, well-tailored dark suit.

He wanted to just stand and watch them, unseen, to try and get them into some perspective but his mother was in his arms and his father pounded his back, took his duffel bag. He introduced them to Henderson and then Henderson introduced his parents and everybody shook hands and spoke at once and he and Henderson swore they'd be in touch when both knew they wouldn't. They hadn't liked each other in Nam and there was no reason why they'd like each other back home.

They all talked at once on the drive home or all fell silent at the same time and then each of them spoke again, as though silence mustn't be allowed to happen. The house looked exactly as he remembered it; it had been large in memory and reality did not diminish it.

He'd been gone for twenty-two months out of his twenty-four years. He caught his father's quick appraising look, which for once ended in a nod of approval.

"Scotch, Patrick?" his father asked, then made two high-balls, which they drank slowly, self-consciously, in the study. "How was the trip? You must be tired. Probably won't really hit you for a day or so."

"I'm fine. This feels good, just sitting here, in this room." Carefully, quickly, he added, "With you, Pop."

His father patted his shoulder awkwardly, fleetingly. They were not used to touching. It seemed almost an intimacy between strangers, false and forced. His father took a deep swallow, moved away from him, settled into his deep leather chair. In the whiskey-warm calmness of the room, Patrick felt a rush of emotion. His head was filled with words he wanted to say but couldn't: Hug me, Pop; embrace me; cry; talk; say what you feel; let me say what I feel. It'll be all right, nothing will fall apart, nothing will shatter.

Christ. Oh, Christ, the honesty he'd learned with his dead buddy didn't apply where it counted most.

"Gee, you look good, kid," his father said. There was depth to his voice and warmth and pride. "Tell me, Pat, how's it been?"

He tasted the drink again, put the glass of whiskey on the table beside the couch, ran the tip of his index finger around the lip of the glass.

"It's not exactly over for me yet. I'm going to Kenyon's wake tomorrow. I told you about Kenyon?"

"Jesus, Pat, I feel like I knew him. It's a lousy thing, a close buddy like that."

"It's a funny thing about Kenyon. He knew he was going to

354

get it. Almost like it *had* to happen because he was so sure of it. I never thought it would happen to me. And here I am."

"A lot of guys are like that, fatalists. I remember—"

Patrick raised his face, moved his head to one side and his gray eyes pierced the space between them. "We gonna compare wars, Dad?"

It was the first sign, the first warning that there were things between them, beneath the safe surface of conversation. There was a momentary silence, sharp and electric, as they regarded each other and found familiarity.

His father's mouth pulled into a smile and he spoke easily. "I was going to say that I remember you wrote us a few months ago about Kenyon, how he wasn't afraid of anything because he felt it was going to happen to him and there was nothing he could do about it."

That wasn't what his father had started to say and they both knew it. Patrick admired the ease with which his father could size up a situation and respond to it in the best way possible, maintaining the advantage at all times.

"There was nothing *anybody* could do about *anything* over there," Patrick said shortly. He stood up with a surge of restless energy. He turned, scanned the large room with the unusually high ceiling, the dark stained-glass window set into the paneled wall. He jammed his hands into the pockets of his fatigues and stared at the window. "I never could figure who that was supposed to be," he said. "When I was a little kid, I used to think it was Grandpa, then I used to think it was the devil. I remember once Grandma Crowley told me it was Saint John of the Cross."

His father's laugh filled the room with a harsh staccato. "I think the first two would hit the mark. I wouldn't put it past the old bastard to have himself mounted in glass. He was a corker all right. Christ, Patrick," his father said, "I think the old man would have given the last ten years of his life for the sight of you right now."

When Patrick turned and faced his father, he was unprepared for the open expression of relaxed and genuine pleasure with which his father regarded him.

"I'm glad you're home, kid. I'm *really* glad you're home." Then, unable to go any further, his father stood up, winked,

355

held his drink toward the window and said in a sharp, tough voice, "I'll drink him welcome home for you, Pat, my lad."

His mother stood in the doorway, small hands on her apron, and said softly, "Well, if you've finished with your drink, the roast is just about ready."

Neither Patrick O'Malley nor any of his friends had ever had any real commitment toward the war. Patrick went because it was his war and his turn to be part of it. His father had had a war; his older cousins had Korea; Viet Nam was his turn.

His friends decided, over beer or a shot of whiskey, that this one was there for them. None of them knew too much about what was involved politically or militaristically or morally or immorally. They knew they were for it and felt superior to those opposed.

They knew, had been taught, believed, that a carefully drawn world-wide pattern existed; their teachers at St. Thomas Aquinas had taught them what to look for; even at St. John's it was pointed out to them. Communism was slipping its strangle hold on the free world. It was up to them.

They sat one night, a bunch of them, spoke vaguely. Except for Tommy Noonan. Over a fourth shot of whiskey, Noonan said bluntly, "My father. My fuck-up war-hero sonuvabitching father. Isn't that what the hell it's all about, Patrick? I mean, ultimately, when we analyze it and get to the ultimate stinking bottom of it, isn't that why we're enlisting, you and me and Sullivan and Flynn and some of the others? Aren't we trying to prove we're as good as the old man? But I think, actually, you know, it's a pretty shitty war they've given us. I mean, hell, *their* war was all big deal and gung ho and all that 'we're in it together' stuff." Tommy Noonan swallowed the shot and said thickly, "I think, my friend Patrick, that you and me and the rest of us are getting a bit of a royal screwing in our particular war, just to prove to our fathers that we got balls too. But what the hell, initiation rites, as the primitives would say, right, O'Malley?"

Tommy Noonan had both of his legs shot off by a gunner in an American helicopter in one of the unfortunate accidents of war which had caused the serious wounding of seven other Americans besides Noonan. He and Tommy Noonan had gone through grade school, high school and a year and a half of college together. They enlisted in the Army together, along with a somewhat reluctant Tom Sullivan, who thought the Marines had better-looking uniforms.

Sullivan ended up in ordnance and spent most of his time in Thailand. Tommy Noonan was assigned to the Corps of Engineers, spent his time building, destroying and rebuilding landing strips for supply planes.

Patrick O'Malley, through no fault, desire or understanding of his own, ended up as a medic. He did not see Tommy Noonan after he was shot up. He was in the field with Pfc. Dudley Kenyon, picking over what was left of a detachment of men who had been sent in to capture a small rise of land known on their maps as Hill 202.

He and Kenyon eyed each other warily. Kenyon, truly dark enough to be called black, rested his hand lightly on his huge Afro, patted at it, pursed his heavy lips, nodded at the tall blond kid with the pale face. He could see the kid hadn't been at it very long but he could also see he wasn't ass-brand-new. There were a few facial muscles set in place so he knew the kid wouldn't come apart at the first piece of meat they stumbled over, but the kid looked soft enough so that Kenyon hoped they wouldn't find any bits and pieces of his friends or buddies out there.

Patrick O'Malley let Kenyon take the lead with a grave respect which Kenyon noticed and liked. It wasn't deference or any of the phony shit some of the whiteys displayed to let you know they considered you their equal, which was shit in and of itself. It was a smart move on the kid's part and showed a healthy regard for his own skin, to let the more experienced man know, right at the start, that he was the boss.

Kenyon stood over an inert, groaning figure, leaned forward just slightly to listen for a particular sound. He nodded once briskly and motioned Patrick away.

"That man is two breaths away from dead," Dudley Kenyon said, "and we ain't got nothin' to waste on a dead man."

Patrick glanced back once as they walked away, heard a harsh, sibilant sigh, saw the body arch and hold rigid for an instant, then go limp.

Kenyon knelt beside a bleeding man whose face was hidden against his buddy, who cradled him.

"He got it in the stomach," the soldier said. His voice was hollow, empty; he hugged the wounded man's head as though it were a pillow.

"Lemme have a look at his face, man, you like to smother him," Kenyon said. He put his hand under the wounded man's chin, jerked his face abruptly. "Hey, man, you with us or you out yonder or what?"

Kenyon gestured impatiently at Patrick for a needle. "Hey, what color your eyes, soldier? Your face sure one helluva gray color. You got eyes to match or what? Come on, open up and show me."

The lids fluttered; the eyes were glazed and unfocused.

"Where's your buddy from, soldier?" Kenyon asked.

"He's from Tennessee."

Kenyon gave a deep growl from his chest. "You from Tennessee, white boy? Well, now ain't that something interesting. My old papa, he was from Tennessee. Buncha them old sheet-wearing night riders, they come and they took my old pap away one night and we never seen him since." Kenyon leaned close to the wounded man's face and whispered menacingly, "What part of Tennessee you say you was from, whitey?"

The wounded man gasped; his eyes flew open; he stared in terror at the black face which bore down on him. "I didn't do nothin' to your pa. I ain't got nothin' against any you Nigras, you could askt anybody, I got lotsa Nigra friends."

Kenyon squatted back on his heels, cleaned a spot for an injection and grabbed the man's arm. He grinned and said, "Well, you just gave yourself a nice good jolt of adrenalin, boy. You gonna be just fine, once I get this nice mama needle into you. You gonna feel so good that hole in your gut not gonna hurt you one bit."

Kenyon ripped torn clothing away, dug into his kit, cleaned the wound, applied a dressing. He signaled for two stretcher-bearers, and as they carried the wounded man down the hill, Kenyon said to Patrick, "Sometimes you gotta jolt 'em a bit to see if they got anything left. What *you* do is, you ask some bleeding black man, 'Ain't you the nigger fucked my sister back home in Detroit city?' I guarantee you'll see an almost

358

dead man come back to life, he got anything left in him at all."

Before he joined the Army, the only black person Patrick O'Malley had ever had contact with was the overweight son of a wealthy physician. He was a beige color, with thick pale lips, tightly kinked hair neatly cropped to his skull, and strange light-gray eyes. He had the unfortunate name of Jeremiah J. O'Hara III. He was in all of Patrick's classes at St. Thomas Aquinas, from freshman year through graduation.

The novelty of a black classmate with the unlikely Irish name of O'Hara was good for laughs when things were dull, but Jeremiah O'Hara didn't make a good scapegoat. He had a naturally easy manner, a long-suffering attitude of one who was tired of waiting for an original joke at his expense. He was also richer than practically anyone else at school, got higher grades and had every intention of attending, first, Harvard, then Harvard Law.

Dudley Kenyon was black in a way that Jeremiah O'Hara could never be. He surrounded himself with a conscious racial tension for it had been just such racial tension which had directed his entire life.

But in his work, which was the saving of life, Kenyon displayed a complete lack of awareness of color.

It was *condition* that spoke to him and he taught Patrick to disregard everything but the possibility of survival when selecting who to attend first.

The dead would wait forever and the dying would die.

It was the living you tried to save.

It became almost a contest, a point of pride at selecting those who could make it and leaving the others for later.

Patrick felt a tough satisfaction when Kenyon would turn to him and say, "Yeah, okay, he looks good," meaning some writhing bloody form who Patrick had decided stood a chance. "Only the winners, man, we pick only the winners."

When they were away from it for a week, moved back from the lines for a few days of rest, it hit Patrick: what they had been doing.

It hit him with the force of doom and instinctively he sought relief as he had been taught from childhood: he found a priest.

He was a Navy priest, young, smooth-cheeked, with longish

sideburns. He apologized for not being an Army priest, laughed to put Patrick at ease, assured him he was a genuine chaplain; despite his apparent youth, he'd been in Nam on and off for nearly five years.

It was hard to put it into words, the sense of what he had been doing. It was as though he'd been playing God. The selection of who would live and who would die overwhelmed him. Faces were beginning to haunt him, to accuse him. Young boys covered with their own blood and excrement, lying in a tangle of torn flesh, with nothing human left but a strangulated cry for help, confronted him.

"I might have helped some of them. God, at least I might have eased some of their agony a little."

The priest—Patrick never caught his name; it was something long and Polish or Ukrainian, though he spoke with an irritating Midwestern drawl—wrapped his long hands around his bent knee, dug his heel into the rung of his chair for greater comfort. His face was serious and pensive and he frowned, almost as though to impress Patrick that he was giving a great deal of thought and consideration to the matter.

After a long silence, the priest coughed slightly, blinked, released his knee and told Patrick about how things are in wartime: choices have to be made sometimes. He was sure that Patrick was doing the best he could under very terrible circumstances and he would pray for Patrick and for all of the poor boys he had had, of necessity, to pass by.

He told Patrick that he should make the most of his short leave, try to refresh his spirit, forget for the moment the horror he had so shortly left behind and so shortly would again encounter.

Patrick O'Malley stood up slowly and smiled his blazing boyish smile so earnestly that the priest felt the warm glow of his own comforting powers. He stood up to take the offered hand with hearty fellowship.

"Gee, Father, thanks. Thanks very much. Boy, you sure made me feel better. I mean, I felt pretty bad when I came in here to talk to you, but just listening to you made me feel a hundred per cent better."

"Well," the priest said, flushed with pleasure, "that's what we're here for, that's what we're here for."

"Yeah, Father," Patrick said, "you made me feel so goddamn fucking good that I'm going out to the boondocks and screw at least six little slant-eyed whores."

For just one instant, the priest's hand held in his, continued pumping, until the sense of what Patrick said caused the priest to yank his hand away.

"What . . . what?"

"And I'll think of you at the very minute I shove it in, Father."

Patrick left the chaplain's office and headed for the bar run by an old Japanese man and his two sons. It was where Dudley Kenyon hung out.

The day that Patrick saved Kenyon's life was the day that Kenyon told him about the five men he'd stalked and murdered.

They were loading the wounded, tied securely to their stretchers, flattened by the protective tarpaulin so that they all looked like cardboard corpses. The heavy blade whirred above their heads, the force of artificial wind prickled along Patrick's scalp, seemed to draw him upward, wanted to suck him into the heart of the machine. The proximity of the invisibly whirling blades was something he could never get used to. The rhythm ran through him as he raised and balanced and handed off the wounded: ma-chete; ma-chete; ma-chete.

The last boy lay patiently waiting, lit cigarette dangling from his lips. Patrick squatted beside him, sniffed and grinned.

"Man, where'd you get that stuff from? From my buddy over there?"

The soldier inhaled, moved his head slightly to indicate that Patrick should take a drag. The sweet familiar odor came slowly in lazy billows from the soldier's mouth. Patrick grinned and inhaled elaborately, then replaced the reefer in the soldier's mouth.

"Sure makes the trip a little easier to take."

Kenyon came over, helped himself to a drag, gave the wounded soldier the last. "This here mother got it made, O'Malley. He got himself a few little toes knocked off his goddamn foot and home again, home again."

"I don't know, man, I don't know." The soldier's voice was thin and far away. "That's what you tell me, brother. But how come I don't like feel nothin'? Don't feel fucking nothin' nowhere, like I don't exist no more."

Patrick caught some quick signal from Kenyon and he realized that this was the kid with the severed spinal cord. He said quietly, "That's 'cause my man here gave you some real a-one special-stock pot like no other shit you ever had."

The soldier's eyes rolled slowly from Patrick to Kenyon and he tried a lazy, heavy smile. "Hey, man, this little whitey boy talk like he soul."

Kenyon flung an arm around Patrick's shoulder, wrapped an arm around his neck in a rough, scraping embrace. "He been hangin' around so long with the brothers, he beginning to talk and walk and roll like soul."

Patrick felt unaccountably happy and relaxed. At a signal, he lifted his end of the stretcher, the head end, lightly and with ease. Kenyon backed up the slight incline and couldn't see what was happening behind him.

Patrick, who did see, couldn't immediately calculate the effect of what he saw, not consciously. Some other, knowing part of himself took over, reacted, dropped the stretcher without thought as he heard the scream of fear from the stretcher. The cold death blade bore down on them. Patrick absorbed only that the helicopter had tipped, slanted, angled into them and Kenyon's head was inches from decapitation.

He lurched, threw himself at Kenyon, knocked him to the hard ground, felt his heavy booted foot smash against the man on the stretcher, felt his arm smash into Kenyon's throat. They rolled together along the ground beneath the terrible gaping hole of the helicopter.

The wounded and their tenders had been dumped indiscriminately, sprayed out in various positions, heads twisted, faces pressed down into earth. The wounded cried out; the corpsmen, wounded now themselves, cried out. Two airmen, stunned, insensible, clutched at each other, pulled at each other. They had one moment been safely inside the body of their 'copter and the next moment, unknowingly, they pulled themselves upright, directly into the irrevocable cutting edge, were dismembered, their flesh tossed in wild unbelievable disarray all over the area, before the pilot, knocked from his seat, was able to cut the engine.

How the accident had happened, why, what caused the solidly resting machine to lurch, was really academic. The damage was estimated and the number of dead attributed to the accident was reduced to the two airmen. It was figured that the three wounded who succumbed when unceremoniously tossed from their safe berth would have died anyway.

The kid with the severed spinal cord wasn't injured further by the accident but he kept whispering over and over again, "Hey, how come I don't feel nothin'? How come?"

Later, Kenyon held Patrick by both shoulders and studied him intently. Patrick noticed that the black face had gone paler, a strange yellow crept along Kenyon's cheeks and around his mouth.

In an exaggerated slurring, Patrick said to him, "Why, man, I just done like I been taught to do. I just picked out the mother who looked to me like he had the best chance."

Kenyon laughed then and called him a few obscene names. and they boxed and tussled wildly and lit a joint and shared it. Later, that night, when things had calmed down and neither one of them could sleep, Kenyon told him about the five men he had murdered. From his old unit, before he'd become a medic.

"You see," Kenyon said, "them five mother fuckers killed like forty-five unarmed civilians. They was all them little skinny old ladies you see along the road sometimes, you know, who run and hide the minute they see us comin'.

"We was out on patrol lookin' to contact an advance unit. We come upon a passel of dead Marines and nobody knew who the Christ they was or what they was doin' up there. This lieutenant, he was one mean sonuvabitch bastard, a short, little round-belly guy. Shit, he always had that scared look on him, like, man, if a little slant kid comes up to him, he ready to blow the kid's head off. You know the kind. Well, the lieutenant, he looked the bodies over and he seen somebody took ears. Three of the bodies had ears that was missing. Now, shit, man, we been takin' ears steady, but see, this was *different*, you know? This lieutenant, he like to went crazy. He started jumpin' up and down and yellin' how's we was

363

gonna get them savages done this and I says, 'Hell, Lieutenant, them Marines don't need no ears where they're at now.' "

Kenyon pulled a long hard drag and held the fumes inside his lungs before he passed to Patrick. He exhaled slowly, lovingly. "That little mother whirled around at me, you know, pointed his fucking a-one number automatic rifle at my head and he says, 'Soldier, don't you turn your back on me!' "

Kenyon hit his long, hard thigh with the palm of his hand and shook his head. "Hey, that's the kind of man you sure don't turn your back on. Well, we collected dog tags, you know, and pushed on till we come to this here little clearing with a buncha them little shacks. Weren't nobody there but little old women and some little bitty babies. Not kids, mind, but babies, little teensy babies in their mamas' arms, crying and sucking out their breakfasts.

"Them old ladies, you know, weren't really old, I guess, just look that way, with troubles they known. Men all gone, run off, and here's this fuck-off yellin' at them like he thinks they got a hutful of gyrene ears they preparing for a feast or something. He's yellin' and the women are cryin' and the babies are lookin' all scared and then, just like that" — Kenyon snapped his fingers and locked his lips and jerked his head up, then spread his fingers in a gesture of wonder — "he just opens up on them, just like that, baby, right on, he rips into them and turns and tells all of us, there was nine of us besides him, he says, 'Open up, kill the Commie slant-eyed Cong bastards.' Some old crippled stooped-over man comes creeping out of one of them hootches and the guy next to me opens up with an automatic and he starts yelling, 'V.C., V.C. You was right, Loot, V.C.' "

Kenyon caressed the last small remnant of glowing marijuana with the tip of his finger, then crushed it. "Little brother with me, little soul brother from Philly, not more than eighteen, he got sick to his stomach and then he started crying, real big tears coming from his eyes. That boy started crying and yelling and the lieutenant turns to him and points his automatic and says, 'You want some too? Then start shootin'.' "

Kenyon rubbed his hand over his eyes for a moment and shook his head. "Oh, shit, Irish, that little black boy from Phila-

364

delphia, with the tears runnin' down his face, he turns and starts shootin' and wastin' them little mamas and their babies, just like that!"

"What about you, Kenyon?" Patrick asked, knowing but wanting to hear anyway.

Kenyon said slowly and precisely, "No way, man, uh-uh. There was ten of us and five done the shooting. One guy, another soul brother, he run away and I never seen him again. A white kid, kid who was planning on going to medical school, he sat down on the ground and covered his face in his hands and like he was frozen and couldn't move from that position. Another whitey, he just walks away and leans against a tree like he been kicked in the stomach, all gray in the face. This other black guy from Jersey, him and me, we just look at each other, see. We got our trigger fingers ready, you know, and without sayin' nothin' we both know it ain't the slants we thinkin' of wastin', but this guy, he looks around and shakes his head, like he's sayin', 'Not now, Kenyon, not here and now, baby.' Which was right, because that lieutenant and his guys, they coulda took us easy as we coulda took them.

"Later on, the white guy who stood against the tree, he went to the company commander, see, and he said it was a massacre and he wanted the lieutenant and them men arrested, you know. Well, baby, I coulda told him." Kenyon laughed at the man's stupidity. "But the poor dumb bastard didn't ask me. The commander, why, baby, he never heard of such a thing; he never *wanted* to hear of such a thing again, you know. And oh, my, that G.I., but didn't he get his balls blown off during a mine sweep. That whitey, he didn't know shit about how you get things done."

Kenyon knew how to get things done. Two of the men who shot the civilians were found dead in a Saigon alley, dead of overdoses of bad heroin. Two men were shot dead: Sniper fire, sir.

And the lieutenant: a couple of hundred pieces of that man's ass forever embedded in jungle rot, since he had the misfortune to step on a mine.

"You see, baby," Kenyon said softly, "you gotta get something done, why, *do it*. Ain't no fuckin' difference between here and home, where I come from." Suddenly, as though it

365

had just occurred to him, Kenyon said sadly, "Oh, shit, baby, how'm I gonna make it back home, you tell me that? Some dude bothers me, gives me some shit I don't want, why it wouldn't mean nothin' to me to waste him. I mean, baby, it wouldn't mean *nothin'*. And the Man gonna come and tell me I gotta be locked up the rest of my life like I'm somethin' in the zoo because I wasted some dude who don't mean shit. Oh, man, it's a fucked-up world for sure."

Through the long spun-out nights, they sat around camp-fires, tried to get dry and free of the damp earth around them. They tried to blot out the days, which were filled with mangled young bodies which in an instant lost youthfulness and acquired the horror of helpless age. The men in the unit were slightly older than the wounded they dealt with. Kenyon, twenty-four, was the oldest; Patrick, twenty-two, was the average. The age of the wounded averaged out to twenty, with some as young as eighteen, some as old as twenty-three.

Sometimes Kenyon shot heroin; some of them took uppers and downers. They all smoked pot. Kenyon said, "What the hell, baby, if it feels good, do it. Learned me a nursery rhyme when I was a little chile: 'Don't matter who you screw or what you screw only *that* you screw.' "

Patrick went through the nights, floated, drifted on pot, but he could snap into reality if he had to; not like the real heads, they went off too far, out too far. In a way, Patrick stood over them as they dozed and spun away from themselves and each other, a kind of guardian in the night. Some of them were hooked on whatever took them out of themselves. Patrick wasn't sure about Kenyon; it was hard to tell with him.

"Hey, you know," Henderson said thickly, "you know what I seen today?" He was a pothead and hardly spoke most of the time, but pot loosened him. "Guy we brought in with the busted right leg, redhead from Virginia, you know? Guy had a string of *ears* on him, hooked onto his belt. Christ Almighty, can you imagine a guy doing something like that? *V.C. ears.* He says that everybody in his outfit does it. He says their C.O. wanted proof of body count. *Ears!*"

Kenyon grinned. "Don't matter shit, you take a dead man's ears or his pecker off'n his corpse. Don't matter shit."

366

"But hell, Kenyon," Henderson protested, "that's pretty rotten stuff. I mean, that isn't Christian. We're supposed to be civilized."

Kenyon laughed out loud and Becker, a small, intense, close-cropped, tense-jawed boy from Iowa, said, "What's funny, Kenyon? You think that anything is okay, nothing's wrong? Well, it's *wrong* to desecrate bodies; it's wrong and I hate to see our men do it."

Wetzel and Hutton, cousins from Tennessee, were flying now, spaced out on pills, eased and floating on pot. They started to laugh uncontrollably and Becker really got sore.

"What the hell, you guys. I mean, if *we* do the same kind of atrocities that *they* do, then what's the difference between us? I mean, that sort of thing makes *us* just as bad as *them*."

For some reason, that struck all the others as funny. They kept laughing, those who were almost too high to keep up with what was being said and those who passed up every second drag as the reefer, a giant concocted by the Tennessee cousins, went around the circle. Patrick wasn't too high but he felt an edge of hilarity and he began to sing "God Bless America" and they all joined in, really giving it force.

For some reason, that made Becker really fly into a rage and they tried to assure him that they were being patriotic, and to prove it, they started singing "The Star-Spangled Banner" but nobody could remember all the words. They laughed and gagged and sucked in the pot and laughed and felt so crazy good they couldn't figure it all out and it didn't seem to matter anyway. Only Becker, between drags, grumbled, and after a while, he didn't know what the hell he was so mad about but he stayed mad because it felt good.

"All I gotta say," Becker mumbled, "is it's a terrible, terrible thing to mutilate a dead body. Even if it is a V.C."

"What I gotta say is that it don't matter *shit* what you do, one way or the other," Kenyon said with a sudden strange vehemence that caught everyone's attention and seemed to cut the mood. It cracked, split, changed, rearranged. Kenyon hunched forward, probed a long black finger into Becker's chest. "You listen, mother fucker, and you listen good to me. Don't matter. Dead's *dead*. Dead's *nothing*. Dead's *shit*. Be general or dog, dead's *dead*."

Becker, sober and bitterly aware now, said, "Nothing matters to you. What matters to you, Kenyon? Tell us, because I've seen you; nothing matters to you."

"Not *death*, baby. Death ain't *nothin'* to matter about."

Patrick leaned toward him intently, with an urgency he didn't understand. "But what, Kenyon," he asked, *had* to know, "what matters, Kenyon?"

They all turned toward Kenyon, waited for him, as though he, Kenyon, had the answer. There was silence around the fire; the flickering red light around them encompassed them in a reality remote from any other.

Kenyon sighed deeply, reached a rough hand into Patrick's shaggy blond hair and shook him. "Don't nothin' matter but stayin' alive, baby. And I'm not too sure that matter shit neither."

Kenyon was married and received letters from his wife, but he never wrote back to her. "She ain't gonna have no stack of letters to spend her life with if 'n she don't get me back."

They went on a four-day R and R together and over drinks in an early-evening bar, Patrick talked to Kenyon more than he'd ever talked to anyone in his life. He talked about his father, because his mother had sent him newspaper clippings which quoted his father at the site of a student demonstration protesting the war: "Deputy Chief Inspector Brian O'Malley made a brief appearance at the site and when asked to comment said, 'Look, my kid is over there. How do you think I feel about these demonstrators?' "

"See, I'm of some value to him now. I'm over here and now, *now* I'm valuable to him. Jesus, I don't know, Kenyon. My old man, well, he's so fucking goddamn great, like what the hell is the use, you know? I mean, he was a real hero in *his* war, not a bullshit armchair hero. You know what kind of hero? The kind who never talks about it. My uncle told me about him when I was ten or eleven. I mean, hell, I never knew that my father took over a whole goddamn unit when all the line officers were killed. Hell, he was about my age, maybe a coupla years older, your age. He wiped out four Japanese machine-gun nests. You know, John Wayne kind of stuff, creeping up with a grenade stuck in his mouth, that kind of

368

thing. On Iwo Jima, his unit was being wiped out and my old man ended up winning the whole damn thing, practically by himself."

Kenyon drank beer and waited with a strange slight smile pulling at the corners of his mouth.

"You know what he is now? A deputy chief inspector. I mean, there he is, no education or anything and he took those tests and kept passing them. One of the youngest captains in the Department's history and now he's one of the real bosses."

"No shit?" Kenyon said, unimpressed. "Well, somebody gotta be fuzz, I guess."

"Hey, Kenyon, I'm a cop. Didn't you know that?"

"For real, Patrick? Hey, for damn real?" Kenyon's head rocked back and forth. "I don't believe that, baby."

"Yeah, really. I had eight months on the job before I enlisted. It's waiting for me when I get back. What the hell. Everybody's gotta be something. But, Jesus, my old man: war hero, deputy chief inspector. You know what I mean?"

"Man, you got big trouble," Kenyon said, amused. "Must be real tough to hafta measure it with your daddy."

"What the hell kinda thing is that to say, Kenyon? What do you know about it?"

"Not shit, baby. I don't know shit. Got no daddy of my own to break my chops. Some dude slipped it to my mama one night, and on his way, and here I am."

Patrick was shocked. Hell, that was his *mother* he was talking about. "You shouldn't say something like that, Kenyon. It reflects bad on your mother."

Kenyon considered for a moment, then said simply, "Hell, my mama got lots a' bad reflections on her. Never bothered her, why the hell should it bother me?"

Another world. Jesus, them colored live in another world.

He'd heard it when he was too small to know who they were and now Kenyon was telling him exactly what he'd heard and overheard from his father and his uncles, his cousins, his friends, men he worked with. But he and Kenyon were buddies and friends. He was closer to Kenyon than he'd ever been to anyone, and yet he had no understanding of Kenyon or of his world.

Kenyon leaned his elbows on the table, tilted his head

369

back, drank from the bottle, the only way he liked beer. He sighed a long beery breath and grinned. "Hell, baby, I done things by the time I was ten that you only just heard about when you was eighteen."

Patrick pulled a shocked face, widened his eyes. "Easy now, man. Don't tell me anything I shouldn't know. I'm just a pure and innocent young boy."

The broad black face went serious. Just the slightly mocking smile played at the heavy lips, but Kenyon's eyes, color of his skin, were still, seemed sad, almost gentle, the way his voice went gentle. "You know, Irish, that's a for-real fact. You truly are a innocent boy. Goddamn, but I think that's half the trouble goin' on, the whole fuck-up business of what's good, what's bad. You know what scares the living shit outta most of you whiteys? I mean, man, it's just basically pure and simple. What the hell I got between my legs. Get down to it, man, that's what it's about. See, you been raised to see it one way; I learned another way."

Kenyon dropped his hand to his lap, caressed his sex, smiled. "It comes alive, baby. I mean, the minute I tell it to, the minute I say to it, hey, I *needs* some *comfort* or I *needs* some *fun* or I *needs* to *fly* or to *feel* or to *prove I'm me*. And nothin', no words or rules or dumb regulations, gonna freeze me down, hold me in. Nothin' gonna turn me soft or melt me away, because, man, this here is *mine*, you know?"

As Kenyon spoke, his face relayed his pleasure, his mouth moved in careful sensuality, his eyes revealed the rising sensation, his shoulders moved forward slightly, large, strong shoulders caving forward.

"Whites, see, you got yourselves about nine million reasons why ain't nobody should get no pleasure, but shit, baby, this is all we got, get right on down to it, and ain't no way I'm gonna let anybody turn this here off. It don't matter, see, don't matter shit how I use what I got." Kenyon stopped speaking, grinned broadly and shook his head in amusement. "Oh, baby, you have turned a bright, bright red in your face. What's the matter, Irish? You gettin' a tingle in your dingle?"

Patrick felt heat sear through him, not just through his face and head, but through his body, down the inside of his thighs, in his groin, across his stomach. As Kenyon's voice played with words and created intimacy, Patrick felt the beginnings of an erection, caught and held and brought down by the beginnings of the terrible, ancient adolescent fear. He picked up the heavy mug and drained the flat beer.

"Relax, man," Kenyon said quietly, his eyes intent, "I don't wanna make it with you."

Patrick flashed anger without a word; the tightened jaw and the hardened eyes turned to steel. Kenyon had touched a boyhood, open, painful, vulnerable nerve ending: one of the most stringent, fearsome of all prohibitions.

Kenyon laughed, not sensuous sound but loud amusement. "There you are, man. I just gave you a genuine live demonstration. See, you all uptight and caught in a strangle. And for what? The way I see it, a man can do any goddamn fucking thing he wants to. Don't change nothin'. Don't make nothin', don't break nothin'. Don't make him a man or unmake him a man. See, if that's the measure of it, just that handful down there, if that's what decides what a man is, well, then it's all really one big bucket of shit, you dig?"

"No," Patrick said shortly, "no, I don't dig this at all. I don't know what the hell you're talking about."

"Talkin' about life, baby. Look, what you believe is, you die and you burn. I mean, that's what *you* believe, baby. But me, see, I *know*, I mean, I *know* for a number-one fact that dead is dead and this is the one and onliest time around. Man, I want to try *everything*. I want to have it *all* before I'm nothin'. I screwed with little girls practically babies and with old whores ready for the garbage can and with women so juicy ripe I'd liked to died just drowning in them with all the lush smells and tastes and feels. I done it with men and boys and everything in between and in ways you couldn't even register. But just you get this one thing straight at the beginning if you ever wanna learn something about life: it ain't no measure of a man, *how* he do it."

"Then what the hell is a measure of a man? To you, Kenyon?"

Kenyon touched his Afro lightly, felt it spring beneath his fingertips; it was a pleasurable touch and he lingered for a moment, then said, "Why just that he keeps trying to find out things, I guess. That he don't go shutting no doors he never has even tried to open. Oh, but you got a sad, sweet, dumb face, white boy," Kenyon said.

He felt sad and he felt dumb. It wasn't just when Kenyon talked about his life; it was when the rest of them, the black guys, sat around and eased into it: always about the same thing, about sex.

The white guys listened, uneasy, unaccustomed, Jesus Christ, *dying* with a combination of emotions ranging from lust to fury. Who the fuck did these black bastards think they were anyway. How the hell did they get away with it? Their sexual liberation underscored his, Patrick's, personal individual bondage to terrors that went back farther than his conscious memory.

Jesus, the misery of his adolescence: the priest-centered, fear-laden, guilt-pounding, stomach-sick terror of his adolescence. The long, lonely, breath-holding dark nights of his desecration made infinitely worse by the too awful to acknowledge knowledge that what heightened his tension and excitement were the sounds he could hear, vaguely but imagined with great intimacy, from his parents' room. The walls were thick and the occasions few, but he, rigid, sharply awakened, senses at the edge of his skin, screaming at the edges of his being, would listen for the sound of bodies against bedsprings — the goddamn bedsprings, couldn't they stop the springs from giving them away? — and the moan, the groan which couldn't have carried down the hall but which carried through the wall or down the hall into him, into his own growing and terrible need.

And carried sin around inside him like a growing, festering wound, to be lanced and seared and torn from him in the clammy confessional, through shame and sweat-bathed agony.

It didn't seem fair, the scars he carried because of his sexuality, and here were Kenyon and his buddies, and they talked about things which would have paralyzed him, literally crippled him.

Sodomy: by mouth by asshole by force by consent.

Incest: little sister big sister; man, that child could go, wanting to teach her little brother something fine; mama, oh, mama.

Rape; masturbation; experimentation.

372

And music. God, they turned music into a sexual experience. Close your eyes, baby, and let it take you take you don't hold back. Slow hard winding grinding brain-shattering torso-twisting pelvic thrusts, tight hard buttocks shoving it shoving it.

Patrick learned how to do that anyway, how to let the music reach inside of himself and become part of his being. Kenyon taught him how, in some whore's house (but a *good* house; Kenyon knew the best). He had gone mind-stoned with pot and music and Kenyon telling him how, Kenyon right there, hell, Kenyon, and the whore, with tiny hands, warm tiny hands and strong little fingers warm and moist, hell, Kenyon, not with you right there *watching*, for Christ's sake.

But why the fuck not, baby? Why not?

Why not?

Now how the hell would his father like that?

Two weeks before their tour ended, Kenyon fell on a mine. There was enough left to ship home; the lower portion of his body was blown away. His face seemed peaceful enough and untouched by what had happened to the rest of him.

The C.O. was a young guy with a skin crew cut, a sawed-off chin, small beads for eyes, thin shoulders, long legs and no experience in combat. He was from Kansas and figured anyone from New York was neighbor to anyone else from New York. Patrick didn't bother to explain the kinds of distance that separated Riverdale and Harlem. The C.O. sent him home two weeks early, along with Kenyon's body and instructions to convey his personal and the Army's generalized sympathy and compliments.

"You tell them the importance of the work done by Private Kenyon; he was a devoted soldier and that knowledge might make their grief easier to bear."

There were several corpses besides Kenyon's aboard the 707 charter flight but that didn't seem to dampen the spirits of the two hundred and forty men aboard, or of the eight stewardesses who raced through the plane with continuously smiling bright faces. The smiles were good, real, not plastic pulling of phony mouths, but warm and generous, given when eye contact was made and attention established.

They wore brown uniforms with light-beige blouses. Patrick preferred to see girls dressed in blue or, best of all, in red. But the girls held up during the long flight; they couldn't possibly have managed to catch more than an hour or two of sleep through the whole twenty-six-hour deal, yet they bounced down the aisle, seemed to have plenty of energy and attention to spare. They didn't give out with any of that stale yes-soldier, no-soldier, whatever-you-say-soldier shit that the U.S.O. staff handed out or any of the quick, on-again, off-again aren't-I-noble crap of the professional entertainers who came over to Nam from time to time.

Patrick was attracted to the girl because her shiny brown hair slipped from its pinnings and she just casually shoved it under the little brown cap, and when it slid out again, she bit her lip and whispered a spirited "Oh shit" to herself, and when she saw that he had lip-read her, she grinned and leaned close to him. Her smell was fruit and flower and the vague essence of soap.

"Don't report that to my captain or he'll have me write out a list of twenty alternatives which would be much more acceptable. He's a Mormon and very gung ho."

Patrick pulled a blank face. "I'm from Salt Lake City, miss . . . er . . . What did you say your name was?"

The little name plate said Eileen and she covered it quickly, stared at him with large, startled dark eyes, then her face relaxed and she shook her head. "Oh, you're really mean. If you're from Salt Lake City, pal, you missed your stop by about a thousand miles." She leaned forward, squinted at his name plate. "Hmm. Patrick O'Malley, that's a nice mean trick for one Irishman to pull on another. Sure, it's Eileen O'Flaherty you're talking to."

"Well, hello, Eileen O'Flaherty. You got a place in New York?"

She put one hand on a nicely rounded, brown-skirt-encased hip, fussed with the waistband for a minute. "Quiet, you'll wake your buddy there. Sure, I've a place in New York, along with four others. Safety in numbers, right, mate?"

"Not necessarily." Patrick watched her cute, pert, alive face, the skin flushed pink and slightly damp from her exertions of serving food, running the length of the plane's narrow aisles, soothing, providing blankets and pillows and small talk.

374

Something so provocatively *alive* about her irritated him suddenly, irrationally. Her ease with him, her ease at the closeness of all of their male bodies, her complete lack of awareness of where they'd been, what they'd done, of what they'd seen and lived with, of how they'd fought death. All of it, with a heavy weight he couldn't understand, obliterated the sense of her femaleness and he wanted to strike out at her.

"Well, Eileen O'Flaherty," he said carefully, aware of the sense of cold calculation which filled him even though he couldn't understand the reason, "tell me, what services do you provide for the passengers to the rear?"

She misunderstood, pulled a mouth at him as though he'd said something with a double meaning, but the boyish face fixed into an expression which puzzled her, held her. She touched her hair lightly and asked him, "What do you mean, O'Malley? Which passengers to the rear?"

"Oh, four or five of them, I guess. You don't have to feed them or settle them down or tuck them in or arrange their heads on pillows or flirt with any of them. I guess they make the best passengers of all, huh?"

He noted with a sudden alarm that her face went white as she realized what he meant. He filled with a regret as sudden and unanticipated as his need to attack had been, but she turned too quickly, was down the aisle before he could extricate himself from his seat and he didn't see her again until they landed.

As they all inched down the aisles, wedged together toward the exit, she suddenly appeared, close against him, surprised and caught.

"Hey, look, Eileen," he said, "hey, look, I'm sorry. I was out of line. Just feeling a little weightless upstairs, okay?"

She studied the expression carefully, thoughtfully. She didn't flick on a quick okay-soldier smile. She bit her lower lip and frowned. "I shouldn't have run off like that. My fault, I take offense too quickly." Then she grinned. "That's very Irish, isn't it? Listen, good luck, O'Malley. I really mean it."

He held her wrist; it was warm in his large hand. She was very short, and he had to lean down to her. "If you really mean it, how about a phone number? Come on, O'Flaherty, I've been gone a long time. I could use some kindhearted company. For a couple of drinks?"

She dug a scrap of paper from a pocket in her skirt and as they moved, their bodies carried along by bodies, down the aisle, she jotted her name and address and phone number, then pressed the paper into his hand.

"I'm a working girl, you know, Patrick. Kind of give me a shove toward the front of the ship, will you?"

The address was in Woodside, Queens, and Eileen winked at his puzzled expression. "I told you I share with four others: my mother, father, and two brothers. Come on down here a minute." When he ducked down toward her, she whispered in his ear, "That's where we *start* from. There *are* places, you know."

She disappeared in the press of young male bodies and when he finally saw her again, some twenty minutes later, and she checked his name on her clipboard, he carefully put his duffel bag on the floor next to his feet, reached for her face with both of his hands and for a long moment held his lips against hers to the cheers of the other soldiers.

Eileen O'Flaherty, freed finally, grinned, adjusted her cap and smoothed her blouse and said cheerfully, "Well, isn't it nice that the soldier enjoyed his flight so much."

THIRTY-TWO

Dudley Kenyon's wake was held at the Armory on Seventh Avenue and 125th Street. It was a misplaced gray fortress with battlements overlooking unworthy terrain.

The hall where the coffin had been placed was huge, a drill hall converted for the purpose, with an arrangement of chairs, banks of flowers, an aisle down which black ushers escorted visitors.

"Yes, can I help you?" The man's voice was powerful and deep and he held his head to one side as a sign of courtesy to the soldier who stood so obviously ill at ease in the surroundings.

"Yes, sir. I've come to pay my respects to Private Kenyon and his family."

The funeral director said, "How kind of you. May I have your name, sir, to relay to the family."

As he gave his name, the funeral director jotted it on a small pad which he held in the palm of his hand.

Beyond the solicitous funeral director, Patrick saw nothing but dark faces. To his left, he spotted flashes of bright color, young men and women decked out in African garb, men and women dressed alike in long, flowing billows of color, topped by huge, fragile, billowy, spun-sugar bubbles of hair. As he went down the aisle, he felt a wave of hostility unmistakably directed at him. He caught the coming together of faces, the folding of arms, the unblinking bright eyes that followed him and made him intensely aware of himself.

He was escorted to the coffin and he could feel all the attention in the room center on him, on the back of his head, along his neck and stiff, rigidly erect body. He tried not to look anywhere but at the coffin, but he glanced involuntarily at the

377

honor guards who flanked the flag-draped box. The tall, thin chocolate soldier at the foot was stoned out of his skull; his round eyes, glazed, looked through Patrick without seeing him; his mouth was slack and he was humming softly.

Patrick crossed himself, bowed his head and stood uncertainly since there was no kneeling bench. He stopped midway through a prayer and opened his eyes and stared at the contours of the coffin. He tried to visualize Kenyon inside, in there, Kenyon dead in there, but nothing came back to him and the bright tomato-red of the stripes of the flag held his gaze to fascination. What the hell any of this had to do with Kenyon or with him he couldn't say.

His elbow was touched lightly and he moved away from the coffin, grateful to be escorted to the side of the room where everyone was dressed in black and seemed older and somewhat less hostile and angry.

"This is Private Kenyon's mother," he was told. "This is Private Patrick O'Malley, come to offer his respects."

Patrick offered his hand and said, "I'm sorry for your trouble, Mrs. Kenyon. Dudley was a friend of mine."

She lifted her face, tilted it to one side for a better view of him and in so doing offered a better view of herself. It was an unexpected face, neither young nor old, ageless, smooth and warm and brown. She narrowed her dark eyes for a moment and her voice was deep and a small smile crept up the corners of her mouth, vague and familiar. She held his hand firmly in her own gloved hand and examined him with interest.

"Didn't nobody call him Dudley," she said softly.

"No. No, ma'am. I mean, we always called him Kenyon. We all did."

She nodded as though he had met some requirement, released his hand and indicated the chair beside her. "Your ears are fire-red. You walk from the subway in that cold wind?"

He touched an ear stupidly and nodded.

"Well, you were good to come all this way," she said without knowing where he'd come from, only that it had to be some distance from where they were now. It was an acknowledgment of a different kind of distance and Patrick bit his lip because he didn't know how to speak to her. "You were together in Nam?"

He nodded again, then realized he had to speak. "Yes, ma'am, same unit. We were, well, Kenyon and I, we worked together for more than a year."

Her eyes, beetle-black, carefully blue-lidded, slightly theatrical, with long fringy lashes, studied his face and accused him of nothing, yet he felt accused. The accusation came from within himself, pounded with his heartbeat, his eye blink, his every awareness of life. He sat here and Kenyon, what was left of what used to be Kenyon, was up there in that box under that flag.

Look, lady, I'm alive. Okay. You don't know anything about it, about how it was, about Kenyon and me and living and dying and killing and getting killed.

A bead of sweat started down along his temple though he didn't feel warm. He felt somewhat short of breath and each inhalation included the heavy, sweet scent, sweet and spicy, powdery, sensuous, which surrounded Kenyon's mother. Her face was broad, with high cheekbones that gave an odd smiling countenance. There was something almost mocking about the way she held her head to one side, the way she studied him and was aware of his discomfort.

She clicked her tongue against her teeth and spoke with an edge of annoyance, as though it was a passing, temporary thing, this whole thing about Kenyon. "I told that boy he was a damn fool for getting into it, but he never asked my opinion or cared a damn for it anyway." She shook her head and stared straight at the coffin for a moment, then back at Patrick as though for confirmation that she was right after all. "Listen, were you with him? Right *then?*"

"Yes, ma'am."

"Don't call me 'ma'am,' honey. Sounds like you fit to choke over it." She watched the blood fill his face and reached for his hand and smiled. "It's okay. I guess you just a little bit out of water here. I know about you, Patrick O'Malley."

He showed surprise and she sighed. "Oh, Kenyon wrote to *me.*" Her voice was husky and she directed a sardonic glare at the coffin, then turned back to Patrick. "He wrote home to his mama, like all good boys do. For a little piece of bread,

379

Mama, a little loan against the future. Well, what the hell, he ain't got much a future now, has he?" Her voice changed, filled with a womanliness, a rich wholeness that encompassed Patrick. "He told me you was a friend, baby, and you came here, so I know he was right. I'm glad you was a friend." Her hand pressed his once, then released him, an acknowledgment of who he was and that he was not an intruder here. She moved her head to indicate the other side of the room, her eyes went toward them, then back to him. "Don't you pay *them* no mind but don't go expecting they're going to thank you for coming like you was King Tut or something."

Her attitude and manner disturbed him. Some essence of her surrounded him, and at the center of himself, he felt a terrible panic and sense of loss for something he'd never had. She created an intimacy with him and he wanted more, wanted some part of herself, some share of the deep world wisdom her bright and weary face revealed. Yet in his uneasiness, Patrick was not unaware that she stirred some fierce and lonely sexuality within him.

This is Kenyon's mother, for Christ's sake.

It didn't matter. She was more; she was someone elemental, who didn't have to be defined or explained or located. She was someone he would never know and he wanted some share of her unknown warmth and amused, ironic, unquestioning understanding and acceptance of unspeakable things.

Kenyon had said, "Hell, my mama got lots a' bad reflections on her. Don't bother her, why the hell should it bother me?"

Patrick understood something about that now. There was a different measuring here, a different meaning for Kenyon's mother. She was of a different reality.

"Oh, Gawd," she said suddenly. "Oh, Lord, here she comes, the old woman. No way to keep her out once she gets it into her mind."

Patrick turned toward the center aisle and watched a small, straight, thin, gray-haired old black woman hurry toward the coffin. The funeral director followed closely and a pruney old man in clerical garb limped after them.

"That's Kenyon's great-grandma," Kenyon's mother told him.

"His *great-grandma?*"

380

Her face beamed with dark, hard pride and her eyes stayed on the old woman. "My own grandmother; eighty-nine years old and full of hell, but I wished she'd a' stayed home."

"Oh, Lawd," the old woman called out in a thin, high, shrill, piercing voice as she arrived at the coffin. She leaned over and whacked the coffin with the palm of her hand for a few resounding thumps and called out, beseeching the high ceiling, "Oh, Sweet Lawd Jesus, have mercy on his poor sinner's soul. Oh, Lawd, have mercy. Sweet Jesus, have mercy. He goin' home now!"

From the other side of the room, the bright African side, came a deep voice, sardonic, mocking, "A-men, sister, a-men. Lawdy, he a' goin' home!"

There was a soft wave of scornful laughter which rolled slowly from that side of the room, swept across them tangibly, heavily.

The old woman whirled around, glared wildly and shook a fist of anger at the direction of the sound. "Shame! Shame on you. Shame! The Lawd see you. He know who you are. Yes, Sweet Jesus, you sees them sinners, don't ya?"

A man's voice called out in answer, "Yah, sister, I sees 'em all right, I does!"

The whole left side of the room began to vibrate with a chanting sound accompanied by the sharp crack of hand-clapping.

"Oh, shit," Kenyon's mother said, "they gonna start *that* again?"

The minister, hardly bigger than the old great-grandmother, and as old, wrapped a wiry arm about her shoulders and directed her toward Kenyon's mother. Patrick stood up quickly to make room for her and Kenyon's mother held her in the chair firmly, powerfully.

"Now, grandma, they just funnin' you," she said. She winked at Patrick, included him in some small and personal conspiracy. "They just mean little bastards, grandma, but don't you go giving them nothing to work with, you hear? You know and I know, our Kenyon, he never did go for your Jesus stuff. So if you'll just knock it off, I'll get them to knock it off, okay?"

As she spoke, she relaxed her grip, relented her strength carefully, once assured the old woman would stay put. The old woman's bony hand poked and dug into the depths of her large, cracked black-leather pocketbook, then withdrew a small, worn, leather-covered Bible. The hand dove again, moved frantically, then emerged with smudged plastic-framed eyeglasses. She put them on, blinked hugely, then confronted Patrick.

"Who this here?" she demanded brusquely. "Who this white boy standing here?"

Kenyon's mother motioned him closer; she caught his sleeve and pulled him toward them. "Why this here is a soldier same as Kenyon was, come to pay his respects."

Under the old woman's accusing, angry glare, Patrick nodded awkwardly and took the small, cold, dry hand in his and was afraid his grip might crush the collection of fragile bird bones. "I'm sorry for your trouble, ma'am. Real sorry about your great-grandson."

She stared with her roundly magnified eyes and pulled her hand free, then shoved the glasses up along her nose. "Gone home to Jesus. Lawd, yes, gone home. Oh, Sweet Lawd, but don't I know trouble. You think I don't know trouble, boy? I've known my troubles and that sweet lamb's gone home to his Savior and his Lawd now. Amen."

Kenyon's mother stood up, spoke privately to the old minister who took her place and bent with the old woman over the Bible. The two of them chanted in thin-voiced unison over the small printed words as the old woman's finger traced along needlessly. Both of them knew the words by rote, yet she pretended to pick them out.

"Well," Kenyon's mother said heavily, "you might as well meet Kenyon's wife. That is, if you've a mind to."

"Well, yes, I guess so." He didn't want to meet any of them. They sat sprawled or stood languidly among the wooden chairs and waited and he felt his intrusion and their resentment. He just wanted to get the hell out of there, but the touch of Kenyon's mother, her hand on his arm, led him toward them.

The mass of color, the wild patterns, the shapeless garments, the rounded full heads, the dark faces, were indistinguishable one from the other. They seemed to him like toys, manufactured dolls in their studied, tight casualness.

She was tall but he couldn't tell if she was heavy or thin

beneath the hang of her brown-and-yellow garment. Her long hands seemed bony as they played with the edges of her sleeves, plucked and pinched as she confronted him. Her face, light brown, skin drawn tight against flat bones, wasn't pretty. It was contorted, nostrils flared with quick-breathing anger, lips pulled back into a threatening smile.

"Who's this?" she asked with a snap of her fingers toward him. "This what the Army sent to make it all come fine?"

"This is a soldier buddy of Kenyon's," Kenyon's mother said and released his arm and stepped back and watched.

"Mrs. Kenyon, I'm very sorry. About your husband."

She stared at his offered hand and slowly, deliberately slid her hands up along her arms, inside her wide sleeves. "Yes, you're sorry. You're sorry, shit. How come you standing here and he's lyin' in that box up there?"

Someone came beside her, a man dressed in a red-and-black robe. He had a neat round Afro and a small mustache and beard. He put an arm around the girl and she tried to shake him off.

"No, let him tell me. How come all these white boys come marching home on their two good legs and how come Kenyon's up there in that damn box?"

There was absolutely no place to begin. He scanned the waiting faces and they blended into the embodiment of his own accusation. He murmured something, some words of regret, turned and left them without hearing what they said.

It had started to rain with a cold, hard intensity. He yanked his cap from his back pocket, jammed it low on his brow, bent into the wind. A street voice called out from the doorway of a tenement but he didn't catch more than the sentiment: Get outta here, you.

He was almost at the subway entrance when he realized he had been hearing his name. He turned and waited as the bearded man in black and red came toward him.

"You got time for a drink?"

Patrick shrugged. "Sure. Why not?"

It was dark in the bar, which was filled with men hunched over drinks, whispering together, laughing, arguing in groups of two or three. Sudden bursts of sound punctured the air; the jukebox shrieked with jangling music. A few heads turned,

383

eyes slid over him with mild curiosity as Patrick followed to a booth in the rear. The man slid in opposite, held up two fingers toward the bar.

"Scotch okay?"

"Fine."

"I'm Kenyon's brother."

Patrick squinted in the bad light and the face did seem familiar, even seen in the dimness, but whether it was because it was the mother's face or brought with it memory of the dead brother, it was hard to say. The drinks arrived and the waiter said, "How's it goin' down, Ed-boy?"

"Yeah, Charlie."

He touched Patrick's glass with his fingertips, moved it slightly toward him. "Look like you need this. Not used to the cold weather?"

Patrick shook his head. He felt the rawness down his spine. The cold wrapped around him and he shuddered, took a good swallow and grimaced. "Wow, that'll kill the cold."

"You in Nam long?"

"As long as Kenyon. Nearly a year. We were medics together. I saw him get it." His fingers wrapped around the glass and he was silent for a moment, then raised his face in resolve. "Look, you want to hear about it? I mean, do you have a *need* to hear about it? Because if you do, I'll tell you. But if you don't, hell, let's let it go at that, okay?"

Kenyon's brother carefully lifted his glass and gestured for Patrick to do the same. He tapped their glasses together and said, "Cheers, baby." He drank, eyes closed, sighed. "*That's* what I *needed*. Look, reason I came after you was this. I wanted to thank you for coming. You didn't have to and I wanted to thank you."

"Goddamn it, I *did* have to and don't you thank me."

Ed Kenyon considered the pale blond kid for a long moment, studied him, searched him, then he nodded slowly and drank again.

"When's the funeral?" Patrick asked.

The brother shrugged. "Well, there's a bit of a to-do about that. Like about everything else in this whole thing. Kenyon's wife wants one kind of funeral; his grandma wants a down-home-style Baptist service. They're kind of pulling it between them. I guess when it gets right down to it, it don't matter what the hell they do at this point."

"It don't matter *shit* what they do at this point," Patrick said. He spoke in Kenyon's voice with Kenyon's inflection. Both men seemed slightly stunned, as though some communication had finally been accomplished without any effort, consciously, on their part.

Patrick emptied his glass and asked if Ed wanted another, but Ed shook his head. "You don't want another drink now, baby. You go on home now."

"Yeah. I guess so." He leaned back and felt empty and directionless. "Jesus," he said softly, "we were *friends*."

"I'm glad you were, O'Malley. I'm glad you were."

There was nothing left of it now. He wanted to tell Kenyon's brother that there should be something left of it, that he wasn't a stranger, that the black faces which regarded him with cold, hostile suspicion, which had declared him an intruder, had no right, didn't know. He felt tired and the Scotch hit him across the forehead. He reached out a hand toward Kenyon's brother, palm upward. There was a slight, awkward hesitation, then Kenyon's brother slapped his palm and turned his own hand for the ritual. With Kenyon it had been a warm and joyous and easy and natural contact. Now Patrick felt embarrassed and self-conscious. He eased himself from the booth.

"You take care now," Kenyon's brother told him.

"Yeah, right."

They watched him leave, the curious, the disinterested. He heard laughter resume behind the door, more natural, relaxed with the intruder gone. He walked into the slashes of rain toward the subway entrance; sleet made long dark streaks on his uniform.

"Hey, whitey."

He glanced up, saw a kid, about nine or ten. He was hanging out of a tenement window two stories up: dark face, round Afro, a dark indistinguishable presence. The kid disappeared for a second, then bounced up and heaved something out of the window. "Go fuck yourself, whitey."

Patrick veered to avoid the rock, slammed into a row of overflowing garbage cans. Some unidentifiable soft matter, colorless, shapeless, squirted from a torn plastic bag and onto the leg of his pants. He stood in the rain scraping the stuff off his trousers with a scrap of torn cardboard. Then he glanced up, caught the kid grinning down at him.

"Hey, baby," Patrick called out softly and without rancor, "*you* go fuck *yourself.*"

The kid stared for a minute, uncomprehending, then his face split into a wide grin and he disappeared from the window with a loud yelp of laughter.

THIRTY-THREE

Patrolman Patrick O'Malley was assigned to the 25th Precinct in the northeastern portion of Manhattan just before the borough narrowed into a sliver of land which was separated from the Bronx by the dirty Harlem River. He was assigned to a patrol car and his partner was Patrolman Jimmy Hughes.

Patrolman Jimmy Hughes had been well built when he was in his twenties; he was showing signs of impending obesity at thirty and would be a fat slob by the time he was forty. He had six years on the job, a wife, three kids, and a house in Syosset, Long Island. He had quick-moving eyes which darted constantly on the alert:

"See that nigger over there? The one with the gimp leg? I busted him twice for indecent exposure. I mean, *twice,* and me in uniform, so how smart could the bastard be? Watch this now, he'll wave to me like we was old friends. Hey, Gimp, you been behavin' yourself?"

The crippled man turned toward the patrol car, squinted, leaned forward, recognized Hughes and nodded vigorously. "Ain't been doin' nothin' at all, officer. No sir, stayin' on the outside, that's me."

"Yeah? Well, watch yourself."

Hughes rolled up the window and said to Patrick, "Ain't that hot stuff? I busted that guy one good shot, almost knocked the balls offa him, the second time I took him in. And he smiles when he sees me like we're old buddies. Yeah, and he better, all right, he fucking well better."

For nearly two months, Hughes instructed him in the lay of the land and the customs and mores of the natives and it boiled down to a few basic, essential facts.

"Let 'em know who's boss. Let 'em see you, ya know, increase your visibility at all times. Let 'em know you're right on top, know what I mean? Christ, during the riots in '64, we did some pretty damn good bustin' up."

Hughes adjusted his cap and leaned back, grinning over memory. "Jeez, I got some black mother-nigger sonuvabitch I been looking to get my hands on. Ya know, one a' them fresh bastards with the wise-guy way of movin'. Jeez, they got a way of movin' their asses, it says, 'Fuck you, buster,' as clear as you'd wanna hear it said. So I been looking to catch this mother fucker at anything. You know the type; you can just tell he's N.G. but you can't get 'im. And so, when the riots was on, I just started to walk toward the sergeant and Christa-mighty, beautiful! There's this black-assed bastard just turning the corner and he walks smack into me and he's carryin' a tape recorder. And the TV and radio store is in the direction he's comin' from and there we are and he ain't so smart-assed now, see, there's just me and him and the sergeant's back. He starts talkin' real quick. 'Hey look, officer, this here is mine. See, I just been tapin' some of the things on the street, like to maybe sell it to the news people, you know?' Oh, shit, I took him so fast it was pathetic. He didn't know what the fuck hit him. Jeez, you wanna get a guy good, one quick one in the balls, then you come up with the end of the stick right in the mother's throat and then he's yours. I mean, then you do whatever the fuck you wanna do, you got dead meat at your feet. Funny thing about that nigger though. I don't know what the hell it was between him and me but we both knew we'd have to meet up someday and have it out. I'm sure as shit glad it was me had the upper hand because he'd as soon cut my throat as look at me." Hughes scratched along the back of his neck. "And for no good reason, you know?"

"Was there any possibility that the tape recorder *was* his?" Patrick asked.

Hughes looked blank. "What the fuck does that have to do with anything?"

Word had gone out on O'Malley, of course: son of a deputy chief inspector. But the kid seemed okay, didn't invoke his father, in fact, rumor was around that they didn't see much of each other. O'Malley had his own apartment and whatever the truth was the old man didn't seem to interfere, and everyone practically forgot who his father was. The fact was, it was the kid they became a little wary of.

On the day that the P.B.A. delegate announced to the cheers of the men being turned out that they had not only been granted permission to wear the little enamel American flags over their shields as part of their uniforms, but that the President of the United States himself had congratulated the man who brought the matter to a court decision, O'Malley's reaction was peculiar. The delegate noticed that he was the only guy on the shift without a flag pin. He figured maybe the kid was a little cautious, what the hell. In a gesture of good will and friendship, he approached the tall, quiet blond patrolman.

"Hey, Pat, I got something for you. Had an extra and I noticed you don't have no flag," Savonese, the delegate, said and handed him a flag pin.

Patrick held it in his hand for a minute, wordless, while Savonese waited for thanks. Finally, he said, "Tell you what, Savonese, let's put it here, okay?" He pinned the flag to the sleeve of Savonese's jacket.

"What are you doin'? Hey?"

It was hard to tell what the hell went on in the kid's mind. He kept his voice soft and his face devoid of any expression. Patrick patted Savonese's shoulder a few times, then said, "You've been wearing it on your sleeve for years, right? So that's where it belongs."

By the time Savonese got the insult, O'Malley was out of the ready room and standing for inspection, calm, detached, remote.

It wasn't the first time he'd insulted the flag. Word had gone around that O'Malley considered it stupid to have a little flag attached to the patrol car.

"We're an American police department in an American city in an American state. We're all citizens or we couldn't be on the job, so what's the point?" O'Malley was reported as saying.

The men in the precinct began to watch him. If he couldn't understand a thing as basic as displaying the flag, if that had to be explained to him, the guy needed straightening out. If it wasn't for his old man, he'd have been straightened out by now.

The fact that he'd served in Viet Nam was all to his credit, but the fact that he never mentioned it, that they found out about his service only through his record, was puzzling. Another mark against.

Patrolman Jimmy Hughes didn't have much to say about O'Malley; the kid seemed to be a good cop, backed him up the few times it was necessary, but he never really *said* anything, you know?

Actually, Patrolman Hughes talked enough for both men and never really seemed to notice that Patrick hardly ever answered him.

"Jeez, you know, I no sooner get the fuckin' snow thrower paid for, the wife starts on me. Now I gotta get an electric lawn mower. I tell her, let the kid move his ass a little this summer, do him good, but her friend next door, she's got an electric with one of them little seats on it, ya know? I'll tell ya, it's one helluva responsibility. Lucky thing I got this friend in the Twelfth Precinct. See, he kinda gets a break on all this here equipment. Jeez, he got me my snow thrower about fifty per cent off list price." Hughes winked and grinned. "Know what I mean? Jeez, this guy got more business going for him. I gotta get after him for the mower."

They were dispatched to the scene of a hit-and-run on 112th Street and Lenox Avenue. By the time they arrived, a small crowd stood clustered around an old woman who was bleeding from the mouth.

"Put in a call for an ambulance, O'Malley. I'll have a looksee."

By the time Patrick joined his partner, Hughes had determined that the woman was in serious condition. He leaned close to Patrick and whispered, "Jesus, watch out, O'Malley. She lost control of herself and crapped all over the place. Christ, just our luck."

She was an elderly black woman dressed in a neat dark dress and an old black coat. Her legs, encased in heavy cotton stockings, stuck out beneath her dress and were shoeless. One of the two black men who squatted beside her held the shoes, which were bent and twisted to the shape of her feet. The other man held her head in his hands and kept whispering to her.

Patrick got to his knees, touched her face lightly with his

390

fingertips and determined that she was conscious. He flipped out his clean handkerchief and applied pressure to the cut mouth. "You got something to rest her head on?" he asked without taking his eyes from the woman's face. "Yeah, good, fold your jacket, that's fine. Listen, I want you to let her head down real easy, yeah, yeah, good." His face went close to the woman and she blinked at him and moaned softly. "Hey, you gonna be just fine, okay? You hear, we're gonna get you all fixed up, okay?"

Hughes looked down at them, notebook in hand. "Hey, get her name, Pat, for the aided card. What's your name lady? She conscious or what?"

Her voice was stretched and thin. "Annie Jackson."

Hughes leaned over heavily. "Okay, Annie, where do you live?"

Patrick smoothed a stiff lock of gray hair from her lined forehead and bent his face close to hers. "Hey, Miz Jackson, don't cry." The woman tried to say something. Patrick turned toward the black man nearest him. "You catch that? What'd she say?"

The black man, young, about Patrick's age, with a scarred fighter's face, leaned over the woman and his tough face went soft. He whispered to Patrick, "She all upset 'cause she messed herself up. She ashamed somebody might know about that."

Patrick realized now, suddenly, why Hughes hadn't brought the blanket from the car. He had assumed it was an oversight. "Hey, Jimmy, get the blanket."

Hughes said, "Look, the ambulance will be here in a minute."

Patrick turned abruptly to the black man who held the old woman's shoes. Tersely, he said, "There's a plaid blanket in the back of the squad car. Get it for me, okay?"

Carefully, without moving her, they covered her and Patrick whispered into her ear, "Don't you worry about a thing now, you hear?"

She nodded and he could see she was in grave pain. He heard Hughes's voice, taut and demanding.

"Anyone seen what happened? Anyone seen the old lady get hit?"

"I seen it," the man beside Patrick said. "Some punk kids out joy riding in a blue Ford, but you never catch up with them. They probably dumped it by now. Man, this poor old woman, she went ten feet in the air, didn't you, Mama?" There was a sudden edge of panic in the man's voice. "Hey, officer, she done gone out like a light. Hey, she okay or what?"

Patrick reached for her wrist, then his hand went inside the coat to her bony chest. Nothing. He leaned his hand on her chest, applied pressure, released. Again. Again. Again. There was a flutter, a quiver, a rasping sound from between her parted lips, but it stopped as suddenly as it had begun.

Patrick pulled off his jacket, which was hampering him, bent to the woman and began breathing into her mouth, pressing her diaphragm: forced breath in, forced it out. Again, the faint soft sigh, the attempt to breathe, to live. And all the time, inside his head, Patrick could hear his own voice saying, "Gonna be just fine there, Mama. You gonna be just fine."

By the time the ambulance arrived she was breathing, painfully, raspingly, but breathing. The attendants lifted her carefully and Patrick watched as they put an oxygen mask over her face. He turned at a touch on his shoulder.

It was the fighter: face ugly, thick-lipped, face of a loser, brown eyes reddened and watery. "Here's your jacket, officer."

"Oh, gee, thanks." Patrick put it on, brushed vaguely, buttoned it. The man picked up Patrick's hat from the curb and handed it to him. Patrick wasn't even aware that he'd dropped it. "Thanks." He put it lightly on the crown of his head, then pulled it forward into place.

"Hey, officer," the man said thickly, then couldn't find words. He reached out and took Patrick's hand in a tight grasp. "You a real man, baby," he said and then he walked away.

Hughes revved the motor the minute Patrick got into the car beside him. For once, he was quiet. Patrick caught the tense stiff set of Hughes's jaw, the throbbing along the temple, but he didn't say anything.

At the precinct, they gave the information to the desk and details to the detectives, who weren't very impressed but had to look into the matter whether it impressed them or not.

392

Patrick went into the men's room to wash up and was surprised at the blood on his face. He washed it away, rinsed his mouth, remembered the blood taste of the woman, the death he tasted inside of her, sucked out of her, the life he breathed into her.

She'd gone into shock; if he hadn't breathed for her, she'd have died. Right then, there, in the gutter, she'd have died. Jesus, he had actually *tasted* death and he'd blown and breathed it away. He felt an elation and joy he couldn't quite contain.

"Hey, listen you," Hughes said. His eyes surveyed the area, made certain they were alone.

Patrick blotted his face with rough brown paper towels, rubbed his hands and tossed the wad of paper into the wastebasket. Hughes's face was quivering and his lips were dry.

"What's your problem?" Patrick asked quietly.

"Listen, don't you never pull that kind of shit on me again, you got that?"

The taste of death was still in his mouth and he regarded Hughes coldly and dispassionately, watched him work up to voice-stretching tension, watched it all come bursting out of the man, growing fuller and larger because he refused to act.

Hughes's face was a deep, dangerous red. The heavy folds of his cheeks shook and his eyes went from Patrick's face to the mirror directly behind him, back and forth.

"Don't you never send no fucking nigger into *my* squad car. Don't you never go right past me, right over my head, and send one a' them apes into my car or so help me Christ, I'll break your ass!"

In his passion, he miscalculated or misread Patrick's reaction, and carried along by the momentum of his rage, which instead of subsiding swelled, he shoved his index finger into Patrick's chest and when that brought forth no reaction, verbal, physical, nothing, Hughes, for emphasis, just to be sure he was properly understood, shoved Patrick against the washbowl.

"Any decent man'd be in here vomiting his guts out right now, he put his mouth on that old nigger woman's," Hughes told him.

The taste of death ran down his throat, deep into his gut,

393

into the center of himself, where all the dead and dying kept their counsel, from where they all accused him.

This once, he had defeated it. There had been nothing but a feeling of triumph and this man Hughes had been repulsed by his act, without having even the slightest understanding, conception of what that act involved: the defeating of death.

There were no words, none that could define his act or explain. There was only a powerful impulse, which he followed. With his two hands locked together he swung and smashed Hughes in the face with a force that stunned the larger man, sent him reeling backwards into feet-sliding, skull-crashing helplessness.

Patrick didn't move in on him, just stood, hands at his sides, watched dispassionately, calmly, remotely as the sergeant burst in, looked from one to the other.

"Hey, what the fuck?"

Two uniformed men came, pulled Hughes to his feet; a couple of detectives came, offered Patrick a cigarette, told him to calm down, take it easy, which was funny because he was the calmest one of everybody. They all seemed shaken as hell, as though something really important, really serious had occurred when it was all really so completely insignificant when measured against the fact that he had tasted death and spit it out.

THIRTY-FOUR

Brian wished Mary Ellen would skip the once-a-month, if-we-can-all-get-together Sunday-dinner ritual. She acted as though she didn't catch any tension between Maureen and her husband, Tim Logan. Christ, even their two kids were practically rigid, could hardly lift their faces from their plates.

"Well, why don't you two kids go outside and play on the swings I put up for you?" Brian asked his grandchildren. They turned worried faces toward their mother and she nodded and rose quickly to help clear the table.

He and Tim and Patrick went across the hall into the study for the customary after-Sunday-dinner drink.

"This is a fine old room," Tim Logan mused, exactly as he did every time he entered the study. He was a pompous, fine-cut little bastard and Brian had the feeling he was calculating the worth of every stone in the house, counting and evaluating. He never did understand why his daughter had married him. A computer salesman, for Christ's sake.

"Well, Pat, how's life in the Police Department?" Logan asked his brother-in-law. "Hey, they let you get away with that stuff, kid? Hair's a little on the long side, isn't it?" He gave a short, unpleasant laugh. "They wouldn't let you get away with that in the company."

Though Brian agreed about Patrick's hair, there was something so irritating, snide, brittle, condescending about Logan that to his own surprise, Brian said, "I think he looks pretty good. You must be getting old, Tim. You sound like a real old company man."

They all turned toward the door, toward the loud shriek and Mary Ellen's worried voice and Maureen's commotion.

Tim stubbed out his cigarette and said tersely, "Oh, shit, here we go again," and he rushed to see what Patricia, his youngest, had gotten into this time.

"He's a real beaut, isn't he?" Brian said to his son. It was at least one thing he knew they agreed on. He didn't feel there was much safe ground lately. "Well, we haven't seen you for quite a while, Pat. How's it going?"

"Okay. You know."

The steel-gray eyes veiled over, looked right through him, as though he were a shadow. The heavy blond hair suddenly irritated Brian. Maybe it was the way the kid casually brushed it off his forehead.

"What are you doing, letting your hair grow so you'll fit in with the hippies down at the Ninth?"

His son's hand touched the hair along his collar. He shrugged, let his hand fall to the arm of the chair. Of course, his father had been informed of his transfer. They just never mentioned it to each other.

"A lot of the younger guys are wearing their hair longer, Dad. Couple of 'em have real handlebars, too. It's funny, some of them look like pictures of the old-timers. You know, right out of the gay nineties."

"Yeah, but these are the swinging seventies, right?" Brian waited for his son to argue, debate, dispute. The damn kid just shrugged, moved his broad thin shoulders easily, pushed at the hair again, dragged on his cigarette. Okay. He'd take his cue from his son. "Oh, well, what the hell, hair is hair. Fads come and go. You look like you've lost a little weight, Patrick."

"I'm a lousy cook, but really, I'm fine."

"You still going to school?" It was a stupid question; he knew Patrick was enrolled in the John Marshall College of Criminal Justice and that he was carrying a heavy load of courses toward his degree.

"Well, yeah, sure. New semester starts in a couple of weeks."

With an inexplicably urgent need to impress his son, Brian said, "You know, I'm gonna give a couple of lectures at the college in the spring semester. I'm preparing a few talks on how to deal with the news media. If we like the way it goes, I might schedule a regular course as part of the curriculum at the Police Academy for the next class."

"Well, that's fine, Dad."

They ran out of small talk, empty words, statements, vague questions. Brian put his glass down and leaned forward and held his son's eye. "Pat, how's it going? *Really?*"

"Okay."

The cool remote gray eyes focused on him with a familiar year-spanning challenge; the pale face sharpened his memory of a child who had confronted him, feared him but confronted him. It would always be between them, preventing them from talking the way other men could talk. For them, it had to be question and answer: father and son. He didn't want it to be that way, didn't think his son wanted it to be that way, yet he felt helpless to do anything to change it. In a sudden burst of anger, explosive, too long held in, he abandoned resolve that he would be careful.

"What do you mean 'okay'? What the hell happened at the Twenty-fifth?"

"You were told about it, weren't you? Why ask me?"

"I *am* asking you."

Absolute circle. Complete. Cut the shit. Father and son.

"Okay," Patrick said. "Some guy pushed me too hard, so I decked him." He said it in a tough, casual, offhand way. "That's it. That's all."

Brian jammed his hands in his pockets, moved his fingers among keys and coins to keep from smacking his son, this steely-eyed kid, this baby-faced, cold-voiced, closed-up stranger. This was who the kid had always been; he'd lived here with him, seen him every day. But he'd just seen his surface, had never been able to get more than a quick fleeting glimpse of what was inside. He wanted to ask Patrick the circumstances, wanted a chance to understand. But the mask was rigid and impenetrable.

"You don't want to screw up, Pat," Brian said softly, surprised by his own sound. It was almost a plea.

"No. I don't want to screw up, Dad."

Impulsively, Brian asked, "What *do* you want, Pat?"

The kid blinked, looked away, bit his lip. His face changed. Unguarded for just a moment, he had that pale weary boy's look of realization that no matter how hard he tried, how much he struggled against it, the two long hot streams of tears would slide down his face and betray him. But there were no boyhood tears; there was a man's quick adjusting of his features. He exhaled through his teeth in a thin whistling sound, stood up, shrugged.

"Maybe just to be left alone."

"Okay," Brian said.

"Hey look, Dad, I hate to eat and run, but I've got a date."

"Yeah, okay. Well, look, make sure you tell your mother good-by. And . . . don't be such a stranger."

"Yeah, well, with the job and school and all . . ."

"Yeah, right, sure."

A brief, mutual but unconnecting shoulder slap, hands quickly withdrawn before they might demand something from each other. He walked into the hallway with his son.

"Pat, listen . . ."

The familiar face set into a resigned neutral pleasantness, a remote polite smile, the dark-blond brows rose patiently, waiting. "Look, Pat, if there's anything I can do, I mean, at any time . . ."

"Right, Dad, thanks."

He tried to draw something from the fact that the kid hadn't come to him. Had handled it himself, even if that meant messing it up, screwing it, blowing it. He'd done it by himself, on his own.

But Christ, Brian couldn't understand why his son was digging his heels in at all the wrong places.

The two kids sat at the kitchen table working carefully with crayons in their coloring books. Mary Ellen and Maureen were doing the dishes, and when he came into the room, mother and daughter exchanged worried glances. He could tell that his daughter had been crying.

"Any coffee left?"

Mary Ellen prepared the coffee for him. She cleared the children from the table. "Come on Patty and Timmy, let's you and Grandma go inside and I'll read you stories from that new storybook I got you."

"Gonna have some coffee with me?" he asked his daughter. Her hands trembled as she folded the dish towel neatly,

398

matching corner to corner. It was funny how he could see himself in her face; she had his features, smaller, finer, modified. She reminded him of a photograph of himself when he was a child. "Okay. Wanna talk?"

She suddenly pressed the damp towel against her face tightly, held it for a moment and when her face emerged it was red and distorted.

She sat across from him and her small hands twisted the towel as though she didn't know she was doing it.

"Daddy, I want to leave him. I can't live with him anymore."

He knew they'd been fighting; he'd heard the car drive off. The little bastard would probably drive around for a while to cool off.

"Come on, honey, everybody has a blowup now and then. It'll pass."

He wasn't prepared for her passion. Her small hand clenched into a fist and she pounded the table. "No, Daddy, it's not just that, not just a blowup. It's . . . it's become a whole way of life. It's become all there is and it just isn't enough. There just isn't anything, not *anything* anymore."

"There are two kids, Maureen," he pointed out quietly.

"Oh, Daddy, it's all turned into a great big blank zero, everything, my whole life. It's as though I'm dead. I'm nobody. I'm not a person anymore; I don't even know who I am or who I was supposed to be."

There was a note of rising hysteria, a glimpse of the stranger who was his daughter, who had been hiding all this time behind a well-known, well-loved, familiar, safe and reliable girl. If his son had shown him too little, his daughter was offering too much.

"You don't know who you are? You're Maureen O'Malley Logan, that's who the hell you are." He pointed at her, then jabbed a thumb over his shoulder. "You're the mother of those two kids in there and the wife of the man who went storming out of here a while ago. You've got a beautiful home in Westchester and your husband has a damn good income and you've all got your health and you don't know what the hell trouble is, Maureen. I mean, you'd really have to go out looking for it because you don't really know."

"Can't you understand?" she asked vehemently. "Can't

you see? I'm just, just . . . I cook and clean and I wipe up and I chauffeur those kids back and forth, back and forth. And I keep my figure"—she lightly touched her tiny neat waist—"and I entertain beautifully. I say all the right things to his friends and he's very proud of me. I do him justice and it's all like being a shadow, like not being a *real* person. Like being without any substance, it's . . . it's all *him* and Daddy," she bit her lip, shook her head, whispered to the table, "there's really nothing to him. Just talk and brag and he doesn't come near me. I mean, I just can't take it anymore." She rubbed her fists into her eyes, then looked at her father. "I'm still young. God, I'm only twenty-eight. It doesn't all have to be over for me, does it?"

"What the hell did you expect it to be?" Brian said bitterly, then aware of what he'd said from the shocked, injured look on his daughter's face, he reached for her hands and softened, as he always did where Maureen was concerned. "Oh, look, honey, we all have ups and downs, good days, bad days. Come on, you're a big girl now. Ride it out. It'll be okay." Then firmly, "Maureen, you've got two kids. You don't break up a home because you're feeling sorry for yourself. You have to think of them before yourself."

In a cold and unexpected voice, she said, "Yes, I guess that's the way you always figured it, Dad." She withdrew her hands, clenched the dish towel.

"What the hell does *that* mean? Look, where do you get off, saying something like that? Your mother and I have a good life together. You and Patrick had a good home."

She nodded and started washing cups and saucers.

Mary Ellen looked up at him and the two kids, large-eyed, expectant, tense, glanced from their storybook, leaned a little closer into her, one on each side of her. Mary Ellen signaled to him, just a slight pursing of her lips to indicate their innocent presence.

"Look," he told his wife, "I'm going to take that TV set down to Mom's. If Maureen wants to stay overnight, she's welcome."

Mary Ellen released her breath slowly, drew her arms tighter around her grandchildren, looked young enough, scared enough, small enough to be their mother. They nestled protectively close to her. "Won't that be fun? Timmy, you and Patty can sleep in Uncle Patrick's room. The room he had when he was just a little boy, like you."

"Mary Ellen," he said carefully, *"just for tonight."*

Brian leaned his head back against the old familiar chair, stretched his legs to the hassock, closed his eyes and could almost feel time slip away. His mother's voice came from the kitchen. There were the scuffling sounds of boys, the warning note in his mother's voice; an argument in high thin voices: "It was him; he did it." "No, it was him, not me."

"Go on in now and tell Uncle Brian good night," his mother instructed and he pulled himself up as the two boys entered the living room.

Jesus, they were practically black: dark-brown faces, bright-black eyes suddenly gone shy when confronted by him. His mother casually shoved them forward.

"Come on now, say your good nights properly."

"Good night, Uncle Brian," said Juan, the oldest, twelve.

"Good night, Uncle Brian." That was José, his brother, just ten.

Uncle Brian. Christ. Well, yeah, I guess they have to call me something and mister was too formal and he'd be damned if they'd just casually call him by his first name.

"Good night, boys. You guys been behaving yourselves? Not getting into any trouble?"

They nodded earnestly, poked at each other, jabbed and chased and darted into the bedroom. His mother smiled and looked after them for a minute, listened to them hit the bed in flying leaps.

"Mind those bedsprings in there, you hear?"

"Okay, Grandma." Giggles, scuffles, punches, grunts.

"Well, they're a fine pair, aren't they?" she said fondly.

He leaned back and considered her. "Aren't they too much for you, Mom? They seem like real live wires."

"Oh, Brian, it was something terrible before they came. The quiet after Maria and Rose and Mathilda went back to their mother. Though I'll tell you, God's truth, I much prefer to have boys about than girls. I don't mind the rough-and-tumble; God knows you boys were holy terrors. But with girls" —she touched a stray lock of white hair and with a firm hand put it back into place—"ah, the girls. It's argue and bicker all day long. Oh, and they can be that mean to each other, and the tears flowing and the hurt feelings. They're good boys, poor little fellas. Kit and Murray had them up to the lake for the whole weekend with their own brood so they're all wound up and exhausted now. They'll settle down in a short while, you'll see."

Kit had brought the first kid home as though it was a wounded bird. A little girl, two years old, no English, no father, the mother put away with T.B. and the kid with nowhere to go. Hell, he told Kit, all the kids in the foundling hospital have nowhere else to go, but Kit said, "This one is something special, Brian," and she said, "Mom needs something too, Brian. That apartment is so damned empty."

Kit's house was never empty. A large, old frame house in the Pelham Parkway section of the Bronx. She and her husband, Dr. Murray Weinstein, filled that house with an assortment of strays, a mixed group of foundlings, some of whom they adopted and some who stayed until ill or departed parents were able to care for them. Kit's career as a social worker among the poor of the Bronx put her in touch with the needy of all kinds. Although she'd quit her job at the foundling hospital, staying home and taking care of stray kids who had a way of collecting stray animals didn't seem enough. Kit became active in politics as a way to combat the problems which caused the abundance of children she found in dire need of services which weren't available or adequate. She was winding up her third term as state congresswoman for her district and planning to run for the state senate.

Brian had been against his mother taking in children. She was too old, for Christ's sake; she was seventy years old. He'd been after her for years to give up the apartment and come and live with them. They had more than enough room, what with Maureen married, Patrick off to the service, then off to his own life. He didn't like the idea of her living on Ryer Avenue anymore. Hell, the way the neighborhood changed, you could hardly see white for black and Puerto Rican. There was talk of closing down St. Simon's because the new parishioners couldn't support it. Hell, they couldn't support themselves, half of them were on welfare.

He'd have thought his mother would be glad to have some peace and quiet up in Riverdale. All her life, she'd been so surrounded by all of them, all their commotion, but Kit said, "Let her try it, Brian. I've just got a feeling about it."

Well, his mother took to it all right and they moved in and out of her life in a steady stream. Let Kit tell her there was a bunch of little sisters or brothers who were going to be split up and his mother somehow managed to find the room: "It's fine; it'll work out. We'll manage just fine. It keeps me busy and, oh, Brian, it fills the house again."

He wondered if sometimes when she sat up at night, her hands busy with the sewing and the knitting and the ironing of small clothes, he wondered if she ever pretended that the soft child noises from the other rooms were her own children: Roseanne, dreaming of romance; Kit, laughing in her sleep at her own secret triumphs; Martin, quiet and peaceful; Kevin, tossing and turning; and himself. He wondered what memory she had of him at ten, twelve years old.

"I got the letter from Roseanne with their Billy's wedding pictures," she said. "It's somewhere around here. Now where did I put it?"

"I know, Ma, you showed me before."

"Did I? Did I now? Isn't that terrible? I must be getting simple, saying the same things twice. Well, she's a nice-looking girl, all tan and healthy. I saw in a magazine the other day, they're all like that in California. They grow up like oranges out there, it said in the magazine, all fine and healthy. Well, Billy's bride looked like one of the magazine girls, and he so tall himself, so I guess it's true enough."

She polished her eyeglasses on her apron, smeared them so that when she put them back on they glistened with something oily. She squinted and said, "You know who I saw, Brian, the other day just outside of Alexander's on Fordham Road?"

"Give them here, Mom. I'll clean them for you."

"Eh? Oh, yes, well. Do you remember Mrs. Phelan? Oh, you *do*, Brian. You remember Buddy Phelan; you were in his class all through school. Go on now, you were."

He shook his head, held the glasses to the light, attacked them with a clean handkerchief. "Kevin was in Buddy Phelan's class, not me."

"Oh," she said thoughtfully, "was Buddy younger than you? That's funny."

"He was *always* younger than me, so what's so funny?"

403

"Oh, *you.*" She reached over and slapped his knee at his teasing. "Well, I saw Mrs. Phelan anyway and she told me that she's living right down the street from Anna Caprobella, Brian. You remember Anna that was sweet on our poor John? They live in Yonkers, the Phelans, and that's where Anna lives now, only of course she's not Caprobella but some other long Italian name I've forgotten. She's four or five children, all boys, Mrs. Phelan said, and her husband is an electrician. I guess her children are mostly grown now." She reached for the glasses, hesitated for a moment before putting them on. "It's a funny thing, isn't it, Brian, how things come out?" She put her glasses on and touched her white hair off her thin cheek. "I'll make you some nice strong tea. You just lean back there now and relax a while. You look a bit tired. I'll bring it when it's ready and some nice nutcake I made fresh just this morning."

He settled back into the chair: the old chair, covered and re-covered, old stuffing ripped out, renewed, replaced. It was funny about the chair, the way she held on to it. All the other furniture had been discarded and replaced through the years, but not the chair and the hassock. He'd never seen his mother sit in it. It had been his father's; then his; then all the kids, whoever got there first; but his mother never sat in it.

Christ Almighty, the ceiling patterns never changed; plastered and scraped and smoothed and painted over, they came back persistent as time, forced themselves back into this room. The minute he saw them, traced and recognized and remembered them, he could be transported back as though the world began and ended here in this room, this apartment, this home base. Maybe that was why she wouldn't leave. It was too filled with familiar patterns; she could travel back and hold on to whatever meant most to her.

He didn't really know what her memories were, what all the events were that centered here in this place. His father's wake, of course. His grandmother died in this room; just she and his mother alone, here, during the war. But there were other events, conversations, decisions, sorrows and pleasures here in this room that only she knew about.

She'd sat at the little lamp table against the wall and written her letters to them all through the war years, keeping them up to date:

404

—Nana died two nights ago, at home. She hadn't been sick and it was peaceful and she seemed to know what was happening. She was very old and the new priest, Father Kelly, said Mass. I'd always thought Father Donlon would be around forever, I guess. But Father Kelly is quite nice.

—Billy Delaney was given a medal over there, somewhere in Italy his letter says.

—Roseanne and the children (her little girl's a beauty, dark curly hair and Roseanne's eyes) are going to live with me the while Billy's at war. There's no sense at all to her keeping her place with the house empty, now you've all gone.

—Kit will graduate school this June and was thinking about nursing school.

—Your cousin Billy O'Malley was killed at a place called Guadalcanal.

—Your brother Martin has been assigned a parish somewhere in Brooklyn; I'm not sure where, it's such a complicated place.

—Your brother Kevin was home on leave and he looks to be taller than you but still too thin, those uniforms make him look so scrawny.

—My brother Jimmie John is dead.

—Matthew's gone. It was his heart. My sister Ellen is not the same, first Billy, then Matt. She's gotten thin, and used to be so hearty.

—Your Mary Ellen had the baby last night, a lovely small girl, and she looks just like you did at birth, Brian, so alike it was amazing. The old man had forty fits, he was that mad for a grandson, the old fool . . .

There were huge gaps in her life that he never thought about, could not account for, periods of time, years, collections of sorrows, illnesses, worries, losses. And all the time, she had lived here, never left. Seen them all leave, her children, her grandchildren, her sister gone off to live with a daughter-in-law and son in Jersey and wasting away and dying. All familiar faces gone, leaving behind change.

Large apartments that had been filled with huge families were divided into small apartments that were filled with huge families and all of them strangers. No one came back, nobody's children came back from their houses in the suburbs.

There was a handful of them left, the old neighbors, and when they met on the street, outside the stores, hurrying along in the late afternoon, anxious to get home before it got dark (there was another lady got hit in the face and her pocketbook grabbed right around the corner on Valentine Avenue, wasn't it terrible though?), they exchanged information and gossip and news and none of it was good. They seized new information voraciously and passed it along at every opportunity to whoever would listen.

"Do you remember Mrs. Hagan, Brian?" She came in from the kitchen, wiped her hands on her apron. "The one used to live at 2108 and had that fat son Michael? Sure you do, you were there when he fell down the stairs and broke the dozen eggs that time, great clumsy boy he was. Well, she was hit by a car and killed, Mrs. Hagan was, right on the Grand Concourse, poor soul. Nearly eighty she was, what a shame."

His mother spoke of people he had not seen or heard of for years and hardly remembered ever existed. Yet they were still a current part of her life, had a place in her existence, and with a sense of shame he would pretend: Yes, of course he remembered Mrs. Kirshner with the lame daughter; Mrs. O'Donnell with the redheaded husband; Mrs. Gallenberg with the funny way of talking.

It struck him sometimes that other sons must listen to other old mothers ramble on, and included in their reflections, his mother's name must evoke a similar reaction.

"Do you remember David Fineman?" He leaned forward and helped her with the tea tray. "Well, I saw Mrs. Farragher, you know, the butcher's wife, and she told me that David Fineman is a very famous plastic surgeon." She rubbed her chin thoughtfully for a moment, head to one side. "Plastic surgeon was it now? That's the one does all the tricks to the movie stars' faces? Yes, that was it, a plastic surgeon."

Brian carefully tested the tea, which was scalding. "Now how would Mrs. Farragher know that? The Finemans moved away from here years ago."

"Well, she saw it in one of the magazines. There was an article about all those plastic surgeons and the things they do to make people look younger, for heaven's sake. And there was this picture of him, Mrs. Farragher said, Dr. David Fineman. She said she recognized him right off the bat. A bit stout, Mrs. Farragher said. Oh, Brian, they've four families living in

406

Dr. Fineman's old house. Isn't that a shame, that house all crammed full up that way? What's wrong? What? You get a scrap of shell in your tooth, dear?"

He dug out the sharp, jagged edge of walnut shell.

She leaned forward anxiously. "Oh, you didn't break a tooth, did you?"

He felt a wave of guilt for her concern. "It's okay, Mom. No harm done, really. Listen, are you sure you don't want me to drop the TV set off at the parish house for you?"

"No, no, it's fine here, Brian, and thanks for donating it. The fair's not for a week yet and in the meantime I'll let the boys have it in their room for the fun of it."

He felt a curious, senseless but painful resentment toward them, those boys, whispering to each other in Spanish, in his old bedroom, laughing and poking and jostling and having their ears and nails checked every day by his mother.

"How will you get it to the parish house then?"

"Oh, there's ways. Now don't you be quizzing me like that," she said sharply.

It occurred to him that she had managed so many things in her life without his assistance. He watched her worn, tired face as she bent over her darning. It was an open, honest, innocent face, her eyes clear and bright beneath her glasses, narrowed a bit as she threaded her needle. Her hands were rough and red and sinewy and callused; her fingers were scarred with innumerable old burn marks and line-thin white marks of knife cuts where blade had gone through bread and flesh when, for an instant, she had turned her head toward a child's cry or a ringing bell.

She was his strongest connection to his beginnings; being her son made him forever her child, for as long as she lived. In no other presence could he feel precisely as he felt when he was with her.

She looked up at him quizzically, her head to one side as though she'd missed something he'd said. "Yes, dear?"

He smiled, rose, glanced at his wristwatch, though he didn't have to do that. She never detained him.

"Well, good-by, dear," she said and then, as always, she added, "My love to Mary Ellen and have you heard from Kevin lately? Why don't you give him a call? And try to drop a note at least to California. Roseanne would be so surprised. Give my love to Maureen and Patrick and . . ." She named them all, recited her litany, reminded him of their remaining connections to each other, made her necessary attempt to hold something of all of them together.

He kissed her cheek and squeezed her hand. His mother never questioned who she was, who she was supposed to be, what life was supposed to mean, what it was all about.

She just lived and that in itself seemed enough for her.

THIRTY-FIVE

It was a fast trip from the neat brick one-family attached house in Woodside where Eileen O'Flaherty lived with her parents and two brothers to the large apartment building in Forest Hills where Eileen shared a four-room apartment, on a rotating basis, with six of her stewardess friends. The small red sports car which she drove was owned jointly by Eileen and two other girls.

"It all works out somehow," she explained to Patrick. "I have a share in apartments in L.A., London, Saigon and I used to have a share in this really dreamy villa in Saint Thomas but I don't do that flight anymore. For the last fifteen months, it's been almost straight back and forth with you boys."

The apartment, on the eighteenth floor, was huge and modern and filled with a curiously impersonal collection of furniture and accessories that clearly defined it as a stopping-off point for transients. It didn't have the cared-for, pulled-together look of a home, though most of the furnishings — sectionals, chairs, tables, lamps, wall arrangements, draperies, carpets — were expensive and in bland good taste. The well-stocked bar and tremendous number of glasses of all sizes indicated that large numbers of people were entertained on a regular basis.

Eileen made quick, casual introductions; each girl in turn introduced whoever she had brought to the party. There were more than twenty people drinking, eating, munching from large trays of dips and steaming platters of exotic foods. They were scattered throughout the apartment in clusters, on the floor, at the informally laid dining table, leaning against the bar, lounging on the terrace.

Patrick noted that the girls were all pretty, almost standardly pretty. They all had the neat trim figures required of airline stewardesses. They all knew the proper way to apply make-up; they all had crisp, short, shiny hair. They all looked like girls who never sweated or had bad breath or had to use the bathroom or became angry or had any feelings beneath their well-polished and vaguely pleasing surfaces.

Eileen worked her way expertly through the crowded room and fetched a drink for Patrick. "Now don't even ask what it is because Susan Farrell is just back from a quick hop to Calcutta and she absolutely refuses to give out with the ingredients. She swears a maharaja gave her the recipe." She sipped, grinned over her glass, wrinkled her short nose. "Remind me never to enter a harem. Tastes like perfumed varnish."

"It's not that bad," Patrick said. "Does this go on all the time or just on weekends?"

She surveyed the scene and shrugged. "We all have different weekends. Our Saturday nights really happen whenever anyone's in town. It's just by chance it really is a Saturday tonight." She smiled at him brightly. "Well, I must say, Patrick O'Malley, I was surprised that you finally got around to calling me. I'd about given up on you."

"I had some settling in to do."

"Has it been rougher than you expected?" Even Eileen's frown was pleasant, a brief raising of beautifully shaped eyebrows which caused an unaccustomed line or two across her clear doll-like forehead.

"It's been a little rough. I guess the transition, you know. Everything's exactly the same back here. Like I'd never been away."

She looked relieved and patted the couch beside her, wiggled a bit against a girl who could have been her twin, and made room for Patrick. "That's a very common complaint, Patrick," she confided. "That's the part that takes getting used to. You leave the combat zone, hop a plane, and zap! twenty hours later, another world and everything you left behind in Nam never really existed."

"But the fact is, it *did* exist. And it still *does* exist."

"Oh, look," she said comfortably, "believe me, it'll fall into place. I know. The first couple of trips back and forth, I thought I'd lose my marbles. I mean, we ferry boys both ways and I used to look at the cargo. My God, three hundred of you guys at a clip. I'd just practically crack up thinking: That redhead with the freckles; my God, I don't want to look at him. I don't want to remember his face because maybe he's marked; maybe he'll get it." She sipped her drink, made a funny face. "Ugh. India."

"How did it 'fall into place' for you?" he asked quietly.

"Oh, well, I was just so upset at the beginning, the captain noticed and he said, 'Now look here, Eileen, you forget the boys we leave over here and you start concentrating on the ones we take on the flight home.' Well, I'll tell you," she said cheerfully, "that's what did the trick. You can feel different on the flight home. I mean, gosh, I can look at a fella and think, Well, he's been the whole route. He might be on his way to Iowa or Kentucky or Chicago or New York or wherever else, but he's not on his way into some stinking V.C. ambush." She sighed and frowned intently. "You know, we had to convert to a hospital plane once and bring the wounded home. I'll tell you, when I saw all those boys with missing arms and legs, I just wanted to drag some of those peacenik nuts on the plane, just have somebody shove them on that plane and force them to look at those poor kids, crippled for life. Huh, and those little bums, living off the fat of the land and causing so much trouble all over the place when here you guys have gone and tried to do the job. I don't know, Patrick, I just don't understand it at all. I'll tell you something, Pat." She leaned closer to him, created an air of confidentiality. "We girls made a vow among ourselves. We date only Viet vets. Here and in our apartment in L.A." She tipped her glass toward him in salute and sipped delicately.

"Sort of like doing your share, huh?"

"Well, that's how we feel about it."

"That's very nice of you girls."

"It's the *least* we can do." She moved close against him and breathed words into his ear. "And the *most* we can do, Patrick, is just about *anything* you'd like. *You know.*"

"No. Tell me."

She poked him in the ribs with her elbow and grinned,

411

a dazzling white smile more comfortable on her face than a frown. "Listen, I'll tell you something, Patrick. A lot of guys have experienced, well, difficulties with girls when they get back. God, no wonder, how can they even begin to communicate with a girl after what they've been through. But see, *we've* been there too. It does make a difference. It kind of cuts through barriers. Like all the things it's hard to talk about, Nam and the gooks and how you feel coming home into this incredible apathy and outright hostility from so many creeps. Well, all this can interfere with a guy's ability to . . . to . . . you know."

"With his ability to fuck you mean?"

She pulled back from him abruptly, eyes intently on his face. "Now, Patrick, don't be crude," she told him firmly. "Oh, I know all about the language gap too but that's one thing I really object to, because you can *certainly* modify your language. I mean, that's only a matter of, you know, respect."

He amended politely, "Sorry. We're talking about a guy's ability to have sexual intercourse?"

"Well," she said, reverting to a coy tone, "we could say his ability to 'make love.' Doesn't that sound nicer?"

"Okay. We're talking about the effect of a guy's experience in Nam on his ability to 'make love' and how sometimes he finds it difficult and sometimes it's helpful for him to have a girl who fully understands his predicament."

"Right." She pressed her hand on his arm and told him earnestly, "Honestly, Patrick, there isn't anything we haven't heard. *We've* been there too. We want to help. *I* want to help."

The stereo bounced music all over the room; someone set a switch and lights flashed in some vague synchronization with sound. Smoke, thick, heavy, pungent, familiar, rose toward the ceiling then drifted lazily back toward the carpet. A group of two girls and three young men lolled against one wall, whispered and laughed and shared first some capsules, then some tablets, all swallowed with liberal amounts of secret-ingredient Indian-maharaja special. A few couples stood up and gyrated to the music: pelvic thrusts, head tosses, bent-knee torso twists, solo orgies.

"Want to turn on?" Eileen asked, eyes hot and bright.

"No. I want to be very clearheaded."

412

She blinked, touched her lips to his lightly, whispered, "Good. I like that. I really like that. Come on."

She guided him across the body-strewn, furniture-packed room as efficiently as though she were walking down the length of a narrow-aisled troop plane.

The bedroom was dark, shadowed by vague dull slashes of light from under the bathroom door. They heard the flushing of a toilet and running water. For a brief moment the room was illuminated. A couple exited from the bathroom with a friendly wave. The girl grinned, ran a hand over her crisp, neatly cut hair and down over her smooth miniskirted bottom. The man, broad-shouldered, fleshy, swayed slightly as he crossed the bedroom. He rested his hand heavily on the girl's shoulder, got his balance but still leaned on her as they entered the living room.

Eileen touched Patrick's lips with her index finger, lightly, then darted into the bathroom. When she returned, she locked the bedroom door.

"Someone will have a fit if they have to use the bathroom, but that's their problem." She pulled her high boots off, sank down onto her feet, tilted her head back. "You are a tall one, aren't you?"

"All six feet one of me."

"You know, you look like Terry of *Terry and the Pirates*. Honest."

"That's who I am, actually. If you saw me in my flying gear, you'd have recognized me right away."

"Well, me Dragon Lady, Terry." She reached her arms around his neck and pulled him toward her. "You tell Dragon Lady what you like and she oblige, very chop-chop."

"That's very Oriental of you. Oblige your man, huh?"

"*Anything*," she said with a new intensity. Her hands quickly unzipped the front of her tiny short pants; she wriggled her hips and let the pants drop to the floor, then stood back a little. "Did you ever wonder what a girl wears under those silly things?" She jutted her pelvis forward to show off her panty hose, which she quickly slid off. She ran a finger down the front of her bright-red tunic and the buttons opened with no further effort. She dropped the tunic to the floor at her feet.

413

Patrick stared at the garments on the floor. "You see," he whispered, "I killed a lot of people over there."

She led him to the bed, eased him down, caressed him carefully and languidly. "That's all right, Patrick. It's all over now. You have to forget everything. Just think of now. Think about how good this feels. How nice, really nice and exciting."

She moved her hands as expertly as she dispensed trays of food or airsick bags. She opened buttons and zippers; her fingers found the slash in his shorts, entered, sought, found, held.

Patrick saw the slight disappointment and the bright quick blink of resolve: the determined acceptance of a challenge. Her eyes moved to his to see the reflection of her own pleasure.

"Listen, Eileen, I killed thirty-five people."

Her fingers tightened momentarily, then relaxed, then tightened more carefully and deliberately. There was a twitch at the corner of her mouth. Her tongue touched her lip briefly, then she leaned to him and kissed his face, his eyes, the bridge of his nose and then his mouth.

"Eileen," he said softly, "*they were all women and children.*"

She nipped at his earlobe and whispered, "Forget it, Patrick. In a war, people get killed."

"They were all unarmed, helpless civilians."

"Don't think about it, Patrick. You're here with me. You're alive. I want to make you feel alive. Don't let them get in your way. *You're alive!*"

Her voice had the heavily muffled sound of growing passion. Her body pushed and prodded him. Her hand, in growing desperation, sought to arouse him.

Patrick pushed her aside and sat up. As he spoke, he buttoned his shirt. "I am the Resurrection and the Life saith little Eileen O'Flaherty."

Her hands went to his neck and tried to pull him down again. "Come on, Patrick, you're not the first to tell me something like that." There was a bright, fresh, pert quality in her voice. She tilted her head to one side, pulled a mouth at him and said in a scolding tone, "You're just going to have to make an effort, Patrick."

He stood up, felt his hands tremble as he zipped his fly.

414

He felt the lightheaded grayness of nausea, the fullness of saliva in his mouth.

"I *am* making an effort, Eileen," he said softly. "Oh, Christ, what an effort I'm making."

He pulled at the bedroom door, fumbled the lock, then yanked the door open and plunged through the swarming living room without inhaling. The narrow carpeted hallway was musty and the smell of tobacco and marijuana fumes floated stalely about his head. He stabbed the elevator button repeatedly to hurry it.

He held his face up, mouth opened slightly; breathe rapidly, rapidly, rapidly to dispel the trap-closing, brain-diminishing, floor-spinning nausea. Get oxygen to brain. He inhaled fumes of poisoned air. He closed his eyes and leaned his head against the frame of the elevator door. He felt the humming click of machinery as the car pulled upward, toward him. Music filled the square Formica box as he entered the elevator; light, tuneless violins whisked him down to the lobby. He crossed the simulated garden, all heavy greenery and flowing fountains set in polished marble. The doorman caught the huge glass door, pulled it open for him and closed it quietly behind him.

THIRTY-SIX

Before his service in Viet Nam, Patrolman Pete Caputo was generally considered a pretty good guy: a little quiet, not too quick on the uptake, definitely not one of the locker-room jokers, but a generally inoffensive guy.

He patrolled his post in the all-white, middle-class, mostly Jewish section of Brooklyn where he was assigned without distinction but without ever drawing a complaint for any dereliction. He issued the required number of summonses for traffic violations; he collared an 1140 or two hanging around a public school; he calmed the mother of a child who had been hit by an automobile, while managing at the same time to recognize that the driver, a trembling elderly man, was on the verge of a heart attack. He recognized the symptoms, as his own father had a cardiac condition. He promptly searched the driver, located the lifesaving tablets, administered the medication, made out the required aided cards on both the child and the driver of the vehicle, assisted the ambulance driver with the necessary information and then called the precinct with details.

The sergeant told him to stay on the scene until a tow truck arrived for the abandoned Buick, and when the Jiff-ee Tow arrived some fifteen minutes later, the overalled driver approached Patrolman Caputo, nodded, winked and reached to shake his hand.

"Ten okay?" the tow driver asked.

"Gee, I don't know," Patrolman Caputo responded. "What do you usually charge?"

The tow driver studied the not-too-bright-looking cop for a moment and scratched the back of his neck. "I mean ten for the call. *You know.*"

416

Caputo looked at the folded bill which the driver had pressed into his gloved hand and slowly shook his head. He handed the money back to the driver and couldn't quite figure it. He called the sergeant to report that the vehicle involved in the accident had been removed from the scene.

"Yeah," said the sergeant. "How much?"

That was when Caputo finally understood. It was the first time the word went out to him: either stupid or a little slow; definitely in need of wising up.

"Look, Petey," the sergeant told him later, "this here is a real nice precinct, know what I mean? I mean, like we are very clean out here. Nothing runs out here, no pushing, no vice, hardly nothing. So if a tow guy wants to show his appreciation, there is nothing wrong with it at all. He's glad for the business. He writes it off as a business expense. Same thing, see, like at Christmastime. If the neighborhood storekeepers wanna show that they're grateful for the sight of us out there, making sure everything's fine and all and that no one is interfering with their lawful business, what the hell? They want to throw a couple a' bucks to the boys in the house, or a couple a' bottles, nothing wrong with that, is there?"

Caputo shook his head. It seemed like there was nothing wrong. He just wouldn't feel right taking a share. The fact that he felt the way he did really didn't mean he felt there was anything wrong about other guys feeling differently. The sergeant accepted that somewhat cautiously, but finally it was decided that Caputo was all right. Just a little stupid.

Patrolman Peter Caputo took a leave of absence from the New York City Police Department in the spring of 1967 and joined the United States Army for a tour of duty in Viet Nam. The men in his precinct threw a going-away party for him and most of them told him he was a hell of a good guy. They were all as proud as hell of him. His action in volunteering obliterated any ideas any of them had that there was something just a little bit wrong about Pete. Yes, he was one helluva great guy and what the country needed was more like old Pete Caputo and less of the goddamn war-dodging, snot-nosed little punks who were nothing but liberal Commie pinko bastards causing trouble all over this country. They all oughta be shot.

When Pete Caputo volunteered in 1967, it was because he felt a deep, if unarticulated, sense of obligation to his country,

417

which had been instilled in the five sons and four daughters of Josefina and Vincente Caputo, along with their love of parents, Church and God.

Vincente Caputo was orphaned at seventeen years of age. His stonecutter father died from some lifelong hacking lung disease and this event left Vincente an unskilled and unwanted apprentice. He had one treasure left him by his father: a picture postcard from an uncle in America. It was yellowed and brown along the edges and the writing had faded but the picture was as clear as on the day it arrived from America. It showed a view of the Statue of Liberty in New York Harbor. That was all Vincente Caputo knew about America but it was enough.

For one year he hired out his body at any sort of labor he could get for whatever coin he could come by. He ate whatever he could steal, forage, beg or obtain without spending money. Through many long winter nights, Vincente slept with a cold coin in his mouth and swallowed the copper taste of despair; but when he awakened the next morning, the coin was still his, to be added to his buried hoard, and not in the pocket of some farmer. After one terrible, degrading, unbelievable year—a year which he never spoke of to anyone, ever— Vincente Caputo bought his passage to America.

After some difficulty, he found his uncle, who was a dour and unfriendly man married to a warm and generous woman. His uncle's wife took him to a place called "the shop" and it was there that Vincente Caputo learned, laboriously, patiently, miraculously, that there was, after all, a kind of magic in his hands. He became, after several years, a highly skilled tailor and a gifted cutter and he was much sought after in the garment industry.

Within ten years, Vincente Caputo had gained some twenty pounds, had acquired a pretty round-faced wife, two sons, three daughters and his citizenship papers. With a passion close to religious fervor, he enlisted in the United States Army on December 8, 1941. On September 6, 1943, Corporal Vincente Caputo marched with the Seventh Army through the towns of the province where he had been born. He was sent as an interpreter along with a lieutenant and a sergeant to seek out information and the cooperation of the local governments and to instruct the population as to how they were to conduct themselves in the presence of American troops.

With a heavy sense of despair, mixed with an incredible sense of freedom, Vincente viewed the town square of his childhood; despair because for one terrible moment the sight of the unchanged, unchanging, barren dusty landscape, the black-clad, dirt-stained women with their scarred heavy buckets lined up at the village fountain, which was their only source of water, the faint whiff of donkey manure, the dry dust of that existence, enveloped him, reached around his body and encompassed him in its possessive grip. But when the village priest, an old, shapeless, pock-marked man, his cassock greening with age, approached Vincente without recognition, respectfully, reverentially, bowing, nodding, hand extended in a form of blessing, then Vincente exulted. This was not his home. He was an American.

In the next twenty-four hours, he visited incredulous cousins and uncles and aunts. Particularly, he was fascinated by the men cousins his own age. Twenty-eight or twenty-nine, they were defeated, scarred, lined, bitter, gap-toothed old men, already bent into the shapes they would forever bear.

Vincente carried their faces and stunted destinies inside himself for all his life as a constant reminder of what he had escaped. After the war, he and Josefina regularly sent packages of food and clothing, and when they could, they sent money to his relatives and never forgot.

There were times when Vincente was nearly overcome with terror at his good fortune. He opened his own small shop in the garment center and soon four people worked for him. Children arrived regularly, healthy and black-eyed and olive-skinned, girl after boy, boy after girl, fine, fat. His family filled the small clapboard house in Brooklyn which Vincente and Josefina's brothers had built. There was a nice back yard for grapes and figs. On any late afternoon, weather allowing, Josefina's father and his old men friends played *boccie* down the long alleys between the yards of their houses and they argued and laughed and hooted in old men's voices. All of the children went to the Holy Visitation school and were taught by the pale Sisters. They learned religion and to love their country and to respect their parents and elders.

Vincente took great pleasure in hearing the clear, sharp

419

voices of his children as they crowded around his table, dark heads bent over heaping plates of food. They switched easily, naturally, without thought or effort from the Sicilian dialect of their parents and grandparents to the quick, pungent slang of Brooklyn and with just as much ease reverted to the musical singsong intonations as they memorized poetry which Sister had assigned.

The oldest son, Ralph, was apprenticed at seventeen into the construction business and set to work with his uncles. When the Korean War started, Ralph enlisted in the Army and it hardly seemed possible to Vincente: the small boy a grown man.

When the telegram came, followed by a letter from Ralph's commanding officer, neither Josefina nor Vincente knew why their son had died or where this place Heartbreak Ridge was or why it was important enough for their son's life. Vincente never really understood why the war was fought or why there was such bitterness in the country because of it. But beneath the terrible wound of his grief there was one tiny glowing sense of consolation; blood of his blood had been spilled for this country and whatever this country might exact of him or any of his flesh, it was a debt of honor, honorably to be paid.

His daughters grew up and married neighborhood boys and stayed close to home for a few years, then began to move out to places on Long Island or out to Jersey.

His sons went into the service, came out, went into Civil Service: one in the Department of Sanitation, one in the United States Postal Service, one in the Fire Department and Pete became a policeman. His second-oldest son built an addition to the house when Josefina died and moved with his wife and two sons from an apartment in Woodside and it was agreed without anything ever having been discussed that this would be their home with the old man.

When his son Pete took a leave of absence from the Police Department and volunteered in the Army to fight for his country in Viet Nam, Vincente felt the old deep pride: yet another son willing to stand up and pay his debt to this great country. If the war and its issues were confusing, it was of little importance. What was important was that his son had respect for his country and its flag. It was Pete's turn to go,

420

as his father had gone and as his brothers had gone before him. Vincente hugged and kissed his son and sent him off to war with God's blessing on his head.

A different son came home from Viet Nam, a stranger, with hollow, empty eyes, and beneath the ragged black beard, a bitter turned-down mouth that seemed to forget how to smile. He had some steel pins in his right kneecap which caused him some pain, but there was something terribly changed and unknown about this son and Vincente would never know him again.

Harley Taylor glanced nervously down the length of the conference table, waiting for the men to settle themselves. He wondered if he'd ever get used to the mix of students; three-quarters of them were older than he was and even the younger ones, under twenty-six, seemed of a different order. He had taught two other classes at the John Marshall College of Criminal Justice, formal English literature classes, but when his students, for the most part working policemen, discussed the various reading assignments, somehow, mysteriously, the closeness of violence seemed to punctuate their every verbal disagreement. Violence to these men was for the most part not some latent, held-in, primitive memory but a very real, active, ongoing life-style. When they discussed the common, ordinary events of their everyday working lives, they made him feel somewhat sheltered and incompetent, even somewhat stupid, though Harley Taylor, at twenty-six, with a doctorate newly received from Harvard, was Phi Beta Kappa, a Fulbright scholar and a thoroughly respected member of the academic community. For when they opened up, these hard-mouthed, shrewd-eyed men, when they revealed what was behind their stiff masks, Harley could feel the small pale hairs along the back of his neck stand erect and the start of an involuntary shudder work its way down his spine.

He looked down the table to the other member of the teaching team for this special, newly devised course. Mel Arden, the balding, middle-aged, pipe-fondling psychologist, radiated a controlled, anticipatory excitement. His intelligent dark eyes slowly circled the table without lingering on any of the men, yet they narrowed or widened momentarily as he made his

421

incisive calculations. He cradled the bowl of his unlit pipe between thumb and forefinger, leaned back, stretched his neck muscles, let his head loll forward, then to one side, then back, then to the other side, then he remained still, chin toward chest, for a few seconds. Finally, yoga exercise completed, he looked up brightly, eager for the seminar to begin.

When everyone who was assigned to the course had arrived and found a chair and settled down, a certain uneasy tension began to descend on the students and on Dr. Taylor. Not Dr. Arden; he merely returned inquisitive glances with a bland, expressionless countenance. After the shifting of bodies, shuffling of feet, scratching of heads, coughing, nose blowing, cigarette lighting and gum chewing had gone on almost beyond endurance, one of the men finally, in exasperation, addressed Dr. Arden.

"Well, now what?"

That was Patrolman Schultz, a large man with gray curly hair and deep shadows under his eyes.

Dr. Arden seemed to enjoy the whole thing, to relish the discomforting curiosity and uncertainty and wariness of the men in this new situation. It was their first experience with a nearly unstructured course and it was by nature of an experiment.

Dr. Arden shrugged easily. "Whatever you want," he said. "You've all received copies of the reading list and the dates for discussion of each book."

They bent over the mimeographed reading list. Some consulted wristwatches; one or two nervously straightened edges of notebooks.

"Well, we don't have any book for discussion this week," another man said. They all turned toward him as though for direction. "The class is scheduled for two hours, Dr. Arden. You intend to shorten the period today, since it's the first meeting and we've nothing to discuss?"

Again, the friendly but noncommittal shrug.

"Could I ask a question?" someone in the middle of the table called out.

"By all means." That was Dr. Arden and Dr. Taylor, both together.

A low tough voice, directed at the surface of the table but

422

calculated to reach everyone in the room, asked incredulously, "*Malcolm X* is on a reading list of American authors? Is *that* what he was?"

"Hey, we got some porno stuff on this list." The man seated next to Dr. Taylor looked up accusingly, first at Dr. Taylor, then toward Dr. Arden.

"Where? Hey, where, Bradley? Which ones? Maybe we could read them first?" The comedian of the class got an anticipated laugh from the others.

Dr. Arden quietly commented, "That depends on what you consider porno, doesn't it, Mr. Bradley?"

Bradley's face came up, he narrowed his eyes, his finger kept to the accused title. "Not what *I* consider porno, Dr. Arden. What the *law* considers porno. Hell, we raided a bookstore not more than two months ago and this here book was one of the books we confiscated."

"Yeah," said the man next to him, "but I bet it got thrown out of court."

"Yeah," Bradley answered caustically, "the courts really give us cooperation. They really make our job a pleasure."

"Well, Mr. Bradley, I trust you won't find the rest of the list too offensive," Dr. Arden said.

"He'll find number six offensive." The voice was flat and deep, almost without inflection. He had long dark hair and the black beard which covered his cheeks and chin was neatly clipped and tended. He wore a light-blue turtle-neck sweater which emphasized the surprising light-blue eyes, incongruous in so swarthy a man. He turned those eyes fully on Patrolman Bradley. "It's *Hiroshima,* by John Hersey."

"Why do you think Mr. Bradley will object to *Hiroshima?*" Dr. Arden asked. He leaned forward slightly, the bowl of his pipe hidden in his clenched hands. "Suppose you identify yourselves when you speak, gentlemen? You're Mr. . . ."

"Peter Caputo. Patrolman Caputo. Or do we dispense with our rank and serial number?"

"I think we ought to keep to civilian status, if that's agreeable with everyone." Dr. Arden looked at each one, waited for dissent or agreement, but no one said anything. "Well, Mr. Caputo, why your prediction?"

Caputo's eyes returned to Bradley, who moved uncomfortably under the force of the stare. Then he smiled, an upturning of thin lips inside the dark beard, and he moved his shoulders just slightly.

"Maybe I'm wrong," he said with a soft emphasis that made it clear he thought he was right.

There was a curious tension in the room. It emanated not just from Patrolman Bradley, who leaned forward, stubbed a cigarette with great force into a dirty ashtray, then leaped up, ashtray in hand, and emptied it into a metal wastebasket. There were a few low exchanges, a few wisecracks, a couple of consultations of the reading list.

"Who made up this list anyways?" a short-cropped man asked sharply. His chin rose slightly, his head went to one side to give force to the accusation of his question.

It was exactly the tone of voice that Dr. Taylor had come to dread: the policeman voice, used to intimidate, badger, refute, deny, insist, demand. He'd seen them in day and night classes, middle-aged men unsuited and unaccustomed to being at the receiving end of instruction.

"Why the hell don't he come right out and say what's on his mind if he wants to make a comment about the times he lives in? Why the hell do we have to wade through all this stuff and try to figure him out? Can you tell me, Dr. Taylor, I mean really tell me, why it's essential for me to go through all this literature in order to qualify for my degree in police science?"
"The well-rounded man, Mr. McCarthy, should have at least a familiarity with the past, a working knowledge of human nature as revealed in the great literary achievements of our predecessors, so that when confronted with changes in our society that seem unprecedented, beyond our comprehension, we can fall back into a certain assurance. We can perhaps expand our frame of reference. We can go back more than two thousand years and discover that great scholars of the Greco-Roman era thought the world was going to hell, that the youth of the day—"
"Well, Dr. Taylor, I'll tell ya. I don't have to go back no two thousand years. See, I can remember back when I was a kid, in the thirties and forties, when kids had respect. All a cop had to do was make his appearance on the block and the little wise guys would straighten out. One whack on the be-

424

hind with a nightstick straightened out more potential mur-
derers and thieves than all the books ever written."

The man with the short hair identified himself as a detective,
name, John Cassidy.

"The reading list, Mr. Cassidy, was made up by a committee
of faculty members," Dr. Arden said reasonably.

"Pretty peculiar list if you ask me," Mr. Cassidy said.

"The selections might seem arbitrary, without cohesive-
ness," Dr. Arden said mildly, deliberately ignoring the implications of the previous comment. He glanced at the list, then
at the men around the table. "We range from Faulkner to
Malcolm X, from Conrad to Mailer, from J. Edgar Hoover to
Richard Rovere. Included are novels, books written by jour-
nalists, some by political activists; we've included some
anthropology, psychology. In short, as the course name im-
plies, a compendium, with hopes that reading any particular
book might lead to an investigation of works that might possibly give another view of the same situation."

"You care to identify the people you refer to as political
activists?" a polite gray-haired, gray-eyed man asked him
quietly.

Dr. Arden ran the stem of his pipe across his lower lip
for a moment, smiled and shrugged his characteristic noncommittal, patient gesture. "That will be for all of you to
decide. This will be the most totally open course you'll probably ever be involved in. No grade, no exams, only pass-fail
and the only qualification for passing is attendance. No pressure to contribute. Sometimes your very silence can make a
statement. The readings merely represent a starting point for
what we hope will be an exciting learning experience for all
of us, faculty as well as student. This will be an entirely unstructured course, a creative experience for all of us."

A neatly groomed, white-shirted, dark-tied and -suited,
closely cropped, clean-shaven, blandly polite man, middle
thirties, raised his hand and waited for Dr. Arden to nod in
his direction.

"That isn't exactly accurate, Dr. Arden, as I understand
the term. You said the course would be unstructured. Well, it
seems to me that it very definitely does have a structure and
I'm not too sure if you're being totally honest with us." It

was not put in the form of an accusation but as a polite, sincere, concerned inquiry.

"Mr. . . . ?" Dr. Arden raised his brows.

"Fraley. George Fraley."

"Mr. Fraley, perhaps you're right. Perhaps I was being a bit too broad in characterizing the seminar as unstructured. Let's just say it will be interesting to see what form of structure tends to build around the seminar hours we spend together."

When it was suggested that each student introduce and identify himself, Fraley quietly stated that he was a special agent attached to the New York office of the F.B.I.; he was a senior at John Marshall; he expected to receive his degree in criminal justice in June.

Seven of the men were seniors; Pete Caputo and Patrick O'Malley and the gray-haired detective assigned to the Manhattan D.A.'s office were juniors; two men were sophomores; two men were absent. They stayed together for an hour and twenty minutes, then by mutual consent they disbanded until the following week.

As they stood up to leave, Pete Caputo's right leg seemed to lock. He lurched forward unexpectedly into Patrick O'Malley, nearly knocking him over.

In confusion, Patrick turned; in a split second he grabbed out and kept Caputo from hitting the floor. "Hey, you okay?" Patrick asked, thinking the man was passing out.

"Hold on for a second, okay?" Pete Caputo, without explanation, leaning against Patrick, bent over and with both hands clutched at his right knee and gave it a sharp jerk. There was an odd metallic clicking sound, then Caputo stood up. His dark face had gone darker with the exertion. "Okay," he said tersely, "thanks."

There was something familiar about Caputo, something recognized, known, some connection Patrick felt instinctively. "You get the leg in Nam?" he asked quietly.

Caputo seemed surprised, then, after a slight consideration, he nodded and said, "Yeah, over in Nam."

Patrick pulled his mouth to one side and said, "That's some fucking old war, huh, buddy?"

That was the beginning of their friendship.

THIRTY-SEVEN

Deputy Chief Inspector Brian O'Malley pushed the button down for a dial tone on his private line. Before he could dial, the light flashed on the extension and Sergeant Dickson's voice announced through the call box on his desk, "Chief Pollack is on four, sir."

He hit the button, heard Dickson hang up before he said, "Good morning, Chief."

"Brian, a couple of things before I see the Man."

"Want me to come down?"

"No, no, brief me over the phone. Hey, before I forget, that was nice coverage you got for those guys in Brooklyn last night."

Two narcotics detectives on a stakeout had spotted a man on the fire escape of the building they were watching. He was holding what appeared to be a package close against his chest and the two police officers, acting instinctively, positioned themselves directly below the man in time to catch the missile which he sent hurtling to the sidewalk.

This "missile" turned out to be a two-month-old child; the man turned out to be a newly released psycho who had just cut his wife's throat. One detective ran, infant in arms, to telephone for assistance while the second raced up the stairs to the roof and proceeded to keep the man from leaping from the ledge for the twenty minutes it took for the emergency squad to spread a net, into which the distraught man promptly jumped.

Brian, briefed at home, made two telephone calls and had TV news people on the scene to interview the detectives.

427

"It was a nice job," Arthur said. "How about their narco case?"

"It's still alive. They gave the impression they were cruising when they spotted the guy."

"Okay," Arthur Pollack said, "what do we tell the Man about these damn articles in the *News?*"

Brian could hear the newspaper rustling over the telephone and he held his own copy flat on the desk and scowled. A young reporter had taken the patrolman's exam, passed, gone through an accelerated training program at the Academy the previous spring when the Department was on emergency status, served as a probationary patrolman for two months, then resigned. From that experience, he wrote a six-part article "telling all" about the New York City Police Department.

Brian rubbed his eyes briskly as he spoke. "Well, if you break it down to what he's had to say in these first two articles, you got: One—the training was insufficient. Okay, we concede that; we were on riot alert. Most of the men have gone back for in-service training. Junior here didn't stick around long enough. Today, when you come down to it, all he's griping about are small acts of kindness on the part of older officers." Brian ran his finger down the column of print. "You got the article there, Arthur? Third paragraph, quote, 'The sergeant poked me in the ribs and said "Just take it easy, sonny. Nobody expects you to go out and fight the wars; stay kind of to one side if anything happens,"' unquote. He was told where he could duck in for a smoke and a cupa. Minor violations when it gets down to being technical."

Arthur hummed into the phone for a minute, then said, "Well, my thinking is that we ought to wait and see what the rest of the articles are like and make no comment until then."

Brian agreed. "In fact, I think the best damn thing probably would be to make *no* comment on any of them at all. If asked directly, I would take the line 'We're waiting for the full series before any comment'; from then on, 'We're checking into the veracity or lack of veracity of various allegations.' You know, that kind of thing.

"Now, to counter whatever impact these articles might have, I would suggest a bit of a stepped-up campaign in print. We could pick a couple of good collars out of the hopper and get

428

them in print. One good 'chase-'em, catch-'em' could grab a headline and shove this crap back where it belongs."

"Right, Brian, I'll see you get a complete list of activities from detectives and uniformed. Oh, yeah, we got a request from *The David Susskind Show* for four guys on a panel. What's your reaction?"

Brian jotted a note on his pad. "I'll look into it. We don't want to walk into a setup. Hell, offhand I can't think of any four guys I'd trust sitting on a panel with Susskind."

"Except you and me, Bri," Arthur said lightly. "Okay, kid, I'm off to meet the Man."

The new Police Commissioner, on first viewing, didn't make much of an impression. He was physically slight, soft-voiced, articulate, didn't resort to the dramatic theatrical pronouncements of some of his predecessors.

The impact came when he backed up his soft words with hard action. When the P.C. said something, he meant it. As the wave of retirements rose, newer, younger men stepped into vacated positions with a slight stir of excitement. Textbooks appeared at Police Headquarters; young lieutenants and captains exchanged course material and crib notes for graduate courses at the City University.

All personnel of the rank of captain and above were required to attend seminars in public affairs; community and minority workshops were held in the various neighborhoods where problems arose. Various programs were initiated whereby unofficial leaders of black and Puerto Rican communities would be able to communicate directly with a superior officer of the Department, bypassing what many found to be a nerve-racking, frightening visit to the local precinct house.

Most of the men attended the various classes because they were ordered to do so.

They sat in the clean square classrooms of the Police Academy and listened, expressionless, while criminologists, sociologists, psychologists and penologists told them how to do their jobs.

The selection of Arthur Pollack to replace the newly retired Chief Inspector came as a shock to everyone, including

Arthur Pollack. He was fully qualified for his position: one of the most decorated police officers on the job; passed every promotion exam he'd ever taken at the top of the list; served every post assigned in an exemplary manner.

But he wasn't one of the boys. It was the first time in the history of the Department that a Jew was included in the highly exclusive inner circle of top echelon. From the Irishmen who were disappointed by the new P.C. came word that for all his Irish Catholic background, the P.C. might just as well be a Chinese Jew.

Down the line, the lower ranks waited to see what new innovations would be inflicted on them.

Brian O'Malley was recommended for his new post of Deputy Chief Inspector in Charge of Public Affairs by Arthur Pollack, his predecessor. O'Malley had a facile mind, an easy way of controlling and guiding and turning a line of interrogation to the best interests of the Department. He had good rapport with the press and other media people; he had many friends and good connections. He could move easily into and out of a wide range of situations and leave behind him soothed egos and a sense of satisfactory responses, whether that was the case or not.

He met Karen Day when he'd been on his new assignment for less than a month.

The crime had been committed on the twelfth floor of a luxury co-op in the East 50's and it was one of the most bizarre murders any of the men present could recall. Two young women and one young man had been bound, mutilated, sexually attacked and slaughtered. The apartment reeked with violence, drapes ripped, furniture slashed, pieces of flesh hacked from the bodies, arranged, rearranged to satisfy some depraved appetite. The stereo had been set full blast as had three transistor radios and two color TV sets in the apartment. It was the electronic noises that had finally annoyed the other tenants. They claimed to have heard nothing else of an unusual nature.

Brian briefed the waiting news people in the lobby of the building; he gave the barest details allowable at the time. Names of victims to be withheld pending notification of next of kin; victims had been sexually molested; all died as result of multiple stab wounds; the Department was conducting an intensive investigation into the matter and would have no further statement at this time.

He politely stared straight ahead and pretended not to hear the repeated demands for more information. What was the relationship of the three victims? In whose name was the apartment held? Were any perversions involved? "Come on, Chief, how the hell can we deliver any copy when we don't know anything more than this?"

"See ya later, fellas." He waved and entered the elevator, which stopped on the sixth floor. Karen Day got into the elevator with him and he nodded at her, as though he knew her, then he stared at her, frankly puzzled.

"Hello, Chief O'Malley," she said in a husky voice. "I'm Karen Day. From NBC."

It didn't register immediately that she was a newswoman and had no right to be beyond the lobby. "Jesus," he said softly, "you're the living image of Karen Duvall."

"I'm Karen Duvall's daughter," she said crisply. "I'd like to ask you a few questions about the victims, Chief. You really didn't tell us anything. White or black? Homo? Lesbo? Was the apartment a setup? What did they do for a living? Come on, Chief, start me on something for the eleven o'clock."

She was very tall and she regarded him with bright dark eyes and a sharp aggressive expression. She spoke rapidly, in a deep, familiar voice, and as she spoke, she ran her long fingers through thick, straight dark hair, brushed it idly from her face.

He shook his head and said quietly, "Jesus, I used to break my neck to see your mother. I must have seen her twenty or thirty times. I remember when she sang with Dorsey —"

"And I bet you collected every record she ever cut," the girl said acidly.

Brian stared at her, at the image of the popular singer whose sad big voice had touched and remained in some vulnerable center of himself. The girl was prettier than her mother had ever been but in a cold, hard way. She spoke and moved and studied him with an assurance and arrogance that destroyed memory of another girl, denied the relationship between them.

431

Karen Duvall, soft, tiny, hurt by the world which both loved and tormented her, had drawn forth collective waves of protecting masculinity. By the time of her death at thirty-eight, she had been four times married, many times beaten and cured and beaten again by drink. Occasionally, some sentimental disc jockey would dig out a Karen Duvall and the powerful voice, lamenting the world, would evoke, for all who had ever been moved by her, other, simpler times.

"What did you say your name was?" Brian asked sharply.

"Karen Day, NBC News." She hooked a thumb under the press card, which was pinned carelessly to the lapel of her suede coat.

"Well, I'll tell you what, Karen Day, NBC News. You get your ass the hell back down to the lobby where you belong or Mr. Jason Harris, NBC News, will get a phone call advising him that in the future you're barred from any and all police calls."

Her mouth fell open for a moment, then she said, "Who the hell do you think you're talking to, buster?"

Brian leaned toward her, tapped her press card with his index finger. "To Karen Day, NBC News. Now beat it."

Within a month, what had been a tantalizing mystery became a sordid, predictable story of perversion, drugs, cultism and various forms of insanity. Through diligent, plodding, methodical detective work, the culprits, two males and one female, were apprehended and subsequently indicted for the homicides. The story played itself out with its explanations and was of no further interest outside the judicial setting. There were hundreds of new sensations of greater interest to the news media.

One morning, Lieutenant Mike Fitzgerald, one of the bright boys, with two college degrees, early thirties, Brian's assistant, called his attention to a request made by NBC.

"What they want to do, Chief," Fitzgerald explained earnestly, "is to have a camera crew assigned to ride with a patrol-car team for a week or two. Format will be to show that with all the modernization and new technology, et cetera, the basic job of policing still involves the man out there, on patrol. The slant is okay, but . . ."

Brian scanned the notes he'd been presented with quickly and looked up. "But what? What's the problem?" There had been similar accommodations in the past. As long as they were handled carefully, a good patrol team in a good location, it could turn out to the benefit of the Department.

"Well, the thing is, the reporter is a *girl*." Fitzgerald clearly didn't think much of the situation.

Brian looked closely at the official request for departmental cooperation. It was signed by Karen Day, NBC News. "I'll look into it myself, Mike," Brian said.

He watched her on the eleven o'clock news that night. She had one quick spot-report about a school board meeting.

He called her the next day and invited her for a drink.

It ran as a three-part five-minute addition to the *Eleven O'Clock News Roundup* and Brian thought it caught the pace of the men who worked the car to advantage. The camera stayed with them through routine patrol, which included answering two crime-in-progress calls, the fortunate apprehension of a liquor store holdup man fleeing the scene of the crime, the delivery of a baby to a bewildered Puerto Rican mother with the incredibly lucky fact that one of the patrolmen had a good smattering of Spanish. It added a nice warm human touch.

After the third part had been aired, Karen Day called him. "Well, what did you think of it?"

It had been a fair, intelligent job and showed the Department in a good light. That was always his first concern.

"Fine. I think you handled it very well."

Her voice came through the telephone clear and sharp. "It was pure *shit*. It was edited down to absolute *shit*. The bastards cut my best footage. They promised me a straight thirty minutes, prime-time viewing. They left me with the merry adventures of Patrolman Huff and Patrolman Puff, five minutes here and five minutes there. It didn't convey any of the feeling I was trying for." Abruptly she said, "Meet me for a drink. I'd like to see you. Come on over to my place tonight."

If he'd expected something exotic, he was disappointed. She looked as though she didn't belong in the expensive, beautifully furnished apartment. She wore faded dungarees

433

and a body-hugging jersey top which emphasized her thinness. She pulled her bare feet onto the sofa and rested her
hands on her knees. She jerked her head vaguely toward the
bar. "Help yourself, O'Malley."

Brian didn't move. "In a little while."

He didn't like the way she sat there, studying him, evaluating, measuring. Deciding. There was a great deal about her
that irritated him, not just her sloppiness and the fact that she
hadn't bothered to put on any make-up, not even a little lipstick. She gnawed on her index finger for a moment and
there was a flash of that familiar face: Karen Duvall, with the
great pain-filled black eyes, the helpless quality of a trapped
animal.

She laughed suddenly and rocked back on the couch, her
face to the ceiling, then she finger-combed the long, straight
dark hair. "Boy, that got to you, right? You really must have
been stuck on Mama, huh? I can do her for you if you want me
to." She stood up, moved toward him. "I can even get that
little 'oh-gee-gosh' catch in my voice. 'Gosh, mister, see, I'm
just so damn open and honest and trusting that I was born to
be a loser, but no matter how many times I fall—'"

Brian grabbed her by the shoulders roughly. "Okay, knock
it off." The parody was too good. It was vicious and bitter,
more so because she had her mother's face and could imitate
the voice perfectly.

Karen pulled away from him. She hooked her thumbs into
the empty belt loops. "Jesus, it's a long time since I ran into a
genuine Karen Duvall freak. It's really funny. I mean, you're
defending her and you don't even know who the hell she was.
Well, O'Malley, she was a fucking *lush*, baby."

He didn't know why he felt so angry but he wanted to hit
her. It made him even angrier to know that she was daring
him, trying to provoke him. Without moving, his voice steady,
he said, "I don't like pretty girls with dirty mouths."

She smiled and shifted her body, took a deliberate, posed
stance, one sharp hipbone higher than the other. Her dark
eyes moved slowly over him, studied, lingered, speculated.
Her voice went low and husky and warm. "Well, what *do* you
like, O'Malley?"

Tersely, he said, "I like to make my own moves, for one
thing."

434

"You scared off by aggressive girls? They threaten your whole male *thing*? *You're* supposed to make the advance? That's the way things should be?" She walked to the bar and poured a drink for herself. As she brought the drink to her lips, Brian took the glass from her and drained it in one steady swallow.

"Thanks for the drink, Karen. Good night."

She folded her arms across her chest and raised her face toward him. "Hey, O'Malley. I'll tell you why I asked you here tonight. I thought you might be good in the sack. I won't say I thought you might be a good fuck, because you don't like pretty girls with dirty mouths."

He cupped his hand under her chin and when she closed her eyes expectantly he turned her face and kissed her lightly on the cheek.

"Good night, baby. *I'll* let *you* know when."

He watched her on the late news every night for a week before he went back to her apartment. She opened the door, stared at him for a moment, then shook her head.

"Uh-uh. I don't think so."

He pushed the door with his shoulder and was inside the apartment before she could stop him. Until the instant he saw her, standing beside the open door, those huge black eyes confronting him, the vaguely forlorn quality beneath the toughness, he didn't realize how much he wanted her. He'd been watching the electronic image for a brief few minutes each night but it wasn't the electronic image that aroused him. It had been the haunting, ghostlike image of her mother which had somehow transmitted itself from the television screen more insistently than through the medium of her actual flesh. It had been the ghost of her mother that had brought him to her apartment. It was the daughter, Karen Day, who aroused him now.

"I told you I'd let you know when."

She stood against the closed door, arms folded over the man's large shirt worn over her dungarees. "Tonight, sweetie," she said with acid in her voice, "you go fuck yourself. That's what *I* had to do the other night."

That triggered his anger as precisely as if she had planned it, but her startled cry was as much of surprise as of pain when

435

he grabbed her arm and pulled her through the apartment. He swung about from the kitchen, found the bedroom door and shoved her ahead of him.

"I told you I don't like girls with dirty mouths, so cut it out."

She started to say something; her mouth twitched but she bit her lip, let her teeth linger on her lower lip until he pressed his mouth on hers. Her teeth went into his lip but he didn't notice until she bit hard and tasted his blood. He pushed her back and touched his mouth, saw blood on his fingertips.

"You little bitch. Get outta your clothes. *Now.*"

She shook her head slowly and smiled. *"You* undress me."

"Your way?" He pulled off his own clothes as she watched, then grabbed her by the shirt. "How about *my* way instead?" He ripped the shirt, pulled it from her, broke the zipper on her dungarees and pushed her onto the bed. She tensed her legs to make it difficult for him to strip her but the struggle changed, took on a different quality. She relaxed her foot when he slid the bikini underpants down and threw them to the floor.

She was bone thin, model thin. His hands could feel the structure of her body through the smoothness of her skin. His mouth moved along her throat, upward along the sharp cheekbones; his tongue tasted her ear; his breath made her shake her head from side to side until his mouth contacted hers; then he pulled away sharply.

"Don't bite. Damn it, that hurts!"

He felt her tense beneath him, saw her mouth set with determination as she tried to force her strength against him. He relaxed, enjoyed her exertions, felt the fullness of her resolve as she managed to slide from beneath him, as she leaned over him, breathing quickly, glittering with triumph. She grinned down at him, leaned toward his face, then twisted suddenly and bit his shoulder and wouldn't let go until he lurched over, his full weight on her, diminishing her now with his own strength.

She struggled against him until he found her moistness, entered her, moved relentlessly to his own rhythm until she began to follow, to become part of it, and he continued until

436

he could feel her response grow, until he could feel her gasp and shudder and stiffen, a soft surprised moan from her mouth, and then, freed of all thought of her, he allowed his own physicality to overwhelm him.

"You know," she mused, "it's so damn strange."

He ran his fingertips along the clearly defined segments of her spine, over the small, neat, hard roundness of her buttocks, under the curve where a buttock became thigh. He explored her quietly while she glanced over her shoulder at him.

"Why are you so thin?" he asked.

She lifted her face, rose on her elbow and started to turn onto her back but he pushed her lightly to her stomach again. "It's part of the whole damn thing. I don't come by this fleshless build naturally. God, I literally starve myself to stay thin for the almighty camera. If I gain so much as one pound, it shows up like ten. Tell me, who'd give a fuck if Cronkite put on twenty pounds?"

He slapped her sharply on the bottom with his open palm. "If you're going to be my girl, you'll talk the way I want my girl to talk."

Karen laughed and rubbed her finger over her mouth thoughtfully. "That's what's so damn strange. You're everything I'm opposed to in a man. There you are, a whole summation, the whole statement, the whole chauvinist thing. What I can't figure out is"—she dropped her head to her arms and slowly stretched her body under his touch, then rolled onto her back—"that you do something to my body that is totally, completely, irrationally removed from my head. I don't understand why I'm so damned attracted to you. Just plain old-fashioned lust, I guess. My God, you've got no subtlety, no love play, no preliminaries, nothing. Just the rough old jump and roll. Chemical, animal, have at it, wham bang."

He moved up beside her. Her tough voice was incongruous; her body was elegant, her face childlike. But her barrage of words, her attempt to pinpoint him, to categorize him, annoyed him.

"That wasn't rough stuff, baby."

437

She pulled her mouth down, her brows went up. "Oh, that wasn't 'rough stuff.' Drag and push and shove and rip the clothes off my back wasn't rough stuff?"

"That wasn't rough stuff, and you know it." His hand caught in the thickness of her hair. "That was all careful and controlled and designed to please the lady."

She had underestimated him and was puzzled by him. He was someone who did have unknown dimension and she felt she had lost the upper hand. Quickly, impulsively, she said, "How old are you, O'Malley?"

He shook the lock of hair. "You're a real little bitch, aren't you? I'm forty-nine."

She ran her tongue along the edges of her lips and grinned. "That's great. No, really, I'm not kidding. I'm twenty-seven and my father is just about your age. Hey, do you have a daughter?"

Carefully he said, "Yeah. Why?"

"How old is she?"

"About your age. . . . *Why?*"

She moved closer to him and jabbed an index finger into him. "That's absolutely great! Don't you get it? I can screw my father and you can screw your daughter without any of the Freudian complications."

He yanked her hair hard enough to force her head to the pillow, then pulled his hand free. "Jesus, you are really some kind of a nut."

She could see it was an effort for him to control his anger, to leave the bed, cross the room for a cigarette. She began to laugh. "Oh, my God, O'Malley, you're a *prude!* That's terrific. I never would have expected it. No, really, don't be mad. I mean it as a compliment. Any man as good as you in bed, well, the whole puritan thing just doesn't go with what you can do. Ah, come on, share the cigarette with me and stop looking like you want to strangle me."

"I'm not mad, Karen, only let's have a few guidelines, okay?"

She started to laugh again, a surprisingly fresh, young, relaxed, spontaneous sound, again reminding him of someone hauntingly innocent and vulnerable. She laughed so hard she began to cough. He pulled her into a sitting position, slapped her back while she caught her breath.

He watched her move from her closet to her bureau as she arranged her clothing casually over the back of a chair. She left the long folding door of the closet pushed back, displaying an array of colors and fabrics. As she came from the bathroom, easily moving naked about the room, seemingly unaware of him, he called to her.

"Karen. Do something for me, if you have time."

"I have time. What?"

"Model for me. Put on some of those things for me. Come on. A private show."

She took off the shower cap and tossed it to him. "Oh, boy, and I thought you were strictly a straight, O'Malley. Why, you're nothing but an out-and-out pervo. All right, if it gives you a kick, I'll parade around with my *clothes on*, for God's sake!"

She moved with a model's expressionless, gliding, stylized quick grace, stared blankly through him as she paraded past the bed. She spoke in a flat voice in a rapid tempo.

"You will notice the daring plunge of backline." She turned, lightly touched the backless dress, which revealed the beginning curve of buttock, then slid around, ran her fingertips across the flat bustline. "Because of the superb construction of Monsieur Clondet's creation, it would of course be sacrilegious to wear anything but oneself beneath this gown."

She slipped into a one-piece outfit with tight little shorts and long narrow sleeves.

"You will notice that for this playsuit, one must possess the contours of a little boy; not necessarily frontwards, but" – she turned and shook her bottom at him – "from this point of view."

Finally, she put on a floor-length bright-blue silk garment, narrow and elegant, with a high Chinese collar and full flowing sleeves. She changed. The blank model's expression was gone. The flirtatious short-pants-clad gamine disappeared. She moved toward him serenely, her expression no longer remote. She took on elegance and cool desirability as she moved. The gown touched and brushed her body, hinted at her contours with subtle sensuality.

She started to speak, but something about Brian stopped her. His expression had changed as she had changed. His eyes moved over her body, then held on her face, and he stood up and came toward her and tilted her face and kissed her gently.

He moved his hands along the front of the gown, pulled each hidden snap, reached along her shoulders and removed the silk from her body and let it drop to the floor. He held her against him and for just one instant felt her tense and stiffen but he pressed her to him and whispered, "It's okay, Karen. It'll be good this way, too. Let me show you."

This time he moved slowly, touched slowly, lightly, whispered to her, caressed her, tasted her skin, explored her, found her slowly rising need and again set a tempo which she at first struggled against but he persisted, encouraged her, controlled and directed and led her into the very center of herself, and this time it was perfect because he was right there with her and it was hard to separate their shared sensations.

"My God," she told him, "I don't know you at all, do I?"

"Maybe I'll even introduce you to yourself." Finally, he pushed her toward the edge of the bed. "Now, get the hell into the kitchen and make me some coffee."

She looked down at him for a minute, then yanked the pillow from under his head and tossed it at him. "Make it yourself, chauvinist. I have to shower and fix my hair. I've a show to do at eleven."

She picked the yellow shower cap off the floor and pushed her hair into it. He heard her turn the shower on, then she came back into the bedroom. "You know, O'Malley, you're a damn good lay." She paused, timed it for the right effect, then added in a tough voice, "For a man *your age.*"

He threw the pillow at her and leaped for her but she managed to close the bathroom door and get into her shower.

"You little bitch," he said good-naturedly. He heard her singing and she didn't sound anything like her mother.

He caught a glimpse of himself in the mirror over her dressing table. For a man of his age, he was in helluva good shape. He put his hand on his flat stomach, admired his long body, which hadn't gone to flab, had remained hard and muscular and responsive.

Christ, for a man his age, he felt like a man of any age. He pulled on his clothes and brushed his hair with her heavy brush.

Then he went into her kitchen and to surprise her, and to his own surprise, he put on a pot of coffee.

It lasted because they made no unrealistic demands on each other. She was absorbed in her career and Brian viewed her achievements with pride. She knew how to channel her energies and she moved ahead steadily to larger and more important news assignments.

He kept his private life separate and apart from her; she never pried but merely surmised. There were times when he was tempted to speak to her about certain things, but he knew instinctively what to keep private. He felt a new joy in his own achievements when he was with her, for she was not easily impressed, yet was impressed by him.

For two years, while neither took the other totally for granted, there had at least developed a sense of reliability. She was not a woman given to wounded feelings. A quick phone call canceling an expected meeting was as easily accepted by her as by him. She'd been in Los Angeles for three weeks on assignment and he felt slightly lonely and unfulfilled. She'd been preparing an hour-long special on sensitivity training centers and she'd called him once to announce that she was involved with the greatest collection of kooks ever assembled in one place at one time.

He was about to dial her number when she called him. It was one of the things that happened between them all the time and if either said, "I was just reaching for the phone to call you," it was invariably true and they both knew it.

"Tonight okay?" she asked. When he said yes, that was all there was to say at the moment, but she added uncharacteristically, "Good. Hell, I think I missed you, O'Malley."

He hung up the receiver and attacked the work on his desk in a lighthearted mood.

THIRTY-EIGHT

The fifth article in the series in the *Daily News* was the one that caused the commotion they had been hoping to avoid.

"I had been at the precinct for four weeks," the author asserted, "when I was approached about going on 'the pad.' "

Lieutenant Fitzgerald was at his desk when Deputy Chief Inspector Brian O'Malley arrived at a quarter to eight. Fitzgerald had read the article in the first edition of the newspaper, which came out the previous evening, and he knew he could expect his boss early. He brought a cup of hot coffee to Brian's desk and waited for instructions.

Brian scanned a list of notes he'd written to himself, glanced at his wristwatch, then instructed Lieutenant Fitzgerald.

"Get Chief Aaron Levine on the phone. If he's not in yet, keep trying. I wanna get to him before Chief Pollack arrives."

Aaron Levine, Deputy Chief Inspector in Charge of Internal Affairs, New York City Police Department, leaned back in the corner of his chauffeur-driven unmarked Department car and sighed. He was running a little late this morning. Probably the Commissioner would want to see him because of this dope's article. As far as Aaron Levine was concerned, the less he saw of the P.C., the happier he was.

Not that he had anything against the Commissioner. The reverse was true. He was a fine man, if a bit of a dreamer, but truly, a better man than the Department he headed.

It hadn't taken Aaron more than a month on his assignment to get the feeling that the Department was rotting from the center on out. He had no great inclination to take on a crusade for honor and integrity within the New York City Police Department. What he had in his mind, actually, was putting in the remaining year and four months that would make him eligible for retirement at three-quarter pay. Then, at fifty-five, he would be able to step into a position as Dean of Law Enforcement at any of three upstate universities which had been bidding for him for the last three years, ever since law enforcement began to excite academic imaginations.

In a way, Aaron regretted his decision to stick it out until the three-quarter pay. At least in this new capacity. It had been pleasant as a captain. He did his supervisory work in a nice, easygoing manner in his nice, easygoing, white, middle-class precinct in Kew Gardens.

He'd needed a promotion like he'd needed an ulcer. He'd never had any reason to anticipate either; now he seemed to have attained both.

The new Commissioner had approached him after a careful study of what the Commissioner called Aaron's "fantastic academic achievements." The Commissioner was known to be impressed by higher education and Aaron Levine, in the course of thirty-three years as a member of the New York City Police Department, in addition to having achieved the rank of captain, had simultaneously earned a master's degree in criminology, a master's degree in social psychology, a doctorate in urban planning and an LL.D. from Brooklyn Law School. He'd obtained his teacher's license; he'd taught a few courses at the Police Academy; and when moonlighting became legal, he'd conducted courses in basic criminology and penology at John Marshall College of Criminal Justice.

He'd managed to raise and educate two daughters and one son; all three were married, professionals with graduate degrees, successful in their respective communities in Long Island, Connecticut and Westchester.

Aaron's wife, a former schoolteacher, was kept very busy in her social involvements in Great Neck. She stressed his academic accomplishments and played down his "connection" with the Police Department among her friends. To her, Aaron was a scholar and an academic; she liked to feel that he was a police officer merely as a means of studying law enforcement at first hand to enhance his professional knowledge. At any rate, she referred to him as a "law enforcement special-

443

ist; one of the few in the country"; as such, her friends were most impressed.

When the new Commissioner appointed Arthur Pollack as his Chief Inspector, Aaron Levine nodded with approval. Good. He had more than just his showcase Jew. He had selected a thoroughly competent man who had always done a good job and who always brought credit to himself and his fellow members of the Sholem Society, which was an important consideration.

When Aaron was offered the assignment of Deputy Chief Inspector in Charge of Internal Affairs, there were two considerations he had to keep in mind. The first was that he, personally, had no ambition to rise to any great heights in the New York City Police Department. He liked his small, cozy, safe office in Kew Gardens. The second consideration was more pointed.

"A *Jew* to head the spy squad, Aaron? You hafta be crazy to even consider it." That was the opinion of Sergeant Sam Markowitz, president of the Sholem Society. "That's all they'd need, Aaron, to point us out as their persecutors. Don't give them any ammunition. Listen to me."

"Bullshit," volunteered Max Chumberg, a lieutenant and vice-president of the organization. "We gotta move when we can, wherever we can. Look, Artie Pollack is right up there at the top. It's time to stop being afraid of making a bad impression with these guys. Aaron, take the job."

"Aaron," their rabbi-adviser said, "do your duty. Go with God."

Aaron took the job. His main tasks were to root out corruption in the New York City Police Department; to institute departmental charges against those derelict in their duties; to investigate civilian complaints. In his new position, he heard plenty and took action wherever it seemed feasible.

Philosophically, Aaron Levine considered his position with a sense of ironic amusement. He'd spent a lifetime in the Police Department attending one course or another, taking one degree or another, often on city time and once, for a year on scholarship at Berkeley, on city money. He'd long ago decided that there was nothing intrinsically dishonest with how he'd spent his life. His accumulation of knowledge and academic credentials served the Department and the city well.

444

He used his knowledge for the good of his job, in a way. Certainly, he tried to bring an enlightened approach to his job. He never harmed anyone.

That was about the only way to view his life: through rationalization, with a grain of humor and a smile at the turnings and twistings of life and fate or whatever it was that decided things for a man.

Patrolman Jacobs, the only other Jew in the office, since Aaron heeded the Society's advice not to load the division with Jews, greeted him abruptly. Jacobs was a very tense young man, eyes always glowing with a sense of excitement and alarm.

"Chief, you got a call already from Chief O'Malley. He wants you to call him back. Right away as soon as you get in he said."

"Okay, Stu. And relax. You're making me nervous and it's going to be a long nervous day. Go, type a report or something for the meeting."

Aaron Levine sat and contemplated the telephone. Call Chief O'Malley. It was funny. He hadn't thought of Brian O'Malley as any connection to himself for years; not since they'd both been appointed captain together had he even realized there *was* a Brian O'Malley in the Department. The son of his father. Well. It was a strange world all right.

He didn't have much to do with O'Malley. They had an occasional conference about how to handle certain corruption issues with the media. O'Malley impressed Levine as being very much in the mold of that still strange, still remote hard breed of men whom Aaron had dwelt among all of his working life, yet had never come to feel anything toward but a sense of alienated wonder and curiosity. He never could figure how little Arthur Pollack had slid right into the midst of them, the strangers, and come up on top.

He dialed, waited for the first ring to be interrupted.

"Hello, Chief O'Malley? This is Chief Levine. You got a minute?"

Karen called just as Brian was leaving his office for the conference with Arthur Pollack. "Listen, Karen, can I get back to you? You at the office or home? I have a conference."

"This is business, Brian."

He hesitated, felt a sharpening sense of awareness. Her voice was businesslike and insistent. Carefully, he said, "What business do we have pending?"

In the past, he'd given her small things, fed her leads if there was a particularly sensational crime current and if she was assigned to it. But it had been understood between them that she'd never initiate any inquiry. Brian had the vague feeling that she was violating some unstated agreement.

"This newspaper article, Brian. What's a 'pad'?"

"Karen, I'll see you tonight."

"Brian, hold it a minute—"

"Tonight," he said tersely and hung up.

At the Chief Inspector's office, there were, in addition to Deputy Chief Inspectors Levine and O'Malley, two inspectors and two deputy inspectors.

"Go ahead, Brian," the Chief Inspector said, "I didn't mean to interrupt."

"Right, Chief. I've sent someone over to the *News* to pick up an advance of the article they're going to run tomorrow, but the gist of it is what I've already gotten over the telephone."

Arthur Pollack rubbed his horn-rimmed glasses with a clean handkerchief but didn't put them back over his tired eyes as he spoke. "So, he doesn't actually name names?"

"Well," Brian answered, "he indicates the position of the men he claims were on the pad. I mean, what the hell. If he's accusing the squad commander of the precinct's detectives, that could be only one guy, right?"

Arthur pinched the bridge of his nose with his slender fingers and closed his eyes for a moment, then put on the glasses and said, "Aaron, you're on top of this?"

Arthur Pollack's tone was more hopeful than authoritative. He hadn't developed the tone of command, yet his reputation for getting things done, all things considered, was strong.

Aaron Levine consulted the list of neatly typed notations which were attached to his clipboard. "We've sent someone over to this reporter's home and someone to his office to interview him. He's not around and nobody seems to know where he is, so we're looking into that." He made a small check mark next to the item and continued down his list, checking

446

as he spoke. "I have a man over at the D.A.'s office to see how he feels about a grand jury appearance for this Jerry Smith. Incidentally, that's his real name, and as Jerry Smith, he was in the Department on the dates and in the locations he's indicated in his articles.

"I have two men over at the Seventeenth Precinct now interviewing anyone he ever worked with. I have an appointment with Lieutenant Cavanaugh, the squad commander of the precinct detectives, scheduled for two-thirty this afternoon, in my office.

"The Legal Department is studying the articles for possible action, et cetera." Aaron Levine looked up finally and ventured, "Along with all the usual possible bases to be touched whenever any allegations such as these arise, that's it to date, Chief."

Arthur Pollack nodded and stood up. The men in his office, taking this for a signal that the meeting was over, stood up too. He glanced at them in some surprise, looked slightly startled, then gestured them back into place. Standing, he looked about as tall as his subordinates did seated.

"No, no, stay put, please. I just wanted to stretch my legs. Oh, one other thing, Aaron. I assume you've thought of this, but just to be sure. Aside from checking out the accusations, you're also checking on this reporter?"

Levine scanned his list, snapped his fingers. That particular notation was neatly jotted on the other side of his paper. "Yes, Chief, I've somebody on his background from day of birth up to the present. We should have that by late this afternoon."

"Well, then let's hope he's a convicted perjurer at least. It would make things easy, wouldn't it? Now, Brian. We'll handle this along the lines we've previously discussed. The Commissioner feels we're still in a position to adopt a wait-and-see attitude."

"No problem there, Chief."

Arthur Pollack stared blankly for a moment; one eye turned in slightly until he blinked, held up his hands, looked around the room as though for confirmation. "Okay, then, that's it for now, gentlemen."

Karen swallowed some Scotch, wrinkled her nose, extended her glass toward him. "Brian, drop a couple of cubes in this for me, will you? Look, I don't know what you're so angry about. I *did* call you first thing this morning and I *did* say it was business."

"Look, babe, if you're going to be stepping on my toes, at least make sure you've got some weight going for you. What the hell kind of crap was that to pull: 'The Police Department was not available for comment on the allegations contained in today's published article.'" He handed her the drink and sat opposite her, his feet on the cocktail table between them.

Karen rolled the drink between her palms. "Look, Brian, you know I'm working up to my own show. It's all set, three nights a week, *Talk About Your City*. I'm going to be dealing with every city agency from the mayor's office down to the Department of Sanitation."

"You ought to reverse the order: Department of Sanitation down to the mayor's office. Look, I still think you hit low tonight and it bounces right back to me."

She shrugged, played a finger over an ice cube. "Okay, want to give me some detailed information? My show's scheduled to start in two weeks. The Police Department might be for openers."

"Forget it," he said tersely. "I'm not kidding, Karen. Don't try to use me."

Slowly, she leaned forward and put her glass on the table. She shook his foot lightly from side to side. "Why not, sweetie? We've been using each other for a long time."

He was surprised at how angry he felt. "Look, kid, I'm serious. If the Department's got a problem, it's internal, and I'm not about to give you a few tidbits to feed your voracious audience and get your show going in style. My job is to keep the lid on. There's nothing involved that requires full-scale TV coverage."

"Well, it's a good story when it involves investigating the investigators, Brian. Your job may be to keep the lid on. My job is to open it all up to the public eye."

"Then I think maybe we'd better not discuss it when we're together, Karen. You do your job, I'll do mine, right?"

She chewed on her index finger for a moment, then grinned. "If I do *my* job properly, you won't be *able* to do yours."

448

Brian leaned back and returned the challenging smile tightly. "Yeah, baby, but if I do *my* job properly, same thing applies. You know, it's so damned nice and comforting to have an understanding woman."

"Screw you, O'Malley."

THIRTY-NINE

Patrolman Johnnie Morrison prided himself on his appearance. He was of medium height, slender build and he knew how to dress and how to wear clothes. He had his hair styled and groomed at an expensive men's salon. He had the look of today and the look of the crowd he most admired and had been assigned to work around. He liked vice assignments; they meant action and a chance to mix it up with the real swingers. Sometimes, he felt he'd been born too early. It was a great time to be twenty-five instead of thirty-five, but for a man of thirty-five, he held his own pretty good.

He didn't think much of Patrolman Pete Caputo. As far as appearance goes, the kid was a slob. Johnnie Morrison had seen guys with beards look dapper and cool. This kid was just plain motley; no style, no class, nothing. He wasn't exactly the kind of partner Johnnie Morrison would have selected for himself, but he was, nevertheless, the partner given him in the new shake-up.

The word on the kid was that he was a little strange but basically okay. If the word was a little vague, that didn't bother Morrison too much. He'd size the kid up in short order. At least he'd heard the kid had moxie and that always came in handy, since no matter how you played it when you worked an unmarked out on the street, you never knew what the hell you might come on and it was good to have a bit of backbone behind you besides your own.

"You got much going out in the Seventy-first?" Morrison asked. "I don't know Brooklyn. I'm strictly a Manhattan boy myself."

"The Seventy-first is pretty quiet, I guess."

450

"Well, the Fourteenth is pretty active," Morrison said. He glanced sideways at his young partner and added, "You know. In lotsa ways. Hey, speaking of which, did you catch that on the radio?"

They both leaned forward and Morrison picked the words out right away. He was attuned to anything that might mean his particular sector. "Yeah, that's us, Pete. Go. Oh, Jesus, Emporium Furs. Hell, I know that place. It's *wholesale*."

There were signs of breaking and entering, but by the time they arrived at the huge store on West 32nd Street, there were no further signs of the intruders. There were three patrol cars on the scene when Morrison and Caputo arrived in their unmarked black Plymouth.

A slightly built sergeant leaned toward one of the patrol cars, which had obviously arrived just moments before the unmarked. "Okay, okay, there's no fucking sideshow to be seen here. You guys can just take off; there's nothing around for all you guys. Go on, go on, it's under control."

"What do you say, Johnnie," Pete Caputo asked, "should we scout the area? They've probably been scared off by now but we could ride around a little and take a look."

Johnnie rubbed the back of his neck for a moment, his fingers lingering on the soft curl of hair, newly styled. "Take it easy, kid. I just wanna go have a look around."

As they got out of the car, the sergeant approached them, his face a tight, questioning glare. "Oh, it's you, Johnnie. Who the hell is this? Bearded Sam?"

"This here is my new partner. Pete Caputo, meet Sergeant Edgar. So, what's doing?"

"The owner's been notified. He'll be here in about forty-five minutes."

It seemed somewhat irrelevant information, but Morrison nodded as though that was what he wanted to know. He scanned the patrolmen on the scene, one stationed at the door, two inside the store, then turned to Pete.

"Hey, partner, look. I'm just gonna have a look-see. You keep on the radio, okay?" He winked and as he walked into the store he casually hung an arm over the sergeant's shoulder.

Pete sat in the car and smoked a few cigarettes. They were parked directly across from the front of Emporium Furs and

451

he had a fairly good view into the shop. The whole block had a middle-of-the-night three-thirty feeling to it. He remembered the summer he'd worked in a dress shop, not two blocks away. Christ, he shoved racks down these streets when they were jammed with trucks and cars and shoving people. Funny, he hadn't thought of that for years, but one day, a truck actually knocked him down. The truck backed up suddenly, and Pete and his rack of cheap dresses barreled right into the truck. Pete went under the truck and all he worried about was the fucking merchandise. Jesus, the boss would kill him if he didn't make delivery.

God, kids were dumb. He'd never told anyone about that, as though it were a terrible fault he should keep private.

Pete flipped the cigarette out the window and wondered who was pulling up in the dark Oldsmobile. Must be the owner of the shop. A tall, slim, dark figure of a man. One of the patrolmen came over to the car and stood beside the man, talking. Then the patrolman touched his cap and went back inside the shop. It seemed a little strange. If he was the owner, why didn't he go inside the shop?

Pete slid down, pressed his shoulders against the back of his seat and watched. After about five minutes, the patrolman came out of the shop. He carried a large box, which the other man put on the fender of the car. He examined the contents of the box and seemed angry about something. The patrolman shrugged, gestured over his shoulder. The other man shoved the box at the patrolman, looked at his wristwatch, lit a cigarette while he waited again.

Johnnie Morrison came out in a few minutes. He carried a huge box in two hands and he and the other man examined the contents. As the taller man bent toward the box, Johnnie's hand patted his shoulder, then they both stood up and Johnnie seemed to be explaining something. The other man tossed the box onto the back seat, said something, listened, said something else, then extended his hand for a handshake. Johnnie looked around casually and watched the man get into the Oldsmobile and drive away.

Pete slumped way down in his seat and watched the driver as his face hit street light. It was the lieutenant in charge of the precinct's detectives.

Pete got out of his car and walked to the front of the store.

The uniformed patrolman stiffened, then recognized him as Johnnie Morrison's partner and he brought his hidden cigarette to his mouth.

Pete jerked his head in the direction that the Oldsmobile had gone. "He's a tough man to please, huh?"

The patrolman hesitated, then grinned. "Well, fuck him. He wants dark mink, he oughta risk his ass and go and pick his own, ya know?"

Pete shoved his hands into his trouser pockets and shrugged. He glanced across the store and noticed that the sergeant seemed very angry and Johnnie Morrison seemed very calm and pacifying as he helped the sergeant make a careful selection of merchandise. When Johnnie looked up and saw Pete, his expression never changed and he continued to pack and tie the large box which he handed to the sergeant, who handed it to a patrolman, who carried it outside and put it in the trunk of one of the patrol cars.

The owner of the store arrived shortly after; he was plump and pale and had the look of a man who had been disturbed by terrible news in the middle of the night.

"The *gonifs*, the goddamn *gonifs*. They'll raise my insurance again. Third time this goddamn year I been hit."

"I don't think it's too bad, Mr. Levin," the sergeant said quietly. "By the looks of it, they couldn't have got much. At least they didn't mess up the place on you this time. And what the hell," he said reasonably, "you're insured for anything that's missing, aren't you?"

Johnnie Morrison began to feel a little more comfortable with his new partner. The kid kept his mouth shut and his eyes open and those were two of the most important qualifications a guy could have. Not that he trusted him completely, but he was easing him along, testing him, trying him out. After all, the kid had to learn the setup and Johnnie had to make sure he learned it right. He'd taken a big chance tonight and the kid still kept his cool, just stood by, waited without a word.

Johnnie indicated that Pete should take the wheel. He settled alongside him and studied the bearded face. "You wondering how come we didn't lock that bastard up?"

Pete turned the key, started the motor. "I figure you got your

453

reasons. I mean, we got him with more than a half ounce of suspicious white powder. We caught him dead flat out, so I figure there must be a *good* reason why we didn't bag him."

Johnnie Morrison considered the bland, expressionless face for a moment, then nodded. "Well, we're gonna see some action in about five minutes. This little bag here"—he held the glassine envelope by a corner—"this here little bag is just insurance. Just in case we need it. See, what we're going to do now is, we're going to teach some little fuck-off a lesson. We got a message needs gettin' around, and when you wanna make a public announcement, you do it in public. You know where Gomez' bar is? On the corner of Ninth and Twenty-eighth Street?"

It was a small, dingy neighborhood bar and they parked across the street from it and sat for a moment just looking around. Morrison narrowed his eyes, seemed able to penetrate the filthy window even from that distance.

"Yeah," he said finally, "the little bum's in there. See that mutt tied to the lamppost? That's Juan-o, Rodriguez' dog, and he always leaves it there. Half the time the dog is crocked. They slip him beer to keep him happy, the stupid bastard." He looked at his wristwatch. "Good timing. We'll get to make Night Court, then we can break. Okay, kid, all you gotta do this time out is, you gotta look and learn."

"That's what I'm here for, Johnnie," Pete Caputo said quietly.

They took him with a great deal of sound and commotion and shoving and yelling. Rodriguez was small and wiry, with ratlike darting black eyes and fluttering hands which went up instinctively to Morrison's huge hands, which wrapped around his throat.

Johnnie Morrison roared, "Hey, what the fuck is this, Rodriguez? You resisting?" He turned and said to Pete Caputo, "You witness this, Pete. This little bum is resisting!" He practically choked the man, threw him against the wall and warned, "You little turd, I'll break your arms and legs, you try resisting arrest."

"No, no, I no resist, no resist."

The others in the bar stood quietly where they'd been told

454

and watched as Morrison crashed into stools, knocked over drinks and with a great flourish whirled Rodriguez against the wall and patted him down.

It was obvious to anyone who was watching closely, and they were all watching closely, that Johnnie Morrison planted the bag on Rodriguez.

"Well, you little spic bum," Morrison said loudly. "Look what he had stashed on him. You here to sell, Rodriguez?"

"Oh, no, hey, man, I'm clean." He turned to face Morrison and he lowered his voice to a loud, hissing whisper. "Hey, man, we can talk, yeah? Oh, don't take me like that, man. Jesus, we can talk, you know?"

Johnnie Morrison leaned in close and rammed his fist into Rodriguez' stomach. "I'm talkin' to you, bum. You understand English good now, huh? You didn't hear me last time I talked to you. This time, you'll hear me real good." He turned to Pete. "Okay, let's get this little piece of shit down to the station house."

Juan Jesus Rodriguez had been arrested seventeen times for a variety of offenses ranging from selling to possession to impairing the morals to assault with a deadly weapon (knife) to gambling and a variety of disorderly conducts; he had three felony arrests and one conviction on the sheet; he had served a combined total of upwards of seven years in various institutions on various charges.

In the squad room, he quieted down and said in a reasonable tone of voice to Johnnie Morrison, "Hey, look, Detective Morrison, you lemme talk to the boss, see, I make things square. Hey, Johnnie, you gimme a break, I make it up to you. See, my lungs been so bad with the asthma, you know, I gotta spend so much as one night in the slam, I'm likely to choke."

"That's okay with me. That'll be one more good spic."

"Ah, come on, don't be like that. Look, I had some trouble at home, you know. The kid been in trouble and it costs."

Morrison went on typing the arrest report with two index fingers picking and tapping. His mouth pursed over the words and he seemed to go deaf.

The desk sergeant was as unimpressed by Rodriguez as was Morrison. "Why don't you just shut the fuck up?" the sergeant asked mildly.

Finally, Rodriguez was reconciled to his plight. He was quiet during the ride to Police Headquarters, where he was photographed, and throughout the court proceedings, where he was held in custody in lieu of a thousand-dollar bond.

"You're okay, kid," Morrison told Pete Caputo. "You been learnin' real good." He cast a speculative eye over Pete. "You know, kid, you oughta take more of an interest in clothes. I mean I guess you dress kind of hippie for the job, like nobody makes you for cop, but Jeez, listen, I gotta guy I go to, you know. I mean I don't own a suit costs less than three hundred bucks, but this guy, he gets them for me for under sixty. Look, you go into any store, good store, you know, and pick out what you like. See this sports jacket? Costs hundred and fifty bucks at Saks Fifth; I paid thirty-five. You pick out what you like, and then you tell this guy, see? Within a coupla days, he has it for you. Listen, kid, you let me know when you're ready, right?"

"Okay, Johnnie," Pete Caputo said, "I'll let you know when I'm ready."

The friendship between Patrick O'Malley and Pete Caputo grew and solidified, not only in the classroom but afterward, over endless cups of coffee. They fell on the same side in all the classroom arguments and discussions and they each noticed that the other clammed up at precisely the same point. It was as though there was a point beyond which neither of them trusted himself to venture. Some of the older men in the course plunged on, blandly sure of themselves, seemingly unaware of the remote, mutual silence among the younger students.

Mel Arden noticed the reticence of the younger students and he didn't think it was capitulation to the more outspoken and boisterous older students. He sensed it with sadness. It was almost a sense of despair, as though they realized, these younger men who'd been to Viet Nam, that they had no common language with this older generation.

Patrolman Kelly grew red in the face with the force of his conviction. "I still say we shoulda used whatever force it took to effect a complete victory. For God's sake, we're the strongest country in the world."

456

Professor Harley Taylor shifted uncomfortably in his chair. The group discussion always got off the topic the minute the war was mentioned. It started this afternoon with a casual remark from one of the men about the students demonstrating against the war. He was one of the men who'd been assigned to a demonstration at Foley Square. From there to nuclear weapons was a fast step in Patrolman Kelly's mind; he felt the demonstrators should be annihilated, the sooner the better.

"Well, one of the speeches made at the rally," Dr. Arden said quietly, "relates to the corruption prevalent in the Thieu Administration, Mr. Kelly. Do you think that corruption is a genuine concern of ours, since we're largely responsible for the establishment and maintenance of that Administration?"

Patrolman Kelly's red face jutted across the table and he said loudly, "We just oughta go and do the job the right way, that's all there is to that."

Pete Caputo smiled tightly and shook his head.

"Mr. Caputo, do you have a comment?" Dr. Arden asked. He didn't miss much.

Pete didn't look up. His voice, soft, aimed at the surface of the table, could hardly be heard. "Oh, no. No. I don't have any comment at all." He looked up finally, turned his light-blue eyes on Kelly, then smiled.

In Viet Nam, Pete Caputo, assigned to ordnance, had had a sickening firsthand opportunity to observe black-market corruption which involved millions of dollars' worth of stolen supplies. He'd seen privates, corporals, lieutenants and captains grow rich through the medium of stolen drugs and materials intended for relief supplies or basic supplies for either the civilian or the military. He'd witnessed an operation so vast and finely tangled that he had no idea where it began or how it would ever end.

One day Private Caputo was shot in the knee by a sniper as he walked toward his office, which was on the outskirts of Saigon. In retaliation for the injury of a good, closed-mouth, cooperative man, his sergeant caught and lined up sixteen male civilians, aged fourteen to sixty-two. All were suspected V.C., therefore all were presumed guilty of subversion, perversion, corruption and murder. Within sight of the suffering Private Caputo, in a planned and well-coordinated action,

457

each man had his right leg shot up by the sergeant and several of his men.

That action was supposed, somehow, to help Private Caputo's leg to heal faster and better. It was his sergeant's contribution to the war effort, outside of the fast fifty thousand bucks he'd made from the black market.

"Well, what the hell are *you* grinning about?" Kelly asked, a dangerous note in his voice.

Caputo shrugged, let his hand fall open on the table, leaned back in his chair. He exchanged glances with Patrick O'Malley, across the table from him. He'd told Patrick his experiences; they'd exchanged confidences. They knew it was no use.

"Speaking of corruption," Professor Harley Taylor, in his innocence and through a genuine desire to know and to understand, asked the class at large, "could anyone explain to me exactly what is 'the pad'?"

There was a stark silence, a few grins, then a series of wise-cracks, insinuations, protestations. The discussion turned sharply to the articles in the *Daily News*, which alleged that pay-offs, bribes and graft were a daily fact of life in the New York City Police Department.

Patrolman Finn, a fat man with the look of a stereotype, asserted flatly, "It's a goddamn figment of that freak reporter's imagination, that's what it is." He glowered around the table in an attempt to control and direct whatever was to follow.

"Yeah, Finn, he made the whole thing up."

Finn rubbed one hand over the other and directed his side-long glare at the young policeman to his left. "Okay, do *you* know of any so-called pad?"

The young policeman pulled a mock-innocent face. "Who? *Me?* Listen, I don't know from *nothing.*"

Dr. Arden looped an arm around the back of his chair and spoke through teeth clenched on the stem of his pipe. "For clarity's sake, will someone spell out exactly what's meant by being 'on the pad'?"

Lieutenant Palmer, a fingerprint specialist from the Bureau of Criminal Identification, young, crisp, sharp, articulate, stated, "The allegation is that there exists a list of personnel within the particular division to whom regular pay-offs are made for a variety of reasons, mainly to prevent the enforce-

458

ment of certain laws. Generally, the nonenforcement relates to gambling and vice but could include liquor-law violations, construction-law violations, et cetera."

Conversationally, Dr. Arden asked, "Would there be a nice line drawn, say for the sake of a kind of morality, where drugs are concerned? Or where a serious crime involving injury is concerned?"

Lieutenant Palmer shifted in his chair and leaned forward.

Before he could answer, Pete Caputo said in a clear, cold voice, "The line isn't drawn anywhere there's money to be had."

FORTY

There was something a little disturbing about Pete Caputo's preoccupation with what was happening around him on the job.

"I'm telling you, Pat," he said vehemently, "there isn't an honest guy in the division. They steal everything they touch. Christ, Morrison told me that it's hot stuff when they get a call on a men's wear store. He says some guys were actually trying on shirts and jackets to make sure they get the right size."

As he spoke, Pete tapped a small black-leather notebook along the edge of the table.

"What the hell is that, anyway?" Patrick asked finally.

Pete Caputo hunched over the scarred wooden table, scanned the coffeehouse quickly and said in a hoarse voice, "This is *it*, buddy. I got it all down here. This beauty, Morrison, is the goddamn bagman. I've been keeping a list of who he collects from. What I haven't got so far is the other side of it, the pad, the names of everyone on the take."

Pat ran his hand over his face and said calmly, "Okay, Pete. Now the question is, What are you going to do with all this? Isn't that what you're leading up to?"

Caputo nodded briskly and slipped the notebook into the breast pocket of his Army fatigue shirt. "You don't think I'm going to anyone in the Department with it, do you? Look, what I figured is, this guy, you know, this reporter, Jerry Smith. He dropped just a few hints compared to what the real story is. I figure I'd go to him and let him open up the whole damn division."

Patrick O'Malley slowly shook his head and in a low and

460

tense voice said, "I think you'd be making a mistake that way, Pete. I really do. Look, from what we can figure, this guy Smith is nothing more than an opportunist. Any guy that thinks he's exposing a city department after spending two months, hell, he's hit and run. I'd bet you anything you want that he wouldn't touch you with a ten-foot pole."

Caputo's expression tightened; his hands played the cup of coffee back and forth until some sloshed over the rim and onto the table. "Jesus, I don't know, Pat. See, the thing is this. I don't trust the district attorney. Hell, I've made some anonymous inquiries, you know? Just kind of scouting it out, and researching past investigations about departmental corruption. You know whose ass gets dragged? Same as always, same as anywhere else, the low man on the totem pole." His pale eyes glazed over, became as remote as glass, as though he were seeing right through Patrick to another time and place. "The brass always gets away with it; no matter what, the higher-ups never get touched. They get theirs and get out, and if anyone gets caught, it's the lowest guy." His hands tightened around the cup as he spoke, spasmodically, with a life of their own. "Sometimes . . . sometimes I think there's only one way to get them. Just that, you know? *Get them.*"

That was when Patrick O'Malley went to his father.

Brian O'Malley had very mixed feelings about the whole thing. He thought his son's friend, Pete Caputo, was very tense and tight and secretive. It was obvious he was distrustful, but for Christ's sake, when you go to someone for something, you have to give a little.

"How about letting me in on what it is you've got, as far as something concrete?" Brian asked.

Caputo pulled on the end of his beard, rubbed his fingers into the furry dark growth. He looked from Patrick to his father, back to Patrick, then he studied the carpeting and shook his head.

Brian crushed out his cigarette and tried to stay very calm. It had been a long time since Patrick had been home; it had been longer than he could remember that his son had come to him with any problem. He wanted to be very careful; he sensed this as an opportunity to build something between

461

them. He only wished to hell it could have been something involving just the two of them.

"Okay, let me get it clear in my mind what it is you want, Pete. You'd like an investigation into your division relative to what you allege is the existence of an operating pad. You don't want to talk to anyone about it."

"Chief O'Malley, it would get squashed at patrolman level; everyone would pull back. You'd end up with a handful of guys and they'd catch it and that would be that. I've read up on this," Caputo said, waved his hand vaguely. "Sure, Internal Affairs would ask me to wear a wire, catch a few guys making admissions. Big deal. They'd take a fall and the whole operation would go on. I'm telling you, Chief O'Malley, the scale is one hundred and fifty a week to start, up to triple shares for brass."

"That's a pretty rough allegation, Caputo," Brian said sharply.

Pete Caputo leaned back in the leather chair and wearily scanned the room and wearily wondered how the hell Brian O'Malley could afford a house like this, in Riverdale.

"Dad," Patrick said, "Pete has his reasons for not wanting to talk directly to Internal Affairs. Couldn't they handle it just on information from you?"

Brian stood up, jammed his hands into his trouser pockets, played some coins between his fingers. "Looks like that's how they'll have to do it if you don't want to 'get involved.' " His sarcasm was lost on Caputo.

He kept the telephone conversation light-handed. He didn't know much about this guy Aaron Levine. He remembered certain allegations from years back, but they didn't have any meaning to Brian. There were always allegations when a guy got a special assignment.

"I would guess there might be *something* to what my informant says, Chief," Brian said carefully. "Of course, he just might have misunderstood certain things said to him, or misinterpreted or something, but I thought I'd pass it along to you."

He'd done it smoothly; no names, just some casual information relative to some alleged corruption within the division that should be kept "within the family."

462

"Chief O'Malley, I appreciate the information. It will be looked into right away and thoroughly. Tell your informant not to worry, it's in our hands now."

Aaron Levine's hand lingered on the telephone receiver for a moment and he stared thoughtfully at the dial. It was ironic; son of the father; and now he had to call Ed Shea, another son of a father; all of them, after all the years between, connected again, one to the other.

On the second ring, Inspector Ed Shea picked up the telephone.

"Inspector Shea? Aaron Levine here. Listen, Ed, I've just gotten a bit of a rumble that there's something going on in your division among the plain-clothes people. I don't know how much there is to it, but in view of the fact that the news media have been stirring things up, I thought you'd want to look into it yourself rather than have me send any of my people on it. You'll keep me informed, right?"

Inspector Ed Shea assured the Deputy Chief Inspector in Charge of Internal Affairs that he would conduct a personal investigation relating to any allegations of corruption in his division.

Ed Shea hung up the phone and softly cursed.

The stupid greedy bastards. They were all getting careless, and if they didn't watch it, they'd all hang together.

Karen Day ran her fingers through her long hair casually as she considered the young man across the desk from her. He leaned forward, lit a fresh cigarette from the stub of another, then forgot to squash the stub. Acrid smoke curled up thinly in front of his face. He had an uncomfortable way of staring; his eyes held hers with an intensity that both interested and disturbed her.

"Suppose you tell me why you've come to *me?* I mean, *me* in particular?"

Pete Caputo's light-blue eyes flickered, narrowed against the smoke he exhaled. His mouth pulled down and he rubbed his hand roughly over his chin. "I've been watching your new show. I've been following the exposé on the housing inspectors. Hell, that's been going on for years. It's been an open secret for years, and it's only just getting some official attention since you put it on TV." He tapped his fingers on her

463

desk; he seemed in need of constant physical movement. He stood up, sucked the cigarette, turned and abruptly stubbed it out. "Look, Miss Day, I've exhausted my resources. I went to a high-ranking superior officer over one month ago and nothing's been done. Absolutely nothing."

"How can you be sure of that?" She questioned him crisply, professionally, sharply. "If there is an investigation, it would be undercover and you'd have no way of knowing about it, right? If it was done properly."

He slumped into the chair, slid down on his spine, put one ankle to his knee, munched on his knuckle. "Look, I *know*, okay. It is wide open." He dug into a pocket abruptly, came up with a sealed envelope on which there was some neat printing. He tossed the envelope to the desk and Karen reached for it, wary but curious.

"What is this?"

"My take," he said tersely.

She picked up her reading glasses and frowned over the words. "May 4, 1972: $150.00 to Ptl. Peter Caputo #1897326; given by Ptl. John Morrison #148790." She looked up at him over the rim of her glasses. "Then you're 'on the pad'?"

"Yeah. Oh, hell, yes, lady. I've rented a safe-deposit box and I've deposited four of those envelopes so far. Marked them just like I marked that one. Evidence for the future, but, Jesus, I don't know who to present it to."

Karen Day felt the beginnings of excitement. The articles by the young reporter had been vague, glib, a cop out. He'd been interviewed by the district attorney and all he'd come up with were secondhand hearsay allegations. Her new show hadn't caught the public's eye; there weren't too many people interested in corruption in the housing administration or the sewer department.

The Police Department was another story.

Brian was annoyed when his son asked him what was doing on the investigation relative to Pete Caputo's charges, but if he was honest with himself, he had to admit that he was less annoyed with Patrick than with Aaron Levine. The least the guy could have done was to have given him a yea or nay. He didn't particularly like having to call Levine, but he wanted to make sure that the assurance he'd given his son was justified.

"It's a coincidence that you're calling me, Chief O'Malley," Deputy Chief Inspector Aaron Levine said. "I had a notation to myself to buzz you today. Listen, that matter that we discussed. It's been looked into and the charge is without foundation."

Ed Shea drained the last of his coffee, wiped his mouth and glanced around the expensive restaurant appreciatively. "Brian, you always did know how to live. For Christ's sake, they treat you like royalty."

Brian winked, nodded at the waiter that everything was to his satisfaction and nothing further was required at the moment. Brian studied Ed Shea and grinned.

"Jesus, I still think we're the two best-looking guys from the Class of '40. Not to mention two of the most successful."

They always wound up their occasional dinner together with a few wisecracks and reminiscences. They always complimented themselves and each other on their rise in the Department and the number of men from their Police Academy class who had risen with them. And those who hadn't.

"Hey, I was down at the Police Academy last week," Brian said, "and I ran into Francis Kelly's youngest kid. He's a cadet, working the switchboard." Brian remembered the heavy-set, thick-cheeked eighteen-year-old. "Christ, he's a ringer for his mother."

"How the hell is Francis anyway? Jesus, I don't think I've seen him since he retired."

Brian shrugged. "Ah, you know, Ed. You lose touch. Especially when a guy goes out. The kid said Francis is still at the bank. That's a hell of a way to go, you know? I could never see it."

Ed Shea lit a long, thin cigar and carefully turned his face to one side as he blew smoke from between his pursed lips. He closed his eyes appreciatively for a moment. "You know, Bri, these younger kids today have the right idea. They put their time in *and* get a college degree. Jesus, they can go out in twenty years and collect half pay plus step right into

465

teaching. Wasn't that way in *our* time. But we were pretty lucky, all in all."

"Yeah, I've got no complaints."

There was a bit longer pause, as though they both were aware of having exhausted through a long and leisurely meal most of the small talk.

Ed Shea said, "Hey, how's Kevin? Jesus, last time I saw you he was having that ulcer taken care of. He ever have that surgery?"

Brian shook his head. "Kevin and his ulcer are going to be together a long time. He's fine once he gets out to Montauk for a month or so. He's been talking about packing it in for a while and moving out to Montauk permanently, but he's still got his youngest in high school. I guess in about a couple of years he will. He's got a nice place out there."

Ed Shea grinned and shook his head. "I can't picture Kevin out of harness. He'd be out with the fishermen two months and he'd be looking to take over as chief of police."

"I won't say the thought hasn't occurred to him," Brian confided.

His younger brother was a lieutenant in the Arson Squad and in fifteen years hadn't had a vacation that wasn't interrupted by a summons to come back for consultation on a case.

"Sometimes I think Kev should have been a fireman. Jesus, I wouldn't have his job for anything. So, Ed, how goes things with you?"

Ed Shea, a large, handsome, well-cared-for man, tilted his head to one side. He was well aware of his appearance: curly dark hair streaked with gray, sideburns longer than he'd ever worn them, sun-lamp tan to add to his good looks. He had the look of a man who was contented with himself and with his lot in life.

"I got a number of good years left, Bri. How about you? I don't think you put on five pounds in twenty years." Ed Shea patted his own stomach and pulled a face. "Jesus, you know I'm always on a diet. If I eat a normal amount of food, I swear I put on fifteen pounds as easy as chewing."

They kidded each other about boyish appearances and it was true; they were both in good condition; each knew it and was pleased to measure himself against the other.

466

"How's Rita?" Brian asked. "Young and beautiful as ever?"

Ed Shea's mouth pulled down for a brief, passing moment before he gave the required assurances that his wife was all she should be. There had always been rumors about Ed Shea's marriage. He'd married a girl from a wealthy background and they lived well beyond a policeman's means: private school for their two daughters, considerable traveling around the world. On the rare occasions that Brian had attended a party at the Sheas', it was always a catered affair and anyone from the job was suitably impressed and awed. Rita had always been proper and polite to Ed's police friends; beneath the tight smile, there was always that slight indication of distaste.

"Rita's fine," Ed said. He shrugged, grinned. "You know women."

Brian signaled for the check; they did some kidding back and forth, but it had been understood that dinner was on Brian and he signed the check and slipped the waiter a bill. Then, instead of leaving, Brian leaned over a second cup of coffee. Ed Shea declined a second cup, relit his cigar, tensed just slightly. And waited.

"Jesus, they make good coffee." Brian carefully put the cup back on the saucer, stared at the black liquid for a minute, then looked up at Ed Shea. "There's something I think you ought to know, Ed."

Ed Shea removed the cigar from between his lips, held the slight quizzical smile, cocked his head to one side. "Yeah, Bri? What's that?"

"Well, just something I think you should look into yourself. If it's gotten to me, it'll travel to other ears."

Several things flashed through Ed Shea's mind, several derelictions, both personal and official, but his expression never changed. He'd caught the tension all during the lunch. There had been a few empty, blank, silent moments and there had been something just behind Brian's quick wisecracking and easy bantering talk. He dropped his hand over the ashtray and carefully, lovingly tipped the white ash off his cigar.

"Okay, Brian, if I should hear something, suppose you tell me."

"It's gotten to me that there is a pad flourishing in your

467

division. Widespread. Wide open. I think the best way would be for you to look into it directly."

Ed Shea narrowed his eyes against the acrid smoke of the thin cigar and studied Brian O'Malley for a moment, then he moved his head just slightly, a fraction of an inch. "Thanks, Bri," he said quietly, and in the silence it was difficult for each of the two friends to know what the other was thinking. "Well, that was a hell of a good feed," Ed Shea said somewhat boisterously as he stood up, extended his hand. "That's one I owe you, kid."

"We gotta keep in touch, Ed, gotta do this more often."

"Right, kid, you bet."

Johnnie Morrison felt a long rivulet of sweat down the side of his temple and he casually wiped it away with the palm of his hand. He was glad it was dark; Pete might have noticed that he was sweating. It was the only outward sign of anything. Hell, it was *the* only sign. Inside, Johnnie was as calm as he'd ever felt in his life; more than calm. He felt almost peculiar, at peace, happy, on top of everything in the whole world. He didn't even wonder how he could feel this way, just accepted it and went with it. Just the damn sweat, on his lip, down his face, along his body. Well, the hell with it.

"I wanna check that Macy's warehouse over on Tenth Avenue and Thirty-sixth Street," Johnnie said quietly. "Uniform guy told me that there was an attempted bust-in last night. You'd be surprised how stupid some of these guys are; they don't score one night, they come back right away. They figure you won't figure they'd do that."

Pete Caputo made a left turn, drove toward Tenth Avenue. He was as tense as Morrison was calm. There was something wrong; he'd known it for days. Nothing had changed, nothing he could put his finger on, yet he knew instinctively that something was very wrong. He'd seen something in Morrison's expression one night, a quick, studying, calculating glance, then he'd looked away, as though he'd been caught at something shameful. He never said anything, never indicated anything; just *something* was wrong.

He'd had the feeling he'd been followed for nearly a week now but he wouldn't let himself give in to that. That was too crazy. He'd been careful of his visits to Karen Day; he'd met her in coffeehouses and at her apartment. He was sure she was convinced he was telling the truth. She'd said she'd been talking to her producers about making some equipment available: vans with cameras and really good audio equipment. He'd promised to wear a wire because he knew she'd do what the D.A. couldn't or wouldn't do: get the bastards at the top.

As they drove up Tenth, Johnnie Morrison hummed softly to himself, then whistled a tuneless continuation of his song. Suddenly, he grabbed Pete's arm, pointed across 31st Street toward the waterfront.

"Did you see that guy?"

Pete shook his head. He'd been staring at the long line of traffic lights along the empty middle-of-the-night street.

"Keep cruising, keep cruising. Christ, if that's who I think it is, this is perfect."

"What? What's perfect?"

Johnnie Morrison bit his lip, shook his head. "Look, go up two blocks, circle back and then we'll come up on him. Hit the left side of the street."

"But who is the guy?"

"Remember that nigger wanted out in Cleveland for killing two cops? I'd swear on a stack of Bibles that's the bastard leaning against that white convertible on the corner."

Caputo was confused; he tried to see if Morrison was serious. "But . . . Johnnie, how the hell could you tell? Did you really get that good a look at him? Gee, I don't even remember the flier. Are you sure?"

"Sure enough to want a better look. Okay, okay, slow down and pull up to the curb and cut the motor. He hasn't even seen us. He's waiting for someone. And there's nothing around here but warehouses so he's up to no good, that's for fucking sure."

They slid from the car silently, slipped into the shadows against the building. He was a tall, dark Negro, dressed in sports clothes, middle-aged, slight Afro, hands jammed into his pockets. He shifted from one foot to the other and looked up, startled, frightened, as the two men confronted him.

Johnnie Morrison held his revolver level with the man's chest.

"Hey? Hey, what is this? What is this?"

He started to pull his hands from his trouser pockets when Johnnie Morrison shot him twice, once in the heart, once in the stomach.

Pete Caputo, stunned, his revolver slack in his hand, turned to his partner. "Johnnie? Jesus Christ, Johnnie, what did you do?"

The strange warm calmness filled Johnnie Morrison, the certainty that things were going to work out just fine. He raised his left hand, pointed a second revolver at Pete Caputo's face.

"Why, buddy, I just killed the fucking nigger who killed my partner."

He fired just once. It was all that was necessary.

FORTY-ONE

Brian drank the black coffee and made a face. It had grown cold in the heavy mug on his cluttered desk. He rubbed his eyes, felt the stubble on his cheeks and chin. He moved his hand around in the top side drawer of his desk and found some shaving equipment.

Lieutenant Fitzgerald tapped lightly on the door and entered the office. His only concession to the long hours was a loosened collar and pulled-down tie.

"I have a copy of Morrison's statement, Chief. And here's a list of telephone calls that came for you while you were on the wire with Chief Pollack."

"Okay, leave them. Listen, I'm going to take a quick shave and then I've got a meeting with Chief Pollack." He scanned the messages, tucked them into the corner of his desk blotter; Karen Day had called twice. "You can tell any media people that a statement will be issued from the Chief Inspector's office this afternoon."

There was a lot of white in with the black of his tough beard and he scraped the dull razor and cursed about the poor light and the flecks of blood along his jawline. He felt seedy and needed a shower. He'd been going since he'd gotten the call from Headquarters at three-forty-five in the morning. It was past noon and all he'd had was a few cups of bad coffee and a slightly stale Danish.

Based on the initially vague facts, in his car on his way to the scene he jotted down the initial statement for the press: standard release under standard circumstances. A police officer was killed in the performance of his duty; suspect was shot and killed by the officer's partner.

It wasn't until he arrived at the scene of the killing that he knew the dead officer was Pete Caputo. Caputo's partner, Johnnie Morrison, told a simple, straightforward story. En route to check out the warehouse on 36th Street and Tenth Avenue, they spotted suspect leaning against a car on the corner of 31st Street and Tenth. Patrolman Caputo remarked that the man bore a close resemblance to one Clarence Phillips, a felon wanted in Cleveland in connection with the shooting of two police officers. They circled back, parked the car, approached the suspect, identified themselves, at which time the suspect raised a revolver, which he apparently had been holding, fired once point-blank at Patrolman Caputo, killing him instantly.

Patrolman Morrison fired his service revolver twice, killing the perpetrator.

Arthur Pollack's voice in their last conversation still puzzled him. It was as thin and drawn as fine wire. "I want you over here as soon as possible, Brian. There's something odd in all of this. Something that doesn't fit."

Arthur Pollack massaged his eyes gently with his fingertips. They were red-rimmed and his complexion was gray. He picked up the mug of tea, swallowed, shrugged. "I have a sore throat," he said, "and according to my wife tea and lemon are the next best thing to bed rest." He felt his hot forehead and sighed. "Frankly, I prefer bed rest. However. Well, Brian, here's what's come up. The 'perpetrator' has been identified as one Martin Osmond of 88 Interwood Terrace, Manhattan; age forty-eight years; born U.S.; married. *Professor of chemistry at C.C.N.Y.*" He looked up from the slip of paper which contained the information. "Brian, he was waiting to take his son home from work. The son is a college student who works two nights a week at the warehouse at Thirty-first Street and Tenth Avenue, a seven P.M. to three A.M. shift. The boy's car was stolen last week and his father didn't want him to travel by subway." Arthur touched lightly along the side of his throat and swallowed painfully. His voice was rasping and dry. "The man felt it was *dangerous* for his son to travel on public facilities, so he drove down to pick him up." Arthur spread his hands in a futile, puzzled
472

gesture. "So what in God's name have we got here, Brian? What was a man like that doing with a loaded revolver which for no reason at all he points in the face of a policeman and fires?"

Carefully, Brian asked, "You got people doing complete backgrounds on both the father and son? Chief, you know as well as I do, sometimes the most seemingly decent people can become involved in things."

Pollack held his throat, swallowed some tea, shook his head. He sounded anguished, but whether from physical pain or circumstance, Brian couldn't tell. "Brian, these were very fine people and I want to know what the hell happened last night."

Johnnie Morrison leaned back in the large leather-upholstered chair and carefully pushed his fingertips through his thick hair so that the effect was casual and ruffled.

"Tell me again, Patrolman Morrison," Chief O'Malley said. "Tell me right from the beginning. Just go over the whole thing like I never heard any of it before."

Morrison glanced at the Chief of Detectives, who nodded, then he sighed, rearranged himself more comfortably in the chair, and in a sad and patient manner, he carefully recited the events of the previous night in an emotionless monotone. There was no slightest deviation from what he had already recited over and over again.

The telephone messages piled up; Karen Day called again. His son Patrick telephoned twice. The Commissioner's office called and Brian was to attend a conference at 4 P.M.

He added the memorandums to the others, lit another cigarette and dialed quickly. Lieutenant Fitzgerald poked his head into the office but Brian waved him away and the young lieutenant backed off discreetly.

"Inspector Shea's office," a bright young voice informed him.

"Put Inspector Shea on, this is Chief O'Malley."

After a moment of background sounds, Ed's voice was in his ear, a little tight, a little forced. "Hey, Chief. Hell of a thing, this shooting, huh? What's up?"

"Ed, I want to see you. Some place where we can talk."

There was a brief silence, then Ed Shea suggested a bar on Third Avenue in the 50's.

Shea looked tired; his eyes were narrowed to slits and what showed was red and irritated. "You want a sandwich, Brian?"

Brian shook his head. "No, just coffee is fine." He waited while Ed consulted the menu and finally ordered a hamburger, which was the house specialty.

"I can't remember when, or for that matter what, I ate last," Ed said apologetically. "Jesus, it's getting a little harder to take the long hours, Brian, don't you find that?"

He closed his eyes for a moment, rubbed them delicately with his well-groomed fingers, sighed and then he became very still, his dark eyes settled now on Brian's face. "Well, what's up, buddy?"

Brian licked his lips, shook his head as though to clear it. His voice was thick from exhaustion and far too many cigarettes, yet automatically, distastefully, he lit another. It tasted bitter and gave no pleasure or comfort.

"Ed, this is a bad one. What do you know about this guy Johnnie Morrison?"

Ed Shea shrugged slightly, a fractional move of his shoulders, but the muscles around his mouth tightened. It seemed that everything about him tightened imperceptibly. Some tension seemed to emanate from him, yet was quickly covered, obliterated by his expression of concern. "What's the problem, Bri?"

Brian roughly rubbed a hand over his face, took a deep unhealthy drag on the cigarette and said hoarsely, "He's lying. His story doesn't hold water."

Ed Shea's voice was steady and calm, as though he hadn't heard what Brian had just said. He spoke softly and rationally, almost persuasively. "We've got a dead patrolman, Brian. Killed in the line of duty. And we've got a dead perpetrator, killed right on the spot by the patrolman's partner." His hand on the table turned palm upward; his dark brows rose simultaneously. "I don't see any problem."

"Ed, this guy, Martin Osmond, was a professor at C.C.N.Y. He was waiting to pick his son up from work. They're both clean, father and son. Upstanding citizens. Why the hell would he suddenly pull a gun and shoot"—Brian snapped his fingers—"just like that?"

"Lots of strange things happen, Brian," Ed Shea said reasonably. "Maybe he thought the officers were trying to hold him up. Maybe he panicked. As far as it being unlikely, Christ, kid, you and I've been around long enough to know you can't vouch for anybody. These days I'd bet ninety per cent of all black people carry one kind of weapon or another."

He leaned back courteously as the waiter put the plate of food on the table before him. He asked for ketchup and waited until it had been brought to him before he spoke again. "Being a college professor doesn't give a nigger, or anybody else, for that matter, the right to shoot a cop, Brian." He carefully seasoned the hamburger and cut it in half.

Brian crushed the cigarette and leaned forward. "Ed, the kid who got killed last night, the patrolman, Peter Caputo, came to me about a month ago and told me there was a pad operating in your division. He was pretty vehement about it."

Ed Shea bit into the hamburger and chewed carefully, then wiped his mouth. "A month ago? You only told me about it last week."

There was some vague accusation, some mild reproof that seemed inappropriate, that registered somewhere in Brian's brain. He felt himself becoming more alert, more tense than exhausted. "I handled it exactly as I would handle any other similar allegation brought to me, Ed. I put it through Internal Affairs."

"Aaron Levine?"

"He claimed the charge was unfounded. That was why I finally came to you last week, Ed. The kid was a friend of my son. I think he was telling the truth. He implicated his partner."

Ed Shea said, "But you said Aaron came up dry."

Impatiently, Brian said, "I don't know shit about Aaron Levine or what the hell kind of follow-up he did, Ed. I *do* know this kid was getting very tense lately. And now this thing last night." He rubbed the back of his neck, irrationally thought he needed a haircut. "I don't know. Too coincidental. I want to know about Johnnie Morrison."

Ed Shea put his hamburger on his plate, carefully opened

his napkin, wiped his mouth and hands. "Brian," he said quietly, "I think we ought to just let this dead police officer have his inspector's funeral. I think, in the best interests of the Department, this ought to be handled quickly and discreetly as a closed matter." He regarded the puzzled, uncomprehending expression on Brian's face, clicked his tongue, sucked out a piece of meat from between his back teeth and waited.

"Wait a minute, Ed. What the hell are you talking about?"

Ed Shea reached into his breast pocket and took out a long thin cigar, which he stripped of its cellophane wrapping. He bit the end off and lit it. He rolled it between his fingers thoughtfully for a moment and then slowly and as though picking his words with great care, he said, "Hell, Brian, let's give the kid his inspector's funeral. After all, the Department did as much for *your father*."

Brian stared incomprehensibly across the table; the words made no sense, were incohesive, as though spoken in another language by a stranger. He stared at his own hands as though to reassure himself of reality, then looked back at Ed Shea with a stupid, puzzled, almost apologetic smile, bewildered.

"Hey, Ed, hold it a minute, huh? What are we talking about?"

Ed Shea held the cigar between his thumb and forefinger, examined it for a moment, then said, "Brian, what I'm talking about is this. Let it alone. The kid is dead. The guy who killed him is dead. All the civil liberties groups in the city can scream from now to doomsday. They've got nothing. We've got the murder weapon and the only witness to what happened. It'll all die down. Now"—he turned his face politely, so as not to blow smoke in Brian's face, then turned back again with a strange, bemused expression on his face—"for the good of the Department, Brian, let it rest there. *Right there.*"

"What the fuck are you talking about, Ed?"

"Why, Brian, what I'm talking about is collection time, kid. Your turn to pay back. The Department took care of you and your family. Gave your old man the hero treatment. Let him into his grave with honor, right? Now you've got to pay your debt and see to it that no dishonor comes to the Department."

476

Brian felt as though he were the observer of some disconnected conversation between two strangers, yet he knew consciously that he was seated across the table from Ed Shea, that he was physically present, that his presence had a basis in reality even if things seemed to be dissolving into unreality, the way a movie scene loses its meaning if your mind wanders and the conversation has been very intense and intricate and clever. He was conscious of Ed Shea watching him through dark slit eyes, with a strange, unfamiliar, unpleasant smile at the corners of his mouth. He tried to find the joke, the prod, the needle, the old friendly familiarity which would enable him to shake free of the irrational yet persistent, growing apprehension that something terrible and inevitable was about to happen and he was powerless to stop it, some act of total destruction that he tried to avoid with a quick grin.

"Hey, Ed. What the hell?"

Ed Shea pursed his lips as though he was about to whistle and blew a thin acrid stream of smoke into Brian's face.

"Okay, Brian," the hard unknown voice told him, "okay, old buddy. I'm gonna tell you exactly how your old man died and how *my* old man and several others took care of you O'Malleys. And then you'll know exactly why you're going to back off on this Morrison thing."

FORTY-TWO

There were too many things for him to think about all at the same time. His mind filled and expanded with vague impressions, fleeting, half-remembered, yet strangely retained vaporous impressions: a glance turned away quickly; a secret amused smile; some sly reference beyond his comprehension. Things directed at him, yet which had bounced off him. Christ. Christ, had *everyone* known, everyone in the whole goddamn Department?

Brian held his hand over his forehead, locked his eyes, leaned his elbows on his desk. No. Just a few of them knew; just a few of them and they had passed it down the line, just in case the knowledge should one day prove useful.

He tried to visualize his father but nothing came, not form or feature or shape or essence. It was ludicrous to try to think of a thirty-nine-year-old man as your father when you were older than he'd ever been. Brian couldn't even begin to come to terms with his father, not now, not yet.

What he felt more vividly, more painfully, with a sense of the most overwhelming loss and grief, was this new concept of Ed Shea. Thirty years of friendship; beneath the warm, familiar, trusted man was someone he'd never imagined existed; someone waiting his time, garnering his knowledge, coldly and unemotionally using it to protect himself when Brian never even knew Ed Shea needed protection.

When the phone rang, Brian reached toward it instinctively, then held his hand in midair. He'd instructed Lieutenant Fitzgerald to take all calls except from the Commissioner or the Chief Inspector. He didn't want to talk to any of the many people who suddenly insisted on talking to him.

478

He didn't want to see anybody. The reporters were holding court in the outer office waiting for his latest statement. The various civil liberties and black organizations had representatives camping at his door demanding explanations. He had an appointment with the district attorney in an hour. His desk was filled with reports and requests for more reports and his head was filled with too many things he felt he just couldn't handle right now. Not here. Not now. He needed a hot shower, a couple of hours of sleep, of total, uninterrupted, uncorrupted blankness.

He needed someone he could trust completely, and suddenly he felt the raw pain of realization: the first person he thought of was Ed Shea.

He grabbed the container of coffee, drained it to the bitter granular bottom and dialed his brother's office.

Kevin's voice, tight, sharp, with that odd policeman's accusation even when answering a telephone, responded on the second ring. "Arson, Lieutenant O'Malley."

"Kev, it's me." His voice sounded strange to his own ears, hollow, false.

Kevin adjusted his tone, didn't quite conceal his surprise. "Hey, Brian, hey, how's things?" And then, to show he was aware, he added, "Hey, you guys must be busy now, huh?"

"Kevin," he said tersely, "I need a job done. Can you come over to my house tonight, about nine?"

"Why, sure, Brian. Sure. What's up?"

"We'll talk then, okay?"

"Jesus, sure, Brian."

They hadn't spoken in a long time. There was more than physical distance between them, more than the distance in rank. They were different from each other, Kevin respectfully remote and impressed by his brother. But that, at the heart of the matter, was where their connection lay; they were, after all, brothers.

At the district attorney's office, Johnnie Morrison was the calmest person present. He leaned easily into his chair, responded politely and at length. Never once did he change his original statement or contradict or in any way alter anything he'd previously said.

479

He adjusted his wide gold tie, brushed imaginary flecks of dust from the shoulder of his dark-gold-and-brown-plaid sports jacket, ran a hand lightly along the curled edges of his slightly long hair, leaned forward attentively when he didn't quite catch a question and requested that it be repeated for clarity's sake.

Brian O'Malley stood against the window sill, arms folded across his chest, and speculatively observed the cool, perfect performance. He formed a definite, sickening opinion: Johnnie Morrison was a man capable of anything.

The D.A. was young and earnest and concerned; the shootings had generated a great deal of publicity and civic interest.

He sat, one leg dangling from the corner of his desk, and said to Morrison, clearly pacing his words for the stenotypist, "Now, officer, is there anything, anything at all, that you'd like to add to your statement at this time?"

Johnnie Morrison pursed his lips, stared thoughtfully at the small diamond pinky ring on his left hand, really concentrated, then looked up and said, "No, Mr. Reeves. Everything was exactly as I told you."

"You understand that I will be going before the grand jury with this matter? You understand that you will have to appear before the grand jury?"

Morrison inclined his head slightly, and when he spoke, it seemed to Brian he was trying to reassure the young district attorney. "Yes, of course, Mr. Reeves. That's routine. Any shooting . . ." He spread his hands to indicate that this was no special matter.

It was Brian's job to be at Morrison's side as he faced the battery of reporters outside the district attorney's office. He was hardly needed. Morrison fielded questions coolly, expertly.

"I have nothing to add to what I've already told you fellows," Morrison said smoothly. "I just went through the whole thing with the D.A. and it's a matter for the grand jury now."

"Come on, Johnnie," one reporter called out with the tough, easy informality of a man impressed by no one and nothing, "how about your own personal opinion as to why this Osmond pulled a gun and shot? You must have *some* opinion."

Johnnie Morrison adjusted his shoulders; his mouth pulled down; his slate eyes narrowed. His voice went low and soft. "Listen, all I know is that my partner is going to be buried tomorrow. These days who the hell can figure out why anyone does anything?"

Brian gave a quick signal and Morrison tilted his head and indicated he had nothing more to say. He stood aside, properly, and let Brian enter the black Pontiac first, then he sat beside him and deftly pulled the door closed.

"Jeez, those guys can get on you like a dirty shirt, can't they, Chief? Man, I'm really beat." He didn't look it and he didn't sound it.

Brian lit a cigarette and blew out the match with his first exhalation of smoke. "What kind of cop was he?" he asked without preliminaries.

"Cop? Oh, you mean Pete Caputo." Morrison played with his pinky ring for a minute, then looked up, his expression sincere and confiding. "He was a good enough kid, Chief, but he shouldn't have gotten shot, if that's what you mean. I wouldn't say this to anyone else, but hell, the kid's reaction was too slow, like he froze when he saw the nigger's gun." Johnnie Morrison shook his head and added, "He lacked that basic instinct to survive, if you know what I mean."

"But you've got that basic instinct, right, Morrison? To survive?"

Johnnie Morrison nodded slowly and said thoughtfully, "Oh, I'm a survivor, Chief. Yeah, I'm what you'd call a survivor."

Mary Ellen waited for him at the door; she must have seen him drive up the circular driveway. It was obvious she had something to say, something immediate, something that couldn't wait. Just like everybody else today.

"Brian . . ." She spoke as though fearful of being overheard in her own home.

"Mary Ellen, look, could it wait a while? Christ, I need a shower."

"Brian, Patrick is here," she whispered, and as she spoke, their son came from the study, stood in the doorway for a moment, then turned away without greeting his father.

It was funny. It struck Brian that it was as though *he* was

481

being summoned into the study by his son. He remembered, years ago, doing exactly that, standing there to make it clear that Patrick was to present himself, then turning, wordless, assured Patrick would do what was expected of him.

"He seems very upset, Brian," Mary Ellen said unnecessarily. "He wouldn't eat anything and he's hardly spoken."

"Okay," Brian told her. She stood there in the large hallway, ghost of her mother, ghost of her past, waiting to be told what to do, to be reassured, her large eyes dependent and clinging.

"Go and make some coffee," he said. He reached out, squeezed her shoulder once and nodded and it was all she needed to lift the burden of confused concern. It was in Brian's hands; it was between the men of her family and she would just keep out of the way.

Patrick stood facing the huge fireplace, staring at the huge log which had been set in place for years because it was just the right size, not for burning but for show. His hands were jammed in his pockets; his shoulders were hunched forward. He wore Levi's and a blue work shirt and his thick blond hair curled over the collar, and when he turned, Brian noted that his sideburns were down along his cheeks nearly to his jaw.

Patrick's face had a thin, gaunt quality, revealed and vulnerable, as though the cool, confident mask had been ripped bluntly to expose the raw pain.

"Pat," Brian said quietly, "I'm sorry about your friend Pete. It was a hell of a rough break."

The gray eyes had the pale, hard, translucent quality of crystal and they impaled him with accusation. His son's voice was a thin, hard stretch of bitter emotion and certainty. "*He was murdered.*"

The accusation didn't have to be clarified; they both knew he meant by Morrison.

Brian poured Scotch, too much of it, into a wide short glass, swallowed it down, felt it hit his stomach then rise to his face. He shook his head slightly as the alcohol jolted him, then he turned to his son. They were the same height; Brian always thought his son was smaller than himself but they were eye level now.

"There's one thing I want to know," Patrick said. His shoulders hunched forward as though that movement, that

482

tightening, held his body together. "Is it going to be *your* job to keep the whole thing under wraps for the Department? Is that what the Deputy Chief Inspector in Charge of Public Affairs does, protects the *Department*, no matter what the hell the truth is?"

Brian rubbed his eyes; Christ, they ached. His throat ached and his head ached. Every part of him ached and his son, an extension of himself, pain-filled, confronted him, accused him. There was so much he wanted to tell him, but it had its beginnings too far back and there was no end anywhere in sight.

He said simply, "The matter is being investigated, Pat."

"Jesus," Patrick said in a tone of wonder. He took his hands from his pockets, placed them low on his narrow hips, shook his head. "Jesus, you sound like you're talking to some dumb-ass reporter. 'The matter is being investigated.'" His laugh was short and bitter. "Jesus jumping Christ, Dad, this is *me* you're talking to, okay? Petey was murdered. And so was that other man, that poor son of a bitch who just happened to be in the wrong place at the wrong time and it just happened to work out to Morrison's advantage and he's going to get away with two murders to protect the whole goddamn corruption that Pete was trying to expose. 'The matter is being investigated.' Nice. Neat. Really neat."

His son's righteousness angered him more than his innocence, which assumed that wrongs could be righted by simple methods.

"Patrick," he said tensely, "*grow up.* For the love of God, grow up. There isn't a fucking thing that could be proved. Accusations are cheap and easy—"

"Did you think Pete's accusations were cheap and easy, Dad?"

"I thought they had some validity and—"

"And you sat on them, right?"

For one quick moment he wanted to justify himself, to defend himself to his son, but the need passed, left him drained and sickened; he couldn't try to defend and explain himself as though he were a stranger. There were too many lifelong strangers confronting him: friends and ghosts and now his son. He clenched his teeth and turned back to the bottle, not wanting it, just automatically pouring the amber liquid into the stubby glass.

"What I really came by for was to give you something, Dad." He turned and Patrick held his silver patrolman's shield in his right hand, extended it. "End of a family tradition. From grandfather to father to son and right back to you." For one brief moment, Patrick's voice went low and sad and a little self-mocking. "The dumb thing is, I really liked being a cop. I didn't realize it. I just went on the job because it was just assumed I would, but for a time, in some ways, I *liked* being a cop." He shook his head abruptly and his voice tightened. "But now, hell, I'm gonna lean back and watch how you real professionals handle things. You'll handle the publicity and the committee hearings and the grand jury investigations and everything else, and by the time you're finished with it, the dead black professor will probably end up the leader of an underground movement to kill all cops caught on the street at three A.M. And Johnnie Morrison will probably make second grade and you'll keep the Department under wraps."

When Brian didn't reach for the shield, Patrick tossed it on the table beside the decanter and said in a soft, mocking voice, "Should I skip the traditional, or should I tell you to shove it up your ass?"

He hit Patrick across the mouth with the back of his hand, not hard, not even unexpectedly. Patrick nodded as though they had completed a transaction, sealed a bargain, brought things to an inevitable conclusion, then he turned and Brian heard him exchange a few quick soft words with his mother before he left the house.

Kevin O'Malley's light-blue eyes searched his brother's face furtively, as though to find secrets which were always denied to him. He was always tense and eager around Brian and the damn gnawing ulcer bit into his gut like a rodent. He tried not to gulp the drink down straight, first because he didn't want Brian to see how badly he needed it and secondly because it went straight to the raw spot in his duodenum.

Brian didn't waste any time on small talk; there was no family stuff, no how are the kids, or have you been in touch with Mom lately. He just led Kevin into the massive room,

484

poured out the drinks, gestured his brother into a chair, sat opposite him, leaned close and said in a thick, strange voice, "I need a job done."

"Jesus, Brian, anything. Name it and you got it."

It was the first time Brian had ever come to him. There had been times, over the years, when he had had to come to Brian, when Brian had bailed him out, smoothed things over, covered things up. Kevin O'Malley was a good cop, one of the Department's best investigators, which surprised even himself; he had a depth of patient perseverance which made him one of the most effective arson detectives in the history of the Department. But that hadn't always been his strong point; in the early days, the unmellow years, Kevin O'Malley's reputation was built on his hair-trigger temper, his quick, impulsive, physical reaction to a situation. Through the years, it had earned him both commendations and reprimands. Once or twice, without Brian's intervention, it might have gotten him into serious legal difficulties.

It had been a long time since Kevin O'Malley had gotten out of line but he was always slightly awed by his brother's position in the Department. He finally gave in to the impulse, downed the Scotch, noted then how bad his brother looked: Christ, like an all-night drunk, his eyes shot to hell, his hand trembling.

Finally, Brian said, "Kevin, I want to get a guy. I want to get him really good, all boxed in."

Kevin's mind raced wildly, could latch on nowhere; they were too far removed from each other's experience, no one came to mind, nothing. He pressed the glass tightly into the palm of his hands and waited.

"This guy Johnnie Morrison."

Kevin bit his lip, narrowed his eyes thoughtfully. "Guy involved in the shooting last night? Guy that killed the nigger that killed his partner?"

"What I want you to do," Brian said without explanation, "is to find someone who will swear on his mother's grave that the gun that killed Morrison's partner was his. That Johnnie Morrison took it off him for a throwaway."

Kevin let his breath out softly between his parted teeth in a whistling sound. He turned the words over in his quick, agile brain. There was nothing incomprehensible, nothing outside the realm of possibility; in twenty-two years, he'd seen it all, knew anything could happen; knew that Brian must have his reasons.

He couldn't resist asking, "You going after this Morrison for murder?"

Brian shook his head and held his hand up. "Don't worry about it. You just get me some mother-fucking pusher who's got a score to settle with Johnnie Morrison. That's all I want from you. Make sure he's good. I got special plans for Johnnie Morrison and the less you know about it the better."

Kevin considered the cold, hard, evaluating glaze of his brother's eyes and nodded once. He pressed his hand against his burning side, then offered it to Brian for a hard, quick shake. "Count on me, Bri."

"I *am* counting on you, Kevin."

He watched himself on the late news; watched and listened dispassionately to the smoothly professional way he avoided direct answers to very direct and probing questions. He dozed for a while, heard Mary Ellen beside him in the bed move, reach for the control switch.

"Shall I turn the TV off, Brian? I thought you fell asleep."

"No. No, leave it on for a while. I'll sleep in a while."

She turned, curled beside him, went back to sleep instantly, the way a child does. He adjusted his pillow so that he had a better view of the TV set. His mind drifted, filled with too many thoughts to focus on anything, and then he heard her clear, crisp, professional voice.

"Good evening. This is Karen Day." Pause, dramatic effect; catch their attention. She'd explained it all to him; whatever he'd thought natural was contrived. There was nothing—no pause, no inflection, no gesture, no expression—that wasn't carefully planned. End of pause, announcement: "And this . . . is your city." Pan on New York; music carrying up and down city streets, through crowds of people, past buildings; the whole spectrum of introduction.

She seemed more vivid on color television than in life. Her lips were redder, fuller; her hair was blacker; her eyes shone with reflected lights and some special eye drops she used to

486

gain just that effect. She faced the viewer directly, unwaveringly. He recognized the red blouse over which she'd knotted a red-white-and-blue scarf with casual elegance. It was flipped over one shoulder; just the right touch.

"I have no guest on my show tonight," Karen Day said carefully, her voice filled with portent. "The guest who was supposed to appear with me tonight is dead. He was killed last night. He was a policeman. His name was Peter Caputo, and according to the New York City Police Department, Patrolman Peter Caputo was killed in the line of duty. Heroically. And so he will be given an inspector's funeral, which is the way the Police Department pays final respects to its heroes. And he *was* a hero. I don't know about what happened last night, but however he died, Peter Caputo was a real hero in the way he lived." Her long hand fondled a lock of hair, shoved it from her face. "Patrolman Caputo was coming to this show to reveal corruption within the Department he served so well."

Brian felt an electric shock wave jolt the length of his body, then surge full force into his brain. Jesus Christ Almighty. Two things, separately, hit him: First, Caputo had gone to her, was planning to take his charges into the public arena; second, she was *using it.*

He could hardly distinguish her words anymore; it was hardly necessary. The impact was what overwhelmed him; she was doing it, really doing it.

". . . I had spoken to Peter Caputo several times before he convinced me that he was indeed aware of a fantastic amount of corruption within the Department and that . . ."

He watched her mouth, was fascinated by the false electronic mouth. He caught a glimpse of white teeth, was aware of the familiar gesture when she flicked the edge of her scarf between long, slender fingers. He was fascinated by the strangeness of her long, lovely, familiar face; he thought of her long and elegant body, which had been so giving and had so delighted in taking. He watched her as though she was part of a remote dream which never had been part of his reality. Karen.

". . . and so the New York City Police Department and its highest-ranking officers will have a lot of investigating and a

487

lot of explaining to do before we can be satisfied that we have been given the true story of the deaths of Patrolman Peter Caputo and of Professor Martin Osmond."

The telephone rang even before she signed off the air. He hit the remote control, watched Karen get swallowed into a tiny white circle and disappear.

Arthur Pollack in his thin, sore voice said, "Brian, I just watched the Karen Day show. What the hell is going on?"

He hunched over the match, inhaled quickly before he answered. "Arthur, will you give me about two days?" Then, suddenly and totally aware of the urgent need he felt, the need to take things into hand, to get things under *his* control, he said with undisguised passion, "Arthur, will you *trust* me for a couple of days?"

"Brian, Brian. I'd trust you forever, but I'm being kept in the dark about too many things and that I don't like. The Commissioner's probably trying to get me right now and I wanted to talk first to you and then to Aaron Levine before the Man reaches me."

"Arthur," Brian said carefully, "*don't* call Levine."

There was a silence and Brian could picture the worried face, gray, thin; turned-in eyes seeking answers. He heard a long deep sigh, filled almost with a shudder, as though Arthur had been punched in the stomach while in the act of exhaling.

"Brian," Arthur Pollack said finally, "for God's sake, don't leave me stranded."

"I won't, Chief," Brian said. And meant it.

It was three-thirty in the morning and he let his gaze wander over the dimly lit room: the old man's room. It was odd but that was the way Brian always thought of the study. Patrick Crowley owned the room, filled it with his presence even though he'd been dead for nearly twenty years.

Brian nodded as though in final acknowledgment and admiration. The shrewd old son of a bitch had been right; he'd always known the score, the way to get things done. Any goddamn way that would work and that was the only criterion.

There had been, throughout his career, great advantages in being Patrick Crowley's son-in-law but Brian never doubted that most of his accomplishments were his own. He knew

488

who he was and what he was capable of; Crowley provided the opportunities but he'd always come through on his own efforts. And he'd paid a price too. Being Patrick Crowley's son-in-law.

Mary Ellen Crowley, his beautiful doll-like wife, had felt dishonored by the act of sex from the very beginning. More, worse, she felt that she dishonored God. Night after night, she had steeled herself against what she considered an act of sacrilege. Christ, it had been hard. The tears, the actual physical revulsion she'd felt. The clenching of her small fists, rigid at her sides; the final agonized and agonizing *submission*. He'd tried. He'd really tried, but something indelible had been engraved on her very bones. Her real avocation had been the terrible Crowley-daughter tradition of virgin nunhood.

During the years of their wartime separation, he'd tested himself on more women than he could remember, had felt his manhood assert and reassert itself as something more than animalistic and shameful and repulsive. Yet, on his return, it was to Mary Ellen, no more mature, no more willing or understanding; only more willingly submissive and suffering in silence and totally, ignorantly, hopelessly unaware of the massive insult her submission caused her husband.

They worked it out through the years of their marriage. She submitted with some slightly better grace; he made fewer and fewer sexual demands on her as he found other women more and more accessible.

His son, Patrick, resulted from what was nearly an act of rape, a passion of anger and despair and self-hatred and hatred for her for making him feel ashamed of his natural lust.

He wondered, sometimes, what the old man knew or suspected. It wasn't an area ever to be discussed or approached. The old man seemed satisfied with life when his grandson was born; he made out a will with Patrick Brian O'Malley as his sole heir but his worldly possessions amounted to a few small properties. His heir would never inherit his true wealth: power and the knowledge of how to garner that power and use it.

That had been Brian's inheritance: "Take care of yourself

489

at all times, Brian," the old man had counseled. "Make sure you always have the upper hand because, for the love of God, you never know."

Brian thought about Ed Shea and felt the pain of loss, the emptiness of sudden, unanticipated death. They'd grown in the job together; they'd been friends for all these years and it was incomprehensible to him that he'd never known Ed Shea beyond the surface of his skin.

Tomorrow, he'd confront Ed Shea and force him out of the Department. He'd had the evidence for more than ten years. It was funny, odd, strange, cold-blooded, the way he'd remembered the old man's words, and without any thought process at all, he'd gotten the upper hand on Ed without Ed ever knowing about it and without feeling the slightest qualm. Brian considered quietly that the reason he hadn't experienced any guilt was that he'd never envisioned himself ever, for any reason, under any circumstance, using what he had on Ed, so that made the having excusable.

Ed Shea took two examinations for the rank of captain in the New York City Police Department. Many men took the examination more than once and there was nothing wrong with that in and of itself. What was wrong, in Ed Shea's case, was that he took two examinations at the same time. The first, the official examination paper, was graded a failure and certain measures were taken, secret, illegal measures, and Ed Shea was given a second paper to fill out with the help of some textbooks and some good advice. This second paper, which received a very high score, was then substituted for the original, failing paper.

Brian O'Malley had photostatic copies of both of these examination papers. He had come into possession of them through a lifetime of careful placing of loyalties and favors and accumulated knowledge of the actions of certain strategically placed people who were glad to advise him of certain potentially useful situations.

Brian's eyes closed but he knew he wouldn't be able to sleep anymore this night. Reluctantly, inevitably, finally, he thought of his father. Buried for a hero, killed by a whore. Unmanned by a whore.

The Department had closed ranks, protected his father and

490

his mother and himself and his brothers and sisters and all of his family. It was an action to be expected. Take care of your own because, Christ knows, nobody else will. And because they had all been men too and the thought had always been close to the surface: There but for the grace of God. For all of its collective faults, Brian O'Malley loved the Department as much as he loved his family. He would protect the Department as much as he could, in any way he could, but he would also clean it up as best he could. In any way he could.

He leaned his aching head back against the chair and thought of all the things he had to do, all the people he had to get, all the wheeling and dealing he had to accomplish.

Christ, wouldn't it be great if he could bring it all out into the open, call a murderer a murderer and a thief a thief and a betrayer a betrayer? All clean and open, the way his son thought it should be. But Brian knew that nothing could be accomplished that way. Absolutely nothing.

He felt the waves of exhaustion across his forehead and way deep along the crown of his skull, and when he exhaled, a sound very much like a sob came from Brian's throat, or deeper, from his chest. The sound surprised him, seemed to drain and empty him.

And then he filled with a strange, calm sense of wonder at his lack of anger. All the years of his youth, he'd been trying to live up to an image of a man who never even existed, had been a myth, a fiction. There was something comforting in finally knowing that his father had been an imperfect human being like everyone else. Just before drifting into a deep, short, dreamless sleep, he wished that his son could accept him for what he was too.

FORTY-THREE

It took Kevin O'Malley less than twenty-four careful discreet hours to come up with Juan Jesus Rodriguez. He noted in the arrest record that Rodriguez was due for sentencing on Morrison's arrest within three weeks. An additional, heavier narcotics rap in the interim could send the bum away for fifteen to twenty years.

Kevin located his man without much difficulty. They were creatures of habit, this breed. They hung out in certain locations, they didn't wander too far, stayed where they felt familiar and reasonably safe, among their own kind. At 2 A.M., Kevin took him in the hallway of the tenement where Rodriguez lived. Startled, the slightly built man thought at first that he was being mugged. He threw his hands into the air, swallowed a cry of fright with a gasp, offered himself without resistance as though to purchase mercy.

Then, in the dimness, his small, shrewd dart eyes saw Kevin O'Malley's policeman face, recognized with certain hard knowledge that he was once again in the hands of the police and he was literally terrified of what this unknown one might want of him.

Johnnie Morrison, impeccably dressed in a navy blazer with brass buttons, expensive turtle-neck sweater, dark-gray slacks, carefully flicked a speck of dust from his sleeve and by his every studied gesture showed distaste for his surroundings. He was deliberate about showing absolutely nothing else; not apprehension, not even curiosity, just calm, respectful if somewhat disdainful interest in whatever it was that Deputy Chief Inspector Brian O'Malley was up to.

492

Morrison received the telephone call in the middle of a deep and erotic dream and he regretted the interruption. The Chief said abruptly and without explanation that he was to come to this location, a dingy dump of a trucking office on the West Side. The Chief specified he was to arrive within thirty-five minutes and Johnnie Morrison, always careful, made it on time.

The legend on the dirty glass door spelled out "The A-OK Trucking Corporation" and Morrison hadn't the slightest idea who the hell the office belonged to but it was immediately clear to him that the location was selected because it afforded the utmost privacy and whatever was going to pass between them required this kind of setting.

Morrison ducked his head forward over his lighter, blew out smoke from the back of his throat and looked up sharply as two men came from the inner office.

Kevin O'Malley had a discreet but definite grip on Juan Jesus Rodriguez and he helped him to step rapidly into the room and to confront Johnnie Morrison.

"This the man?" Kevin asked tersely. Apparently, he applied some greater physical pressure on the man, for there was a gasp and Kevin said louder, "I didn't hear you. Talk."

"Yes, yes, sí, yes, that's the man," Rodriguez said quickly.

Deputy Chief Inspector Brian O'Malley turned from his perch on the corner of the cluttered, battered old desk. "This is the man who *what?*" he asked. "Spell it out."

Juan's voice was dry and his tongue clacked but he spoke quickly and clearly with the weight of a pound of pure heroin held over him. "This here is the man who arrested me last month. And took my gun away from me."

Brian's eyes moved to Morrison, fixed on Morrison, caught the uncontrolled paling, the tension, the doomed awareness of what was being done to him. He spoke to Rodriguez but looked steadily at Morrison. "Tell me the make and caliber of the gun this officer took away from you when he arrested you for possession of narcotics. Tell me the registration number."

Rodriguez reeled off the make, the caliber and the serial number.

"You ready to testify to this in court?"

Kevin moved suddenly and Rodriguez' head bobbed up and down. "Yeah, okay, sure, yeah, Christ, you break my arm there."

Brian jerked his head and Kevin took Rodriguez from the room.

Johnnie Morrison's lips barely moved as he said, "That fucking little shit."

Brian said coldly, "That fucking little shit can connect you to a double murder, Morrison."

Slowly, Johnnie Morrison inhaled, exhaled, studied the smoke before his eyes, fingered the diamond ring on his pinky carefully, then looked up at Chief O'Malley and shrugged slightly. It was a gesture of acceptance, nonchalant, an almost elegant acknowledgment of his predicament. It was a mild salute, one operator to the other. He turned his situation over in his mind, examined it minutely, quickly, expertly for possibilities. In spite of the heavy, thick, lumpish roiling of his intestines, he felt reasonably calm. He knew that something could be salvaged, some bargain struck. Hell, that was why they were meeting in this shithouse of an office instead of at the district attorney's.

He turned his candid slate eyes on Brian, held his hands palms up, questioningly.

"Okay, Chief. What is it you want?"

"We're going to do some house cleaning, Morrison," Brian said.

Aaron Levine took off his uniform jacket and hung it on the rack in his office. The collar left marks along his throat; it had always been just a bit too tight and he had felt slightly choked all through the funeral service, but he had stood at military attention along with the others and was, as always, impressed by the precision and impact of the ritual.

There was so much work to do that he didn't know where to begin. The mayor had acted swiftly in response to the television allegations of widespread corruption. He appointed an interim committee with which Aaron would have to work. He'd tried to speak to Ed Shea, to ask Ed what the story was, but Ed had avoided him at the funeral service. In fact, he'd looked sick. Aaron thought back to Brian O'Malley's request

494

that he look into allegations of a pad in Caputo's division. He'd turned it over to Ed Shea directly because Aaron learned a long time ago that there were certain people you let handle things for themselves; they leave you alone, you leave them alone. Now, for the first time, he wondered, without much emotion, if Ed Shea had been on the take.

It used to be a patrolman would shake a shopkeeper down for five, four of which was passed on to the sergeant and distributed from his hand up. Okay, hell, the shopkeeper got an extra bit of protection, an extra presence. Usually they didn't complain about it; it was like death and taxes, inevitable. But this whole ritualized thing that was being alleged on TV and in the newspapers and on the radio, it could split the Department wide open. Aaron Levine, for one, did not particularly care one way or the other. His main goal had been to just stay in place long enough to get out at three-quarter pay. He'd never touched a dirty dollar, did his best to stop it when he could, either through direct action or a word to the wise. Like a word to Ed Shea. And if Ed Shea was someone wise, God, Aaron couldn't understand a man like that. And this whole thing with the young patrolman they buried today, Peter Caputo. How his death could be caught up in this whole corruption allegation was beyond Aaron.

The buzzer interrupted his thoughts and he depressed the button on the intercom. A nervous patrolman's voice advised him, "Chief O'Malley is here to see you, sir."

"Oh, yes. Yes, send him in."

Aaron stood up to greet Brian O'Malley, who pointedly ignored his outstretched hand. Aaron immediately felt guilty of some terrible offense, some mistake in some unknown code. God, these hard Irish faces; no matter where he encountered them, under what circumstances, they made him feel an intruder.

Wordlessly, O'Malley took a large manila envelope from beneath his arm, opened it, withdrew some lined legal papers which were covered with small neat words: entries, listings. He dropped the sheets to Aaron's desk.

"What is this, Chief O'Malley? This something for the meeting we have with Chief Pollack this afternoon?"

O'Malley dropped into the chair in front of Aaron's desk,

leaned back, pressed the sole of one shoe on the edge of Aaron's desk. His face had a frozen, waiting expression, tight and expectant.

Aaron just glanced at the first page, skimmed the second, knew immediately what it was: a complete record of Aaron Levine's career in the New York City Police Department. A line-for-line report of where he was assigned, what tour of duty, what scheduled hours of work, and aligned with that information was a complete rundown of the time, days, hours that Aaron Levine spent in various institutions of higher learning. During working hours, on city-paid time, in violation of not only departmental regulations but in the commission of fraud involving enough money to be classified a felony.

Aaron sat down behind his cluttered desk. His hands moved restlessly over the papers; stupid questions filled his head relative to how this information had been put together so precisely. How could *they* always manage to compile things when he found it so difficult? What did any of this have to do with him, now, at this time, at this point, after all these years?

Finally, O'Malley pressed with the sole of his foot and the heavy desk moved just slightly, just an inch or so, but enough to make Aaron look up.

"Put your papers in, Levine," O'Malley said quietly. "Get going on it today. Advise Chief Pollack you're retiring at the meeting today."

Aaron spread his hands over the record of his life. Why at this particular point? His mouth opened, but there were too many questions and not enough protestations. O'Malley's eyes were dark and cold. He rubbed his thumb under his lower lip for a moment, considered Levine, seemed to be giving great thought to something, then finally said, "I really don't believe you know what the fuck has been going on. I really think you've been nothing but a goddamn patsy but the shit is going to hit the fan and my job is to keep it from flying too far. We're all going to have to testify before the mayor's commission, Levine. Now if all you want to be accused of is extreme incompetence"—he jutted his chin toward the documentation of Aaron Levine's double life—"you get your papers in. I don't care what the fuck you tell Chief Pollack. Tell him you feel you've let the Department down by not

496

being on top of this whole pad deal. Tell him you got an ulcer or a sudden urge for country living or whatever the hell else. But get your papers in today."

Aaron nodded. He watched Brian O'Malley shove himself back from the desk, stand up, shake his head with an expression of disgust and leave the office. Aaron sat at his desk, the work piled up, the demand for reports from the Chief Inspector and the Commissioner and the demands for explanations.

Thirty-three years and he sat surrounded by his own ignorance, finally beaten by them. An odd thought struck Aaron: It was the father, Brian O'Malley, who had made it all possible for him. It was the son, Brian O'Malley, who brought it all to an end.

Brian felt absolutely nothing toward Aaron Levine; for some strange reason, intuition maybe, he believed that Levine knew nothing at all about the corruption within the Department. He didn't even feel anger at Levine's total incompetence, just a vague, hollow sense of disgust.

He caught sight of Ed Shea before Ed was aware of his arrival at the small, intimate Third Avenue spot they'd agreed upon. He watched Ed down the shot, hold his head still for a moment, then react with just a slight, barely discernible shudder. Brian turned toward the bar, held up two fingers, V sign, nodded toward the booth in the rear where Ed sat.

Ed looked up, face neutral, but his eyes gave him away; there was a searching, questioning, puzzled intensity, as though if they remained wordless and if he studied Brian thoroughly, he would find the answers to all the terrible questions he would rather not frame.

The waiter brought the drinks and Ed seemed somewhat surprised, reacted slightly, then tilted his toward Brian, went carefully on this one, needing to keep clearheaded.

"Well, Bri," Ed Shea said, "I'm here."

Brian searched for Ed Shea, for thirty years of friendship, but he was a stranger, curious, expectant, uncertain. Brian rubbed his hand roughly over his eyes, felt the weary exhaustion of too much betrayal, too much realization. He hoped Ed would make it easy for both of them; Christ, it was little enough to hope for at this point.

497

Brian grasped the tall, cool glass within his palm, studied it for a moment, finally raised his eyes to meet Ed's. Softly, he said, "Throw your papers in, Ed. Today."

That small shudder, as though he'd just downed a powerful shot of raw liquor, uncontrolled, barely noticeable, except that Brian noticed it, took Ed Shea for a second; then he sloughed it off, adjusted his handsome mask, pulled the tight smile, showed the good white teeth, head held to one side, flushed face almost relaxed because he was a pretty good actor.

"Now why would I do that, Brian?" he asked lightly, as though this was all part of banter, a continuation of years of insult, playful banter between friends who knew and could penetrate each other with the confidence of knowledge.

Brian wanted to do two things simultaneously. He wanted to rise from his seat opposite Ed, to strike out at him, to batter his face to pulp, to physically, powerfully, personally destroy him; and he also wanted to throw an arm over Ed Shea's shoulder, clasp him, tell him, "Christ, what a stupid mistake I almost made."

He did neither; didn't move; instead forced himself to become pure policeman, observing the slightest giveaway sign, capable of penetrating, noting, calculating, evaluating the slightest gesture, blink of eyes, movement of fingers, twitch of lips. Coldly, impersonally alert for the reaction, Brian O'Malley said, "We got Johnnie Morrison." There was no reaction, none whatever. "We got him so cold that he is waiving immunity and is willing to testify before the grand jury. It's going to be one hell of a circus, with all the publicity and committees, but it's going to be done the only way we can still at least salvage something, Ed. He's going to detail the whole pad operation. All the way to the top of the heap."

Nothing showed except some slightly relaxed breathing, which confirmed what Brian had somehow anticipated, that Ed Shea had been smart enough, clever enough, careful enough, corrupt enough to keep himself so far removed from the actual operation that when and if it ever hit the fan, he couldn't be touched.

Ed moved his head slightly to one side, shrugged. "I'm sure you'll do the best job for the Department that can be done, Brian."

"I'm doing the best job I can, Ed." He stood up slightly,

498

enough so that he had access to his rear trouser pocket, removed an envelope, sat down again. He held the envelope between his two hands for a moment, as though the act of holding it might somehow negate the contents. He felt an actual physical reluctance until he again confronted the man across the table from him. He tossed the envelope to Ed Shea.

"These are photostats, Ed. The original and other photostats are in safekeeping." Brian pulled himself from the booth and gave in to the deep savage urge to strike out. He grasped Ed Shea by the lapels of his suit jacket, leaned close enough to inhale the odor of fear, clenched his hands tightly enough to hold back the violence that pounded through his chest and head and arms. "You put in your fucking papers by this afternoon or so help me God, if I have to lie from here to next Christmas to do it, I'll box you in on the murder of that poor sonuvabitch Caputo."

He didn't use the key. After all this time, he pressed his finger on the small black brass-encircled buzzer and listened as the chimes echoed throughout the apartment, softly, melodiously, insistently. He stared straight at the small round mirror, caught the slight change in its consistency as she peered at him before opening the door.

She was more beautiful than he had ever seen her: sleek, scrubbed, dark hair pulled back from her face casually with a clip. She'd been doing exercises and she wore a dancer's leotard and tights. She was one long sinuous lean tight fine-boned vision of perfection.

"Brian? Why did you ring the bell?"

He leaned heavily against the door and felt his age and his weariness and his deep regret as he looked at her. She was so lovely. Finally, he reached into his jacket pocket, fingered the key he had detached from the others, then gently took her right hand and put the key in her palm and closed her hand within his with a gentle pressure.

Karen whirled from him, tossed the key furiously to the floor.

"Goddamn it to hell, Brian, come on! You can't be this childish. You absolutely cannot be this stupid damn childish. It has nothing to do with you and me."

All the way to her apartment, in the taxicab, he thought of

what he would say to her but all of it was pointless. None of it would penetrate; none of it would be comprehensible to her.

Basically, he finally decided, it was the difference between them, between their time. Her world was right now, this minute, the quick and flashing sensation devoid of sentimentality or ties of any kind. She was riding the crest of her own career; singlehandedly, she had caused the explosive public scandal, she had accomplished the great coup. Her producers would take her more seriously now, would give her better time slots, more operating expenses.

Her public outrage, night after night, had been really good: controlled, righteous, determined. But beneath the performance, Brian knew there was a total, cold lack of concern. The whole area of police corruption was something that would play itself out and she'd move to whatever was more timely, more exotic; on to the next great story.

There was no more connection between them; it had always been tenuous and based on their differences rather than their similarities. They had amused and puzzled and delighted each other and through each other themselves. But it was the basic difference now which separated them: her insistence that nothing between them had changed, that they could remain aloof and remote and apart from something that really meant nothing to her and that was in the process of destroying a part of him.

"Why don't you at least *say* something, for Christ's sake? Don't stand there looking so . . . so . . . God Almighty, you *knew* I was after the story. That Caputo boy came to me because your people failed him. I handled it the way I *had* to handle it, Brian."

She stopped speaking abruptly, held her long hands behind her neck, stared down for a moment, closed her eyes, raised her face to him.

"There's no way to keep it under wraps, Brian. I've been served with a subpoena from the grand jury. God, I've been interviewed by two assistant district attorneys and some people from the mayor's committee have been calling. Bri, they've given me an hour, prime Sunday-afternoon talk-show time, this week. Work with me." The idea suddenly encompassed her. "You could come off looking good, get the Commissioner to come on the show. Brian, it doesn't have to all fall apart. You could be instrumental in salvaging something if you'd work with me."

He knew exactly which part of her was real, which part performance. He was oddly touched at the slight edge of panic which crept into her voice at his failure to respond. That was real. He watched and knew exactly when the realization came to her that she wasn't going to have it her way. That in gaining whatever she felt she had gained professionally, she'd lost something too.

She came to him, anger and panic exposed; she pulled his head down, forced her lips on his as though this was the answer to everything, this was what put them in a separate existence, apart, could maintain them and keep them untouched.

He responded because her mouth was familiar, had been part of him for two years, and because he was tired and drained and emptied and in need of safety. She pressed her lean body against him, down the length of him; her hands slipped inside his jacket, encircled him, moved into him. He felt her sigh of relief as she rubbed her cheek against his, whispered something about his needing a shave.

Finally, he pushed her back, held her by the shoulders, examined her with deep regret.

"You want me," she insisted in a husky whisper, "damn you, you know you do, Brian."

"What I want and what I get are two different things, Karen. It would be just like making it with a whore." He reached his hand to her cheek, gently fitted his palm to the contour of her face and said quietly, sadly, "That would really be a lousy last memory for both of us, baby."

Then he left.

FORTY-FOUR

Arthur Pollack looked the way Brian O'Malley felt, fatigued beyond any sense of his own being. He spoke mechanically in a dull hoarse voice; occasionally, his hand touched his throat as though to comfort an ache.

He waved Brian across the broad expanse of the Chief Inspector's office, leaned forward, hunched over the desk which practically devoured him. He peered over the rim of his reading glasses, then searched the array of papers on his desk, held up first one memorandum, then a second.

"Brian," he said, "these were handed to me within the last hour. First, Aaron Levine. Then, Ed Shea. Brian, you knew all along these would be submitted?"

Brian flung one leg over the arm of the wooden chair and shook his head slightly, then said, "Only as of a few hours ago, Arthur."

"Brian, how much is there to tell? How much are you going to tell me?"

"As much as I know, Chief."

Carefully, slowly, wearily, meticulously, he told Arthur Pollack exactly as much as he felt Arthur Pollack needed to know.

The staff meeting lasted for nearly two hours, as Arthur Pollack outlined the various procedures of cooperation that would be established between the New York City Police Department and the interim investigating committee established by the mayor. Each top staff member was assigned to a specific area.

"The main concern at this particular time is that we not only give the *impression* of internal house cleaning, but that we actually become totally involved in this activity."

It sounded to every man present in the room like a direct quote from the Commissioner. It probably was. What the hell other line could they take?

When the meeting ended, Brian O'Malley and Arthur Pollack labored far into the night preparing the tone of the news releases and how the matter of Patrolman John Morrison's sudden and unexpected contrition and willingness to expose himself and his fellow officers had come about.

Late that afternoon, Arthur had received word that the grand jury had exonerated Patrolman Morrison with a finding of justifiable homicide. There was no other finding possible under the prevailing circumstances.

"You think the media will buy this story, Brian?" Arthur asked.

"Fuck the media, it's what we've got to go with." He stood up, pulled his loosened tie farther downward, rubbed one bare forearm, adjusted his rolled-up sleeve. He picked up the rough draft, paced up and down as he read softly, almost to himself, "Patrolman John Morrison, grief-stricken by the death of his young partner, Patrolman Peter Caputo, and after much soul-searching and struggling with his conscience, has come forward to the Manhattan County District Attorney with an offer to testify before a special grand jury now being formed to investigate corruption in the New York City Police Department. He has also offered to appear before the Webb Commission just formed by order of the mayor. He has further agreed to waive immunity before the grand jury."

Brian shrugged. "More or less, that's it and we'll stick with it."

Idly, Arthur picked up the resignations of Deputy Chief Inspector Aaron Levine and Inspector Edward Shea. "And these resignations represent a form of apology for not having properly done their jobs." He shrugged, let the papers fall on his desk. "I don't know, Brian. Such a sudden surge of morality in the midst of all this immorality." He shook his head sadly, and his weak eye turned inward. "Well, I'll have the Commissioner go over these first thing in the morning. I have to get top clearance on this, Brian. It's unusual, but, God, this whole thing is 'unusual.'"

Brian rolled down his sleeves, fumbled with the buttons on his cuffs, seemed unable to manipulate his fingers. He took his suit jacket from the back of a chair and put it on, adjusted his tie.

"Brian," Arthur Pollack began tentatively.

Brian held a hand up, then let it fall heavily to his side.

Pollack came beside him, searched his face earnestly. He put his hand on Brian's arm. "Brian, how did you get Morrison to turn himself in?"

Brian leaned forward, brushed his fortieth cigarette of the night into the overflowing ashtray. He could hardly see Arthur Pollack's face through the heavy smoke and his overused, agitated eyes.

"Christ, Arthur, you look like hell, kid. Whyn't you get home and get some sleep?"

Mary Ellen was waiting for him in the kitchen. She sat over a cup of coffee and there were two half-smoked cigarettes in the ashtray, which was unusual since Mary Ellen rarely smoked.

"Brian . . ."

He kissed her lightly and said, "You didn't have to wait up for me, honey. How come you're drinking coffee this time of night?" He glanced from the kitchen wall clock to his own wristwatch as though in confirmation. "Jesus, it's two-thirty. Come on, let's get to bed."

She rose slowly, grasped both of his arms as though to steady herself. She seemed about to speak, but unable, and her large blue eyes filled with tears.

"Mary Ellen? What is it?"

She licked her lips quickly, then said in a shaking whisper, "It's your mother, Brian. Kit telephoned an hour ago."

"My mother?"

Mary Ellen shook her head, shuddered, held him tighter. "Heart attack, Bri. She's gone."

There was a cool, remote, unreal quality about the room. It

504

was large and subdued and theatrical. Groups of well-dressed men and women stood speaking in well-modulated whispers, careful of sound and gesture, as though they'd all been rehearsed in proper behavior.

Brian played his part too, stood, hostlike, greeted those who'd come to pay respects on his behalf. It seemed so peculiar, so strange, that all these hundreds of people who had never known his mother, never seen her, spoken to her, touched her, been touched by her, came to this midtown Manhattan funeral parlor, nodded with deference, expressed regret, looked sad, approached the coffin, offered the quick automatic prayer, then, duty done, quickly scanned the crowd for a familiar or sought-for face.

She lay all but forgotten, his mother, Margaret O'Malley. The banks of flowers which nearly stifled them in their profusion seemed limitless and bore cards from all the various organizations which he or his brothers and sister Kit belonged to as well as offerings from relatives and neighbors and friends.

Martin arrived from his parish in Chicago, his leave quickly arranged, and was there in time for the first night. He embraced Brian and Kevin, hugged Kit, inquired about Roseanne, who was flying in from California. His hair was still fair, but gray now instead of blond, and he wore it longer than Brian remembered, unpriestly, but then Brian remembered that Martin worked with the young people in his parish and had said something about hair being one of the minor but important bridges. And rock Masses. Christ, the last time he'd seen Martin was two years ago at Christmas and Martin played the guitar for them all and said he played in his parish's rock Saturday-night Mass.

Martin was thin and tall and the gathered spectators identified him to each other with some sense of awe and respect: the priest-son. They watched as he went to his mother's side, leaned close to the open coffin, privately whispered something no one was ever to hear. Then he knelt for a long, long time, then turned and gestured for his brothers to join him, and when they knelt by his side, Martin did a strange thing. He placed an embracing arm around each of them, totally mindless of the audience. He joined them together, her sons, for a brief prayer, then he pressed his hands to their shoulders, then into his eyes to smear away the tears without shame.

Kit had arranged everything in her quick and orderly way. Thin, intense, efficient, she consulted with the funeral directors, gave instructions, greeted and introduced and thanked the vast numbers of visitors from her political sphere. Martin was to say the Rosary on the third and final night. Then Margaret would be transported from Manhattan to the Bronx for the funeral Mass at St. Simon's, then burial would be in Woodlawn, next to their father.

Beside Kit, dark eyes filled with apprehension and awe, fingers nervously working, stood Juan and José. Kit put her arms around them both, confidently introduced them to judges and state senators and district leaders as her "two youngest brothers who are going to live with Murray and the rest of our brood now."

After many numbing hours, after the endless walking back and forth from the center of the room to the small alcove where, discreetly, unobtrusively, the coffin was under soft indirect lighting, people seemed to forget where they were, for what occasion. Voices rose a little, conversations picked up, crisscrossed, photographs of children and grandchildren were shown, stories were exchanged, laughter was heard from time to time.

At one point, Brian heard one of Kit's political friends say shrewdly, "You're a real cutie, Kit. Not only have you tied up the Jewish vote with that beauty of a name of yours – Kit O'Malley Weinstein – now you've got the Puerto Rican vote with these two little brothers of yours."

Two old women came on the last night, two shy, old neighborhood women who had known his mother as a person, contemporary, human being, rather than as the mother of one or the other of them. With gentle gratitude, with renewed awareness of the occasion, Brian escorted them, studied them with some odd memory as they perused his dead mother's face. They nodded, prayed, briefly held his hand and left for there was no one else present for them to speak and whisper with.

Francis Kelly and his wife, Marylou Delaney Kelly, came toward Brian, carefully picking their way through the crowded room. He hadn't seen either of them for several years. It was difficult to see them now, to recognize them, to find some memory of them.

Francis Kelly had retired after putting in his twenty years and he had gone fat and bald and diffident from years of messenger work in a bank. He offered a large moist hand to Brian, briefly reached for his arm, then dropped his hands quickly, as though he'd taken a liberty. He'd always been intensely aware of and uneasy about the differences in their departmental rank, for Francis Kelly had never gone beyond patrolman.

"Chief," he said, as though to a stranger, "I'm sorry for your troubles. We just heard about it and came as soon as we knew."

"Well, thanks for coming, Francis."

Marylou embraced him clumsily; she seemed overwhelmed by the number and importance of the people present. "Sorry for your troubles, Brian."

He inclined his face toward the alcove and they went, regarded the doll-like figure, knelt briefly, said their prayers, stared again and withdrew. Brian felt a surge of memory and affection and emotion when he saw the tears glisten in Francis Kelly's innocent blue eyes and he felt a gratitude: there was still some memory of his mother alive.

Roseanne O'Malley Delaney arrived just as Francis and Marylou were leaving and the two women embraced and tried to examine each other after nearly twenty years, but in the dimness and under the circumstances, it was nearly impossible.

Kit reached her sister first, then Brian felt her shudder as he embraced her tall, thin body. She pulled back, searched his face, her eyes wide and dry with apprehension, and he realized with a dull shock of wonder that beneath the facade of mature woman was Roseanne, still his young sister, and though it was in some way absurd, he whispered to her, "It'll be okay, Roseanne."

It was absurd for their mother's death affected none of them, did not threaten or change any of them or assign them other roles in life for they, her children, were all middle-aged and parents, adults with their lives already mostly in the past, yet

507

Brian found something still remembered in Roseanne and for one brief instant they were each of them who they had been so many years ago.

Roseanne swallowed dryly, glanced at all the strangers and asked her brother, "Will we have some little time alone with her, Brian? All these people . . ."

He nodded. "At the end of visiting hours tonight, we'll stay on. Just the family. And you can be alone with her."

He and Martin and Kevin went with her then and Roseanne knelt, her face tightly drawn and pale, and she couldn't seem to rise to her feet again and her brothers helped her. Mary Ellen and Maureen led her to a quiet corner of the room and sat with her on a velvet couch and after a while the three women fell into quiet conversation about children and weddings and cousins and grandchildren.

Patrick O'Malley stayed at his father's side throughout the three days of the wake. He was close-shaven and neatly cropped and fair and handsome in a dark suit and white shirt and black tie. They didn't say much to each other, there was little occasion, but Patrick filled in, took over for Brian easily, naturally, without being asked. Brian felt a bond with his son he'd never felt before, but couldn't examine it, just wondered if Patrick felt anything toward him or was just doing his family duty as his cousins did for their parents.

The family hour with their mother was an anticlimax; they were all too exhausted for any real feelings and it had all been extended too long, dragged out until they felt no connection with the presence in the coffin. Brian's mind wandered and drifted and couldn't seem to fasten on his mother because she was nowhere present in this artificial setting. Only Roseanne cried finally, neared hysteria, was quickly controlled and briefly apologetic: the long flight, the lack of sleep, the anxiety as well as her held-in grief. She hadn't seen her mother for nine years. Margaret had flown out to California for two weeks and they'd gotten on each other's nerves, but they corresponded regularly and spoke on the telephone every month and got on well enough on that basis.

The day of the funeral was clear and autumn-crisp. There were twelve cars in the procession. It was a Low Mass and the graveside service was simple and swift and they all returned to Brian's house for something to eat.

508

Mary Ellen had hired a very capable couple to prepare and serve food to the mourners. Everything was ready for them; everyone was hungry and filled with surprise at their appetite: their affirmation.

Martin and Roseanne left together for Kennedy; he would see her on her plane for Los Angeles an hour before his flight to Chicago. Kit would see to Mom's apartment. Since no one really wanted anything, she'd see that it was all dispensed to people who could use what little she'd left.

Finally, they all left, his brothers and sisters, his daughter and son-in-law, the close friends and distant relatives who returned to the house with them. Mary Ellen worked with the catering couple, cleaned up and put away and tidied.

Just he and Patrick remained, alone, for the first time since Margaret died.

"Let's have a drink," Brian said.

Patrick loosened his tie, gestured for his father to sit down while he poured for both of them.

Brian leaned back and studied his son and he didn't need the taste of Scotch, the warmth of alcohol, to relax him. "It meant a great deal to us, your mother and me, Pat, to have you with us these last few days."

Patrick nodded. "I'm really sorry about Grandma, Dad."

"I know you are, Pat. Christ, the whole thing kind of turns into a circus after a while, doesn't it? It doesn't really have much to do with the person who's died. Well, cheers." He drank deeply, then put his feet up on the table between them. "Want to talk, Pat?"

"Is this a bad time? I *do* want to talk to you, but if you'd rather let it ride a while—"

Brian shook his head. "No, go ahead. Christ Almighty, Pat, let's talk. Let's get it out or try anyway."

"Okay." It was the serious, earnest face of a man who confronted him. "I've been following what's been happening in the newspapers and through . . . other sources. You got two at the top, Levine and Shea, to turn in their papers. You got Morrison to turn himself in and agree to testify. That was *you*, right?"

Brian shrugged but didn't answer.

"And the investigation will go deeper than just skim the surface, right?"

Brian looked up at his son, steadily held his eye. "That was the goal, wasn't it?"

Patrick put the glass on the table and leaned toward his father. "Okay, the goal is being reached, or at least approached. But what about the *methods?* I don't know how you got two top men to retire. I don't know how you got that bastard Morrison to turn. I *do* know that it had nothing at all to do with the corruption at hand."

"Which means what?" Brian asked softly.

"Which means *more* corruption." Patrick held his hands up, his mouth fell open, he shook his head. "Christ, isn't there a *moral* way to commit a *moral* act?"

There was a ragged, pained edge in his son's voice and the pain showed on his face, which had lost the boyish soft innocence, had acquired the beginning hardness of knowledge. Brian felt sad for his son and for himself.

Gently, he said, "Patrick, I am fifty-one years old. In all of my life I've found that morality counts shit when it comes to getting a job done. What counts is doing it any goddamn way you can, but get the job done. Your way, Pete Caputo's way, nothing. Absolutely nothing. No proof, just charges. We examined the contents of Caputo's safe-deposit box. He kept nice, neat, *uncorroborated* records: dates, names, places, amounts paid, et cetera. Okay. Now Morrison will corroborate. Never mind why or how. The fact stands. Yeah, I got Morrison. That's what counts."

Patrick held his hand over his eyes for a moment, shook his head. His voice was hollow and helpless. "Johnnie Morrison murdered Pete Caputo and that other man. You got him as a crooked cop, acting as a cooperative witness. He'll get away with everything; he'll turn everybody in and walk away."

Brian whistled for a moment between his slightly parted lips, then said, "For a while he'll seem to get away with everything. But I'll take a bet that within a year you'll see Johnnie Morrison up on homicide charges."

"What do you mean?"

"Oh, Pat. Christ. He's going to screw so many people; he's going to upset so many standard operating procedures. He'll get his. He won't get away with murder. They'll pin something on him and make it stick."

510

"So it'll all come out even, then?" Patrick demanded bitterly. He stood up abruptly, jammed his hands into his pockets, strode up and down the room before he stood absolutely still. "Does that make it all come out even?"

Brian shrugged. "Jesus, don't you stand there and criticize *me*, buddy. I mean, what the hell, kid, you've walked away from it, right? That's damn easy, to just walk out and the hell with it. Okay, I think the whole system stinks too but I'm not willing to just let it go on. I've done what I can, the only way I've ever found to work. Okay, we can be very technical: fighting immorality with immorality; ends justifying the means and the means are maybe worse than the ends. But you don't have any platform to preach at me, Pat. *I'm* not the guy who said this whole thing is too rotten, therefore I'll condemn it from outside. I don't know if I *can* change it from inside, but I'm trying. Don't you get up on your holy little ladder and look down and condemn me, buddy, not when you haven't got any other way but to turn tail and run."

Patrick stood and stared at the fireplace, turned when he heard his father at the desk, heard the metallic sound of the patrolman's shield which Brian extracted from the top drawer and tossed on the desk.

Brian jutted his chin toward his son and his voice was bantering now, challenging. "Go ahead. Pick up the gauntlet. Show the old man. Christ, you can't prove anything unless you can beat me at my own game using your own rules."

Patrick picked up the shield, held it in the palm of his left hand while he idly stroked the lettering and embossed numbers with the fingers of his right hand. When he looked up finally, there was an odd, sheepish smile on his lips. He looked somewhat embarrassed and flushed. "I guess I didn't mention this to you, but I took the sergeant's exam last month. I guess I didn't want to mention it until I found out where I stood on the list."

Brian said tersely, "Number seven out of a list of one hundred and twenty-four."

Patrick's hand tightened into a fist over his silver shield, he tensed and tightened for a brief moment, then, as though making an important decision, he sighed and nodded.

"What the hell, you're my son, right?"

"I figure to make captain by thirty," Patrick said.

"You won't even make sergeant by twenty-five with five days A.W.O.L. against you," Brian said.

Patrick studied his father for a moment, then smiled with a strange acknowledgment. He scraped his chin with the metal shield. "Have I been assigned to your office for those five days?"

Brian shook his head. "For the first two days, special assignment, office of the Deputy Chief Inspector in Charge of Public Affairs. The next three days were death-leave days because of your grandmother." Brian lit a cigarette, carefully tossed the match into the fireplace. "Well," he asked softly, "do you feel corrupted or corrupt?"

Patrick reached into his father's breast pocket, helped himself to a cigarette. "In a way, that's how it starts, though, isn't it, Dad?"

"God knows how it starts or how far it goes before it has no way of stopping. It's life, kid. It's a gamble. I do the best I can, Patrick. I *try*. Maybe I'm a corrupt man, maybe not. Maybe there are circumstances none of us really knows how to cope with, but I *do* try. Now *you* start doing the best *you* can. If you can teach me, okay, kid, I'm willing to learn. But let's both keep open minds, Pat, okay?"

Patrick reached for his father's arm and pressed it tightly and swallowed hard and studied his father as though he was just becoming familiar with his face beneath the hard and mocking mask.

"That's a deal, Dad. Let's see where it takes us."